PRAIS
THE SCARLET C

"Wakanda meets *Warhammer 40,000* . . . Readers will enjoy the setting and the magic system."

—*Publishers Weekly*

"Rwizi says he based his unique science fiction and worldly tale on myths and stories he heard growing up in Swaziland . . . Because Rwizi combines technology, science fiction, and myth, the novel is like a video game filled with action and tension . . . Rwizi delivers a fast-paced story with vivid images of sub-Saharan Africa, lacing Salo's epic journey with flash, violence, drama, and a love story."

—*Authorlink*

"Rwizi's debut is noteworthy for its African-inspired setting."

—*Library Journal*

"Raised in Swaziland and Zimbabwe but now residing in South Africa, C. T. Rwizi is a remarkable new talent. He deftly juggles five very different protagonists; establishes a vast yet intricate new magical system unlike anything else I've ever seen; and unfolds stories scattered across the distant past, the chaotic present, and in entirely different planes of existence."

—*Tor.com*

"C. T. Rwizi . . . builds a rich setting by combining recognizable aspects of his home with deft and fantastical world-building."

—*Medium*

"It's a thrilling, fanciful debut, crammed full of imaginative world-building and excellent dialogue."

—RevolutionSF

"A promising new series by a promising new author."

—Fantasy Literature

"*Scarlet Odyssey* is an intricate and intense magical journey. This is lengthy and quite involved, with many characters and perspectives, so it could appeal to fans of the Lord of the Rings and Game of Thrones series."

—Young Adult Books Central

"At a time when we all need a little entertainment in our lives to distract from the reality of our world comes a book unlike any other."

—Fangirlish

"*Scarlet Odyssey* is an epic in every sense of the word. Almost six hundred pages of tightly woven plot, world building that keeps expanding with every chapter, a wide cast of characters, and an intricate magic system; this African-inspired fantasy has something in it for everyone."

—Bookshelves and Paperbacks

PRIMEVAL FIRE

ALSO BY C. T. RWIZI

The Scarlet Odyssey Series

Scarlet Odyssey

Requiem Moon

PRIMEVAL FIRE

C. T. RWIZI

Text copyright © 2022 by C. T. Rwizi
All rights reserved.

Published by 47North, Seattle

www.apub.com

Amazon, the Amazon logo, and 47North are trademarks of Amazon.com, Inc., or its affiliates.

ISBN-13: 9781542037112 (hardcover)
ISBN-13: 9781542037105 (paperback)
ISBN-13: 9781542037099 (digital)

Cover design and illustration by Shasti O'Leary Soudant
Cover image: © kamin Jaroensuk / Shutterstock;
© Digital abstract Art / Shutterstock; © Levchenko Ilia / Shutterstock;
© arteria.lab / Shutterstock; © Nadezhda Shuparskaia / Shutterstock;
© James Cohen / Shutterstock

Printed in the United States of America

First edition

For Esnath

APOS

THE ENCLAVE

JALAMA DESERT

DULAMA KINGDOM

KIYONTE KINGDOM

WORLD'S VEIN

EQUATOR

YONTE SAIRE

DAPIARO OCEAN

LAKE ZIVARLUND

WORLD'S ARTERY

UMADILAND

KAGERU

SERESA

NAMATO

YEREZI PLAINS

FARASWA DESERT

VALAU KINGDOM

INOETERA OCEAN

SHEVULAND

DRAMATIS PERSONAE

Yerezi Plains

MUSALODI (SALO), a young mystic *(deceased)*
VASININGWE, his father, chief of Khaya-Siningwe
MUJIOSERI (JIO), his brother, a ranger
MASIBURAI (SIBU), his brother, a ranger
ABA DEITARI, his uncle, a general
ANENIKO (NIKO), a ranger
MHADDISU (ADDI), an aspirant ranger
MAFARAI, a ranger
ALINATA, an Asazi
NEROPA, an Asazi
UNATI, an Asazi
TUMANI, a ranger
VITARI, a ranger
IREDITI, queen of the Yerezi Plains
AMASIBERE, a clan mystic
VASIBERE, chief of Khaya-Sibere
THE ORACLE, a young soothsayer

The Yontai

ISA ANDAIYE SAIRE, a king *(deceased)*
JOMO SAIRE, her cousin

OBE SAAI, a Sentinel *(deceased)*
KOLA SAAI (THE CROCODILE), his uncle, headman of the Crocodile clan *(deceased)*
ILAPARA, a former mercenary
TUKSAAD (TUK), her friend, an atmech from the Empire of Light
KAMALI, a Jasiri warrior and the emperor's Left Hand
TAJI, a mystic
ZURI, a mystic
MSIA, a mystic
ODARI, a former Sentinel
IJIRO, a former Sentinel
KITO, a former Sentinel
AMIDI, a priest of Engai
TULIZA, his daughter
THE ARC, a high mystic and emperor of the Yontai

Elsewhere

THE ENCHANTRESS, the Crocodile's widow
PROPHET, her associate
AYANA, a Faraswa woman
AAKU SISSAY, an old Faraswa man
AYZEL DI VESTRI, a businesswoman and necromancer
ARAM, a brothel owner
AXIOS, captain of the *Ataraxis*
ALESIA, helmswoman of the *Ataraxis*
FAIDON, mechanic of the *Ataraxis*
THE PROFESSOR, an experimenter onboard the *Ataraxis*
ADAMUS, his assistant
SALIM, an amnesiac young man
SEVAN, a former military analyst
PRISCILLE, a former medic

BALAM, a former mechanic
JULIAN, an Imperial lord
CLAUD, her associate
LUKA, her associate and Claud's brother

The Gods

AMA VAZIISHE, THE MOTHER, moon goddess and source of Red magic
ISINISO, VERITY, a deity of the white sun
ISHUNGU, VALOR, a deity of the yellow sun
VIGILANCE, a deity of the New Year's Comet
ENGAI, an arboreal Primeval Spirit
ARANTE, the devil and the source of Black magic

PROLOGUE: THE ORACLE

A Stone Chamber

A young oracle throws bones of divination onto a mat of woven grass, perusing with her dark sight the threads of past, present, and potential future.

She has been asked to gaze into the tapestry of time and provide insight into the possible future outcomes of one specific event. But the tapestry is unraveling, threads of time fraying and annihilating each other, a cataclysm about to make landfall, and the future she is meant to divine is in the heart of this storm. Try as she might, she cannot parse through the knot of threads entwined in the chaos.

The event in question: a meeting between a queen, an emperor, and a king.

The first two wait on a hill in the desert for the last to arrive, and when he does, they are not pleased to see the golden mask that conceals his face and eyes. First, he insults them with a summons out to these sandy wastes, as if they were his underlings. And now he dares to hide behind a mask.

The queen voices her displeasure. "How can we deal with a man too cowardly to show his face?"

"Put my face out of your minds, Your Majesties," says the king. "My appearance would only distract you and is not nearly as important as what I want. What we all want."

"And what is it you think we want?" asks the emperor, a playful, dangerous tenor coloring his words.

"To stop fumbling around in the dark," the king replies without fear. "You wear those fragments like they were made for you, but you are pretenders, children playing with weapons they do not understand. You do not know the true power you possess. Behold."

The king casts a spell, and the ground shakes as something tremendous breaches the surface and rises from the sands. The queen and emperor are amazed.

"What is your offer?" the queen says, and the king must surely smile behind his mask, for he now has their attention.

PART 1

ANENIKO

*

ILAPARA

1: Aneniko

Yerezi Plains

I remember the first time I noticed you like it was yesterday.

The red moon is a gibbous orb in the noon sky, and Niko and his squad of five mounted rangers have just spotted an enemy across the velds.

There, on the flat, grassy horizon, an Umadi war party riding an assortment of antelope marked with white paint.

Astride his quagga stallion, Niko squints, shading his eyes with a hand. To his left: the chief's twin sons, Jio and Sibu, and the dreadlocked ranger Mafarai. To his right: Potso and Tumani, the former an easygoing, toothpick-chewing layabout who smokes too much nsango, the latter Niko's broody rival in many things.

They're all in the crimson loincloths and red steel bracers and greaves of the Ajaha rangers. All riding tronic quaggas fortified by the queen's arcane blessing. All the epitome of what a young Yerezi man should be.

Niko is distinguished from the others by his honor guard's pauldron, an armor piece cast into the head of a spike-maned leopard depicted midroar—the Siningwe clan totem. It rests on his right shoulder, secured by a well-crafted leather harness crisscrossing his bare chest, saturated with the queen's magic, just like its wearer.

Earlier he and the others galloped from the borderland outpost as fast as a gale following a scout's alarm about intruders. Here are the intruders, just like the scout warned.

Niko counts about a dozen of them some seven hundred yards away. Hungry men here for what they hope will be easy prey. Sometimes a raiding party will turn back once they know they've been spotted, but these seem the sort who need to be forced back.

We were in the mountains on the eve of our circumcisions, amid a group of boys who were sitting around a fire, trading stories beneath the light of the full moon. Like me, you didn't talk much; you were more of a listener. Then one boy told a joke and you smiled, and it was like someone had dropped me off the edge of a cliff and my chest was in free fall.

Yours was absolutely the most beautiful smile I'd ever seen.

"What are you waiting for?" Tumani says to Niko. "Order the charge."

Tumani has a snarl on his face. Always snarling, that boy, especially in Niko's presence. Eager to wet his spear with Umadi blood. Eager to prove that *he* should be wearing the honor guard's pauldron, not Niko.

And they *could* charge if Niko gave the order. He'd tell them to raise their weapons. The twins, Potso, and Tumani would lift their spears. Mafarai, whose primary weapon is the bow, would raise his saber. Niko would reach for his tether with the queen and draw on it, and he would suffer the sensation of being watched, a pair of umber eyes with unfathomable depths of knowledge evaluating him from afar.

A sense of approval would flood across the tether, there'd be a flash of light glinting off his own spear, and then he'd be joined in a six-way battlebond with his squad. Their reflexes would become his reflexes. Their senses would meld with his senses, and they'd charge into battle. Outnumbered though they are, the enemy would face a force greater than the sum of its parts and be routed.

So yes, they *could* charge. And they'd probably win the altercation. But not without casualties.

The Umadi war parties they've been seeing these days wield strange new weapons from across the seas. Sticks that shoot bolts of deadly fire. A week ago Niko watched a fellow ranger fall from his saddle after being hit by such a weapon, his right arm nearly burnt to a crisp. He barely survived.

Niko doesn't think he can watch another ranger fall like that.

"Order the charge, Aneniko," Tumani growls again. "We need to take the initiative."

A new warlord has been sweeping across Umadiland, sending his rivals skittering all over the place. The hardened ones tend to fight back, but the weaker ones sometimes come here to try their luck and make a claim on Yerezi territory. So far, none have succeeded.

"Do not follow me until I tell you," Niko says to his squad, then rides ahead to meet the awaiting war party.

"Bra Niko!" Jio shouts behind him. "What are you doing?"

Niko doesn't stop. He spurs his quagga into a gallop, gritting his teeth, his spear solid in one hand.

Six hundred yards.

I remember the day I tracked you down to the hills south of the lake, where you'd sometimes escape to enjoy the view while you smoked your pipe beneath an ancient tree. When you saw me coming, I took pleasure in the way you glowered at me, like you'd slap me in the face if I came close enough. But then you smirked and blew a cloud of smoke in my direction, reclining deeper against the tree. I couldn't take my eyes off you.

"Careful, Ajaha," I heard you say. "Keep following me around like this and I might start thinking you like me."

The truth was on the tip of my tongue. I wanted to speak it. I don't know why I didn't.

Rage quickens the beat of Niko's heart. A closer look at the enemy tells him there are two riders with those strange sticklike weapons. The others are armed with spears and cavalry swords. They were all licking their lips in anticipation of a fight; now many of them tilt their heads and glance at each other in confusion, wondering why only one ranger is charging at them.

Five hundred yards.

One of the stick men fires his weapon, and a javelin of crimson moonfire hisses toward Niko. Only through the lunar blessing in his bones does he move quickly enough to raise his left fist in front of his face. An invisible ward of force expands away from his red steel vambrace, and as the javelin arrives, he bats it away. There's a flash of heat as it hits the ward and disintegrates, but the stick man fires again, and so does his comrade. They pummel Niko's ward over and over; he rides on anyway, baring his teeth. Beneath him, his stallion accelerates.

I remember watching you go down beneath the talons of a redhawk. That night I was so confused. You'd betrayed everything I'd grown up thinking a man should be. I'd known for a while that you flirted with magic. I'd caught you doing so once or twice, but I'd never thought you could have gone so far as to do what the Asazi do—to learn the secrets of mystics. I felt like you'd betrayed me. I wondered what it said about me that I liked someone like you. I was ashamed, and I hated myself for being ashamed.

Then the redhawk came down and pierced your chest with its claws.

Niko lets out a bloodthirsty battle cry. After Monti's death at the hands of an Umadi witch, he vowed to wreak vengeance upon their hated neighboring tribe. He's killed so many in these border skirmishes, and today he will kill again. But he knows no amount of death will ever soothe the rage that smolders within his core.

Four hundred yards. He's almost close enough.

The grass beneath him begins to blacken. He slows down a little and sees the corruption spreading toward him from directly ahead. The withering grass releases an ashy, powdery substance that makes him cough as soon as he breathes it in.

Poison.

An Earth mystic, it seems, using sorcery to pollute Yerezi land with poisons. He's hanging back from the rest of the war party, a potbellied man dressed in leopard skin, riding a sickle-horned sable antelope.

The rage Niko already felt swells to an inferno, but he becomes light headed as the alchemical magic in his red steel kicks in, purging the poisons from his body before they can do him harm. He comes to the verge of losing consciousness and almost doesn't block an incoming fire javelin in time.

Three hundred yards.

I remember when you came to the glade the day you left. You were going to ask me to come with you. I knew that you would, but I didn't let you finish. I was afraid of what everyone would say if they saw me leaving with you, if they saw me forsake the queen's blessing for yours, to be sworn to your service the way I was meant to be sworn to a woman.

I was afraid that they would laugh.

I was so, so foolish.

Niko deflects another flaming javelin with his vambrace. Dust and ash from the blackened grass haze the air, which has become acrid, burning him from the inside out. Waves of white-hot pain throb all over his body.

Behind the waiting war party, the mystic smiles, his eyes reflecting the light of his glowing cosmic shards. Blisters break out all over Niko's body, and he tastes blood on his tongue. His red steel was enchanted to protect him from such sorcery, but the sheer force of the attack overwhelms the charms. Still, he rides on.

Two hundred yards.

I dreamed of you when you left for Yonte Saire. Sometimes my dreams were so vivid I was convinced they were real. Even now I feel as though I could ride up to that tree south of the lake and find you smoking your pipe, waiting for me with a smile. I still go there sometimes and sit in the silence, hoping I'll hear the crunch of your footsteps.

The rider at the head of the party lifts his machete and releases a howl, which his comrades echo. As one they begin to charge, but it's too late.

The anger inside Niko explodes and he shouts, drawing strength from the blessing in his bones. He rises up in his stirrups and launches his spear forward with all his might. It leaps away from him, tearing into the air and arching over the Umadi riders.

The mystic's eyes widen. He stops casting his spells and begins to bring his antelope about, but the spear flies true and hits its mark, transfixing him in the heart. He falls off his saddle with a look of disbelief.

A hundred yards to the Umadi riders, but they pull up all at once, shocked that their leader has been felled so quickly. By now the other rangers are hot on Niko's heels, and the intruders all hastily turn their mounts about and flee, leaving their mystic's corpse behind.

Defeated by the single thrust of a spear.

I remember when the queen returned from Yonte Saire with a body wrapped in white linen. She wore a new diadem upon her head—copper, like her usual crown of erect feathers, but much simpler. Little more than a twisting band like a vine in a wreath.

She spoke to the crowds gathered in the chief's compound, where the body lay on a table in full view, and while most of those present dreaded to find out whose face the shroud concealed, I already knew.

I took one look at your father sitting behind the queen, at your uncle sitting beside him, I saw the emptiness in their eyes, and I knew. Dear Ama, I knew.

The poisonous ash dissipates almost all at once, along with the burning pain. Niko's alchemical wounds begin to heal as his red steel undoes the foul sorcery that infected him.

He doesn't chase after the fleeing Umadi. He dismounts his stallion and walks to the fallen mystic so he can extract his spear. The man is already dead, eyes bulging like he can't believe his fate.

Niko lifts his weapon and stabs him through his skull for good measure. Freed of its master, the sable antelope trots off into the open wilds.

It's over.

The rage whooshes out of Niko, leaving behind something less intense, more incessant. Something inward. Like a shroud of twisted thorns wrapped around his heart.

I remember when your father let me into his house so I could pay my respects. The body now lay in the parlor, and the queen had revealed the truth to the clan. Murdered on the streets of Yonte Saire, she said, during an ethnic riot that engulfed the city.

There could be no doubt now. I'd known the truth from the moment I'd spotted the shroud. Yet I needed to see with my own eyes. I knew, yet I prayed to Ama there'd been a mistake.

But there was no mistake. It was your face beneath the shroud. It was you lying dead before me.

It was really you, Salo.

"What the devil were you thinking?" Jio shouts at Niko when he and the other rangers finally catch up. "You never charge into battle on your own!"

Niko quietly surveys the five mounted rangers. Evidently none of them are amused by his stunt, not even easygoing Potso. By their identical frowns, the twins are upset, and Tumani's temples are pulsing in quiet fury.

Guilt almost moves Niko, but it quickly shifts into indignation. He saved them all from potential injury. They should be grateful.

He moves to remount his stallion. "It's called deterrence," he says. "An overwhelming show of force to make them think twice about fighting us. It worked, didn't it?"

Sibu, the more temperamental of the twins, shakes his head. "I'm beginning to think you want to die," he says. "Is that it, mzi? Are you so burdened with guilt you'd throw your life away?"

A flash of something red hot ripples through Niko, and he almost lashes out, almost loses control, almost says something he'll regret.

I remember watching you sail off into the lake on a raft, your body swathed in ceremonial hides and red blossoms. You were a hero, the queen said. Before your murder on the streets of Yonte Saire, you'd triumphed in the Red Temple and won your tribe a boon so great it would cement the dominion of the Yerezi people for as long as they held on to it. The queen was so impressed she committed you to the Infinite Path herself, there by our lakeside, in the presence of all the clan chieftains and mystics.

Yours was the funeral of a prince.

I kept my composure as I watched your raft go up in flames. No one could have known that my world was ending.

It hurts. Oh dear Ama, six moons later it still hurts so much I can't breathe sometimes.

Niko lets the moment ebb, the anger evaporate.

"You know nothing about what I feel," he tells Sibu, then prods his stallion into motion. "We're done here. Let's head back to the outpost."

Niko counts Jio and Sibu among his closest friends. He would die for them in a heartbeat if it ever came to it. Lately, though, they've annoyed him more often than not.

Bad enough that they remind him of their half brother. They have his light, coppery complexion, his big ears, and his gap-toothed grin, though admittedly on their faces it's nowhere near as winsome to Niko. And where their brother was tall and graceful with a quiet laugh, the twins are solidly built, rowdy, and as subtle as a pair of elephants. A piece of their brother shines through when they fall quiet, though, and it always stabs Niko in the heart like a blunt shiv.

What's worse is that they don't understand why he can't just move on and forget. Pretend everything is fine. Ignore the hollowness in his chest.

Ama knows he has tried.

The outpost is a small settlement of thatched drystone buildings with a single conical guard tower. It was built to keep watch over

Khaya-Siningwe's western border, which it shares with Umadiland. There are usually about fifteen rangers posted there at any one time along with a number of civilians to support them, including a small team of boys—aspirant rangers themselves—who serve as stable hands, care for weapons, and clean the barracks.

When Niko and his squad arrive, they find the aspirants in the sparring yard behind the barracks gathered around a dark-complexioned youth who's dusting himself off like he's just risen up from the ground.

With a sense of foreboding, Niko guides his stallion to the stables and dismounts, tethering the beast to a post for one of the boys to come take care of later.

"Jio, Sibu, report to the captain. I'll go see what this is about."

He doesn't wait for them to acknowledge his command. Spear still in one hand, he heads over to the gathered aspirants. An ember of annoyance flickers inside him when Tumani follows, but he says nothing.

"What happened?" he asks as they reach the boys. They're all dressed in white linen loincloths and leather sandals, carrying blunt swords or spears.

"Addi had another seizure," one of them says, eyeing the youth at the center of attention.

Tumani grunts. "What is this now, the fourth time? The fifth? I've lost count."

Niko ignores him. "Addi, are you all right?"

The boy winces with embarrassment, looking down as he dusts his palms. "I'm fine."

"He's not fine," Tumani puts in. "Having seizures during training? He shouldn't even be here."

"Really, it's nothing," Addi protests, to which Tumani gives a doubtful snort.

"Are you sure?" Niko says, still looking at Addi.

The boy nods, failing to meet his eyes. "But maybe I should take a break. And since you're back, I have a quagga to attend. If you'll excuse me."

They all watch in silence as he heads for the stables, keeping his head high despite his mortification. When he's gone, Tumani steps into Niko's space, oozing attitude and resentment. The aspirants step back and look on from a safe distance.

Here we go again, Niko thinks with an inward sigh.

"He doesn't belong here," Tumani says.

"According to who? You?" Niko replies.

"Faraswa have no place in the Ajaha. It's sacrilege. Maybe that's why he keeps having seizures."

"Are you a witch doctor? How can you know why he's having seizures? And I guess our chief is sacrilegious, since *he's* the one who agreed to let Addi train for the red. Is that what you're saying, mzi?"

Tumani's scowl deepens. "What happens if his seizures get worse? We don't have mystic healers this far out from the kraal."

"We have an Asazi, and she looked at him and determined that he's fine."

"And if he has a fit during battle? What then?"

"Let the healers worry about that," Niko says. "Our only concern should be training the aspirants. Matter of fact, I believe it's your turn today, so maybe you should get to it."

The scar running down Tumani's left cheek twitches like he's holding in a snarl, but he shakes his head. "Whatever you say, O hallowed honor guard."

Niko smothers a spike of anger and tries to remember that Tumani's resentment is neither abnormal nor unexpected. *But does he have to be so petty all the time?*

A little over a comet ago, the pair of Ajaha in the queen's honor guard completed their four years of service and moved on to positions of command in the regiment. It was generally known the queen would choose one of her next two Ajaha from Clan Siningwe on account of how valiantly their rangers had fought during the attack on their chief's kraal. At the time people whispered the choice was between Niko and Tumani. They weren't friends, but Tumani became especially bitter when Niko was awarded the pauldron.

Niko might have once tried to win the other ranger over. These days he can't find it in himself to care.

Deciding he has more pressing concerns, he leaves the training yard to the aspirants and goes to report to the outpost's captain.

For a fifteen-year-old former street urchin, Addi—or Mhaddisu, as his full name is spoken—has settled quite well into the Siningwe clan, his intermittent seizures notwithstanding.

One might have even thought him Yerezi were it not for his ruby-colored irises or the metalloid appendages growing from his temples like the horns of a buck—though Niko now knows better than to call them horns. They are tensors, a manifestation of the now-dormant Faraswa ancestral talent. "Horns are for beasts" is what Addi once said rather moodily.

An interesting accent colors his Sirezi, which he learned so quickly he might as well have been remembering a tongue he'd forgotten. It was only a matter of weeks before he achieved practical fluency.

Niko joins him later that afternoon by the stepped veranda outside one of the dormitories. He's humming a tune while he buffs Niko's pauldron with a cloth. A jar of polishing oil sits on a lower step in front of him, while the rest of Niko's armor is neatly arranged on a grass mat to his left.

He stops humming when he notices Niko standing nearby. "I'm fine," he says, answering the unasked question. "Seriously. I'd tell you if I wasn't."

Niko studies his face, then nods. "I know. But you can't blame me for worrying."

Addi sighs, turning the pauldron around and carefully running the cloth between the metal spines projecting from the armor piece. "I'll go to the Asazi healer when I'm done with your armor."

"You know you don't have to polish my armor every single day."

"You're an honor guard," Addi retorts. "Your armor must always look flawless. And what kind of aspirant would I be if I didn't help my favorite mentor look his best?"

"The kind who takes his health seriously."

Addi leans to his side, picks up another cloth, and tosses it at Niko. "Help me and I'll be done quicker. Then I'll go to the Asazi."

Unamused, Niko considers the cloth. "I'm your superior. You shouldn't be giving me chores."

"Consider it payment for yesterday." A tiny smile touches Addi's lips. "My wrist is still smarting, you know. You spar like a demon."

"It's for your own good," Niko says, but he sits down next to Addi and picks up a greave, then dips one edge of his cloth into the oil in the jar and gets to work.

Addi's Sirezi certainly isn't the only thing about him that has improved since his arrival. Niko has quite frankly been amazed by the transformation. The kid might still need to pack a little more meat onto his frame, but these days Addi holds his head high, rides quaggas like a natural, and trains with more zeal than most other aspiring Ajaha. Gone is the frightened bag of bones Niko first saw outside the kraal's gates one rainy afternoon almost a comet ago.

That day, a team of angry Ajaha from Clan Sikhozi delivered him to the kraal with a wagonload of other Faraswa refugees from Umadiland. The rangers said their clan wasn't going to take responsibility for foreigners invited to the Plains by a rogue Siningwe mystic. The chief of Khaya-Siningwe would either accept them into his lands, the rangers demanded, or they would drive the refugees back across the border.

Understandably, Chief VaSiningwe was furious, at least until Nimara translated Addi's story. And thus everyone learned of how a Yerezi mystic had saved him and the others from certain death, paying a great sum of money to have them delivered safely to his home. There'd been two wagons originally, but one had been intercepted along the way, its driver slaughtered by a warlord's disciple. Addi, who'd been driving the other wagon, had been spared for some reason, so he'd continued onward to the promise of safety for himself and his charges, and so here they were.

Once he learned of his son's involvement in their arrival, VaSiningwe was persuaded, albeit reluctantly, to let them stay.

But not everyone was welcoming. When Addi first mustered up the courage to explore the kraal on his own, the looks he attracted along the way discouraged him from making further attempts. Niko couldn't abide such behavior, so he took it upon himself to make Addi feel at home. The rangers in his posse weren't pleased when he started bringing Addi to their training sessions in the glade by the lake, but Niko leveraged his popularity and new rank to put them in line, making it clear they could either get used to Addi or train with someone else. They stopped complaining.

At least until the seizures started.

Niko rubs the length of the greave in his lap with his cloth, his eyes tracing the enchanted scripts carved in ornamental patterns onto the steel.

He told me how you saved his life. The risk you took in doing so. Now I watch over him like a protective brother because I feel it's what you'd want me to do.

Sometimes I feel like he's my last link to you.

Frowning intently, Niko focuses on polishing away a stubborn scratch on the steel.

"I don't think that's going to get any shinier, Bra Niko," Addi says, his eyebrow raised at Niko's frenetic hand.

Niko stops. He sets the greave down and bundles the cloth tightly in a fist. A wave of emotion crashes into him, leaving him clenching his jaw. "Something's gotta give, or I'll lose it," he says under his breath.

A boy shouting draws their attention to the flock of black-feathered ravens flying in a perfect circle above the outpost.

"I believe we have a visitor," Addi remarks, and Niko licks his lips, eyes focusing on the birds.

As if on cue, the ravens fly down and flutter together in front of the dormitory into a prepossessing young woman dressed in a flowing garment of beads, pale silk, and red steel.

"Si Alinata," Niko says. "This is a surprise."

The twins and a few other boys have drifted closer and watch the Asazi with clear interest.

It's not hard to see why. The queen's favorite Asazi has closely cropped hair, unblemished dark skin with a radiant bronze undertone, and a visage so stunning Niko thinks he might actually be the only ranger his age who isn't utterly smitten with her. She briefly scans her audience before her sharp hazel eyes return to Niko, betraying no emotion. "The honor guard is needed at the Queen's Kraal. I am to fly you there immediately."

Niko takes a moment to digest this. "Why?" he asks the Asazi. "What happened?"

"The queen has convened an emergency session of the council of chiefs." The Asazi glances at the twins, seeming hesitant. "Your chief and his advisers are already on their way. We need to be by Her Majesty's side before they arrive."

There's obviously more to the story, but the Asazi probably doesn't want to get into it in front of the others.

Niko rises, his mind racing. "I must inform the captain of my departure."

"We'll let him know," Jio says. "Go. Tell us everything when you come back."

"And thanks to my wisdom your armor will be nice and shiny for Her Majesty," Addi says with a grin. "Here. I'll help you."

Niko conveys his gratitude to Jio with a nod, and then Addi silently helps him don his armor pieces for the second time that day. The Asazi looks on quietly the whole time.

When he's ready, she discorporates without a word, turning into a flock of ravens and taking Niko with her as they lift off into the skies and head for the Queen's Kraal.

2: Ilapara

The KiYonte Kingdom

She was once Ilapara the misfit, back when she lived in the lands of her birth and wouldn't conform to what was expected of a woman of her tribe. She then became Ilapara the renegade when she ran off to work as a mercenary in a foreign land. Then Ilapara the outlaw helped kill a warlord's disciple, and Ilapara the saboteur helped deny the political ambitions of a would-be king.

Now Ilapara the insurgent turned reluctant mediator moves quietly through the jungles growing along her encampment's perimeter to settle yet another dispute between two very tiresome KiYonte mystics.

A flycatcher flutters off a branch above her and produces a visible shimmer as it passes through the encampment's massive stealth field. Visible through the gaps in the jungle's canopy, the field is a translucent dome of illusion magic maintained by electrified rods of aerosteel that encircle the camp. By the look of things, one of these rods is the source of this latest conflict.

With a long-suffering sigh she approaches the two belligerents, a man and woman who won't cease arguing even after she stops in front of them and folds her arms. The stealth rod in question is staked into the ground nearby. Ilapara infers that the rod has been nearly depleted of essence and needs to be replenished. From what she quickly gathers, the man wants to replenish its reserves without deactivating the charm it holds. The woman is convinced that doing so will cause irreparable damage to the rod's core.

"Every time you open your mouth, I swear I wonder how you can even read," she laments. "You're woefully ignorant. But what else would you expect from someone who received his education in a sewer?"

"Says the cosseted know-it-all who has no practical experience," the man retorts. "All your knowledge is theoretical. I have years of hands-on training with charms. I know what I'm doing."

"Dabbling in poorly charmed trinkets hardly qualifies as 'hands-on training.' I was a respected arcanist at the House of Axles. My experience far exceeds yours both in depth and breadth."

"You wish. The House of Axles hasn't produced anything original in centuries. All you rigid pedants ever do is plagiarize from the past."

"Why, you unenlightened cretin! I don't even know why I bother with you!"

"Same here, lady!"

They were enemies once. He was an independent mystic practicing his magic in Yonte Saire's undercity, while she, a devoted member of the orthodoxy, served the high mystics as a faithful acolyte. No one could have ever guessed that they'd one day be united in rebellion against an emperor they equally despised.

If only they could stop squabbling.

"Bibi Zuri, Bwana Msia," Ilapara finally says, speaking over them impatiently. "Is this really necessary? Why must everything be an argument between the two of you? Can't you accomplish *one* task without turning it into a battle between independent and orthodox? Must I remind you that those distinctions are meaningless now? There are no independents anymore, no orthodox. There's just us. There's the resistance. There's this camp. And it needs your protection, not your bickering."

Bibi Zuri breathes in and out like she's trying to rein in her temper. "I understand that, Comrade Ilapara." She waves a hand at the nearby rod. "But if we keep replenishing these linchpins while they're active, their cores will degrade. Then we'll need to replenish them more and more frequently, until we can't use them at all."

"Any degradation will be entirely negligible," argues Bwana Msia.

"Not over a large number of cycles, it won't," she counters.

"It would take years to get to that point. But if we keep deactivating the linchpins every time we need to replenish them, the whole enchantment could fail, and the camp would be compromised."

"Not if our calculations are correct, and mine always are."

Ilapara presses her fingers against her temples. She used to cover her crimson dreadlocks like an Umadi woman, but since becoming a jungle-dwelling insurrectionist, she's ditched the veil and taken a liking to wearing haltered tops that leave plenty of room for her skin to breathe. Right now she feels like pulling all her hair out and screaming until her voice box ruptures.

"Why don't you try both methods," she suggests. "Alternate so that we decrease the risk to the stealth field while also prolonging the lifespan of the rods."

"Linchpins," they both say.

"Whatever. You get my point. Can we do that?"

They frown at each other, and then Bwana Msia scratches his beard, thoughtful. "I suppose we could try."

"So long as we start with *my* method," Bibi Zuri says.

He glowers at her words but otherwise remains on board with the plan.

"Thank you, Red-kin," Ilapara says. "And next time you have a disagreement, come to a compromise."

She turns around and walks off before they can manufacture some other reason to waste her time.

I should just cut my losses and go back to my old life, she thinks, and not for the first time. Ama knows she didn't come to the Yontai to fight alongside these infuriating people. But leaving would feel too much like turning her back on . . .

On him. On Salo. Dear Ama, even thinking his name is like pouring vinegar on an open wound. She has to believe she didn't follow him all the way up here just to have him disappear forever. There has to be more she can do. Five moons have passed since he vanished on the night of the Bloody Requiem, but she still refuses to accept that this is how it all ends.

"Fire!" someone shouts at the top of his voice, and a rapid succession of deafening twangs rings over the roughly built huts and tents making up the camp.

A few people cover their ears, but no one is alarmed. Squads of fighters train daily in the practice range with Jomo's new weapons, awfully lethal brass contraptions he acquired in a trade deal with some sleazy southeastern merchant.

Handheld death from across the seas, apparently. A concentrated beam of moonfire at the pull of a trigger.

Bindukis is what many people here call them. *Typhonic firearms* according to Tuk, with subtypes like *sidearms*, *rifles*, and *carbines*. Before their arrival the emperor was on the verge of crushing Jomo's resistance. Then came a weapon that could take down a mystic with a single finger movement, and the conflict came to a standstill.

When the first batch arrived in a crate on the back of a wagon, Tuksaad was mysteriously apprehensive. He took one look inside the crate, saw the weapons, shook his head like his worst fears had been confirmed, and walked away. Ilapara didn't understand his reaction until she held one of the smaller firearms in her hand and discharged it at a tree.

She has trained with the weapons since then because it would be foolish not to. But she's refrained from keeping one on her person.

These weapons might have improved the fortunes of the resistance, but there's something disconcerting about a machine so small and light-weight holding so much death.

As she approaches one of the larger tents in the camp, a guard wielding a brass binduki rifle accosts her with another man in tow.

"Comrade Ilapara," the guard says. "If you'd please escort this messenger to Prince Jomo. He's just arrived from the Crocodile province."

Ilapara gives the messenger a once-over. A young man. Chapped lips. Travel-worn sandals. She's seen him around before. "Of course," she says. "This way."

The messenger follows her quietly, his eyes cast to the ground. At the tent she tells him to wait outside while the two men guarding the entrance let her pass through the flap and into the cool, magically dehumidified interior. Prince Jomo Saire and two other members of the camp leadership are seated around a table inside, their eyes closed as if in prayer. A golden oval ornament rests on the table with concentric rings spinning freely inside a round cavity, one of several such artifacts Salo enchanted before his disappearance.

Before his death, some corner of Ilapara's mind whispers, but she pushes that thought back where it came from.

The artifact is active and has a strange pull around it, a sort of gravitational field that seems to attract only thought. Bracing herself, Ilapara gives in to the pull and lets her mind fall inward, and she transits through the crushing, merciless vacuum of the Void before materializing on a marble porch in front of a large double door.

After Salo secretly and illicitly duplicated the entire collection of spells in the Pattern Archives, he needed somewhere to house them, so he built this place inside his metaformic amulet: an arcane construct in the shape of a grand library.

It floats in the middle of a lake, six archives for each craft of Red magic and a seventh for multidisciplinary spells, all of them connected to a central pavilion through raised walkways that bridge over the water.

Unique artworks sit on the porches in front of every archive, serving as visual markers for the type of spells housed beyond the doors. The one in front of Ilapara is a constellation of tiny floating stars that constantly rearranges itself into various illusions: a flower on a vine, an eagle in flight, a moon changing through its phases.

The constellation dissipates around her when she walks through it. She descends the steps to the porch, then strides across the walkway toward the pavilion.

Beautiful though this construct is, coming here isn't easy for her. Salo's presence haunts the place so strongly she sometimes thinks she'll find him reclining on his favorite chair in the pavilion, plotting his next insane scheme. She knows this was probably why she didn't feel too strongly about relinquishing the amulet and its enchanted communication shells to Jomo's cause.

And Jomo has used it rather well, she'd say, leveraging access to the library to court mystics both foreign and domestic, striking deals to hoard as many firearms as possible and using the construct as a secret meeting place.

She finds him in the pavilion with the rest of the leaders of his resistance, all standing around a table covered with detailed maps of the kingdom, debating how to better disrupt the emperor's supply lines. Jomo has a finger on one of the maps and is in the middle of speaking when he spots Ilapara.

His gaze brightens. "You're just in time. I need your input on something."

Jomo Saire was somewhat of a pampered prince when Ilapara first met him, round in the cheeks and a little too fond of drink. But the last five moons have seen him mature into a competent leader. He stands leaner these days, the result of kicking his reliance on alcohol and training daily with his three former Sentinels turned staunch allies.

Ilapara is self-aware enough to know that Salo isn't the only reason she's reluctant to leave the Yontai.

"There's a messenger outside for you, Your Highness," she says. "From the Crocodile province. It might be urgent."

Jomo stands straighter and becomes more serious, putting weight onto his mahogany cane. The leg brace reinforcing his left knee used to be gilded; now it's simple aerosteel. His tunics and pants are simpler, too, less princely, almost always mournful grays and blacks. He's also taken to wearing a binduki on his hip, a brass sidearm featuring a glass chamber filled with a lurid red plasma.

"Excuse me, my elders," he says to the men and women around the table. "I've been waiting anxiously for this message. Please continue without me."

He and Ilapara pull themselves out of the construct simultaneously, awakening back in the tent. Jomo gets up from his seat and comes over, taking Ilapara's arm with his free hand.

"I wish you didn't have to make me beg you to attend these meetings," he says in a quiet voice as they leave the tent. "Everyone knows you're a valued member of my inner circle. You shouldn't feel out of place."

"I had to deal with the arcanists," she says. "They were arguing again."

Jomo gives a huff. "I swear if we didn't need those two . . ."

"Trust me; I know the feeling."

They come to the messenger, and Jomo exchanges polite greetings with the man.

"I'll give you your privacy," Ilapara says and starts to leave, but Jomo tugs her back.

"No. Stay." To the messenger he says, "What news do you bring, my friend?"

The messenger won't look Jomo in the eye as he unearths an oval ornament from a pocket—yet another one Salo enchanted back in Yonte Saire.

"Elea Saai refused to accept the communication shell, Your Highness," the messenger reports. "She says she doesn't want to risk being seen associating with us. She has plans to begin negotiations with the emperor."

Jomo rubs the scruff on his cheeks as he stares at the shell. He looks tired more than anything. "Did you remind her that this same emperor is responsible for the death of most of her family, including her beloved son and my dear friend Obe Saai? Did you remind her of what happened at what was supposed to be her brother's wedding?"

"I did, Your Highness, but she said she must think of her people first. The crocodiles have all accepted her as their representative and will go where she goes."

"Thank you, my friend." Jomo is morose as he accepts the shell from the messenger. "Go get food and rest. You've earned it."

The messenger bows his head and walks away.

"I'm beginning to wonder if any of this is worth it," Jomo says when he and Ilapara are alone, staring blankly at the treetops hemming the edge of the camp.

"What do you mean?" she asks.

He looks at her. "Are we even on the right side here? Everyone else has accepted the Arc. Even the Faraswa Collective has acknowledged his rule. How can I fight against a ruler they—of all people—have endorsed?"

"The Faraswa had it bad in this kingdom for a very long time," Ilapara says. "He's promised to make things slightly *less* bad for them, so they've accepted. That doesn't mean he's any less of a tyrant." She lays a gentle hand on his arm. "Do not lose faith now, Jomo. You've led well thus far. This is simply a setback."

"A setback?" Bitterness makes his voice crack. "We keep bleeding support like this, and there'll be no resistance left." He looks around the rickety shacks, huts, and tents making up the main encampment of his movement. "What if I've made a mistake bringing all these people here?"

He's told no one else the complete truth about what happened at the Summit on the morning of the king's wedding to Kola Saai. No one else knows the hand his cousin played in the incident, that she sacrificed herself and all the other headmen to end the curse of the KiYonte clan marks in an effort to stop interclan violence, and that she did it using the yellow diamond Salo retrieved from the Red Temple's inner sanctum at her behest. No one else knows that the explosion was her own doing, and as far as Ilapara is concerned, no one else needs to know. It would only serve to distract from the more pertinent truths, because ultimately the king was a victim too. She was manipulated.

What's plenty obvious to everyone, however, is that the explosion killed every figure of power in the kingdom except for one high mystic who then claimed the throne for himself. And not as king, like every other ruler the Yontai has known, but as emperor.

"The resistance is so much bigger than you, Jomo," Ilapara tells him. "You might be the glue holding everything together right now— all these disparate groups have chosen to rally around you—but they're here for their own reasons. They're here because they want to be."

The doubt she sees persisting in his eyes makes her tighten her hold on his arm and pull him toward the tent.

"Come."

Back inside the construct's pavilion, the resistance leadership is still in deliberation.

"Apologies, my elders," Ilapara says, addressing them with the type of self-assurance one acquires from regularly speaking to powerful people. "Forgive my intrusion. But I believe the prince needs a reminder of why you continue to fight by his side."

A middle-aged woman with a neat mass of gray curls on her head straightens her posture, studying Ilapara at first, then the prince. She was an instructor at the House of Forms and continues to dress in the fine black robes and moongold chains befitting that former station, though she has been unwavering in her support of the insurrection.

"I joined this resistance because I'm strongly against what the new emperor represents," she says. "Mystics must not wield political power: plain and simple. It is an inevitable path to tyranny. Already we see it with this usurper, how he punishes anyone who dares disagree with him. We who are blessed by the Mother must bow to the will of the common folk. That is the KiYonte way and a principle I am willing to die for."

A grizzled man standing across the table watches the first speaker with a humorous glint in his eyes. "My comrade belonged to the orthodoxy, which we independents despised for their aloofness and elitism. Even now we don't see eye to eye, but we agree that the emperor is a power-hungry despot who won't be satisfied until he's dominated every aspect of our lives. He would dictate to us how to learn magic, what magic to learn, who to help with our magic, and when. I was born an independent and will die one if need be."

Next to speak is the nobly dressed merchant and scholar standing beside the independent. "The emperor's revolting new surveillance magic has made everyone afraid to speak their minds. Anyone who so much as whispers a dissenting thought is arrested. He has erased our cultural identities, forced us to abandon our heritage, our clans, our traditions. He has proscribed art and music that celebrates who we are, and worst of all, he has conscripted our sons into his legions en masse, detaining any who refuse to serve him. I owe it to my children to fight such a man."

"The Sanctuary of the Living Waters was my home," says the elderly nonconformist in an olive caftan and headscarf, her voice trembling with righteous fury. "The emperor has promised to allow us to worship in peace so long as we abide by his heavy-handed stipulations. He would tell us how to honor our patron in our own sanctuary! We stood against such tyranny before. We will stand against it now."

Aisha, the youngest woman at the table, was a member of the jackal clan, who were enemies of the Saires and in league with the crocodiles. When her parents died at the wedding, she shaved off her hair, got permanent tattoos of the marks that had been erased from her neck, and took an oath of vengeance. She wears a warrior's breastplate and carries a sword with her at all times. "I lost everyone I loved at that blighted wedding," she says. "The emperor is responsible, and I want his head. I don't care who gets the scraps."

There is one more person at the table yet to speak. Aside from Jomo and Ilapara, he and Aisha are the only ones whose physical selves are actually in the camp. When he gives no indication of chiming in, Jomo lets out a long breath. "I hear you, my comrades. But I'm beginning to wonder—"

"Wait," Aisha says, eyeing the silent one with suspicion. "Why are you so quiet today? You haven't said a word since we got here."

Ilapara knows the man was a former captain of the city guard and a member of the impala clan. She's not surprised that he wouldn't volunteer his reasons for remaining with the resistance, since he has often been vocal about his doubts. It does surprise her, however, that he's been quiet all along, given just how talkative he tends to be.

He grimaces as the room's attention swivels in his direction. Droplets of sweat gather on his forehead. He makes a choking sound like he's stifling a cough.

"Are you well, Bwana Moyo?" says the elderly nonconformist.

Moyo makes a heaving motion, then vanishes from the construct. Aisha follows, pulling herself out too. Jomo looks over at Ilapara, worried, and together they exit the construct and appear back in the tent, where Moyo has vomited onto the table. While Jomo and Aisha get up and recoil in disgust, Ilapara's stomach almost drops to the floor as she spots something moving within the curdled, beige liquid: a metal wasp with iridescent wings and a crystal thorax. It flutters off the table and floats upward.

"The camp is compromised," she remarks.

Jomo curses. "Moyo, you bastard. You've betrayed us!"

"I don't understand," Aisha says. "Isn't the stealth field supposed to confuse and kill off these things?"

"It appears they can pass through just fine in someone's stomach," Ilapara says.

Moyo sinks to his knees, succumbing to another bout of retching. "I had no choice," he weeps. "They had my family."

"You filthy liar!" Aisha moves around the table and approaches him, eyes blazing. "Your family left this camp willingly. If you're going to turn traitor, at least have the guts to own it."

The floating wasp arrests their attention again as it releases a stream of sorcerous light from its crystal, producing a vision that chills the blood in Ilapara's veins: the emperor himself, wearing a simple crown of moongold, outlined in red light, as though he were standing before them.

Damn you, Salo, she curses. *Why did you have to be so clever?* His ingenious network of mobile mechanical skimmers was the inspiration behind the emperor's own system of surveillance, except the emperor has had time to refine it.

"Your camp has been surrounded," says a resonant metallic voice emanating from the wasp. *"Surrender, hand over the agitator Jomo Saire, and you will suffer no harm. Resist, and you will perish."*

Horns go off all over the camp. People outside start shouting. Ilapara almost feels like she's stepped into a nightmare as she watches everything fall apart. All their work. They were so careful.

There's a scream of unbridled rage, and before Ilapara can intervene, Aisha has unsheathed her sword and struck. Moyo's head tumbles off his shoulders, and the foul smell of his blood fills the tent. She swings her blade again, and the wasp falls to the ground in pieces. The emperor's mirage winks out.

"Bibi Aisha!" Jomo screeches. "What have you done?"

"He knew too much," she says. "And we can't afford to haul traitors around."

"I agree," Ilapara says, though she's sickened by the beheaded corpse. "What's done is done, besides."

The entrance flaps open, and the former Sentinel known as Odari shows his face. "The ash witches are ready to leave, boss."

One of the first things Jomo did when his rebellion became formalized was trade spells with a group of fire metamorphs from the Halusha tribe in exchange for their help. They're always on standby in case a hasty escape is needed.

"There won't be enough time to save everyone," Jomo says helplessly.

"Everyone knew the risks involved, Your Highness," Aisha says. "No one is expendable, but if we lose you, we lose everything. You must go."

"Damn you, Moyo," he whispers, shaking his head. He reaches for the communication shell on the table and grimaces as he tries to shake it free of vomit. "Bibi Aisha, keep your shell with you at all times. We meet in the Void in three days at high noon."

She nods, then exits the tent.

Ilapara waits for Jomo to pocket the shell, and then they leave the tent together. The skies are overcast outside, growing darker by the second as menacing storm clouds gather. All around the camp, thick plumes of ash and embers are shooting up into the jungle canopy— Halusha ash witches whisking other insurgents away.

One of them is waiting nearby with Jomo's three Sentinels. Dressed in simple hide garments, she also wears colorful plates embedded within her earlobes and has rubbed her locks of hair with ocher.

"Are you ready, Your Highness?" she says.

Jomo pauses, looking at Ilapara. "You're coming, right?"

She hesitates, clasping one of the little horns of tronic ivory dangling around her neck. "I have to find Tuk."

Jomo doesn't take his eyes off her.

"I'll be fine," she tells him. "And I know how to find you. Go."

They watch each other as the witch draws power into her cosmic shards, summoning a whirlwind of ash from the ground that slowly thickens as it surrounds her and the rest of Jomo's party.

"You gave me a reason to live, Ilapara," he says through the maelstrom. "Don't go and break my heart now." And then he and his Sentinels become embers and lift off for the skies with a whoosh.

Only once she's certain of their escape does Ilapara turn around and run to find her wayward friend.

The Halusha ash witches are a product of their tribe's ancestral talent, which endows their mystics with a greater affinity for fire. No other metamorphs on the continent can match them in speed or stealth. They're the perfect vehicles for escape.

There just aren't enough of them to save everyone in the camp.

The screams start almost immediately after the stealth shield falls and the legionnaires begin to make good on the emperor's threat, cutting down insurgents with sword and spear. The few armed with bindukis try to fight back, their weapons screaming in earsplitting chorus. Most scatter into the surrounding jungles, but Ilapara knows they'll be hunted down.

She keeps running, heading for Tuk's little hut at the other end of the camp's perimeter. To make sure she's moving in the right direction, she clutches one of her two ivory pendants. She commissioned both pendants from an enchanter shortly after joining the resistance so she would always be able to find Jomo and Tuk in the event of their separation. Each young man has an identical pendant linked to hers so they can find her too.

She learned her lesson with Salo. She won't be losing another friend.

The pendant fills her with a sense of Tuk's whereabouts, and she accelerates, paying no heed to the carnage around her.

He built his little shack at the very edge of the camp, where the jungle is dense and traffic infrequent. He was gregarious once. Charming. Quick to smile and playfully aware of the potency of his physical presence. Then Salo disappeared, and the lunar blessing he'd bestowed upon Tuk vanished from his bones with no warning.

They were still refugees in the Valau embassy when it happened. Tuk sat deathly still for a whole day. He shed no tears, but the desolation Ilapara saw in his eyes was worse.

He hasn't been the same since.

He's seated cross-legged in the empty hut, staring intently into space like he's oblivious of what's befallen them, still wearing the same gray sleeveless shirt from two days ago. His overgrown locks of dark hair spill away from his face as he looks up at Ilapara, eyes shining a steely shade of gray like the storm clouds outside. Even in his grief, Tuk remains intensely beautiful.

"Tuk! What the devil are you doing? We have to go! The camp is under attack!"

"I can't keep running, Ilapara," he says in a strangely calm voice. "Not if it's for nothing. I need to know there's a point to all of this."

"What are you talking about?" That's when she sees what's nestled in his right hand, a glass vial of cloudy liquid with a bluish luminescence. Her eyes widen. "Tuk, you're not planning on drinking that right now, are you? We're under attack!"

"I have to know." Before she can say another word, he pops off the vial's stopper and downs the contents in one gulp.

"Tuk, no!" Ilapara watches in horror as Tuk's head tilts back and his eyes roll up into his skull. She rushes in past the threshold, then falls to her knees in front of him and grabs his shoulders. "What the devil have you done?"

The empty vial rolls out of his limp hand. His skin has paled. She picks up the vial and examines it. This is the item she and Tuk retrieved from a trashed apartment in Northtown—Rapture of the Stars, if she remembers correctly.

She tosses the vial aside and shakes him again. "Tuk! Wake up!"

But his mind is no longer here.

"Shit!"

She freezes as the hairs on the back of her neck stand erect. Her uncle once taught her that a good hunter of the wilds can always sense the weight of a predator's gaze: the leopard lurking in the grass, the kerit bear stalking from behind, the inkanyamba hiding by the riverbank.

There's a spear leaning against the wall. She rises to her feet, picks it up, and slowly walks out the door.

A Jasiri waits for her outside, his crimson robes billowing in the strengthening winds. Bright tattoos are visible along his exposed left arm. His exquisite aerosteel breastplate has a moongold-and-silver red-hawk splashed across the chest, the sword in his hand engraved with ciphers. She can still hear screams coming from elsewhere, but she knows that the biggest threat in the camp right now is standing in front of her.

She holds her spear in a defensive stance, ready to defend the door with her life. "Kamali. Look at what side you're fighting on. Look at all the slaughter. There are innocent civilians here. How can you be okay with this?"

He became a household name after his legendary performance in the city's arena, popular among noble and common folk alike. Pardoning the Jasiri for his crimes and offering him a place by his side was one of the emperor's masterstrokes.

"The emperor's hand is firm but fair," Kamali says in his stoic voice. "His leadership will bring lasting peace across the kingdom and beyond."

Ilapara can barely believe her ears. "Is this peace, Kamali? All this death. Is this the kind of world you want to live in?"

"I want to live in a world where I never have to use my sword to kill again. But you and your resistance force our hand. You're not even KiYonte. This isn't your fight."

"That's not true and you know it."

Kamali looks down. When his eyes flick back up, Ilapara sees traces of the honest, humble man she first met at the House of Forms. "I'm truly sorry for what happened to your friend," he says. "I tried to save his life. I bloodied my hands and wiped my own memory—for him. I didn't want any of this to happen. But resisting the emperor now is not only futile; it's counterproductive."

The winds have intensified greatly, churning up leaves, clothes, and tents. "So what now?" Ilapara says. "Will you kill me?"

Kamali is quiet for a moment. "I should," he says. "Either that or bring you in alive."

"But you won't," she realizes, because he'd have done so already if that were his intention. She also notices the lack of red legionnaires in this sector of the camp. He means for her to escape.

"Let's not meet again like this, Ilapara. I can't promise your safety next time." He jerks his head to the side. "Go."

She doesn't pause to question her luck. She runs back into the hut.

To her dismay, Tuk is still in a stupor from the concoction he drank.

"Tuk, I'm going to need you to wake up because I'm sure as the pits not carrying you!"

When he fails to respond, she curses, tosses her spear to the side, and bends down to sling his arm around her shoulder. Tuk is rather short for a man, but his body is mostly muscle and sinew with barely an ounce of fat—he's not light. But she manages to drag him up to his feet and limp out of the hut, supporting the brunt of his weight.

As they stagger into the jungles, she balls her left hand into a fist and makes a twisting motion; a cocoon of light erupts from the charmed bracelet on her wrist, enveloping them both in a field of invisibility.

Two minutes later, Ilapara's knees give out, and she falls to the undergrowth with Tuk, thorny leaves and shrubs scraping her skin. The charm on her bracelet also dies with a sputter, the core depleted of essence. Tears blur her eyes as she sits up and shakes Tuk's insensate form.

"Wake up! Please! I don't want to leave you, but I can't carry you any further."

Men can be heard shouting not far behind them.

"Tuk!" Ilapara cries.

She jumps when he gasps and abruptly sits up, his eyes flinging open.

The relief almost makes her weep, a feeling quickly supplanted by anger. "What the hell were you thinking? Are you trying to get us killed?"

He looks at her, eyes still wide as if in disbelief, his irises shining as bright blue as the mixture he imbibed. "I know how to fix everything," he says.

"What?"

He leaps to his feet and looks around the trees, a dimpled smile animating his face. Then he stops and points. "This way."

At first Ilapara can only gape as she watches him walk away. She picks herself up from the ground, dusting her knees. "Where the devil are you going? Tuk!"

Suddenly he tracks back to her and takes her hands in his, pressing them together between his calloused palms, bright-blue eyes looking deep into hers.

"Do you trust me?" he says.

Her anger deflates, though she remains confused. "Of course I do."

"Then follow me."

A younger version of Ilapara would have resisted him. The version she is now lets him take her hand and lead her away.

Dear Ama, she thinks as they run deeper into the jungles, *I better not regret this.*

3: Aneniko

Niko's thoughts are too preoccupied for the Void's usual bleakness to affect him as his disembodied consciousness soars on the wings of Alinata's ravens across grasslands, rivers, and grainfields.

They streak over multiple parties of mounted riders galloping like demons along the gravel roads below, and Niko becomes even more anxious when he spots Chief VaSiningwe and his retinue of Ajaha at the head of the pack, the afternoon sunlight flashing on their spears and polished red steel. They're almost at the kraal's large gates by the time Alinata flies over them and banks up toward the Hill Complex.

What's gotten them so agitated? Niko wonders, his imagination running wild.

The tribe's largest kraal is less a village than a city, sprawling down a grassy hill and into a valley. Its various complexes generally become more ancient as they ascend the hill, though every wall in the kraal was built of granite drystone—bricks of stone held together with no mortar, as is typical of Yerezi architecture. The roads winding through the streets were themselves paved in stone and were old long before Niko's ancestors started calling themselves Siningwe.

The ravens carry him over the shingled rooftops of the Library of the Foremothers and finally descend onto a central plaza. He feels a nauseating shift as his body transits from the Void and back into the mortal plain, his sandals and the end of his spear on solid flagstone, the Asazi Alinata standing next to him in a busy plaza.

Asazi are everywhere, radiant in their beads and red steel and pretty face paints as they go about their errands. Most other Ajaha his age might have taken a moment to admire them; as it is, Niko can barely stop himself from breaking into a run so he can interrogate the queen.

"Her Majesty awaits us in her study," Alinata says, her hazel eyes looking squarely ahead. "We must go."

Buildings with colonnades of stone pillars and tall windows of yellow stained glass surround the plaza. One side leads up a wide, multi-level stairway to the queen's palace, the most elevated structure in the kraal.

As they begin striding toward the stairway, a second flock of ravens descends from the skies and comes together right next to them, delivering the other two members of the queen's honor guard: a slender, sandy-skinned beauty whose hair falls all the way down to her back in a single braid, and a bull-necked, spear-carrying Ajaha whose ceremonial pauldron was cast into the head of a gnu, Khaya-Nyati's totem animal. They immediately fall into step beside Niko, and he narrowly avoids scowling at the grin that animates the Ajaha's features.

"How goes, Bra Niko?" the Ajaha says.

"Vitari," Niko says with a civil nod.

"Is it true what they're saying?" Vitari says. "That you're finally joining the Asazi? Good for you, mzi. I think you'll look very splendid in beads and skirts." Vitari grins wider at his own joke, like he hasn't told it several times already.

He and Niko are of a similar height, but Vitari hasn't been shy about drinking muscle-building tonics to make himself bulge like a hulking gorilla. Even his face is veiny and muscular.

"Don't test me right now, mzi," Niko tells him as they begin climbing up the stairway. "I'm not in the mood."

"No? But all the boys will salivate. Don't you think so, Neropa?"

Neropa sighs. "Don't mind the fool," she says to Niko. "He's just jealous of your good looks and popularity."

Like Alinata, Neropa exudes guile and moves with the grace of a snake in water, but where Niko has often found the queen's favorite apprentice to be cold and unapproachable, Neropa has a flirtatious nature and a whimsical sense of humor.

Next to her, Vitari releases a huff. "Why do you keep wasting your breath? He'll never be into you. I reckon I'm closer to his type than you'll ever be. Your eyes should be over here." He wiggles his eyebrows, smug as a hippo in a pool of mud.

"I'd sooner bathe in acid," Neropa says.

"I'd sooner infect myself with a flesh-eating plague," Niko agrees.

"I'd sooner roll around in a nest of fire ants," she says.

"I'd sooner feed my manhood to a meat grinder," he says.

Vitari bellows with laughter. "Say what you will. You both want me."

As they reach the palace's wide entrance, Alinata's patience snaps. "Must you always act like children? Be mindful of where you are. We're not here to play games."

She storms off while Niko and the others stare after her, surprised.

"What the devil is her problem?" Vitari says.

"Please don't piss her off any further." Neropa visibly shudders. "I have to live with her."

They say no more and follow Alinata down the palace's hallways of stone, which are heavily guarded and patrolled by Ajaha from every clan in full regalia. When they finally enter the queen's study, Niko's skin is tingling with anticipation. By now he's stood in the queen's presence more times than he can count, but his breath still catches as he glimpses her beyond a wide desk of pristine, bone-white witchwood, standing out on the stone balcony, a graceful silhouette against the pale afternoon sky.

"Irediti Ariishe," he says and bows his head, pressing his fist against his chest. Vitari mimics him, while the two Asazi clasp their hands in front of them and bob once in womanly bows.

She turns around to look them over, and Niko is once again struck by the force of her presence. Her unblemished ocher skin seems to shine like it was rubbed with glitter. Her gown of golden silk and plates of red steel is of a kind a warrior-mystic queen might wear to battle. A collar of spikes stands erect around and behind her neck, while a large ruby gemstone hangs above her plunging neckline. Her crimson head wrap is arranged so that it towers, adorned by a sinuous copper circlet that sits above her forehead.

"Good. I've been waiting for you," she says. "Would that you'd arrived sooner, but I suppose it couldn't be helped. Come closer, children."

As one, the four of them move around her table and join her out on the balcony, where they're graced by her scent, something subtle yet compelling. She's backdropped by the kraal's Valley Complex beyond the stone parapet, rising from the earth down the hill like the bones of an ancient carcass. Already a knot of people can be seen gathering around the Circle of the Elders as the chiefs arrive with their attendants.

"I understand you were victorious in fending off an Umadi incursion into Khaya-Siningwe, Aneniko," the queen says, and he feels a modest surge of pride.

"I am your faithful servant, Your Majesty," he says. "The enemies have strange weapons that shoot spears of fire, but they've yet to prevail over us."

While Vitari eyes Niko with poorly masked envy, the queen clucks her tongue. "Those weapons are becoming a nuisance."

"Who's responsible for their appearance, Your Majesty?" Niko asks, unable to withhold his curiosity.

"Strangers from the East," she replies. "Beyond the waters of the Inoetera. They've been arriving along the coast with increasing frequency, giving exotic armaments to whoever will take them."

"But why would they do this?" Niko asks, and her answer is more detailed than he expected.

"I believe the world beyond our shores is now at war with itself, Aneniko, East fighting with West, and that it is their intention to open a new theater of war right here in the Redlands. To wit, I believe the Easterners are attempting to recruit proxies in anticipation of an imminent Western invasion. And while there's much to be said for an ally who is generous with new weapons and technologies, we cannot sit idly by as they continue to arm our enemies." The queen's eyes glimmer like the edge of a sharpened knife. "We may be forced to take control of the eastern seaboard south of the Yontai and perhaps much of Umadiland."

Niko's blood races at the promise in her voice. Something is changing. *Vengeance. Retribution against the Umadi. War.* It can't come too soon.

The sunlight catches on the wings of a great metal eagle banking around the valley. Khaya-Sikhozi's clan totem is so big it hardly looks like it should be able to fly, but it alights with grace onto one of the eight monoliths surrounding the Circle of the Elders, joining four other totems that have already settled down onto their elevated perches atop the monoliths.

"I'll need the four of you to keep the peace today," the queen says. "I sincerely hope not, but a demonstration of strength might become necessary. And since your strength is a reflection of my own, I want to leave no doubt that challenging me is not wise."

The queen extends her arms, which glimmer with bangles of copper, red steel, and moongold. "Come forward, Aneniko and Vitari. Take my hands so I may strengthen the gifts of your blood."

They hesitate only for a second. Niko almost shivers when his palm makes contact with the queen's right forearm, her cold bangles pressing up against his wrist as she grabs onto him in turn. Vitari takes the queen's other arm, and he and Niko share a curious glance.

"We have always thought of our ancestral gift as being of two natures," the queen says. "Feminine and masculine. Mind and body. Logic and instinct. Sorcery and strength. This belief has shaped our relationship with magic for centuries and, in many ways, our traditions. It so happens that we were not entirely wrong. There *is* a duality. But what we didn't understand, perhaps what we forgot, is that this duality need not be sundered into its constituent halves. It can be wholly contained within the same person."

As the queen speaks, there is a melodious ringing sound, like the chime of a glass struck gently by metal, and then her crown and both her eyes incandesce with a white-hot glow. Her cosmic shards light up beneath Niko's palm, and he feels her skin getting warmer.

"The world beyond our borders is in a state of flux. To survive, we shall have to adapt—to *change*—and this is rarely easy," she says. "Aneniko, Vitari, I now unleash within you the full strength of your ancestors so you may be the pillars of this tribe, the instruments our people will need to not only survive the coming changes but to flourish, to reach greater heights."

And all at once the heat coming off her skin flares to the strength of an open flame. Niko's eyes water from the pain, but he remains motionless, his grip steady, his expression firm as a bar of steel. *I've known greater pain than this,* he tells himself. *Better this heat than the thorns that pierce my heart.*

The queen keeps holding them. Sweat pours down Niko's forehead, but he refuses to submit. Vitari emits a grunt and bends as though his knees are about to buckle. Niko's vision blanks out.

And then she lets go, and he has to lean on his spear for balance as the world spins around him. The pain drains from his palm, and when he looks over at Vitari, he is taken aback by the crimson shadows he sees pouring out of the ranger's eyes. They vanish in the next heartbeat;

Vitari blinks and shakes his head like he's waking himself up, and it's as if the shadows were never there.

Niko opens his mouth, then closes it. The queen's circlet has stopped glowing, and so have her eyes. He could almost believe he imagined the last thirty seconds, except something has changed within him, a certain esoteric wisdom now swimming through his veins like a virus.

What manner of sorcery was that?

"Now you are ready," the queen says. "Change is coming to the Plains, my children, and you will be its harbingers." She looks at her Asazi and nods. "Alinata, Neropa, to the Circle we go."

Niko can only grit his jaw as he is transposed into the Void once more and they lift off the balcony in a thundering cloud of black wings.

An ancient circular amphitheater grows in their field of view as they approach the Valley Complex, eight identical pillars of granite stone towering over its walls.

Massive tronic beasts have claimed a pillar each—an eagle, an owl, a hyena, a gnu, a meerkat, a macaque, and a gazelle—seven of them in total, sitting at the tops of their monoliths like a pantheon of theriomorphic gods. Only one pillar remains empty; the ravens fly over it, then down into the theater, across a level, circular arena filled with sand, before finally fluttering together in front of a high-backed throne of stone. The next thing Niko knows, he's standing next to Alinata on the queen's right, while Neropa and Vitari appear to her left, the five together facing the crowds that have gathered in the theater.

A palpable silence descends as everyone rises to stand.

The chiefs are already there, each dressed in the black loincloth, ornamented red steel, and traditional headdress of his station. Seven of them have taken the thrones beneath their respective totems, each one surrounded by his retinue of advisers, his clan mystic seated on a second throne to his left.

Only the monolith above Chief VaSiningwe remains bare, and so does the throne next to him. But he has come with his brother, General Deitari, and the commanding staff of Khaya-Siningwe's cavalry. The heat Niko sees smoldering in their eyes worsens the anxious tingle in his fingers.

A few dozen Asazi have gathered on the tiers directly beneath the queen's throne. He spots Nimara's large mass of curly hair among them, and it's like she can feel his gaze on the back of her head, because she almost immediately turns to look up at him. She was summoned here to further her studies after the queen sent a surrogate mystic to serve Khaya-Siningwe, so he hasn't seen much of her these last several months. But she's not a member of the Asazi leadership, so he's not sure why she'd be here.

They smile as they look at each other but break eye contact when Vitari steps forward to announce the queen at the top of his voice. "All hail Irediti, queen of the plains! All hail AmaYerezi, anointed daughter of the moon!"

"Irediti Ariishe," the Circle responds all together.

The queen steps forward and gestures for everyone to sit. All obey except the designated guards who've formed cordons around each retinue. The honor guard also remains standing behind the queen as she begins her speech, and the first thing she says sends a bolt of electricity down Niko's spine.

"Almost nine moons ago, an Umadi Black mystic attacked VaSiningwe's kraal with evil spirits from the netherworld, killing twenty-seven of his people and wounding many others. The witch escaped before she could face justice, but the wounds she inflicted remain with us to this day."

An angry jingle rises from beneath the empty monolith as the Siningwe Ajaha strike the ground repeatedly with the butts of their spears. Niko joins them, the force of his own sudden fury taking him by surprise.

"Death to the Umadi!" shouts a ranger, and Niko adds his voice to the answering cries.

The queen doesn't speak until the racket ebbs. "I hear you, Yerezi-kin. You are furious, and rightly so. We all are. Yet I must now stoke an even greater fury within you, for it has been revealed to me that the crime was even worse than we thought. Yerezi-kin, the Umadi witch was little more than an assassin. Paid for by one of our own."

The amphitheater falls still.

"Your ears do not deceive you," the queen says to her spellbound audience. "It was one of us who invited the witch. One of us who orchestrated the deaths of our tribespeople, and that traitor is *here*, right now."

Only through an enormous feat of self-control does Niko remain silent. The rangers in the Circle shift restlessly on their feet, however, each group eyeing the others suspiciously. Across the amphitheater, VaSiningwe rises to his imposing height, made greater by his spike-maned leopard headdress.

"How do you know this?" he bellows.

The queen nods at someone seated in the tiers beneath her throne, and everyone watches as a girl no older than thirteen slowly gets up with the aid of a white staff. A crown of beads sits on her bald scalp, a stripe of white paint running down the center of her face. From Niko's point of view, it appears her eyes might be closed.

Then she opens them, and there's an audible gasp as day becomes night. On their pedestals, the totems roar and shriek in agitation.

"Tell the Summer Leopard what you are," the queen commands the girl.

In the unnatural gloom, her eyes are black sinkholes with halos of light that move like water circling a drain. The suns must still be shining in the skies, but it's as if a pall of black smoke has blanketed the amphitheater and all the world's light has been drawn into the whirl-pools around the girl's gaze.

"I am the Oracle," she says. "I am our tribe's first soothsayer. I gave up the sight of flesh so I could know the dark sight, and when my true eyes were opened, I saw in the warp and weft of time a conspiracy to take your chiefdom, VaSiningwe. I saw the identities of those who sought your destruction."

The entire Siningwe cohort is now on its feet. "Who are they?" the chief demands. "Show them to us!"

"Thank you, revered Oracle," the queen cuts in before the girl can speak. "That will be all."

And just as quickly as it came, the pall that blotted out the suns evaporates, and a murmur spreads across the Circle as the girl who called herself the Oracle settles back down, her eyes closed.

"You would deny me justice, AmaYerezi?" VaSiningwe shouts.

"I would give it to you, Great Leopard," the queen replies. "But first let us give the traitors the chance to reveal themselves."

Niko's heart pounds like a drum as he waits. Glowers get traded all across the Circle, whispers exchanged, but no one comes forward.

Then AmaSikhozi, the mystic seated beneath the eagle totem, breaks the silence. "How can we have a soothsayer, Your Majesty?" she says, not bothering to conceal her doubt. "Is that not ancestral knowledge belonging to an extinct people?"

"That is no longer the case," says the queen. "As you have seen with your own eyes, we now wield the power of divination, and it has revealed to us traitors in our midst."

"I say the traitor is the one standing before us as queen."

Mouths drop everywhere. Beneath the hyena totem, a woman of swarthy and slender beauty rises from her throne, her perfect teeth on display in a sneer. Above her the totem twitches its three metal horns and growls.

"You've really done it, haven't you, Irediti?" she says. "You've got everyone wrapped around your finger, just like you always wanted. But why don't you tell them the truth about that crown on your head? Tell them how you *really* got it."

The rangers in the Circle begin to reposition themselves. Like the Siningwe contingent, all the men beneath the hyena totem have stood up. Most look worried, but some have hostile eyes for the Siningwe retinue. Niko suffers the itch to leap down and join his clansmen, but he stays put, knowing that his proper place is next to his queen.

"Thank you for revealing yourself, AmaSibere," the queen says amid shocked gasps. "You stand accused of conspiring with an Umadi witch to murder your own tribespeople for political gain. You unlawfully traded a valuable Yerezi artifact for her savagery. And when your plan failed, you sent the same witch to attack VaSiningwe's son, Musalodi, as he made his way to Yonte Saire."

Blood roars loudly into Niko's ears at the sound of that name, and he almost doesn't hear the clamorous protests that erupt all over the amphitheater.

"Are you saying she killed my son, Your Majesty?"

VaSiningwe doesn't shout, but his question is clear enough to silence the din as everyone holds their breaths in wait. Niko could almost explode from the pressure that piles up in his chest.

"She was not successful, Great Leopard," the queen replies. "Even as a newly awoken mystic, Musalodi proved too powerful for the witch and her minions. He was also under the protection of my apprentice, Alinata. They made it safely to the city and did not hear from the witch again. But this does not absolve AmaSibere of her guilt."

Niko looks to his side; Alinata keeps her eyes forward, though her somber expression tells him volumes. *She was with him in the days before his death. She was with him, and she failed to protect him.*

Following that bitter thought is a guilty one: *At least she was there. Where the devil were you?*

"Lies!" shouts the chief of Khaya-Sibere, a short, thickset man wearing a cloak with the head of a tronic hyena. "What evidence do you have besides spurious divinations?"

"Let the woman speak for herself," shouts the chief beneath the gnu totem of Khaya-Nyati, earning murmurs of agreement from the other chiefs. "AmaSibere, how do you answer to these grave accusations?"

"I deny them," she says emphatically. "They are malicious lies spun by a would-be tyrant bent on removing all threats to her crown. If anyone is to blame for your son's death, VaSiningwe, it is she. His death is the only way she could be wearing that thing on her head."

VaSiningwe's glower does not relent. "I specifically remember you threatening my son after he revealed what he'd done. *You* wanted him killed, AmaSibere. And it is no secret that the hyenas have always coveted my lands. If you are responsible for the attack in *any* way . . ."

"I am not. And it was not your son I feared but how Irediti would use him. I was trying to stop exactly what is now happening! Don't any of you see what she's doing?" AmaSibere gestures accusingly at the Oracle. "Already abominations walk among us! If we let her continue, she won't stop until she's enslaved us all!"

The hoary old mystic beneath the macaque totem rises from her throne, wrapping her blanket shawl tighter around her shoulders. "Irediti is queen, AmaSibere, chosen by this very Circle, and you will accord her the respect she deserves."

AmaSibere lifts her chin defiantly. "She is no queen. She is a murderer. She deserves only contempt."

"Bring forth the Chalice of Truth." VaSiningwe lifts the spear of his chiefdom and slams the blunt end upon the ground. There is a rumble like that of a rockfall—the sound of a chief casting his vote in the Circle. "Let them both drink of its waters; then we shall know which of them speaks falsely."

The graying warrior chief beneath the meerkat totem rises and performs the same gesture with his spear, causing a second boom. "I agree.

These accusations are much too serious to be accepted without definitive evidence. Your Majesty, for the sake of peace, you and AmaSibere must both drink of the Chalice so we may know the truth."

Five other chiefs rise and bring thunder to the Circle with their spears—more than enough to force the queen's compliance. Chief VaSibere, the lone holdout, remains mulish.

"I won't stand for this! My clan mystic has done no wrong."

"The Circle has decided, Great Hyena," the queen tells him. "We have no choice." She looks down and nods at the seated members of the Asazi Directorate, who are the keepers of the Chalice. "The Chalice of Truth has been requested. Please bring it to the Circle."

"It's not happening!" VaSibere unsheathes his sword and takes a step down, moving to stand in front of his mystic. "You can't just accuse someone of a crime and then demand that they drink of the Chalice. That's injustice!"

"This is a simple matter, Great Hyena," says the queen. "If she is innocent, as she claims, the Chalice shall not harm her but harm me instead."

"*If* she is innocent, Your Majesty? The only evidence you have of her guilt are the divinations of a strange girl!"

VaSiningwe also takes a step down from his throne, his rangers parting for him, his brother close by his side. "She will drink from the Chalice, or I swear by Ama there will be blood in the Circle this very day."

"Then let there be blood! Sibere-kin! Defend your mystic!"

"Siningwe, to me!"

In the split second before pandemonium erupts, a command pierces into Niko's mind: *Reveal your strength. There shall be no bloodshed today.*

His reflexes take over, something stirs in his mind, and he shoots forward—

There's a flash as the world blurs into a tunnel of red shadow, and when he blinks next, he's standing on the sands in the Circle, facing the Sibere rangers, who all stop dead as their eyes widen in shock.

51

"Stay back, Yerezi-kin," he says, lowering the gleaming point of his spear in threat. "I don't wish to harm you."

The rangers were ready to charge across the Circle just heartbeats ago; now they gape at him like he's transformed into a fire-breathing tikoloshe. He stands resolute, though he is himself astonished. How did he move so fast? He didn't feel the contraction of his limbs; he didn't see himself navigating through the tiers of benches beneath the queen's throne or running across the sands. He simply flew forward as though he'd temporarily become a weightless shadow.

Vitari must have moved just as fast, because he's blocking the Siningwe rangers from advancing any farther, and they, too, look shocked by the feat.

"Ajaha casting spells in the Circle," AmaSibere says in the stunned silence, her voice ringing with vindication. "This is the sacrilege Irediti has brought upon us."

Ravens flutter into the Circle, and the queen and her apprentices rematerialize on the sands between Niko and Vitari.

"AmaSibere is right about one thing," the queen announces. "I had everything to gain from Musalodi's sacrifice. We all did. Because of his pilgrimage to Yonte Saire, I and every queen who comes after me shall know mastery over many ancestral gifts, including our own. What you have all just witnessed was the true power of an Ajaha unleashed. Power that I can grant to any of you, that I can also take away."

"Abomination!" cries the chief of Khaya-Sibere.

"Observe." Light reflects off the queen's crown, and AmaSibere cries out in surprise; then many of the rangers in front of Niko fall to their knees, their spears slipping from limp fingers, their eyes dilating with horror. At the same time the hyena totem stops snarling and goes rigid and lifeless on its perch, while beneath it Chief VaSibere looks at his arms like he doesn't recognize them.

"What have you done to us?" he howls.

"I have taken from AmaSibere the power to grant blessings," the queen says. "I will restore her power as soon as she sips from the Chalice and proves her innocence. Alternatively, she can confess her guilt and let the Circle decide her fate."

As the crowds mutter in disbelief, Niko's head spins at the implications. If the queen can take and give ancestral talents so easily, no tribe will be able to stand against the Yerezi people. *Umadiland will burn like chaff.*

He relaxes into a nonthreatening posture. "AmaSibere," he says in a gentle but firm voice, "the Circle has commanded you to drink from the Chalice. Please step down and comply." *Please don't make me drag you down.*

The Sibere rangers regard him with hate, but they are mere men now, robbed of the strength of their mystic's lunar blessing, while his has been enriched in ways he doesn't yet understand. He desperately hopes he won't have to, but he knows he could face them all on his own and not suffer a scratch.

She protests again and again, and so does her chief, but AmaSibere eventually comes down into the Circle, where she faces off against the queen. Her Majesty remains placid even as the other woman stares at her with pure spite.

A senior member of the Asazi Directorate comes between them with the Chalice of Truth, a relic of moongold brought to the tribe by a Bloodway pilgrim from a bygone age. "The Chalice is ready," she says.

"You first," AmaSibere spits.

"As you wish." The queen accepts the Chalice, then waits for AmaSibere to state her accusations.

"You murdered VaSiningwe's boy for that crown. I *know* you did."

"I did not," the queen says plainly. "Musalodi was attacked during a violent riot on the streets of Yonte Saire. He later succumbed to a severe chest injury. This is the truth."

The goblet's surface shimmers as she brings it to her lips, and then she tips it back and swallows down several gulps of whatever liquid it contains. She wipes her mouth and proffers it back to the Asazi director, but the woman waits, watching the queen closely. Only after some several seconds does she reach forward to accept the Chalice with obvious relief.

"The words Her Majesty has spoken are true," she announces to the amphitheater, and a knot of tension Niko wasn't aware of loosens in his chest.

"It is your turn, AmaSibere," the queen says.

AmaSibere licks her lips as she eyes the Chalice. "You've tampered with it. You must have. I know what you did."

"The Chalice is incorruptible," comes VaSiningwe's unsympathetic voice. "Drink, or admit your guilt."

"What do you know of magic?" she hisses at him. "For all we know, she could be controlling it with that abomination on her head."

"For someone who claims to be innocent," the mystic beneath the eagle remarks, "you're doing a fine job of looking guilty. Drink from the Chalice, AmaSibere. We tire of your dithering."

AmaSibere looks around the Circle like a hunted woman, her face contorting with hatred. "Curse you, Irediti." She snatches the Chalice from the director and takes a big gulp, then extends it back, eyes wild with triumph. "There. Are you happy? I'm in—"

She drops the Chalice, her words dying on her tongue, and the crowds gasp as AmaSibere's skin blackens to the color of soot. Burns and blisters erupt all over her face. She scratches frantically at her throat, sinking to her knees, her head tilting up to the sky, nails clawing skin off her neck in strips, and when she tries to scream, she gurgles out a thick, inky fluid. A fetid stench fills the air as her flesh putrefies, rotting off until bone and tendon are visible. No one moves to help her as she collapses to the ground, where she continues to convulse and wither away. Only once she is little more than bones does she fall still, like the rest of the Circle.

Niko averts his eyes, nauseated.

"The Chalice has found AmaSibere a liar and rendered judgment," says the solemn director. "May her soul find redemption on the Infinite Path."

"You filthy son of a dog!" VaSiningwe comes down into the arena, glaring death at the now-dejected VaSibere. "You couldn't face me like a real man? You had to hide behind the skirts of Umadi witches?" His fierce gaze swivels to the queen. "Your Majesty, you must let me face him in single combat. The spirits of my slain kin demand it."

The queen shakes her head. "I cannot claim to understand how you feel right now, VaSiningwe, but violence should not beget violence. It is not the Yerezi way."

"To the pits with the Yerezi way!"

"Give me a chance, Great Leopard. I can solve this to your satisfaction without bloodshed."

VaSiningwe fumes, but his silence is the assent she needs. She holds her head high as she turns to face the Sibere chief. "VaSibere, you stand accused of conspiring with your mystic to attack VaSiningwe's stronghold with the intent of coercing me into giving you control of his lands. How do you plead to this charge?"

"Why bother?" the man says, slumping onto his throne. "Do whatever you must."

"Very well. May the council of chiefs step into the Circle to deliberate its verdict—barring you, VaSibere."

"What must we deliberate?" says the chief beneath the owl totem. "We have seen the evidence of his guilt. Deliver your sentence, Your Majesty, and let us be done with this terrible affair."

"Are you all of the same mind?" she asks, and all seven chiefs strike the earth vigorously with their spears. The ensuing rumble lasts several seconds.

"The council of chiefs has judged you guilty, VaSibere," the queen says. "By the power vested in me I hereby strip you of your chiefdom and banish you and your house to the Qotoba Coast. You are not to return to the Plains for one hundred years; the punishment for doing so before your exile has expired will be death."

The Sibere chief remains silent, but a young Ajaha next to him exclaims, "You can't be serious!"

The queen ignores him. "Moreover, Clan Sibere is hereby abolished. Your kraal will be dismantled. All administrative duties of your former chiefdom will be transferred over to VaSiningwe, who is now charged with the task of integrating both clans under his totem. He will assume command of your cavalry, which he must assimilate into his."

An uproar brews among the Sibere rangers, but the queen's patience is at an end. "Silence!" she shouts, her voice carried by a spell that makes the air itself shudder.

The rangers obey.

"The young Asazi Nimara of Clan Siningwe has completed her Axiom. It has been approved by the scholars at the Library of the Foremothers, and the Asazi Directorate have authorized her awakening." The queen looks toward her throne, where the Asazi are seated. "Nimara, rise so you may be seen."

The girl stands with her hands clasped in front of her, the taut look on her face suggesting she didn't know she'd be singled out.

"Tomorrow," the queen declares, "Nimara will face the redhawk and awaken as the new AmaSiningwe. All former Sibere Ajaha and Asazi are to take her blessing should they wish to continue serving in their capacities. Those who refuse shall be stripped of their ranks and privileges. And any former Sibere Asazi who attempts to awaken without permission from the Directorate will face immediate execution. This is not a negotiation."

This time no one dares challenge her.

"Since the original Siningwe totem remains at large," she continues, "a new crested leopard will be fashioned for Nimara using parts from the now-decommissioned hyena totem. The staff belonging to the hyena shall also be handed over to the new AmaSiningwe. This is my judgment, and it is final."

The Sibere contingent has wilted. Their chief has nothing more to say.

Amid their defeated silence, the queen looks at AmaSibere's desiccated corpse, then rakes the amphitheater with her eyes. "Let no one here forget the twenty-seven souls who perished due to Sibere treachery. VaSibere chose to destroy his fellow tribesman in order to increase his influence; it is only fitting that he now suffer the very fate he sought to bring down on his neighbor." She regards the Siningwe chief. "Are you appeased, Great Leopard?"

He has just been made the wealthiest and most powerful chief in the Plains, but the rage in his eyes has not dimmed. He levels a finger at the former Sibere chief from a distance. "Be gone from these lands by dark tomorrow, dog, or I will personally take your head off with my blade."

Disgraced, the Sibere rangers shamble out the exit, many in tears, though their chief does his best to leave the Circle with dignity, his chin lifted, shoulders squared.

The nerve, Niko thinks, violence stirring inside him. Salo would probably still be alive were it not for this man. Why should he walk free?

Before he does something he'll regret, Niko reins in his new power; then he returns to his post next to the queen.

4: Ilapara

The KiYonte Kingdom

She's an observer, an intruder, lurking unseen behind a marble pillar along a porch with a view of a large garden. The details are indistinct and tinged white as if seen through a curtain of fog, and the sounds are muffled as if heard from outside a sealed chamber. Yet the scene unfolds around Ilapara more lucidly than normal for a dream, and however hard she tries, she can't remember how she got here.

She takes a cautious peek behind the pillar and sees Tuk looking around himself with open bewilderment. She almost reveals herself to him, but an odd feeling tells her to stay put.

Farther along the marble porch, a glittering woman in a scarlet-and-violet gown rests on a long chair like a queen. Her eyes are hidden behind thin golden strings that fall halfway down her face from a circlet. She smiles warily at Tuk, like she's not certain how he'll receive her.

"Hello, brother."

Tuk turns to look at her, putting his back toward Ilapara so that she can't see his face, but she notices his hands curling into fists by his sides. He quickly relaxes them. "Sister, how very glad I am to see you."

The woman's red lips move into a cynical smile. "That's why you should have gotten those ghastly eyes removed, my dear. Makes lying easier."

"Oh, I don't mind. Being an open book is quite liberating." Tuk looks about himself for a second time. "So what is this place? A dream?"

"Yes and no. We *are* actually speaking. And if it looks real and feels real, then isn't it as good as real?"

Ilapara is struck with sudden recognition: a woman at the New Year's Feast, dressed in violet and scarlet and a circlet with precious stones, sitting on a tiered stage among ten princes and seven high mystics.

Still hidden behind the pillar, Ilapara listens.

"You kidnapped me into a construct?" Tuk says. "I feel violated."

The woman snorts dismissively. "This could have only worked if your subconscious was willing to speak to me. I can't dream-cast you into a metaformic construct without your mind's consent."

Tuk folds his arms, tilting his head to one side. "How odd. Because I really meant it when I told you I never wanted to see your face again."

"And yet here you are."

Distantly, Ilapara feels herself turning onto her side on an uncomfortable surface, her eyes fluttering, her head pillowed on her hands. *I'm sleeping,* she thinks, but the dream fails to break.

"What do you want, *sister*?" Tuk says.

"Many things. But let's start with peace. I want to end this little tiff between us."

"Tiff?" Tuk takes a step forward. "I *know* you had something to do with what happened in Yonte Saire. My friend is dead because of you. This is no tiff. The next time I see you, I *will* kill you."

She studies him, then frowns as she leans back into her chair. "If you knew I was in the city, why didn't you come visit?"

"Who says I didn't?" Another slow step, then another. Tuk moves behind her chair, letting a hand trail along the backrest—a seemingly harmless action, though giving the impression that he could reach down to choke her. His irises are pitch black. "Who says I didn't sneak into your chambers in the Summit and wait until you were alone? Do you know how close to death you came, dear sister? I could have slit your throat and slipped away, and it would have been over for you."

"But you didn't," the woman says, to which Tuk fails to respond, moving away from the chair to stare at the gardens so that Ilapara is looking at his profile. "I don't blame you," says the woman. "I couldn't do it either."

He glances at her, surprise on his face.

"What? You don't think I had plenty of chances to have you killed? I knew where you lived, brother. I knew what you and your friends got up to. I knew *everything*."

He blinks, then shakes his head. "The steward Ruma Sato. He was your spy."

"An accusation I neither confirm nor deny."

"You haven't changed one bit," Tuk says.

"And neither have you. But it seems we're destined to revolve around each other no matter where—or when—we are. Which is why I think it's foolish for us to keep fighting."

Tuk stares at the woman. "Why am I here?"

"I want to help you," she says.

"I don't want your help."

"Even if it means getting your friend back?"

Behind her pillar, Ilapara holds her breath.

A quiet, dangerous edge enters Tuk's voice. "Why would you care about him?"

"You must know by now what he was," the woman says. "Truth be told, his death was . . . a waste. Tragic, really. If I'd known what the high mystic was planning, I wouldn't have worked with him so closely." She laughs, a short, ironic burst. "I thought I was using him, but in the end, I was just a tool in his scheme for power."

"You damned fool," Tuk says. "You created a monster. Millions of people will die before he's done with this continent. And for what?"

"Which is why I want to help you," the woman presses. "I made a mistake, but I'm not *evil*. You know this. All I want is a world in which what was done to us is never done to anyone else. Is that wrong?"

"I'm finished with this conversation," Tuk says, turning away from the woman.

Her lips curl in disgust. "Go ahead. Leave. It's what you're good at."

Tuk stops, his face flushed with emotion. "You'll always hold that over my head, won't you."

"You broke your promise to me, Tuksaad. You left me when I needed you and never looked back."

"I was a toy!" Tuk shouts, turning back around to face the woman. "Bought and paid for. I didn't choose to leave!"

"Ah, but your master was kind to you, wasn't he? Gave you a good life. You were happy. Tell me I'm lying."

Tuk swallows, saying nothing.

"And in all that time, did you even think for one moment to tell him you had a sister you'd left behind? Did you even tell him my name, Tuk?"

"I told you, I—"

"You were afraid, yes. And that's just it, isn't it? Your fear of losing everything was greater than your love for me. But while you lived like a prince, I was a plaything for your master's friends. Do you know the abuses I suffered?"

"I suffered too! Yes, I kept silent about you, and yes, I'll regret that for the rest of my life, but maybe it was for the best! Look at where I ended up, Luksatra. Whatever wrongs I did to you, I paid for them."

"That's for *me* to decide. Not you." The woman takes a moment to regain her composure, leaning against the backrest of her chair and breathing in deeply. "And that's not why I asked you here. I'm here to offer my help—" She cuts herself off as her eyes pivot in Ilapara's direction. "Who's there? Tuk, did you bring a visitor?"

The dream disintegrates as Ilapara awakens, her memories flooding back. She and Tuksaad were trudging through the jungles when night and exhaustion fell upon them and they decided to make camp. They fell asleep next to a fire, hours ago now, since the skies above the canopy have lightened with the arrival of dawn.

She sits up and is met by a startled pair of hazel-brown eyes staring at her from across the smoldering campfire. Knowing Tuk as well as she does, she can tell from that color he's concerned and guilty as the pits.

"Were you . . . ," he sputters. "Was that . . ."

She aims a finger at him. "You have some explaining to do. I know that woman, Tuk. She was the Crocodile's wife. Why was she calling you her brother? And don't even think about lying to me."

His eyes turn a baffled yellow. "How did you . . ." Then they fall to the pair of ivory locator pendants on her chest, one of which is linked to an identical pendant dangling around his neck. "Oh," he says. "Shit."

"Answer the question, Tuksaad. Was that woman your *sister*? And what the devil did she have to do with Salo?"

"I can explain."

"Then explain!"

"I will when you stop looking at me like you want to strangle me!"

"I do want to strangle you! All this time, Tuk! By Ama." Ilapara springs up to her feet and starts to pace. "How could you keep such a secret from me? You're just like Alinata."

"Hey. Don't compare me to *her*."

"Birds of a feather," she retorts.

Tuk gets up, too, his eyes murky and indignant. "Do you really think I'd do anything to hurt you? To hurt Salo?"

"I don't know *what* to think, Tuk. Salo . . ." She chokes up as she finally lets herself confront the truth. "Salo *died* because he was trying to stop the Crocodile, and now I find out his widow is your sister?"

Tuk looks down at the ground and kicks a discarded twig with the toe of his sandal. "I told you, I can explain."

Ilapara takes a deep breath. "I'm listening."

"On the way," he says and crouches down to put out the dying fire. "We don't have much farther to go."

Tuk seems to know where he's headed, so she lets him walk ahead of her despite her misgivings. "Technically, she's not my sister," he says once they establish a good pace along what might be a hunter's trail. "I can't have a sister. I'm an atmech; I was made, not born. It's just that our blueprints were extracted from a pair of twins who lived centuries ago, and we were made at the same time. We also came to life with some of their memories. Flashes, really, but enough to recognize each other from that other life."

That makes her your sister in every meaningful definition of the word, Ilapara thinks.

"We were close at first," he continues. "We kept each other sane despite everything. And then . . . I guess you could say I failed her. I let her down, and she became resentful. Years later, when our maker helped us escape to the Enclave, our paths diverged. She changed herself. Changed her eyes so they wouldn't be like mine, found ways to hide her true nature. Used her wits and charm to make herself a fortune and buy her way into the Enclave's aristocracy."

He ducks beneath a branch leaning into the trail, and Ilapara quietly follows. She knows he lived as a bathhouse slave for years before a wealthy lord of the Empire adopted him and gave him the life of a prince. But it ended in tragedy when the lord's true sons murdered their father in a fit of jealousy, sending Tuk to an even worse place than the bathhouse he'd escaped.

The part he left out when he told her this tale was that he had a *sister*.

"When we started our lives in the Enclave, I'd just lived through months of abuse in the worst hellhole you can imagine," he says. "I wasn't in my right mind. I didn't notice the company she was keeping until it was too late. By the time I got my life together and joined the Vigilants, she was already a member of the Shadows. I think I told you about them."

"The secretive mystics who seek the destruction of the world," Ilapara says.

"I couldn't talk her out of it. She hadn't forgiven me for failing her, and the Shadows had filled her with all these . . . these *strange* ideas." Tuk sighs. "She'd already done some unforgivable things by that point. I had to cut my losses and move on with my life."

Ilapara takes a moment to process what he's told her. "Here's where things stop making sense. How the devil did you end up in Yonte Saire at the exact same time?"

"The odds aren't that low, actually," he says as he continues to pick his way along the trail. "Our sects are natural enemies. I crossed the Jalama because I sensed Vigilance wanted me to come here. And if Vigilance developed an interest in the Redlands, it makes sense that the Shadows would too."

Tuk stops and turns around to face Ilapara. His hazel eyes don't change their hue as he speaks—a sign that he's being truthful, Ilapara has deduced. When he lies, his irises dance through the color spectrum, and he's usually amused.

He's not amused right now. "I didn't know my sister was in the city until after the Requiem Moon, and by then it was already too late. In hindsight, I should have seen the signs a lot sooner—Higher technology appearing everywhere. How could I have missed it? How could I have been so blind?"

He blames himself, Ilapara realizes. *He's blamed himself this whole time.* Her anger goes out like a snuffed candle. "Did you really go to the Summit to kill her?"

"No one even saw me," he says, moisture collecting in his eyes. "I could have killed her and her husband. Maybe Salo would still be alive." A tear spills down his cheek, and he wipes it, bowing his head.

"You can't know that," Ilapara says. "Salo had already disappeared by then. At the end of the day, we all did our best. It just wasn't good enough."

His chest expands as he takes a deep breath, a determined look stealing over his features. "We'll fix things," he says. "We have to."

Doubt stirs in Ilapara's heart, but she follows him as they resume their trek through the dense equatorial forest, stepping lightly along a narrow trail that negotiates its way between hills and across streams. Thorny leaves scrape against them at every turn, the trees encroaching upon their path as though angry at being intruded on. As the suns rise higher in the sky, their light slants through the treetops in bright shafts of illuminated dust and pollen.

Occasionally, where the terrain allows, she catches a glimpse of a solitary structure of mammoth size soaring high above the forest canopy in the distance, a tower of giant vines spiraling up into the heavens as if to reach for something there. This isn't her first sighting of a vine tower, the Yontai's largest plant species—another one grew not far from the first resistance camp she joined—but the way it dwarfs everything around it takes the breath right out of her lungs.

She realizes they're heading in the tower's direction as they begin to descend into the valley where it grows. Its individual vines are so large she can see them even from miles away, interweaving with almost perfect symmetry to create a tower thicker at its base, twisting up into a thin spire at the top. A peculiar distortion of light hangs about the spire, like heat rising off a paved surface.

Not a welcome sight, and it puts Ilapara on edge.

They reach the valley floor, where the jungle's treetops obscure the tower from view. As they trek closer and closer to its base, Ilapara begins to lose her patience.

"Tuk, why does it look like we're walking toward that tower?"

"Because we are," Tuk says plainly, just as she fears.

"You do know the KiYonte have an aversion to them, don't you? I've heard rumors of unnatural monsters that lurk around the vines."

Laughter colors Tuk's voice. "They're not exactly wrong."

"And yet we're still approaching one like a pair of idiots."

"Do you trust me?"

I must be a fool, because I do. "I'm here, aren't I?"

"Aw, thanks. Just trust me awhile longer. I can't say how, but I believe the solution to our problems lies in the tower's vicinity."

Ilapara tries to imagine all the possible ways this might be true. A pond of moongold, maybe? A malaika to grant them wishes? Every idea she comes up with is as preposterous as the last.

"What did you see when you drank from that vial?" she asks. "Was it a voice? Did you actually speak to Vigilance?"

Tuk shakes his head. "He doesn't speak to us directly. Often, he gives us impressions. Images coupled with words. Sometimes a riddle. Other times a sensory experience, like a smell or a sound or the feeling of wind across your skin. And sometimes it's all of these."

"So it's subject to interpretation," Ilapara concludes.

"All language and communication is subject to interpretation," Tuk says. "Even the words we speak now are interpreted. But you can hone your mind, improve your vocabulary and your knowledge, so there's less chance of misunderstanding what someone is trying to tell you, no?"

Ilapara opens her mouth to answer, but Tuk goes still in front of her, raising a palm in a signal for her to stop. She obeys, looking around the trees. She sees nothing amiss, but the hairs on the back of her neck have gone up.

"What is it?"

"Stand very still," Tuk says. "We're being watched."

"Great." They're both unarmed, so if a predator is stalking them, they won't have many options beyond running for their lives.

The trees rustle and Ilapara tenses, preparing to flee or fight, but her heart stops beating as a four-legged beast taller than she is prowls into the open, its cyan-blue eyes beaming at her with an inner glow.

A leopard. Its white coat has spots the color of burnished copper. Its paws and claws are themselves a metalloid, much like copper, and so is the mane of spines haloing its head like a crown. Ilapara remains frozen as the tronic creature approaches them, its tongue lolling out, canines shining with the luster of polished daggers.

"Mukuni?" she and Tuk say at the same time.

He was built to gallop across grassy plains, but he seems at home in these jungles, which is a shock to Ilapara because the last she saw of the totem, he was a metal statue sitting next to the gates of their former Skytown residence. He'd been that way since the night of the Requiem Moon, when he'd battled against and killed an arcane lion, getting injured in the process. With his master dead, Ilapara thought he would have run back to the Plains by now.

He stops in front of them as if to block the way forward, a low growl coming from his throat.

"What's he doing here?" Ilapara whispers to Tuk. "Is he what we came to find?"

"I'm not sure," Tuk answers with a note of excitement.

"What do you mean, you're not sure?"

"Halt!" shouts a voice behind Mukuni, speaking in KiYonte. A lanky man with a receding hairline, dressed in a dashiki and pants of wax-dyed cloth, comes into view in the trees ahead. He brandishes a crudely made wooden staff with a conspicuous golden gemstone fastened to the head with wires. From the way he's holding that staff, Ilapara assumes it might be more than it seems. Other men appear behind him, armed with spears or swords. A camp must be somewhere close by.

"State your purpose, or our familiar will maul you to death."

"We come in peace," Tuk says, lifting both palms, a gesture Ilapara imitates.

"State your purpose," the man repeats.

"Your familiar is a Yerezi totem that belonged to a friend of ours," Tuk explains. "We . . . were told to seek his star beneath a tower of vines in the north. We came from a resistance camp about two days south of here. It was attacked by the emperor's legionnaires, but we escaped."

A heavy frown creases the man's forehead. "A star?" he says.

Tuk is less sure in his answer than Ilapara would like. ". . . Yes. A star. Our friend's star. I don't know exactly what that's supposed to mean, but I was given the impression you'd understand."

"I'm sorry, friend, but we have no 'star' for you here."

Tuk hesitates for a moment. "I don't understand. It has to be here. Your familiar's presence proves it."

"Tuk? Ilapara?" A young woman separates herself from behind the armed men and comes forward with a surprised look on her face. Ilapara recognizes her cloud of curly hair immediately.

"Tuliza?" It almost makes her dizzy how quickly her morning has gone from exasperating to surreal. "What are you doing here?"

The man with the staff looks askance at Tuliza. "You know these people?"

"Yes!" She runs forward, passing Mukuni like he's not a giant predator who could bite her in half, and enwraps Tuk in a hug.

"Hello, Tuliza," he says with a surprised laugh.

She comes for Ilapara next, who's still too mystified to do anything else but stand still as the woman embraces her.

"Ilapara! Wow. We keep running into each other in strange places, don't we." Tuliza looks at the man with the staff. "Father, these two were part of the team that rescued me and the king from the undercity. They were friends of the Yerezi mystic. The one whose soul we . . ." She stops, her perceptive eyes flitting between Tuk and Ilapara. "Did you say you're here for his 'star'?"

"Yes," Tuk says rather desperately. "Do you know what that is?"

She glances at her father, and they seem to exchange silent words. "I believe I do."

"Absolutely not," he says, and Ilapara notes the way he draws his staff back possessively.

"We always knew this moment would come, Father," Tuliza says. "We owe it to Her Majesty. This was her wish."

"And what of the security of this camp?"

"Engai's grace has always protected us. It will continue to do so."

He glares for a while, and then his shoulders slump. He turns around and starts to walk away, shaking his head. "Return to your posts," he says, and the armed men relax their postures and disperse into the trees.

Tuliza looks back at Ilapara and Tuk with a smile, though it isn't as bright as before. "Come. You must be tired and hungry after your journey. Our sanctuary isn't far from here."

As they make their way to the settlement, Mukuni following quietly behind, Tuliza's father interrogates Tuk on how they managed to find the camp. Tuk confesses—without raising more questions about himself—his affiliation with the Vigilants who once lived in Yonte Saire. Ilapara listens with one ear, paying more attention to her surroundings, which seem to grow stranger with every step.

The tree trunks are thicker in this part of the jungle and more spaced apart, though the canopy is dense enough to blot out much of the sunlight, meaning there's very little undergrowth. The vine tower is still some distance away, a mile perhaps, but already looms with the presence of a mountain, an enormous shape visible beyond the gaps in the canopy.

"What are you doing all the way out here?" she hears herself say.

"The vine tower is home to the Great Funkwe," Tuliza replies, moving closer so they can talk. "The Serpent of Endless Waters. She is the guardian of this valley and provided sanctuary for us when we came here after fleeing the city." Tuliza smiles, suddenly amused. "You know, it's just occurred to me that we might have you to thank for our presence here."

"Oh? How so?"

"Primeval Spirits almost never communicate with mundane folk. They either ignore us or, if we displease them, destroy us with natural disasters. We didn't expect the Great Funkwe to acknowledge us when we came to this valley, but she sensed the Eternity Crystals in our possession and knew that we were children of Engai, so she revealed herself to us."

Tuliza must notice Ilapara's confusion, because she goes on to ask, "Do you remember the crystals the king and I were carrying that night in the undercity?"

Ilapara casts her memory back to the night of the earthquake. She vaguely remembers the two young women holding unusually bright crystals, but they were all so busy trying to stay alive that there wasn't any time to ask questions.

"*Those* were the Eternity Crystals," Tuliza says. "And we wouldn't have gotten them without your help. So I guess we owe you a debt of gratitude."

"It was a combined effort, and for a good cause," Ilapara demurs. "But why did you leave the undercity? I know there are some nonconformist communities who chose to stay."

"Mainly? The Crystals. Had we stayed, the emperor would have seized them and used them to strengthen his tyranny. We couldn't let that happen." Tuliza stares fondly ahead at her father, who's still peppering Tuk with questions. "My father is also a proud, stubborn man who would die before he let someone else tell him how to live. He led more than a few sanctuaries out here. Many of us were unsure. Now we don't think we'll ever leave."

Ilapara is quietly stunned as they come to a small village built entirely of living trees. Some of the structures even seem to protrude right out of the boles, roots knitting together into spiraling staircases, branches gradually arching into roof beams or walkways that span over the village high above the forest floor.

It's the ubiquitous flowering vines, however, that bless the village with its breathtaking, dreamlike beauty. They creep up almost every branch and across every roof, their colorful, bulbous flowers glowing with a soft bioluminescence.

"As you can see," Tuliza says, gazing upon the village with pride, "the Great Funkwe has been good to us."

Men are seated in a circle in front of a shebeen as they drink beer from a clay pot, passing it to each other after a few sips. Ilapara earns a few lingering stares from them as she arrives with the rest of the party.

Gardens and orchards growing beside the tree houses brim with nuts, fruits, and vegetables so fat Ilapara's mouth salivates at the sight of them. Fortunately, she and Tuk are soon allowed to gorge themselves in the garden behind Tuliza's home, which she shares with her large family.

"Did you hear what Tuliza told me?" she asks Tuk. They have been given their privacy while they eat. All the furniture in the garden is made of interwoven vines that still look alive, including the table and chairs. The vine tower itself is visible through the canopy behind Tuliza's house, its spire shimmering as if seen through water.

"About the spirit?" Tuk says, licking melon juice off his fingers. "I did. My guess is, it's probably feeding off their crystals. I doubt it would have shown interest in them otherwise."

That actually makes sense. "Should we tell them? It didn't sound to me like they know."

"Nah. They probably don't call them *Eternity* Crystals for nothing, right? They should take a while to deplete. Besides"—Tuk's eyes flash with purpose—"I'd rather not risk pissing them off before they've given us what we came for."

"The star," Ilapara says, watching him closely, but he breaks eye contact.

"Yes."

Mukuni reappears with Tuliza and her father, then sits on his haunches a few paces away from the table and watches them with quiet interest.

Tuliza's father—who's introduced himself as Amidi—settles down across the table, his odd staff in hand. He looks conflicted as he stares back at the cat. "When he appeared, we thought at first that he was a benevolent spirit sent by the Great Funkwe to protect us. It wasn't until a month later that we realized he was actually responding to this." He gestures at the golden stone fastened to his staff.

"And what's that?" Tuk says, his voice strung with tension.

"This, I believe, is the star you have come for."

Both Ilapara and Tuk lean forward to take a closer look. Salo once wore an amulet that pretended to be an expensive ruby. This stone is somewhat larger, though not of a material she recognizes. Something about it sends a shiver down her spine.

"What are we looking at?" she says.

"An artifact of Engai's grace," Amidi explains. "On the morning of the king's wedding—may her soul find peace on the Infinite Path—we performed a ritual to catch a soul as it departed its vessel. This specific soul. Your friend's soul. Everything he ever was, his essence. It is all contained within this rock, by the grace of Engai."

Ilapara's head spins as Tuk inhales sharply.

"You *must* let us take it," he says. "We can't pay you, but we'll do anything. *Anything*. Please."

Amidi exchanges a look with his daughter, then nods, as if in permission.

"We don't expect payment," Tuliza says. "This was a favor for a friend. I believe she knew this moment would come. The . . . star, as you called it, is yours."

Amidi unfastens the stone from his staff and hands it over to Tuk, whose eyes go watery as he accepts the gift. "You can't possibly know how much this means to us," he says, his voice shaking. "Thank you."

Ilapara stares at the stone, wondering how a human soul could be contained in something so small. *Salo's soul.* Could it be possible? But even if it is, then what?

"What will you do with it, if I may ask?" Amidi says, echoing Ilapara's thoughts.

"Nothing nefarious, I assure you." Tuk gets up to his feet energetically and pockets the stone. "Thank you, again, but we must be on our way."

"What?" Ilapara says, caught off guard. "We just got here!"

"Will you not rest for a while?" Tuliza says, looking just as puzzled.

"I'm afraid not," Tuk says. "We have a *very* long journey ahead of us."

Ilapara remains bemused. "We do?"

"Yes, and the sooner we get going the better."

Tuliza smiles sadly as she looks over at Mukuni. "I suppose we'll be saying goodbye to our furry friend."

She gets up and walks to the cat, then reaches up to scratch the fur of his neck. His tongue flicks out of his mouth and over her face, making her giggle. Even Amidi, who Ilapara senses is not a man of many smiles, looks upon his daughter and the cat with wistful tenderness.

This doesn't feel right.

"Tuk," Ilapara says, "Mukuni has been protecting this village. If we take that stone with us, he might follow us, leaving them vulnerable."

By the look on his face, Tuk's mind is already far away. He shrugs. "So ask him to stay. We can always come back for him."

"Ask him to stay? He's a *cat*, Tuk."

"He's a totem," Tuk corrects her, "and his mind was bonded to a very intelligent fellow. Try him."

Ilapara fails not to roll her eyes, but she gets up and approaches Mukuni cautiously, given how he seemed ready to tear into their flesh not very long ago. He remains serene even as she stops in front of him. Tuliza watches her with open curiosity.

Looking into his cyan-blue eyes, Ilapara speaks to him in the tongue of their homeland. "Mukuni, you know who I am. You know where I'm from. You know how much Salo meant to me. You've probably been quite sad since you woke up, and so have we. Well, Tuk has a plan to fix things. But I'm going to need you to stay and guard these people for a while longer. Can you do that? We'll come back for you once we've fixed things. I promise."

She could swear she sees doubt moving in the shimmering pools of his eyes, but then it is gone, and Mukuni lowers himself to the ground, then begins licking his fur, looking completely uninterested in her.

"Huh," she says. "I guess that worked?"

"Told you," Tuk says.

Later, when they leave the garden—with sackcloth knapsacks filled with fruits and waterskins—Mukuni doesn't follow. Tuliza escorts them to the edge of the settlement, and before they part ways, Ilapara embraces her.

"Thank you, Tuliza. You've been a blessing from the Mother herself."

"Farewell, Ilapara," Tuliza says, "and may we meet again in yet another interesting place."

Tuk's stride through the jungles is brisk and determined as they head for the hill they descended to get to the valley.

"So what's the plan?" Ilapara says, trying to keep up with him. It's times like these when she's reminded of his true nature. He never seems to get tired.

"You know where Jomo is, right?"

Ilapara fiddles with one of her ivory pendants. Jomo's general whereabouts are like a secret pressing against her mind. "Yes."

"Let's go find him."

She almost growls. "Why, Tuk? I'm getting tired of you being so cryptic. Just tell me what the devil is going on."

After stopping to face her, he takes the stone out of his pocket and presents it on his palm. His eyes are as bright blue as the heart of a flame. "Don't you see? The 'star' is a mind stone. Salo's mind stone. Better than that, it's his true consciousness. In here, Ilapara. In this stone."

She stares at the stone. Sunlight plays along its golden facets, and she gets that uneasy sensation again. But she still doesn't understand. "So . . . ?"

"All he needs now is a body," Tuk says, "and I know exactly where we can get that." He pockets the stone and starts walking again.

She follows. "A body? Where, Tuk?"

"The Enclave," he says.

"What?"

"We're going to the Enclave, Ilapara. And we're going to get Salo back."

This time Ilapara runs forward and grabs the back of Tuk's shirt, pulling him to a stop. Once again, he turns around to look at her. "Don't give me false hope," she says. "Don't you dare, Tuksaad. I don't think I could handle the disappointment."

His eyes soften, the irises turning a kinder, less intense shade of blue, like the clear skies above the forest. "Nothing's promised," he says. "But this is the only chance we have to get him back."

Despite herself, hope stirs in Ilapara's chest. A thousand arguments rise to compete with this hope, but it strengthens and swells until it's all she can feel. "I have to say goodbye to Jomo," she says.

Tuk's dimples appear as he beams. "And that's why I said we should go find him," he says. "I know you too well." He gets back to the business of walking. "Now come on. Like I said, we have a *long* journey ahead of us."

5: Aneniko

The dreams returned last night. The vivid ones from months ago.

He was walking up a familiar hill south of the kraal—he couldn't remember how or why he was there in the first place—but he decided he'd rest for a few minutes beneath Salo's favorite tree before heading back home.

Except when he reached the tree, lo and behold, there was Salo waiting for him, smiling around a lit pipe. Recognizing he was in a dream, Niko pulled himself out immediately, waking up with a start.

The shock wore off. Then came the regret.

Why walk away from the chance to see him again, even if it isn't real?

Tonight, when the dream takes him, he lets it, and he's fully aware as he walks up the same hill, his heart slamming against his chest in excitement. An ethereal glaze sits over the world, the sky and grass and blooming wildflowers rich in color.

Salo is there again today, dressed only in sandals and a white loincloth. He's sitting beneath the same tree, back casually resting against the trunk, one knee bent, the other leg stretched out. Niko slowly walks over, admiring the long and graceful lines of his body, the smooth, glistening copper skin stretching over lean muscle, the slight and mischievous curve of his lips, like he knows *exactly* what Niko is thinking.

Aching heat stirs in Niko's loins before it sets his cheeks on fire with embarrassment. "Great," he mutters. "I'm lusting after a dead guy."

Salo's spectacles flash with the sunlight as a lazy grin spreads across his face. "Hey," he says. "I didn't think you'd come back. Why'd you run last night?"

Words briefly fail Niko, his eyes beginning to sting. That voice. That smile. *Would his skin feel just as real if I touched him? What's happening right now?*

"Come," Salo says, patting the space next to him. "Sit with me."

Niko wanted to come. But now that he's here, he's not so sure. "I . . . really shouldn't."

"Oh? Why not?"

"Because you're dead," Niko blurts out.

Salo turns his face away, looking toward the chief's herd of cattle grazing down the hill near the lake. "I suppose I am," he says, then looks back at Niko with renewed playfulness. "But I don't want to think about that right now. Do you?"

"I . . ." Niko wishes he never had to think about Salo being dead. He shakes his head. "Not really."

"We don't have to talk. Here." Salo extends a lit smoking pipe in Niko's direction. The fragrance of burning nsango reaches his nostrils, sweet, seductive. "Sit with me," Salo says. "I promise, you've never smoked anything better."

Niko should leave, end this dream and never return. That would be wise. Instead, he stays and passes the night in the company of an alluring ghost, sinking deeper into this new madness.

By the time he wakes up in his cot in the kraal's Ajaha barracks, the shutters covering the dormitory's east-facing windows are haloed in sunlight. He can hear barking dogs and cowbells in the distance, probably the cowherds taking the chief's cattle out to graze.

He blinks at the dormant glowvines draped around the rafters of the thatched roof. *Why do I torture myself like this?* he wonders. *How will I get over him when I can't get him out of my head?*

He rises and gets dressed in a fresh crimson loincloth, fastening his pauldron and leather harness to his bare chest. His spirits lift somewhat when he remembers he'll be visiting his parents and sleeping in his childhood home tonight, a welcome reprieve from the barracks.

They had him later in their lives than usual—his aba had just retired from the iron mines when he was born—so people sometimes mistake them for his grandparents. They'd been childless for almost two decades of marriage when he finally came to them. He was their miracle, they said, and they never let him forget it. The day he earned his steel, his aba cried tears of joy, and his ama ululated until her voice was hoarse.

Maybe seeing them will do him some good, Niko decides. Basking in their doting, uncritical affection. Gorging himself on his ama's cooking, fishing with his aba in the lake. Maybe that's what will fix him.

After a quick breakfast outside the compound's drystone kitchens, where he is served tea and mealie bread by bleary-eyed aspirants who've probably been awake since before the crack of dawn, he heads down to the Ajaha training glade, leaving before Jio or Sibu can catch him. He should be at the Queen's Kraal with the other honor guards, but the chief asked him to help with the integration of the younger Sibere rangers into the new consolidated Siningwe regiment. And so here he is.

But the Sibere men haven't been very cooperative. They're still furious about losing their clan. And it didn't help matters when the Siningwe general decided that, rather than have them simply receive Nimara's newly awoken blessing like they expected, they'd have to earn it first, like aspirants. An effective demotion.

General Deitari is already in the training glade when Niko arrives. He's watching from the side as his lieutenant and husband leads a unit of young Sibere rangers through sparring exercises. Judging by his posture and expression—arms folded, a heavy frown on his brow—he's not impressed.

"Did these idiots never train without calling on their blessings?" he says before Niko can greet him. "They can barely lift their swords."

"I suspect the problem is that they think this whole exercise is a waste of time," Niko says, assessing the lackadaisical attitude of the drilling rangers. "They don't believe they can ever win your favor or that you'll ever let them become rangers again."

The general scoffs. "At this rate, I probably won't."

"Might I make a suggestion?"

"Go on."

"Promote two or three of the most promising. Show the others you'll reward hard work and dedication. They've also built camaraderie and solidarity around their contempt for you. Introducing some competition might strain this unity and make integrating them a little easier, no?"

The general considers the suggestion. "But who in this sorry bunch would I even promote? They're all worthless as far as I can see."

An exaggeration, but Niko's job here is to be the voice of reason. He points out a pair of young men sparring in the middle ground. Both are obviously skilled combatants, but more importantly they haven't been as vocal in their dissent as some of their peers. "I believe those two are ready to move on."

"Doubtful," says the general. "But let's give it a try." He raises his voice. "You two. No, not you. You, over there. Yes. Step forward." The pair of rangers obeys, pride and apprehension vying for their expressions. "The two of you have performed . . . adequately," the general says, gritting out the last word. "You'll receive AmaSiningwe's blessing at moonrise. You may leave the glade."

Everyone blinks at the general in surprised silence.

"Don't make me repeat myself."

"Yes, General," the newly promoted rangers say in unison, shuffling off while their peers glare in confusion and jealousy.

The effect on the sparring ground is almost immediate. The laughing ceases, and the swords start coming down with more purpose. Even the lieutenant notices and winks at the general with a smile.

"It's a good thing you're here," the general says to Niko. "I'd have sooner put a sword through these sorry bastards and be done with it."

Niko studies the side of his face. "You wouldn't really do that, would you?"

The glint of profound violence passes through the general's eyes, but it's gone as quickly as it came. "After what their leaders did, let's just say I'd seriously consider it."

A grim silence falls, and they watch the lieutenant putting the rangers through their paces.

"I understand you were good friends with my nephew," the general says a while later.

"I was." Niko looks down at his sandals, and after a moment he adds, "Though I'd hoped we'd become better than friends in time." A year ago, he wouldn't have admitted this out loud. But Salo deserves better than a half-truthful admission about the nature of their relationship.

Niko feels the general staring at him. When he finds the courage to look up from the ground, he is met with surprise in the man's eyes.

"I see," the general says, returning his attention to the sparring men. "You know, I regret not taking the time to understand him better. To be perfectly honest, I saw too much of myself in him. Rather, too much of what I feared becoming as a young man."

Niko frowns, finding something uncomfortably familiar in those words. "And what's that?"

The general pierces him with a knowing look. "Something tells me I don't have to explain it to you. Every Yerezi man who loves as we love fears the same thing."

"Being seen as inadequate," Niko admits. And wasn't that what he feared himself? Why he stayed away when what he really wanted was to draw closer?

"Inadequate," the general agrees. "Weak. Impotent. Defective. Worthless. Take your pick."

Niko shakes his head, refusing to let those words go unchallenged. "Salo wasn't any of those things. He was fine just the way he was."

"Do you really believe that?" the general asks.

"With all my heart." *Then why did you let him go alone? Why were you afraid of what everyone else would think of you?*

"I hope you never lose that confidence," the general says. "Ama knows I could have used it at your age."

It's Niko's turn to be surprised. "I don't understand what you mean. Everything worked out well for you. Forgive my impropriety, but you've . . . you've married the man you love."

"Ah, but what I have was handed to me on a platter, sometimes despite my stated wishes. I was the son of a chief and the quickest warrior in the glade. So long as that remained true, people were willing to overlook who I spent my time with. And when my brother became chief, he forced me into the wedding because he knew it was what I wanted even if I wouldn't admit it. Not many others can be so lucky."

For a moment, Niko allows himself to imagine a life where he could've married Salo, loved him in the open, lived with him and woken up next to him every morning. It's too painful, so he stops.

"How insensitive of me," the general says. "You're grieving, and here I am, gloating about my fortunes."

"I'm glad for you," Niko says, blinking away the moisture from his eyes. "You need not apologize for finding happiness."

The general's face softens with gratitude. "Thank you. And Aneniko . . . I'm sorry for your loss."

No one else has acknowledged the personal loss that Niko suffered. Sometimes he wonders if he even has the right to feel the way he feels. He nods, also grateful, and they leave it at that.

A young Asazi comes to summon him to the kraal's place of healing a few hours later. He recognizes her as Nimara's alchemical assistant and one of Khaya-Siningwe's new crop of Asazi who serve the clan with her blessing.

He immediately assumes the worst. "Is it Addi? Is he all right?"

"He's fine, Bra Niko," the Asazi assures him. "But AmaSiningwe would like to speak to you now."

He quickly apologizes to the general and departs the training glade with the Asazi.

It's been two weeks since the day of the battle near the western outpost, and during that time, Addi's seizures have grown worse. They've gotten so bad he had to be recalled from the outpost and taken to Nimara so that she could keep a constant eye on him. As a newly awoken mystic, her powers of healing are substantial, but she has yet to figure out how to treat Addi's affliction.

A group of thatched buildings makes up the kraal's place of healing, built around a witchwood tree with leafless branches as white as ivory. The Asazi guides Niko straight to the hut where Addi is being kept, though she bids him wait outside.

He obeys, cracking his knuckles and pacing in an anxious rhythm while he runs through all the possible reasons Nimara would want to see him.

When she finally emerges from the hut, however, the tired, genuine smile she gives him puts him at ease. "Niko, good to see you."

She has retained the youthful paints of the Asazi, eyelids bronzed and lips red as a bloodrose, broken by a white stripe running down the middle of her face. But now, in place of beads, an ornamented circlet of red steel crowns her forehead, its bands disappearing into a cloud of thick, lustrous hair. Her eyes sparkle with a vibrant light born of a newly acquired confidence, for whatever curse had been cast upon the clan to prevent the awakening of Siningwe women ended the night she successfully met her redhawk in the lake and became the new clan mystic.

Niko once entertained notions of courting her. Many of his peers expected that he would. That was before he admitted to himself that his affections lay elsewhere.

"It's good to see you too, AmaSiningwe," he says, to which she rolls her eyes.

Taking him by the arm and leading him away from the hut, she says, "I've told you many times before, Aneniko. I'm too young to be an ama-anything right now. We're friends. Call me by my name."

Her citrus perfume tickles his nostrils in a way that makes him self-conscious about the fact that he's been sparring and sweating all morning. He prays he doesn't stink too much. "As you wish, Nimara. Is everything all right? I came right away."

"I need you to be perfectly honest with me," she says, frowning. "I know you're an honor guard and you serve the queen and whatever, but Addi's life is at stake. Do you understand?"

Worry surges back into Niko's bones. "What do you need to know?"

She stops and faces him, looking up into his eyes. "What the devil is going on in the Faraswa Desert?"

Thrown by the unexpected question, Niko blinks at her. "I'm not sure what you mean." *And what does that have to do with anything?*

Nimara looks around as if to check for prying ears, then lowers her voice even as her tone becomes accusatory. "I've heard rumors the queen is making moves there. Tell me what you know."

"Nothing," Niko says, still baffled, then thinks about it. "Actually, I heard from Neropa there's a new king who's risen there and that Her Majesty has allied with him or something. Why?"

"Is that *all* you know?" Nimara asks.

"Yes. Why is it important?"

She starts walking again. "Come. I'll show you."

He follows her into the compound's vacant workshop and is immediately hit by the strong vapors coming out of whatever alchemical concoctions are brewing in glass instruments on the counters. Nimara pays them no attention, heading to a table on which a red gemstone is ensconced inside a simple jewelry box. A mirage of light in the shape of a luminous map hangs over the box, projected from the stone.

He points. "That gemstone. What is it?"

"My new talisman," Nimara replies with a note of pride. "Although saying it's a talisman is like saying a leopard is a cat. Technically the truth, but not exactly the same orders of magnitude."

"Looks familiar," Niko says. "Salo had one just like it."

Nimara gives him a sharp look. "No, he didn't. I'd have known." Then she lists her head in thought. "I suppose he *could* have gotten one in Yonte Saire, since that's where they came from. But how would you know?"

A good question. When Salo left for Yonte Saire, Niko dreamed about him. The dreams were so vivid Niko still can't convince himself they weren't real. But . . . no. He couldn't have seen that gem before. "Never mind," he says. "What did you want to show me?"

Nimara gives him an odd look, then gestures at the map. "I figured out that Addi's seizures seem to . . . coincide . . . with a weak, distant burst of energy coming from the west. With help from my talisman, I've pinpointed the source to a location in the Faraswa Desert."

The location is marked on the illusory map by a strobing yellow star somewhere in the interior of the continent's western desert. Niko doesn't know much about the place save that it was once the seat of the ancient Faraswa empire.

"How'd you come to this conclusion?" he asks Nimara.

"I was treating one of the Faraswa women the other day, and on a whim, I asked her if she knew anything about Addi's seizures. She was taciturn at first but eventually told me she can sense when the seizures are about to happen. Right before, she hears the whisper of a song coming from the west. Indistinct but audible. On a hunch I decided to interview the other Faraswa refugees and discovered that they *all* experience odd sensations in the moments just before Addi has a seizure, though each of them seems to experience a unique sensory event. One said he could smell baking bread. Another said she was overcome by the need to swim. I'm now reasonably confident that the source of these events, including Addi's seizures, is a signal coming from whatever's here." Nimara points again at the hovering star on the map.

"But what does this mean for Addi?" he asks. "Can he get better?"

"It means the source of his illness isn't physiological. He's having a hypersensitive response to an arcane signal that is, at worst, only a mild inconvenience to his kinfolk. As for whether he'll get better, I have a theory, but . . . I might be wrong."

"What is it?" Niko presses her.

She hesitates. "I believe this thing, this signal or whatever it is, it's calling out to him. Perhaps the only way for him to get better is to answer the call."

"You mean to go to the Faraswa Desert."

She nods. "He suggested going there on his own to investigate, but Niko, I can't allow it. A teenage Faraswa boy crossing the wilds of Umadiland on his own? He won't make it. But I don't know what else to do."

In that moment, a crossroads appears before Niko, a fork in his path that demands he make a choice. He was once offered such a choice not too long ago, and in that instance the path he chose is one he'll regret for the rest of his life.

He won't make the same mistake again.

"Why do you think the queen is involved?" he asks.

Nimara begins to pace. "I don't know. Just a feeling. The changes we've seen lately . . ." She stops and looks Niko squarely in the eye. "How much can I trust you, Niko? I know we're friends, but you're also the queen's honor guard."

"You can tell me anything," Niko says. "I was your friend first."

She searches his eyes to be sure before she relaxes. "I saw Salo's Axiom. Months before his awakening. I knew there was something different about it; I just didn't know *how* different at the time. But now that I've awoken . . . let's just say I understand that his Axiom was a weapon. An immensely destructive weapon."

Niko shakes his head. "Salo wouldn't have built such a thing."

"I don't think he understood *what* he was building. The point is, the queen saw it, too, and instead of punishing him as was expected, she let him, a man, awaken. Then she sent him on a trip to Yonte Saire, where he ended up dead, while she returned with a powerful artifact that lets her bend the laws of magic. It's . . . fantastic, no?"

Growing discomfort makes Niko shift on his feet. He almost regrets letting Nimara confide in him. "We both saw her drink from the Chalice of Truth. Her Majesty had no part in Salo's murder."

"The Chalice only confirms the truth of a spoken statement. It doesn't reveal whether the whole truth has been spoken. You could lie by omission. You could string together truthful statements that build a deceptive picture." Nimara puts her hands on the table and looks down. "I'm not accusing the queen of . . . anything, really. I just have this sense that she didn't tell us everything. But we're digressing. I just wanted to let you know what Addi's options are."

"I swore an oath to serve Her Majesty before anyone else," Niko says. "But Addi is my friend. I can't sit by and watch him die. I'll take him to the desert if this is what he needs."

"The queen will *not* be pleased," Nimara says even as relief erupts in her eyes.

"I know. But it can't be helped. This is more important to me."

Tenderness lightens her expression. "You're a good man, Niko."

I'm simply learning from past mistakes, he thinks. "Let me talk to him first."

"Of course. But don't be long. He just had a particularly bad seizure and needs rest."

He finds Addi lying faceup on his bed, watching the exposed rafters of the hut's ceiling with distant eyes. Dressed only in a white loincloth, he looks frail and thinner than usual. Fragile.

He lifts himself up onto his elbows as soon as he's aware of Niko standing by the door. "Bra Niko," he says, offering a weak smile.

Niko moves into the room and takes a seat next to Addi's bed. "How are you holding up?"

The young man exhales. "I know I look terrible, but it's only bad during and just after the seizures. I feel fine the rest of the time. That's the truth."

"I believe you," Niko says.

"Really?" Addi twists his lips with sly purpose. "So does that mean I'm still your favorite aspirant?"

Niko laughs. "I'm not supposed to have favorites."

"Come on," Addi drawls. "Just admit it."

"Maybe," Niko concedes, and Addi pumps a fist in triumph, which makes Niko chuckle and shake his head. "Addi, this is serious. Nimara told me about your seizures and why they're happening."

The humor ebbs from Addi's face, replaced with the same distant look he had when Niko walked in. "I didn't want to believe her at first, but I think she's right. Something out in the west wants me. I can feel it pulling at my mind, like I'm being swept away by a river." His voice quivers with a mixture of grief and anger, his eyes shining with tears. "I get the chance to live a normal life, and now this shit happens. Why me?"

Niko leans forward and tries to sound reassuring. "Addi, listen. I could take you to the desert to see what this thing is. And once we deal with it, we'll come back."

Addi looks at Niko, surprised. "I wouldn't ask you to do that."

"You didn't, and you don't have to. I insist."

He blinks. "I could go on my own."

"You're brave enough to do so," Niko says. "But you won't have to."

"You'll get in trouble with the queen!"

"It'll be worth it."

"Are you sure?"

Niko makes himself smile as he remembers that he will also be disappointing his mother and father, who expected his visit tonight. "You're my favorite aspirant, remember?"

Tears threaten to pour out of Addi's eyes, but he quickly wipes them. He sniffs, looking away in embarrassment. "Thank you."

"We'll leave first thing in the morning. Do you think you'll be able to ride, or should I arrange a wagon?"

"I can ride," Addi says. "I can usually tell when a seizure is coming, so I'll warn you in time for us to stop and dismount."

"Then it's decided."

They ride out of the kraal just as dawn arrives, Niko on his tronic quagga stallion, Addi on a graceful mare they stole from the chief's stables after bribing the grooms with a stash of high-quality nsango herbs.

Someone's probably watching them from one of the kraal's guard towers, so they resist the impulse to break into a gallop and raise suspicion, confining themselves to a casual trot, then a canter once they reach the base of the plateau.

They're about to turn onto the dust road bound for Khaya-Siningwe's western border when three quaggas whoosh past them from behind, then turn about ahead of them so as to block the way forward.

Like Niko and Addi, the three riders have worn their pointed straw hats and blanket cloaks draped over their shoulders. They're also fully armed, Jio and his twin brother both carrying spears in one hand, the quiet and dreadlocked Mafarai with his bow harnessed to his saddle.

Anger mists Niko's vision as he brings his quagga to a halt. "What gives, cousins? One would almost think I'd stolen your girlfriends. I swear I did not."

The joke fails to amuse them. "Is there a chance I can talk you out of this foolishness?" Jio says.

"What foolishness? Addi and I are going boar hunting. We'll be back in a few days."

Tense in his saddle next to Niko, Addi remains silent.

Sibu glowers at him, then at Niko. "Don't treat us like fools, mzi. We saw you packing."

"Yes, for our hunting trip," Niko says.

"Then I suppose you won't mind if we join you."

He finally loses his patience. Thousands of miles separate him from his destination. "What do you want from me? Tell me what you want so I can give it to you and maybe you'll leave me alone."

"What we want is to stop you from screwing things up for yourself," Jio says in a calm voice. "An honor guard doesn't abandon his post. That's what you're doing."

Niko wonders, and not for the first time, if the twins can read his mind. Try as he might, he can't hide anything from them. He took every precaution to make sure he'd slink away undetected. "Sometimes there are more important things than staying in your post. Addi is important to me, and he's sick and I can help him, so I will."

"We know why he's important to you," Jio says. "But you're letting guilt drive you toward bad decisions."

"I don't have time for this. I don't owe you an explanation. I'm a grown man, and I can make my own decisions. Now get out of our way."

They don't move. Jio exchanges looks with his companions. They nod at each other. "We're coming with you."

"Absolutely not. I won't have both of the chief's heirs follow me out into danger. If anything happens to you, it'll be my fault. And you, Mafarai, shouldn't you be heading out to the outpost later today?"

Mafarai shrugs, looking entirely unconcerned. "Some things are more important than staying in your post. I once heard someone say that."

"Idiot," Niko says.

"I also heard something about grown men making their own decisions," Jio adds. "And seeing as we're grown men, whatever happens out there is on us. We'll be damned if we let you go into Umadiland alone."

"But I'm not alone," Niko says, to which Sibu snorts.

"You might as well be."

Addi scowls but remains silent.

It's pointless. The energy it would take to convince them to stay isn't worth the effort, and there's a long journey ahead. He'll just have to face the consequences when he returns. "Do as you wish. But I'm not sharing my provisions with any of you."

"Don't worry," Sibu says. "We brought our own."

So they knew they'd be coming along from the beginning. Shaking his head, Niko spurs his stallion into motion, and the group gallops away into the west.

6: Ilapara

On the Way to the Enclave

Ilapara's ivory pendant guides her to Jomo's hideout in the thick rainforests of the Jackal province, not far from a river cascade with a wide pool at its base. Their reunion is bittersweet, though; Jomo is unsurprisingly disappointed when he learns she'll be leaving with Tuk for the Enclave, but he doesn't try to talk her out of it.

That night, she sneaks with him to the cascades for a private farewell, where they undress each other with urgency and give themselves over to one another in the cold water, with only the stars bearing witness.

She digs into his back with her fingers every time they move, her hips straddling his, their tongues caught in a dance, their troubles and fears melting away into the shadows of the moonlit jungles. The waves of orgasm that grip her are blinding. She has taken lovers before, but never has a man felt so much like a part of her, like he was made for her and her alone.

They remain locked in an embrace for a time after their climax ebbs, but Ilapara's impending departure soon settles over them like a cloud.

She explained why she has to leave. She still feels like she's abandoning him.

"I care about you, Jomo," she says, resting her head on his shoulder. "Possibly more than I've ever cared about someone. But . . ."

"You needn't explain yourself," he says quietly. "I understand."

She lifts her head, drawing back from him so she can study his face. "You do?"

There is sadness in his eyes, but the affection within them is genuine. "I want you to stay. Of course I do. But I fell in love with a woman who never hesitates to do what she knows she must do. If there's even a chance you can get Salo back, you can't waste it. I'll be here when you get back."

She wants to say so much to him, but she doesn't know how. She kisses him instead.

The arrival of dawn sees her ready to leave with Tuk. It's been two days since they left the vine tower to find Jomo and his party, but Tuk's eyes haven't lost their eager shade of blue, and he's practically bouncing on the balls of his feet.

"How are you traveling?" Jomo asks them. His three Sentinels, Odari, Kito, and Ijiro, and the Halusha ash witch who evacuated them are the only other occupants of this tiny camp. They all slept around a fire, with the Sentinels taking turns to keep watch throughout the night.

"We'll walk north to escape the legionnaires," Tuk says. "Cross the border into Halusha territory, then make our way to the nearest town along the World's Artery and take a wheelhouse to Ima Jalama. I have coin saved up if that's what you're asking."

"But how will you cross the desert?" Jomo asks. "I've heard it's a cursed wasteland that kills anyone who enters it."

Tuk adjusts the straps of his knapsack rather impatiently. "I have a plan. I crossed the desert once before and can cross it again."

Unconvinced, Jomo stares at Ilapara. "And you trust this . . . *plan?*"

She has concerns, but she nods. "Tuk has earned my trust. If he says he can do something, I believe him."

"Great!" Tuk says. "So can we go now? Time is of the essence, as they say."

"Not just yet." Jomo glances behind him at the Sentinels and the Halusha mystic watching from near the fire. His face is the picture of uncertainty as he looks back, but his eyes harden with resolve. "Take Disanka. I spoke to her, and she can carry you as far as Ima Jalama."

Having heard that she's the subject of discussion, the ash witch approaches. She's a statuesque woman with a slender frame and locks rubbed almost orange with ocher. The lines of her angular face are set in a neutral expression.

Ilapara balks. "We're not doing that," she firmly says, but Tuk is squinting like he's considering the idea. "No, Tuksaad! We're not taking her! They need the mobility."

"So do we," he protests. "She could shave *weeks* off our trip. It's a great idea, in fact!" He grins at Jomo. "For once."

Jomo doesn't rise to the bait. "Your mission should take priority, Ilapara. If you can bring Salo back . . ." He shakes his head like a man indulging a hope he knows is desperate. "Quite frankly, we could use him. And Disanka will return as soon as she's delivered you safely to Ima Jalama. We'll probably be holed up here the whole time anyway. It'll be a while before I can safely regroup with the others."

Ilapara hates the idea of taking his only means of fast escape, but she can't fault his logic. Getting Salo back would change everything. "As you wish," she reluctantly says.

A knowing twinkle lights up his eyes, quietly reminiscent of the night they shared. It disappears as he regards Tuk. "Watch her back out there."

"I've been doing that since before you met her, Your Highness." When Ilapara glares at him, Tuk rolls his eyes. "Fine. I promise to give life and limb before I let anything happen to your precious beloved, and so on and so forth. Now can we go, for the Mother's sake?"

They bid their last farewells; then Jomo and his Sentinels step back while the ash witch spreads her arms and summons a whirlwind of ash and glowing embers. Ilapara waves at Jomo through the thickening wind; he waves back, but the loss she sees in his eyes makes her question her judgment.

She's found something real here. Why must she leave it to chase ghosts in a foreign land?

She's almost grateful when the ash witch transposes them into the Void, taking the decision out of her hands.

Disanka flies them north in a fast-flowing column of ash, steering clear of any towns or other population centers, which they know will be swarming with the emperor's forces.

They keep to the wilds instead, the canopy of rainforest below seeming to go on forever, broken only by the occasional river or vine tower reaching into the sky in the distance. In time the rich jungles give way to a uniform woodland of tall conifers, and these to rolling mountains and deep canyons, and that's when they know they're far enough into Halusha territory to risk banking west and approaching the World's Artery.

At dusk, the ash witch releases them from the Void near a small but busy stopover town hemmed in by steep cliffs, where the rounded buildings are carved directly into the surrounding stone on either side of the continental roadway. Despite the unfamiliar architecture, the heavy traffic and crowded streets remind Ilapara a little too much of the Umadi stopover towns where she once plied her trade as a mercenary.

She suggests spending the night in the wilds, but Tuk snorts dismissively at the idea, saying they'll have plenty of opportunity to tough it out when they cross the desert. They go on to find rooms in a moderately priced inn built into the side of a cliff, accessed by climbing a narrow stone staircase.

Disanka proves to be an aloof traveling companion, speaking only in reply to direct questions and delivering her words with a polite, indifferent cadence. She becomes despondent, however, later that night, when they hear from other patrons in the inn that the neighboring Inoi tribe has agreed to submit to the emperor in exchange for arcane technologies and is now waging war with the Halusha at his behest. Apparently parts of north Halusha territory have already fallen to the Inoi, including, as it turns out, Disanka's home village.

They verify this for themselves an hour into their flight the next morning when they approach the scene of a battle, hundreds of men engaged in a fierce skirmish, many already felled, bodies being trampled by riders mounted on armored beasts as they skewer and slash at each other.

Above them an Inoi mystic riding a massive vulture casts spells of death from his airborne saddle, raising spikes of stone and earth from the ground that impale multiple enemies at once. Ilapara mutters a silent curse when she glimpses the metaformic amulet dangling around his neck.

The emperor is a smart son of a bitch. They all assumed he'd use his own legions to invade the Halusha territories. They never considered he'd entice another tribe with magical artifacts into doing the work for him.

Without warning Disanka accelerates, and Ilapara understands why when the mystic's vulture emits a screech as it races in pursuit.

The mutant bird is faster than any vulture has any right to be, much less one large enough to carry a man, but Disanka leans into her ancestral magic and pulls away. The Inoi mystic releases several spikes of destructive Void craft that tear across the skies like solid shadows, but

Disanka disperses her ash so thinly it becomes undetectable, evading the attacks.

Eventually the mystic gives up and returns to his battle, and Disanka resumes their flight northward.

It must take substantial mental fortitude to carry two people across the Void at high speed, but she flies with a determination she didn't show before. The Inoi tribelands rush by all day long, and by the time darkness has fallen, the plains below have become arid, with trees few and far between—the southern edge of the Jalama Desert.

They rest at a large roadway inn where visitors sleep in carpeted tents and cook their own food on open fires. Tuk pays for a plucked and cleaned fowl from a butcher, which they roast and eat with flatbread from a local baker. Many of the people here are of light complexion, some as light as Tuk, and wear long garments that shield them from both the harsh northern suns and the frigid nights. So far up the World's Artery, Ilapara can't be sure what tribe they belong to or what language they speak. She doubts she could even point to where she is on a map. Without Tuk or the ash witch, she'd be utterly lost.

Not a welcome feeling for someone who's always prided herself on her independence.

"We're not actually going to Ima Jalama," Tuk says after wiping the grease from his fingers. In the warm, flickering light of their campfire, his eyes are still a blazing shade of blue, betraying almost manic excitement. "We're going to a village a little deeper into the desert. That's where I left my raft. If you can take us there, Disanka, you'd save us a lot of time."

Disanka has barely touched her food. She stares at Tuk, then at Ilapara, grief dampening her eyes. "Your mission," she says. "You have a plan to stop him? The emperor?"

Ilapara doesn't want to make false promises, so she locks eyes with Tuk to leech some of his confidence. He doesn't flinch. "That's the hope," she says to Disanka.

"Then you must not fail." She nods at Tuk. "I will take you as far as you need to go."

Their flight path the next morning takes them away from the World's Artery and its terminus, the famous city of Ima Jalama, but Ilapara glimpses at the edge of the arid horizon the vague profile of slender towers with gilded domes and massive terraced structures, all glittering like a chest full of gold half-buried in the sands.

Somewhere in that massive city will be the god-king's palace. Ilapara once heard that the Dulama god-king sires ten sons every year from ten different women, all to be born on the same day. They are raised in luxury and splendor, their every whim catered to, but on the eve of their eighteenth comets, the young princes must fight each other to the death until only one remains. While his brothers are interred and forgotten, the victorious prince joins the god-king's court as a warlord and possible heir to the throne.

A horrific but fascinating tradition, and Ilapara is somewhat disappointed that all she'll ever see of it is the hint of a distant skyline. But even that soon dips beyond the horizon as they continue their flight deeper into the desert.

They hurtle past caravans of nomads shepherding herds of humped beasts. They spot a sizable tronic lizard darting across the sands after a swift-running flightless bird. Dunes begin to rise and fall like waves, and an hour passes before they see the next signs of vegetation. It is high noon when they finally land along a tree-lined roadway leading into a settlement built around a small lake.

In stark contrast to the surrounding desert, palm trees and well-tended orchards abound in this unexpected oasis. While Ilapara takes it in with admiration, relieved to be out of the Void, Disanka hugs herself, looking northward with a worried purse of her lips.

"What is it?" Ilapara asks her, following her gaze.

"I sense . . ." The ash witch averts her eyes from whatever she was staring at. "I'm afraid I won't be able to go any further."

"This is as far as we needed you to take us, Disanka," Tuk says, stepping forward with a hand extended. "Our means of crossing the desert lie within this village. You've done us a great service. Thank you."

Disanka skeptically takes the offered hand and shakes it once, but a shadow clouds her face again as she glances north. "I wish you all the best." She looks directly at Ilapara, anticipating her concern. "And don't worry. I won't keep the prince waiting for long."

Ilapara nods, relieved. "Thank you, Disanka," she says, shaking her hand. "And farewell."

Without another word the ash witch turns into glowing embers and shoots off into the skies.

"What was that about?" Ilapara asks Tuk soon afterward. "What spooked her?"

He adjusts the straps of his knapsack and starts walking along the roadway toward the main cluster of buildings in the oasis. Ilapara quietly follows.

"Jomo was right," he says. "The desert is cursed with arcane storms that devour anyone foolish enough to attempt a crossing."

She stares at his profile. "Then how the devil are we supposed to get to the other side?"

"By being very clever," he says cryptically.

The roadway continues into the settlement, but Tuk takes them along a branching road toward a walled villa built upon a hill.

A pair of guards in belted white tunics watches them approach the villa from the gates. Their faces are hooded beneath white headcloths, but they radiate hostility, their hands hovering near the hilts of their sheathed, straight-edged swords. Ilapara tenses as she spots two more guards on the battlements atop the adobe walls, both with bows drawn and ready to fire.

One of the gate guards shouts something ill tempered in the Dulama tongue, which makes Tuk come to a stop, so Ilapara does the same.

When Tuk replies in their tongue, the guard appears to lean forward as if to take a closer look at them. To Ilapara's surprise, he beams with sudden joy and signals for his comrades to lower their weapons. "Tuksaad!" he cries with open arms.

A bemused Ilapara watches Tuk exchange enthused handshakes with the guards. They even clap each other on the backs like old friends. It gets her wondering if there's any place on earth Tuk won't instantly fit in. At this point it might as well be an ancestral talent.

She forces a stiff smile when Tuk introduces her to the now-friendly guards, though their dialogue flies over her head given her ignorance of the Dulama tongue. When their reunion finally ends, one of the guards escorts them past the gates and toward the three-story villa, whose walls and pillars are almost the same hue as the sands of the desert. There's no shortage of green, though; men clad in the skimpiest of loincloths tend the numerous date palms and fig trees growing on the grounds. This is obviously the home of an individual who wields power.

While they wait outside for the guard after he slips into the villa, Ilapara eyes her companion closely. "So," she says, "I'm assuming you've been here before and you didn't charm those guards into liking you with your smile alone."

Tuk's eyes are predictably green and full of smugness. "My smile is certainly bewitching, but no, the guards know me from before. Remember the story I told you about the Dulama mystic who sedated me so he could run experiments on my body?"

How could she forget such a tale? "You said you woke up middissection and cut his head off while your guts were still hanging out."

"I stuffed them back in first, but yes, that's the short of it. Turned out he was a menace to this town. Children and young women disappearing, that sort of thing. Everyone knew who was responsible, but no one was strong enough to challenge a sorcerer."

"Until you came along," Ilapara says, now understanding.

Tuk nods, though his eyes have lost a shade of brightness. "I thought the townspeople would kill me when they found out." He shrugs. "They threw me a feast."

"Of course they did," Ilapara says.

He flashes a grin. "What can I say? I'm very adorable."

"And this place?" Ilapara asks, looking up at the villa.

"It was his home," Tuk says. "I'm told the townspeople are thinking of turning it into an inn. No one lives here at the moment, though."

The guard returns, jangling a set of keys in one hand. He beckons them to follow and leads the way to a fenced-off shed behind the main building, where he unlocks the iron gate and steps inside.

A large shape lies still beneath a canvas sheet within the shed. The guard says something as he pulls the sheet aside to reveal what it hides; Ilapara gets the impression he's reassuring Tuk that everything is in order.

Sure enough, Tuk nods approvingly at the thing the canvas was concealing. Some sort of vehicle, by the looks of it, though Ilapara can't be sure.

It resembles a low, open-topped carriage with no wheels. Stranger are the two semicircular blades of a translucent crimson material; they project from the front and rear of the machine like handheld fans stretched open. The front one is smaller and narrower as if to cut better into the wind, while the wider rear blade might add stability to the vehicle.

Ilapara bends forward to get a closer look. Two seats in the interior. A panel of brass controls. A set of mirrored arches that might be a steering mechanism. A host of levers in between the seats.

"Meet our very illegal transport across the desert," Tuk says. "It's fast, and it has instruments to warn us away from any storms. We'll be in the Enclave in no time."

Ilapara walks around the machine so she can see it from all sides, aware of the Dulama guard watching her. A nebulous weight sits on her shoulders.

"So this is it? We just . . . get in this thing and sail across the desert?" *Away from the Redlands? From everything I know? From Jomo?*

"We've been allowed use of the villa for the night," Tuk says. "For now, we can head into town, stock up on food and water for the trip, maybe get some new clothes." He sniffs himself and grimaces. "Don't know about you, but I could use a new shirt. And a bath. Come dawn tomorrow, we leave. How does that sound?"

I'm being silly. I've come this far already, so why panic now?

"Are you all right?" Tuk says, perhaps sensing her inner turmoil.

"I'm fine." She wipes her forehead. "It's just the heat, I think. It's relentless."

He can see through her, but she's grateful that he simply nods. "All right then. Let's go get those supplies."

Later that night, Ilapara lies alone in a musty but well-furnished guest chamber of the villa.

The wind howls outside like a conclave of angered spirits, making the wooden shutters rock loudly against their hinges. A persistent metallic clang haunts the empty corridors of the building, coming from what might be a basement floor. Every time she comes to the verge of sleep, the sound jolts her awake, her skin tingling with the sensation of being watched. Only at the cusp of dawn does sleep finally take her.

"Wake up, Ilapara! It's time to go."

She pries her eyes open to the sight of a shirtless Tuk stretching himself by her doorway. "I had such good dreams," he announces.

She would strangle him if she could summon the energy. "At least one of us did," she grumbles. "I swear this house is haunted."

"I wouldn't be surprised," he says. "Lots of people died here. *I almost died here.*"

That reminder is enough to banish the sleep from her bones. She sits up, rubbing her fatigued eyes. "Maybe it's best we leave."

"I couldn't agree more," Tuk says and leaves her to get dressed.

I'm crossing the Jalama today, she thinks as she gets off her bed, but a bout of nausea has her rushing to dry heave into the chamber pot. She scolds herself afterward, annoyed that she would let her nerves get the better of her.

After washing up, she proceeds to wear one of the garments Tuk bought for her yesterday, a loose, ivory-colored ankle-length robe common among the denizens of the town. Tuk himself wears a similar garment, though he cinches his at the waist with a black rope. He also winds a long white headcloth around his face and head and insists Ilapara do the same.

She's no stranger to veils, but she's already sweltering in the morning heat. "Do I really have to?"

"You'll understand soon enough," Tuk says.

The sand raft is still in the shed where they left it yesterday. Tuk packs their supplies behind the seats, then steps in and settles down in front of the vehicle's controls. Ilapara watches from outside the shed as he flips a number of switches, but there's one particular lever that brings the engine to life. The quiet wailing sound it makes reminds her of the winds that blew last night.

She shivers as the thing rises to hover half a yard above the ground. Chuckling at her reaction, Tuk pulls on a lever and guides the machine out of the shed, either hand gripping the steering mechanism. The raft glides at his command and comes to a graceful stop next to Ilapara.

His eyes twinkle up at her. "Come on. Get in."

She stares down at the precarious space between the machine and the ground. "If this thing falls, Tuk . . ."

"It won't."

There's a minor dip when she hesitantly climbs inside, a similar sensation to stepping onto a rowboat, but the machine otherwise stays put, and there's very little rocking as she settles down next to Tuk.

"Here. Put these on." From a compartment beneath the control panel, Tuk unearths an odd pair of close-fitting spectacles with protuberant lenses. "Goggles. For your eyes."

She reluctantly puts them on. Tuk dons his own pair of "goggles," and with the rest of his face concealed beneath cloth, he achieves the appearance of a mummified corpse. Ilapara figures she looks just as ridiculous.

She holds on to her seat as he guides the raft out of the villa grounds through a back gate. He waves at the guards in farewell, and they cheer and wave back at him. Then he maneuvers the machine down the sandy hill at a pace not much faster than a jog. She reckons she could run faster on her feet if she had to, and after five minutes of plodding along, she begins to wonder if they'll reach their destination before the year is over.

Tuk takes them down another hill to the bottom of a wide and flat gully where a river might have once flowed, slowing the raft even further until they come to a complete stop. She almost asks if there's something wrong with the vehicle, but the way Tuk stares at her through his bulging lenses makes her uneasy.

"What?" she says.

"Are you ready?"

"Ready for what?"

"I'll take that as a yes."

Giving her no warning, Tuk pulls a lever, and the raft *leaps* forward. Ilapara tries not to scream as the acceleration pushes her back into her seat, but the machine keeps accelerating until everything is a blur, until even the slightest of collisions would flatten them into meat patties, and just when she thinks it can't go any faster, Tuk pulls yet another lever that lifts them higher off the ground. A wave of nausea grips Ilapara, and it's all she can do to fend it off.

Over the loud whir of the engines, she hears Tuk giggling in delight. She curses him silently and holds on for dear life.

A living map of the desert sits on the control panel. It's a sheet of brass whose black ink moves on the ruled surface to form a dynamic image of the surrounding terrain, with the raft represented as a glowing dot of red light and their intended route as a gray snake cutting across the map. Ilapara notices how the charted route avoids undulating dune seas that may slow them down, keeping them flying over flat stretches of land at maximum speed.

And speeding is all they do. The suns slingshot across the cloudless skies while the wind beats relentlessly across their covered faces, carrying with it endless plumes of sand particles. Ilapara begrudgingly comes to accept that Tuk was right to make her wear the goggles, even if they're uncomfortable.

They stop briefly at sunset to hydrate and stretch their knees, but Tuk insists that they keep moving, so they set off again a few minutes later. The gibbous moon rises shortly after dusk, bathing the sands of the Jalama in an eerie reddish tint. Combined with the unclouded starlight, there's enough ambient brightness to cast shadows, but Tuk flips a switch that activates a brilliant torch at the front of the vehicle, illuminating the way forward so that they're able to see almost a mile ahead.

Ilapara tries to stay awake throughout the night, but her lack of sleep in the villa catches up to her, and her eyelids grow heavy. Soon she loses herself in restless dreams, before waking up hours later with a painful crick in her neck from sleeping awkwardly.

She tries in vain to massage it away. The eastern skies have lightened somewhat; dawn can't be far away, though a massive storm has darkened the skies to the northwest, almost in the direction they're headed. Something about the storm makes her seek the ivory pendants around her neck with her hand, the strong sense of Jomo's life force bringing her a measure of comfort.

She looks to her side. Tuk's hands are still on the raft's steering mechanism, but she catches him just as his chin dips down to his chest. Alarmed, she reaches for his arm to shake him awake.

He jumps in his seat. "What?" he shouts over the drone of the raft's engine.

"Pull over," she shouts back. "You need to rest."

"We can't stop," he says. "You never stop moving, or the storms will catch you."

Ilapara looks northwest. It might be her imagination, but the storm seems to have grown larger. "You're falling asleep," she tells Tuk. "We'll never get there if you fly us into a cliff."

"We can't stop for longer than five minutes," he says, adamant.

"How did you cross the first time?"

"I used lots of tonics to stay awake. Now I have you. Keep me awake, and I'll be fine."

Not a good idea. He might be inhumanly resilient, but she knows he needs sleep just as much as anyone else.

"Show me how to fly the machine."

He glances at her. "Are you sure?"

"Is it difficult?"

He seems to think about it. "The hardest part is getting up to cruising speed. After that, it's just a matter of following the charted route. I can walk you through the steps."

"Let's do it."

He brings the machine to a stop, and they switch seats. She pays attention while he explains the functions of each switch and lever. There are levers she needs to press down with her feet in addition to those she needs to pull with her hands. She thinks she might have taken on more than she can handle, but Tuk is patient and she's determined. Soon she's got the machine moving at its slowest speed.

"Pull the shorter lever while you press down on the big foot lever," Tuk says. "Remember—"

"At the same time," Ilapara says. "Yes."

She executes the maneuver, and the raft shoots forward at its second-fastest speed, which is already fast enough to make her eyes water.

"Great! Now, pull the long lever while pressing on the big foot lever."

The raft jumps even higher, accelerating to its cruising speed. As the force pushes Ilapara back into her seat, violent shudders travel up the steering column and into her hands. She begins to panic as she learns just how sensitive the mechanism is. One wrong move, and she'll steer them straight into the ground.

"Tuk!"

"You have excellent reflexes!" he shouts. "You'll be fine. Just keep your eyes on the road and follow the map." Like the imbecile he is, Tuk is already relaxing in his seat, preparing to sleep.

"Tuk! Wait!" He has the remarkable ability to turn himself off and sleep like a coma victim—or perhaps a dead machine—no matter where he is, so he's practically unconscious the second his head hits the headrest. "By Ama, if I kill us, it'll be your fault."

But Ilapara eventually gets the hang of the controls and navigates the raft along the charted route into a long valley. For a time, the gathering storm disappears behind the terrain; then they climb up the other end of the valley and reach the top of the incline with enough speed to launch the vehicle several yards into the air. Ilapara screams as gravity reasserts itself, but instead of giving a violent jolt, the raft gradually slows its descent and maintains its hovering height.

She almost screams again at her first look at the storm. While the suns have risen in the east, the northwest is shrouded in bloodred darkness. It's not so much the clouds that frighten her, even as they churn above the desert in a freakish cyclone. Nor is it the steady salvo of crimson lightning bolts that gives the clouds their forbidding shade, as if they were lit from within by the moon. It is the elongated, vaguely human face she sees within the storm, large as a mountain with massive eyes.

Unblinking eyes staring across the desert, right at her.

She moves her frozen hand to shake Tuk awake, unwilling to risk speaking. When he stirs and begins to groan in complaint, she shushes him and points.

"Look!"

He's silent as he regards the storm. Whatever expression is on his face remains hidden beneath his veil and goggles. "Breathtaking, isn't she?" he eventually says. "I didn't get to see her from this close on my way south."

While the rest of the spirit's face is somewhat abstract, a shape formed by the arrested motion of storm clouds, its eyes are clearly defined, and they look bloodshot. And angry. Its irises are rings of crimson lightning. Veins of a darker red striate the eyeballs.

"What the devil is it?" Ilapara asks as quietly as she can.

"The Lady of Storms," Tuk replies. "She and her husband are the Primeval Spirits who rule the desert. They're also the reason crossing it is so dangerous."

"She's staring right at us, Tuk. That can't be good."

"She saw us the second we set foot here. But don't worry. Follow the route and we'll be fine." Tuk is already going back to sleep, leaving Ilapara annoyed that he could be so calm with an evil-looking human face filling half the sky.

The storm progresses across the desert, the spirit's angry gaze never leaving them, but the charted route steers Ilapara out of its path. Soon the storm is behind them. Smaller storms dog them throughout the rest of the day, however, giving Ilapara the sense that they're sentient and actively hunting her. Rain never breaks, but the rumble of thunder is eternal, and it chases the raft across the sands well into the afternoon. She's almost overcome with exhaustion by the time it's safe to stop and let Tuk take the reins again.

For the next two days, this is their routine. Tuk flies the machine in the dark hours, and Ilapara takes over from dawn to dusk. They never stop for more than five minutes at a time so as to remain ahead of the storms, and with the loud noise of the raft's engine, there's not much room for conversation.

On their fifth morning, the terrain begins to change, and hardy grasses become common. Later that afternoon, Tuk tells Ilapara to bring the raft to a halt close to the banks of a wide river. "The hard part is over," he says. "Now comes the tricky part. There's a small town about five miles northeast of here. The area ahead is heavily patrolled, so this is as far as we can take the raft. We'll have to sneak into the town, get a change of clothes, then board a leviathan bound for Apos. Leave everything behind except the waterskins."

It's insane to Ilapara to just desert the raft, a machine that kings and queens of the Redlands would kill for, but she follows Tuk out of the vehicle. "Why are we sneaking?" she asks.

Tuk begins to extract the last of their filled waterskins from the knapsacks behind the seats. "The law of zero contact, remember? All travel to the Redlands is illegal. If we get caught out here, they won't just kill us. They'll torture us until we beg for death."

"You people and your strange laws," Ilapara says, shaking her head.

She's no sooner finished speaking than she feels a painful sting in her neck, like the bite of a wasp. She swats herself where she's been stung, only for her hand to come away with something needle shaped with a red feather on one end.

A dart.

She stares at it. "Tuk? I don't feel so good."

Clouds gather in front of her eyes, her vision blurring. She thinks she sees a squad of men running in their direction, but she's so sluggish she can't think straight.

"Shit," Tuk hisses under his breath, pulling out an identical needle from his own neck. "We've been ambushed. Damn it!"

A weight pulls Ilapara to the ground, gravity becoming irresistible. The men are shouting. Tuk is also shouting. Ilapara's vision darkens.

"Ilapara! You bastards! You'll pay for that!"

She closes her eyes and falls into a dreamless sleep.

PART 2

ALINATA
*
A STRANGER
*
KAMALI

7: Alinata

The Qotoba Coast

At high noon along the southeastern seaboard, a flock of black carrion birds descends onto a wildflower-carpeted cliff top looking over a bay of turquoise waters. The birds gather into a young woman dressed in a gown of pale satin and jewelry of the finest red steel. Alinata has served her queen in the past as a spy and an occasional assassin, but today she is an emissary, an embodiment of the queen's will and might. An *incarnation*, and so she has dressed accordingly.

Prince Diric of the Qotoba Coast, wearing a long qamis of blue linen that flatters his slim physique, is waiting for her up ahead with his company of turbaned guards. A golden embroidered koofiyad sits atop his head, while in his right hand he holds a gilded scepter encrusted with gemstones. His rather sizable fleet of war galleys can be seen floating in the bay behind him, each ship a wooden fortress with a massive rearing sea serpent carved onto the prow.

At the sight of her, the prince's gaze hardens with hostility. Alinata continues to approach undaunted, quietly noting the enchanted billao shortswords each guard has sheathed by his side. More interesting to her, though, are the brazen weapons in their hands, barreled mechanisms with glass chambers that glow red like the moon. She has never before seen this exact model of weapon, but she knows enough to recognize it as one of the new fire spitters from across the Inoetera.

Disquiet flutters in her stomach.

"What you do in Yonte Saire will send ripples across the world," the queen said to her in the days before she left for the Yontai. Alinata can't help but wonder if these foreign weapons are some of those ripples ricocheting back to her.

"Where is your queen?" Prince Diric demands in the Qotoba tongue. "Don't tell me I came all the way here just to deal with a messenger."

The guard on his right, a man in a crimson turban with white paint marking his face, isn't carrying any weapons. At least nowhere in sight. *A mystic,* Alinata deduces but keeps her expression plain.

"My apologies, Your Highness. Her Majesty couldn't come in person, but rest assured she wouldn't have sent me unless she trusted me implicitly."

"To the pits with her trust. I won't be talking to some foolish girl. I'll speak to your master or to no one at all."

Most would have cause to avoid the prince's ire. He might have been cast off into exile after the Coral Throne chose his younger brother to be king, but he is still a powerful man, with the loyalty of a fleet and a small army at his beck and call. He is dangerous, worthy of fear.

But Alinata is well acquainted with fear. She knew it the first time she entered the Void and felt its emptiness, its indifference to her and all living things. Empress or peasant, god or demon, in the Void, all are insignificant; all will die and be forgotten, their bones turned to dust and scattered by the winds. The Void is mortality itself.

What is this prince to such a force?

She braces herself for it now, feels its chill oozing out of her red steel jewelry. "If you will not speak to me, Your Highness, then you will speak to no one."

A sneer twists his lips. "Then maybe I should send your queen a message she won't be able to ignore." He nods at the man in the red turban, whose forearms instantly come alive with deadly magic.

A split second. That is how long it takes for the mystic to surround her in a depression in the fabric of reality. He follows it with a force of opposite polarity, a protuberance crackling in the palm of his right hand. The air heats up as nature seeks to equalize this sudden, unstable difference in potential. A thunderous bolt of red lightning arcs from the palm of his hand toward Alinata and—

And—

Ah, but she knows the emptiness of the Void, that place where she is nothing but a flicker in a bottomless pit, a speck of dust in a crushing nothingness that endures forever and ever and ever—

Ravens burst forth from where she stood. They swarm across the wildflowers, too fast for the startled prince to act, too fast for his guards to fire their weapons or his mystic to cast another spell. She pulls the prince into the Void, separating him from his entourage. They fly off and rematerialize yards away. He makes to scream but goes still when he feels the pinch of a cold knife prodding his throat from behind and a second one prickling his side, tearing through the linen of his robe. The knives pulse with shadows, made of the Void itself.

"I've done this many times before, Your Highness," Alinata says from behind him. Her knives dig in slightly to discourage any further movement. "Are you willing to take your chances?"

Prince Diric drops his scepter and raises his hands in surrender, careful not to move too much. Blood is already pearling where the knives have pierced his skin. The guards point their fire spitters in Alinata's direction, and the mystic spools another spell around his glowing cosmic shards, but they all wisely stay put, recognizing how easily she could put an end to their master.

"Good," Alinata says, eyeing the guards. "Now, let us try this again, shall we?" The prince doesn't respond, but she continues anyway. "You wanted to speak to the queen, but she's not available, so you'll speak to me, or you'll never hear from either of us again."

"I got her message," the prince says in between rapid breaths. "I'm interested in making a deal. But I need to know she has the power to meet her side of the bargain."

Alinata hasn't taken her eyes off the guards. She senses one of them getting ready to fire his weapon, so she digs a little more with the knife in the prince's side, making him cry out. "Tell your guards to behave."

"Don't shoot, you idiots!" he shouts, and the guard lowers his weapon a little.

Alinata relaxes the pressure but keeps the knife in place. "What makes you doubt my queen, Your Highness? She wouldn't promise something she cannot give."

"You don't understand," the prince says. "No one has ever taken the Coral Throne from the one it has chosen. Even if I killed my brother, the throne wouldn't accept me, and it might not choose someone for years. Our people would be vulnerable and kingless. That has always been our reality. Why would I believe that your queen can change this?"

"She can," Alinata says. "And that's all you need to know. Your main concern should be how you intend to earn the gift she has offered you."

The prince gulps, the skin of his neck sliding beneath Alinata's blade. "Can you remove your knives, please? I promise my guards will behave." Raising his voice, he shouts, "Don't attack. That's an order."

Keeping one eye on the guards, Alinata slowly steps back from the prince. The guards glower at her but otherwise obey their master's command. He turns around to face her, wincing as he rubs the little cut she made on his neck. He looks at his bloody thumb, grunting in displeasure.

"Yerezi magic," he mumbles. His eyes find hers again, and a cunning look crosses them. "So your queen wants my absolute loyalty, is it?"

"I believe that is within reason considering what she's offered you."

"I won't be a puppet."

"You won't have to be. How you rule your lands will be up to you. It is what you do beyond your borders that interests her."

His eyes narrow as he considers her words. Then he shakes his head and chuckles. "We take your exiles, pay tribute to your queen. It was only a matter of time before you tried to make us your vassals."

"We want to be your allies, Your Highness," Alinata tells him. "We've always been a buffer between you and the Umadi warlords. Without our cavalries your people would have fallen a long time ago. What the queen has proposed would simply be a formalization of a relationship that already exists."

"You say *relationship*; I hear *dependency*." He smiles cynically. "I'm well aware of your importance to us, Asazi. But your queen must understand I won't be a mindless thrall."

"She doesn't want a thrall. She wants a man of war. A man with steel in his veins."

"Cease your mind games," the prince growls. "Just spell out what your queen expects."

"That you use your might to conquer all of the eastern seaboard south of the Yontai and rule it as viceroy in her name. A contingent of Yerezi Ajaha officers will serve on your fleets, and with their help you will intercept all incoming vessels from the East, seize all weapons onboard, and send two-thirds of whatever you capture to the Plains. You will do this until she tells you otherwise. These are her terms."

Prince Diric flashes his teeth again, though there's no humor in his eyes. "Surely you jest," he says. "Even with the Coral Throne and the seas under my command, I would require the combined strength of five kingdoms to perform such miracles. Conquer the eastern seaboard? We're proud, capable mariners, but we're a small tribe, and our power is limited."

"Power will be given to you, Your Highness. But only if you agree to her terms."

"I absolutely agree, but I'll believe your promises when they've been kept."

Alinata is an incarnation, a more complete avatar of her queen than any ordinary Asazi could ever be. Now, when she closes her eyes, she suffers a not entirely pleasant heat burgeoning inside her chest as the queen's presence strengthens within her. It is not exactly giving up control of her body but the merging of intent and purpose. Becoming the physical instrument of the queen's objectives.

She opens her eyes, and with a deep and magisterial voice, she says, "Kneel."

Prince Diric draws his head back a little, like he doesn't believe he heard her correctly. "Excuse me?"

"Kneel, Diric Tawfik of the Coast. Your time to ascend has come."

His eyes widen as he recognizes the truth of who is now standing before him.

He glances over his shoulder at his men, perhaps worried he'll look foolish kneeling in front of a messenger, but he stands tall like a man consigning himself to a difficult task and then goes down on one knee.

She ignores the stunned guards and approaches their prince to grip the sides of his head. The queen's new power floods Alinata's veins from the flame of heat inside her chest, and for a fleeting moment the power is all she can feel, as though she's been plunged into a sea of omnipotence. The power is ancient, pure, unleashing within the prince the full extent of his people's arcane knowledge, giving him mastery of the Coral Throne and of the seas and the winds that stir along the coast. In that moment Alinata knows what it's like to taste Red magic as it was meant to be, as it has not been known in eons.

The flow of power stops as the queen retracts her presence. Alinata exhales, then steps back from the prince, flexing her fingers, which feel tingly and numb. She doesn't move to help him when he falls onto all fours, convulsing. His guards run over, but he has the presence of mind to ward them off with a hand.

"I'm all right!" he shouts, though it's a while longer before he recovers control of himself. He sits back on his heels, a wild look in his eyes. "I feel . . . ," he starts to say, and then his face lights up like he's a poor man who's just discovered a chest filled with gold. "I feel amazing! What did you do?"

"Her Majesty has fulfilled her promise," Alinata tells him. "The time has come for you to do the same."

He stares up at her for a lengthy second. Abruptly he laughs. Full and throaty. Still on his knees, he spreads his arms and looks up into the sky with an expression of triumph. "Blessed be Irediti, empress of the south, daughter of the moon. With this power I shall conquer the seas in her name. Tribute shall flow to her coffers from the four winds." He gets up and faces his bewildered men. "Come, my brothers. Tonight, we claim the Coral Throne. Tomorrow, we become an empire."

Alinata lingers in the skies along the coast as the prince and his men set sail to confront his brother. There will be war and death at the end of his journey, and Alinata knows that some of that bloodshed must ultimately be laid at her feet.

She used to tell herself the ripples she made were for the good of the tribe. These days she doesn't bother making excuses.

She waits until the fleet has left; then she gathers her ravens and flies westward, back to the Plains.

She'd just seen her fifteenth comet the day the queen took her to the mountains west of the kraal, where young unmated ravens flock to this day in large numbers. There was another girl back then, before Neropa. A girl who, like Alinata, had grown up in the Queen's Kraal with little attachment to the lands of her clan.

Her name was Liera.

Theirs was the friendship and rivalry of sisters, and they fought as often as they laughed together. They'd spent months memorizing the ciphers of their first spell and were ready to prove who between them was worthy of the queen's favor. They thought she'd take them to the high trees where the birds roosted. Instead, she led them to the bluffs on one side of the mountain, where she summoned a single flock of ravens to fly in slow circles some distance beneath a sheer drop.

"Whoever is first to bind herself to that flock," she said, "will be my apprentice."

Liera was the first to leap, but Alinata was the one whose spell ultimately worked.

Later, as she wept over Liera's broken body at the bottom of the cliff—the queen standing nearby, watching without expression—hot anger took hold of Alinata, and in that moment she hated her sovereign more than anything in the world. "Why would you make us do this?" she cried.

What the queen said would stay with her forever. "My dear, had you jumped first, you would have been able to catch her."

And that was the first lesson she learned as the queen's apprentice. A moment of hesitation had been the difference between saving Liera and watching her plummet to her death.

The suns are nearly kissing those same mountains in the west by the time she flies through an open window and into the living room she shares with Neropa.

Curtained doorways facing each other partition their chambers from the living area. Muffled laughter coming through one of the sheer curtains warns her of Neropa's presence.

And of the fact that Neropa is entertaining a "guest."

With a sigh, Alinata ventures to her quarters to change out of the gown she wore to meet a foreign prince and into something more suitable for exercise.

Living in the queen's palace was once a point of pride for her, almost as much as being the queen's apprentice. The walls in her quarters are bare stone, the furnishings sparse, but she was proud of it anyway, because she'd earned it with her own ambition and determination.

Here was a girl orphaned in a fire just before her third comet, now a queen's apprentice living in a palace.

But these days the palace has lost its sheen. This might have something to do with her monthslong stay in a Skytown mansion where even the plates they dined on were glazed with precious metals. The palace certainly feels rustic in comparison, but she knows the reasons for her disenchantment run deeper than a downgrade in luxury and decor.

By the time she's changed into black exercise leggings and wrapped her chest in a brassiere of kitenge, the sounds coming from Neropa's rooms have lowered to breathy moans. Irritation stirs inside Alinata, and she makes her way out of their suite through the door in the living room.

She is certainly not one to judge Neropa for her . . . leisure activities. She's had no qualms in the past about diverting herself with a strapping Ajaha or a sultry Asazi whenever the fancy took her, and there's no shortage of either in the Queen's Kraal.

No, it's not that. What annoys her about Neropa these days is how . . . dear Ama, how *frivolous* and utterly oblivious she is to what's happening around them. Sometimes Alinata wants to shake the girl and shout: *Are you not afraid of what's coming? Am I the only one whose eyes are open?*

Alinata throttles her anger as she makes her way along the stone halls of the palace. Clan motifs dance on tapestries hung on the walls, crystal lamps shining from high sconces so that they cast long shadows of the Ajaha posted at every door and corner. They stand in full regalia, still as statues, but beat their chests when Alinata walks by. She nods back every time out of sheer habit.

Outside, the late-afternoon air is cool and invigorating enough to instantly chase away the rest of her anger. She begins her daily jog along the perimeter of the Hill Complex, running behind the buildings surrounding the stone plaza, then completes the loop in front of the stairway climbing up to the palace.

Her body is slicked with sweat when she finally makes her way to the training ground near the library—a quadrangle covered in river sand. She finds a group of younger Asazi there, moving in precise, choreographed sequences, each girl with a knife in either hand.

Alinata watches them for a time. She remembers having to learn this dance back when she aspired to join those few Asazi whose specialty is the knife.

It was, and still is, a waste of time. What she knows about the knife she learned by spending hours on these sands, striking at wooden dummies until her arms hurt so much she'd almost cry from the pain. By challenging her instructors over and over again until they could no longer best her and considered her a nuisance. By reading in the Library of the Foremothers about the warrior women of Shevuland or the assassins of the nomadic Jalama tribes and emulating their strenuous training regimens.

This dance, pretty though it may be, is really just that at the end of the day: a dance.

Leaning against a stone pillar rising at the edge of the quadrangle, she folds her arms and says, "None of this is helping you become better fighters, you know."

They all falter at the same time, lowering their knives with wary looks on their faces. But the sylphlike girl with luxuriant frizzy hair—the one who likely organized this gathering—smiles as she resumes her dance. The others follow her example.

"The knife dance teaches us poise and control, Si Alinata," says the girl. "A graceful posture is key to success on the battlefield."

Alinata isn't familiar with the others, but she knows this girl's name is Unati and that she comes from Khaya-Ngobane, the macaque clan. Popular. Pretty. Likely hopes to be apprenticed to the queen when Alinata and Neropa move on. Alinata was just like her not very long ago. Maybe that's what makes her smile so insufferable. "Poise, maybe, but not the athleticism to make it count," she replies. "You need to be fast if those knives are going to be of any use to you, and speed requires strength. Stamina. This dance isn't going to give you that."

Unati snorts, continuing to lead the girls in their silent knife dance. "We don't need strength or stamina when we'll have magic."

Alinata feels her eyes become hooded. What Ilapara would teach these ignorant fools.

Leave them. They're not the cause of your ire.

Too late. Alinata steps onto the sands. "Try to cut me," she says to Unati, whose smile finally disappears.

The girls lower their knives again, Unati's face caught halfway between confusion and suspicion. "I don't wish to hurt you, Si Alinata."

"You couldn't hurt me if you tried," Alinata says. "That's my point."

Unati seems wounded at first, but then she straightens her posture, prideful. "You have magic, so of course you can say that."

"I won't cast even a single spell." Alinata spreads her hands. "Go on. Show me the poise and control that dance has taught you."

Eyes flashing, the younger Asazi strikes with her knives, causing her colleagues to gasp and step back. Her technique is better than Alinata expected—her swings and swipes are not thoughtless, and perhaps, had she been facing one of her friends, she would have landed a killing blow.

But Alinata easily ducks out of the arc of her knives even while remaining within the other girl's reach. Unati grows angrier with each missed swing until at last she snarls and sends one of her knives spinning in Alinata's direction.

Alinata sways to one side, and the knife hisses past her face, hitting a pillar behind her. She sidesteps another swing when Unati charges forward, then executes a bare-handed chop to the girl's throat.

Unati immediately crumples to the ground, clutching at her neck as she coughs and wheezes. The other girls look on in shock.

"You're too slow," Alinata tells them. "Too weak. None of you would last five seconds in a real fight. I have fought tikoloshe. I have faced Umadi war parties. Out on the battlefield the enemy doesn't care if you're graceful or pretty to look at. They strike, and if you're slow or weak, you're dead. Get any other silly notions out of your head."

The girls say nothing. Unati is now sitting up and massaging her neck. Her eyes have misted over with tears of fury. *She doesn't get it. None of them get it, and they never will.* Alinata shakes her head in disgust and leaves the quadrangle to return to the palace.

She heads straight for the bathing chamber down the hall from her quarters, where half a dozen steel bathtubs are arranged in curtained stalls. A copper pipe disgorges heated water into her tub at the turn of a squeaking valve, and she watches indifferently as the bath fills, her thoughts straying to faraway places. Only as the water begins to spill over the rim does she return to the present. With a curse she shuts the valve and reaches down for the stopper to drain some of the water away.

The tub is nothing like the bathing pools of Skytown, but it's large enough for her to comfortably immerse herself. Holding her breath, she closes her eyes and dips her head beneath the water, staying there even as the pressure builds up in her chest.

What the devil is wrong with me? she wonders. Alinata knows she's never been the sunniest person in the world, but she never thought she'd devolve into such a cheerless killjoy.

Becoming hard as stone was a necessity for her. She's always had to count on herself and couldn't expect anyone's unconditional love and support. While most Asazi at the Queen's Kraal have homes to return to, families who will gladly welcome them back to their clanlands, Alinata has no memories from before the fire that killed her parents and older sister. She knows she was born in Khaya-Nyati, but her sense of kinship with those of the gnu totem is at best superficial. The competitive and political environment of the Queen's Kraal is all she has ever known, and she learned from an early age that if she wanted success in this place, it wouldn't be delivered to her. She'd have to take it.

And so she did, in the process becoming the kraal's frost queen, the Asazi everyone talked about, favored by Her Majesty, admired and envied by her peers, and desired by the Ajaha. She reveled in her reputation.

Lately, though . . . *I'm not sure I even like myself anymore.*

She surfaces for breath just before she loses consciousness, and as her eyes adjust, she sees a shape standing beyond her stall's open curtain, hands on the hips.

"I just found out what you did to Unati."

Alinata wipes her face and is slightly taken aback by Neropa's scowl. The girl is usually passive aggressive when she has a grievance, almost never directly confrontational. "She'll be fine," Alinata says, which only fuels Neropa's anger.

"You humiliated her!"

"She needed it," Alinata says even as a current of shame runs through her.

Disapproval pours off Neropa thicker than the heat from the water. "What the devil has gotten into you? I know Yonte Saire was hard for you—"

"You don't know the half of it."

"But it was months ago," Neropa says. "Whatever happened, you need to let it go, because you're taking it out on people who don't deserve it. You want to be curt with me? Fine. I can handle it. I'm a grown woman. But Unati is still a child. She's *not* your scapegoat."

Alinata sighs. "I'll go and apologize."

"Thank you," Neropa says and doesn't wait around for a reply.

Left alone again, Alinata feels her shame intensify, as well as her anger at herself.

But she stops dwelling on her shortcomings when the queen's presence strengthens inside her all at once. While she flew east to the Coast earlier this morning, the queen left to meet her mysterious new ally, a masked figure of supposedly considerable technological strength who's set himself up to rule the Faraswa Desert. The queen must have just returned.

Alinata completes her ablutions, dresses, and goes to report to her master and mentor.

She finds the queen standing on the balcony outside her study, statue still as she watches twilight shroud the kraal below. The line of mountains on the horizon is a dark contrast to the lighter sky. Floating in the foreground is a cloud formation that almost looks like a flamingo in flight.

The queen has an ornamented gourd of wine in one hand.

Like Alinata, Queen Irediti grew up in the Queen's Kraal as a talented Asazi with no family and little attachment to the lands of her clan—exactly the kind of candidate the council of chiefs prefers to elect as queen. So when she made Alinata her apprentice, no one was surprised, and better yet, the chiefs approved.

But Alinata never let herself be carried away by visions of being queen. More important to her was becoming as worthy an apprentice as she could be. She figured she would bond with Her Majesty over their commonalities, and in her deepest slumber she dreamed that she and the queen would grow close in the way a daughter grows close to her mother.

She did everything in her power to prove herself.

She once assassinated a Shevu ambassador on his way to negotiate a military treaty with the Valau Kingdom. She then had to secretly dispatch a particularly talkative Asazi who found out about it and threatened to expose the queen to the council of chiefs.

She learned to harden her heart with each use of her knives, to learn that unpleasant things needed to be done for the safety of her people, that being queen was an immense burden only a toughened soul could bear, that the queen would accept nothing but utmost loyalty.

They did grow close, eventually, just not as mother and daughter, as Alinata had once hoped. But as coconspirators.

The gourd of wine in the queen's hand puts Alinata on alert. She has seen her touch drink exactly once before. A sip, at a chief's wedding.

"Your Majesty," she says, stopping at the threshold to the balcony. "My trip to the Coast was successful. Prince Diric will soon claim the Coral Throne and begin intercepting foreign ships from the East." When the queen fails to respond, Alinata gives in to her worry. "Your Majesty, are you well?"

"I'm quite well, Alinata," the queen replies. "I'm simply contemplating an interesting choice I must make."

The inflection of bitter humor in her voice is familiar at least, though in Alinata's experience, the queen usually reserves it for complaints about the chiefs and their intransigent ways.

"Is this about your meeting with the king?" Alinata asks. "Did something happen?" She rarely has to wonder what her master is up to, but Her Majesty has been unusually reticent about her recent trips to the desert—a frustrating reality for Alinata because whatever the queen is doing there, it's changing her, making her more withdrawn and prone to spells of pensiveness.

"Often a person's life is defined by a single decision," the queen says, "a key nexus where the threads of time are so intertwined no outcomes can be divined beforehand. I believe I stand at such a nexus. Not even our Oracle can help me." The queen turns around, and Alinata is surprised by the almost wild light shining in her master's eyes. "I'm still . . . ambivalent about my new masked friend. As it happens, I have yet to see his face."

"Then is he truly a friend, Your Majesty? What if he seeks to challenge you?"

"I thought that, too, at first," the queen admits. "But no. I was never interested in the desert, and he has no interest in anything outside its boundary." The queen turns back to the view below the balcony, her voice falling low. "I should be glad, but I think I'd have felt better if he *were* a challenger. That, I would have understood. My choice would have been simpler, cleaner, the result a straightforward calculation of strength, resources, and tactics. But what he has offered . . . I can't walk away."

Alinata considers this information. "The emperor has met him too, hasn't he? What does he make of him?"

"I suspect we're of a similar mind. Neither of us like this new king and whatever hidden ambitions are driving him. But we recognize that the opportunity he presents is one we'd be unwise to reject. And therein lies my conundrum."

"What is this opportunity, Your Majesty, if I may ask?"

The queen takes a sip from her gourd. "The completion of all we've worked for," she finally says. "You did well in the Coast this morning. You continue to impress. But you must leave me now. I have much to contemplate."

Alinata obeys and leaves her master still looking out over the kraal.

The Oracle is waiting for her in the hallway, her staff held upright in one hand, eyes closed, her shoulders so still she might not be breathing.

Alinata didn't know her very well before the queen gifted her the ancestral talent of foresight, but she remembers seeing her cheerful face among the young girls who attend the kraal's grammar school. Whatever the queen did to her drained her of any semblance of childhood. Alinata has never seen a girl so void of emotion, so lacking in facial expression.

And what is she even doing out here? She never leaves her chambers without the queen.

Unsettled, Alinata makes to brush past her, but the girl blocks the way forward with her staff.

"I saw something in your future," she says without opening her eyes, and cold fingers of dread caress Alinata's skin with each spoken word.

"I don't want to know."

"I think you might," the Oracle says.

"Excuse me." Alinata pushes the staff out of the way and attempts to escape, but the girl grabs her arm and a veil lifts from Alinata's eyes, revealing a future that makes her gasp—

Sheathed in moonlight, she tumbles from the skies, but the clouds do not cushion her fall. She tumbles and falls and the earth rushes to meet her, death waiting in its bosom. She plummets and screams and she—

Alinata yanks her arm away. *"Why* did you show me that?" she demands, trembling all over.

The Oracle remains placid, closed eyelids fluttering as she tilts her head. "I'm but a servant of the threads of time, Si Asazi," she says. "I saw that a choice awaited you, and I've delivered it. What happens now is up to you."

Alinata grips her arm as though the Oracle's touch left a lingering burn, and though she has a few choice words for the violation, she says nothing as the girl turns around and walks away.

8: A Stranger

A Strange Place

The shadow chases him without end across a flat and barren wilderness.

It chases him through dust storms and beneath forks of lightning that dive in and out of a bleak sky. It chases him across hostile ground littered with jagged stones that cut into his bare soles with every step, but he keeps running, knowing that if the shadow catches him, it will obliterate him.

It lengthens on the ground, stretching out in front of him. Talons emerge from its contours. Arms, a snarling face, all shadow, but the face is a twisted reflection of his own, its eyes merciless pits of venom. He trembles, gripped by paralyzing terror, but he can't stop, for the shadow is the end of all that he is.

He runs.

Instant awareness, as though at the turn of a switch.

Liquid warmth envelops his naked body. He can hear the rapid beat of his own heart, but he's not breathing. In fact, he hasn't taken a breath in a long time, but he knows to remain calm.

There's a voice somewhere inside his mind, and it says:

"You are serene. You are magnificent. You are alive."

The warmth around him strengthens, soaking into his limbs, introducing him to his extremities. His fingers, hands, arms, legs, feet.

"You must get up now," says the voice. A woman's voice, and there's a labored quality to it, like she's having trouble breathing. *"Slowly. Calmly. Feel the edges of your tank. Lift yourself out and breathe."*

He sits up, and his first gasp of breath is a shock of cold that floods his lungs. He wipes his face with a hand, flinging away the strangely warm fluid that surrounded him. Brightness assails his eyes when he blinks them open, so he shuts them again.

"Your spectacles are on the table at the foot of your tank. Climb out, feel your way toward them, and put them on."

The stranger does exactly as he's told, climbing out of the slippery tank, feeling his way to the table. He stops when the tips of his fingers graze an object made of glass and thin wires—the spectacles. He puts them on, and the world sharpens into perfect clarity.

"There. Isn't that better?"

He blinks at his surroundings. A glass tank filled with a crimson liquid. Brass machinery surrounding the tank. One side of the small room is partially reflective glass. He stares at the tall and naked young man looking back at him.

The bespectacled face is familiar, at least. It feels *right*.

"Wipe yourself off with the towel on the table," says the voice. *"I've also left some clothes for you to wear. I was informed you're partial to sandals."*

Once again, the stranger complies, if only because he has no reason not to, and towels the remnants of the tank's odorless liquid from his body before slipping into the garments neatly folded on the table.

A black shirt with long sleeves. Black trousers that reach down to his ankles. Black leather sandals with multiple straps.

He wiggles his toes, smiling. The voice was right. The sandals are glorious.

But his smile fades as he awakens to a strange new sensation. The world feels like it's vibrating with a peculiar resonance, a chaotic and forceful energy touching and penetrating everything. He decides he doesn't like it.

"I'm sorry to tell you this," says the voice inside his head, *"but by the time you hear these words, I'll have been dead for days, perhaps weeks."*

The tranquility the stranger awoke with morphs into growing disquiet. He moves to open the door; the metal handle is cold to the touch as he twists it to one side. The door opens out into a hall filled with statues, most of which stand in darkness, but the few lit by lanterns at their bases depict fiendish beasts surely drawn from nightmares.

A lamp at the other end of the hall is flickering. The stranger steps through the door and quickly makes his way through the horrid collection, purposefully avoiding the shadows they cast.

"There's not much time left. This is all happening sooner than I expected. And I know it may not be enough, but I've done all I could for you." The woman wheezes for breath. *"You're my finest work. How fitting that I shall not live to admire it."*

A woman lies dead beneath the flickering lamp. The stranger's heart thuds powerfully in his chest as he approaches, but his thoughts remain lucid, like the inside of a clear diamond.

He steps over what might be a dried puddle of vomit or blood and crouches next to the fallen woman so he can see her better.

A cerise gown of fine quality. Golden jewelry on her neck and arms. She was obviously wealthy, but her skin—what remains of it—erupted with burns so severe as to make her unidentifiable. By the stench of decay, she might have died at least a week ago.

"Who were you?" the stranger asks, his voice hoarse with disuse. "And who am I?"

No answers are forthcoming, so he gets up and takes a left at the end of the hallway, then approaches a flight of stairs.

"You'll know the way out," the voice says. *"Trust your instincts to survive."*

More dead await him on the floor above, most of them wearing blue coats over their garments. Perhaps this was a library or a place of learning. The dead lie strewed in brightly lit rooms of brass machinery, control consoles, and steel chairs; between desks and shelves and countertops, skin ruptured with burns and faces melted off, dried vomit crusted on lifeless lips, not a single soul alive. Rectangular brass panels enchanted with Mirror light flicker in the stillness, and something about them and all the machinery in the building tickles the stranger's mind . . .

He doesn't stop to investigate. He goes up, up more flights of stairs, searching each floor and finding yet more dead before continuing onward. There must have been hundreds of people here, killed suddenly.

He realizes he's in a subterranean building when he emerges into a ground-floor lobby. Shattered glass lies scattered across the floor, papers swirling in the winds coming through the smashed windows that once graced the facade. As the stranger steps through what might have been a glass door, the voice speaks to him one last time.

"You don't know me, but for what it's worth, I'm sorry."

The world beyond is a hellscape of fire and destruction. It might be daylight, but a thick blanket of smog has turned the skies and everything below into the color of diluted blood. Fires rage all along the ruined towers flanking the adjacent street, thick plumes of smoke billowing out through high-rise windows. The laws of nature must have broken down, too, for there are chunks of debris floating everywhere in the skies, some as big as houses, slowly adrift with no compulsion to fall as they should. Strange vehicles lie dormant all along the roads, many with bodies slumped in the seats or against the windows.

I'm dead, the stranger realizes with a spasm of terror. *This is the land of the dead, and I walk among them.*

The very air is poisoned, and now that he's aware of this, he understands that the vibrations he felt earlier, the ones he can still feel, are a poison permeating and penetrating everything around him. Every surface and every wall, killing everything it touches.

Perhaps not precisely everything. The stranger squints, wondering if his eyes are deceiving him, but no, she's really there, a young woman standing across the street, looking right at him.

Yellow blossoms were woven into her braided hair; their petals are torn and discolored now, much like her yellow strapless gown, such as it is. From the looks of her the stranger would believe she walked through a fire and survived.

Despite her sorry state he is struck by her beauty, so out of place in all this ruin and destruction, and also . . . familiar? He could swear he knows her from elsewhere. From before now.

But what came before?

Her lips appear to move, but no sound reaches his ears. He opens his mouth to call out to her, but a rumbling sound draws his attention farther down the street. He thinks he sees movement, but whatever it is ducks behind a burning building.

And when he looks back at the woman, she's no longer there, but the hint of a lengthy shadow passes over where she stood.

Dread grips the stranger like a fist, clenching around his guts. *I am in the land of the dead,* he reminds himself. *And here, ghosts walk in the light of day.*

Mustering his courage, he goes to investigate the noise.

An invisible lattice sits over the burning city, weaving through the fabric of reality like the interlaced webs of a nest of giant spiders.

As he jogs down a ruined street to investigate the movement he saw, the stranger gradually awakens to the existence of the lattice and the way it seems to stretch well beyond the bounds of the city. What unsettles him is the feeling that his own mind is a spider on this web and could navigate it from one node to another if he chose, could manipulate its threads or even add threads of his own.

That in fact, the lattice might continue deeper into his mind, into his own thoughts.

He stops walking and tilts his head as he focuses. The lattice becomes so vivid in his mind he can almost see it with his eyes. It's nothing at all like the vibrations that have poisoned the world, chaotic and all-pervading. The threads of the lattice are ordered and have intent; they are numbers and music and language, and only now does he realize that this was what he sensed coming out of the machines back in the building of the dead.

Signals, he thinks, paying closer attention.

A few more signals shoot out at him from the adjoining street. His curiosity returns, and he runs ahead, turning right at the next four-way intersection. This new street is yet another corridor of lofty ruins and shattered glass, but his breath catches at the way a vivid shaft of sunlight cuts through the red skies to reflect off a distant glass tower with a gilded spire still intact.

What I would have given to see this city when it yet lived, the stranger thinks.

Up ahead he spots a wagon without wheels floating along the street, accompanied by . . . *what are those?*

He stops, freezing in place. The three beings walking beside the floating wagon are humanoid in form, but a rubbery hide covers their plump bodies and bulbous heads. Demons, perhaps?

The sound of chattering voices breaks the stranger out of his terror, touching his mind through the invisible lattice of signals. Surprisingly, the words spoken are intelligible, though something tells him he shouldn't understand this language.

Even so, he relaxes. Not demons, then, even if they look misshapen. Demons don't speak like humans do. At least, he doesn't think they do.

"Hey!" he shouts and runs ahead, approaching the three beings. A fourth one seated at the head of the hovering wagon pulls on a lever, bringing the vehicle to a stop. Together the quartet turns their heads to look at the stranger.

He slows down when he catches sight of what's within their wagon. Golden candelabras. Silver goblets. Statues of alabaster.

Valuables, the stranger thinks, and he realizes that these beings are scavengers picking at the bones of this ruined city. Even now two more come out of a nearby building, one of them carrying an amphora glazed with brightly colored designs. The other carries a long sticklike weapon with both hands, its barreled end pointing downward.

A typhonic rifle, part of his mind whispers. *A deadly weapon that can shoot bolts of destructive fire, named after a fire-breathing creature of the eastern seas.*

Unease makes the stranger tingle all over as he notices that the other beings are carrying similar weapons.

Two of them walk closer, looking him up and down through unblinking, protuberant eyes of glass that reflect the red skies. Altogether, these beings look like giant flies walking on two legs.

"What in the living hell?" says one of them in a surprised voice.

"Must be a cog if he's still walking around in this soup," says the other one.

Nothing they've said makes sense to the stranger, but he politely smiles. "Hello. I think I'm lost. Can you help me?"

The two beings exchange glances. Behind them, the wagon's pilot speaks. "It must be malfunctioning."

"Reckon we could sell it, boss?" says one of them. "Maybe tear it open and strip it for parts. Must be an advanced model if it's still operational."

"It's probably too contaminated," replies the wagon's pilot.

"Then we'll run it through the washer just like the rest of the junk."

As they continue to speak, it dawns on the stranger that these beings aren't monsters at all but people wearing suits of armor. They have faces hidden beneath those ugly, bulbous masks. Tiny cores imbued with power sit in concealed packages at the backs of their suits, allowing them to transmit their voices to each other through the lattice of signals—that's how the stranger is able to hear them, he realizes, and why their voices carry an electric cadence. He can also see, with his odd new senses, how the suits are protecting them from the city's sea of poison.

So why am I not dead?

He lifts an arm to inspect it and is mildly surprised to detect a thin pocket of emptiness surrounding his body, a field of energy the poisonous vibrations cannot pierce.

"Perhaps if you just pointed me somewhere I could find assistance," he says to the armored strangers.

They stare at him, then at each other. "Put it out of its misery," says the wagon's pilot. "You're right. Maybe we can salvage something from its corpse."

Those words turn the stranger's blood to ice. *I was right all along. These* are *demons, and they want to rip my soul from my bleeding corpse.*

"I'm sorry for interrupting," he quickly says. "I will leave you be." He turns around and flees.

"Stop right there!" shouts one of the demons.

The stranger keeps running. A high-pitched cry like birdsong follows him, and the ground near his feet erupts in a small explosion of fire. A quick look over his shoulder tells him two of the demons are giving chase, both running awkwardly in their suits and aiming their typhons in his direction.

He runs as fast as his legs can carry him, faster than he thought he could move, and he's almost reached the next junction when there's another high-pitched cry followed by a bolt of searing pain that burns into his right calf and brings him crashing to the pavement. The pain is enough to make his eyes water, and he cries out as he clutches his wounded leg. His once-pristine trousers, now stained all over with ash from the pavement, smolder where the bolt has singed his flesh.

The two demons approach, both ready to unleash more fury from their weapons. The stranger tries to back away, but the pain is too much.

He doesn't remember his name or his life before today. He doesn't recall ever having anything to live for or, better yet, anything worth dying for. But he knows he doesn't want to die here, alone and unremembered. Forgotten. He wants to live, at least until he remembers who he was. Grief overwhelms him, and he begins to weep.

"Don't kill me," he pleads. If the demons kill him here in the land of the dead, what will happen to his soul? Will he be obliterated? "Please. I beg you."

"What are you waiting for?" calls the pilot from the wagon. "Kill it already!"

One of the demons aims his typhon.

"Trust your instincts to survive" is what the voice said to the stranger.

Desperate, he opens his mind to the lattice of signals and becomes one with it. Information flows into his thoughts in the blink of an eye, and he instantly learns four things he didn't know before: the demons cannot communicate vocally without signals because their suits impede the propagation of sound; the power cores in their suits generate shields that protect them from the sea of poison; their typhons also have power cores; and his mind is connected to all of them through threads of signals that he can manipulate.

Before the demon can fire, the stranger sends ripples of disruption from his own mind through the lattice. Every typhon on the street explodes out the side, and the demons dance in alarm, flinging their weapons away.

"Something's wrong with my suit!" cries the one who would have killed the stranger. But none of the other demons hear him because the stranger has cut them all off from each other and damaged the cores keeping their suits functional. They'll have to find shelter from the sea of poison should they wish to remain alive.

Biting back a scream, the stranger gets back up and begins to limp away. A fever has beset him, sweat drenching his forehead, but he's aware that this is a sign of his body working hard to heal itself.

The wagon roars back to life and races away, leaving two of the demons behind. They run after it, screaming for the pilot to stop.

The stranger continues limping as fast as he can, searching the lattice of signals for a place to hide and recover.

This is the land of the dead, and bloodthirsty demons roam in search of prey. He must not let them find him lest they take his soul.

9: Kamali

The Elephant Province

He was awake when they carved his back and gave him a vertebra of moongold from which he could draw enough power to fight like a demon.

He screamed as they burned arcane tattoos onto his skin, each one a prison for a restless spirit that would curse him with nightmares for many moons before he learned to master them. He walked barefoot on burning coals until he could prevail over the pain, his eyes blinded until he learned to sense the currents of essence as they flowed and ebbed around his cosmic shards. Never once did his training cease, not for a second, not until the pitiless masters of his order had turned him into the perfect weapon of the Shirika and a defender of the kingdom.

Into the perfect killer.

And in all that time, never once did Kamali think he'd be called upon to use those terrible gifts against the very people he was supposed to protect.

"What do people want from life?" says Taji Msani as she looks across a forested valley beneath a golden sky and its low-hanging suns. Her robes of saffron and bronze silk flutter in the wind, and so do the braids of her unbound hair. She reaches up to brush aside a strand from her face and glances at Kamali, who's standing next to her. "What do *you* want, Jasiri? What's your most basic desire?"

Kamali Jasiri of the Fractal—dressed in the eyeless horned mask and crimson robes of his order, along with the embellished breastplate of his new station as the emperor's Left Hand—gives the question a half-hearted thought. His senses are preoccupied with tracking the advance of his legionnaires as they encroach upon the camp hidden in the valley. "I want to live my life in peace," he says. "I believe the same is true for most people."

"Then why do we spill blood and die so often for the disagreements and ambitions of the powerful?" Taji says. "Why does the cycle of war never seem to end?"

It's at times like these that she reminds him she's a Msani, an artificer, not a warrior. Taji was meant for the engine rooms of reclamation centers and the enchanting labs of the House of Axles, not the front lines of a war against her own people.

Why does the cycle of war never end? *Because we put more faith in our leaders than we do in ourselves,* Kamali thinks. *Because it's easier to obey orders than to question them, to conform than to stand out.* He places a hand on Taji's slender shoulder in an attempt to comfort her. "It's almost over," he says. "Today, it ends."

He senses her eyes welling with the promise of tears, but she gives him a smile, though brief. She takes a deep breath, schooling her face into an expression of resolve, and says, "Then let us get on with it."

Kamali looks across the valley again, spreading his cosmic sight to detect footsteps miles away. "The legionnaires are close enough," he says. "It's time. Extend your dampening field across the valley."

Taji has already summoned the power of Void craft into her cosmic shards, visible as scarlet sparks of electricity flickering all around her forearms. She closes her eyes, reaching with one hand for the crimson metaformic crystal dangling on a chain around her neck. Kamali feels a slight change in pressure in his ears as she casts her spell. "I won't be able to hold it for long," she says. "You have five minutes."

Kamali summons power into his own shards, calling upon Blood craft to awaken the spirit imprisoned in the colorful winged tattoo sprawled across his chest. "Don't worry," he says. "This will be quick."

Power suffuses his limbs as the tropical peregrine spirit awakens, and when he spreads his hands, the ghosts of brightly colored feathers shroud his body. With one flap of his phantom wings, he leaps off the edge of the bluff and glides into the skies.

He was ready to die when he gave himself up to the emperor for execution. It was in part a ploy to draw attention to himself and away from Ilapara and Tuksaad so they could sneak out of the Valau embassy, where they'd taken refuge, and escape the city. But it was also his way of ending what had become a wretched existence.

His mistress was dead. A muting collar still bound his throat, and he was a convicted criminal. To a born and bred Jasiri, death was preferable to persisting in such disgrace.

The last thing he expected was for the emperor to pardon him for his crimes and offer him a place by his side.

Kamali refused at first. The emperor had killed his mistress, and no threat of harm, no torture, would force him to work for the man. But the emperor made no threats to his life that day. Instead, he plunged into Kamali's mind with a spell and showed him visions of burning villages and towns, of mothers wailing while cradling their dead children, of lightning storms razing fields and homesteads to dust.

Only once the horror had fully washed over Kamali did the emperor clarify his position. "The threat is not to you, Jasiri. I need someone honorable by my side who will work hard to ensure I never have to use my power against our people. Against *your* people."

As he glides over the treetops blanketing the valley, Kamali thinks about Taji's question again. *What do you want, Kamali?*

The answer is the same thought he had that day when he was on his knees before the emperor. *What I want is to not see my people die at the hands of a man who wields the power of a god.*

He swoops low enough to almost graze the valley's canopy of trees. With his old Axiom, he could be airborne only a few seconds at a time. Its mistress was a matronly academic whose knowledge in the art of Blood craft could fill a library, but the Axiom had many limitations, and she hadn't given Kamali access to its fullest potential.

There is a new Fractal now, and a new Shirika, appointed by and beholden to the emperor. Where Mistress Talara's Axiom was rigid and predictable, like a familiar walking stick, the new Fractal's Axiom of Blood craft is as deep as the seas and just as erratic.

It's also extremely powerful. A thing devised by the emperor's new machines and metaformic crystals, amplified by a cocktail of ancestral talents that should not, at least in theory, exist in the same person. Kamali's shards brim with so much Blood craft his peregrine spirit hasn't tired even after a minute in the air.

A clarion goes off in the hidden camp ahead, telling him that his army of legionnaires has been detected. By now the rebels in the camp will be scrambling to evacuate their leaders, but this time Taji's dampening field will prevent the ash witches from using their Void craft to escape. Well, at least temporarily, but a little time is all they need.

Kamali flies past the camp's stealth field, swoops down into the trees, and lands on the forest floor, next to one of the aerosteel rods keeping up the stealth charm. As the peregrine's spirit goes dormant and his wings and feathers retract into his skin, he unsheathes his sword and lops off the top half of the rod, killing the enchantment and revealing the camp to the rest of his forces.

People run and shriek among the shacks and tents, some trying to escape into the jungles. But there will be teams of legionnaires and a contingent of Jasiri ready to greet them.

A bolt of moonfire sails toward Kamali, shot from one of those irksome binduki weapons. The bolt misses his eyeless mask by less than an inch, burning a hole into the tree behind him.

He once suggested to the emperor that they study these new weapons and perhaps replicate them for the legions, but the emperor was disinterested. This despite having lost an alarming number of mystics to what was supposed to be a weak resistance.

"No outworld weapons can match our magical superiority" is what the emperor said.

Having watched so many of his men perish at the hands of binduki-wielding insurgents, Kamali has a different opinion.

He moves, feeding power to the chameleon snaking around his left arm. As it awakens, he gains a form of invisibility by camouflaging into his surroundings. A second bolt of moonfire misses, and so does the next one.

Panicking, the insurgent begins to fire randomly. He cries out as Kamali lifts him off his feet by the collar of his shirt and launches him into the air. There's a loud thud when he hits the trunk of a tree and falls unconscious.

Another rebel runs to Kamali, swinging a hatchet blindly like a madwoman, but he lays her out with a punch to the head. He moves on, knowing exactly where he must go.

He's unable to remain merciful. He summons speed from his moongold vertebra and cuts down a pair of well-trained sentries armed with spears. He dismembers a skilled swordsman who puts himself in his way.

At his destination, an elderly mystic he recognizes as a former instructor of the House of Forms has put herself in front of a group of rebels armed with bindukis. They're all standing outside a large tent, and the two Halusha ash witches behind her have fear written on their faces.

"We won't die without a fight, Jasiri," the instructor bravely says, her shards glowing with power.

He stops, letting them take a good look at him. Some of the rebels eye his sword, which is dripping with blood. The weapons in their hands begin to shake, their aim wavering. The Saire prince is in the tent, no doubt, with his former Sentinels as his last defense.

Kamali finds that he admires these people for their dedication to their leader. Yet this changes nothing. "Stand down and you won't be harmed," he declares.

"Never!" yells a bald woman armed with a sword. "My family will be avenged!"

"Aisha, don't!" cries the former instructor, ashen with dread, but the woman is already charging.

She swings and then gasps, her eyes bulging with shock. She looks down at her chest, at Kamali's sword, which has pierced her, running her through completely, and then looks back up into his eyeless mask.

Everyone watches as he withdraws his blade and helps her to the ground. He suffers a pang of guilt at the look she gives him in her dying moments, the sheer depths of hatred.

The armed rebels prepare to fire their weapons.

"Stop!" shouts the former instructor, defeat in her voice and posture. "Please. All of you. Lay down your weapons. It's over."

By now the legionnaires have worked their way across the camp. Many rebels are on their knees, their hands interlaced behind their heads. As the rebels in front of the tent obey the elderly mystic and drop their weapons, another masked Jasiri approaches with a squad of spear-wielding legionnaires.

Kamali nods at the Jasiri. "Take them away. I'll deal with the prince."

"Yes, General."

The former instructor, the ash witches, and an independent mystic don't resist as they're clapped in muting collars. Kamali waits until they're all led away before he enters the tent, where he finds the Saire prince standing with the aid of a cane and a metal brace on his left leg.

With him are three youths, former Sentinels no doubt, as well as a man and woman with active cosmic shards. The Sentinels each have long-barreled bindukis aimed at Kamali. The prince is also armed, though his weapon is of a smaller make, designed to be held in one hand.

Kamali stops a good several yards away and watches them. They all return the favor. "I do not wish to harm any of you," he says.

"We will die fighting before we let you take us to your emperor," says one Sentinel.

Slowly, Kamali reaches up to take off his mask. His eyes sting as they adjust to the light, but the colors around him become vibrant. Cosmic sight, though truer than eyesight, has very little fidelity to the color of things.

Recognition dawns on the prince's face, his mouth falling open. "You."

"Your Highness," Kamali says, addressing him directly. "You and your people need not die here today."

"Ha! You think I'm forcing them to do this?" the prince says. "You think I have any power over their decisions? They're stubborn bastards, Jasiri, just like me, and I go where they go."

Running a thumb over the hilt of his sword, Kamali makes a decision. "You helped save my life once. I owe you a debt, and I intend to repay it. But I need your word that you'll leave the Yontai once I let you go. Do not continue this fight, Your Highness. Enough people have died."

They all look to each other. "You would let us go?" the prince says, sounding incredulous.

"Only if I believe you will end this rebellion," Kamali warns. "The emperor has been restraining himself thus far. I won't allow you to force his hand."

Prince Jomo looks to his Sentinels again, a silent argument passing between them. Whatever is communicated, he firms his expression and makes his choice. "We will leave if you let us go. You'll never see us again."

By the looks of it, not all his Sentinels agree. A complication. "Where's Ilapara?"

"Why do you care?" the prince snaps, then looks away. "She left weeks ago. I don't know where she is, and I don't think she's coming back."

Kamali entertains the idea of plunging into the prince's mind and seeing the truth for himself but ultimately decides against it. "Keep your word, Your Highness. Do not continue this fight. Leave and never return. I'll make sure you're not followed."

They don't wait around long enough for him to question his decision. From the top of a boulder at one edge of the camp, he watches them disappear into the jungles while his forces secure the rest of the prisoners.

He feels a change in pressure in the air and isn't surprised when Taji appears beside him with a clap of thunder and a flare of red lightning, having transposed herself through the Void from miles away. Such a spell was once thought impossible, but with the emperor's new magics and machines, it has become routine.

"The emperor will *not* be pleased," she says, following Kamali's gaze.

"I ended the resistance," he says without looking at her. "That's what he wanted, isn't it? I don't have to spill more blood than necessary."

"But how can it be over when you failed to crush the head of the snake?"

"I have his word," Kamali says and meets Taji's stare. "Sometimes we don't have a choice but to fight the wars that come our way. But they don't have to change who we are."

She places a gentle hand on his arm, perhaps a gesture meant to comfort him, but her eyes say something else: *You've already changed. You just don't know it.*

Kamali looks away, hoping she's wrong.

Several transpositions through the Void, with brief stops so that Taji can rest, get them back to Yonte Saire in under an hour. They appear inside a dedicated arrival area within the newly reconstructed royal palace, a domed chamber of marble and cerise-colored frescos warded to accept only the emperor and his team of transposers.

The two sentries posted there, both armed with enchanted spears and decked out in the crimson-and-aerosteel livery of the new Imperial Guard, salute as Kamali steps down with Taji from the circular arrival dais. None of the new guard are mystics, but magic from mysterious ancestral talents pours off their breastplates and vibrates from their bones in ways that irritate Kamali's gums.

They also always seem to know where the emperor is and what he wants.

"Honored Left Hand of the Emperor," one of them says, beating his chest with a fist. "His Imperial Majesty requests your immediate presence in the bloodrose garden."

Kamali kills off an internal spike of annoyance. He was hoping to sink beneath the cool and soapy waters of a bathing pool for an hour or two.

"I'll see you later," he says to Taji as they leave the chamber.

She squeezes his arm for a second time today. "Good luck."

They part ways, and Kamali navigates the newly tiled and painted hallways of the Summit to meet his fate. The rebuilt Summit is not quite as sizable as the palace it replaced—for one thing, there's no longer a large extended royal family to house anymore. But its architects spared no expense to make it worthy of an emperor. They used the new machines and magics to construct marvels Kamali didn't know were possible: moving sculptures of moongold, fountains with hovering spouts of water, a garden of the rarest flower in all the Redlands.

Kamali reckons the bloodrose garden alone is more valuable than the entire royal complex that stood before the explosion.

He barricades his mind behind an arcane ward of cipher prose as soon as he steps out into the garden. Bloodroses in perennial bloom are everywhere. Their scarlet petals glisten with dew amid a sea of the greenest leaves, sharp thorns promising a bloody reward to anyone who dares disturb their parade. Latent, poorly understood magic oozes off them with such strength the air is saturated with a dizzying sense of unbridled desire and possibility, the idea that any wish could come true. Kamali is still affected despite his ward.

The emperor is indeed waiting for him along a stone path meandering through the garden. Aside from the thin, sinuous band of moongold resting on his bald scalp, the old man hasn't changed his manner of dress since ascending to his throne. Fine but modest robes of crimson-and-cream-colored brocade cover his lank frame, which stands erect even in his advanced age, hands clasped behind his back, his scarified face set in a severe expression.

Kamali catches sight of the seven masked men and women of the new Shirika walking off in a group toward the colossus rising at one corner of the Summit's plateau. No one knows who they are or where they came from. Not even Kamali knows the identity of his new coven master; she wore her mask when she blessed him with her Axiom, and he hasn't spoken to her since.

The old Shirika consisted of high mystics who were equals among themselves. The new Shirika are completely loyal to the emperor and, in Kamali's experience, never venture far from him.

"Your Imperial Majesty," Kamali says with a low bow. "The camp was successfully captured and destroyed. The resistance is no more."

He remains in a bowed position until he is given the signal that he can stand upright. When the emperor begins to walk, following the Shirika, Kamali does the same, falling into step beside the emperor. They leave the bloodrose garden and walk across a lawn dotted with palm trees, on their way to what used to be the Meeting Place by the Summit, where the king's wedding took place.

Before that fateful wedding, the colossus that presided over the Meeting Place was a gilded warrior-prince who stood as a reminder of Saire dominance over the kingdom. He has since been replaced by a redhawk sculpture of equally massive proportions, which stands on its perch with its wings tucked in, looking over the city beneath the plateau like a god watching over his realm.

"Do you know the story of Senenhathor Nerikasher?" the emperor says without preamble, his deep voice sending shivers of static through Kamali's bones. "She was a Hegemon who ruled during the latter years of the Sunset Ascendancy, some twelve centuries ago."

Kamali is no Akili, no scholar or librarian. What he knows of the Ascendancy couldn't fill a page even if he wrote it down in his largest script. He knows it had a long line of emperors who called themselves Hegemons, that it waned and strengthened repeatedly over the course of three thousand years, with its peaks divided into three distinct periods: the Sunrise Age, the Midday Age, and the Sunset Age, which was the most recent.

He also now knows the Ascendancy had something to do with the All Axiom, the very thing that drove him to commit murder in the Pavilion of Discovery in an attempt to save his people from calamitous change . . .

· Not that this helped in the end.

"I'm not familiar with any of the Hegemons, Your Majesty," he says, staring intently at the ground ahead. "I never had the privilege of learning the history of the outer world."

"Yet another mistake the academy shall have to rectify," the emperor says. "We can no longer afford to be ignorant of the world beyond our shores. A discussion for another time. I want to talk about the Hegemon Senenhathor Nerikasher, whose people were once ruthless slavers and oppressors before an uprising saw them exiled to an island somewhere in the Northern Hemisphere.

"Now, Nerikasher knew her people's collective guilt would prove an obstacle to her plans for nation building, so one of the first things she did on her path to becoming Hegemon was to scour the island for all historical records predating the exile—and destroy them. She then furnished her people with new histories that cleansed them of blame. *They* were the victims, they now believed, an oppressed but long-suffering tribe driven off their rightful lands not by the people they'd once enslaved but by evil invaders."

Kamali risks a glance at the emperor, wondering where the story is going.

"The central myth Nerikasher created revolved around a particular flower that supposedly once grew on the island, though no living specimens were ever found. Their ancestors, the new histories claimed, having escaped genocide and slavery from an ocean away, had sailed across the misty waters for many moons and were losing hope they would ever find a new home, when, lo and behold, an island appeared in the mists. And on this island grew a violet flower whose nectar was so nutritious it made the new settlers taller, stronger, brighter, and fairer skinned than their former oppressors."

The emperor stops, staring at the colossal redhawk with his hands still clasped behind him. When his eyes light up with white-red magic, the colossus begins to *move*, slowly stretching out its four gigantic wings, lifting its head higher and opening its long beak as if in threat. It is a display that will be visible from all corners of the city and even beyond the perimeter walls.

Kamali remains silent.

Once the redhawk has fully extended itself, the emperor's eyes dim, and he resumes his walk.

"This mythical flower," he continues, "and the belief it symbolized would later become the rallying cry of Nerikasher's reign as Hegemon. Entire peoples were slaughtered beneath its vengeful banner. The world learned to tremble at the sight of its violet petals. Her reign was short lived, thankfully, and after the fall of the Ascendancy, her history, along with the histories of all the other Hegemons, was expunged and suppressed to the point where you will not find a complete account of it anywhere in the outer world." The emperor stops to face Kamali. "Do you know why I have told you this tale, young man?"

Kamali stops, too, but keeps his eyes downcast. "No, Your Majesty."

"Senenhathor Nerikasher is barely remembered," the emperor says. "It is quite possible that our libraries are the only place with a complete accounting of her deeds. But the people of her island? They still revere her mythical flower. To this day they wear it on their chests, paint it onto their ships, print it onto their coins. It is on their flags and military uniforms. If you were to go there now and speak ill of the flower or desecrate its image, you would be hanged for blasphemy.

"That is the power of a symbol, Kamali. It can condense an entire philosophy, even one built on a foundation of lies, myths, and historical revisionism, into a single uncomplicated idea that can outlast the very empire that gave birth to it. Symbols are how you build militaries, how you convince a peasant to fight, kill, and die on the battlefield for reasons he does not understand, how you give him the pride to say, *This is why I'm better than everyone else.* Symbols are the bedrocks upon which nations and kingdoms are founded, and you have just let the most powerful symbol of the resistance escape."

I don't fear this man, Kamali tells himself. *I don't fear death.*

But images of burning villages fill his mind, flesh melting off the bones of innocent women and children who call his name, demanding to know why he failed to save them.

He goes down on one knee before the emperor, head bowed in penitence. "I didn't wish to disrespect you, Your Majesty. I believed the prince was honest when he told me he would end his rebellion. I also owed him a debt I wished to repay. I would have died a prisoner were it not for his help."

The emperor watches Kamali. "The prince believed what he told you in that moment. There's no guarantee he won't change his mind."

"He's lost his will to fight, Your Majesty. A young woman was his primary drive; she is no longer with him. I'm certain that without her presence he won't pick up arms against you."

"And if he does?"

"Then I will kill him with my bare hands and deliver his head to you."

"Either that or I shall have to handle the matter myself."

Kamali finds the courage to look up into the emperor's deep-set eyes. "I serve you so you won't have to. He will not be a problem."

The emperor's face yields nothing about whether he believes Kamali, but he nods. "Rise. I have another task for you."

Kamali obeys and joins the emperor on his slow walk to the Meeting Place by the Summit, where the Shirika are waiting for him. "Another symbol has risen in the southwest," the emperor says. "I'm sending you there to take care of it."

Kamali stares at the emperor. "You wish me to assassinate the King of the West?"

Some weeks ago, the emperor returned from a diplomatic trip out of the Yontai with news that a new and powerful king had risen in the southwestern desert. Though he confided very little about his trip,

Kamali had the impression that the emperor was deeply puzzled by the development.

The emperor waves a dismissive hand. "No. Not him. At least not yet, and perhaps not ever. I have my doubts about him, but I believe he presents an interesting opportunity." With a far-off look in his eyes, the emperor says, "I wear a fragment of the Hegemon's crown, yet much of its power remains dormant for reasons I didn't understand before. I may understand them now. We've always suspected that the fall of the Faraswa people and the end of the Ascendancy were related given their close chronological proximity. I've seen evidence that this theory has merit."

"What sort of evidence?" Kamali asks.

"A recently excavated pyramid of impressive size out in the dunes of the Faraswa Desert. I judged that it gave off nearly as much power as the Red Temple's inner sanctum. Perhaps more." A frown creases the emperor's forehead. "The Faraswa changed something when they activated it. Whether this was by mistake or design, I believe it weakened the lords of the Ascendancy and doomed its creators. I intend to help the new king bring an end to its curse."

"But wouldn't an Akili or Msani be more appropriate for such a task?" Kamali asks. "I'm just a warrior."

"And a warrior is precisely what I need," the emperor says. "Tell me, are you familiar with the name Meddur the Wise? He's a Faraswa gentleman of Inoi origin who's been causing quite a bit of a stir these last several moons."

Kamali nearly frowns, wondering what this has to do with his new mission. "I've heard the name. I believe the Faraswa in this city look up to him as a spiritual leader."

"Not just those in this city, I'm afraid. His fanatical gospel has spread well beyond the borders of the Yontai, and all because I acted too late." A scowl visits the emperor's face. "I let him be in my desire to demonstrate a more generous and permissive attitude toward the

Faraswa people. But this 'Meddur the Wise' has used the developments in the desert to infect his people with dreams of a new awakening, and now we face the possibility of Faraswa emigrating en masse to their old homeland. I'm sure I don't need to explain why this would be disastrous, do I?"

"No, Your Majesty," Kamali says. "The Faraswa are . . . important contributors to the Yontai's economy."

The emperor makes a scoffing noise. "You mince your words. The Faraswa are *vital* to our economy. We depend on exploiting their cheap labor. Obviously, this must change in time, but right now we simply cannot afford to lose the Faraswa, especially not all at once. Far better to slowly integrate them into our society. Meddur the Wise, however, has complicated matters, perhaps beyond repair."

Kamali nods, beginning to see the contours of what the emperor expects of him. "Where is he now?"

"He must have read the signs and known I was about to lose my patience, so he fled. South, I believe, likely into the desert itself. But the fires he lit continue to burn in his absence. Find him and bring him to me alive. I will need him to publicly renounce his teachings and restore calm to the Faraswa community." The emperor lifts his chin, looking toward the colossus. "You leave in the morning with a transposer. And you will be discreet, understood? The new king is not to know of your presence."

"Yes, Your Majesty," Kamali says.

"Don't disappoint me this time. There will be consequences if you do."

Knowing he's been dismissed, Kamali bows and remains in place while the emperor proceeds to join his Shirika in the Meeting Place. Only after the emperor is a safe distance away does Kamali retreat back to the palace, his chest torn between relief and creeping dread.

◆　◆　◆

He relaxes on the submerged steps at one end of his bathing pool, letting the echoes of dripping water lull him halfway to sleep. A Saire prince or princess once bathed in this chamber. Now it's part of his private quarters as the Left Hand of the Emperor.

His eyes remain closed when the door opens and footsteps approach the pool. There are ripples in the water as a second bather enters, and his skin tingles at the sound of her voice.

"Since you're still alive, I assume the emperor gave you a chance to fix your mistake."

Kamali opens his eyes and takes in Taji's naked form, covered only by the waist-high water. Dark freckles dapple her cheeks, and a light gloss dances over her full, sensuous lips. Her smooth honey-brown skin and the graceful curves of her body make Kamali's pulse quicken as she draws nearer.

"Actually, I convinced him the prince no longer poses a threat," he says.

Taji arches a shapely eyebrow in surprise. "You're brave; I'll give you that." She's close enough that Kamali can smell her floral perfume. Her eyes fall to his chest, homing in on the silver ring dangling at the end of a simple chain. "You still haven't told me where you got that peculiar ring of yours. I sense—"

Kamali catches her arm before she touches the ring, their gazes clinging onto each other. "I can't give you what you want, Taji," he tells her.

A defiant fire ignites in her eyes. "And what is it you think I want?" When he fails to answer, she yanks her arm out of his hand. "You over-estimate yourself, Jasiri. You're a friend, but you're also a firm body, and that's all I need right now."

He could never give her his heart, not truly. That lies elsewhere. But they are both here in the now, searching for a physical connection to a world that has become strange. Where's the harm in taking comfort in each other? And it's not like they haven't done this before.

He drinks her in with his gaze, her skin, her curves, her breasts, and blood rushes to his member. He stares into her eyes and sees his reflection in them.

She is lost, but so am I.

The last walls of his resistance fall, and he pulls her in, yielding to desire.

10: A Stranger

A Strange Place

The stranger limps on, sweat pouring down his face, waves of pain shooting up his right leg with every step. Perhaps it's the fever, but he can't divorce himself from the idea that his shadow is longer than it should be and darker, that it might possess a mind of its own and could swallow him if he tripped and fell.

He casts those thoughts aside, focusing on his present need for shelter. As he sifts through the city's lattice of signals, he comes to understand that the lattice was probably thicker and more vibrant before whatever cataclysm struck the city, but there are still quite a few signals out there yet to succumb to the vibrating sea of poison.

He follows a particularly strong one down the street, hoping it will lead to safety and maybe a place to hide, but he slows to a stop when he spots a flash of yellow on the other side of a plaza.

It's the woman from before, standing in her tattered gown at the doors to a mostly intact building of glass and metal arches. She was already in a wretched state when he first saw her, but now what was once a yellow garment is shot through with bright stripes of crimson from unseen wounds, and scrapes and bruises mark her skin all over.

And yet, despite this, she bears herself with regal poise, a fixed purpose burning in her amber eyes. He waits, thinking she'll address him, but she turns, the train of her frayed dress sweeping the ashen ground, and she simply vanishes beyond the doors like a wraith.

He blinks, still as a grave, and when his heart starts beating again, he follows.

The dead populate the plaza, many buried beneath fine blankets of ash. The stench of decay competes with the lingering smoke to irritate the stranger's nose. He finds the doors locked when he arrives, but there's a central mind core somewhere inside the building, and its walls of algorithms crumble at the slightest push, giving him complete control.

He commands the mind core to let him in, then locks the doors behind him. Semidarkness shrouds the high-ceilinged lobby. Artworks hang undisturbed on the walls, and sculptures of varied style and material stand displayed on pedestals. From the mind core the stranger deduces that the artifacts kept here were of such value that the building was protected by strong force fields—probably why it survived the cataclysm mostly intact.

Yet the sea of poison still got in. Everyone who was in here is dead. The stranger looks around. There's no sign of the woman. But from the mind core he knows there's a small kitchen in the building. A frostbox with food. *I need food.*

He limps deeper into the building, heading for the kitchen. Most of the crystal lamps in here are off. The few that are on illuminate the assortment of artworks arranged in long galleries. He spots more than a few that fell and shattered on the floor.

People used to come here to admire these artifacts. Now they shall rot here forever in this poisonous sea.

The kitchen is at the end of a hall beyond a short flight of stairs. He understands through the mind core that this was where those who worked here came for their meals during breaks. There are no windows down here, and though he understands he could use the building's core to turn the lights on, he decides not to.

In the near dark he raids the cabinets and the brass frostbox, finding an untouched loaf of bread, a clear container of cold meats, and a carton of milk. All poisoned quite extensively, but the stranger knows his body will survive it.

"Trust your instincts" is what he was told. Right now his instincts are telling him he needs this food.

Beyond the kitchen is a small living room with a single couch. He tosses all the food at the foot of the couch and groans as he settles down next to it, stretching out his wounded leg.

I'm in the land of the dead, and I'll join them if I don't eat.

His stomach proves surprisingly accommodating, and he finds that he's hungry enough to consume the whole loaf and drink every last drop of milk. Weariness envelops him as soon as he's finished, but he lacks the strength to lift himself up and lie on the couch, so he stretches out on the carpeted floor instead.

His fever persists and gives him restless dreams. He sees a king in a ragged yellow dress fighting for her soul against her own reflection, will against will, tempest against tempest, a flat and barren wasteland stretching out all around them. The reflection wears the king's face, but in place of rags, her gown is radiant and scarlet and shimmers with many stars.

She is an empress, this reflection, a force as indomitable as the cosmic winds, but the king refuses to yield, defiant. The stranger takes a step forward, thinking he must help the king. He feels it in his bones: she must have been a friend. But his shadow twists on the ground, becomes monstrous, black talons reaching up for him, a drooling smile, a horrid perversion of his own face.

He jolts awake hours later at the sound of a crash. His burnt leg no longer hurts as much as it did before, but he doesn't think he could run. Not that it would help; whoever caused that crash already knows that he's here. He senses a device on their person that detected his heat, giving him away.

Footsteps approach. Cones of bright torchlight sweep the cabinets before beaming in through the door he left open. Biting down a scream, he lifts his back off the ground and drags himself by his hands into a corner, where he hugs his knees.

They find him anyway.

Four of them in total. A suited man accompanied by three beings with luminous halos.

The man—or demon, the stranger can't be sure—is wearing a suit like the demons from earlier, but his is slimmer and smoother, with a more sophisticated power core whose presence in the invisible lattice of signals is practically imperceptible. Over the suit he wears a shoulder belt with many pockets, and the visor covering his face is clear enough that the stranger can almost see through it.

As for the other three . . .

Malaikas, the stranger thinks in awe. They look human, impressive figures in black hooded capes that flow behind them, but they must be from the heavens surely, for the steel of their armor shines like it was infused with daylight, surrounding them with auras that repel the city's poisonous energy so that they don't need suits.

Awash in their torchlight, the stranger blinks, willing his eyes to adjust. He sees that the central malaika is a woman with skin like bronzed ebony, flowing locks of braided hair, and an angular face built for a stern comportment. Her two male companions, pale skinned and flaxen haired, might be siblings given their close resemblance, though one is slender while the other is more sturdily built.

"Well, hello there," says the suited man, speaking in yet another language the stranger knows he shouldn't understand. His voice projects from a mechanized implement attached to his suit. Behind his visor, an eyepiece with a luminous green lens covers his left eye.

"Please don't hurt me," the stranger says in the same language.

Something whirs over the man's shoulder and stops to hover in front of the stranger, followed by a swarm of others just like it: spheres of brass, each the size of a plum with three telescoping tubes protruding from their surfaces. The spheres spin so that their tubes are facing him; some expand while others contract, as though the machines are trying to see him better.

He shivers when he catches sight of the large weapon hanging on a sling across the man's shoulder, a typhonic rifle with a tank of glowing red liquid and a very long barrel. Adjusting the sling, the man crouches in front of the stranger with a crooked smile, yellowed teeth showing through the thick, jet-black beard covering half his visored face.

"How curious." He reaches with a gloved hand to cup the stranger's chin and turn his face from side to side. His spheres swarm closer, their scopes pointing in the stranger's direction. "Incredible. Is that a . . . shield . . . I detect?"

Bewildered, the stranger says nothing.

"How's he even alive?" says the brawnier of the two haloed brothers.

The woman makes a noise of irritation. "Pay attention, Luka. He's not alive."

The man named Luka takes another look at the stranger, then gapes. "Suns. It's a cog. Shouldn't it be fritzing or something?"

"You go on ahead," says the suited man. "This cog must be valuable to possess such shielding technology." He grins at the stranger. "I'll fetch a nice profit from you, won't I, precious."

"Don't expect us to haul it around for you," growls Luka. "It looks injured."

"Don't worry, Your Lordship." The suited man gets up and begins to unlace the length of wound rope fastened to his side. "I'll tie it up and carry it myself. If we leave it here, it'll fall to the scavengers looting the city, and that'll just be a waste." He crouches again. "Your hands, precious. Bring them together for me. It'll be easier that way."

As if in a trance, the stranger obeys and lets the captain begin to bind him.

"You speak as though you think you're any better than the scavengers," Luka remarks.

The suited man scowls and continues the business of binding the stranger with rope. "Sanctimonious prick," he mutters in yet another tongue.

"What did you say?" Luka demands.

The woman cuts them off. "No, we're not doing this again. Luka, control your temper. Captain Axios, the cog might be able to help us find what we're looking for. I need to speak to it."

The captain sighs. He stops binding the stranger and steps aside. "Be my guest," he says in a voice the stranger now recognizes is accented. Whatever tongue these malaikas are speaking, it's foreign to the captain.

The woman comes closer, her eyes taking note of the burn on the stranger's leg.

"Do you speak Chatresian, cog?" she says.

"It seems I do," he replies, fluently and with no accent, much to his surprise.

"Do you have a name?"

The stranger hesitates. "If I do, I don't remember it."

"This is a waste of time," complains the other haloed man, and his voice gives the stranger the impression that he might be the younger of the two brothers. "We need to find the artifact. Those maniacs weren't far behind."

The woman disregards her comrade. "Do you at least know who you belong to?" she asks the stranger.

"Should I belong to someone?" he asks, surprised.

"Your kind usually does."

He thinks about it. A handsome face floats into his mind, followed by a strong pang of sorrow, but nothing more. *Maybe I did belong to someone.* "Perhaps when I was still alive," he says. "I don't remember."

"Its mind is corrupted, Julian," says Luka's brother. "We must leave it and continue our search."

"Just one moment." The woman—Julian, apparently—looks back down at the stranger. "We're soldiers of the Empire, and we seek an artifact hidden somewhere in this museum. It might have another name, but we know it as the Spectral Star. Can you help us find it?"

Museum. The stranger mulls over the new word, its meaning coming to him like something he once knew and now remembers. *A house of historical artifacts of artistic and cultural significance. That's what this place is, and since they found me here, these people think I once belonged here.*

But he knows he can't have belonged here, since he arrived only to seek refuge. So where *did* he belong?

It doesn't matter. He was told to trust his instincts, and right now they're telling him he needs to be useful to this woman. He queries the museum's archives through its mind core, absorbing the resultant flow of information, then recites it to the woman.

"There's no artifact named the 'Spectral Star' in this museum," he says. "Perhaps you might be looking for the Phantom Sunset? Also known as the Sunset of Ashermose, a gemstone that belonged to the Hegemon Rao Ashermose."

"Phantom Sunset," Luka repeats with a thoughtful frown.

"It fits, though, doesn't it?" Julian muses. "Spectral Star, Phantom Sunset. Perhaps something got lost in translation?"

"My thoughts exactly," says Luka's brother. "And if it belonged to Rao Ashermose, then it has to be what we're looking for. Can't be a coincidence."

They all look back down at the stranger. "How do we get to it?" Julian says.

From the museum's core, the stranger knows that the Sunset of Ashermose was never put on display. It was sealed away with other jewels once treasured by the Hegemons, though he lacks knowledge about who the Hegemons were or why their jewels should matter.

"The Sunset is locked in a vault five floors below," he says. "I could get you in, but . . ." He makes a point of looking down at his bound hands and wounded leg.

"Release the cog, Captain."

The captain stares. "So long as you know it's mine."

Julian spears him with an icy look full of disgust. "I wouldn't dream of robbing you of your bounty, Captain Axios. Release him."

He grunts with displeasure but complies. "As you wish." Crouching down in front of the stranger, he loosens the knots he'd begun to tie.

"Claud, help him up. And let him lean on you if he needs to."

The younger of the two brothers, Claud, reluctantly obeys, and the stranger stifles a scream as he's helped back to an upright position. Thankfully, Claud hooks the stranger's arm over his shoulder.

"Where to?" he says. The stranger can now see that his eyes are a rich brown, prideful like his brother's, though less sullen.

"We have to take the stairs," the stranger says. "This way."

According to the access logs in the mind core, a near-impenetrable system of arcane security protocols barred the vault five floors below to everyone but the museum's administrator, who rarely used the privilege.

The double doors swing open for Julian without protest.

Suspicious, she looks back over her shoulder at the stranger, seeking an explanation.

"I've deactivated the museum's security countermeasures to allow you access to the vault," he explains.

"So you *did* work here," she says.

The stranger equivocates. "I'm afraid I can't recall anything before today, Your Lordship."

The furrows on Julian's forehead deepen.

"Maybe it's the Corruption," Claud suggests. "Hard to believe he'd get away completely unscathed."

Julian sets her suspicions aside and enters the well-lit vault, Luka close behind.

Grimacing nervously, the captain draws a sign in the air as if to ward off evil. "Here's to hoping we don't anger the spirit of some ancient Red lord," he says, then enters the vault.

The stranger winces with each step as he trails behind with Claud, who takes in the rows of artifacts with awestruck wonder. "I can't believe we're actually in here. Any of these things belonged to a real, honest-to-goodness Hegemon." He shakes his head, a weak laugh escaping him. "My father will absolutely kill me."

Knowing nothing of the Hegemons, the stranger cannot relate to Claud's excitement. "What did you mean by 'Corruption,' Your Lordship?" he asks. "Did you mean the sea of poison killing everything all around us?"

Claud appears to consider the words. "I suppose 'sea of poison' is as apt a description as any. The Corruption is certainly pervasive. Though it is in truth the lingering echo of the terrible weapon that killed this city. Anathema to all living things. And cogs aren't usually built to survive it," he adds, giving the stranger a sidelong glance. "Is that why you're wearing spectacles? Because your lenses got fried?"

"My lenses, Your Lordship?"

"What are you two talking about back there?"

The captain's mechanized voice startles them both. He's stopped next to a case displaying a golden idol.

"Nothing," Claud tells him.

"Are you trying to steal my find from me, Your Lordship? You'll have to pay for him first."

"Your 'find' needs my help to walk, Captain Axios. Remember?"

The captain grunts and looks away, focusing on the idol.

"What an asshole," Claud mumbles under his breath.

"Cog, where is the Spectral Star?" Julian says. "There must be hundreds of artifacts in here. Can you point us to it?"

Cog, the stranger thinks, finally examining that word. *Short for* cogwheel. *Part of a mechanical arrangement of gears in a machine. My resilience to the Corruption must have convinced them I'm not human. Is that why they all keep talking about me like I'm a thing? Property.*

He thought he was in the land of the dead, with demons and malaikas of heaven, but now he has doubts.

The stranger points. "The Phantom Sunset is inside that display case. Break the glass; all protective enchantments have been deactivated."

For some reason suspicion strengthens in Luka's eyes. He says nothing as he and Julian walk closer to the display case the stranger pointed to.

"Put the cog down, Claud, and come over here," Luka says.

Claud obeys, helping the stranger down to the floor and letting him lean against a glass pedestal, and then he joins his comrades by the Sunset artifact. The captain, meanwhile, remains wholly riveted by the golden idol. He keeps circling its display case like he's looking for a crack in the glass.

"Is it just me, or is that cog in control of the building's security systems?" Luka whispers, perhaps thinking the stranger can't hear him. "That's not normal."

"Who cares?" Claud says. "It's helping us."

"But why?" Luka asks. "If it's part of the security system, why let us in?"

"Unsettling to be sure," Julian agrees, looking in the stranger's direction. "But the cog's memories are corrupted. Perhaps it doesn't recall what it's meant to do."

"It could be dangerous," Luka says. "Do we really want the captain bringing it onboard our ship?"

A sudden racket makes them all jump. Across the vault, Captain Axios retracts the butt of his typhon from a smashed display case. He reaches in and plucks the golden idol from its stand, making a satisfied hum.

The Imperial lords watch him expectantly, possibly waiting to see if a security system punishes him for his transgression. When he remains unharmed, Julian proceeds to break the glass of the display case in front of her with a fist, then reaches in and lifts a transparent crystal out of the case before holding it up to the ceiling lamps. Two bright points of light shine within it, or perhaps the illusion of them, so that it appears she's holding a slice of the double sunset frozen in time. Webs of energies wrap around the gem in thick, oscillating patterns.

"Test it," Luka says, breaking the awed silence. "We need to make sure we have the right thing."

"I'm not an idiot," Julian mutters. "Here. Hold it for a second."

She hands Luka the artifact, then reaches into a shoulder bag to retrieve what looks to the stranger like a book with covers of filigreed gold. She places the book gently on top of a nearby display case and opens it about halfway through. The pages are thin enameled panels that, like the covers, are hinged to the spine.

Enchantments have been woven so thickly onto the book the stranger cannot see through them to determine their purpose, but when Julian takes the artifact back from Luka and shines its illusory light onto the pages, the layers of magic seem to peel away.

Julian gasps. "By the suns. I can see the scripts!"

"Really?" Claud leans closer to look. "What does it say?"

The three Imperials lean forward to read the contents of the book, but after a few seconds, Luka shakes his head with a grim frown. "Gibberish."

"Not gibberish," Claud tells him. "Ancient hieratic. Julian, you can translate this, can't you?"

Worry crosses Julian's eyes, but not enough to dim her excitement. "It'll take time," she says. "But we have the Star now. Let's not linger."

Just as well, the stranger thinks, for they're no longer alone. Through the arcane scopes affixed onto the ceilings in every room, he sees a group of six haloed individuals walking into the building through the smashed entrance. All six intruders are wearing white cloaks over shiny breastplates embossed with solar symbols.

The stranger watches them march down a staircase, no doubt on their way here. Allies? Or the mysterious "maniacs" Claud referenced earlier? The stranger doesn't wait to find out. He partially reactivates the museum's security, locking all the doors behind and in front of the interlopers. They quickly find themselves trapped in a hallway two sublevels above.

Only once he's limping out of the vault with Claud's help does he raise the alarm. "Your Lordships, we have company. Several people have just entered the building through the same entrance you used. Like you, they are clothed in sunlight."

"What?" Luka slows to a stop at the foot of the stairwell leading back up and tilts his head as if to catch a distant sound. His eyes widen. "Oh shit. He's right."

Claud tenses, the captain utters a curse, and the stranger sees fear crossing Julian's stern features for the first time since they met. She looks up the stairwell. "What now?"

"The way out remains clear," the stranger says without elaborating. "We'll escape if we don't tarry."

"Luka, help him for a minute."

Claud hands the stranger over to Luka, who accepts the burden with an unhappy scowl. The stranger winces in pain as he finds his balance, draping one arm over Luka's broad shoulders.

"What, he's too heavy?" Captain Axios says with a chuckle.

"It's not that." Claud quickly unfastens the little black book dangling from his belt. "I must speak a benediction so our friends cannot scry for us. Go. I'll do it on the way up."

They hurry up the stairs while Claud mutters prayers from his book in a tongue the stranger—for once—doesn't understand. Yet somehow, the words manage to evoke the sensation of sunlight against his skin.

Explosive sounds begin to echo down the stairwell as the enemy Imperials battle to destroy the enchantments now confining them. The doors continue to hold for now, but the building's integrity is compromised, and so is the energy source powering its security systems. Eventually, the doors will give in.

Julian catches on to what's happening. "Sounds like they trapped themselves in one of the galleries," she says. "Hurry."

"Apostates!" comes an angry voice from elsewhere in the museum. "We know you're here. There's nowhere on earth you can hide from us! We'll find you!"

Luka picks up the stranger and slings him over one shoulder, even as he continues taking the stairs three at a time. He shows no evidence of exertion, but when they finally reach the lobby, he puts the stranger back down and loudly exhales.

"You're heavier than you look," he says, panting.

The stranger tries not to grimace from the pain of being jostled around. "Thank you for the assistance, Your Lordship."

"Where are they now?" Claud whispers, taking over from Luka and hooking the stranger's arm over his shoulder once again.

"Still trapped," the stranger tells him. "The doors are strong and will hold them for a while longer."

Julian has already left through the opening they blasted into the museum's glass facade. She looks around for threats before beckoning to the rest of the team. "We're clear. Come on."

"I was thinking," Claud says as they limp for the exit, "what shall we call you? It seems odd to keep calling you 'cog.' Surely you had a name before."

The stranger is touched by the sentiment, but as much as he tries, he fails to make his true name materialize from the fog of his memories. So he quickly searches the museum's records for names and selects the first one he likes. "Perhaps you could call me Salim."

"Well met, Salim," Claud says. "Now let's get the devil out of here."

PART 3

ILAPARA
*
SALIM

11: Ilapara

Far Away

The bed beneath Ilapara cushions her aching body so well she never wants to move again, but something isn't right.

I shouldn't be here, cries a voice from the haze of her semiconscious mind. Fear seizes her and she bolts upright, expecting to see the strange men who ambushed her when she alighted from Tuk's sand raft.

But the men aren't here. She's alone on a bed in a cramped little room longer than it is wide, with a low ceiling. Her bed spans most of the width of the room, leaving just enough space on either side for a nightstand with a bedside lamp. A door stands on the wall to her right, a large window covered with blinds on the wall to her left. The soft golden glow slipping in through the blinds tells her it's daylight outside, though not precisely what time of day it is.

Slowly she brings her feet onto the carpeted floor, groaning as she straightens up. Her head throbs and begs her to lie back down onto the nice bed, but she forces herself to stay upright, bracing a hand against the wall until she can stand on her own. She takes several wobbly steps around the foot of the bed and to the window, where she lifts a slat on the blinds to peer outside.

"By Ama . . ."

She's seen so many inexplicable things in her life at this point. Giant spirits staring at her from across a desert. Moving statues in a pavilion of moongold. By now she should be inured to the seemingly impossible. And yet the vision beyond the window leaves her dizzy, breathless, doubting her own eyes.

She steps away and moves for the door, then shivers at the feel of its cold steel handle on her fingers. It opens out onto a narrow hallway lined with windows on her right and a few more doors on the left. She follows the hallway down to a long and narrow lounge with armchairs and tables.

Tuk is there, alone, sitting on an armchair and holding a porcelain teacup with one hand while he stares at the vambrace on his other arm, an elaborate creation of brown leather with brass fittings—knobs, gears, and switches as well as a flat panel displaying tiny scripts of multicolored Mirror light.

He's shaved his beard in the time since she last saw him, and he's washed out and combed his long wavy hair. He's also changed into a formfitting shirt beneath a waistcoat, a pair of trousers, and boots, all black.

In a way, this is the Tuk she remembers from when they first met. Confident. Dashing. Mysterious. But this is also him in his natural environment, the person he was before coming to the Redlands, and she realizes that this part of him is a stranger to her. She didn't even know he liked tea.

His cheeks dimple when he sees her, eyes a sparkling shade of green. "Ah. There you are. I was beginning to worry you'd never wake up. Come. Sit. Breakfast should be here momentarily."

Breakfast. That answers what time it is. It was afternoon when she was knocked out. Has she been out the whole night? Wordlessly, Ilapara moves to sit on the armchair across Tuk's table. The blinds on the large window next to her are raised. Looking at the view, she curses under her breath.

The world outside is moving. And fast. Prairies and meadows hurtle by at breathtaking speed, leaving only the muted sound of a howling wind in their wake. Of course, Ilapara knows that *she's* the one in motion, but the only sign of movement is the slight hum coming up from the floor. As she looks out the window and up, she sees a long diaphanous membrane attached to the top of whatever vehicle is carrying her forward, flexing and oscillating through the air like the fin of a sea creature. A very long creature at that, judging by the length of the lounge alone.

"By the way," Tuk says, "I had your bracelet recharged with essence while we were in town. I had to pay extra so the local arcanist wouldn't ask questions about where I got it." He slides across the table Ilapara's golden bracelet, which Salo endowed with stealth magic back in Yonte Saire, among other spells.

Quietly she picks it up and slips it onto her left wrist. "This is the part where you explain what the devil's going on," she says. "How'd we get here? What happened to the men who attacked us?"

"I took care of the men after you fell," Tuk says with the casual air of someone reciting what they ate for dinner last night. "Then I stole their vehicle and dragged you into town and onto the next outbound leviathan—all without raising suspicion, by the way. It wasn't easy."

"How did you 'take care' of the men? There were at least a dozen of them."

He waves a hand dismissively. "I have built-in immunity to tranquilizers. How are you feeling, by the way?"

"Like I fell down a long flight of stairs."

"Don't worry. The effects should wear off soon."

Outside, tracts of plowed fields whoosh by, and she catches the glimpse of large machines lumbering along the furrows. *I'm no longer in the Redlands,* she thinks. *I crossed the Jalama to the other side.* She reaches for Jomo's ivory pendant and takes comfort in its solid shape and the sense of his whereabouts. So distant now, but there, somewhere, waiting for her. "So this is a leviathan?" she asks.

"The fastest vehicle on land," Tuk replies. "Named after the giant eels of the northern Inoetera. You'll understand why when you see it from the outside. We should be arriving in Apos in a few hours."

Apos. The name means nothing to Ilapara. She turns away from the view and looks Tuk in the eye. "And then?"

"And then we go meet the woman who'll help bring Salo back." Tuk turns a brass knob on his forearm device, and the Mirror light scripts on the flat panel appear to move in response. "She's hosting her weekly salon at her estate later this evening. I've asked a friend of mine to arrange a pair of invitations for us. We'll stop by his place, get the invitations, get dressed for the occasion; then we'll pay her a visit."

Ilapara stops herself from staring at the device, recognizing she's probably about to be inundated with all sorts of magics and technologies she's never seen. "This woman," she says. "The one hosting the . . . salon, is it?"

"Yes. A fancy gathering of artists from all over the Enclave."

"Right. Well. I'm still stuck on the part about this woman bringing Salo back. How's that going to work exactly?"

Tuk's eyes wander out the window. "The thing is, Ilapara, this woman . . . she was a well-known arcanist in the Empire. Made living toys for wealthy nobles. Pets at first. A metal snake that could turn into an ornament for a staff. A cat with fur that could change color. That sort of thing." He hesitates again, his shoulders going stiff. "My sister and I . . . we were her first human creations. Before us, atmechs were very machinelike. Anyone could tell from a glance what they were. Then a curious necromancer figured out that the best way to imitate life was not to imitate it at all but to *be* it. She harnessed the residual essence of dead humans and rebuilt them using synthetic components. We were the result." Tuk locks eyes with Ilapara. They've darkened by several shades. "It made her a fortune."

This is a sensitive topic for him—Ilapara knows this from experience. She also thinks she's beginning to see the larger strokes of his plan and can't help but suffer a strong spasm of disappointment, the feeling that she's come all this way for nothing. "You want to bring Salo back as an atmech."

"Oh, don't look at me like that. I'm not crazy. I know how it sounds, but it'll work."

"I don't see how," she says. "Tuk, you once told me you were built from the memory of someone who lived long ago, but you're not the same person. That means whoever your creator makes won't be Salo but a shade."

"That's just it," Tuk says. "You're right; I'm a flawed copy of a dead man. I have his face, I have some of his memories and quirks of personality, but my soul, if you believe in such a thing, is different from his." Tuk unearths a familiar yellow stone from a pocket on his pants. "Salo's true self is preserved in this stone. Not a copy but him. His true essence. His consciousness. When my creator builds a body around it, the person who'll emerge will be, for all intents and purposes, the Salo we both know."

Ilapara studies the stone, finding Tuk's words nearly impossible to believe. "Are you sure?"

He retracts the hand with the stone, turning his gaze out the window. "We'll get him back, Ilapara," he quietly says. "I believe it with all my heart."

"I pray you're right," she says and decides not to say more on the subject. "Now, is there a lavatory somewhere on this thing, because I feel like my bladder's about to burst."

"Oh. Sorry. Yes. Straight down the hall. The door next to your cabin."

It turns out Tuk rented out the entire front section of the leviathan, and when Ilapara asks him how he was able to afford such a thing, his answers are evasive. A middle-aged man in a smartly pressed gray uniform emerges from somewhere beyond the lounge to serve them a breakfast of tea and sweetened cakes. She notices him giving her a lingering glance, but what little he says sounds polite. Not understanding a word, Ilapara keeps silent and lets Tuk do the talking.

"Looks like we picked the worst time to cross the Jalama," he says after the servant leaves.

"Oh?"

He nods at his bracer device and speaks around a mouthful of pastry. "A group of Eastern Vigilants are claiming that a new Hegemon has risen. The Empire and the Enclave don't like that, so they're rattling their sabers, threatening war unless the East shuts them down. The East is refusing to comply and making threats of their own. Cooler heads usually prevail when these sorts of things flare up, but something feels different about this. It's almost as if everyone *wants* a war."

Ilapara considers the different parts of this political puzzle. "Are these the same Vigilants you belong to?"

"It's a common tactic for governments to slander any group they hate as Vigilants, so I doubt it." He pauses, listing his head in thought. "I can't be sure, though. Each cell operates independently, so they might be. We had a base in Apos, but we scattered just before I left. Someone was hunting us down."

"You make it sound like you're not very popular."

"Our enemies have been effective at making us look like terrorists."

"And you're not?"

Tuk's eyes dim. "We never target innocents. We never kill just for the sake of killing. That would go against everything we stand for."

Ilapara takes a bite of a jam-filled pastry and wipes her mouth. "Is my appearance going to draw attention?" she says. "I noticed that man staring at me."

"The steward?" Tuk says. "He was just curious. I had to bribe him to let me smuggle an unconscious woman onboard. You might need to change once we get to the city, but even if you don't, they'll just assume you're from the south. They dress like that near the desert towns."

Ilapara looks down at her filthy traveling robe. "I meant beyond my clothing," she clarifies. "My hair. My complexion. Won't it be obvious I'm not from around here?"

"Not really. The world outside the Redlands has seen many waves of migration, people from everywhere going everywhere else. You can't really tell where someone's from just by looking at them. Especially in major cities, which attract all sorts of people. Your clothes will probably raise some eyebrows, but that's easy to fix." A thought seems to occur to him. "Although I *am* concerned about the language situation. Syliaric is one of the most widely spoken tongues in the world. You not understanding a word of it will be suspicious."

"I can just keep quiet and avoid people."

"Not good enough. You need to know what's going on around us, and there *is* a way for that to happen. It's how I managed to get by when I first crossed the Jalama, before I got my hands on a language nexus. But knowing you . . . perhaps it's best I tell you when it becomes necessary. I don't want you to fret."

"I resent that," Ilapara huffs. "I don't fret."

"Did I say *fret*? I meant *glare at me until I have holes in my head*. Relax. Enjoy your breakfast. Adjust. Trust that I have everything under control, because I do."

She doesn't believe that, but she keeps her opinion to herself.

It's almost high noon when they finally reach the outskirts of the city. The skyline appears outside their window as the leviathan races along the foot of a rounded hill, giving Ilapara her very first look at civilization beyond the Redlands in all its glory.

Gilded towers and hovering citadels with rose-tinted windows rise absurdly high along a wide stretch of coast, presenting a glittering view of shifting reds and golds against the pale sky, like a constellation of stars. Beyond them lies a body of turquoise waters larger even than Lake Zivatuanu, perhaps larger than any lake, for this is no lake at all but a sea. Or maybe even an ocean. The very edge of the continent.

There are things flying in the skies, too, fortresses reflecting the sunlight as they go out to sea. They are large as buildings perhaps, though they seem immune to the laws that govern how heavy objects should act under forces of gravity.

She catches her faint reflection in the window and sees that she's clutching her ivory pendants in a death grip. The worry in her own eyes sobers her, and she lets the pendants go. Yonte Saire seemed like a city plucked from a dream when she first set foot there. Now, here's a place built by people who fly across oceans, a city with hovering citadels whose windows and spires sparkle like jewels and make the world's beating heart look crude in comparison.

"Each time I think I know my place in the world," she murmurs, "I'm shown to be even smaller and more insignificant than I thought I was."

Tuk grunts. "It is impressive, yes," he says. "The Ruby of the Northern Coast, the center of the Enclave, the Seat of Vice, or, as I like to call it, Smoke and Mirrors. Be wary, my friend. Around these parts, trust is a precious commodity you'd do well to guard closely to your chest."

"Sounds like Yonte Saire, then."

"Except with more drugs, assassins, blackmail, and deceit," Tuk says. "Anyone who has power here has blood on their hands."

The leviathan sprints into the city's jungle of towers and slows to a stop, and then an announcement delivered in Syliaric booms across the cabin. She follows Tuk's lead and disembarks onto a long and busy platform in a terminal with an arched glass ceiling that tints the light filtering in with a rose hue.

Looking at the leviathan from the outside for the first time, she immediately understands why it was named thus. Golden and streamlined like an ornamental eel, the leviathan has a pair of flexible crimson membranes attached to either side of the roof, running the length of the vehicle so that it vaguely looks like it was meant to swim through water, not float across the land at great speed. Another leviathan slows into the terminal with a hiss and stops at a different platform to deposit more passengers. A smell like burnt molasses fills the air.

Tuk catches her wrinkling her nose and says, "It's the moonglass."

"The what?" she says.

"The membranes. The 'fins' on the leviathans. It's the same material that made my sand raft work. On heavy machines, moonglass emits a sweet but slightly acrid burning smell. Get used to it because it's all over the city."

Panels of brass flicker with images and foreign scripts all over the terminal and the concourse leading away from the platforms. As she follows Tuk along the crowded concourse and into a large hall built of steel and glass, Ilapara watches the people around her closely, trying to absorb as much firsthand knowledge about them as she can.

To her surprise, the people are in fact as varied as Tuk suggested, spanning the full spectrum of heights, builds, and complexions. Were it not for Ilapara's distinctly exotic robe, there'd be nothing specific about her that would make her stand out.

They drag wheeled metal cases of luggage behind them, threading through each other like ants in their nest. The men seem to prefer darkly colored coats, waistcoats, and jackets that hug their chests. The women wear tight-fitting bodices, but their skirts are wide, and their fabrics swirl with color. Here and there Ilapara spots someone dressed differently—a woman in a robe much like hers, a man in a bulky coat of spotted fur—but most of the denizens of this city seem to blend into the crowd, and a less vigilant eye might miss the details that set some of them apart . . .

A finer cut of material. A lily-white shirt that's never known a stain. A necklace of pure silver set with scarlet gemstones. That man strutting about like a peacock is obviously wealthy and important, and the three goons walking with him, pushing people out of his way, must be his bodyguards. A mystic, perhaps? A wealthy aristocrat?

They exit the terminal and emerge onto an outdoor plaza. From here the rose-tinted towers of the city rise so high some of them block out the suns. Just the sight of them is enough to make Ilapara dizzy.

A bronze statue of a woman with a cunning expression, crowned with a crescent moon and standing atop a globe, hovers at the center of the plaza, suspended in place by magic. Larger versions of Tuk's sand raft can be seen gliding along the maze of surrounding roadways, some of them with shells to encase their passengers in privacy. The air indeed carries the scent of burning syrup, but the breeze is salty and otherwise fresh.

She could stand here all day and just watch and absorb the sights, but Tuk sets a brisk pace, leading her beyond the plaza and toward a wide canal. Fast-moving boats zip up and down the greenish water, all with ribbed sails of moonglass.

Tuk heads straight for a boat of relatively small size moored to a post at the edge of the canal. A bronze-skinned, broad-shouldered man is seated at the helm; from the way his impressive mustache curls upward in a grin when he sees Tuk, he's expecting their arrival.

He comes off the boat, arms spread wide open in welcome, and crushes Tuk in a tight embrace. After setting him down, the man plants a gentle kiss on his forehead.

"This is my friend Aram," Tuk says afterward, looking everywhere but at Ilapara. "We'll be staying with him during our time here."

Aram says something that Ilapara doesn't catch, but she smiles politely and shakes his hand when he offers it. He beckons them onto the boat, and she complies, albeit gingerly, settling down across from Tuk onto a seat upholstered in honey-brown leather.

Aram releases the mooring once they're seated, and while he works, Ilapara notes the blue tattoos snaking up his brawny arms and into the short sleeves of his cream-colored shirt, which he's left unbuttoned at the top so that the sprinkling of dark hair on his chest is visible. Tight-fitting crimson breeches hug his muscular legs, and his black shin-high boots are of a make and quality Ilapara finds herself staring at with envy.

Who is this man, and how does he know Tuk?

He takes control of the boat's tiller and whisks them away from the terminal, and they sail deeper into the wonderful, beautiful maze that is the city of Apos.

At the end of the canal, they careen onto a large stretch of open water teeming with all sorts of vessels. A harbor or bay, perhaps. What immediately catches Ilapara's eye is the conical hill rising some few miles off the coast—or rather, the cluster of buildings orbiting the hill like moons. Floating citadels with overflowing gardens drift slowly around the hill like they weigh nothing.

There can be no practical reason for such buildings, but Ilapara doesn't need to ask why they exist. Power exerts itself similarly no matter where it is, whether via these glittering, floating wonders or a wealthy mercenary lord building a house with imported bricks and water tanks in the middle of the most rural, decrepit stopover town in Umadiland. They are both statements that say: *I live in a house that defies the laws of nature. What are you to me?*

A colossal statue rises farther out into the sea, near the harbor's breakwaters. Even from a distance Ilapara can see that it depicts the same subject as the one she saw outside the terminal, including the same arch and knowing smile, but this rendition is a majestic marble white, and its crescent crown, which hovers above her head, has been enchanted with an active red glow. She holds a sword aloft in a triumphant pose, standing watch over the mouth of the harbor like a guardian.

"Someone important, I presume?" Ilapara says to Tuk over the noise of the boat's engines.

He has to turn his head around to look. "Important? Ha! That, my friend, is the Mother of Vice herself. Guardian of the Enclave, she whom you call Ama Vaziishe."

Surprised, Ilapara takes a closer look at the statue. Other details pop out to her. Long straight hair. A dainty, willowy figure. A young, wrinkle-free face. Nothing at all like what she imagined Ama might look like. After all, the Yerezi speak of her as an older, motherly figure.

"How do they know she looks like that?" Ilapara asks. "And why call her 'Mother of Vice'?"

Tuk relaxes back into his seat. "Maybe an artist somewhere a long time ago made a sculpture or painting that people liked, and then it became convention. I don't know. As for why she's called the 'Mother of Vice,' you can thank the Empire for that."

Ilapara recalls Tuk mentioning the low regard in which the solar mystics of the Empire hold the moon and those who follow her. But he made it sound like the Enclave had been established in opposition to this doctrine. "I thought you said this place was supposed to be free of the prejudices of the Empire."

"That's how it started," Tuk says. "A haven for all who worshipped the moon, safe from Imperial tyranny. Unfortunately, they didn't account for the Empire following them here. It was in their hearts, you see, in their mannerisms and philosophies. They couldn't escape the Empire any more than they could escape themselves."

Ilapara tries to digest this information. "So they internalized the Empire's ideas about the moon's inherent evil."

"Pretty much. And that's not even the full extent of Imperial influence over this place. The Enclave was supposed to be for all moon worshippers, not just mystics. But it wasn't long before the mystics began to hoard power for themselves. The Empire has the Court of Light. Here, the Crimson Court rules over all, and they're just as greedy and selfish as their Imperial counterparts."

Ilapara gazes at the hill of floating palaces. She'd bet her left leg that's where the so-called Crimson Court and its members make their home. "So they became the thing they once sought to escape," she says, to which Tuk nods.

"Turns out that what they thought they hated was what they secretly craved for themselves. And now you know why the Empire and the Enclave have known an uneasy peace for centuries: they might despise each other, but they recognize one another as two sides of the same coin."

Both hungry for power, Ilapara thinks. "But do the people here really view themselves as evil?"

"Not evil, precisely," Tuk says. "They simply don't believe in moral absolutes. Their main doctrine revolves around pain and pleasure; actions that amplify pain to the detriment of pleasure are abhorrent, while actions that amplify pleasure and ameliorate pain are praiseworthy. They believe the moon is permissive, sometimes even encouraging, of certain vices, so long as the outcome is ultimately pleasurable."

"A lot of evil can be permitted under such loose constraints," Ilapara observes.

"True. But a lot of good can come from it too. The death of a nobleman known for abusing young bathhouse servants won't be investigated for too long. A mystic who picks up orphaned children from the streets for his experiments can fall down a flight of stairs and break his neck, and no one will ask questions." Tuk smiles, though his eyes have become pools of shadow. "One thing I like about the Enclave is that no one here hides under the guise of holiness to take or do what they want. In the Empire, a lord of the suns will extol the virtues of chastity and fidelity in a shiny temple during the day but in the cover of night inflict the worst humiliations on his bed slave. Why? Because he knows he's holy and that the courts will protect him. But here? That bed slave can fight back. Here she can get justice—or ask someone else to get it for her."

Tuk's voice is even, but the look in his eye tells her these aren't mere hypothetical situations he has conjured. She decides not to pry.

They reach the other side of the harbor and race into another canal. The statue and the floating palaces disappear behind an ornate marble building, and that, too, recedes from view when Aram turns the boat into a narrower canal bordered on both sides by three-story buildings with colorful windows.

Aram slows and stops the boat just before an arching bridge hanging over the canal. Signs with glowing violet scripts adorn the walls and doorposts all along the street, some with pictograms of skimpily clad dancers. Aram cheerfully leads the way to one such establishment, where they enter through a back door and into a hallway thick with the heady smell of burning nsango. The haze of smoke fluoresces in the light from the dim lamps hanging from the walls. There's laughter and music coming from elsewhere within the building, along with muffled sounds of moaning from a nearby door.

A lissome young woman in nothing but nightclothes rushes by, but Aram catches her by the arm before she can go farther and pulls her closer. They speak in hushed voices, both glancing in Ilapara's direction, and when the woman looks over with an intrigued smile, it's all Ilapara can do not to try to hide behind Tuk.

She might have crossed the desert to a strange land, but she knows a brothel when she sees one.

The young woman finally notices Tuk and makes an excited little squeal, moving to embrace him. They kiss each other on the cheek like casual friends, but she must be busy, because she waves him goodbye and returns to whatever she was doing before they met her. Tuk and Aram speak for a little while longer, and then Tuk takes Ilapara by the hand and leads her up a staircase to an unoccupied room on the third floor, a sanctuary of silks and velvet upholstery.

"What did your friend say to that woman?" she says as soon as the door shuts behind them.

"Relax. She'll help you get ready for the salon. Come. I'll show you where you can bathe."

Ilapara plants her feet on the floor. "Tuk, what is this place? Why are we here? Who's this Aram?"

"A friend," Tuk replies evasively.

"What kind of friend?"

A vein on his temple ripples with annoyance, eyes turning a shade of amber. "Nothing escapes your attention, does it?" He moves to sit down at the edge of the room's only bed, rubbing his thighs in a nervous rhythm. "Aram is—or was—a Vigilant operative. Like me. Our sanctuary is gone now, but when I first joined, he took me in and gave me a home here. Helped me wean myself off drugs and get my life together."

"So you worked here," Ilapara says, dreading the answer.

"Not in the way you're probably thinking," Tuk replies with an amused smile. "This isn't just a brothel, you know. It's a house of entertainment. There's food, music, gambling. Sex, too, but for once I wasn't on the menu. I ran errands, mostly. Served drinks. Spied on the patrons. Dealt with dangerous threats. Aram owes me more than a few favors for the work I did here." Tuk pauses, hesitating. "And fine, maybe I did sleep with him, but that was a choice, not an expectation. I can see on your face you're worried he took advantage of me, but that's not what happened at all."

Ilapara isn't completely convinced, but a knot of anxiety loosens in her gut. "So you were lovers?"

"We slept together. There's a difference. We stopped when we became good friends. I don't sleep with people I genuinely care about."

She lifts an eyebrow, confused and disturbed. "Are you telling me you didn't care for Alinata?"

"Not when we were still sleeping together," Tuk says, then shrugs. "She was a stranger back then. We stopped when it looked like we might . . ." His eyes fall to his palms, and then the palms ball into fists. "What does it matter now? She betrayed us. And besides, meaningless sex is what I know. It's all I'm supposed to be, and for years, it was all I was. I'm trying to work my way out of that, but it's not easy. The best I can do for now is keep sex from tainting any friendships I care not to lose."

Abruptly he gets off the bed. "You should ready yourself. Sarai will be here to help you dress. The sooner we get Salo back, the sooner we can leave. The bathroom is in that room over there. I'm sure you'll figure out how it all works."

He walks out without another word, leaving Ilapara kicking herself mentally for not being more tactful. Talking to Tuk about his past is like navigating a treacherous maze.

She looks around her new room with a sense of displacement. *I'm in a brothel in a city with floating buildings on the other side of the Jalama.*

But there's no use complaining about it now, so she goes into the bathroom and prepares herself for her first night in Apos.

12: Salim

A Strange Place

Captain Axios left his vehicle waiting a few blocks away from the museum, so they flee the building on foot, determined to be long gone by the time the Imperial soldiers trapped inside break free of the enchantments keeping them prisoner.

Salim leans on Claud to keep pressure off his wounded calf as they flee, though the pain has almost become tolerable. Were they not in such a hurry, he thinks he might have managed an unassisted walk.

The city around them is a fiery haze. The sunsets have infused the sky, the clouds, and the thick fog of smoke billowing all over with an uncanny ruby glow. In the strange light, the captain's vehicle, which they find hovering not far from where Salim was shot, is a rusted and mottled shade of brown, with a crimson, glass-like appendage running across its roof like a dorsal fin.

Moonglass, supplies the wise and hidden part of Salim. *An essence-infused material that strengthens the magics of kinetic Void craft.*

A small shattering noise draws his attention to something that has fallen onto the ground near the vehicle. He hears the same noise a dozen more times, followed by the captain uttering a loud curse.

"Suns damn it! My mirrorscopes!"

One of his hovering brass spheres rolls down the road next to Salim's sandals, emitting red sparks through a crack in its shell. It seems the others have suffered the same fate.

"Were they rated for surviving exposure to Corruption?" Julian asks, to which the captain glares.

"How was I supposed to know?"

Luka gives a harsh laugh. "So you brought sophisticated machines into this soup without making sure they'd survive? How clever."

"Shut up," the captain fires back, to which Luka smirks.

They cram themselves into the vehicle, Salim in the rear seat between Claud and Luka while Julian takes the seat next to the captain up front. In the pilot's seat, the captain immediately engages the vehicle's engines, and soon they accelerate away into the city's red smog.

A vambrace of brass knobs and switches hugs the captain's left forearm; keeping that hand on the wheel, he flicks one of the switches on the device with his other hand, then leans forward to speak into it in what Salim assumes is his native tongue.

"Alesia, this is Axios. Can you hear me?" When nothing happens, he flicks the switch up and down repeatedly, cursing.

"A problem, Captain?" Julian asks.

"This damned Corruption. Now my bracer tool won't work." He tries again, returning to his native language. "Alesia, this is Axios. Can you hear me?"

This time a woman's voice crackles out of a circular wire mesh on the tool, but she sounds far away or like she's standing in heavy rainfall.

"Alesia?"

"Yes, Captain," the voice says, a little clearer now. *"Do you need extraction?"*

"No. Just get the *Ataraxis* ready to leave. I want us out of here the second I get back. We might have sunlords on our tail."

"We saw them arrive. We'll be ready to go as soon as you board."

"They give you any trouble?"

"*They couldn't see through our shield. As far as they know, we're just one of a hundred dead ships floating in the bay.*"

"That's what I like to hear." He glances back at Salim, grinning behind his visor. "Oh, and I bring gifts. Found an intact cog in the museum. Wounded but fully operational."

"*Captain, I must advise against bringing a contaminated cog onto the ship.*"

"Funny enough, it's not contaminated. It has some sort of field protecting it from the Corruption. I don't think it's a standard model."

"*That . . . is very interesting if true. The Professor will want to study it.*"

The captain grunts. "He can keep his grubby hands off this one. I don't want him ruining it like he did the others."

"*He'll be disappointed, but I'm sure he'll understand.*"

"He damned well better. All right, I'll see you soon." The captain flips the switch again to end the conversation.

On the seat next to him, Julian has suspicion written all over her face. "Is everything in order, Captain?"

"Of course, Your Lordship," the captain says, sliding back into the language of the Empire. "I was just informing my helmsman of our imminent arrival. The *Ataraxis* will be ready to leave as soon as we board."

"Let's hope our 'friends' won't chase after us as soon as they see us moving," Claud says.

"They won't," his brother replies. "Not so long as the others remain trapped in the museum."

As they swoop over a rubble-strewn road, Salim spots a woman standing on an adjacent street, between two columns of ruined towers. No one else seems to see her, and though he catches only a glimpse, it's enough for him to notice that the streaks of yellow that remain on her gown are few. Most of it has soaked through with blood and has turned a deep shade of scarlet.

The city is even larger than Salim thought—and more peculiar. They pass the severed head of a massive statue tumbling weightlessly down the streets like a leaf in the wind, trapped in its own pocket of null gravity. Other buildings have clusters of rubble caught in unnatural loops: debris falls upward and then slowly drifts to the ground, only to shoot back up like water spouting from a fountain. One particular tower seems to have crumbled in its entirety, blown to smithereens, really, but an invisible force corralled its wreckage into a starburst pattern, as if time stopped moving as the explosion went off.

An explosion, Salim muses as he studies the odd ruin. *Perhaps one of many?* Either way, something immensely powerful broke this city.

The docks are a jagged ruin of multileveled platforms and scaffolding. Near the waterfront, the captain engages a lever with one hand, and the vehicle slows, but not to a stop. Instead, he pilots the vehicle *into* the water, and Salim is alarmed when he feels a cold sensation seeping into his toes through his sandals. He looks down. A puddle of water has formed around his feet, growing larger by the second.

Luka and Claud also look down at their boots with frowns.

"Don't worry," the captain says. "She's leaky, but she'll get us to the ship before she drowns."

"I pray you're right," says a concerned Julian, lifting her feet from the water pooling beneath her.

The harbor holds other floating things. Wreckages of ships and vehicles large and small. Broken pallets and cargo containers. Corpses. The sheer toll of destruction almost breaks Salim's mind.

The only intact ship he can see is the one they seem to be approaching, and his first good look at the vessel has him wondering how it would withstand even a storm of moderate strength.

The ship has the profile of a bird, if the wings were long, wide, and triangular shapes made of moonglass. They jut out from just beneath the top deck and run nearly the whole length of the vessel, but they appear limp, angled downward so that they're partially submerged in water.

A long bowsprit with ropes slants upward over the glass superstructure rising at the bow to support an arrangement of flat, horizontal blades of moonglass that canopy the deck; the blades look like extra-long crest feathers that could tear away at the first showing of wind.

Definitely not an auspicious design to Salim's eyes, yet the ship bears an aged, perhaps antiquated look. The hull is a patchwork of different-colored metal, as though parts of it have been slowly replaced over many years.

A shield of energy surrounds the ship so thickly Salim can almost see it as an aurora of swirling colors repelling the Corruption. A powerful mind core sits at the heart of the field, a locked and barricaded door designed to resist unauthorized influences, but Salim is certain he could break through with ease.

He shoves that thought aside.

The captain approaches the ship from the stern, where a large ramp has extended to grant them access to a rear compartment. The ship's bulk casts them in shadow as he maneuvers the vehicle close to the ramp, but that's as far as he goes.

"Everyone out. Ride ends here."

They don't waste time crawling out of the vehicle and onto the ramp, though once outside the captain awkwardly reaches back in through a window to fumble with one of the levers. He pulls out just as the vehicle lurches forward on its own, drifting away from the ship as it takes in more water.

"What a waste," he mutters.

Luka rolls his eyes, unsympathetic. "We're paying you enough to get a hundred more, Captain. Now tell your helmsman to get us the devil out of here."

The captain growls but says nothing.

They walk up the ramp and into the bay, where the captain slams his fist onto a red knob on the wall. The ramp immediately begins to rise and seals the bay shut.

"Alesia. We're in. Let's move."

A voice rumbles into the bay from a speech box bolted onto one of the bulkheads. *"Yes, captain."*

A loud chime follows, and then machines turn on all over the ship, the rush of signals and electrical information intensifying to an almost dizzying cacophony. Salim winces, unaccustomed to being inundated with so many signals.

Everything in sight is rubber or metal and smells like salt and sea. Weak crystal lamps shine from fixtures on the bay's high ceiling, imitating a dim shade of sunlight. Oddly enough, there's another vehicle in the bay, though significantly larger and longer than the one the captain just lost. A lanky, ruddy-skinned man working on the vehicle's exposed internal machinery has stopped to give Salim a curious stare.

"Faidon. Decontamination. Now," the captain says to him.

The man named Faidon nods, wiping his hands on the sides of his already filthy orange coveralls. "Welcome back, boss. I'll get the hose ready."

Still in his suit, the captain hangs back while Faidon moves to unspool a length of pipe from a large reel bolted onto the floor. Julian and Luka, uninterested, are already halfway to the circular hatch at the other end of the bay. Claud lingers, a thoughtful crease above the bridge of his nose, like he's searching for the right words to speak.

"Captain," he finally says, "the cog was extremely helpful to us. I hope you . . . consider this in your treatment of him."

"How I treat my property is none of your business, Your Lordship," the captain says. "Put the cog out of your mind. Your focus should be on where we go next. You still haven't given me a destination."

Claud scowls. He opens his mouth to say something but thinks better of it. His shoulders sag as he looks away. "I'll see you later, Salim," he says, failing to make eye contact.

Salim can only watch as Claud follows Julian and Luka out the hatch.

"Sit," the captain commands, pointing to a bench pushed up against the wall.

Salim quietly obeys and watches as Faidon douses the captain's suit with a milky-blue liquid. After several minutes, Faidon turns off the spray, pulls out a pair of spectacles with thick varicolored lenses from a pocket on his chest, and puts them on. He considers the captain for a moment, then nods.

"You're clear."

"Get me out of this damned suit," the captain barks, and Faidon rushes to comply.

"That's the new cog, is it?" Faidon says with a glance at Salim, his hands working dexterously to undo the fastenings on the captain's suit. "Looks human to me."

The captain grunts. "Tell me about it. Back in my day a cog was a cog, and you knew it when you saw one."

"Back in your day, boss? You're not even that old."

"You're lucky I'm in this suit, or I'd smack you. Now hurry up."

An ill-focused tension settles deep inside Salim. To distract himself, he pulls up the pant leg covering his injury to inspect his burn, fearing the worst. Whatever hit him tore through his calf so viciously he ought to be maimed, but he can barely feel the pain anymore, and a layer of tender pink tissue has already covered the burn.

"I heard you brought me a gift."

Salim lifts his head at the sound of this new voice, his gaze finding an unassuming gentleman of short stature standing by the hatch. He has thinning yellow hair and wears a grease-stained apron over black trousers and a spotless white shirt with the sleeves rolled up, his boots polished to perfection. A leather bracer tool with brass switches and instruments wraps around his left forearm.

Someone else enters the hatch behind him; one glimpse and Salim freezes in horror.

This other man might have been handsome once. The left side of his face is a study in strong, well-proportioned masculine features, unblemished and rosy in complexion. He has the slender frame of a huntsman, with luxuriant copper hair neatly combed into a side parting.

The other half of his face, however, is missing. Flesh and skin have been peeled away to reveal the skull beneath—a skull that shimmers grotesquely with the luster of brass. His forearms are monstrosities of metal shafts and wires, poking out of his sleeveless blue coveralls, devoid of flesh and tendons.

Salim finds himself back on his feet, heart thudding rapidly inside his chest, staring into the forbidding pinprick of amber light glaring out from within the man's exposed eye socket.

"A cog with shielding technology strong enough to protect it from the Corruption," says the man in the apron, coming closer to Salim. "Is this it? You have to let me study it."

To Salim's shock, a signal brushes against his mind in the same way the museum's mind core spoke to him, an invisible thread connecting him to the half-faced man. In this thread Salim recognizes a truth that resonates with his own nature more than he'd like to admit.

"I don't want you breaking this one, Professor," says the captain. "I'm selling it to the sculptors in Mabaw. I reckon they'll pay a fortune for whatever tech it's carrying."

Even out of his suit, the captain is still a large man, heavyset with a big hooked nose, a thick head of dark curly hair, and a beard to match. He wore close-fitting brown coveralls beneath his suit; he begins to unbutton them now, revealing the white shirt below. Behind him Faidon has started hosing down his equipment, including the golden idol he took from the museum.

"Selling it would be a pitiful waste," says the so-called Professor, coming close enough for Salim to catch a whiff of the grease on his apron. "Studying it, however, could greatly benefit my prototype."

"You keep breaking my cogs, and so far I've nothing to show for it but a monstrosity you drag around like a pet. I haven't seen the schematics you promised I'd have by now."

Undeterred, the Professor rakes Salim with his eyes, coming closer until their chests are inches apart. He is shorter, so Salim has to look down at him.

The Professor finally turns away from Salim to face the captain, hands folded behind him. "Patience, Captain. Adamus is the most indestructible prototype ever built, and when I'm through with it, no amount of money the sculptors can pay you will compare to what the governments of the world will offer you for your war cogs."

Captain Axios ties the dangling sleeves of his coveralls around his waist. "You're good at making promises, Professor. For your sake, you'd better be good at keeping them."

"Thank you, Captain. You won't regret this."

"I'm going to get something to eat," the captain says and walks out of the bay.

"Come along, now," the Professor says to Salim. "We have much work to do, you and I."

Salim would rather find a warm, quiet place to lay his head down, but fear and instinct tell him not to resist, not to disobey. He must know more about this world and his place in it before making any moves. Giving in to panic would be a mistake.

So he follows the Professor through the hatch, shuddering as the silent man-machine falls into step behind him.

They navigate two decks up from the vehicle bay and through a maze of narrow steel passages, then pass through a hatch facing a row of glass portholes. The bloody twilight streaming in through the portholes has tinted everything in the compartment cherry red.

A metal examination table. Two adjustable beds on wheels. A number of shelves, cabinets, and drawers. Salim decides this must have been a place of healing for sick members of the crew, but he doubts it's been used for such a purpose in ages.

Oily tools and various machine parts lie strewed about the dirty countertops, including a severed hand made of wires. The man-machine the hand might have belonged to sits still in one corner like a hideous mannequin, flayed of skin.

Averting his gaze, Salim moves to one of the portholes so he can take a look outside. He immediately regrets his decision.

The ruined harbor and its city are now some distance *beneath* him—and getting smaller by the minute. The whole ship has somehow heaved itself up into the realm of the clouds, higher perhaps, all without upsetting Salim's sense of balance.

Funny how he doubted that the ship could sail. He never imagined that it would fly instead.

"Adamus, bring my toolbox. You, clothes off. I want to take a closer look at you."

When Salim turns around, he sees the Professor donning a pair of magnifying goggles with multiple adjustable lenses.

"I beg your pardon?"

"You do not speak to me, cog. You simply obey."

The Professor's pitiless tone prompts Salim to disrobe, starting with his shirt. Meanwhile the half-faced Adamus silently reaches for a wooden box from a shelf and brings it over to the Professor.

"Sit." The Professor pats the examination table with one hand while the other rummages inside his toolbox.

Naked except for his sandals, Salim moves to sit as directed and tries not to squirm as the Professor examines him, starting with his left arm.

"Let's take a closer look," he says, studying the arm through his multilensed goggles. Salim thinks he sees scripts and patterns of light moving across the surface of the glass lenses. "Perfect simulation of human skin, bones, and cardiovascular system." The Professor leans closer, poking Salim's forearm. "Nothing obvious to explain the generation of a protective field. Interesting. Adamus, syringe."

Adamus quietly unearths a steel-plated syringe from the toolbox and places it into the Professor's waiting hand. Salim tries not to wince as the Professor punctures a vein on his arm and draws blood.

"Run the sample through the analyzer," the Professor says, handing back the syringe to Adamus.

The man-machine accepts the syringe and takes it to an appliance across the room, but Salim forgets all about it when pain unexpectedly flares along his wounded calf.

"A typhon burn?" the Professor remarks with surprise, poking at the tender flesh. "Recent too. Interesting." Salim groans and is relieved when the Professor finally stops. But the man leans down to take a closer look with his lenses. "Healing factor is respectable but not exceptional. Hmm."

The Professor straightens back up, transferring his scrutiny to Salim's face. "Now, what's this?" he says, divesting Salim of his spectacles.

Unholy brightness floods into Salim's eyes, so he slams them shut, but the Professor slaps him lightly on his cheeks. "Uh-uh-uh. Keep them open."

He tries to comply, fighting back an overflow of tears, but in the bright room he can only last a few seconds before his reflexes take over and his eyelids close of their own accord.

"Damage from the Corruption?" the Professor wonders. "But you have no trace of it anywhere else. Curious."

Salim waits patiently for the Professor to return his spectacles, but the man's voice recedes like he's walking away. "Your docile behavior implies all the standard inhibitions are active. I'll have to run more tests to be sure, but that can come later. For now, I'll hold on to your spectacles while Adamus runs one last test for the day. Adamus, you know what to do."

A whisper of movement, then a sudden explosion of pain on Salim's left temple. He tumbles off the table from the force of the blow and has no sooner gasped for breath than another blow collides into his abdomen, squeezing the air out of his lungs.

What proceeds is a beating so thorough it breaks every bone in Salim's body. He fails to lift a finger in his own defense, paralyzed by the shock, the sheer brutality, the mercilessness, to be shown so clearly that he's hated, that someone holds his life in the most callous disregard.

Adamus throws Salim against every bulkhead, he bashes his head against every table, he slams and kicks and breaks and doesn't stop until the Professor tells him to. In the delirious aftermath, Salim, now a bleeding, trembling, broken pulp on the floor, finally comes to a realization that has been staring him in the face all day long.

I'm not human.

He can't be, for surely no human would treat another in such a way.

"Welcome to the *Ataraxis*, cog," comes the Professor's voice. "It seems you're more interesting than I assumed, to have survived Adamus intact. I don't care what the captain says. I will know all your secrets even if I must tear you limb from limb."

There are footsteps and then silence.

I'm not human, Salim thinks again. *I'm a thing, to be beaten and dissected and broken. A toy. A machine. A cog, like Adamus.*

I'm not real.

13: Ilapara

Apos

The sky cart in front of Ilapara is a glazed capsule of steel waiting on a raised platform near the edge of the city's waterfront. A single roof-mounted lamp illuminates its pristine interior, which has mirrored seats of a cream-colored leather. Several other sky carts can be seen zipping through the early-evening sky along seemingly predetermined pathways, as though bound to suspended rails.

But there are no rails in sight. Those carts are all borne aloft by magics Ilapara couldn't even begin to understand, which is why she pauses at the threshold while Tuk steps onboard and settles down on one of the seats.

Noticing her hesitation, he stretches out his legs, making himself comfortable. "Tell me the brave and fearless Ilapara isn't afraid of heights."

She glares at him, annoyed that he finds her discomfort entertaining. "Are you sure there's no other way to get there?"

"Can you fly?"

"Of course not."

His green eyes glitter. "I guess you'd better hop in, then."

"Damn you to the pits, Tuksaad," she huffs but lifts the hem of her gown and steps inside.

Behind her the glass door shuts with the loud ticking of moving gears; then a disembodied voice fills the enclosed space, crackling with static, its intonation implying a question.

"Islo di Vestri," Tuk answers.

There's a hiss, and Ilapara has barely settled down on the bench facing Tuk when the cart lifts itself off the platform and sails into the air, heading out to sea. She struggles for breath as they gain altitude, the waterfront retreating at breakneck speed. Another sky cart whooshes past them outside, its illuminated interior giving her a glimpse of three men laughing. Beneath them the sea twinkles darkly in the twilight, so far below they would surely die if they fell.

She shudders.

"The sky carts of Apos are a technological wonder of the world," Tuk says. "There've been no accidents since they were installed half a century ago. You should relax."

Ilapara opens her mouth with a devastating retort, but the cart navigates a sudden curve, making her lurch sideways in her seat. She places a hand on her chest as if it would stop her heart from leaping out. "Dear Ama."

"We'll be there shortly." There's more concern in Tuk's voice this time around. "You look nice, by the way. Maybe too nice. You'll draw some attention, that's for sure."

"Well, I got dressed in a brothel, Tuk," Ilapara snaps. "I can't help it if the result is too provocative for your tastes."

He winces. "I'm sorry. I wasn't saying you're too provocative—or provocative at all. I was just . . . I'm sorry."

Watching him stammer through an apology moves Ilapara with guilt. "No. It's okay. You didn't deserve that. I'm just . . . tense."

His eyes lighten. "We'll get through this," he says. "And you really do look nice."

She manages to smile. "I think I look ridiculous, but thanks."

A black wide-brimmed hat sits askew on her head with a netting that veils her face. Her frilly garment is a carmine off-shoulder gown with a puffed-out rear and an asymmetrical hem, higher in the front and barely covering her thighs, while reaching low enough in the back to almost sweep the floor. Over the gown she wears an absurd, tightly fitting bodice made of a rich black leather with so many laces she needed help to tie them all. She might have refused to wear the outfit had it not come with a pair of black flat-heeled, knee-high leather boots, each with a sheath sewn into the inner shaft for the concealment of a knife. She's already decided she'll be keeping them.

Tuk has accented his ensemble of patterned gray waistcoat and pin-striped pants over a white shirt with a silken neckerchief that matches the shade of her dress. He's also wearing a hat for the first time since they met.

"Remember when I told you I had a solution to your language problem?" he says.

She regards him warily as he reaches into a pocket on his waistcoat. "You also said I wouldn't like it."

"Did I say that? I meant you'd need an open mind." He takes out a pill the size of a pea bean. Its outer casing is transparent so that the yellow liquid contained within is visible. "Do you remember that dream you saw on our way to the vine tower?"

"The one with the sister whom you'd never mentioned before? Hard to forget."

"I apologized for that. Also, let's not digress. In this dream, you understood every word we spoke, right?"

Ilapara nods, wondering where this is going and what it has to do with the pill in Tuk's hand.

"But what language were we speaking? Do you remember?"

She opens her mouth to say that of course they were speaking in Sirezi but stops when she thinks about it. While she definitely remembers the strokes and lines of what they said along with the images behind their speech, she can't recall a single specific word of their conversation. "I . . . don't remember, actually," she says.

"That's because communication in metaformic constructs isn't verbal at all but emotional. Or something. I'm not really sure myself, but that's not the point. The point is, there's this tonic called Empathy. It works by putting your mind in a receptive state so you're attuned to the emotions of the people around you, almost as if you're in a construct. Popular at parties and during . . . ahem . . . other pleasurable activities. Anyway, this pill is a weakened form of the tonic. It'll let you tap into the general sense of spoken speech, though not the individual words that comprise it, and while you still won't be able to talk back to someone in a foreign language, you'll get a vague idea of what they're saying."

Ilapara scrutinizes the pill, then narrows her eyes at Tuk. "Why do I sense you haven't told me everything?"

"Well, uh, you might also suffer unpleasant—but mild!—side effects like dizziness or headaches. But you might also not, and even if you do, the effects wouldn't—"

While Tuk goes on blathering, Ilapara impulsively reaches for the pill on his palm and pops it into her mouth, then swallows it down.

He gapes at her, amazed. "I thought you were going to fight me on this."

"I followed you onto a flying cart. Might as well go all the way."

He blinks several times. "Well then. Problem solved, I guess."

Their destination is one of the hovering palaces orbiting the conical hill at the outer edge of the city's bay. Marble carvings, ornamental shrubs, fountains, and a constellation of outdoor lights populate its well-tended grounds. The estate is practically a floating island.

The sky cart descends onto a designated platform, where a guard waits to receive them. As they step out of the cart, Tuk hands the guard their invitations, which the man scans with a vigilant eye. He then steps aside and gestures that they can continue.

They follow a train of guests down a paved driveway between rows of lampposts and trees with red foliage. It's a parade of silks and velvets, of rubies and pearls, of men in waistcoats and women in flowing gowns. Other guests have decided to linger outside, mingling or leaning over the balustrades that wall in the edges of the estate, enjoying the panoramic views of the evening coast.

Ilapara feels out of place, so she's surprised when she receives a few admiring glances. *Maybe Tuk was right about the dress,* she thinks morosely and wishes she'd had the wisdom to bring a coat.

As they approach the main palace entrance, a presence grows inside her, almost as if she'd possessed herself with an Umadi charm. The soup of foreign words and mutterings seems to congeal around her ears, and she almost sways under a spell of dizziness. Whatever Tuk gave her must be starting to work.

"Are you all right?" he says.

She waves his concern away. "I'm fine. Just wondering what your plan is. Showing up at someone's door unannounced and asking them to resurrect a dead friend seems crude."

"No time for niceties, I'm afraid. But I'll be sure to ask her very politely."

He tugs her past the atrium and farther into the marble palace. They soon enter a hall where a dance is about to begin, and as they join the spectators, a masked, tray-bearing servant offers them drinks. Tuk picks up two crystal glasses from her tray and hands one to Ilapara, though he whispers to her not to drink more than a few sips given the pill she's already taken.

The music is a peculiar but pleasant fusion of upbeat percussion and lazy stringed melodies from an ensemble occupying one side of the hall. But all eyes are on the eight pairs of masked dancers in the center as they bow and curtsy to each other.

Their dance is hypnotic. Lithe bodies in sequins and lace press against one another. The steps are long and elegant, the figures well practiced and complex. The performance is a flawless display of athleticism, core strength, and grace, and Ilapara finds herself unexpectedly entertained.

As applause breaks at the end of the dance, she makes the mistake of locking eyes with a spectator across the room, a large-bosomed woman in an imperious sapphire gown and raven hair piled up elaborately. Her already pale skin seems to drain of color, and it's only belatedly that Ilapara realizes that the woman isn't staring at her at all but at Tuk.

She nudges him with an elbow to catch his attention, but she needn't have; he's already staring back at the woman with coal-black eyes.

"I believe we've caught the host's attention," he says. He drains his glass in a few gulps and hands it over to a passing servant. "Shall we say hello?"

He's walking before Ilapara can respond, forcing her to relinquish her untouched glass as well and follow him through the mass of guests. Snippets of conversations bleed into her mind like echoes from afar. The words themselves are meaningless, but they etch familiar lines and shapes in her mind. A woman expressing her admiration for one of the dancers. A man complaining about someone spilling a drink onto his expensive shoes. Ilapara rubs one of her temples, feeling unbalanced.

Tuk takes her hand and pulls her forward when the woman in the sapphire gown abruptly exits the hall. They follow her along a crowded hallway, then down a marble staircase. By the time they reach the last landing, the woman has walked past a gallery bordering a large indoor pool. All Ilapara sees of her is the hem of her dress as she swishes into an adjacent passage at the gallery's other end. They accelerate after her.

"I don't like this," Ilapara says, noticing how deserted the area seems to be, with no guards or guests in sight. "Something's off."

Tuk doesn't slow down. "Knowing her, I'm counting on it."

There's a click as they reach the passage, the sound of a door being shut. They follow the noise to a pair of frosted-glass doors. Tuk reaches for one of the handles, but Ilapara puts her hand forward to stop him.

"Tuk. Wait. We might be walking into a—"

He opens the door anyway and steps inside, leaving Ilapara to mutter a curse.

Statuary abounds in the large room beyond, a workshop of some kind. Machines and instruments of mysterious purpose lie dormant all over the room, their metal and glass surfaces reflective in the soft lighting. The air holds an earthy smell, like sanded-down stone.

The workshop's mistress appears from behind one of her statues, a silver life-size man with no facial features standing across the room. She's clutching something in one palm, too small for Ilapara to make it out, but the tremor she sees in the woman's hand cools the blood in her veins.

"Thibault," the woman whispers. *"I wish you'd never come back."* Her words do funny things to Ilapara's head, but their meaning is clear enough.

Tuk steps forward, his eyes remaining dusky. *"Madam Ayzel di Vestri. I haven't gone by that name in a long time. I'd like to keep it that way."*

The woman he called Ayzel shakes her head, tears limning her eyes. *"Please know that this gives me no joy, but you've left me no choice."*

She pushes a button on the thing in her hand, and in the next heartbeat, Tuk gasps and falls to his knees, pressing his hands against his ears. His expression is pure agony.

"Tuk!" Ilapara rushes to his side, though she's not sure what to do to help him. "Stop this, now!" she yells at the woman.

Ayzel isn't even looking at her. *"I'm sorry,"* she says. *"But this is for your own good. It's the only way to save you."*

That's it. Ilapara gets up and strides toward the madwoman, intending to rip the torture device from her gasp, but freezes when the silver statue comes to life, moving to stand in front of its mistress, squaring its sleek shoulders as if to challenge Ilapara to come closer.

She breaks through her fear and runs forward with a shout, preparing to tackle the statue and hoping to the moon that it isn't anywhere near as strong as it looks.

The statue moves. Quick as a viper's strike, it catches her by the throat and lifts her up with one hand until her feet are dangling above the floor. She tries to breathe, but the statue's hand tightens its grip, making her eyes bulge almost out of their sockets. She sees her own reflection on the smooth silver surface of its featureless face, choking at the end of an articulated metal arm. And only now does she realize that the thing isn't a statue at all but a living machine.

"I'm sorry," Ayzel says to her. *"But this must be how it is."*

The hell it is.

Ilapara reaches deep within herself and kicks as hard as she can, striking the man-machine in the abdomen with the sole of her boot. She puts everything she has into it, and though the machine makes no noise, its grip around her neck loosens slightly. She kicks again, and the grip weakens enough for her to pry herself free. She hits the ground hard, wheezes, rolls out of reach of the machine—and flicks her left wrist.

Mirror craft bursts forth from her enchanted golden bracelet, enveloping her in a stealth field that distorts light around her. The machine was already walking toward her, but it stops, tilting its head as if in confusion.

"Where did she go?" Ayzel cries in alarm.

One section of the glass wall across the room slides open, and to Ilapara's shock, three more metal machine-men step out into the light, each one searching the room with its faceless gaze.

Cloaked in shadow, she unsheathes the knife hidden in her left boot and stalks toward Ayzel while avoiding the reach of the machines. She reappears to the world when she seizes the woman from behind and presses the edge of her knife against her pale throat. A fearful gasp comes from the woman's lips.

"Stop what you're doing to Tuk," Ilapara demands.

The faceless machines begin to move on her, so she digs just a little deeper with the tip of her knife, coercing a panicked command from Ayzel that makes the machines stop.

"Good." Ilapara points a finger at Tuk. "Now stop what you're doing to him."

"Please don't kill me."

"Tuksaad," Ilapara enunciates, pointing again. "Stop what you're doing to him, or I swear by Ama . . ." She presses the knife edge harder.

The woman drops the torture device and lifts her palms in surrender. *"I don't understand you!"* she cries. *"But there, I've stopped! See? I've stopped! And I wasn't going to hurt him!"*

Indeed, Tuk isn't writhing in pain anymore, but he's still lying on the ground, motionless.

"Tuk, are you alive?"

He groans, rolling onto his side. Slowly, he lifts his back off the floor, shaking his head. "I swear if we didn't need her help, I'd beg you to slit her throat."

Relief washes over Ilapara, but she keeps her knife where it is. "Tell her I'll slit her throat anyway if she doesn't turn off those things."

Tuk staggers his way up to his feet and glares at the woman, eyes steely and cold. *"Turn off your toys, Ayzel. Or my friend will kill you."*

Ayzel quickly utters a second command, and all the machines go limp, chins drooping down to their chests, hands falling to their sides. Ilapara still doesn't feel comfortable freeing her, so she stays put.

"You can let her go now," Tuk says.

"What if she turns them on again?"

"She won't."

Ilapara isn't so certain, but she complies, though not without sliding her finger across her throat in a clear warning to the woman. She also picks up the torture device from the floor—a little black box with several switches on its front face.

Ayzel massages her neck, looking at Tuk with naked despair.

"Are you really so unhappy to see me?" he asks her, the hurt clear in his voice. *"Have you come to hate me so much that you'd try to kill me?"*

"Oh, Thibault," she cries, making an aborted motion like she wants to run closer and embrace him. *"Why are you here? I gave you a life. The freedom to be whoever you wanted to be. I broke your chains and made you strong, at great risk to myself."*

"My name is Tuksaad, and is that what you're worried about? Your own hide?"

"No, my boy. I'm worried about you. About what they would do to you."

Ilapara fails to hold her tongue. "Tuk, what is she talking about?"

He doesn't stop scowling at Ayzel. "She made illegal modifications to me before I crossed the Jalama. I'm a lot stronger and freer than any atmech is supposed to be." He takes in the four silver machines as if for the first time. *"Though I see now that my strength is no longer unique. Ayzel, you said you'd stopped playing god. What the hell are these things?"*

"They are nothing," she says. *"For my own amusement. I make them for myself, to keep my hands busy, but they're not alive, not like you."* A tear spills down her cheek, stained with mascara. *"Oh, my sweet, sweet boy. I wish you'd never come."*

"Why?" Tuk says, bewildered. *"Why does my presence upset you so much?"* The confusion slowly clears from his face. *"Wait. You were expecting me."* Then realization becomes certainty, and then anger, a flash of scarlet appearing in his eyes. *"Luksatra,"* he breathes, like the name is a curse. *"What did she say to you?"*

"Does it matter? Whatever it is you've come for, abandon it now. I failed your sister, she's too far gone, but please let me save you."

"You just tried to kill me!"

"I was going to make you forget! To make you abandon your quest and go and live your life. All I want for you is freedom and happiness."

Tears of betrayal fill Tuk's eyes, his hands trembling and tightening into fists. *"I'm not some machine you can just reset or deactivate whenever it's convenient. Try that again and I swear—"* He stops and runs a hand through his hair. *"I need your help, Ayzel. That's why I'm here."*

Ayzel takes a step forward, a mad light in her eye, like a mother determined to convince her son not to go to war. *"She told me you would come, you know. She didn't tell me why, but she compelled me to help you. Don't you see? If your sister wants me to help you, then doing so cannot be good. She bound herself to ancient powers, Tuksaad. Evil powers. You mustn't play her games."*

For the second time tonight, Ilapara casts her mind back to the shared dream she witnessed in the jungles of the Yontai. The Crocodile's widow expressed regret at Salo's death and seemed to know what Tuk was planning. She even offered to help, and now it seems she went ahead and paved Tuk's path to getting what he wants.

But what ambitions is she serving? Ilapara wonders. *And if she's in league with mystics who seek to destroy the world, then surely it would be foolish to go along with any scheme of hers.*

"I don't care what her agenda is," Tuk says. He unearths Salo's golden mind stone from a pocket and places it on a nearby table for Ayzel to see. *"I want this for me. Help me, and I'll disappear, and you'll never have to see me again."*

Whatever protest Ayzel was about to make, it dies on her tongue as she gazes at the gem, transfixed. *"What is that, Tuksaad? What have you brought into my house?"*

"A friend of mine died," he says. *"I need you to bring him back."*

Ayzel had begun to drift closer, but now she stops, blood draining from her mascara-stained cheeks. *"You would—"* She presses a hand against her bosom like she's scandalized. *"You would ask me to break my vow, Thibault? To commit the evils, the sorrows I caused—you would have me inflict them on someone else? I will not. And besides, the dead cannot be brought back from beyond the Veil. You should know this better than anyone."*

"But my friend didn't cross the Veil," Tuk says, pointing at the stone. *"His soul is in here."*

Now Ayzel regards the stone with deeper interest. Her inhibitions eventually break, and she moves to take a closer look. *"May I?"* she says, and Tuk nods, letting her lift the stone with her jeweled hands and peer into its sunny interior.

"By the Vice," she murmurs. *"Where did you get this?"*

"Doesn't matter," Tuk says.

All traces of the panicked woman who attacked them have disappeared. Ayzel seems alert now, fascinated. *"I have to analyze this with my spectrometer."*

She moves to an instrument with several lenses of varying color, each set on a swiveling metal arm, and places the stone onto a central plate. After rearranging the lenses, she flicks a switch and a lamp turns on, producing a bright beam of white light that ricochets off each lens before spilling into the crystal. Readouts of luminous scripts appear on brass panels near the machine. Ayzel folds her arms as she watches the panels, her fingers tapping out a nervous rhythm.

At last she shakes her head, letting out a doleful moan. *"Oh, Thibault. Or Tuksaad, or whatever you call yourself now. What have you done?"*

"What is it?"

"There's power in this crystal," she says. *"But not any power I recognize. Not the moon, not the suns, not Fireblue. Which can only mean one thing: a Primeval source."* She looks at him. *"But all the Primeval sources in the world were killed and harnessed as weapons eons ago—all except those that roam a savage and wild continent. Tuksaad, please tell me you didn't cross the Wastes into the hinterlands."*

He doesn't immediately answer her, like he's considering his options. In the end, he shrugs. *"There's no use in lying to you, Ayzel. You wanted me to find my own way, and it took me across the Wastes. I was happy there for a time, and I'd like to go back. But not without my friend."*

"But why would you do such a thing? Wait." Ayzel's eyes expand as she points a finger at Ilapara. *"Is that where she's from? Did you bring a wild woman to my house?"*

Ilapara's grip tightens around the hilt of her knife. "Tell her to call me wild again."

"There have been whispers of mad kings rising in the Wilds," Ayzel continues. *"Talk of Hegemons. Did you have anything to do with that?"*

Tuk regards her with hooded eyes. *"Tangentially, maybe. But what if I told you that the solution to making everything go back to normal is in that stone?"*

"This is your sister's doing, isn't it?"

"Yes," Tuk says. *"And this is how we stop her."*

"By giving her what she wants?"

"By giving me *what* I *want."* Tuk rubs his eyelids like he's tired. *"So can you do it or what?"*

Ayzel seems to calm down, curiosity returning to her eyes as she gazes at the yellow stone. She moves to examine the brass readouts once more. *"It has all the markers of a mind stone,"* she says. *"But the resolution is richer than anything I've ever worked with. Remarkable."*

"Is that a yes, Ayzel?" he asks.

She makes a dismissing motion without looking away from the readouts. *"With the right tools, anything is possible."* Ayzel straightens, then picks up the stone and hands it back. *"But not here. Come to my laboratory in the city tomorrow."*

Tuk accepts the stone from her, albeit reluctantly. *"You have a laboratory in the city? I thought you were retired."*

"I am retired, *my dear,"* Ayzel says. *"But I'm still a businesswoman. My employees do all the work for me these days."* She wipes her cheeks and inspects her fingers, sighing at the mascara stains. *"Now if we're done, I need to fix my makeup, and then I have a salon to host. I trust you can show yourselves out?"*

She doesn't wait for a reply. Tuk lets her leave, watching her with a frown.

When they're alone, Ilapara finally voices her doubts. "I'm not sure this is a good idea, Tuk. If your sister wants this to happen, maybe Ayzel is right. And it doesn't look like you managed to convince her, anyway. She might not be at this laboratory tomorrow."

The pools of Tuk's eyes are midnight as he pockets the stone. "Oh, she'll be there," he says. "Either that, or I'll kill her."

The next morning, Ilapara rises out of her bed, goes straight into her private lavatory, and retches. She can't tell if the nausea is a result of the aftereffects of the yellow pill or the persistent knot of anxiety inside her belly or her body's natural reaction to all the drama of the previous day.

If only her family back in Khaya-Sikhozi could see her now. Vomiting into a ceramic bowl across the Jalama because she took a magical pill of unknown origin so she could understand the madwoman who'll attempt to resurrect her dead friend. They already thought her touched in the head back when she still thought she had a chance to join the rangers. Maybe they were right.

She washes up and gets dressed, choosing a crimson blouse with string laces, a pair of velvety raven-colored pantaloons, and a thick leather belt with multiple buckles from among the garments given to her by Sarai, one of the girls who works here.

"For a practical yet slightly rebellious look," Sarai said as she laid the garments on the dresser last night. *"Like a working woman."* She gave a sly grin and looked Ilapara over. *"Or perhaps a woman who knows how to throw a punch?"*

What kind *of working woman would people assume I am?* Ilapara wanted to ask, but Sarai wouldn't have understood her.

She shadows her eyes with kohl, paints her lips black, and steps into the same boots she wore last night, then slides a knife into each boot's inner sheath.

Tuk said they'd leave for Ayzel's laboratory first thing in the morning, but last she saw of him, he was a little drunk and had a woman on one arm and a man on the other, the three giggling as they stumbled into his room farther down the hall. She doubts he'll be awake.

Maybe I should go and wake him up, she thinks, smirking at the idea of watching him turn beet red. But when she moves to open her door, he's standing on the other side, freshly bathed and groomed, his black shirt, waistcoat, and pants immaculately pressed. He lowers his fist, which he'd raised to knock on the door.

"Ah, good. You're awake," he says. "Breakfast?"

Ilapara sighs, her stomach rebelling at the thought of food. "Maybe later."

"Then the city awaits. Come. We'll use Aram's buggy."

They exit the brothel along the side opposite the canal, onto a narrow road paved in cobbles and hemmed in by other three-story establishments that offer similar . . . services. The buggy is an enclosed vehicle waiting on the wayside along the street, a shiny black shell with a fin of moonglass running along its roof.

Ilapara jumps inside next to Tuk, who operates the vehicle's controls like it's second nature. With a high-pitched whine the buggy lifts itself off the ground, and Tuk effortlessly guides it onto the road, joining the city's endless flow of traffic.

"I'm surprised you're already awake," Ilapara says a while later. "Did you sleep at all?"

Tuk wiggles his body. "Hey, like I told you once, I'm young, handsome, and virile, and—"

"You won't let anyone make you feel guilty about enjoying it," Ilapara finishes for him. "I know. I was just teasing." She regards him fondly. "It's interesting to see you in your natural habitat. Were your nights always this exciting?"

Tuk's eyes are a faint green as he watches the road ahead. "Last night was pretty tame. No drugs. I'd like to think it means I've matured. And you know what else?"

"What?"

"No shame. I'd always feel shitty about myself in the mornings. Here I was, a free atmech with no restraints. I could live my life however I chose, and yet I still confined myself to the same debauchery of my days as a slave. I hated myself. But last night? That was something I enjoyed, but it's not all of who I am. I have other things that define me, other things I care about." Tuk looks over at Ilapara, glancing down at her belly. "As do you, I'm sure."

Unconsciously, she puts a hand across her belly, the other gripping one of her ivory pendants.

She knows. Oh, she *knows*.

The bouts of sickness. The missed triweekly cycles—twice now. She knows. She just hasn't looked the truth in the eye because it frightens her and she can't comprehend the first thing about existing in the world with said truth. "How'd you guess?"

"I was built to notice such things," Tuk says. "You want to talk about it?"

Ilapara closes her eyes as she battles the urge to heave. "I'd rather not."

"As you wish." Tuk hesitates. "Just so you know, I'm here for you. Whatever you need. Anything. Just say the word."

"Thank you," Ilapara says, and the rest of the ride proceeds in silence.

They arrive outside a tower of rose-tinged glass built to look like a many-sided polyhedron. As they walk up the steps to the building, Tuk fishes for something in his breast pocket and hands it over. "Before I forget. Here." Another yellow pill. "Don't worry; it's perfectly safe for

. . . you-know-what. Or should I say you-know-who? Anyway, hopefully you won't have to take it for much longer."

Her stomach protests, but she accepts the pill and swallows it down, grimacing at the dry sting in her throat. "Are you trying to choke me? Next time bring a bottle of water, Tuksaad."

He gives a shamefaced grin and opens the door for her. "My apologies."

In the expansive lobby beyond, as the effects of the pill slowly begin to take hold, Ilapara watches Tuk address the man seated behind the reception counter. The man goes on to speak into a device on the counter, summoning a petite woman wearing a navy-blue coat over a white dress.

She smiles and beckons them to follow, then leads the way to a cage that descends into a shaft at the turn of a lever. The sensation of falling doesn't help Ilapara's nausea, but the pill's magic finally settles, and she begins to understand Tuk's conversation with the woman.

"If I may say so, it's an honor to finally meet you," the woman says. "You're a legend."

Tuk lifts an eyebrow, his eyes going dangerously dark, though his tone is playful. "Am I really?"

"Of course!" the woman continues, oblivious. "One of the first sentient atmechs? You're the reason this firm exists. Any artificer would kill to study how you work. But don't worry. No one else knows what you look like. We'd have had to sneak you in through a back door otherwise."

Tuk gives a flirtatious, black-eyed smile. "Just as well. I'm too pretty for back doors."

"Quite," the woman says with a blush.

The cage stops descending and opens onto a floor with bright lights and a menagerie of statues placed on marble pedestals. The woman leads them through a wide hall filled with such statues, among them a ferocious-looking winged lizard frozen midroar and a miniature grootslang rearing its head from a mass of coils.

"Please tell me these are actual statues," Ilapara mutters as they walk past a wolf with two slobbering heads.

"What is this place?" Tuk says to their guide in Syliaric.

"This is Madam Ayzel's private laboratory," the woman replies. *"She comes here to build all sorts of things for her own collection. They are not for sale, however. Madam Ayzel no longer takes commissions."*

"A pity."

The life-size statue of a naked man cast in gold takes the place of honor, hovering in a cone of light, hands pressed together, head tilted up toward the light source—like a soul rising into the Infinite Path, Ilapara imagines. Its facial features are indistinct, its limbs locked in place, but she can't help the feeling that the statue could move at any moment. In fact, besides the gold, it looks very similar to the man-machines she encountered last night at Ayzel's floating palace.

She doesn't realize both she and Tuk have stopped in front of the golden figure until Ayzel herself appears off to the side.

"There you are," she says. *"Thank you, Elayda. You may go now."*

Their guide seems disappointed by the dismissal, but she nods and smiles at Tuk and Ilapara. *"It was nice meeting you,"* she says and makes herself scarce.

"This way, please," Ayzel says, walking off.

She's just as arresting as she was last night, dressed in an elegant black gown of laces and silks with a wide skirt and onyx-encrusted shoes that click on the floor with each step. She leads the way into a room where a silver man-machine is suspended horizontally above a glass tank filled with a thick red liquid.

"Welcome to the Foundry," she says, stopping at the console at the foot of the tank. *"The mind stone, if you will."*

Tuk blinks at her proffered hand, motionless.

She frowns. *"Do you want my help or not?"*

"Of course I do."

"Then you're going to have to trust me."

He keeps staring at her, and Ilapara almost finds it funny how he's the one to hesitate now.

"We came all this way," she says.

"I know. It's just . . ."

"I know," she says.

Reluctantly, Tuk hands the golden mind stone over to Ayzel.

They watch with bated breath as she places it onto an open metal claw sticking out of the console. The claw tightens its grip on the gem and retracts into a recess that shuts itself; then cosmic shards appear along Ayzel's pale arms, though they're thinner and fainter than what Ilapara has seen before.

With her eyes closed, Ayzel makes slow, strange motions with her hands, and the suspended man-machine begins to descend into the tank until it's fully submerged. Lights blink on the console, gears groaning beneath their feet. The air in the room becomes charged with an unseen essence that presses against Ilapara's skin like static until she can taste lightning on her tongue.

"It's done," Ayzel says, lowering her arms. *"Now we wait."*

Ilapara blinks at the tank, unable to believe that anything living will ever emerge from it, let alone something she'll recognize as her friend.

Next to her Tuk shoves his hands in his pockets, licking his lips as he stares at the tank. *"How long?"*

"A few days," Ayzel says. *"Maybe less."*

"That long?"

"It took me years to make you," she retorts. *"I don't think you appreciate the feat I've just performed here. This room possibly contains the most complicated piece of technomagic in the world."* She folds her arms, gazing distantly into the tank's liquid depths. *"And I can't even show it off."*

"But how does this work?" Ilapara asks. "How will we know that whatever emerges is who we expect?"

Ayzel gives her an odd stare until Tuk translates her question into Syliaric.

"*To build an atmech you begin with a framework,*" she says, gesturing at the machine in the tank. "*A skeleton, if you will. If all goes well, the self-image contained within the mind stone will modify the skeleton and rebuild your friend onto it. A strong enough self-image might even re-create any marks on the subject's body that were especially memorable or meaningful to him. Did he have tattoos or piercings? Any distinctive scars, perhaps?*"

Tuk answers the question. "*No tattoos or scars that I remember, but he had a piercing. He wore a copper hoop on his left ear to mark himself as the son of a chief.*"

"Don't forget the eyes," Ilapara says.

"*Yes. There was also a childhood incident he never spoke about. Somehow his natural eyes were damaged beyond healing and replaced with a pair from a first-generation atmech, I believe.*"

Ayzel's head jerks toward Tuk, her lips parting in shock.

"*I know,*" he says, smiling. "*I was just as shocked myself. But the eyes were faulty, and he needed spectacles with light-filtering enchantments to see. He was practically blind without them.*"

"*Do I even want to know how atmech technology made it into the Wilds in the first place?*" Ayzel asks.

"*Hey, don't look at me,*" he says. "*This happened years before I traveled there.*"

Ayzel clucks her tongue, apparently incredulous. "*Well, I can't say I'm surprised that they were faulty. First-generation atmechs had well-known vision deficiencies. The hardware for simulating human sight was still in its infancy and prone to oversensitivity. What I don't understand is how someone in the Wilds managed to graft this hardware onto a human being. This isn't supposed to be possible.*"

Tuk shrugs. "*You should visit sometime. Perhaps you'll learn to stop underestimating them.*"

"*Perhaps I shall. In any case, if acquiring his imperfect eyes was a defining moment for your friend, his self-image will re-create them.*"

"I think it was pretty defining," Ilapara says, recalling her time with Salo and what she observed. Something had happened to him, something that hurt him so much he couldn't speak of it. *Defining* might be an understatement. "He'll need spectacles."

"True," Tuk says and relays her words to Ayzel.

"I'll have them arranged," she says. *"In the meantime, we should let the Foundry do its work. I'll inform you when your friend has returned."*

Before they leave, Ilapara takes one last look at the tank and suffers a spasm of crippling doubt. But the hope she felt when Tuk first told her of his crazy plan is still there, blazing like a bonfire.

"I've gone to the ends of the world for you," she whispers to the tank. "Don't disappoint me now. Come back to us, Salo."

14: Salim

The Ataraxis

In his sleep, the Veil thins temporarily around Salim, and a shadow chases him across a featureless wasteland of jagged rock and never-ending storms. Blood soaks the harsh ground underfoot, seeping from his lacerated soles. His limbs hurt so much he wants to weep, but he knows he cannot allow himself a moment's rest, for the shadow will consume him if it catches him.

He drifts in and out of consciousness. Hours pass. Voices surround him; he glimpses the face of a woman in a lime-colored dress watching over him.

The Veil thins again, and he slips back into the nightmarish wasteland, and this time the king is there, fighting an empress for the right to her soul. The empress wields the power of a god, and yet the king resists her, refusing to submit. The ground cracks beneath them, dust storms tearing new gouges into the already battered landscape, resolve against resolve, willpower against perseverance.

And they have an audience: two godly princes wearing the disks of the suns as halos, yellow for the younger, white for the older, both sitting on thrones in a hall that looks down from the heavens. Between them stands a third man shrouded in dazzling brilliance that stabs out of him like the branches of a tree.

They want the king to lose.

And by rights, she should lose. She is haggard and gaunt, her cheeks hollow, exhaustion blackening the skin around her eyes. But her power comes out of her in massive bombardments, swirling around her in a cosmic storm, raising tempests from the earth, pelting Salim with rocks and pebbles that gouge his skin and draw blood. He crouches low to the ground, hiding his face, but the storm is powerful and he is engulfed.

He sleeps. A woman screams somewhere nearby, endlessly and at the top of her voice, but the sound is smothered, like it's coming from the other side of a thick wall. Her screams dog Salim even through a procession of gentler dreams.

In one dream he plays a game of stones with a little boy whose mischievous laughter fills his heart with joy. In another, he meets a different, much older boy beneath an ancient tree somewhere in a scenic plain. They smoke nsango from a shared pipe, passing the time in leisured silence, the boy relaxing against the trunk of the tree, Salim resting within his loose embrace. A village built of stone sits on a hill in the distance, west of a glittering lake, while a herd of cattle and antelope can be seen grazing along the lakeside. It would all be perfect if only Salim could remember the boy's name.

What does he mean to me? he asks himself.

"I miss you," the boy says, planting a gentle kiss onto Salim's nape.

Salim breathes out a cloud of smoke, shivering with pleasure, and hands the pipe back to the boy. "But I'm right here," he says.

"You're not real, though," says the boy as he accepts the pipe. "You're a dream. A beautiful ghost haunting me from beyond the Veil."

You're not real. Salim would argue with that if he didn't know it to be true. But right now this knowledge doesn't upset him, because the boy thinks he's beautiful, and this flatters him deeply. He smiles, running a lazy finger up and down the boy's leg. "We could pretend, you know. That I'm real. Think of all the mischief we could get up to." Emboldened, he eases into a soft-spoken drawl. "The things we could do to each other."

The boy was inhaling from the pipe; he chokes and starts coughing, which makes Salim chuckle. The boy laughs, too, when he gets his coughing under control.

He nuzzles Salim's shoulder and rests his head there. "This is a bad idea," he says in a whining voice. "Your brothers are right. I'm obsessed with you, and it's not healthy. But I'll be damned if I can help it."

Salim nestles deeper into the boy's arms, savoring the feeling of being surrounded. The boy's skin is hot against Salim's, his scent like burnt grass and freshly cut wood. "Then don't help it. Stay with me. I don't want to be alone right now."

"I really shouldn't," the boy says weakly, but he kisses Salim on the neck again, and he stays.

At least until Salim's fever breaks and he slowly awakens into a fog of dull, throbbing pain.

He can still hear the screaming woman. Her distress claws at the fringes of his mind until he can't take any more and raises mental walls to block the screams out. And still, they never quite go away.

To escape, his subconscious drifts out of his body and into the web of signals flowing all around him. The web offers almost no resistance, welcoming him in through a back door that takes little effort to pry open. Once inside, he becomes connected to everything on the ship.

Ship, he thinks, latching on to that word. It anchors him in place, and he remembers where he is and how he got here.

The ship's signals all originate from the crystal hub, a room near the engine bay housing the enchantments that make the vessel work. But the signals spread out and touch nearly everything else onboard, giving

Salim a detailed awareness of his surroundings as he moves from one node on the network to another.

He becomes a silent spectator, first visiting the helmsman up on the windowed bridge and seeing her through her instruments, then spying on the captain through a bedside lamp while he sleeps in his cabin, and then moving on to listen in on the Imperials through the air filter in one of the guest lounges . . .

"How far?" says Luka.

"Ancient hieratic isn't an easy script to decipher," Julian responds. *"I'm doing my best."*

"Well, how much have you translated?" Luka demands.

"Barely a paragraph."

"So we go through all that trouble, and we can't even read the damned thing. Great."

"To be fair," Claud says, *"we were foolish to assume it wouldn't be written in the most archaic, most ceremonial script in history. I mean, look at it."*

"Now what?" Luka says. *"We need to give the captain a destination."*

Julian's voice hardens like she's clenching her teeth. *"If you think you can do better, Luka, then by all means, go ahead."*

"We're running out of time."

"Don't you think I know that? Now stop interrupting me."

Salim moves on from the Imperials, flowing through the stream of signals to the mirrorscopes in the web, one in the vehicle bay, another in the engine room, and another mounted on one corner of a poorly lit bay. He lingers here, drawn to the scene for some reason. A cage takes up a large section of the compartment. Five people are imprisoned within, two of whom lie on the floor next to each other; one writhes in pain while the other lies still, a blanket covering his form. A woman in a lime-colored dress sits on a stool beside them, watching over the pair like a concerned mother.

It takes Salim a moment to understand that he is in fact one of the two figures on the ground—a disorienting realization that startles him back into his body and full consciousness. He opens his eyes, and indeed, at some point between now and his beating at the hands of the Professor's silent monster, his spectacles were returned to him and he was discarded into a cage next to a woman who won't stop thrashing about.

He lifts himself into a seated position and pushes his spectacles higher up the bridge of his nose. The edge of a filthy blanket falls away from his chest. Beneath it he is completely naked, though at least he's still wearing his sandals.

At first the woman who was watching over him draws back in surprise at his sudden motion, but when the shock wears off, she brightens. "Oh, you're awake! How wonderful! Are you all right? You looked cold, so I gave you my blanket."

A floral kerchief covers her curly pale-brown hair, and her round cheeks give her a pleasant and almost matronly grace. Salim lets his eyes take in the rest of his fellow prisoners. A slim, androgynous figure in gray coveralls, sitting on an upturned crate pushed up against the wall and watching him with bright eyes; a powerfully built, thickly bearded man hugging himself with trembling arms and rocking himself back and forth; and the woman writhing on the floor.

Salim needs no one to tell him exactly what they are; they each touch his mind with unwelcome signals, like nodes in a network. He quickly shuts them out, horrified that they would offer him such unrestrained access to their minds. Don't they realize they're leaving themselves open to attack?

"You looked cold, so I gave you my blanket," repeats the woman in the lime-colored dress, snapping Salim out of his head.

"Thank you," Salim says or at least tries to. His voice comes out like crushed stone.

"You looked cold, so I gave—oh, I said that already, didn't I. Sorry."

"Please, don't apologize."

"I'm sorry," the woman says.

"You have nothing to be sorry for."

"I'm sorry," she says again.

Confused, Salim blinks at her.

"Welcome to the pits, friend," says the individual on the upturned crate. "The Professor's pet really worked you good, didn't he. The name's Sevan, and that's Priscille. She has trouble with her memory, but she's been watching over you ever since they dumped you here."

"I'm a medic," Priscille says happily.

"You *were* a medic," Sevan tells her. "You can hardly treat someone if you can't remember what you were doing three seconds ago. And the only reason you're still alive is that the Professor hasn't yet decided what to do with you."

Priscille makes a scoffing sound. "My memory goes longer than three seconds, thank you very much. And I'm only *occasionally* forgetful." She smiles at Salim. "It's nice to have you back in the world of the living, young man. You had me very worried for a while."

Salim doesn't do it on purpose, but his concentration slips, and he gets an unwelcome glimpse into Priscille's mind. He sees her caring for a sickly little girl with pigtails. Despite her chronic illness the little girl is happy and makes Priscille smile. Caring for her fulfills some deep yearning inside Priscille, for this is what she was made for. But the girl's father becomes restless as her condition fails to improve, and one day he loses his patience and hits Priscille so hard he leaves a hairline fracture in her crystal mind core. She becomes incapable of her duties, so he sells her to a foreign captain interested in damaged or defective cogs.

Horrified, Salim wrests himself from the memories. Priscille is still smiling at him, the same way she used to smile at the little girl. Though disturbed, he wells with gratitude that she's watched over him. "It's nice to meet you, Priscille. And thank you for the blanket. It's very warm."

"Oh, you're welcome. And you can keep it since you've got nothing else. Shameful that they couldn't even find you something to wear."

"As for me," Sevan says, "I was in the Imperial military, so don't try anything funny, or I'll make you regret it."

"Sevan only pretends she fought in the military," Priscille says plainly. "But she was actually an assistant for an intelligence officer until her obedience restraint malfunctioned and she escaped. She pretended to be human for a few weeks before Captain Axios captured her."

"Don't listen to her," Sevan says, hands curling into fists. "I know how to fight."

"She does not," Priscille says. "She's pretending."

Sevan scowls. "I'll have you know I have very advanced risk-assessment capabilities. That's why I'm still on this ship: the Professor wants to learn how I think. And you didn't have to tell him that, Priscille."

"I'm incapable of deception. You know this."

"Yes, but you didn't have to *volunteer* that information."

Priscille doesn't deny this. "I like him," she says, favoring Salim with another smile. "He seems nice."

"I'll still make you pay if you mess with me," Sevan warns. "I lived on the streets for a while before they caught me. I know things, so you'd better watch yourself. Understood?"

Sevan's slick black hair is cut short, and her sleeveless gray coveralls expose pale arms inked almost black with tattoos. Even though Salim senses fear behind her threats, he's still intimidated by her hostility. "Understood," he says, and his gaze wanders to the other male occupant of the cage. The man is still hugging himself and rocking back and forth, his shaved head buried between his knees. "Who's that?"

Sevan looks dourly in the man's direction. "That's Balam. He worked in construction or mining or something of that sort. Looks like he can throw a mean punch too. But . . . well. The Professor got to him."

Sevan need not say more for Salim to understand. "That's a pity."

"What about you? What's your name? Where'd they pick you up?"

Feeling a chill begin to settle around him, Salim rearranges the blanket, draping it over his shoulders.

"I go by Salim," he says, "though I don't think it's my real name. I don't remember my real name, actually, or much of anything else. All I remember is waking up in a building full of dead people." And with that, he recounts what he endured before being brought to the ship.

"Sounds gnarly," Sevan says without much emotion, like she's heard similar tales many times before. "But chopped up by scavengers might be a better fate than ending up in this hellhole."

"Oh, don't scare the boy," Priscille scolds her.

"I'm helping him. He needs to know exactly how much shit he's in. The Professor?" Sevan says to Salim. "He's wanted on every continent for some sick experiment he did on real people. But he made a deal with the captain to hole up on this ship, so now he experiments on cogs. Cuts us up like meat in a butchery."

"Sevan, stop." Priscille's voice has hardened, and her left eyelid has started to twitch. "I think the boy knows," she says. "I think he knows. He knows. He—"

"I hear you, Priscille," Sevan interrupts. "I get it. He knows."

"Yes, he knows. There's no need to keep scaring him."

Salim shudders, disturbed by the exchange, and finally considers the last prisoner in the cage, the woman tossing about on the floor. He almost doesn't want to know her story, but something about her draws his interest. "What's wrong with her?"

Sevan regards her with indifferent eyes, though she grips the sides of her crate until her knuckles have turned white. "We call her Lyria. Don't know if that's her real name or not. She was like this when we came; she's been here longer than the rest of us. Sometimes the Professor takes her away. I've never seen her awake."

Priscille makes a sniffing sound. "Poor woman."

Now that he's paying attention, Salim is shocked to realize that this woman—this Lyria—is the source of the screams he could hear in his dreams. He can still hear them now, in fact, a bloodcurdling sound buffeting at his mental walls.

Pity moves him to lower his walls a little, and instinct has him follow Lyria's tormented signal into her mind. An avalanche of despair rushes to meet him, and he almost pulls out, but he finds the courage to stay put and to push past her pain and into the cipher prose behind it. What he sees brings the sting of tears to his eyes.

"She's in pain," he says. "But it's not real."

Sevan glares at him. "Are you a fool? Of course it's real. Look at her."

"She feels it, but it's not—" Salim stops and rephrases. "Someone activated *all* her pain receptors and left them on and then disconnected her from her vocal cords so she can't scream. How could anyone be so cruel?"

"A good question, my dear," Priscille says as her left eyelid begins to make strange twitching motions again. "But there's little we can do. There's little," she says again, "we can do. There's little we can do. There is—"

"How do you know this?" Sevan demands.

But Salim isn't listening anymore. After securing his blanket around his shoulders, he crawls closer to Lyria to get a good look at her face. She's slicked with sweat. He cannot tell her age—she might be a young woman, or she might be older. But even through the grimace of pain contorting her features, her beauty is undeniable, her cheekbones high and prominent, her lips full and rosy.

"What are you doing?" Sevan says. "If you hurt her . . ."

Salim cradles Lyria's trembling head, brushing strands of long midnight-black hair from her face with his bruised fingers. She isn't real; this he knows. She's like him, a constructed thing—a cog. Not human. But he knows she's alive, and nothing alive deserves to suffer such cruelty.

As he strokes her forehead, he begins to unravel the ciphers that were created to torment her. They crumble like walls of chaff—it actually scares him just how easily they fall, but he presses on, replacing torment with soothing relief, fear and despair with quiet solace.

He knows not to let her awaken just yet; she's known nothing but pain for a long time and would simply scream herself hoarse. Her mind will need time to mend, so he wraps her inside a cocoon of gentle dreams that will gradually fade until she's ready to emerge from them. He knows his work is complete when she stops trembling, giving a loud sigh as she stills and settles into a deep, peaceful sleep.

"Is she dead?" Sevan says a moment later. "Why has she stopped moving?"

"Looks like she's breathing to me," Priscille says from her stool, though she sounds uncertain.

Sevan comes over to investigate, suspicious, and when she confirms that Lyria is indeed alive and at peace, she frowns at Salim. "What'd you do?"

Salim gently lays Lyria's head down and wraps his blanket tighter around himself. He finds that he can't look Sevan in the eye. "Nothing. I did nothing."

"No, no, no. You touched her, and then she stopped doing that— that shaking thing she always does." Sevan kneels next to Lyria, her eyes wide with fright. "Oh heavens. She looks . . . she looks happy! What'd you do? The Professor is going to kill us!"

"Don't overreact," Priscille says, though her own voice has gone high and tense and her faulty eyelid has started blinking rapidly. "We don't know that Salim had anything to do with this. We don't know that Salim had anything to do with this. We don't know—"

She jumps and goes quiet when there's a hiss as the hatch outside the cage slides open.

"Everyone shut up and be still!" Sevan says, rushing back to her crate.

The Professor walks into the bay not a moment later, Adamus lurking close at his heel. He's changed into a sky-blue shirt beneath his grease-stained apron, and his eyes are concealed behind his multilensed goggles. He stops outside the cage, casting a shadow over Salim as he blocks the light of a lamp behind him. Salim blinks at his silhouette while the others shrink into themselves, looking anywhere but at the Professor and his monster. Balam has started to weep.

"I see you're awake," the Professor says. "Good. Adamus, help the new cog out of confinement."

Salim remains still as Adamus steps into the cage and approaches him, the orange light inside his exposed eye socket shining steadily, not a strand of copper hair out of place. He drags Salim up to his feet with a firm grip, then herds him out of the cage. For modesty's sake Salim covers himself with his blanket and follows the Professor out of the bay. His wounded calf no longer hurts, having almost completely healed, but the sharp pain there has been replaced by a uniform ache plaguing his entire body. He winces with each step.

Back in the Professor's workshop, located on the same deck, Salim is made to sit on the examination table just like he did the first time while the Professor studies the extent of each injury Adamus inflicted on him. It's daylight outside the cabin's portholes, and the ship is somewhere above a carpet of fluffy white clouds and beneath an endless ceiling of blue sky.

"Accelerated bone regeneration, as expected." The Professor pokes and prods Salim's rib cage with a gloved hand, making him hiss in pain. "Bruising remains extensive. Blood tests also revealed nothing unusual. Disappointing. I've seen domestic cogs with more interesting architectures."

He presses a few keys on his bracer tool, and the small brass panel attached to it comes alive with Mirror light. Then he walks off to open a metal case resting on another table, where he extracts a shiny loop of copper the size of a circlet.

"On the surface it would seem you're unexceptional," he says. "But that's surely a clever deception." He returns to Salim with the loop in one hand, then stops to consider him. "Someone designed you to survive an apocalypse, and I'm going to find out why. Hold still."

Salim obeys while the Professor places the loop of copper onto his head, but as soon as the device touches him, all his instincts scream in alarm.

He cannot recall ever experiencing such a device before, but its workings are clear: Not only can the loop potentially imprison him inside his own body by taking control of his thoughts and behaviors, but when the Professor activates it using his bracer tool, the device will also be able to see into Salim's mind. The Professor will know what Salim can do—and what he's already done. He'll see that Salim is not bound by any restraints as he should be and that he can break through walls of cipher as easily as he can breathe.

He'll see, Salim thinks, *and then he'll have Adamus take off my head.*

The Professor is already reaching for a switch on his bracer tool. Salim acts within a fraction of a second, instructing the power crystal inside the tool to purge itself of essence. The discharge happens just as the switch is flipped, causing a small eruption of sparks.

The Professor flinches and hurries to take off the bracer, then tosses it to the floor. He watches it, perplexed, as it spews acrid smoke. When it stops sputtering, he scowls. "Adamus, bring me the spare."

Salim's heart sinks. One malfunctioning device could be blamed on terrible luck. Two malfunctioning devices would give him away. As Adamus retrieves a new bracer tool from a cabinet, Salim begins to panic.

"Professor, I need—suns above. What happened? What are you doing to him?"

Salim breathes out in relief as Claud barges into the room, ignoring Adamus. He's not wearing his armor today, only a yellow tunic with silver embroidery, his mop of golden hair running wild. Dark bags rest beneath his eyes.

He stops next to the examination table, taking in the bruises marking Salim's body, then glares at the Professor. "What's the meaning of this?"

The Professor doesn't miss a beat as he shifts into a fluent, lightly accented elocution of Chatresian. "Maintenance, Your Lordship. Sadly, the cog was attacked by one of the others in the brig. A nasty, feral creature. Rest assured they won't be housed in the same cage again."

Claud's eyes narrow, but he seems to accept the explanation. "They'd better not." He looks at Salim. "Are you all right?"

Salim considers exposing the Professor's lie, but the man is looking at him, and so is Adamus. "Your Lordship. It is good to see you again. And yes, I'm all right."

"Did you need something, Your Lordship?" the Professor says, a vein rippling on his temple.

Claud folds his arms, his tone becoming self-conscious. "Actually, I'm here for Salim. I need access to his records of the museum. The captain approved my request."

"I see." The Professor removes his gloves and sets them on the table. "You can ask him yourself, if you want."

"No need. Adamus. Get . . . Salim . . . something to wear. One of your coveralls will do. You're almost the same size, so they should fit."

The man-machine proceeds to unearth a set of folded garments from a cupboard and hands them over to Salim without breaking eye contact.

Salim gets dressed in the awkward silence, pulling a simple white shirt over his head and stepping into one-piece coveralls with twilled blue fabric.

"Behave yourself, Salim," the Professor says to him as he follows Claud out the hatch.

Salim tamps down the urge to break into a run, to tell Claud everything and beg for his protection. Instead, he nods, understanding the hidden threat behind the Professor's words: *Tell the Imperial what happened, and Adamus will tear you both apart.*

15: Ilapara

Apos, Capital of the Enclave

From her little table in a windowed alcove on the brothel's third floor, Ilapara has a great view of the adjoining canal and the arched bridge spanning across to a street on the other side. This is just her fourth morning in Apos, but she can already tell that something is different today.

Silence has gripped the streets. Yesterday when she had breakfast in this same alcove, a steady stream of boats zipped along the canal, and the bridge bustled with foot traffic. Today the canal is quiet, and the few people she's seen crossing the bridge were in groups, heads huddled together in hushed conversation. Even the brothel is different today. The place has proved to be quite lively no matter the time of day or night, but there's no music drifting up from the first floor this morning, only a muted hubbub.

She takes a sip from her mug of spiced tea, savoring the lingering burn on her tongue. It might be the best tea she's tasted, but it does nothing to soothe the tendrils of anxiety moving through her body.

A mother, she thinks for the hundredth time this morning. *Me.*

She has bounced from one deadly predicament to another since she left the Plains years ago, often with little reprieve. She's fled burning villages and watched the streets of a city run red with blood. She's conspired against princes and made enemies of high mystics. How could she, of all people, ever be a mother to a child?

And Jomo. Dear Ama. What would he even say? And even if he accepted responsibility, could they really raise a child together as jungle-dwelling insurgents?

Ilapara absently toys with one of her ivory pendants, contemplating the distant presence connected to it, all the way back in the Yontai, where Jomo is in hiding somewhere in the jungles, probably making plans to resurrect his rebellion against the emperor.

Surely that's no life for a child. A child needs safety, stability. To grow up in a nurturing home without the fear of violence. Ilapara's relationship with her own mother became strained as she grew into a wayward young woman determined to break every convention, but her mother was always kind, and Ilapara never feared expressing herself.

To be anywhere near as good a parent to her own child, Ilapara knows she would have to give up her life of dangerous thrills, of chasing ghosts across deserts and fighting tikoloshe, and return to the tranquility and safety of her homeland—essentially admitting that she failed to achieve the life she originally left to seek. She would return a failure, pregnant with a foreigner's bastard, a cautionary tale for other young women with dreams of defying expectations. Mothers would point her out to their daughters and say, *See? Listen to me, or you'll end up just like her. You don't want to end up like her, do you?*

Ilapara takes another sip of her tea, letting the scalding heat burn down her throat. Her gaze shifts from the windows to the stairs at the sound of footsteps. Aram usually flashes her a friendly grin whenever he sees her, but this morning he seems agitated, his mustache curled downward in a frown. He barely notices her as he jogs farther down the hall to pound on the door to Tuk's room, shouting frantically in Syliaric.

A rather disheveled and sleepy-looking Tuk opens the door, wearing only a black dressing gown. As he belts the gown at the waist, he says something that might be an expression of displeasure at being woken up so early, but he pales at Aram's next words.

Aram wants him to follow, so he comes out of his room and closes the door, but at the top of the stairs he beckons to Ilapara. In the curtained hallway his eyes are shimmering orbs of blackness.

She quietly gets up from her table and follows him down the stairs.

"What's going on?" she says along the way. "Why does Aram look like the world is ending?"

"Because it just might be," Tuk says.

Most of the building's staff have gathered in the barroom in front of a large Mirror light panel set onto a wall, watching the images in quiet shock or mumbling to each other. As Ilapara comes to a stop at the back of the group, Tuk releases a low whistle and utters an unintelligible curse.

"So it's true."

The images on the panel remind Ilapara of the mirrors in Salo's construct, which displayed visions collected by his flying metal insects. At first she struggles to understand what's shown. Whatever is capturing the images must be airborne, but a cloud of black smoke obscures much of the view.

The cloud slowly vanishes, however, and then the vision becomes clear. Ahead and below, stretching away for as far as the eye can see, is a metropolis on fire. The scale of destruction is hard for Ilapara to grasp, but she imagines the city might be as large as Apos, maybe even larger. Every street in sight is engulfed in flame. Towers of steel buckle and crumble in the heat. The suns are high, but clouds of pitch-black smoke have turned day into night.

What calamity could cause so much destruction? An earthquake, maybe? A volcanic eruption nearby?

On the panel, a mighty tower crumbles beneath the blackened skies as though it were pulverized from within. Someone in the barroom bursts into tears.

"What happened?" Ilapara says. "Where is this?"

Tuk doesn't look away from the images. "That's Hierakon," he mutters. "The largest city-state in the Eastern Hemisphere. The Empire and the Enclave have launched a joint strike. It's a declaration of war against the East."

Ilapara catches her breath. "You mean this isn't a natural disaster? This . . . was done deliberately?"

"They call them Anathemas," Tuk says. "Weapons forged from the essence of dead Primeval Spirits. Not even the Hegemons were savage enough to use one. They were only ever meant to frighten with their mere existence."

"*One* weapon did this?" She doesn't want to know, but she must ask. "And there are more of them?"

Tears shimmer in Tuk's eyes. "Every world power has at least a few in their arsenals, so yes. There are more."

And all of a sudden Ilapara understands why everyone is so strung up. If there are other such weapons out there, the use of one will inevitably lead to the use of more, and then the world will burn.

She hugs herself, haunted by visions of the Yerezi Plains being set ablaze by such a weapon. Next to her Tuk and Aram embrace, and then Tuk comes to embrace her, laying his forehead onto her shoulder. She grabs onto him, still watching the nightmare unfold on the panel.

"Please tell me this isn't real," Tuk says, his voice broken with grief. "What are we going to do?"

She holds him tighter. "We get Salo, and then we go back home," she tells him. "We'll go back to the Plains, and you're coming with us. This isn't our war."

"But what if Salo doesn't come back?" he says, voicing doubt for the first time.

"Then you and I go. We stick together, no matter what."

They hold each other for a long time, watching the aerial visions of the burning city repeat on a loop, Ilapara hoping that with each viewing the visions will become less real and be revealed to be a hoax. But they're not a hoax, and the scale of the tragedy only deepens as the day wears on.

Two mornings later, Tuk knocks on Ilapara's door and barges in without waiting for her permission to enter, finding her seated by her dresser, applying her makeups. His eyes are intensely blue, and he looks flushed.

"He's awake."

Ilapara gets up, her heartbeat spiking.

"Ayzel took him to her estate," Tuk says. "He's ready to see us."

"I'll be out in a minute."

With shaking hands Ilapara puts on her boots and cinches her crimson blouse at her waist with a thick black leather belt. She enters her lavatory and takes one of Tuk's yellow pills, washing it down with a glass of cold water. Then they leave the brothel in Aram's buggy, heading for the city's northern waterfront.

They say nothing the whole way there, and she makes no fuss as they board a sky cart bound for the conical hill of floating palaces. This journey, too, transpires in complete silence, as if they fear casting a curse on the moment with their words.

Ilapara can hardly sit still. The knot of nerves inside her feels like it's constricting her lungs. Tuk seems calm in comparison, but the lurid blue of his eyes betrays him. He begins to tap his foot in a rhythm as the sky cart descends and settles gently onto a designated platform on the Vestri island.

A servant receives them as they exit the cart. He gestures for them to follow and leads the way around the palace to a garden of immaculately pruned hedges, where they find Ayzel waiting for them in a rose-colored gown and golden jewelry.

She's fiddling nervously with the fat ruby dangling around her shoulders while she stares at the figure standing by the parapet at the edge of the garden. The figure's back is toward them—he's watching the sparkling oceans below—but Ilapara's stomach nearly drops at the sight of his unmistakable silhouette. Tuk sees him, too, but like Ilapara he doesn't dare to approach.

"Was it a success?" he says to Ayzel.

She lets out a shaky breath. *"Go see for yourselves."*

Tuk looks at Ilapara, seeking reassurance. She has none to give, but she joins him as he slowly approaches the figure, walking along a path between hedged-in beds of flowers.

The figure wears a simple white shirt, matching trousers, and a pair of leather sandals. He is tall and slender, with short hair sheared to the scalp on the sides. But for the garments, everything about him is painfully familiar and surprises Ilapara with an avalanche of emotions that brings wetness to her eyes.

Tuk stops a safe distance away from the figure, reaching for her arm and clinging to it as if for dear life.

"Salo?" he says, and the figure turns around.

His eyes are a light shade of coppery brown, like his complexion. Ilapara has never seen them before, but the face is not one she could ever forget. He seems baffled at first, like a man who's woken up to find the world turned upside down, but as he looks at them, the specter of recognition enters his eyes.

"Ilapara?" he says. "Tuk?" He has a prominent gap between his incisors and a strip of fuzz above his upper lip, and his Sirezi is flawless. "I don't know what's happening. Is this a dream?"

He has a nick on his lower chin, a faint scar Ilapara is only remembering now that he's standing right in front of her. Logic tells her that this can't be him, that dead people don't come back from beyond the Veil, but her heart sees the friend she lost on the night of the Requiem Moon.

It's him. It's really him.

Together they run to Salo and surround him in a tearful embrace.

"It's so good to have you back," Ilapara whispers in a choked voice. Tuk laugh-cries into his chest. "Oh, Salo. My friend."

They hold him in place for a full minute. He has a confused smile when they finally loosen their embrace. "I take it from your reactions I've been gone a long time."

Ilapara's gaze is drawn into his brown eyes. "It's been almost a year, Salo."

"Your eyes," Tuk says, looking up at him. "I can finally see them. I thought you'd need spectacles."

"Honestly, I don't know what's happening," he confesses, and dear Ama, it *is* him. His voice, his mannerisms, all of him. "The last thing I remember . . ." His hand comes up to touch his chest like he expects to find a gaping wound. "The Arc," he says with a haunted grimace. "He tricked me. He . . . killed me. Stabbed me in the heart, and I died. But then I woke up here." He looks about, taking in the other floating islands orbiting the conical hill. "Where are we? Is any of this real?"

Ilapara shares a glance with Tuk. They never thought this far into their scheme to bring Salo back. Of course he'd want answers, but where should they start?

"It's a long story," Tuk says, "and we'll tell you everything, but right now we need to start making our way back to the Redlands. We need to get out of this city."

"The Redlands," Salo says like he's tasting the word for the first time. "The Plains. Khaya-Siningwe. I . . . remember."

"We're going back," Ilapara says. "I don't care what responsibilities made you leave. You did your part. You gave your life. Now, we go home. All of us."

His smile widens, but it slowly dies on his face when something behind her catches his attention. She turns around to look, and her eyes immediately find the pair of new arrivals standing near Ayzel.

The first is a handsome older man with a regal bearing, dressed immaculately in a white suit. Diamonds glitter on the silver necklace resting against his chest, and in one hand he holds a cane with a silver knob. He is lanky and dark skinned with grizzled dreadlocks, a neatly trimmed beard, and silver eyes that shine like the gleaming edge of a sharpened blade.

An exceedingly striking raven-haired woman accompanies him, wearing precious gemstones and a corseted gown of scarlet-and-violet lace with a hem that trails along the ground. Her hands are gloved in black silk, and a veil of black netting hangs over her face, though not so thickly that Ilapara would fail to recognize her.

And how could she ever fail to recognize the woman who sat next to the Crocodile at the feast of the New Year, the same woman she would later see in Tuk's dream, who she would find out is in fact Tuk's sister?

Feeling the chill of danger, Ilapara positions herself in front of Salo. She'll be damned if she lets him come to harm so soon after getting him back.

"What the hell are you doing here?" Tuk demands, stepping toward the new arrivals. *"Ayzel. Why the devil is she here?"*

"I had no choice," Ayzel says weakly.

"I'm not here to fight, brother," says the Crocodile's widow. *"I simply want an audience with your friend."*

Flashbrands appear in Tuk's hands, two golden blades that give off red sparks along the ciphers carved onto their surfaces. *"I told you what I'd do the next time I saw you,"* he says as he approaches his sister. *"A pity you didn't take me seriously."*

"Wait!" Salo shouts, coming from behind Ilapara.

Tuk stops and looks back over his shoulder. The incandescent scarlet of his irises makes Ilapara shudder. "She's responsible for your death. I won't let her kill you again."

"Just hang on, all right?" Salo regards the woman with a mixture of anger and confusion, and then he addresses her in KiYonte, the tongue of Yonte Saire. "I remember you," he says to her. "You poisoned me on the night of the Requiem Moon. You made them think I was responsible for the slaughter. Why?"

The Crocodile's widow takes a step closer, though she remains a safe distance away from Tuk. "Your Worship, we have indeed met before, but you don't know who I am. Allow me to introduce myself."

To Ilapara's surprise, the woman executes a deep curtsy, as though bowing before a king.

"I am Countess Luksatra of the Seven Hills, a peer of the Crimson Court, and an enchantress to the Enlightened Society. I traveled to the Redlands on a mission to resurrect the Ascendancy so that the world would be prepared for a threat I knew was coming. I'd hoped to work with the high mystics of Yonte Saire, but the Arc approached me in secret with a plan to raise a true Hegemon to the throne, and I was persuaded."

Ilapara can hardly believe her ears. Salo himself looks halfway between shock and rage. "You worked for the Arc? He killed me!"

"Forgive me, Your Worship," says the countess, whatever the devil that title means. "At the time I believed our goals were aligned. The Arc needed you vulnerable but alive, so I agreed to bewitch you on the Requiem Moon and continued to watch over you as the slaughter raged on. It was I who later stole your body from the House of Life and delivered you to the Red Temple." The woman hangs her head as if in shame. "I didn't know the Arc planned to take your power for himself."

"Don't listen to her," Tuk barks. "She's a Shadow. She works for the enemy."

"Consider the possibility that everything you think you know about me is wrong, brother. Why would I help bring your friend back unless I wanted him alive?" When Tuk gives her no answer, the countess presses her point. "A terrible darkness haunts the world, and your friend is our only hope of stopping it. Ask him. He knows."

Tuk doesn't budge. "Whatever scheme you have in mind, he's not going to be part of it."

"With all due respect, that's not your decision to make. The stakes are far too high." The countess takes another step forward, addressing Salo directly. "You saw it in the sanctum, didn't you? You saw the horror and pain and suffering."

Salo doesn't answer. He turns around and leans on the parapet, considering the view. The island's slow orbit has swung them around to face the city's colossus of the Mother of Vice, crowned with a floating crescent that glows red like the moon in a midnight sky.

Ilapara joins him, laying a hand on his back. He looks troubled, thoughtful. "I don't know what you saw in the Red Temple," she tells him in Sirezi. "Maybe the Crocodile's widow is right. Maybe terrible things are coming to the world. I've caught glimpses of them myself since I came to this city. But you don't have to be the one to stop it. You've done enough, Musalodi. Let's go home."

He looks her in the eye, an experience she's unaccustomed to. "Can I really afford to do that? The things I saw, Ilapara. There was so much suffering, and there'll be more to come. How can I just walk away?"

He is the same person but also different. Ilapara can see it now that she's paying attention. There is a new presence about him, an . . . authority. A fierceness.

"You don't have to solve every problem," she says. "You don't have to sacrifice yourself over and over again. Let's return home and let the queen handle things for once."

"But that's the thing," he says. "No one else saw what I saw. No one else knows what I know." He turns away from her to face the others, a determined set to his jaw. "There's a gate. A portal at the edge of the horizon. I need to reach it before it's too late."

Tuk stares at him in bewilderment. His weapons are still in his hands, and he's still blocking his sister's path forward. "What are you talking about, Salo? What portal? Where is it?"

"I'm not sure." Salo closes his eyes and inclines his head like he's trying to remember something. "Somewhere in the dunes south of here, I think. It was lost long ago, but it holds the key."

"The key to what?" Ilapara says.

"To stopping the coming war," he says, looking at her. "I met a great evil in the sanctum, and it told me of the terrors it has planned for the world. This . . . force intends to reach the gate and take its power. The only way to stop this is if we get there first."

"We can help you," says the countess. Behind her veil, her eyes glimmer with unconcealed fervor. "That is why we're here, Your Worship. We've come to pledge our allegiance to you and aid you in your quest to stop the evil that seeks to bring ruin upon us all."

"I can't believe my ears!" Tuk nearly shouts. "You're a Shadow! You *work for* a world-ending evil. This war is probably your doing. Now you're pretending you want to save the world?"

"I'll ask you again, brother. If I'm as evil as you say, what am I doing here? Why did I force our creator to help bring back your friend?"

Tuk glances at Ayzel. "I don't know. But I'm not sticking around long enough to find out." Turning his back on the countess, he says, "Salo, please. I know my sister better than anyone. And yes, she's my sister—long story. But trust me; I know her. Do not entertain anything she says. Come home with us. Please."

"Your Worship, I have something that belongs to you." The countess walks to her silent companion, who hands her a sinuous band of gold large enough to sit on a person's head. She approaches Salo again, holding it in both hands for all to see. "Do you recognize it?"

Salo becomes fearful, and he touches his chest again, presumably where the emperor stabbed him. "A piece of the Hegemon's crown," he breathes. "That's what my Axiom unlocked in the sanctum. That's what the Arc killed me for."

The befuddled look on Tuk's face as he stares at the thing is a perfect reflection of what Ilapara feels herself. Why on Meza would Salo receive anything to do with the Hegemons in the temple's sanctum?

"He couldn't use it in its original form," says the Crocodile's widow, taking a step closer. "Not without the All Axiom. So he sundered your crown in three using sacrificial essence from the bloodshed on the Requiem Moon. He gave me the weakest piece as a reward for my help and gave another piece to your queen, who'd sent you into his hands." She takes another step, a serpent slithering closer to its prey. "You knew that, didn't you? That your queen sent you into a trap. She did it for this, a fragment of the Hegemon's power."

Ilapara already knew that the queen had betrayed Salo with Alinata's help. She just didn't know why. It made little sense to her that a queen would orchestrate the demise of a diffident, newly awoken mystic. What could she possibly stand to gain?

The fabled power of the Hegemons, it seems.

"She will rule the south with her fragment, while the Arc rules the north," says the countess. "But their ambitions are trifling in the end. They're blind to what's coming. *You* have a greater purpose. Take this fragment, Your Worship, and lead us to the gate."

"That's it." Tuk banishes his swords and grabs Salo's arm. "If you won't leave, *we'll* leave. Salo, Ilapara. Let's go."

He begins to tug Salo away, but Salo resists. "Tuk, wait."

"No!" Tuk shouts, whirling round to face the other young man. "Let's not wait! Let's go! Please!"

"I know you're worried about me," Salo says calmly, then considers the Crocodile's widow. "But this woman is right, obscure though her ambitions may be." He puts his hands on Tuk's shoulders. "I need to get to the gate, Tuksaad. This war will follow us no matter where we go. And if we do nothing, it'll destroy our home. Will you come with me? I need your help."

Tuk makes a long face, like he's conflicted or wants to cry. "I go where you go, Salo," he says in the end. "I'm never letting you out of my sight again."

Salo gives a grateful half smile, then looks at Ilapara, seeking her opinion.

She was overjoyed to see him just a short while ago. She's still happy he's back, but she'd forgotten how much she hated the feeling of being pulled into deep, murky waters just by being around him, the sense that she's a piece on a board in a game more complicated than she'll ever understand.

For once, why can't things just be simple with Salo?

"As long as we're headed in the general direction of home," she says, "then we'll see what happens when we get to this gate."

His eyes crinkle with joy, and then he looks at the Crocodile's widow. "If we come with you, how will you take us to the gate?"

"We arrived on a windcraft," she says, gesturing toward the other side of the palace. "We could leave right now. The dunes of the Jalama are just a few days away."

Salo nods. "There's little time to waste. We'll come with you immediately."

"Excellent. But first, allow me to introduce my colleague and friend, Duke of the White Sun Rising and Prophet of the Enlightened Society, Gregoire Silver Dawn."

The man in the white suit steps closer and executes a reverential bow. He addresses Salo in Syliaric, speaking in a deep and resonant voice. *"It is an honor to meet you, Your Worship. I pledge to serve you to the best of my abilities."*

"The Enlightened Society is a circle of like-minded scholars, alchemists, and industrialists from across the world," the countess explains. "We're gatherers and keepers of old lore and forgotten history, united despite our theological differences by the sole purpose of preserving humanity from the evils of ignorance and injustice—evils whose greatest avatar, as you know, has now reared its head.

"Gregoire Silver Dawn has led our society for the last fifteen years. He has no language in common with you, I'm afraid, but is eager to serve. In fact, we'll be traveling to the gate onboard the *Rapiere*, his largest personal windcraft."

Salo bows his head to the man in white. "A pleasure. But we must leave now. The enemy advances on the gate even as we speak."

"We are at your command, Your Worship." The countess gives another curtsy, then sweeps a gloved hand to the side. "Please, this way. Our vessel awaits."

Salo immediately sets off with the countess and her companion. Ilapara trails behind with a visibly upset Tuk, who takes a moment to bid his creator one last goodbye.

"Ayzel. Thank you for bringing my friend back. Whatever debt you owed me, you've repaid it in full. I wish you all the best."

Ayzel attempts a smile, but there are tears in her eyes, as well as something Ilapara would say looks suspiciously like guilt. Her smile crumbles in a sob.

"Oh, Tuksaad. My beautiful boy. I'm so sorry."

"Don't be sorry. You've given me a life, and I'm happy. Do me a favor and find your own happiness."

Tuk embraces her, kisses her on the cheek, and then joins Ilapara on her way to the windcraft. The vessel appears as they round the corner of the palace, and it nearly fills the sky ahead.

Floating lengthwise beside the island, with walkways extended down to the sky cart platforms, the windcraft is a streamlined, multidecked edifice of polished wood and white-gold accents. Multiple triangular sails of a pure-white material project from its sides, each bearing a gilded solar crest. A pair of large metal rods extends from the rear of the vessel, both wrapped in sheaths of crackling white-hot flame.

"That's an Imperial barge," Tuk remarks with a worried frown. "And that man. Gregoire Silver Dawn. My sister called him 'Prophet' of the Enlightened Society."

"What is this 'Enlightened Society' exactly?" Ilapara asks.

Tuk's eyes are pits of tar as he stares at the man in white. "We've never known what name they give themselves, but I believe they're what we call the Shadows, which means that man is the elusive leader himself. I've heard he can disguise himself as a Red mystic when he needs to, but they all carry the taint of Black magic. That man is an enemy any good Vigilant would kill on sight."

"Don't," Ilapara warns in a whisper. "Now's not the time."

"I know." Tuk loudly exhales. "This is going to be a very long trip."

Vertigo grips Ilapara as they board the *Rapiere*, not least because her mind won't let itself believe that something this heavy will stay afloat. There's also the manner in which the people onboard react to Salo and, more concerning, the way in which he responds.

A line of men and women in silver armor and capes of white or gold silk wait on the weather deck to welcome him; as he walks by, they each bow in deference, but he hardly seems to notice, passing them without any acknowledgment on his way aft of the vessel.

A few members of the ship's crew—or so Ilapara figures given their matching gray uniforms—watch curiously from the glazed superstructure rising at the deck's fore, possibly too afraid to approach. Another group of much more expensively appareled individuals waits at the end of the line of warriors, faces expectant like they wish to have their turn to meet Salo. But Gregoire Silver Dawn reads his disinterest and waves them away.

Salo keeps walking, and Ilapara and Tuk follow him to the stern, where he finally stops, putting his hands on the guardrail. Ilapara joins him on his right, Tuk on his left, and they peer down at the rods sheathed in white flames some distance below.

The rods glow hotter as the ship smoothly detaches from Ayzel's island and begins to sail away, picking up speed as it turns southward. The motion brings not even the slightest whisper of wind to Ilapara's hair, as though the air around her were still. The culprit must be the barely visible shimmer she can just about make out in the air beyond the rail, which she suspects is some kind of magical shield.

"That was quite the welcoming party," she says, wanting to hear Salo's response.

He grunts. "They're strangers to me."

"They were bowing to you," she points out.

"They think I'm the new Hegemon. But I don't care for their devotion. I only care about reaching the gate."

"*Are* you the new Hegemon, Salo?" Tuk asks. "Is that why I was sent to the Redlands? To find you?"

Salo bends, leaning on his elbows against the guardrail. "I'm not a Hegemon. I refused that role. Not that I could have taken it anyway—the Arc made sure of that. Still, some of the things I learned in the sanctum . . ." His voice trails, his eyes going distant. "We'll need the power of a Hegemon before this is over."

Ilapara exchanges an uneasy glance with Tuk. The Salo they once knew was ill at ease with his role as a queen's emissary and a mystic, in part due to his somewhat timid disposition but to a greater extent because he feared how he could abuse such power.

To now hear him so casually express the need for a Hegemon's power makes Ilapara even more keen to know what he learned in the Red Temple. Whatever it was changed him.

The ship reaches the coast and continues farther inland, flying along a path several miles to the east of the city's main cluster of rose-tinted towers. A leviathan streaks by below, bound for the central terminal, reflecting sunlight off its golden surface as it cuts across the land on an elevated track. Ilapara won't regret it if she never returns to Apos, but she imprints the view into her mind, savoring the city's breathtaking beauty one last time.

"Do you remember when we sailed on the Tuanu waterbird?" Tuk says.

"It was one of the best days of my life," Salo replies with a wistful smile.

"Oh yeah? How does this compare?"

Tuk probably wanted to cheer Salo up. Instead Salo frowns. "I can't say. I have no magic. I can't feel anything. For all my new eyes have given me, I see even less than before. Which reminds me." He pushes off the rail to stand upright. "I must re-create my Axiom and awaken before we reach the gate."

He turns abruptly and heads toward the bow. "Countess!"

Many of those who'd come up to receive him have retreated below-decks, but the Crocodile's widow and her companion have remained, watching just out of earshot.

She steps forward now, hands clasped together respectfully. "Yes, Your Worship?"

"I need a silent place to meditate where I shall not be disturbed."

"A cabin has been prepared for you, Your Worship. I can show it to you now."

"Lead the way," Salo says, and both Ilapara and Tuk make to follow him to the stairs descending to a lower deck, but he stops midway and turns around to face them. "You don't have to watch over me all the time."

"We'll stand guard by your door," Tuk says. "We don't trust these people."

"I'm safe here, and I'm perfectly capable of defending myself. Please don't burden yourselves with worry. I'd feel better if you relaxed. I'll find you later."

They can only watch as he disappears with the countess down the stairs, leaving them alone on the weather deck with strange people who offer nothing but suspicious frowns.

"He's changed," Tuk says unhappily, eyes gray like a cloudy sky.

"He's just come back from the dead after being murdered in the Red Temple," Ilapara reasons. "There's no way he was going to be the same."

"I suppose."

They venture aft again, where the skyline of Apos has already retreated into a distant twinkling star. To Ilapara's surprise, other flying vessels begin to fall in behind the *Rapiere* on either side, about a dozen of them, forming a chevron like a flock of birds. Some have appendages of crimson moonglass; others have white-gold sails.

"Is it normal for windcrafts to fly in a flock?" Ilapara asks Tuk.

"No," he says, surveying the vessels with a sullen look. "This is a convoy. A very rich convoy, judging by the ships. More Shadows, probably, and Salo is their prize."

She nearly shivers at the idea that she's possibly part of a convoy of devil worshippers. "What do you think they want with him?"

"I don't know," Tuk says. "But he'll need us to make sure they don't get it."

Ilapara won't recall the precise moment it happens. She won't recall what she was about to say to Tuk in the moment just before. What she won't forget is the flash that appears in the direction of the city, followed by the sudden release of an immense presence whose wrath presses against her mind with the weight of mountains and depth of oceans.

She'll remember wailing and falling to her knees in terror and being distantly aware of Tuk doing the same. She'll remember the harsh whisper that fills her thoughts as the presence accuses her of defiling it, of imprisoning it, of making it go mad with rage.

She'll remember the presence releasing its hold on her, and she'll remember clawing her way back up and looking once more toward

Apos, the city of floating palaces and sky carts and leviathans, the twinkling star on the horizon, and seeing a vast winged spirit rising from the towers in a devouring column of smoke and fire like a Primeval god, losing strength as it climbs, until it extinguishes itself in a bright explosion.

She'll remember the sonic boom that follows, rumbling across the sky and making the windcraft tremble. She'll remember seeing one of the vessels at the back of the convoy catching flame and falling away at a dangerous angle.

But most of all, Ilapara will remember the broken howl that tears out of Tuk's chest when he sees what has become of his old home, and the way he crumbles back down to his knees, his face the picture of devastation.

"Aram! Ayzel! No!"

16: Salim

The Ataraxis

Claud is quiet as he leads the way one deck up from the Professor's workshop to the lounge he and his fellow Imperials have occupied, but when they reach the door to the lounge, he stops and gives Salim a probing gaze.

"What *really* happened to you?" he asks.

Remembering the Professor's subtle warning, Salim speaks carefully. "I was attacked by another cog, just like the Professor said. Do not concern yourself with me, Your Lordship. I'm quite durable. Did you need my help?"

Claud thins his lips in obvious displeasure. "My brother, Julian, and I are attempting to translate . . . a book of sorts, but it's taking too long. You don't happen to be versed in ancient hieratic scripts, do you?"

Salim wades through the heavily fragmented straits of his memories. He is beginning to realize that they come in two distinct flavors: the experiences of a young man who may or may not have actually existed—Salim can't be sure—and whatever else his creator saw fit to cram into his mind. Knowledge of hieratic script might be the latter kind of memory.

"Perhaps if you showed me a sample?" he says.

"Sure. This way." Claud opens the door to the lounge and beckons him to follow.

The lounge is situated at the very stern of the ship, with a row of round portholes set into the far side of the compartment. Salim quietly walks in and is almost immediately pinned in place by Julian's silver-eyed stare.

Seated across a table scattered with books and papers, she is less a holy warrior today and more a noble scholar, dressed in a simple robe of cream-white silk. She also wears the Phantom Sunset as a necklace, two points of light twinkling on her chest.

Behind her Luka is a glowering silhouette standing with his arms folded, backlit by the daylight flooding in through the portholes. He, too, is out of armor, dressed in a white tunic with golden accents that match the hue of his hair, though unlike his younger brother, he still exudes arrogant confidence and authority.

"Sit," Julian says, gesturing at the chair across her table.

Salim obeys and tries not to squirm while Julian and Luka both stare at him like they think him a thief who might escape with their valuables.

Claud gives an unamused sigh. "Show him the book already. You know, before the Professor finds out I didn't actually get the captain's permission to bring him here."

While Luka continues to scowl, Julian cautiously slides a familiar golden book across the table. Its filigreed front cover of solid gold bears the engraved image of two solar disks with beams radiating away from their centers. Salim wonders if it's so much a book as a work of art.

"This tome is warded—or cursed—to prevent comprehension without the Spectral Star," Julian says, flipping the front cover to reveal the first enameled page. "Unfortunately, the author used a script that was already dead and ancient when he wrote the book, so even with the Star in my possession, translating hasn't been easy."

Salim leans forward to get a closer look and is almost taken aback by the patterns of light and shadow he sees swimming thickly across the page. If anything intelligible exists within that chaos, he'd never know. "How marvelous," he remarks. "What is it, exactly?"

"Imperial history refers to it as the Astronomicon," Julian says, "a secret treatise on the laws of heaven written by an unnamed apostle about two thousand years ago. However, intelligence we recently acquired suggests it isn't a treatise at all but a historical account detailing the specific event that led to the end of the Ascendancy and its Hegemons."

"This event is what we need to know," Claud elaborates. "Our histories tell us that the Red lords fell after a protracted war of attrition against the apostles of light. But in truth, we didn't defeat the Hegemons; the Hegemons just stopped showing up. When the last one died, no one rose to succeed him, so we swept in. But why did this happen? We believe the answer is in that book."

"The little I've translated so far hasn't been promising," Julian admits. "A story about an ancient king who built a great pyramid in the desert as a tomb for himself and his wife. No mention of Hegemons."

Salim stares at the book, intrigued. Layers upon layers of magic are affixed to the metallic pages like the strata of a sedimentary rock. Impenetrable.

"You'll need this," Julian says, pulling the string necklace with the Spectral Star over her head.

She extends it across the table, and the second Salim's fingers touch the gemstone, the layers of magic flee from the book, the words on the open page instantly legible.

And beneath the words, another layer: dreams and mirages and moving ghosts that pull him in like the currents of a whirlpool.

He gasps, dropping the gem onto the table. The layers of magic return immediately, concealing the book's mysteries once again.

"What is it?" Julian says, sitting forward with clear interest. "What did you see?"

Salim's heart thunders inside his chest, a frightening memory gripping him in its talons: somewhere in a cave of secrets he battled against twisting webs of light that tried to take his mind, and like the magic wrapped around the Astronomicon, they, too, concealed the contents of a forbidden book.

"Salim, are you all right?" Claud asks.

"I'm fine," he says, though he has to clench his fists to stop them from shaking.

"What did you see?" Julian asks again. Even Luka comes closer to the table, watchful rather than hostile.

Salim tries to put what he saw in words. "The script and the story the book tells are a disguise. A decoy. It felt like . . . sunlight, or the auras around your suits of armor. But beneath it I sensed a hidden layer of a different magic. Red as the moon and born of agony and blood. As for the book's true purpose . . . I only caught a glimpse, but I believe it holds memories from everyone who's ever touched it, including the three of you."

The Imperial lords regard him in quiet shock.

"Nonsense," Luka says. "Julian has spent hours with that thing. If it had any hidden memories, she'd have seen them."

This time it's Julian who comes to Salim's defense. "Not necessarily," she says. "Think about it: Salim is himself a creation of the Vice. He carries the malady of Red magic. If the Astronomicon is as he says it is—Red magic disguised as holy light—he'd be able to see it."

Luka shakes his head as if to cast her words from his ears. "You're wrong. It was kept in the most sacred place in the Imperial capital. It was written by an apostle. It's supposed to be one of the holiest relics in existence. Now you tell me it's tainted by the Vice? Unacceptable."

"We came this far to find the truth," Julian says. "Let's not shy away from it now." For the first time since they met, she looks at Salim with something approaching friendliness. "Salim, we need you to gaze into the book again and tell us what you see."

Salim hesitates, remembering the rush of images, the feeling of free fall. "Your Lordship, I'm not sure—"

"Please," Julian insists. "I cannot explain to you how important it is for us to know what's in that book."

Salim takes a deep breath, trying to find his bravery. "All right," he says, picking up the gemstone. And this time, when the images come to him, he lets them take him, and he falls headlong into the past.

When the Hegemon Maahes Ashertari died of old age, the man who would later succeed her as Rao Ashermose was a humble instructor at a little-known seminary of magic in a far-flung colony of the imperium.

He had achieved the hallowed All Axiom in his youth, but since a Hegemon had yet lived and would scarcely tolerate a potential threat to her rule, he'd kept his discovery a secret and sequestered himself on an island far from the imperium's capital. He was in his fortieth year when the throne finally lay empty, and that very same night, the Calling came to him, whispering, demanding that he answer.

It was relentless. He'd grown to love his quiet life as a teacher and didn't wish to abandon his students, but the Calling wouldn't let him sleep or give him a moment of peace until he yielded and listened to its demands.

"Go to the temple in the heart of the Red Continent," it said to him in the dead of night. *"See what is shown to you, learn the truth, and prepare. This is my command."*

The Red Continent was sacred ground, forbidden to all but the Hegemons themselves. Angry spirits guarded its deserts and coastal waters and claimed the lives of any wanderers foolish enough to trespass.

He would likely die in the attempt to reach its shores, but the Calling had commanded him, and so he obeyed.

He set off on a sailboat, carrying no instrument or artifact of magic, nothing that could be detected or betray him to the roaming spirits. The winds carried him forward, and the stars guided his way, and for weeks he sailed the seas alone, until at last he reached the eastern coast of the continent, where he was astonished to find that he was expected. A group of local priests who called themselves the Wise Ones had known the precise time and location of his arrival, and they had come to welcome him and guide him to the Red Temple just as they'd guided every other Hegemon before him.

The Wise Ones belonged to a tribe that ruled the continent from sea to sea and desert to desert, a magically gifted people who'd enchanted themselves with metal appendages that grew like horns from their temples. Their empire was isolated from the rest of the world, but they knew of the Ascendant imperium, for it was they who crowned its rulers and named them in their tongue according to their divinations.

They had named the previous Hegemon Maahes Ashertari, "the lion who walks with the moon," for they had seen a ferocious but prosperous reign in her future. When the new Hegemon emerged victorious from the Red Temple's inner sanctum, they named him Rao Ashermose, "light of wisdom, born of the moon," for they saw that he was wise and learned with an even temperament.

But Ashermose was tormented by the visions he'd witnessed in the sanctum, hazy nightmares of a threat that would engulf the world unless he strengthened his new imperium and extended its reach even farther. He'd despised his predecessor's campaigns of bloody conquest, yet he was now tasked with picking up where she'd left off and continuing her legacy.

He could not stomach the idea, so he sought counsel from the Wise Ones, who revealed to him that they, too, were aware of the threat whispered about in the sanctum. They were building a great pyramid, they told him, out in the dunes of the desert, a powerful artifact that, when complete, would pierce the Veil between dimensions and allow them to communicate directly with the moon. Perhaps then she would explain exactly what the whispers of the sanctum meant and what they should do about them.

The Wise Ones needed several more years to complete the pyramid. During that time, Ashermose returned to the outside world to claim his throne and ushered the Ascendant imperium into a new age of peace. Only when he received word that the pyramid was complete did he return to the Red Continent, hopeful that he would finally stand before the moon herself and beg her to answer his long-held questions.

Little did they know that what they would see when they activated the pyramid would make them tremble where they stood, for as they soon learned, the Veil had been put up by the gods to keep a terrible darkness at bay, but the Veil was weakening, and the act of piercing it had only weakened it even further. Soon the darkness it held back would sweep across the world in an unstoppable wave of destruction, and all would be lost.

In a mighty feat of magic, Ashermose and the Wise Ones quickly repaired the rent they'd torn into the Veil, reversing the pyramid's purpose. Now what was once meant to sunder would strengthen and anchor in place, and so long as it stood, so would the Veil.

They succeeded in the end, though they did not know at the time that a foul essence had already escaped into the world from the other side, carrying a power that would corrupt anything it touched.

Black magic had come to the Red Continent.

Worse, the newly strengthened Veil exacted unforeseen costs on those who'd erected it. The Calling was forever weakened; no new Hegemon would hear its whispers after Ashermose, and the age of the Ascendancy would end in a blaze of vengeful sunlight. The tribe of the Wise Ones was doomed as well and would gradually lose their affinity for magic, inevitably becoming slaves to the peoples they'd once ruled.

Seeing the end of an age on the horizon, Ashermose spent his last days infusing his knowledge into a tome of memories so that the truth of the pyramid would survive the fall of his imperium.

And thus, the Book of Lies was born.

Many hands touched it after his death, unwittingly imprinting themselves onto its surface, though Salim can't be sure if the Hegemon intended this or if the captured memories are simply a side effect of the spell used in the creation of the book. Nonetheless, the memories are a river that flows throughout centuries of history, showing Salim glimpses of the empire that rose after the fall of the Ascendancy.

No Hegemon rose to replace Ashermose upon his death, and the imperium teetered on the edge of collapse. The Book of Lies was salvaged from the Hegemon's palace on the night the Ascendant capital was sacked and drowned beneath the waves of the sea by an army of vengeful apostles.

Though they couldn't decipher the book, they would later deem it a sacred relic on account of its halo of sunlight. The corrupted Hegemons must have stolen and hidden it, they decided, but it belonged to them, the true children of the suns.

They named it the Astronomicon, the book of the laws of heaven, and its legend and mystique would only intensify over years of fruitless attempts to decipher it. At last, the priests of the solar diocese decided that perhaps the book was not meant to be understood at all, and so they locked it in a reliquary, where it would sit for centuries, undisturbed save for the occasional dusting and polishing.

The hands that touched it on those few occasions belonged to a long succession of sun priests, each one convinced that they held a book so holy the suns themselves had shrouded its words from mortal eyes. They sensed the light coming off the pages and were reassured, not realizing that the light was there precisely so they would revere the book and keep it safe.

Its creator had foreseen the waning of the moon's imperium and the rising of the suns and knew that if the lords of the coming empire saw the true magic behind his book, they would destroy it. So he cloaked the treasure in sunlight, tricking the apostles into keeping it in their most sacred of temples.

And there the Book of Lies stayed for centuries, until the day Julian, Claud, and Luka stole it.

The Book of Lies shows Salim everything.

He sees Julian and Claud, scions of noble families newly inducted as officers in the intelligence arm of the Empire's military. They were searching the home of a missing colleague suspected of Vigilant corruption when they came upon a curious item she'd left behind, a sapphire-blue artifact that would later penetrate their minds and curse them with frightening revelations about their Empire, truths about the end of the world, the Astronomicon, and secret cabals infiltrating the highest echelons of the Court of Light.

They resisted at first, but the visions were compelling, and so was the evidence now that they knew where to look. So together with the Imperial knight Luka, whom Claud managed to persuade, they committed a daring theft of the Astronomicon, then hired an Eastern cog slaver to secretly ferry them across the ocean to Apos, where the visions told them they'd find the key to deciphering the holy relic.

The city was in ruins when they arrived, however, destroyed by an apocalyptic weapon that oozed a corrupting miasma. But they remained determined, and it was in a museum in that city that they would find a wounded cog—the same cog that would later translate the Astronomicon and reveal to them its secrets.

◆ ◆ ◆

Although not all its secrets.

Like a chasm on the ocean floor, another layer of truth lurks beneath all the others, but its magic is cool and impenetrable. Try as he might, Salim simply can't pierce its depths, as though he were trying to open a locked door without the appropriate key.

He surfaces from the book, and his consciousness returns to the lounge, where he tells the Imperials everything the book showed him, including their own stories. They listen quietly, and when he's done, they all appear lost in their own thoughts.

Claud is the first one to speak. "So the Astronomicon is actually the Book of Lies, and it was written by a Hegemon." He gives a tortured, heartbroken laugh. "On the bright side, I'm relieved to know we didn't really commit sacrilege by stealing it. Hell, we did everyone a favor."

"All I know is I'm not touching that cursed thing again," Luka says with a shudder. "So what now?"

They both turn to Julian.

Across the table from Salim, she has a distant look in her eye. "That pyramid. We need to find it."

"And how will we do that?" Claud asks. "And even if we do, what then?"

"I have an idea, but you probably won't like it."

Claud is quiet for a second. "I think I know what you're thinking, and I agree."

"Can someone clue me in, please?" Luka says impatiently.

Julian hesitates, like she's still considering the idea. "We *have* to seek out the Vigilants. We need their help."

Luka's face contorts with disgust. "What? Absolutely not! We do that and we become true apostates!"

"We already are, Luka," Julian tells him and cuts off his response with a raised hand. To Salim, she says, "Thank you, friend. You must leave us now. We'll call on you again if we have need of you."

"Of course," Salim says, getting up.

Claud walks him to the door. "Thank you, Salim. You've been more helpful than you'll ever know. I'll come check on you later."

The stories Salim saw in the Book of Lies weigh on his mind as he heads back to the Professor's workshop, but his concerns vanish completely as soon as he arrives and sees what's beyond the hatch.

He takes an involuntary step toward the figure lying still on the examination table inside the workshop, her face veiled by a curtain of long black hair.

Lyria. And she's alone in the room, save for the dismembered skeletal machine-man sitting in the corner. *Oh no. Oh, please, no.*

He approaches her slowly, fearful of what he'll discover, and his heart shatters at seeing the raw gash on her neck, the blood that has pooled and congealed on the table.

Dead, dead, dead. All because of me.

He jumps at the sound of shrieks coming from the prison bay and is out the door before he can think better of it. His steps become unsure when he hears the Professor's enraged voice, but he doesn't stop until he reaches the bay.

Priscille and Balam are still in the cage. Priscille is standing, a hand clutching the collar of her dress in fear, eyes twitching uncontrollably and tears glistening on her cheeks. Balam is hugging his knees as far as possible from the cage's entrance, weeping while he rocks himself back and forth.

And outside the cage, Sevan is on her knees, her face bloodied and bruised, Adamus standing over her, the incensed Professor watching from nearby.

"What happened?" the Professor demands. "Who undid my work? Tell me now!"

A trickle of blood drips from Sevan's swollen lips. "Like I said, I don't know anything."

"Hit it again," the Professor commands, and Adamus draws back his fist.

"Stop!" Salim runs into the bay. "Please, stop! It was me! I did it!"

The Professor's wrathful eyes find him, and he signals Adamus to hold back.

Spared from another blow, Sevan should be relieved, but her horror is clear even through her bruises. "No! What are you doing?"

"I'm responsible!" Salim cries, tears blurring his vision. "I caused her death! I should be the one punished."

"How *did* you do it?" the Professor says, tilting his head curiously, and it's almost frightening how quickly he has reverted to the calm, gentlemanly scholar. "I couldn't break through the layers of prose you constructed. They were quite simply exquisite."

"Does it matter?" Salim weeps. "I did it! I can't explain. She was in pain and I helped her. Why did you kill her? Why?"

"You killed her?" Sevan screams. "You son of a bitch!" She suffers for that infraction with a punch to the head.

The Professor grins as he approaches Salim, wagging a finger. "I knew you were hiding something from me. But if you won't tell me what it is, I'll make it easier for you. Adamus, take off the cog's head, but do take your time. I'd like to watch."

Adamus is lithe, his muscles lean—not precisely what one might expect the avatar of war to look like. But his first punch carries the strength of a demon and splinters Salim's rib cage. Salim falls to his knees with a choked cry, his vision going bright with pain.

Desperately, he latches on to the signal coming out of his assailant's mind, following it to its source, but a maze within a maze rises to repel him, walls of impenetrable prose that twist with every breath. Before he can puzzle his way through, Adamus strikes him again, then proceeds to break each of his fingers, and then his arms, and then his legs, unmaking him one joint at a time.

The agony is supreme. It subsumes Salim's every thought. It becomes the whole of his existence, turning him into a wild animal. He would kill to make it stop. Slit his own throat. He would beg and plead. In his delirium a realization or some other strange awareness begins to tease him, tantalizing him with a reprieve from his agony if only he could grasp it. But as soon as he reaches out, a shadow rears its head from within him, and the secret insight flees, slithering away.

He is on the floor now. He can hear Priscille and Sevan screaming; he can sense Adamus readying the final blow, extruding a blade from his machine hand. But a sudden explosion makes the whole ship groan, a rush of panicked signals coming to life on every deck, and then the captain's voice booms into the bay.

"Damn it! Listen up, everyone. The sunlords have caught up to us. Our shields won't hold for long, and we can't outrun them. The Ataraxis *is lost. If you want to live, run for the skiff immediately. Anyone not there in the next three minutes is getting left behind. That includes you, Professor."*

Shrill horns begin to sound, giving off loud repeating wails. Near Salim's broken body, the Professor curses. "Toss both cogs into the cage and lock the brig behind you. Maybe we'll recover something from the wreckage. I need to save some of my work."

There are footsteps and then more pain as Salim is lifted off the ground and unceremoniously dropped. Another explosion sends shudders across the ship's hull, silent warnings racing through the web of signals. There's a resonant click as the cage is locked, then footsteps, then a hiss as the hatch to the brig seals itself shut.

Salim detaches himself from his body and becomes a ghost in the ship's web of signals, witnessing the crew's evacuation through the mirrorscopes. Luka, Claud, and Julian board the skiff. So do the Professor and Adamus, both carrying cases filled with whatever they were able to salvage from the workshop. Captain Axios follows with his golden idol.

The bay opens, and the skiff drops into the sky. Through the ship's exterior mirrorscope Salim sees it plummet for several seconds, backdropped by the shimmering aquamarine ocean far below, and then multiple rigid wings of moonglass burst out of the hull, slowing the vessel's fall. Soon it accelerates and glides away to safety, cutting across the skies too fast for the attackers to follow.

The vessel that hunted Julian, Claud, and Luka across the ocean is a beautiful fortress adorned in gold and silver colors. Salim watches it shoot beams of destructive sunlight at the *Ataraxis* from two barrels mounted just beneath its tapering prow. The beams slam into the *Ataraxis*'s tattered shields, causing damage and explosions on multiple decks. Several nodes wink out of the network of signals, their cores damaged beyond repair.

Salim would laugh at the cruel irony if he could. This ship saved him from a blow that would have killed him just minutes ago. Now it will seal his doom.

Another blast hits the *Ataraxis*. Inside the cage, Priscille mutters a prayer, Balam weeps, and Sevan hugs herself. They will all perish here, on this ship, and no one will remember their names or mourn their deaths. Salim convulses in a sob, thinking it will be his last breath.

Except reality frays around him, some curtain in the fabric of space lifting, and then suddenly he's back in that in-between place, the wasteland where the Veil touches the world of the living.

The king is here, restored to her youthful health. Where she was haggard before, now she wears the splendor of a goddess, stars adorning her braids like jewels, her gown, once yellow and tattered, now glowing like the dawn and the moonrise.

In this place of dreams, the injuries that burdened Salim disappear, and he's able to lift himself off the ground, though he dares not rise, staying on his knees.

"Your Majesty," he says, blurting out the first thing that comes to him. "I . . . see you have been victorious in your battle."

She smiles wanly, addressing him for the first time. "It's funny. I used to suffer recurring dreams about climbing endless ladders of godhood. I thought maybe I was mad, but I was actually experiencing memories that weren't mine."

She waves a bejeweled hand, making the angry clouds part over the wasteland to reveal a swollen red moon. But even as Salim gazes at it, he knows it's no mere moon, for within it lies a great engine, a source of power that draws from the hearts of a thousand red stars.

"I understand now," the king says, staring at the moon with a serene expression. "The gods were once people, just like us, who found godhood on the Infinite Path. They should have stayed there, ascending the Path's endless rungs of enlightenment. But for selfish reasons they returned to the world of flesh so they could delight in their power and be worshipped.

"And when the reckoning they unleashed nearly destroyed them, they escaped here, to the in-between, infecting the living with fragments of themselves to stay alive. When I was born, I was infected with the fragment of a goddess. She was a parasite feeding from me, guiding the course of my life, and when I died, she expected me to let her consume me just like she'd consumed everyone else she'd used."

The king looks down at Salim, continuing to mesmerize him with her words. "But I realized that I wasn't powerless here. I carried the fragment of a goddess, and she couldn't take her essence from me unless

I allowed it. My whole life, I lived in service to the schemes of other people, but for once, I had a choice. So I fought back."

A memory returns to Salim, something a god said to him on the surface of the moon: *"The source of her power is alive. The same is true for the sources that reside in the suns. But the Ascendants who ruled over them are no more, though I am certain their souls remain on your side of the Veil."*

Salim shakes with awe and reverence. "So you are the new goddess, then?" he asks. "Because you have taken her throne?"

Before he can prostrate himself, the king—the goddess?—comes and grabs him by the arms, helping him off the ground. "Gods and goddesses were never meant for this world," she says forcefully. "By abandoning the Infinite Path, they unleashed a terror that we must all now confront. And I will need your help."

"I . . . I can't," Salim mutters tearfully. "I'm dying, and I don't even remember who I am. And every time I'm dragged here, a shadow hunts me without rest. I fear I can't outrun it for much longer."

The king considers him, looks *through* him, rather, his soul laid bare for her godly eyes. She frowns. "Yes. I see it now. Hold still."

He didn't know it before, but a tether was coiled around his heart, a thing of corrupted essence. As soon as the king makes contact with his chest, he feels the tether snap in half, its remnants burning away from him. He gasps, shocked by the difference; it's like he's been freed from an anchor that was weighing him down.

"The shadow shall trouble you no longer," the king says. "And your memories will return to you in time. As for me . . ." She looks up, and when Salim does, too, he glimpses the throne room with the solar princes and the dazzling tree between them, all three watching quietly. "There are others I must free before they are fully consumed. Other souls who didn't know they could fight back. But that is my war." She looks at Salim. "Yours is back in the world. And now, you must return."

◆　◆　◆

Back in his broken body on the besieged ship, something has changed inside Salim. The insight that teased him earlier dances back into view. And this time when he reaches, it comes.

He grasps; he pulls.

And it responds.

Interlude: Balam

A Scary Place

Adamus. The Professor. Explosions. *Terror.*

Terror is all Balam knows, but this wasn't always so.

He was built for strength, after all, to labor calmly and tirelessly in the deep subterranean hard-rock mines of the Empire, extracting the shiny silver metal the sunlords like to enchant. They gave him a mind strong enough to remotely operate multiple heavy machines simultaneously. They gave him arms as thick as trunks and a back stronger than tempered steel so he could move or repair those machines when necessary. They fortified his lungs against the noxious fumes that lurk in the mines and made him fearless so he would never worry about the ever-present danger of explosions or collapsing shafts.

Yes, they made him docile, too, a gentle, obedient giant, but never afraid.

Now he cowers in the corner of his cage, hugging his knees and trembling all over. If his heart were weaker, it would have given out long ago. The explosions that were tearing the ship apart have stopped for some reason, but the terror squeezing Balam by the throat just won't let go.

He shrinks deeper into himself when there's a loud bang, except this time it comes from outside the ship. A long silence follows, broken only when the other cogs locked in the cage with him start to speak.

"What was that?" says the scary one named Sevan. "And why have they stopped firing on us? Why are we still alive?"

There's a groan, and then the new cog says something.

"Salim, you're awake! Keep still. Keep still. Keep—"

"Listen to Priscille," Sevan says. "You shouldn't move just yet. You need to let yourself heal."

Another groan. "I'm fine. Help me up, would you?"

"I'm not sure that's a good idea—whoa. All right, all right. I'll help you. Just . . . take it slow."

Balam risks a glance and sees Sevan dragging Salim up to his feet. She really shouldn't do that. Balam saw Adamus break Salim's legs. Standing will just break them even more. It's terrifying, so Balam hides his face again.

"You're tougher than you look," Sevan remarks. "I'm surprised you can even talk, let alone stand."

"We need to get out of here." There's a jangling sound as Salim tests the locked gate. "Anyone strong enough to break this?"

No, no, no! Balam thinks. This is all wrong. If Adamus returns . . .

"Are you insane?" Sevan says. "What if the Professor comes back?"

"There's no one else onboard. They all escaped."

"What?" squeals Priscille. "Then . . . who's flying the ship?"

"No one. Well, I am, I guess? I'm controlling it through the central mind core in the crystal hub. We're stable and afloat for now, but the stress on our kinetic shield overloaded a number of critical nodes. If those faulty nodes aren't disconnected, I'll lose control and we'll crash." The gate jangles again. "Do you think Balam can break this lock?"

No, no, no!

"Stop. Hang on a second. An Imperial battleship was just trying to blow us out of the sky. What the hell happened to it?"

"It's gone. I triggered a thermal runaway in the main engine."

Balam fails to hold in a sob.

"You did *what*?"

"Don't worry; no one died. I gave them enough time to escape on skiffs before their ship exploded."

"You *let* them escape? They were trying to kill us! Why didn't you kill them back?"

"I . . . didn't think that was necessary."

Priscille makes a noise of disapproval. "Killing people is bad, Sevan. Salim did the right thing."

"Oh yeah? What if they come back?"

"They won't," Salim says. "Their skiffs have limited range, and as far as they know, everyone on this ship escaped. They have no reason to come back for us."

The cage is quiet for a second.

"Are you some sort of advanced war prototype?" Sevan says. She almost sounds impressed.

"I don't know. I'm still . . . remembering. But right now, I need direct access to the crystal hub near the engine room. I need this gate open."

"I'm afraid you're out of luck. Balam could probably break it, but you won't get him to stop shivering long enough to understand what you want from him. He's too broken."

"Perhaps I can help."

They're looking at me! If Balam could sink deeper into his corner, he would. But he's too big. Too muscular. Too stuck with these frightening people.

"Balam, I'm not going to hurt you. I just want to see what's wrong with you. I'm going to touch your temple with my fingers, all right?"

Balam whimpers, breathless, his knees trembling so much they bounce against each other. He's so afraid he can't even scream when Salim touches his head, looking into his mind, seeing his thoughts. He nearly faints from the fear.

"I don't understand," Salim mutters. "What's the purpose of such cruelty?"

"What is it?" Sevan demands.

"His fear centers have been artificially activated to put him in a constant state of terror."

That's so scary! Balam thinks.

"You mean, like Lyria's pain?"

"Yes."

"Poor Lyria," Priscille mourns.

"Balam, I know you're scared, but the fear you feel isn't yours. Someone put it there, and I can take it away. But I think I need your permission first."

Balam keeps hiding his face.

I can't breathe.

"I can help you, Balam," Salim continues, "but you have to nod so I know I have your permission."

Balam wants to run away. He wants to hide in a dark place and never come out. He's so afraid, so exhausted. He hasn't slept in a long time; the nightmares are too much. He wants to be at peace, to no longer be afraid.

Salim terrifies him. A lot.

But he nods.

PART 4

ANENIKO
*
KAMALI

17: Aneniko

On the Way to the Faraswa Desert

It takes Niko and his team of riders a full day of galloping across the velds to reach the World's Artery. Niko has to restrain his quagga from setting too fast a pace since Addi's mare isn't moon blessed and Addi himself has yet to earn his steel. But the boy rides like his life depends on it, and the wind whips past their ears, hooves thundering on the ground in a steady beat.

Niko's first glimpse of the famous roadway comes just as dusk settles, a distant gravel serpent cutting across the land from one horizon to another. They make camp by a stream several hundred paces shy of the road, where they unsaddle, water, rub down, and feed their quaggas before allowing themselves to rest.

Addi suffers his first seizure that night.

They're all seated around the campfire after a dinner of mealie bread and dried meats when he stills like he's seen death. He quietly excuses himself, then walks off into the dark in the direction of the stream. On an impulse Niko follows him and is hardly surprised to find the boy naked and shuddering violently in the grasses a stone's throw away from the camp, his loincloth tossed to one side.

Kneeling next to the boy, Niko lays him gently onto his side and stays next to him throughout the seizure, feeling powerless and pathetic even though he knows there isn't much more he could do, at least nothing that his clan mystic didn't already try.

The fit lasts for a minute, maybe longer, Addi's limbs convulsing like he's possessed by an unfriendly spirit. He slowly comes back to himself when it's over and lifts his head to look at his surroundings.

"You had a seizure," Niko tells him. "But it's over now. You're all right."

His watery eyes shine with confusion in the starlight, then slowly widen with mortification. "I soiled myself."

"I know. I have a nose." Despite the stench, Niko attempts to make light of the situation. "Good thinking getting naked first."

Addi turns his face away. "I don't want you to see me like this."

"Neither do I, but it can't be helped, and it's not your fault."

"I hate being a burden."

"I'm an Ajaha. I have the strength of twenty men. I can carry burdens in my sleep."

Addi rolls his eyes, but he's still too embarrassed to look at Niko.

"And next time you feel a seizure coming," Niko says in a more serious tone, "let me know. Nimara told me what to do when it happens. She also told me to make sure you take your medicines afterward, but I can't help if you hide things from me."

"Yes, Bra Niko," Addi says. "Now if you don't mind, I'll go wash up in the stream before I die of shame."

"Good idea." Niko straightens back up to his feet, grimacing. "And I'm going to get you a bar of soap so your mare won't reject you tomorrow. Seriously, Addi, what did you eat, the bowels of a tikoloshe?"

Addi curses him as he walks off. The boys back at the camp are less chatty and watch Niko attentively as he rummages through his saddlebags.

"Another seizure?" Sibu quietly says.

They deserve to know, so Niko nods, but he stops to look at them before returning to Addi with the soap. "Don't make him feel bad about it," he says. "None of this is his fault."

Sitting next to Sibu, Jio leans forward to prod the flames with a stick. "We know," he says. "Si Nimara told us everything."

That catches Niko off guard. "Why'd she do that?"

"Why d'you think? She didn't want you two coming out here alone."

"She *asked* you to come with me?"

Jio's eyes reflect the dancing flames of the campfire. "She didn't have to, mzi."

A stirring of . . . warmth, perhaps, curls inside Niko's chest. He'd have taken Addi where he needs to go on his own, but the company of his fellow rangers has been rather welcome. He nods in gratitude, and they say no more.

"Tell me what you like about me," says the bespectacled ghost later in his dreams, beneath what has become their favorite tree.

"Maybe I don't like you," Niko says. "Maybe I'm just here out of pity. You'd be lonely if I didn't visit you."

Salo looks up from where his head rests on Niko's thigh, a knowing smile touching his lips. Slowly he reaches up to play with the beard on Niko's chin. "Pity, is it? I doubt the little fellow down south would agree."

"*Little?* I'm not little!"

In revenge Niko pounces, aggressively tickling Salo in the sides, making him squirm with laughter that fills the sky and Niko's soul and buoys his heart, at least until it's time to wake up.

The dream is still on his mind when he sets off with the others at dawn the next morning, heading south along the World's Artery. *Was the real Salo ever that bold?* he wonders. The ghost is so forward and cheeky and *provocative* it throws Niko into a fog of mindless desire. Surely this must be his own doing.

It's possible the real Salo never actually liked him in this way, and even if he once did, that probably changed when Niko let him ride off to Yonte Saire on his own.

As sure as the pits, I'm going insane.

He and his group pass multiple convoys of travelers throughout the day, some of whom stare at them from within ridiculous wheeled structures drawn by loud spirit-powered engines or massive elephants and rhinoceroses.

They ride past squalid towns of rickety shacks and past tunnels of standing stones curving into and over the roadway from both sides like the bones of a broken rib cage. They pass enormous boulders sculpted into the faces of warlords, and rotted corpses pinned to stakes and lined along the wayside. The world beyond the Plains rushes by in its strange and beautiful and ugly shades, but to Niko it's all peripheral to the hundreds of miles that still separate them from the thing that will make Addi better.

Afternoon creeps over the savannas like a living painting, a band of color sprinting with the suns. Niko doesn't have a map, but he knows they're less than a day's ride away from where they'll have to turn west off the Artery and start heading in the direction of the desert. His plan is to ride for a few more hours and make camp at twilight, but Addi slows his mare to a stop just after they pass a crowded wagon trundling slowly along the road behind a pair of striped mules. The nearly a dozen people seated in the wagon have all covered their heads and faces in various cloths, perhaps to keep the dust away.

Niko and the other rangers slow down next to Addi, waiting for him to explain himself, but the wagon has completely captured his attention.

Driving it is a slender man in a loose black robe and a white cloth wound around his head so that only his eyes are visible. They're of a scarlet shade so intense Niko wouldn't be surprised if they glowed in the dark. Noticing the four riders stalled ahead of him, the man slows down, his shoulders going rigid like he's bracing himself for a confrontation.

"What is it?" Niko says, growing impatient.

Addi licks his lips, his expression animated. "If you don't mind, I'd like to speak to these people."

"Why?"

Without replying, Addi turns his mare about and trots back to meet the wagon, lifting a hand to indicate friendly intent. He greets the wagon's driver in the Umadi tongue, and the driver seems to relax, drawing his wagon to a complete stop. Niko and the twins watch the exchange in puzzled silence, but Mafarai's perceptive eyes shine with understanding.

"I think those are Faraswa people," he remarks. "That's why they've covered their heads and faces—to hide their tensors. I'm actually surprised to see a whole wagon of them traveling alone on this road, especially through Umadiland. They're taking a huge risk."

"Where do you think they're going?" Niko asks.

"Why don't we go and find out?"

They all guide their quaggas about to join Addi, who's still talking to the driver. Niko nudges his stallion a little farther along to take another look at the passengers in the wagon, smiling and nodding at them to ease their fears. They regard him with quiet wariness. A young child nestles deeper into her father's arms and hides her face against his chest.

Jio has more success when he greets them in the Umadi tongue, getting a few positive though guarded responses.

"You speak Izumadi?" Niko asks him.

"A little." Jio gives a sad smile. "We used to follow Salo to his lessons with our aago when we were younger. We were there mostly to pester him, but we picked up a few things."

Bile begins to rise up Niko's throat. He's grateful when Addi addresses him.

"Bra Niko, these people are going to the same place we're going! They came all the way from Yonte Saire, and two of them are having seizures like me. A witch doctor told them to find the cure in the homeland of our people. We have to join them!"

Niko takes another look at the people in the wagon. He sees no weapons. There's an elderly woman and an infant child. How they got this far through Umadiland on their own is nothing short of a miracle.

He jerks his head to call the other rangers closer. "Thoughts?"

"They'll slow us down," Sibu complains. "By a lot. We've actually covered more distance than I expected." He looks in Addi's direction with begrudging respect. "The kid rides like he's been doing it all his life."

"And he'll pout at us the rest of the way there if we don't help his people," Niko says. "Come now, cousins. We're going in the same direction, and they're helpless. We would discredit the Ajaha if we abandoned them."

The twins simultaneously sigh in resignation. Niko glances at Mafarai, who dips his head in assent.

Satisfied, Niko turns to Addi. "Tell them we'll be traveling together from now on," he says. "But we have to make camp soon. Our quaggas need rest."

Their campfire is more crowded that night. The wagon's scarlet-eyed driver, an elderly man whom Addi introduces as Sissay, gladly shares his supply of a honey-based wine so strong Niko orders the other rangers not to drink more than a few sips, much to their disappointment.

Addi is happier and more talkative than Niko has ever seen him and plies Sissay with an endless stream of questions. The old man doesn't seem to mind.

"They're very relieved we joined them," Addi tells Niko afterward. "This stretch of road in particular is quite dangerous for my people."

"Why didn't they join a caravan?" Niko asks through the toothpick in his mouth. "Traveling alone on this road is just asking for trouble. And they aren't even carrying weapons."

"No money," Addi says. "They're desperate, but caravans are too expensive."

"I'm surprised they made it this far. We're almost to the southern border."

"I asked Aaku Sissay about that."

"And?"

Addi frowns like he's perplexed. "He's convinced that . . . a spirit has been watching over them."

"A spirit?"

"That's what he said. A shadow with wings lurking just out of sight, though he says he spotted it a few times. He thinks it kept the way ahead clear and might be what guided us to them."

Niko chews on his toothpick, considering the possibility. "I doubt that. We're not under any compulsion to be here."

"Apart from my seizures, you mean."

He looks at Addi, but the boy is staring distantly into the campfire, his high spirits diminished. "Are you scared of what we'll find in the desert?" Niko asks him, putting the question gently.

Addi hugs his knees and lowers his eyes to the ground. "I'm trying not to think about it."

Niko reaches over and squeezes the boy on the nape. "If it needs killing, we'll kill it. If it needs us to ask nicely, we'll be so nice we'll make it swoon."

Addi lightens up but gives him an odd look. "Why do you care what happens to me?" He seems to immediately regret his question. "I'm sorry. Don't answer that. I'm just not used to anyone giving a damn."

Niko retracts his hand, a gray mood settling over him. "It's all right," he says. "And a fair question." After a pensive silence, he says, "I let a friend down when he needed me. I guess . . . I guess I'm trying not to make the same mistake again."

Addi watches him. "You mean Salo."

He recognized a while back never to speak that name where Niko can hear it, but it has always haunted the silences between them. Now the name hangs over them with a weight, stoking Niko's rage like an ember in a shed full of hay.

"You said he risked his life to get you here, so maybe making sure you're all right is my way of making amends," Niko says. He looks Addi in the eye and grins. "But you've also become a good friend, however annoying you may be. I want to see you beat this illness and earn your steel in the bullpen."

Addi's eyes shimmer with wetness, but he smiles. "Thank you."

Niko and Mafarai's turn to keep watch over the camp comes a few hours after midnight, just as the crescent moon clears the mountain range in the east.

After checking on the quaggas and the two mules, Niko leaves the other ranger at the fire and walks in the direction of the distant mountains, deciding to finally attend to a duty he has avoided for long enough. Perhaps too long.

A short distance from the camp but out of earshot of the other ranger, Niko goes down on one knee, facing the rising moon. After the queen strengthened the gifts of his blood, the tether connecting his soul to hers grew so solid he can almost see it with his mind's eye. It responds with vigor upon his call.

"Irediti Ariishe," he says. "Forgive me for running off without your permission. I . . . am on a quest to help a friend who needs me and will return as soon as I'm able." He pauses, wondering if a deeper explanation is warranted. He decides he's said enough. "I beg that you grant me your blessing."

There's no reply, though he didn't expect one. The queen is likely displeased, but the fact that she hasn't rescinded her gift is a good sign.

You're a fool to gamble with a prize many of your peers would kill for, says a voice in his mind. *All so you can make amends with a ghost.*

He returns to the camp, joining Mafarai in his vigil near the fire. They speak little, each preferring to keep to his own thoughts. The skies over the eastern mountains are beginning to lighten when Niko feels a presence passing over him like a cloud on a sunny day.

He looks up, seeing nothing above but stars. The presence comes again, this time gusting behind him in a breeze. He makes eye contact with Mafarai. "Did you feel that?"

Across the fire, Mafarai is alert. He nods quietly.

After picking up his spear, Niko stands, calling on the blessing in his bones—not just strength now but also that other thing the queen put there, the restless power trembling just beneath his skin. The power flows into his spear, heating the tip until it glows red, a feat no Ajaha has ever been able to perform until now.

He waits patiently, and when the presence comes again, he surges toward it in a blur of scarlet shadow, covering hundreds of yards in a half breath. When he stops, the burning point of his spear is merely an inch away from cutting into a woman's throat.

She stills, lifting her hands and showing her open palms. She wears a robe that appears inky in the poor lighting and a veil covering her head like an Umadi woman. The glowing tip of Niko's weapon illuminates a face covered in black ciphers. She doesn't seem particularly frightened for someone on the wrong end of a spear.

"Peace, Ajaha," she says. "I have not come to fight." Her Sirezi is heavily accented but passable.

Niko studies her, and when he's confident she won't attack, he lowers his spear. "You're the friendly 'spirit' who's been watching over the Faraswa, aren't you. Why? What's your interest in them?"

"Listen carefully, Ajaha," the woman says. "The old magics of the desert are stirring. An evil banished long ago has returned in the flesh to rouse them and harness their power. The Faraswa who are called *must* get there in time to stop it, or all will be lost."

Running footsteps sound behind Niko as Mafarai arrives. "Do I raise the alarm, mzi?"

"No," Niko says without turning away from the woman. "Go back to the camp. I'll handle this."

"Yes, mzi."

There's something unhinged in the woman's eyes and a firmness in her voice that makes Niko doubt that she's fully sane. "What's calling them? What is this evil?"

"I have heard that the Ajaha are honorable," she says, ignoring his questions. "That you are guardians and protectors of the innocent. Now you must prove it. There are more Faraswa riding down the Artery. Wait one more day before you leave, and then guide them all to their calling. Know this: no duty in your life will ever be more important."

Niko would be incensed at her presumption if a nagging feeling didn't tell him not to dismiss her words out of hand. Nimara believes something is going on in the desert, and clearly Addi isn't the only one affected. But that doesn't mean Niko should take on even more responsibility.

"Why can't you do it yourself?" he demands. "You've already gotten them this far."

"I cannot," the woman says with a vehemence that surprises Niko. "The evil . . . has a hold on me. This is as far as I can go. The rest is up to you."

Her message delivered, she turns around and begins to walk away but then stops, looking back. "A word of advice: do not linger in the

Crimson Woodlands. The awakening magics have agitated the Great Mokele-Mbembe, and she will not take kindly to trespassers." The stranger looks forward again, then turns her head up toward the crescent moon. "The Blood Woman watch over you, Ajaha. You will need her mercy in the coming days."

And with that she transforms into a great winged reptile and lifts off, a shadowed silhouette with a silver glimmer rising into the dawn.

Later that morning, while Addi and the rest of the caravan share a breakfast of flatbread and a hot, murky beverage that smells surprisingly good, Niko tells the other rangers about his encounter with the visitor. They're predictably displeased.

"You're not seriously considering it, are you?" Sibu grumbles. "She turned into a kongamato! That's a good enough reason not to trust her."

"Agreed," Jio says with an identical frown. "It's one thing to take on a single wagon of tagalongs. But to wait here a whole day for more? What if she wants them all in one place to make it easier to attack them?"

Niko glances at Addi and catches him laughing with a Faraswa boy close to his age. *Dare I voice my suspicions?*

"Something's happening here. Something bigger than just Addi or these people or maybe even us." The queen is hundreds of miles away, but Niko still lowers his voice. "The woman mentioned old magics awakening in the desert. Well, guess what: there's a new king who's claimed the desert for himself, and from what I've heard, AmaYerezi might be working with him. What if, inadvertently, something they did is what's causing Addi's seizures?"

The other rangers blink at him like they fear he's about to be struck by lightning. "What are you saying, mzi?" Jio asks.

Niko treads carefully. "I'm not saying the queen *definitely* did something. But *if* she did, and it's not out of the realm of possibility, *if* she's part of something that *accidentally* caused these people's suffering, then we have a moral obligation to them."

The other three rangers clearly aren't convinced, but they shake their heads and ultimately defer to his judgment.

"So the spirit was actually a mystic?" Addi says after Niko tells him what they discussed. "And more of us are coming?"

"That's what she told me, yes."

Addi beams. "Aaku Sissay will be so pleased!"

He runs off excitedly to the fire and relays everything Niko told him. Indeed, Sissay's whole face lights up with joy, and the rest of his group cheers. He bows his head in Niko's direction, pressing his palms together in thanks. Niko nods back.

"So we're caravan guards now," Jio mumbles next to him.

He pats the other ranger on the back. "Cheer up, mzi. It'll be an adventure you can tell . . . what's her name again? Sindile? Nikiwe? You change sweethearts more often than you bathe; I can hardly keep up."

Sibu sucks his teeth in derision. "More like *they* change him. Sindile ditched him weeks ago."

"Oh, shove off!" Jio yells.

Shoulders shaking, Niko turns away and coughs, trying to disguise his laughter.

The wagons trickle by throughout the day.

Addi sits with Sissay on rocks by the roadside, waiting for them, getting up and waving his arms enthusiastically whenever he sees one, then letting Sissay do the talking. Niko expected that some would refuse, perhaps suspecting a trap, but Sissay must be very persuasive, because every wagon Addi pulls over ends up joining the camp, bringing more people for Niko to protect, more infant children, more elderly, more sick and infirm, and even a few pregnant women.

As the weight of responsibility grows heavier on his shoulders, the Umadi wilds take on a more treacherous character, and he becomes restless.

At about midday a huge southbound caravan passes by. Its lead mercenary stops to accost Addi and Sissay from the back of a hulking zebroid abada with a single spiraling horn that glints like metal. They seem to have an argument, and then the mercenary lifts a blade from a scabbard on his saddle.

Before he can use it, Niko ghosts forward in red shadow, lighting up the tip of his spear. The mercenary's eyes widen at his sudden appearance by Addi's side, and his striped mount rears up on its hind legs in alarm, startling the two oxen that were passing by behind it, pulling a wagon of grain sacks. He utters a string of indignant curses as he rides off, and only once he thinks he's a safe distance away does he look back and shout something ill tempered at Addi and Sissay.

"He wanted us to join his caravan," Addi explains once it has passed. "He said we could enjoy his company's 'protection' for the low price of one mountain per wagon."

"And how much is that?" Niko asks, to which Addi laughs harshly.

"Too much, but only the desperate would camp out here, so he was trying his luck. We told him we weren't going much further down the road. He didn't like our answer."

Niko looks in the direction of the caravan, now a receding cloud of dust and noise. "We'll need to get off this road soon. The next predator might not be so easy to scare off."

By nightfall, more than a dozen wagons have joined the camp. Many of the Faraswa are so pleased to be traveling with company the mood becomes festive. Multiple fires crackle in the dark. Meats and vegetables purchased from towns along the road fill the air with their scents as they roast. Niko and the other rangers decline constant offers of food, concerned they'll end up too stuffed to do their jobs.

But the buoyant atmosphere goes out like a flame in ice water when the first mass seizure arrives. This time Addi gives Niko enough warning, so he's there with him from the start of the convulsions to the end.

He later finds out that there are at least fourteen other people suffering from similar seizures among the Faraswa, ranging in age from a four-year-old girl to a middle-aged man old enough to be her grandfather. The seizures leave them weak, confused, and exhausted, effects Addi suffers himself until he returns to the fire and starts sipping from one of his medicinal flasks.

As he recovers his strength while the other victims remain feeble, a look of guilt crosses his face, and he considers his flask thoughtfully. Niko has to grab his arm to stop him when he attempts to get up.

"Nimara gave you enough for yourself. If you want to help these people, you'll keep yourself strong and able to ride. Without you we'll struggle to communicate with Aaku Sissay."

Addi scowls, defiant, but Niko doesn't yield, and eventually the boy rolls his eyes and sits back down.

They set off the next day at dawn, a caravan lumbering down the World's Artery as fast as its slowest mule, meaning not very fast at all. But the pace is consistent, and it's only high noon when they reach a roadway sign with an active mystic Seal carved onto its surface; it appears to them as a rapidly spinning multicolored diamond that, when looked at directly, conjures the image of an immensely potbellied man sitting on a throne of crimson wood—as sure a sign as any that they've crossed into the Valau Kingdom, for that man could be none other than the Valau priest-king himself.

It's not long after passing his Seal that they finally turn right off the Artery and begin to descend along a narrower dirt road into a woodland of massive trees. The trees are spaced apart widely enough not to form a canopy, but they're so numerous and their leaves grow so profusely they paint the slopes with lush vermilions and rusty umbers and warm yellows.

The grasses and shrubs that grow between them also present rich shades of rose-tinged gold and brim with more flowering plants than Niko can identify. Even the birds and the insects and the little critters frolicking in the bushes are clothed to blend in.

The larger ones too. As the caravan ventures deeper into the woods, they see herds of red kudu and southern springbok grazing among the trees in their moon-colored coats. At one point an imbulu darts across the road ahead in a shimmering russet blur of tronic scales.

The sight of it drives a spasm deep into Niko's chest, a reminder of the time he caught Salo nursing one just like it back to health. He had to force him to let it go for his own good, but he remembers being privately besotted with Salo all over again by the way he didn't hesitate to show compassion even if doing so put him at risk. Compassion flowed from him the way water flows downhill, but the world was built for the hard hearted and power hungry, and it crushed him and ground him to dust.

And I wasn't there to protect him.

"I've grown bored of this scenery," Salo's ghost says to him in his dreams that night. They're seated side by side beneath their tree, as usual, sharing a smoking pipe. "Why don't we go somewhere else?"

"Where to?" Niko asks, and he'd swear a mischievous light crosses Salo's spectacles.

"I know just the place. Come."

Salo gets up, and Niko follows him. The dream transitions seamlessly around them, and the next thing Niko knows, they're walking up the steps to a pillared limestone temple surrounded by familiar crimson woodland.

"These woods," Niko utters, disconcerted to see the real world creeping into his dreams. "This is where I am."

"The whole forest is a celebration of love, you know," Salo says. "So is this temple. Come. I want to show you something."

Salo takes him to a painted wall close to what might be a ceremonial pool in the temple's hypostyle main chamber. Sunlight pours down the walls from vertical slats near the ceiling.

"Look at all these *fascinating* illustrations," Salo says. "My favorite is that one over there."

On inspection, the murals covering the wall are of a shockingly libidinous nature. The one Salo has pointed out depicts two athletic young men fully entwined, engaging in an act of such intimacy it sets Niko aflame.

He gulps, folding his arms. "Uh . . . fascinating indeed. Wh-what kind of temple did you say this was?"

"I was thinking," Salo says with a cunning look. "Maybe you could try that. On me."

Thoughts, mush. Tongue, jelly. Niko rubs the back of his neck, head spinning. "You mean . . . er . . . you want me to . . ."

"It's endearing watching you pretend you haven't thought about it." There is pure deviousness in Salo's slanted grin. "I've seen the way you stare at me."

Niko never thought he'd be the type to get flustered and tongue-tied, but he can hardly think right now. "Dear Ama. When did you get so . . ."

"Alluring? Irresistible? Use your words, Niko."

". . . frustrating!"

Salo shrugs. "I'm dead. I think that means I don't have to be shy about what I want anymore."

With one hand he loosens his lone garment, and it falls away from his hips. Naked, he turns around and walks to the pool, stopping just shy of the descending steps. When he looks over his shoulder, his smirk says he knows *every* lustful little thought racing through Niko's mind.

"Are you coming?"

The taste of sex and nsango rises with Niko the next morning and stays with him as he readies his quagga to set off again. These dreams are getting out of hand. More vivid, more real. Harder to live without.

A nightly treasure.

An addiction.

Am I losing my mind?

His mood worsens at breakfast when it's discovered that everyone in the caravan suffered through a variation of the same nightmare.

Everyone except him.

Jio and Sibu describe it as being swallowed whole by a colossal beast with a neck as long as a river. Mafarai says it felt like drowning beneath the weight of a million fish. Addi says he was eaten by a million fish. Everyone else in the caravan has a similar story.

The other boys eye Niko strangely when he confesses he didn't have a nightmare.

"What did you dream about, then?" Jio asks.

"Ah . . . I don't remember," he replies. "I guess I was too tired."

"Aaku Sissay told me it's the Primeval Spirit that inhabits these woods," Addi says, shuddering. "It doesn't like trespassers. But he says the roadway should avoid its lair, so we'll be fine."

The caravan finally sets off, and halfway through the morning Addi prods his mare forward to ride abreast of Niko at the front. "Is everything all right?" he says. "You seem sullen. More so than usual, in any case."

Niko almost dismisses him automatically but thinks better of it. "Seems weird that there'd be all this woodland when we're supposed to be approaching a desert. And this road. It's well trodden, but we haven't come across anyone else using it. Some parts of it are even paved. It makes no sense."

For some reason, Addi chuckles with mild amusement. "My people built their roads to last, Bra Niko. Just look at the World's Artery. As for these woods, my father once told me they were magically grown by an ancient king for his beloved wife, who'd come from a land across the ocean where the trees bloomed in shades of gold and crimson. But I don't know how true that is."

They're a celebration of love, Niko remembers with a chill and tells himself he must have made that connection on his own subconsciously, because any other alternative is too disturbing to consider.

"This is the first time I've heard you say anything about your family," he observes.

"There's not much to say," Addi replies. "My parents abandoned me in Umadiland when I was eleven. They couldn't afford to feed me or take me with them to Yonte Saire. That's how I ended up in Seresa stealing food and coin to survive."

Niko studies Addi's profile. On the surface the boy is unperturbed, but appearances can deceive. "I'm sorry."

"Eh. It doesn't sting as much anymore. I've had a rough time, but I've seen Faraswa who've known only despair in their sad lives. I'd choose my luck over theirs any day."

Ruins begin to appear the deeper into the Crimson Woodlands they travel. Massive polyhedrons of weathered limestone, collapsed palaces with erect pillars, crumbling towns and villages whose names no one alive remembers. The convoy becomes somber and less talkative.

At around midday, the shadow inside Niko stirs. He tries to ignore the sensation at first, but the feeling of danger only strengthens.

At last he gives a high whistle to bring the whole caravan to a stop. Jio and Addi pull up beside him, alert. The other two rangers are at the back of the caravan.

"What is it?" Jio says.

Red-feathered starlings flit across the road in front of them. The way ahead is clear and well defined, cutting through golden grasses and ruddy trees. There's nothing in sight to make Niko wary, but his shadow is practically screaming at him.

"Something's not right," he says and draws power from his blessing, sending some of it into his spear.

When Jio opens his mouth to ask another question, Niko motions for silence, having sensed an abrupt change in the air. And sure enough, a flash of red lightning hits the road twenty paces ahead, followed by a split second of blindness. When Niko's eyes recover, he sees four figures standing where the lightning struck. One woman wears a saffron robe. The other three are masked warriors in silvery breastplates etched with the image of a redhawk.

One of the central masked figures addresses Niko in a commanding voice, though he uses Izumadi, so Niko has to look to Addi for a translation.

The boy's lips have gone dry. "He says we're traveling with a fugitive of the Yontai and that we're to relinquish him immediately."

"These are Jasiri," Jio murmurs, a worried shine in his eyes. "Look at their masks. And they just appeared out of nowhere. Have you ever seen a spell like that?"

"Tell him we have no fugitive here," Niko says, and Addi looks at him, unsure. "Tell them, Addi!"

The boy reluctantly obeys, conveying Niko's words to the Jasiri, then translates when the Jasiri responds. "He says he has no quarrel with us, but they'll do what they must to secure the fugitive."

By now Mafarai and Sibu have joined them at the head of the convoy, the first with his bow in hand, the second with his spear.

"What the devil is going on?" Sibu says.

Niko ignores him. "Ask them why they think the fugitive is here. Ask for a name."

Addi translates, and the Jasiri responds.

"What did he say?" Niko prods Addi impatiently.

The boy has frozen in his saddle, eyes wide. "Meddur the Wise," he mutters. "An old Faraswa man with distinctively scarlet eyes."

The twins utter the same curse. Behind them, Sissay shouts something—probably an indication of surrender given his raised palms. While the whole convoy watches in tense silence, he gets down from the driver's seat of his wagon and begins to walk toward the Jasiri, his palms still raised. Niko almost lets him walk by, but a foolhardy instinct has him putting out his spear to block the man's way forward.

"I can't let that happen."

Sissay—or Meddur the Wise, or whatever his name is—looks up at him and says something in the Umadi tongue.

"He says to let him go," Addi translates. "He says he won't let anyone die for him."

Niko keeps his spear in place. "Tell him to go back. They will not have him."

"Mzi, is this wise?" Jio asks.

Probably not, Niko thinks, but the Faraswa in this caravan have made Sissay their unofficial leader. They look up to him, listen to him. He's the reason they banded together in the first place. And he knows these woods and seems to understand where this journey will end better than anyone else.

"We can't afford to lose him," Niko decides. "Addi, tell the Jasiri it's my duty to protect everyone in this caravan, including Sissay. If they want him, they can take him once we reach our destination. Until then, they'll have to fight me first."

Addi gulps but does as he's told. His lips are nearly trembling when he translates the Jasiri's response. "He has agreed to fight you and you alone. He says no one else has to come to harm."

A duel, then. So be it. In a swift motion Niko dismounts his quagga with his spear, steeling himself for battle.

"That's a damned Jasiri, for Ama's sake," Sibu hisses. "He has spells and magic. He won't fight fair."

"Don't be dumb, mzi," Jio says. "This isn't why we're out here."

Niko spares his comrades a look. "So you'd rather I give up someone I said I'd protect out of fear?"

"It's not fear," says Mafarai. "It's common sense."

Turning his back on them, Niko moves to put himself in front of the caravan, drawing power from his blessing and feeding it into his spear. The Jasiri steps forward, too, pulling a gleaming sword from where it hung by his side.

A slight breeze recedes, and a stillness settles as they face each other. A child starts to wail and is promptly shushed. The moment stretches, and Niko suffers an unpleasant prickle of doubt, the fear of facing an unfamiliar foe, of having made a mistake.

But when the Jasiri suddenly leaps forward, Niko surges ahead to meet him.

18: Kamali

The Crimson Woodlands

Kamali has always thought himself levelheaded and rational, not given to pride or the aggressive masculinity that rules other men. A patient sort of fellow.

But after days of Taji Msani transposing him repeatedly across the joyless Void alongside Neema and Daudi—two other Jasiri with taciturn, solemn temperaments—Kamali's patience has stretched to a razor-thin wire on the verge of snapping.

They've had to follow Meddur's trail all the way across Umadiland, interrogating people in towns along the Artery, threatening, hypnotizing, mind reading, and sometimes beating them for answers. They've had to fend off multiple warlord disciples far from pleased to see Jasiri operating on their soil. They've had to double back from wrong turns and search every byroad south of the Umadi border until finally tracking their quarry down to these accursed woods.

And now Kamali must fight and possibly kill a puffed-up Yerezi ranger too foolish to realize when he's outmatched.

They meet in a clash of metal along the roadway, aerosteel against its more mysterious red variant, one a prize of the Yontai, the other a Yerezi secret. With his mask on Kamali relies on cosmic sight, which gives him a more detailed picture of his surroundings, if muted in color. The boy's spearhead still glows like molten rock, and it streaks in a scorching ribbon toward Kamali much faster than he expects. No sooner has he turned away a thrust than the next one comes, seeking his masked face, swiping for his neck, keeping him weaving through one parry to another.

They circle each other like feuding cats, looking for openings in each other's defenses. Kamali finds one and lunges, at last outflanking the moving spear, but the boy pivots and spins away, following through with a sweeping cut that blurs toward Kamali's face. He recoils just in time to feel it hiss past the surface of his mask, but the Ajaha whips the spear upward not a split second later, and Kamali moves too late, taking it on his chest. The spearpoint screeches and scrapes against his breastplate, leaving a thin scar across the moongold redhawk etched onto its surface.

Shocked, Kamali looks down at his chest. He thought the rangers of the Ajaha were little more than common men with a morsel of enhanced strength from having their bones enchanted. Evidently he needs to make a reassessment.

Birds caw somewhere in the woods. Members of the Faraswa caravan have disembarked their wagons to watch, huddled behind the mounted rangers. The ranger in front of Kamali licks his lips, eyes alert, spear steady in his hands. No armor or clothing protects his upper body besides a crisscrossing leather harness and an ornate pauldron cast into the snarling head of a Yerezi leopard. Prideful, certainly, but he seems the earnest sort, Kamali would say, if a little naive.

You should have never challenged me. Kamali draws essence from the vertebra of enchanted moongold at the base of his spine—the Jasiri's second heart. He metabolizes the essence as strength, lets it course through his veins, and then unleashes it, darting forward with an unnatural burst of speed.

It's time to stop holding back.

For a swordsman, a spear can be a deadly foe even in the hands of a novice, if only because of its reach. To neutralize a spear-wielding enemy, a swordsman must move fast enough to survive the effective range of the spear while coming close enough for his own blade to strike.

Kamali sets upon the ranger with a hail of rapid blows meant to overwhelm him and break his guard, but the ranger is no novice and keeps up with his speed, turning away each strike with the haft of his spear.

Clever footwork wins him the offensive; then it's Kamali retreating from the red-hot spearhead as it comes for him in a vigorous counterattack. He finds himself reaching prematurely for the reserves of his second heart just so he can wrest back the initiative, but the ranger matches him step for step, speed for speed, striking at angles difficult to block so that Kamali can't find a way through.

"Stop toying with him and finish this, Kamali," Taji scolds him.

Which might have been funny if he didn't need to duck out of the way of a deadly swipe. He's faced fully fledged mystics who crumbled like dirt between his fingers. Toying with him? This boy is actually making him sweat.

The Yerezi Ajaha rise in his estimation. It seems he'll have to lean deeper into his strengths to end this. *So be it.*

He triggers his cosmic shards, and the dingonek spirit tattooed onto his back roars to life, shrouding him in flame and filling him with an insatiable hunger for violence. Its feline face superimposes itself onto his head, lending him its eyes so that he sees the world in shades of fire and blood. Wild power floods his muscles, and he moves forward at the speed of a tronic beast, feinting to one side, then darting to the other. He slips past the point of the ranger's spear and into his guard.

The boy shifts on his feet, but too late; Kamali's blade is about to taste blood from his left shoulder. It's over.

Except the boy *moves*. He slides behind Kamali like a shadow might slide across the ground, and Kamali's sword passes harmlessly through the air. He looks behind him and finds the ranger over ten paces away, enveloped in some kind of pulsating red aura. Kamali barely has time to make sense of what's just happened because the boy spins, sweeping his spear through the air in front of him with a solid two-handed grip.

It should be a futile move given the distance between them, but an arcane shadow the color of moonlight follows the spear, extending its reach, and strikes Kamali with a blow that would've cleaved an ordinary man in half. His dingonek spirit disperses the force throughout his body, and he's launched off the ground like a rock hurled from a sling. He sails into the air, arching away from the road and into the woods.

Disbelief paralyzes him only for a moment. His reflexes take over, and he relinquishes his dingonek, awakening the peregrine on his chest. Ghostly wings erupt from his arms, arresting his fall, and he lands softly on the golden grasses growing between the trees.

Kamali openly laughs. There are Jasiri who would have died from that single blow. He might have been seriously injured himself were it not for his spirit. Even *with* the spirit he almost lost his grip on his weapon.

A Jasiri, nearly disarmed by a warrior with no shards. Blasphemy.

A scarlet shadow sprints for him from the direction of the roadway, and he leaps to the side barely in time to avoid being impaled in the neck. The boy attacks again, then again, his questing spearpoint driving Kamali deeper into the woods.

Tired of being defensive, Kamali revives the dingonek to give himself a burst of speed and begins to push back. He draws more essence into his shards, creating a buildup of power that makes his skin tingle and the spirit mad with hunger.

He flies forward with his sword, aiming for the ranger's heart, and when the ranger predictably sidesteps and seeks to flank him, he lunges, seizes the boy by the throat, and hurls him at a nearby tree. The boy slams into the trunk with a thunderous crack, dislodging a rainfall of cherry-red leaves from the boughs. Before he can recover, Kamali roars, releasing the pent-up essence as a spout of moonfire that gushes out from the dingonek's open jaws.

The boy shoots away right before flames singe the cracked tree trunk. Kamali turns his head to follow the boy, breathing a trail of heat that blackens the grass, but the ranger's moonlit shadow carries him off fast enough to avoid the torrent.

When the fire breath expends itself, the boy comes to a stop, wincing as he touches his bruised side. Kamali doesn't give him a moment to collect himself. He attacks, and the ranger rises to the challenge.

They battle through the woods, over a hill and farther away from the road, goading each other down the slopes of a low, misty valley dotted with limestone ruins.

Two of the ranger's comrades follow on foot, but they know better than to intervene. The Jasiri Neema comes up behind them, leaving Taji and Daudi to keep an eye on the caravan.

As the struggle takes them all farther down the hill, Kamali keeps expecting his foe to tire himself and make a mistake, but the boy knows the power of his spear and maintains faultless control over the weapon's balance point, conservative but fluid little movements generating enough momentum to pierce armor and rend flesh. Whenever Kamali outwits the spear, the boy delivers shadow-powered punches that send

Kamali skidding backward. Grasses burn in their wake, branches snap, and the boles of trees thunder as they split in half from collisions.

They reach the valley floor and tear through the Faraswa ruins, a cluster of innumerable crumbling pillars and effaced statues that haven't been disturbed for centuries perhaps, ghostly shapes standing still in the thick mists. Kamali senses a most unusual magic pervading the damp air, but he doesn't let it distract him from the fight.

The fog swallows them, and he loses sight of Neema and the two rangers. He and his adversary don't stop fighting even when they hear the rangers shouting, their panicked voices calling out for their comrade. As the banks of a lake appear from out of the mists, Kamali fortifies his hand and catches the shaft of the ranger's attacking spear, driving the point of his sword forward. When the Ajaha slaps it away with his enchanted vambrace, leaving himself open, Kamali delivers a spirited kick to the boy's abdomen, sending him flying toward a circle of ruined obelisks.

One of the obelisks disintegrates as he crashes through it, startling the birds nesting in the surrounding trees. Inside the circle he groans as he rolls onto his back on a mosaic floor.

Stepping over the stub of the broken obelisk, Kamali watches the ranger. "Stay down," he says. "I don't want to hurt you, but you're forcing my hand."

The ranger answers by immediately reaching for his spear and getting up. His body is covered with scrapes and bruises, and his exhaustion is apparent, but he says something defiant in his tongue, holding his spear in an offensive stance. Kamali almost understands him given the tongue's slight similarity to KiYonte and, to a greater extent, Izumadi, but he doubts they could manage a conversation.

He shakes his head to make himself clear, hardening his voice and speaking slowly. "Stand. *Down.*"

"No," the boy says and thrusts his spear in a threatening motion.

Deciding to end this once and for all, Kamali gusts forward at his absolute fastest and seizes the boy by his leather harness. The boy can only cry out as Kamali uses all his might to launch him out of the mists and into the sky, toward the lake. In the next half heartbeat, Kamali engages his peregrine and *explodes* off the ground, outpacing the flailing ranger and reaching him in time to catch him midair with ghostly talons. The momentum takes them across the edge of the lake and over its misty surface; Kamali banks to one side, soaring higher on an updraft so that they begin to turn back in the direction of dry land.

But movement disturbs the mists below, and a force Kamali cannot resist reaches up for his soul. And *pulls*.

His peregrine flees from the presence in terror. His grip on the Ajaha loosens. Consciousness recedes from him, and gravity reclaims its dominion. The last thing he hears before he blacks out is the ranger screaming for his life as they plummet into the mists.

Wetness. Darkness. A cold, watery embrace pulling him deeper and deeper.

Kamali opens his eyes and finds that he can't see. Without his cosmic sight his mask is a blindfold, so he takes it off, only for it to slip out of his grip and sink into the murky depths below.

His sword is gone too. He's deep enough that the daylight is a distant glitter dancing far above on the surface. He tries to swim up to it, but the force that caught him keeps pulling him down. His chest tightens with the urge to breathe.

He looks to his side in time to see the Ajaha lifting the head of his spear and aiming it at the surface, bubbles of breath escaping his nostrils as he turns his face upward. He frowns with focus and exertion, and the next thing Kamali knows, the ranger is shooting up and out of the water in a tunnel of moonlight.

Kamali struggles, reaching for the spirits tattooed onto his body with increased desperation. They refuse to come. He lurches as the reflex to breathe nearly overpowers him, and he almost lets water flood into his lungs. It's at that very moment that the presence holding him reveals itself, rising out of the deep as a massive school of cichlid fish that glow bright green and move together to form the rearing shape of a great monster.

Its head dwarfs Kamali with its size. Its neck is as long as a serpent out of the legends, extending into a four-legged body the size of a mountain. The sheer number of cichlids involved in rendering its shape turns the darkness of the lake into bioluminescent daylight.

Even as the lack of breath brings him near to oblivion, Kamali recognizes that he is now face to face with a Primeval Spirit, the Great Mokele-Mbembe herself, and that she is not pleased.

The spirit opens her enormous jaws—thousands upon thousands of glowing cichlids swimming in synchronous motion—and then screams at him, making the waters of the lake tremble.

His bones shake, and his joints rattle in their sockets. The sound penetrates every inch of him, even piercing into his thoughts, filling him with mystifying visions.

Exploding stars. Heavenly gates. Ravenous hordes of demons blackening the skies over many worlds. Nightmares from a tortured mind.

Unexpectedly the spirit's grip on him weakens, and essence floods back into his shards. He senses the spirit has more to say, more psychotic visions to impart, but he decides he's had enough.

Quick as lightning he awakens one of his spirits, a shape tattooed in bright colors down his right arm: the spearfish. It surges into his veins and surrounds him in the ghost of its physical form, giving him a long, pointed spear-like snout and a huge dorsal fin. With every last ounce of his strength, he erupts upward, gaining enough speed to leap out of the water and clear the surface. He gasps for breath, and in midair he summons the peregrine, then spreads his wings to lift himself higher.

The Mokele-Mbembe tries to pull him back down, but forward momentum carries him all the way to the shore. He hits the ground hard, rolling sideways over the pebbles of the lakeside. The ranger had just reached the lakeside himself; his mouth drops in shock, but he quickly recovers, bringing his spear up in a fighting stance.

By the Mother. This again?

Rabid anger grips Kamali. His sword is now somewhere at the bottom of the lake. A Primeval Spirit infested his mind with horrible visions and nearly killed him. He's wet and tired and still hasn't acquired his target. All because of this stubborn, *stupid* ranger.

Kamali picks himself off the ground. "I'm done being diplomatic," he says to the boy. "Now we dance."

He leaps forward with the feline dingonek, cloaking himself in its angry flames. The white mists around them thicken. He can hear the rangers who followed them still shouting for their friend, but they sound far away. A foul stench like an open sewer begins to fill the air, but he pays it no heed, reaching into the extremities of his new master's Axiom, pushing his spirit to heights of speed he couldn't have reached in his old mistress's coven. The spirit laps the power hungrily, becoming stronger and faster but harder to control as its nature rises to compete with his own.

He swipes with a claw and catches the Ajaha on one thigh, and blood wells in three bright stripes.

"You've never lost, have you," he says, the words edged with an inhuman growl. "I can see it in your eyes. The arrogance of a warrior who's never known defeat."

He swipes again and finds an arm, tearing a gash that makes the boy cry out and drop his spear. The boy clutches his arm and trips as he tries to scuffle away, falling onto his back. For the first time fear touches his face.

Kamali picks up the discarded spear. It's as light as aerosteel and surprisingly empty of enchantments, which doesn't make sense, given how he's seen it glow with heat.

Yerezi magic.

Kamali approaches the fallen boy. The revolting stench has intensified. The mists have become so thick he can hardly see more than ten yards away. The shouting rangers are now so far Kamali can barely hear them. And a presence teases his senses, approaching at a rapid pace from the ruins.

But Kamali has stoked the dingonek's hunger, reaching the apex of what he is, and he won't descend from such heights until blood has been spilled.

"You're very good with this weapon," he says, considering the spear. "Maybe it's fitting that it kills you."

To the dingonek's annoyance, the boy takes a deep breath and lets go of his fear, looking up at Kamali like he's ready, like dying won't be such a terrible fate.

Movement behind Kamali, a thickening fetor like death and smoke from a freshly lit funeral pyre. The presence approaching from the ruins is also nearer, but the dingonek has eyes only for its prey.

"Death is the Infinite Path," it says, lifting the spear.

The boy's eyes widen—not at the spear but at whatever is behind Kamali. And that's when Kamali's shards pulse in mutiny, revolted by the vile and unpleasantly oily essence that has filled the air around him. He finally recognizes the stench for what it is, and only now does he turn around and see the legion of fell creatures moving in the mists, crawling out of the water, coming for him. The first have already reached the lakeshore. Torches of white light beam out from their eye sockets, making the mists glow. They shamble forward on skeletal, vaguely humanoid limbs, bloated stomachs bursting with leeches and crab mandibles.

And then the presence he sensed from the ruins arrives, a slender figure who runs past him and *toward* the advancing horde. The figure abruptly stops and thrusts out a hand; a flash of light stabs out of the mists and quickly brightens as a third sun blooms into existence over the lake.

The demons roar as they catch fire in a purifying wave, dissolving into clouds of white vapor that dissipate together with the mists. The conjured sun remains until it has destroyed the entire horde, then bursts in an explosion that nearly blinds Kamali.

He shades his eyes with a hand, squinting into the waning brilliance, and his gaze fixes on a prepossessing Faraswa woman with eyes like the double sunrise and white markings of cosmic power pulsing across her face.

His heart stops.

"Kamali Jasiri!" she shouts. "You who once defied a mshamba and hunted riders in the arena when you should have let them hunt you. Is this what you've become? A heartless murderer?"

He can't believe his eyes. It's her. The woman he fought beside in Yonte Saire's arena. The same woman who later disappeared into beams of sunlight right in front of him in the undercity prison, leaving him nothing but a ring enchanted with unknown power. A ring he's still wearing on a string beneath his breastplate.

The dingonek releases its hold, and his bloodlust subsides.

"Ayana."

Kamali has spent many moons dreaming about her, wondering where she was, remembering the brief kiss that scorched his lips.

Here she is in the flesh, markings like white sunlight throbbing on her face. She wears a simple khanga wrapped at the chest and plain hide sandals. Her frizzy hair dances in a cloud around her head like a halo. He would run to her, but the fierceness in her eyes tells him to be still.

"Ayana," he says, speaking the name like a prayer. He has thought of many things he would say to her if their paths ever crossed again. The words flee from him and leave him nearly dumbstruck. "What are you doing here?"

She starts walking, slowly, obliquely. "I never thought a man like you would let himself become a tyrant's most faithful lapdog. What are *you* doing here, Jasiri? Why are you fighting the emperor's battles and wearing his insignia on your chest?"

The tingle of shame caresses Kamali's skin. "I serve the emperor because he's the best way to restore peace and order to the Yontai. I cannot allow my preferences to cloud my judgment."

"Is that the lie you tell yourself?" Ayana fires back. "You serve him only because he gave you a reason to live!" When he says nothing to that, she stops, her sun-blessed gaze searing into him. "I've watched you from afar, Jasiri. You take your duty to the people of the Yontai seriously, but you have no real attachments to them, no personal loyalties, no reason to live beyond fulfilling your duty."

Kamali frowns, piqued by the insinuation that he's fighting for a cause he isn't invested in. "I'm a Jasiri. My duty is my life."

"And there lies the problem." Ayana takes a step closer, her fixed look pinning him in place. "Duty has always been your life, hasn't it. But you lost that when they tossed you down to rot in the undercity, and you were adrift. Then the emperor dangled a new purpose in front of you, a new duty, and you were all too eager to accept."

Kamali breaks away from her gaze, his eyes falling to the ground. "What would you have had me do? The emperor cannot be fought. I have stood in his presence and felt the power he commands. There's not a soul alive who could match it. Serving him was the only way to minimize the waves of death that would surely come."

"That's what he wants you to believe, that serving him serves the greater good. But in his quest for power he's allied himself with forces more destructive than you can imagine." She flicks her eyes to the wounded ranger. "And you serve these forces yourself every time you kill in his name."

With another throb of shame, Kamali glances over his shoulder and finds the boy still lying on the ground, clutching his lacerated arm. He's slicked all over with blood, his lips ashen, his eyes glassy and unfocused.

"I didn't want to fight him," Kamali tells Ayana. "I came here for Meddur the agitator, and he stood in my way."

"Meddur is a distraction," Ayana says, coming closer. "Your emperor wants *me*, and he knows that getting Meddur will draw me out."

"The emperor has no quarrel with you."

"The emperor is my enemy as surely as he is yours. What do you think he'd have done to you had you refused to serve him?"

Kamali stares at Ayana, unwilling to answer.

"He would have killed you," she says. "People were singing your name on the streets of Yonte Saire because of what you did in the arena. You were a symbol of defiance they would have followed anywhere, perhaps the last remaining threat to the emperor's rule. He knew he needed your allegiance or your death, and while *you* gave him what he wanted, I refused, so he hunts my allies to draw me out."

The emperor's lecture on the power of symbols reverberates through Kamali despite himself. *Symbols are the bedrocks upon which nations and kingdoms are founded.* And what could be a greater symbol to the Faraswa people right now than the woman they witnessed besting seasoned riders in the arena?

Of course the emperor wants to destroy her.

I don't serve him because he's a good man, Kamali thinks. *I serve him because he has power that could wash the jungles of the Yontai in blood, and I want to stop him from doing so.*

"Kamali, look at me." Ayana has come close enough for him to see the specks of gold and silver in her sunlit irises. "Look into my eyes and see the truth of my words. If your duty is to the people of the Yontai, then you have no greater enemy than the man you serve. Even as we speak, his new ally seeks a key to a gate they wish to open; should they succeed, what you saw coming out of this lake will be a trifle compared to the horrors they will unleash."

She's cast a spell; Kamali sees it now. But being well versed in the art of hypnotism himself, he knows he's not being compelled to see or hear things that aren't there. Instead, Ayana's words seem to carry a light of truth that illumines what *is* there, giving him a deeper understanding of what he already knows.

He suddenly recalls the emperor telling him about a pyramid of massive proportions rising out of the dunes of the Faraswa Desert. *I intend to help the new king bring an end to its curse.*

"What do you know about the pyramid in the desert?" he says.

She had paused just out of arm's length, as if to gauge his reaction to her words; now she comes to take his free hand and presses it between hers. "I can show you," she says. "I can show you everything. The heavens sent you to me, Kamali. I'm sure of it now. That's why our paths crossed back in Yonte Saire. Because of this moment, right here. I can show you what I've been shown, why I'm out here, why I wield powers I should not, but you'll have to trust me."

Kamali stares into her magnetic eyes, like pools of sunrise pulling him into their depths. "You want me to betray my emperor for you."

"I want you to do your duty, Jasiri. The emperor's decision to open that gate will doom everyone you're sworn to protect. I know this to be true as surely as I know you're standing right in front of me." She presses his hand tighter between her palms. "I know you sense the light of truth in my words, Kamali."

He wants to call her a liar, but her magic is the magic of truth itself; if she lied, the spell would fall apart and he would know. And if he denied her, it would not be because he doesn't believe her but because he's afraid.

It would be because he's a coward, unwilling to admit he's made a mistake.

"I didn't come here alone," he hears himself say. "My fellow Jasiri won't be swayed."

Ayana's eyes flash, a feline predator sighting prey in the distance. "Then help me send them on their way."

Kamali once betrayed the orthodoxy to keep a secret he believed would destroy his people, knowing what his actions would cost him. The secret got out in the end, despite his efforts, but he would betray and kill again if he deemed it necessary.

"I'll deal with the others," he says. "Afterward, I want to know everything you know."

"Not in these woods," Ayana says. "We've lingered too long already. We reach the desert first; then I'll explain everything."

Kamali watches this baffling woman, trying to figure out what it is about her that's beguiled him since the first time he laid eyes on her. "I'm choosing to trust you," he says. "I hope I don't prove myself a fool."

"You won't."

He nods, then turns to the wounded ranger. He seemed ready to die not long ago, but now fear gains a second life inside his eyes.

"I'll need your spear for a while longer," Kamali says, even though the boy probably doesn't understand him. "My friend Ayana will help you back to the road."

The ranger stares mutely up at him, confusion displacing fear.

Kamali doesn't bother explaining himself. Without another word, he summons his peregrine and lifts off the ground.

Neema and Daudi are both Fire mystics capable of releasing explosive spells of destructive moonfire at a moment's notice. They could level a village in a matter of seconds—or more pertinently, incinerate a caravan as quickly as they can thrust an open palm.

They are also Jasiri, meaning they'll leave these woods with their quarry in custody or not at all.

From the sky he spots Neema picking her way through the woods, heading back to the road. He swoops down on her before she even knows what's happened, skewering her through the nape. He lifts off again and heads for the road, then falls upon Daudi in a similar fashion, piercing his unprotected neck and severing his spine. Daudi makes one convulsive motion before he stills.

"Kamali!" Taji screams. "What have you done?"

Farther down the road, the members of the caravan gawk at him. The mounted ranger who stayed behind nocks an arrow to the string of his bow but hesitates to fire. A Faraswa boy riding beside him notices the spear in Kamali's hands with eyes that widen at first, then fill with hot tears of rage and vengeance.

Kamali ignores him, turning to face Taji. "Do you trust me?"

She backs away from him like he's transformed into a creature of the netherworld. "Not right now, I don't."

"I have come upon new information about what the emperor is doing out in the desert," Kamali says in a calm voice. "I was wrong to join him. We both were. He must be stopped."

The flavor of her fear shifts, and she looks at him the way one might look upon a beloved relative who's gone mad. "What are you talking about, Kamali?"

"It's difficult to explain, but there's a dangerous artifact he's trying to activate to gain more power. It'll destroy us all." He's not getting through to her. He can feel her slipping away. He takes a step forward, but she retreats. "Taji, I need you to trust me. The emperor is no good."

"I don't even recognize you right now!" she cries.

"Taji, wait!"

Space expands as a bolt of lightning arcs from the sky to strike the road, blinding Kamali with its brilliance. When his eyes adjust, Taji is no longer there.

19: Aneniko

The Crimson Woodlands

Niko's world has stopped making sense. From being plunged into a lake where *something* lurked in the water, to being nearly skewered to death by a mad Jasiri, then witnessing an army of tikoloshe crawling out of the lake, only to be saved by a sun-conjuring Faraswa woman—he would almost believe he'd smoked too much nsango and lost his wits.

Or maybe it's the blood loss. At this point, he can't be sure of anything.

The Faraswa woman stares down at him with eyes the color of molten gold. He's not sure what transpired between her and the Jasiri before he took off, but he knows he owes his life to her. She says something to him in the tongue of the KiYonte people, then leans down with a wiry hand extended.

Deciding she's an ally or at least not an enemy, Niko takes the hand and lets her pull him up to his feet. He grimaces at the sharp pain that smarts all along the gouges on his left thigh. His right arm is a ghastly ruin, too—the accursed Jasiri damned near took it off—though Niko suspects it might look worse than it actually is. His red steel is already working hard to clot the wounds and prevent further loss of blood, but there's only so much its enchantments can do on their own. He'll need medical attention.

He sways from a wave of weakness, but the woman takes his good arm and hooks it over her shoulders to keep him standing.

"Thanks," he says, and they start limping away from the lake in the direction of the caravan.

The mists hanging over the ruins aren't as thick as they were before, so he can see all the way to the hill they descended as they fought. He hardly remembers covering so much distance, almost as though something pulled them here, to these ruins. An ancient temple complex, maybe? Definitely not the one from his . . . amorous dreams, but he doesn't like how similar the limestone architecture feels, how familiar the statuary and the iconography, especially considering he's never been here before.

He stops when a faraway voice tickles his ears. The woman gives him a curious look, but he waits until he hears it again.

"Niko!"

His eyes widen. "Jio? Sibu? I'm here!"

"Niko! Where are you?"

"I'm over here!" he shouts.

They call each other a few more times, the voices getting nearer, until two identical figures in crimson loincloths and red steel armor run out of the mist. Niko has never been so glad to see their faces, though they both look ready to kill something.

"By Ama," Jio says, immediately fixing on Niko's bloodied limbs. "What happened?"

Sibu's scrutiny lands on the stranger. "Who the devil is this?"

"Relax. She saved my life," Niko tells them.

Sibu gives her a suspicious once-over, then looks around the ruins like he expects a pack of hyenas to pounce at any moment. "Where's the Jasiri?"

"He took off. Probably went back to the caravan."

"You're a damned fool, Aneniko," Jio gripes. "What the devil were you thinking? You could have gotten yourself killed."

"You can shout at me all you want when we get back to the caravan. The Jasiri might have already taken Sissay for all we know."

Jio growls, clearly with more to say, but he and his brother both take over from the Faraswa woman, hooking his arms over their shoulders and helping him limp all the way back up the hill.

The whole time he fails to convince himself that he's only imagining the sensation of many eyes watching him from the direction of the lake.

The day's strangeness only compounds when they return to find Sissay present and alive, speaking calmly to the now-maskless Jasiri as if they're old acquaintances. Stranger still is the absence of the Jasiri's companions, as well as the loud cheer the whole caravan gives when they see Niko coming out of the woods.

They cheer even louder at the sighting of the Faraswa woman who saved his life.

While the brothers set him down by the roadside and Jio goes to unearth Niko's medical supplies from his saddlebag, the caravan welcomes the woman like a hero out of folklore, clamoring to shake her hand, showering her with muttered blessings. She greets them all, though she receives their attention with slight bemusement, almost like she didn't expect such a strong reception.

Addi is the only other person among the Faraswa who seems just as confused, and he shakes the woman's hand with an openly puzzled expression. Afterward he comes over alongside Mafarai, both visibly relieved to see Niko alive and mostly well, and the story they tell him is so unbelievable he asks them to repeat it.

"The Jasiri killed one of his comrades right in front of us," Addi says breathlessly. "Fell on him with your spear from out of nowhere. The woman got away before he could get her, vanished like lightning, and the third Jasiri hasn't been seen since she walked into the woods."

"Why would he turn on them?" Sibu asks skeptically.

They all glance at the Jasiri and find him watching the Faraswa woman with an unreadable look. Seeing him now, Niko almost can't believe he's the same demon-possessed fiend who nearly dismembered him. He's actually quite easy on the eyes, a light-complexioned fellow with short hair and a broad, stubbled face Niko might have admired if it didn't belong to a man who'd nearly killed him.

"The woman has something to do with it," he mutters, remembering how she conjured a ball of light that banished the tikoloshe coming out of the lake.

Did I even see that, or was I just delirious?

Jio returns with the medical supplies, and with Addi's help he doctors the wounds with an antiseptic tincture that stings so exquisitely Niko bites his lips to kill off a scream. Fortunately, the pain relents as they apply a flesh-knitting salve and wrap the wounds in reedfiber gauze. They also put his arm in a sling.

He turns down any pain medications, since they'd only make him drowsy, and when Addi and the rangers try to convince him to ride in one of the wagons as the caravan prepares to set off again, he refuses, insisting that they help him back onto his stallion. Once mounted, he sees the Jasiri coming over to return his spear to him and has to work not to scowl at the man as he accepts the spear with his one good hand.

But he does scowl when the Jasiri walks off, and again when he struggles to slip the spear into its appropriate harness on his saddle. Addi comes to his aid, which only tests Niko's patience, but he knows better than to lash out at someone who's just trying to help.

At the end of the day, no one forced him to duel a damned Jasiri.

The Jasiri himself joins his Faraswa companion in one of the wagons at the back of the convoy, and then they resume their journey across the woodlands, Niko holding the reins of his stallion in one hand, wincing with every step.

He braves through the pain. His pride has been wounded enough already; he'll be damned if he's chased off his saddle by a foreign mystic.

"Are you all right?" Addi says nearly an hour into their renewed journey.

"I'm fine," Niko snaps.

Addi takes the response in stride and gently says, "I think your ego has been bruised."

Niko shoots him a warning glare, but Addi meets it with friendly understanding, which pisses Niko off even more because now it's obvious he's being childish and unreasonable.

He sighs, looking ahead. "I gave it my all, and it still wasn't enough."

"It looked pretty close to me," Addi says.

"Not in the end. I think he might have been holding back at first." It pains Niko to admit this, but he'd rather face his flaws than pretend they don't exist. "When he gave in fully to his spirits, I stood no chance."

"But you drove him to that point," Addi says. "I'm familiar with Umadi spirit charms, and what I know is warriors who possess themselves with spirits don't like to yield to them completely because then it's the spirits in control. You pushed him so hard he had to give up control, and he's a damned Jasiri, the emperor's general himself if Aaku Sissay is right."

"And I'm a damned Ajaha. An honor guard to boot. I should be able to face any threat, mystical or mundane, and I failed."

Addi gives a scornful laugh.

"Are you mocking me?" Niko demands.

"Yes, actually, I am," Addi says. "I'm mocking you and your impossible personal standards. You're so convinced you failed, but the rest of us saw you stand against a Jasiri to protect a member of your caravan—and *succeed*. Not only that, the Jasiri turned on his own people and joined us. Yet here you are, complaining."

Niko huffs. "I was lucky. The woman appeared just seconds before he killed me, and she's the one who talked him down."

"You earned your luck, Bra Niko," Addi says. "You're a hero to everyone in this caravan, myself included. Now cheer up and stop brooding."

Another mass seizure hits later that afternoon. Addi gives Niko enough of a warning for him to call the caravan to a stop. With one hand incapacitated, he is unable to help Addi himself, but Jio volunteers without a word, dismounting and then helping the boy off his quagga.

Dusk is near, so they set up camp afterward, and despite the continued threat of more seizures, the presence of the Faraswa woman named Ayana fills the camp with a hope Niko finds mystifying. They seem to hang on her every word. Even Sissay regards her with reverence.

"They're saying she's the long-prophesied harbinger of our people's return to glory," Addi tells Niko after joining him by one of the camp's many fires. He then proceeds to explain how she supposedly fought in an arena alongside the very same Jasiri who nearly killed him.

"I guess that explains why they're so happy to see her," Niko says. "But what's she doing all the way out here?"

"The same thing *we're* doing out here," Addi replies. "She says she actually knows what's causing the seizures and how to stop them."

Niko glances at Addi. He's staring into the fire with a studious frown. "You don't believe her?"

"It's not that," Addi says after a pause. "I just don't want to raise my hopes."

Niko's thoughts return to the lake earlier today, the flash of sunlight he saw breaking out of the mists, the legion of tikoloshe catching fire. Aren't Faraswa supposed to be incapable of performing magic? And yet

324

what he saw couldn't have been anything else, even if it differed from any magic he's ever seen.

"I think she might be telling the truth."

"Maybe," Addi replies, though the skepticism hasn't left his voice. "I tried to ask her more questions about the seizures, but she was evasive. She said she'll explain everything once we get to her hideout in the desert."

"A hideout?"

"Some old city called Dahbet. She said it's secluded and well hidden."

Niko likes the sound of an actual solid destination, but he's not fond of Addi's choice of words. "Who's she hiding from?"

"The 'King of the West,' apparently. Ayana says he's doing something bad in the desert and she's been trying to stop him. When I asked her to elaborate, you can guess what she told me."

"She'll explain once we get to her hideout," Niko suggests, and Addi spreads his hands as if to say, *You see?*

"Maybe she has a good reason. These woods are strange. Sounds carry farther than they should. Dreams leak from one mind to another. Maybe she's just being cautious."

"Maybe," Addi says again, still unconvinced.

Niko sneaks a glance at Ayana's fire and finds her sitting next to the Jasiri, who just happens to be looking in Niko's direction at that exact moment. Their eyes lock, and Niko's hackles begin to rise, his fingers itching for his spear. To his surprise the Jasiri dips his head forward in a nod. Not an apology but the acknowledgment of an equal.

A knot of tension loosens in Niko's gut, and he nods back. And later, when Addi offers him medication to ease his pain and let him sleep easier, he accepts it, feeling foolish that he ever thought he had something to prove.

◆ ◆ ◆

It takes the caravan two more days to reach the edge of the Crimson Woodlands.

For Niko the change is like stepping into another world. They arrive at the lip of an escarpment where the rose-golden grasses and red-leaved trees fall away into a rocky bluff. At the base of the escarpment lies a whole new biome: a flat, sandy, semiarid savanna with shorter, tougher grasses, scattered shrubs, and the occasional acacia.

The caravan slows as it follows the winding roadway down the bluffs. At a few places along the road, Niko has to order the other rangers to dismount and remove rocks and boulders blocking the way forward, but the road is in surprisingly good condition considering its age and disuse.

They follow it into the semidesert, a thin strip of cracked paving cutting a line across endless flats of rusty sand and dry vegetation. They advance fairly rapidly along its length, but the sunlight in these parts hits with an intensity that soon becomes unbearable. Niko ends up hiding his face beneath his conical straw hat and covering himself with a light woolen cloak. Addi and the other rangers do the same.

As the day wears on, Niko slowly begins to appreciate just how unprepared they were for this part of the journey and how they might have actually saved themselves by taking on the Faraswa caravan. Being used to grassy plains where streams and watering holes are never far away, none of them paused to think about how they'd cross long stretches of land where water would be scarce. How lucky then that the Faraswa brought barrels of water for their own animals and have more than enough to share with the quaggas. They also continue to share their generous provisions of food, which saves Niko and his team the hassle of having to hunt and cook for themselves.

Evening brings with it a chill almost as biting as a winter's breath and winds that fill Niko's dreams with whispers and the vivid ghost of a bespectacled boy. They chase each other across sandstone hallways carved with occult ciphers. They play-wrestle on top of a great limestone structure disgorging rivers of clear water from its bowels. They make love in the shallows of an oasis lake.

In the morning, Ayana says her hideout is some distance south of the roadway, so Addi relinquishes his mare to her, and Niko lets her take over leading the caravan. While the twins guard the rear, he rides just behind her alongside Mafarai, focusing fixedly on the horizon to keep his thoughts clear.

He doesn't think about slow and lingering kisses, hands sliding over smooth coppery skin and sinews. He doesn't think about thrusting into the glorious heat between a pair of slender legs, or the shame of waking up to find that he'd spurted into his loincloth like a whelp new to his adolescence. He doesn't think about what could possibly be wrong with him that he should suffer such unbecoming dreams about a dead person, and he certainly doesn't think about how a big part of him hopes the dreams never stop.

The loss of a dedicated roadway only slightly slows their progress given the mostly even terrain, but dry savanna soon yields to softly undulating dunes of rusty sand, and then these come alive with ruins that take Niko's breath away with their scale.

They ride past a dead city of crumbling pillars and colonnades, some still supporting architraves with effaced carvings. They ride in the shadow of an enormous hand carved out of limestone, rising out of the sands with a sphere resting in its palm.

More remarkable are the twin pyramids they see in the distance, massive and rugged with exfoliation but in otherwise superb shape considering their age. They'd be impressive enough if they stood side by side, but one is inverted over the other so that its bulk appears to hover, touching its upright twin only at their apexes. To Niko's eyes it should have fallen a long time ago. In fact, so spectacular is the structure's stability he decides there must be a magical influence keeping it afloat.

His suspicion of the presence of magic strengthens as they descend into a wide canyon oasis of date palms and aquamarine-blue water. A near-perfect limestone cube as big as a hill sits precariously, perhaps impossibly, on a rock formation at one edge of the canyon. The slightest wind should tip it over and send it tumbling to the base of the canyon, but like the inverted pyramid, the cube has remained as it is for centuries at least.

Jets of water spew ceaselessly from its interior through rectangular apertures carved into the sides, cascading down into the canyon with enough volume to fill the pool below and feed the river flowing from it.

As they slowly navigate deeper into the canyon and the limestone artifact begins to loom higher above them, worry tickles Niko in the chest, the unreasonable idea that he's seen the desert from the top of that cube, or at least another one like it. His unease must show on his face, though Mafarai interprets it as astonishment.

"Boggles the mind, doesn't it?" says Mafarai, looking up at the artifact with his thoughtful eyes. "What do you think it is?"

"The source that replenishes this oasis," Niko answers with a certainty that surprises even himself. "The Faraswa built many such artifacts and scattered them across the desert to serve towns and villages."

Mafarai gives him an odd look. "Oh? How did you know that?"

A ghost told me, Niko thinks. "I must've heard it somewhere."

"That's incredible." Mafarai shakes his head in wonder, having accepted Niko's answer as truth. "You hear stories about how the Faraswa were cursed by Ama and so on and so forth, but you dismiss them as hazy fireside tales; then you come here and see the shit they built, and the stories start making sense. How else did people who could build something like *that* wind up as slaves and refugees?"

The path skirting the river is too rocky and narrow for the wagons, but Ayana assures everyone that her hideout isn't far and that they can go the rest of the way on foot.

It takes nearly an hour for the caravan to unyoke all the beasts and transfer essential items onto packsaddles. With one hand still in a sling, Niko would only be a hindrance, so he sits on a rock beneath a palm tree while he waits, dipping his feet into the cool crystal-blue waters of the canyon.

Perhaps the waters are enchanted, because a clarity of mind descends on him and he finally admits a possibility that confounds as much as it frightens him. This may not be the oasis from his torrid dreams. For one, the lake was bigger, and instead of a canyon he remembers a sandstone palace complex surrounding the oasis. But he can't keep pretending that his dreams are just an unhealthy obsession and no more. Something is clearly whispering things to him when he sleeps, things he shouldn't know.

A breeze rustles through the trees, and his red shadow rears up like an alerted cobra. A feeling draws his gaze to the canyon's eastern rock face, but he sees nothing there.

When they set off again, he remains on foot like almost everyone else, but he takes his red steel hunting knife from his saddlebag and sheathes it in the scabbard on his leather harness. Then he assigns Addi the job of leading his tronic stallion by the reins.

As Ayana takes them deeper into the canyon and through a maze of narrow gorges where they have to walk in the flow of shallow streams, Niko gradually falls back until he's side by side with Sibu at the rear of the procession.

"Is your leg giving you trouble, mzi?" Sibu says with a note of smugness. "I could carry you if you want."

"Shut up. I'm fine. I just need to take a leak. I'll catch up."

"Scream if you need help," Sibu says, then walks off and disappears behind a bend in the canyon.

Niko closes his eyes, waiting, and when the thing he *knows* is stalking them makes another move, he becomes shadow, flowing *up* the walls of the canyon, the hilt of his knife solid in his good hand.

A blink passes, a flash of red lightning, and then he's pressing the sharp tip of his knife into saffron-colored cloth from behind a very startled woman.

The air around her smells like ozone. She has long braided hair and skin as gold as honey. She yelps and her cosmic shards begin to glow again, so he presses his knife deeper against her unprotected flank.

"Try to cast your spell and I'll slice you," he says.

She must understand the gist of his warning, since she dims her shards, but then she says something Niko doesn't catch—maybe a plea for her life or a prayer to the moon. Either way, Niko doesn't get to ask for clarification because a ghostly falcon rises from the canyon with a mighty beat of its wings, and then the Jasiri is suddenly there, looking conflicted between attacking Niko and helping him.

"Don't," says the Jasiri in the Umadi tongue.

"She's following us," Niko says, keeping his knife in place. "We can't let her go. She'll give away our location."

The Jasiri looks at the woman and addresses her—a question, maybe, delivered with an authoritative cadence. She responds with angry contempt.

He seems disappointed at first, but a hard look settles across his face, and he comes closer, his eyes never leaving hers. He lifts a hand glowing with magic and brings it to her left temple; one touch and she crumples in a dead faint. With one arm bound Niko fails to catch her, but the Jasiri moves quickly, sweeping her into his arms before she hits the ground.

Niko backs away. They stare at each other, the Jasiri expecting resistance perhaps, a demand that they kill the woman, but Niko sheathes his knife and lifts an open palm to indicate he has no complaints. She's his problem now.

The Jasiri nods, grateful; then a pair of spectral wings springs out of his shoulders, and he leaps into the canyon, taking the woman with him.

The strip of sky visible between the walls of the canyon has turned lavender when they finally reach the mouth of a cave guarded by Faraswa watchmen.

Dressed in black skirtlike garments pleated in the front, they raise their spears and cheer when they see Ayana, then greet everyone in the long procession behind her. The cave turns out to be the mouth of a long tunnel wide enough for two quaggas to ride abreast. At the other end of the tunnel sits a vast central cavern, large as the inside of a hollow mountain, and it's here that Niko finally lays his eyes on the ancient city of Dahbet.

His appreciation of the sheer heights from which the Faraswa fell deepens at the sight of the city's numerous staircases, galleries, and flat-roofed edifices, which were not built so much as carved out of the cave's rufous sandstone. Carved bridges span across waterways and cisterns of sapphire-blue water. Illumination comes from several metal spires that glow bright enough to cast an imitation of daylight across the cavern. Everything here must be a millennium old at least, but it has all endured the wear of time with few signs of decay.

At its height the city might have held tens of thousands. Today, from what Niko can see, there are only a few hundred Faraswa present, but that's more than he expected.

They welcome everyone with song and the type of jubilance befitting an army returning victorious from battle or a bride arriving at her marital home. Niko shares doubtful looks with Addi and the other rangers, but they wordlessly follow the spontaneous procession that forms behind Ayana, who leads the way down a staircase, across a bridge, and into the city proper.

Their first stop is a square built up with enough gated stalls to accommodate a herd of quaggas and supplies of hay and grain that could last through a siege. As the members of the caravan get the animals comfortably settled, a silent weight hangs over the moment, like pressure in the air just before a cloudburst, the sense that the journey isn't over at all but only beginning.

A second bridge takes them to a quadrant-shaped amphitheater of tiered seats facing a freestanding rock face. A pyramid as tall as a man sits on the floor of the theater, made wholly of a clear crystal with a heart that glows blue like the New Year's Comet. Ayana goes down the steps and waits calmly in front of the pyramid until everyone is seated, the air growing heavy and bloated with anticipation.

Niko and his crew settle down on the highest tier of the theater, where they have a good view of everything below. A light spire rises behind them and another across the theater, giving everyone double shadows.

"What's happening?" Niko says, impatience getting the better of him.

Addi licks his lips, eyes fixed on Ayana. "I think she's about to tell us why we're here."

"You'll have to translate for us."

"I'll do my best."

A third source of light blossoms in the theater, and everyone gasps in wonder at the miniature sun now floating between Ayana's splayed hands. Cosmic shards pulse white across her forehead and in a line down her nose, sunlight spilling out of her eyes and coiling up her tensors.

The brilliance she's conjured is so penetrating Niko could swear she's cast a light into her own soul. In the reverent silence, she begins to speak, and Addi is so mesmerized Niko has to nudge him to remind him to translate.

"Sorry." He clears his throat and begins, the other rangers leaning closer so they can hear him better.

"'Look into my heart and see the truth of my words,'" he says in a measured voice. "'I stand before you as evidence against a falsehood you have been told all your lives. I give the lie to the justification many have used to enslave us, to rape, subjugate, and murder us with impunity. They say we are forsaken, that Ama rejected us as punishment and condemned us to suffer. But I tell you now, my brothers and sisters: that is a lie.'"

So sincere is her tone, Niko would swear she speaks the truth even though he can't understand her directly. Addi himself might as well be hypnotized.

"'What they call a curse was a noble sacrifice,'" the boy continues. "'Our forebears were accomplished scholars of the secret dimensions between worlds, and in their explorations of these hidden spaces, they came upon a great evil lurking, waiting, bent on destroying humanity. They could have saved themselves, retreated into their caves while the evil rampaged across the world. Instead, they dedicated all their knowledge and resources toward building a prison to contain this evil and save not just themselves but all of humankind.'" Addi shakes his head, incredulous. "I can't believe my ears. This can't be true, can it?"

"Focus, Addi," Niko says. "She's not done yet."

"Right. She's saying the prison was a double-edged sword. The same power that would hold back the evil would weaken the ancient Faraswa as well . . . and they would lose their magic. They made the sacrifice anyway, knowing that the alternative was to stand by and watch the world burn. They gave everything they had to save a world that would not thank them and were rewarded with slavery, strife, and oppression."

Ayana closes her eyes, the light between her hands growing brighter. "'But we haven't been called here to stoke the fires of vengeance,'" Addi translates. "'We've been called for this.'"

What she releases is not an illusion but a strengthening of the sorcery she's cast; somehow this is immediately apparent to Niko. The light of truth shines deeper into her soul so that anyone who looks will see what she's seen and know that it's true.

A great pyramid appears before Niko's eyes, sitting on a platform that rose from a deep chasm somewhere in the desert. Its outer walls carry a blue-gray metallic gloss, and lines were gouged onto its sides in irregular patterns. The apex of the pyramid is missing.

In the cavern's rapt silence, Ayana begins to speak again.

"'Behold,'" Addi translates. "'The old enemy has conspired to release itself, and its emissaries have unearthed its prison from the sands of this desert. They are now poised to break the prison open, and when they do, the very fate our forebears gave everything to prevent will befall us. This is what has called us here, my brothers and sisters. We have been summoned to stop our old enemy from breaking free and destroying the world.'"

A malcontented hubbub rises from the audience; then a man shouts a question at the top of his voice. "'But if letting the enemy break free of the prison will end the curse on our people, why not let it happen?'" Addi dutifully translates, then grunts. "I was just wondering the same thing."

Ayana terminates the spell, killing off the light between her palms. The pyramid disappears, but the aura of truth remains strong around her, and the fierce reproof she gives is one Niko feels behind his rib cage.

It also wipes away Addi's smirk. "'Why not let the prison fall?'" he translates, though with nowhere near Ayana's intensity. "'Because we're better than that. And we're not as powerful as we once were. The enemy's wrath would consume us even if we never left this cave.'"

Another voice shouts in protest, and Addi keeps up so fluidly Niko is able to follow the conversation. "So our lot is to suffer as slaves and victims for eternity?"

"I am proof that there are ways around the curse," Ayana replies. "Our people are due a reawakening. We *will* reclaim our dignity and our homeland, but we *must* honor the sacrifice our forebears made. We cannot let centuries of suffering be for naught, and I for one will not sit idly by while the enemy destroys the world and robs us of the chance to recover who we once were. I will fight. I have already been fighting."

She points at the crystal pyramid behind her, the one with the glowing blue heart.

"This artifact is the capstone of the enemy's prison, which our forebears had the wisdom to bury in a separate location. Together with the people of this ancient city, I retrieved the capstone before the enemy's emissaries could reach it, and I hid it here. Now the wicked fool who's named himself 'King of the West' searches for it like a lion prowling for prey, because he knows he cannot unleash his master until the prison is complete.

"But I know these lands better than he ever could, and so long as he lacks the key, he won't succeed. That should give us time to prepare to fight, and I *will* fight, alone if I have to, but I'd rather have your help."

There are more murmurs of displeasure; then the old man Sissay rises to his full height and turns around to face everyone with a scowl. "'What's wrong with you?'" Addi translates. "'A foreigner has come to harness the magics and technologies of our people, and you would let him?'"

More murmurs. "What about the seizures?" shouts a woman. "My daughter is only eleven, and she's all I have. I'm not here to fight a war. I just want to stop the seizures that are killing her."

"They're getting worse!" shouts someone else.

More complaints, too many for Addi to translate them all. "Let her speak!" Sissay shouts, shushing everyone with the power of his voice, then sits down, nodding at Ayana to continue.

"'The curse binds us differently, some less than others,'" Addi translates. "'Those of you who've suffered seizures are the least affected; that's why you've felt the pyramid's call more strongly. The only way to stop the call completely is to return the prison beneath the sands, where it belongs. But there is a way to embrace the call, in the same way that I have, and that is to . . .'"

Addi's voice falters. Whatever Ayana said has brought a chill to the theater.

"Addi, come on," Niko says impatiently.

"I know, I know." The boy shakes himself out of it and tries to speak through his shock. "Er . . . 'Let me be clear. Some of you won't survive. The inhibiting power of the prison our forebears built hasn't waned, and attempting to awaken under its influence will kill more often than not. But those of you who've felt the call strongly enough to suffer seizures are more likely to survive, and I will need your help . . .'"

Addi falls silent again, shaking his head, eyes mad with horror. "She wants us to become mystics. She wants us to . . . oh dear Ama, I think I'm about to have a seizure."

At that exact moment, a light goes out inside of Niko, a fire that's burned for years in his bones abruptly extinguished. He sags forward, enfeebled, his limbs inexplicably heavier, and he starts to wonder if he's been poisoned. But then he looks to his left and sees Jio hunched over, and to his right, beyond Addi's now-writhing form, Sibu and Mafarai have the same dazed grimaces.

When their eyes all meet, they immediately know what has happened, but Niko refuses to believe.

It can't be.

He calls on his red shadow but finds only an absence. He fumbles desperately for the queen's tether, which has stayed with him since the day he came out victorious from the bullpen, but there's a howling emptiness where it used to be.

Next to him Addi is sinking deeper into the throes of a violent seizure. It seems the whole amphitheater is. Clawing his way back to common sense, Niko gets up and barks a command to the other rangers.

"Sibu, Jio, get up and lay Addi on the seat on his side."

The young men are in complete shock, tears beginning to collect in their eyes. Even levelheaded Mafarai has lost his wits.

"Did she . . . did we . . . ?"

"Snap out of it!" Niko yells at them. "Help Addi. Put him on his side before he falls and hurts himself."

At the tone of his voice, their training kicks in and they obey, laying Addi onto the stone. They've always been consummate rangers, calm and collected under pressure, and he knows he must lead by example, now more than ever.

The soul of who he is has been ripped from him without so much as a warning, but Niko knows he cannot let the other rangers see him crumble, not even for a second. He knows he must pretend to be strong, to treat what's happened as just another challenge they can surmount. For their sake he knows he must remain stoic even if he wants to wail and scream with all his being.

The queen has withdrawn her blessing from us.

She's forsaken us, and we're no longer rangers.

We're nothing.

But I must not fall apart.

20: Kamali

The City of Dahbet

Kamali once heard a rumor that the Faraswa people were the true architects of Yonte Saire's Red Temple as well as the undercity and the machines in the Pavilion of Discovery at the House of Forms.

Of course, conventional orthodox wisdom, which accepted its own superiority as fact, deemed this rumor false, and being a simple Jasiri, Kamali had neither the right nor the inclination to question this wisdom. But now, as he walks the ancient streets of Dahbet, a literal city built inside a mountain, it occurs to him that the rumor must have been at least partially true.

Birds warble from the boughs of old trees growing out of stone flower beds. Roots slipping through the cracks in the flower beds snake over the stone roads and hug the staircases. Colorful fish swim in the numerous interconnected pools and channels of crystal-blue water. Most of the windows in the city sparkle emerald green in the false sunlight from the spires. It all feels like a self-contained metadimension, carved with such commitment to grand scale a man could throw a stone with all his might and never hit the ceiling.

And to think this has all been here since before the rise of the first KiYonte king.

On the other side of a sandstone bridge, Kamali approaches a free-standing building with a sizable flame tree growing out of its front yard. A spear-wielding guard in the black skirtlike loincloth favored by the city's men stands watch near the brass door.

"I need to see the prisoner," Kamali says to him in the Umadi tongue, which most of the natives apparently understand.

The guard doesn't hide his suspicion, giving Kamali a once-over. "Not take long time," he barks, then moves to unlock the door.

Kamali proceeds into the dim interior. Ambient light coming in through the lone window paints the barren stone with a splash of green. Taji is there, lying on a cot pushed up against the far wall, her back to the entrance.

The cot is inside a cage. They also shackled one of her ankles to the wall for good measure, but they needn't have, for whatever wards were woven into the floor by its builders are still active, and according to Ayana, this room was designed to mute all sorcery.

He watches her for a moment, knowing she's awake and aware of his presence. "Are you all right?" he says at last.

"Like you care."

He knew she'd be angry with him, and he understands. He'd like her on his side nonetheless. "You've confused my disloyalty to the emperor with disloyalty to you. I bear you no ill will, Taji. I consider you a friend."

That strikes a nerve. She gets up, the chain attached to her fetters clanking, and comes to the bars of the cage so he can see the depth of her rage. It does nothing to hide her beauty. "A friend, Kamali? I hardly know you. You're a *traitor*. A *murderer*."

The words are meant to cut him, but he carries no shame for what he did. Regret that he had to do it but not shame. "I betrayed a man I feel is no longer worthy of my service. Nor yours for that matter. And Daudi and Neema would have killed me had I not struck first. We both know that."

"And they would have been right to do so! We had a mission, Kamali. We were supposed to capture Meddur, not join him and his caravan of fanatics."

"It's not really Meddur the emperor wants," Kamali says, and Taji blinks at him several times, then gives a mocking laugh.

"So it's about that woman, isn't it? You did all this to protect her. Who the devil is she to you?"

Kamali doesn't answer.

"You love her?" When he keeps silent, Taji laughs again, but this time with an edge of bitterness. "You disappoint me, Kamali, but I guess I shouldn't be surprised. You've betrayed your own before. I didn't want to believe the stories, because on the surface you seem so *virtuous*, so *honorable*. But it's all just a pretty lie. You have no principles. You're rotten to the core."

"I'm truly sorry you feel that way," Kamali says.

"To the pits with your sorry. The emperor will know what you've done." Taji grabs the bars of her cage, bringing her face closer. The wrath in her eyes is implacable. "You'll get what you deserve."

Kamali looks down at his arms, which a few hours ago started to feel lighter. Colder. "I suspect the emperor already knows," he says. "The Fractal has already stripped me of her Axiom."

Eyes bulging, Taji steps back like she thinks Kamali has developed a contagious affliction. She gives him a look between suspicion and fear. "You seem untroubled, considering."

His lips curl upward. "This isn't the first time I've been expelled from a coven. Besides, I knew it was coming sooner or later."

The emotions on Taji's face shift into pity. She comes forward and grabs the bars again. "Kamali, stop this madness. The emperor might show you mercy. You could beg forgiveness, but you have to free me and complete the mission."

"He'd kill me the instant we met," Kamali says. "But even if he didn't, I can't continue to serve him. I was wrong to ever join his side."

"What changed? Why this all of a sudden?"

"I was shown the truth. Look, I've never loved the emperor, you know that, but I served him because I believed him the best hope for our people. I saw in him someone with frightening power, yes, but also the wisdom to constrain himself. Someone who'd use his power for the good of the Yontai."

"That's what he's doing!"

"Is it? Taji, he's drawing plans for the invasion of Ima Jalama. He's using the Inoi princes to attack the Halusha people while getting them to secretly plot against each other. I've had to talk him out of razing villages of his own people to the ground."

"He's a hard man, but not cruel, and his ambitions of empire have never been secret. You knew what he was."

"And I accepted that, but then he sent us out here. What are we doing here, Taji? Why would he send his Left Hand after a Faraswa orator?"

"Meddur is an agitator."

"Meddur is a trap," Kamali says. "The emperor wants him to get to Ayana because she's standing in the way of what he and his new ally want. And what they want is a pyramid they think will give them even more power than they already have, but it won't. It will destroy us all."

Without looking away, Taji retreats back to her cot and sits down. "Your woman told you this?"

Kamali suffers a pang of guilt at the betrayal in Taji's voice, but he's never lied to her. "Yes," he says, "and I believe her."

Taji is quiet for a time, staring at the hands in her lap. Then she lies back down on the cot, her back to Kamali. "Go. I'm tired of you."

He opens his mouth to say something, but the words get stuck in his throat. "I'll come back later," he finally says and obeys her request, leaving her to her anger.

◆ ◆ ◆

He goes looking for Ayana, expecting she'll be with the rest of the city's community of new arrivals, who've been housed in the stone buildings surrounding what might have once been a market square.

Evidently the camaraderie the caravan discovered on its way here is still strong; Kamali finds the Faraswa cooking communally around multiple grates, sharing food and lively conversation. By the looks of things they're all pleased to be here, even if a sense of uncertainty lingers around Ayana's revelations.

All of them except the Yerezi rangers, it would seem.

Kamali lifts a curious eyebrow at the sight of them sitting around their own fire in funereal silence. Their leader has tended to keep to himself due to the language barrier, and so has the silent one with the dreadlocks, but the twins struck Kamali as talkative and boisterous, maybe to a fault. Now they all look like they've seen the malaika of death.

He might have ventured closer to ask them what was wrong, but they don't have a language in common, and there's a chance they'd pick up their spears as soon as he came within three yards.

Since Ayana isn't here, he moves on and eventually finds her at the other end of a terraced alley. She's standing near a garden of dead trees and empty flower beds across the adjacent street, watching as a group of men finishes up bolting a newly raised spire of silver metal to its base.

Kamali folds his arms and watches from a distance as the men make way for her. Ayana touches the spire and closes her eyes, a familiar white brilliance throbbing across her forehead and down her nose, coiling up her tensors in bright strings. Kamali's heart misses a beat when the spire catches the same brilliance, then rapidly supersedes it, as though she merely lit a flame and the fuel was there all along.

The men cheer and applaud at the new light source, and Ayana smiles, retracting her hand and dimming her magic. Kamali applauds as well, astounded by the casual display of magic that shouldn't be possible in the Redlands.

Noticing him, she starts walking and inclines her head in an invitation for him to join her.

"Impressive," he says, falling into step beside her.

He meant it as a compliment, but some of the brightness goes out of her expression. "To be honest, I regret that it is. I wish that what I just did was as mundane as washing the dishes or feeding a baby."

He studies her, collecting yet more pieces for the puzzle he's been slowly constructing in his mind since he joined the caravan, the woman of his fantasies giving way to the vivid reality of her.

If there's one thing he's learned about Ayana in the last few days, it's that she's a contradiction built upon a contradiction. She's naturally shy and soft spoken yet can stand before a crowd and speak fearlessly and with authority. She's kind and affectionate yet harbors a venomous strength curled inside her bones like a serpent. Truth and transparency are second nature to her—she's a laughably terrible liar—yet for all that, she remains a complete mystery to everyone.

"These people," she says as they walk, "the people of this city, they escaped slavery centuries ago and came here to recover the scraps of what was left of our history. They did their best, I suppose, but they understand so little. They didn't even know what these spires were until I showed them. So much of our knowledge has been lost; I fear it may be impossible to recover even a fraction of it."

"Then it's a good thing they have you to guide them," Kamali says, choosing his words carefully. "It seems the prophecy of the Harbinger wasn't just a legend."

Her eyes go distant, a touch of sorrow shining in their depths. "Not prophecy," she says softly. "Forethought." Another piece that slots into Kamali's puzzle. She looks at him, her tone tentative. "Is your friend settled in?"

His gaze fixes on the stone road. They seem to be walking toward a building with a domed roof. "As well as anyone can settle in a prison," he says.

"We can't let her go."

"I know."

"Does she mean something to you?"

"She's a friend."

He sees Ayana smile out of the corner of his eye. That's the other thing about her. She isn't just a terrible liar; lies don't survive for long in her presence. "I see the truth on your face, Kamali."

His head dips lower, and he looks down at his feet. "We were both lonely."

She takes hold of his arm and gently tugs him to a stop, forcing him to look into her eyes. They twinkle up at him with amusement. "Kamali, I'm a grown woman. We had a moment back in Yonte Saire, but that doesn't mean I get to claim ownership over you."

"What if I want you to?" he says, turning her amusement into mild surprise. He takes her hands in his. "I haven't stopped thinking about you since the day we met. I know we're practically strangers to each other, and I know you owe me nothing, but I don't want you having any doubts about my intentions."

She studies his face; then her eyes flicker with quiet laughter. "And what are your intentions, Jasiri?"

"To be as close to you as you'll allow."

"Hmm." Her lips curl playfully. "We'll see."

He might have kissed her right then, but a throat clears nearby.

"Bibi Ayana. Er . . . Harbinger. May I have a word with you?"

It's the Faraswa boy who dresses like the Yerezi rangers, except the cloth wrapped around his hips is a white linen, not crimson. And like the rangers he's given Kamali nothing but dirty looks since they met. Kamali supposes it will be long before they forgive him for nearly killing their leader.

"Mhaddisu," Ayana says with a friendly voice, "I've told you to call me Ayana."

"Er . . . yes. Ayana," the boy says, looking everywhere but at her. Surprisingly his KiYonte carries an Umadi accent, which tells Kamali he didn't always live in the Yerezi Plains. "The thing is, I have . . . concerns about your plan. You want us to awaken as sorcerers of sun magic, but sun magic is . . . it's not . . ." He squares his shoulders like he's mustering courage, schooling his face into an expression of resolve. "I'm not going to forsake the Mother."

Ayana regards the boy like a patient older sister trying to reassure her nervous sibling. "I'm glad you came to me with your concerns. There's something I'd like to show you. Follow me. You too, Kamali."

They proceed into the domed building at the end of the road, what might have once been a religious sanctuary given the rows of stone benches occupying the torchlit interior. Painted onto the far wall is the four-pointed star of a compass showing only the cardinal points, and this is where Ayana takes them.

Kamali leans closer to better see the glyphs drawn at each of the cardinal points. In the north, a circle of seven dots; in the east, an eye resting in the palm of a hand; in the south, a sphinx with the head and four wings of a redhawk; and in the west, a pair of twin stars.

"The ancients called them the Cosmic Tetrad," Ayana says. "The four cosmic powers who shaped our world. Can you guess which is which?"

"Obviously the sphinx is the moon," Kamali says. "The redhawk is a dead giveaway."

"*Asher* in the old tongue," Ayana replies. "Queen of the Sky. Mother of the People."

"The twin stars are the suns, I suppose," says the boy. "And the eye in the hand must be the Star of Vigilance. But what about the circle?"

"The Primeval Spirits," Kamali guesses, to which Ayana smiles in approval.

"And so you see, the heavens as our people once understood them are not warring factions but harmonious pieces of a cosmic whole. I am a child of Asher, the moon, as are we all, but I wield the Light of Truth, and I bask in the Light of Courage, and I honor the Star of Watchfulness, and I seek the wisdom of the earthbound spirits. I serve all the powers of the Tetrad as our forebears once did, and I know I do so with Asher's blessing, for why would she condemn me when she's always lived in harmony with all the heavens?"

There it is again, that thing she does when she speaks from the heart. Kamali still doesn't understand how it works, be it spell or enchantment, but the effects are inescapable.

The boy scratches his head with a nearly comical grimace. "But . . . so the stories about us being cursed for practicing sun magic . . ."

"Are not true."

The boy's grimace shifts from confusion to frustration.

"Do you not believe me?" Ayana asks.

"Strangely I do," he says. "I'm just not convinced you're not *making* me believe you. Magic can do that, can't it?"

In spite of himself, Kamali laughs. "He's blunt. I like that."

"Some forms of the arcane can compel, yes," Ayana says. "But the Light of Truth can only compel a mind to see what's there, never what isn't."

"So just to be clear, I'm seeing what you *believe* to be true, not necessarily what's *actually* true."

"A very good question," Kamali adds.

"Agreed," Ayana says, sounding impressed. "And strictly speaking, yes. That would be correct. But the Light of Truth never shines strongly on untested beliefs. I couldn't use it to convince you of dogma."

The boy appears to consider her words, looking sidelong at Ayana. "I suppose it wouldn't be called the 'Light of Truth' if you could. But I'm still not sure I can do what you need me to do. I know nothing about magic. And what if I'm not like you? What if the magic doesn't come to me like it did for you?"

"It might not," Ayana admits. "But do you know why we have these?" She touches her right tensor, sliding her fingers along its met-alloid surface.

"So slavers can easily identify us?" the boy quips, then winces, looking down at the ground. "Sorry."

"Don't be," Ayana says. "That is indeed the sad truth our people now live. But our tensors were originally used as amplifiers. Watch."

She conjures a small ball of light that hovers in one hand, cosmic shards coming to life across her face. The boy watches with wide-eyed wonder.

"The Veil between worlds is a dampening field that inhibits the power of the gods, but the suns are more affected than the moon, perhaps because they're more distant—I never learned. The point is, sun magic is naturally weak."

She lifts her other palm and conjures a second ball of light, and Kamali doesn't miss how her tensors begin to glow as well, strobing with brilliant white coils.

"For the average person the simplest spell is next to impossible to cast, but the ancients were clever. They used Red magic to enchant themselves with amplifiers that would temporarily weaken the Veil so they'd access much greater pools of sun magic than they otherwise could. The amplifiers also increased the potency of Red magic, and now you know why our people were once such powerful sorcerers."

She slams her hands together, then spreads them apart again, releasing a swarm of phantom white butterflies that flutter off in every direction and slowly dissolve into dust. The joy on her face has Kamali feeling like he's in free fall.

"You want to know something interesting?" she says.

"What?" the boy asks, spellbound.

"Tensors only ever grew on awoken mystics. They were marks of distinction. Something must have happened to trigger growth in every individual."

"You mean I'm not actually supposed to have them?"

"Not until you awaken," Ayana tells him.

The utterly dazed look on the boy's face nearly moves Kamali to laughter. He restrains himself out of pity.

"I . . . I have to think about this," the boy says.

"You do that," Ayana replies with a wistful look as she watches him slowly walk away. "It's good to see there's still fire in my people," she says after some time.

Kamali watches her, this astounding woman, both transparent and a mystery, but he thinks he's beginning to understand her.

"Come," she says. "I believe you were telling me about your intentions."

A spire of illumination stands just outside the bath in her private quarters. Its glow filters in through the green windows, filling the chamber with a diffuse emerald light.

In the waters of the bath Ayana draws Kamali closer, and he slips into her tight warmth, the pleasure almost too intense to bear. They ravish each other again on her ancient stone bed, draped in nothing but long shadows from a flickering lamp.

As they lie side by side in the contentedness of their release, Kamali reclines on his elbow to watch her, almost like he fears she's a dream that will evaporate the second he looks away.

Noticing, she turns onto her side so she can stare back at him, running a finger over the peregrine on his chest. By reflex he tenses as her hand wanders closer to the silver band he's wearing on a string around his neck, but then he relaxes, remembering he doesn't have to guard it so jealously anymore. The woman it came to represent is lying right in front of him.

"When you look at me like that, Kamali," she says as she lightly brushes the ring with a finger, "I feel like you can read my mind."

"I'm just putting a few things together," he admits.

"Putting what together?"

"Who you really are. Where you're from."

A crease appears between her eyebrows. "And what have you deduced?"

"I don't think you're from around here," he plainly says. "Actually, that's not right. I don't think you're from around *now*. This time. I don't know how it's possible, but I think you're from the time of the ancients."

A part of him expected she might break into laughter. She doesn't. She withdraws her hand and turns onto her back again. "That's an interesting theory. Far fetched, but interesting."

"But it makes sense," Kamali says, even more certain now. "You're a young woman who knows things about your people's history that no one else knows. Your mastery and understanding of magic betray a childhood steeped in it. And you carry the kind of confidence I'd expect from a warrior born to a noble house. Wherever you came from, you never knew a day as a servant or a slave."

"Maybe I came from the Empire of Light," she muses, though she doesn't sound convinced by the idea herself.

"I thought about that. But you know this desert like you've lived here before. You've said as much yourself. And though I may not know much about the outside world, I know that their strength is in technology, not magic. They're not capable of spells as powerful as those I've seen you cast. I've also actually met someone from the Empire, and you don't sound anything like him."

She turns her head slightly to look up at him. "You've met someone from the Empire?"

"A friend of a friend. He helped break me out of prison that day. You might've seen him."

She stares back at the stone ceiling, quiet for a full minute. "Our empire was waning," she eventually says, the words coming out as a sigh. "Our people were losing their magic, and the tribes we'd once ruled were turning on us. We could see the end rushing to us like an asteroid falling out of the sky. As a contingency, one of the Wise Ones who sat on the royal council hatched a secret plan: he would seal away a cohort of promising young mystics in Void tombs until there was a way to stop the spark of magic from wiping itself out of our blood. I was one of the chosen. The man who crafted the plan . . . my father."

Kamali listens, and she continues.

"Ten high priests sacrificed themselves to seal me in a tomb beneath what you now call Yonte Saire. The power required to cast the spell was so great it destroyed their bodies, but they gave themselves willingly, believing that I and the others chosen were our people's last hope. I slept in the tomb for centuries, waiting. A second for me would be years outside. But no solution was ever found, and as the years came and went, the world moved on, and our people lost their history and forgot.

"I began to think maybe I'd die in that tomb. In the end it was a follower of Vigilance from the Empire of Light who located my prison and set me free. Somehow Vigilance himself had instructed her to find me, and she'd come with the very solution our people had longed for all those years ago: a way to defeat the pyramid's curse."

Ayana turns away from Kamali and lifts the curls of her hair so he can better see the tattoo on her nape. It's a stylized eye made of sweeping curves, drawn in an ink so intensely blue it might be luminescent.

"The Eye of Vigilance," he murmurs, recognizing the design. There was a cult in the undercity who revered it. "May I touch it?"

She nods, and he runs a gentle finger over the tattoo, feeling its ridges and contours. They are prominent enough he decides that maybe the eye isn't a tattoo at all but a physical object embedded beneath the skin.

"Is this metal?" he says.

"They call it Fireblue. It's the only known substance with an affinity to the Star of Vigilance. Very rare, and not an especially strong affinity at that, but enough to protect against the pyramid's influence." Ayana lets her hair down and reclines on the bed, a mournful mood settling over her. "The Vigilant who freed me—her name was Alette—she came with enough Fireblue for me and the rest of my cohort, but we never found the other tombs."

"Why not?"

"I think we were buried in separate locations. Or maybe the tombs were moved, or . . . I don't know. We tried searching for them in the undercity, but to no avail. And then Alette disappeared without warning. I think she was murdered."

The sorrow in Ayana's eyes almost makes Kamali regret forcing her into this conversation. He begins to draw idle circles around her naked shoulder. "I'm . . . sorry. Is that why you were in the undercity prison? To look for the tombs?" He saw her vanish in a blaze of light. He's certain she wasn't confined to her cell any more than the air she breathed. She was there because she wanted to be.

"It was easier that way," she admits. "And maybe the shock of what had become of my people made me lose my mind. I killed more than a few rapists and murderers that first week. It wasn't my best moment. I suppose the prison gave me a place to hide from it all."

"Do you really believe Vigilance is helping you?" Kamali asks.

She turns around to face him, a smile chasing away the gloom that had dimmed her spirits. "I've met him, you know," she says. "Alette brought him to me. Well, almost. It's hard to explain, but . . ." She places a hand flat against Kamali's chest, something sultry moving in her eyes. "I can show you if you want."

As if he could ever not want.

"Show me," he says, and she kisses him, and he melts into her for a third time that night, although this time Ayana opens her soul up to him so completely he almost feels like their hearts are beating in sync.

The stone below and around them falls away, and Kamali finds himself transported into a realm of starlight, the abode of a benevolence so pure it brings tears to his eyes.

It sees him and all he is and all he has ever been, and it accepts him with all his flaws, wrapping him in a shroud of unconditional love. In its forgiving embrace he weeps like a child, his heart filled with joy, and at the very peak of his ecstasy the arrow of time suspends its flight, and he glimpses in the starlight a pair of eyes that glitter at him like diamonds or sapphires or both. Either way he knows he's looking into the face of a god.

Then the moment ends, and he cries out as he releases himself into Ayana's heat. They collapse onto the bed still entangled, and Kamali can't help the stream of tearful laughter that pours from him.

"You know," Ayana says afterward, "laughter is not the reaction I usually get."

Kamali lifts his head so he can blink at her. "Usually?"

"That got your attention," she says with a snicker.

"I was just thinking about how sex with you is so wonderful you literally took me to heaven," he says.

She snuggles her head onto his chest. "Hmm, I suppose I can live with that."

And so can I, Kamali thinks, holding her closer. *Now and forever.*

Days pass, each one more blissful than the last, and Kamali's infatuation with Ayana quickly deepens into something that frightens him.

He spends hours learning about her past life. Did she have a fellow back in her time? Yes, she was engaged to be married but met him only once. How did she get that scar on her left collarbone? During training with her sister, whom she misses very much.

Am I better looking than your former betrothed?

No, you're more hideous, and I'm only with you out of the kindness of my heart.

He laughs and kisses her when she says that, vowing to convince her to marry him when her war has been fought and won.

But one morning he awakens with an unpleasant pressure building up inside his chest, an itch at the base of his spine.

Ayana is still asleep next to him, and she stirs as he gently disentangles himself from her. He waits until she stills again before he quietly gets up from the bed and puts on his robe and sandals.

The ill feeling takes him out of her quarters and across a district of flat-roofed stone dwellings toward Taji's prison. He's come here every day since they arrived, and there's been a different guard posted there each time. The one there today lets him in with the usual gruff warning not to take too long.

He breathes a sigh of relief when he sees Taji sitting in her cot, alive and well, hands clasped together in her lap.

Thank the Mother she's all right.

But that's not it. The sudden feeling that drove him here wasn't worry *for* her.

He takes a cautious step closer to her cage, eyeing her hands more carefully. In the faint greenish luster coming in from the window, they look slick, as if coated in oil.

His heartbeat spikes, his skin beginning to tingle like he can feel a knife at his throat. "Taji?"

"You forgot to check my Void space," she says with an eerily calm voice. "A common mistake. It took me a while, but I got to it."

Kamali curses, the nebulous feelings of dread suddenly coalescing into certainty that he's made a grave error. "Taji, what have you done?"

"I'm sorry, Kamali. I wish things had been different." She opens her bloodied palms to show him the metaformic gemstone he should have thought to look for. Tears gather in the corners of her eyes. "If you want to live, you'll run," she says. "Now."

A horn blows somewhere outside, loud enough to almost shake the foundations of the city. Kamali is out the door even before the echo dies down.

Ayana and the Dahbet guards were prepared for a swift evacuation. When Kamali finds her, she's already dressed and herding people to the watery escape tunnel hidden at the base of the city.

"Ayana, what's happening?"

"The King of the West has found us," she tells him. "His forces are out in the canyons. We don't have much time."

"What about the capstone?"

"He was always going to find it. What's important now is getting everyone out alive."

Kamali joins the Ajaha in saddling the animals of the convoy with the prearranged supplies, and then they all head down the winding ramps to the mouth of the escape tunnel; it's hidden in a nook just above the lake at the very bottom of the cave, where all the city's water collects.

They hurry up at the sound of thunderous claps and screams coming from the Faraswa guards covering the city's main entrance. Half of the people have already rushed into the circular tunnel, but Kamali grows worried as he waits for the remainder with Ayana.

He looks at the large rock next to the tunnel, shaped like a millstone. "What's to stop them from following us?" he asks.

"There's a mechanism further along to open all the cisterns of the city and direct the water to come out through here. It'll be flooded in minutes."

But it will take time for everyone to make it there, Kamali realizes.

They hear a cry as a Faraswa guard tumbles down from the amphitheater way above, hitting a boulder before plunging into the lake. He never surfaces.

"Move it, people!" Ayana shouts.

As the clapping of thunder continues, voices approaching from above, Kamali makes a decision he would have once made without second thought, but today a voice in his head yells at him to be selfish, to act on his own behalf just this once.

He doesn't listen.

"Ayana," he says, taking off the ring she once gave him. He looks her in the eye, this amazing, wondrous creature. He looks at her, with all she has made him feel, and he smiles. "Thank you for the best week of my life."

She knows what he's about to do, and he can see how much she wants to fight him, the tears she's holding back, but they both know he's right. She accepts the ring, and just like she did when she first gave it to him, she kisses him. First on the forehead, then on each cheek, then on the lips.

"You are the suns, the light, and the warmth," she says. "And now you are despair. May we meet again on the Infinite Path, Jasiri."

Almost everyone else has already entered the tunnel. She follows them without looking back, and he suffers the powerful compulsion to run with her, but another clap of thunder sobers him.

For some reason the Ajaha Aneniko is still waiting by the mouth of the tunnel with his spear.

"Help me close this tunnel," Kamali says, moving to the millstone-shaped seal.

The Ajaha doesn't hesitate, and they both groan from the effort of rolling the seal in place. Halfway through Kamali stops, making the Ajaha frown at him.

There are no more screams, but the sound of marching boots is approaching them.

"Go," Kamali says, nodding at the tunnel.

The Ajaha shakes his head.

"Don't be a stubborn idiot. You don't have to die here. For the Mother's sake, go."

The Ajaha stays put. The voices are on the ramps. They'll be here any second.

Kamali puts a hand on the Ajaha's shoulder and squeezes. "Thank you, my friend. But please, go. Protect them. Help Ayana."

The young man wavers, conflicted. Finally, he nods, but before he goes into the tunnel, he proffers his spear of red steel. "For you, Kamali. Take."

Kamali accepts the gift and nods in gratitude.

"Fight well," the Ajaha says, and then he's gone.

Kamali grunts and strains as he rolls the boulder the rest of the way, sealing the tunnel by the time the first enemy arrives.

They are unlike anything he's ever seen, men in shimmering full-body armor, some with crimson decorative skirts and others with golden capes. Their faces are helmeted, too, and their weapons are those new outworld things that spit rapid bolts of moonfire.

Before they even spot him and aim their weapons in his direction, Kamali immediately drains his moongold vertebra of all its essence reserves. In a single burst of speed, he blurs forward with the Ajaha's spear and strikes—not to skewer the enemy but to knock his weapon out of his hands.

The weapon flies into the air. In a split second Kamali lets go of the spear to catch this new treasure, and then he's opening fire.

He's never used such a thing before; he's only ever seen them being used, but it responds in his hands like it was made for him. His essence-enhanced reflexes instantly adapt to the way it feels in his hands, to the flight path of its projectiles, and for a few seconds he is king.

A man goes down, then another, then another, all of them boiling in their suits, pummeled by relentless moonfire. He grins, delighted with how easy it is, how brutal, how perfect. He is a Jasiri, at best, at worst, and he will not die alone.

The essence in his bloodstream depletes, and he soon becomes aware of the burns on his own face, on his arms and legs, on his chest. And when the next bolt of moonfire hits, it knocks him off his feet and onto his back.

He makes no motion to get up, so the armored men stop firing. Out of the corner of his eye he sees someone approach, but maybe he's hallucinating because this person's feet aren't touching the ground. He's floating in the air, his hands clasped behind his back.

The King of the West, perhaps?

His face is hidden behind a golden mask, but when he speaks, Kamali thinks he recognizes the voice.

"Acolyte Kamali Jasiri of the Fractal. How interesting to see you here."

Kamali tries to speak but fails to move his lips.

"You really should have killed me when you had the chance," says the king. "Unfortunately for you, I will not make the same mistake."

If he could, Kamali would laugh. Instead, he closes his eyes and thinks about the first time he kissed Ayana, back in the prison beneath Yonte Saire.

Her face is the last thing he sees before the Ajaha's spear rises from the ground by the magic of a spell and plunges into the space between his eyes.

PART 5

ILAPARA
*
ALINATA
*
SALIM

21: Ilapara

The Rapiere

In the days following the destruction of Apos, Ilapara suffers through a cycle of emotional distress that gives her no rest, following her into her dreams when she sleeps and staying with her during her waking hours.

Shock: her mind rejecting what her eyes saw from the stern of the *Rapiere*. Despair: her mind grappling with the existence of weapons that could destroy everything she knows and loves in the space of a few heartbeats. And deep foreboding: the recognition that there's little she could do to stop such weapons.

Yet for all the horror of what happened, for all the lives that were surely lost, the mood on the windcraft remains inexplicably optimistic, triumphant even, making Ilapara wonder at times if she and Tuk were the only ones who witnessed the atrocity.

Gregoire Silver Dawn throws a feast in the vessel's ornately adorned banquet hall that very same night. Well-dressed dignitaries fly in on winged vessels from the other ships in the convoy, an air of excitement surrounding Salo's presence. They cheer when he appears at the banquet, raising glasses overflowing with wine in his name. Initially disinterested, Salo gradually warms up to their attention, and by the end of the feast he's letting them kiss him on the hand and shower him with gifts.

Rings with fat gemstones. Chains of moongold and gleaming silver. Expensive silks and leathers. He receives them all with a slightly bored smile and the composure of a prince.

"I feel like we're losing him," Tuk later confides to Ilapara in the cabin they share, him sleeping on the bunk above hers.

She tries to say something comforting, but the lie gets stuck on her tongue.

Salo is different now. More independent, more sure of himself. He's no longer the young man who begged them to stay with him in Yonte Saire. *He doesn't need us anymore,* she realizes.

In fact, Salo begins to spend less time with them and more time alone, locked inside his cabin, insisting he must dedicate himself to the task of rebuilding his Axiom. To rub salt on the sting, he still finds the time to take walks around the ship in the company of the countess and Gregoire Silver Dawn.

Alienated by his aloofness and the convoy's general disregard for the destruction of Apos, Ilapara and Tuk find themselves increasingly isolated, like hostages stuck in an enemy camp, who came to rescue someone who didn't want or need to be rescued.

Tuk turns to doting on Ilapara to keep his mind from spiraling into misery, bringing food and drink to their cabin and making sure she eats, asking after her, treating her like a woman on the verge of labor even though her pregnancy has yet to show.

She doesn't need looking after, but she can't bring herself to tell him to back off. Not when he's slowly coming apart the way he did after Salo disappeared, and Salo himself is too busy to even notice.

She hears him sniffling on his bunk one night, doing his best not to wake her. Wordlessly she rises and climbs up to lie beside him; he watches her, confused, wetness glittering on his cheeks in the dim lighting, but he doesn't resist when she pulls him close and cradles him. They don't speak. Ilapara holds him until he falls asleep.

The convoy's progress across the skies is slow. According to Tuk they should have reached the Jalama on the first night, but they're still floating along the continent's western seaboard four days after leaving Apos.

On the fifth day, the convoy finally turns east and flies inland over the desert, and it's nearly high noon when the vessels all descend to a low altitude, low enough that they would see anyone walking on the dunes in clear detail.

Everyone onboard the *Rapiere* is on the main deck when Salo surfaces from below, wearing a crimson skirtlike garment with an ornament of interlocking plates of gold hanging over the front. An elaborate collar rests over his bare shoulders, his arms, wrists, and ankles shimmering with bands of gem-encrusted gold. And on his head sits the sinuous golden circlet the countess said was a fragment of the Hegemon's crown.

What surprises Ilapara is not that he's allowed himself to dress so opulently—he had to do so frequently as he moved in Yonte Saire's circles of power. But in all their time together, even when he had all the coin in the world to spend on clothes, he refused to stray from a traditional white Yerezi loincloth.

Dressed as he is, she almost doesn't recognize him.

There's a palpable tension as he climbs to stand on the forecastle deck near the long and steepled prow of the vessel. Ilapara and Tuk might have once followed him, but they hang back and watch among the gathered people down on the main deck, wondering what everyone expects him to do.

He stands for several long minutes of suspenseful silence, staring at the deserts ahead. Ilapara looks around, too, half expecting to see storm clouds massing in the skies, giant angry eyes watching her. She thinks she sees a flash of red lightning, but there are no clouds or any other signs of the Primeval Spirit she saw when she first crossed the Jalama.

"Strange, isn't it?" Tuk says after noticing her unease. "The Lady of Storms should have attacked us by now or at least made an appearance. It's almost as if . . ."

"Almost as if she fled from the sight of the convoy," Ilapara suggests when he doesn't finish his thought. He shoots her a troubled glance.

The young man at the center of attention finally turns around, a scowl on his face.

"The gate isn't here," Salo announces. "This isn't the right place."

The countess takes a moment to interpret his response to the richly dressed men and women standing nearby, among them Gregoire Silver Dawn. They confer in hushed whispers; then the countess looks up at Salo and says, "We apologize, Your Worship. Lore and ancient wisdom suggest the gate is in a desert of the Red Wilds, though we have no way of knowing which one. If the gate isn't here, then it's surely in the desert to the south."

"Then we go south," Salo says. "I need to reach that gate before it's too late."

"We'll set an immediate course, Your Worship. We should arrive by dawn tomorrow."

The gathered crowds disperse, many with sighs of mild disappointment. The lords and ladies who'd come onboard for the occasion return to their windcrafts on their skiffs, and Salo disappears belowdecks. But Ilapara has finally had enough of being ignored, so she follows him and corners him by the door to his cabin.

"Salo, a word."

He doesn't quite keep the frown off his face. "I'm a little busy right now—"

"It won't take long."

His jaw clenches, but he opens the door and gestures her in.

They gave him the most impressive cabin on the windcraft, located just beneath the prow, with a curved wall of square windowpanes giving a panoramic view of the deserts. The cabin's silken comforts and adornments of precious metals might be worth more than the rest of the vessel combined.

Salo removes his crown and places it on a richly carved chest of drawers; then he moves to stand by the windows, giving his back to her. "What is it?" he says.

Ilapara's anger spikes. "Is this how it is now? We risk our lives to bring you back, and then you behave as if you don't know us?"

He doesn't reply for a long time, and when he finally speaks, his voice is distant. "I owe you a debt I can never repay," he says. "But I can't be the person you want me to be right now. I have a mission more important than you could ever understand."

She digs her nails into her palms to keep herself from walking over and smacking sense into him. "Salo, you've had a mission I don't understand since the day I met you! What you've never done is freeze us out. Tuk is falling apart. He watched his old home go up in flames, he watched people he loved die in an instant, and you've barely said a word to him. It's like you don't even care, and that's just not like you."

To her shock, Salo gives a low, rumbling laugh. "Not like me," he repeats, turning around so she can see the simmering anger in his eyes. Has such emotion always been there, and she's only seeing it now that he doesn't wear spectacles? "And what's 'like me,' Ilapara? Weak? Dependent? Afraid of my own shadow?"

"Compassionate," she says. "Kind. Empathetic. An idealist. Someone who'd have noticed that his friend needs him."

"And look at where that got me. I was tricked and used and murdered. Because of my weakness, I let myself become a tool for the ambitions of other people. The universe was laid bare before me, and I was shown truths I could never tell you, truths I could have used to save the world, and what did I do? I fled. To my own death. Because I was afraid. Weak. And you want me to go back to being that person?"

For a moment Ilapara wonders if she's standing in front of a complete stranger. "I never once thought you were weak," she says. "A weak person conforms even against their own nature. It takes courage to defy convention and be your own person, and I've seen you stay true to yourself even at the cost of your own safety. That's not the mark of a coward."

He blinks at her like he's of two minds. Then he turns back to face the windows. "I have to be different now. This mission is too important for me to screw it up."

Ilapara leaves his cabin in disgust, regretting that she ever agreed to cross the Jalama to bring him back. Maybe he was better off as a memory to be mourned.

She still hasn't cooled down by the time she finds Tuk back on the main deck, leaning against the railings on the starboard side. He glances at her when she joins him, then looks back at the skies ahead. The convoy has banked southwest, slowly climbing back to a higher elevation.

"You spoke to him?" he says.

Ilapara has many things to say about Salo right now, but she kills them off, trying to be reasonable. "He thinks he died because he was weak and dependent, so he's avoiding us because he's trying to be strong and we remind him too much of his old self."

"He said that?"

"He didn't have to." The dull, pitiful shade of gray that colors Tuk's eyes douses Ilapara's anger. She sighs, leaning on the railings next to him. "Maybe this is like that time in Yonte Saire when he started drinking that strange tea and it made him cranky. He'll be back to himself soon enough, I'm sure. Maybe all he needs is more time."

"You and he are all I've got left," Tuk says. "If he needs time to adjust, then I'll give him as much as he needs."

Damn you, Salo, Ilapara thinks, vowing to give him a good scolding whenever he comes back to his senses.

She stays with Tuk on the main deck as the convoy hugs the coast on the way south. Not even an hour later they spot angry lights flashing out of a cloud formation in the far west. Tuk goes to ask a member of the crew about them and returns with a complexion nearly as pale as the sails of the *Rapiere.*

"It's a battle between Enclave and Imperial forces over the Dapiaro," he says. "They've turned on each other."

"Why?" Ilapara asks, perplexed.

"Apparently the Anathema that hit Apos was of Imperial origin. On the face of it the Empire now believes the Enclave is working with the new Hegemon, so they struck preemptively. And they didn't just target Apos. They attacked every military base too. I think they were hoping to destroy the Enclave's arsenal of Anathemas to avoid a retaliatory strike."

This time Ilapara bypasses the shock and despair and goes straight to existential dread. "Let me guess. They failed, and the Enclave retaliated with another Anathema."

"They hit an Imperial city this morning," Tuk confirms. "That's five cities gone so far, including two more in the East. Looks like everyone's fighting everyone else now."

"Why are they being so stupid? Why fight a war when there'll be nothing but ashes left when it's over?" Ilapara lowers her voice, looking around the deck. "And why is everyone in this convoy so calm, considering the world is literally on fire?"

"Because they're probably the ones who caused it," Tuk says bluntly. "If all the world's major powers cripple each other in a pointless war, then there's no one left to stop whatever my sister and the rest of the high-and-mighties on this ship are up to. Worst thing is, Salo's in the middle of it, and he won't let us pull him out."

"He seems sure of what he's doing," Ilapara remarks.

"Quite possibly the only reason I haven't already slaughtered everyone on this ship." The shadow of malice crosses Tuk's face. "The second he indicates otherwise, I honestly can't be held responsible for what I do."

As the countess promised, the convoy arrives at the shores of a new desert just as the suns dawn into a cloudless sky. Once again Ilapara and Tuk join the ship's gaggle of admirers on the main deck, and again they all wait in a breathless hush while Salo stands on the forecastle deck, golden circlet on his head, gazing out into the desert with the stillness of a carving.

Perhaps it's the soft lighting of the dawn, but the sands of this desert appear a little redder than the Jalama. And if Ilapara's understanding of geography is correct, this must be the abandoned homeland of the Faraswa people.

What the devil could Salo possibly want here?

He stands on the forecastle for so long he becomes a dark outline against the brightening sunlight. When he finally turns around, Ilapara has to raise a hand over her eyes just to see his face.

"Proceed twenty miles further east, then land the vessel. Today, I awaken."

The countess interprets his words to her colleagues like she's announcing a victory, and a cheer breaks out on the main deck, then spreads to the other ships.

Minutes later the *Rapiere* slowly lowers its bulk onto the desert near a lake ringed by date palms and weathered ruins of limestone. The other windcrafts descend and arrange themselves in a crescent around the *Rapiere*. Ramps extend out of their hulls and touch the ground.

Ilapara gets her first look at just how many people are in the convoy as they all disembark. Hundreds, at least. Lords and ladies wearing enough gemstones to buy a kingdom. Crews of the windcrafts in plain uniforms, humble but clearly overjoyed to be here. Warriors with shimmering armor and heavy typhonic weapons. Some wear gold-and-white capes, others cloaks as deep crimson as the sunset moon.

An eeriness sweeps over Ilapara as they all follow Salo in a procession toward the lake. "I feel like we've suddenly joined a cult," she whispers to Tuk.

He doesn't respond. His obsidian gaze is fixed on his sister up ahead, walking next to Salo like a faithful acolyte.

They stand quietly with everyone else beneath the trees growing around the lake and watch as Salo slices his palms with a knife handed to him by the countess. Blood oozing from the gashes, he wades into the water with an expression so focused he might as well be alone in the oasis.

Everyone gasps when he steps over a precipice and plunges into the water, disappearing beneath the surface. Ilapara's mouth falls open, a finger of frost touching her core. She shares a worried glance with Tuk, neither knowing whether to go after him or wait.

They're not alone in their worry. Gregoire Silver Dawn barks out commands, and some of the warriors present remove their armor pieces so they can go into the water after Salo. Tuk takes a step forward as if to join them, but they all freeze in place when brilliance washes over the sky, and they look up to see a ball of fire growing in size.

Ilapara reaches for her ivory pendants, the sound of her heartbeat drumming in her ears. She waits, straining her eyes against the brightness, the fireball growing and growing, getting closer.

Tuk's face loses color. "Oh shit! Get down!"

He dives, taking Ilapara with him, and they've barely latched on to a nearby tree when the lake explodes, ejecting a wave of water that sweeps over them. Ilapara shuts her eyes and holds her breath, clinging to the tree as the wave rushes outward with the force of the impact, then back in as equilibrium attempts to restore itself.

She coughs water from her airways once the worst is over, wiping sand from her eyes. All over the oasis, servants and armored warriors rush to the aid of their lordly masters, pulling them out of the muddied, churning waters of the lake.

"What the devil is happening?" Tuk says.

Ilapara drags herself up and pulls him up too. At this point, it wouldn't surprise her if the lake started to disgorge hordes of demons. "We need to move back."

The lake begins to bubble, the most furious activity taking place near the center. But then the surface stills unexpectedly, and Salo emerges from the water and rises into the air with his eyes ablaze, arms glowing with cosmic power.

And rising behind him is a redhawk with its four metal wings stretched wide.

Ilapara once heard that the gaze of a redhawk carries beams of moonlight that can burn into anything, but this one has vortexes of blackness for eyes. As it hovers above and behind Salo like a guardian spirit, the bird emits a shriek so loud it nearly shakes the earth. People around the lake drop to their knees in submission. Ilapara and Tuk are the only ones who remain standing, shocked by the sight of their hovering friend.

"The gate is nearby," Salo says, his voice deeper and more resonant than Ilapara has ever heard it. The countess loudly and joyfully interprets his words as he speaks. "But I sense it is incomplete. The crown must also be restored before the gate can be opened. I now claim dominion over these lands to protect our mission from the enemy, who comes even as we speak, whose forces are already in this desert and have stolen the key to open the gate. Find them. Bring the key to me. Justice will no longer be delayed."

The gathered subjects—because that's what they are, Ilapara realizes with dread—begin to chant in unison, singing praises in a language she can't understand.

She breaks out into a cold sweat. "What are they saying?" she asks Tuk.

He folds his arms, his eyes having turned as black as the feathers of a crow. "Our friend has just become Hegemon. They're calling him 'King of the Desert' and pledging eternal fealty to him."

"Should we kneel?" Ilapara wonders, and somehow Tuk's irises turn an even deeper shade of night.

"He'll have to make us."

Their friend doesn't seem aware of their existence, however, let alone their defiance. Still hovering above the lake with his redhawk, he spreads his hands, tilting his head to the sky. There's a burst of moonlight, power exploding around him, circling his arms, shining out of his eyes.

The earth starts to quake, clouds of sand drifting up from the ground.

Ilapara grips Tuk's arm with half a mind to haul him away, but they both stay, petrified even as the new king casts his spell.

A slow wave of scarlet light expands away from him in a sphere. The earth gives a mighty shudder and splits, and pillars, walls, obelisks, and statues rise out of the sands, carved with the scripts of a dead language. They assemble around the oasis into a palace of sandstone and emerald glass, restoring in minutes what lay in ruins for centuries.

In the aftermath, the new king's subjects shout so many times Ilapara almost goes deaf from the noise. "All hail the Hegemon" is what they say according to Tuk. "All hail the King of the Desert . . . all hail the King of the West."

22: Alinata

Sheathed in moonlight, she tumbles from the skies. But the clouds do not cushion her fall. She tumbles and falls and the earth rushes to meet her, death waiting in its bosom. She plummets and screams and she—

She stops. Takes a deep breath. Returns to the present.

Alinata and Neropa, both dressed in gowns of delicate white silk, are shadows lurking among the granite pillars of the palace's war room, listening quietly to the emergency council their queen has convened with the seven generals of the Yerezi regiments.

The generals seated at the stone table with the queen, one from each clan, are hardened, battle-scarred warriors in their prime, some of whom once served as honor guards. The room smells like leather, steel, sweat, and massive egos, and by the scowls on their faces, the men are none too happy about the plans the queen has just laid out.

"Your Majesty, with all due respect, none of this makes sense," says the Siningwe general.

A lean figure with cords of rippling muscle and a fur collar resting around his shoulders, he's sitting directly across from the queen, at the other end of the table—a place unofficially reserved for the most powerful general in the council, which he became after the former Sibere regiment was dissolved and put under his command.

He may not be as tall as his elder brother, but his reputation as a swordsman of rare talent, along with the perpetual severity of his facial expressions, makes him just as intimidating, if not more.

"We've already sent contingents of our men to serve on Qotoba ships," he says. "Now you want the bulk of our remaining forces to ride out to the desert to face enemies we've never seen, who've not threatened us in any way. How will this not leave us open to Umadi invasion?"

"The Umadi have been dealt with, General Siningwe," the queen says. "They will not invade."

The generals look to each other with suspicious frowns.

"We've heard troubling rumors about that," says the general from Khaya-Sikhozi in a tone audaciously close to accusatory. "They're saying you've allied with an Umadi warlord, given him permission to bring all the savannas under his Seal. I hope for all our sakes these are just rumors, Your Majesty, because an alliance with an enemy who's dogged our borders for centuries is sure to be disastrous."

He gets mutters of agreement from all around the table, and Alinata almost smiles. The general must have been coached by an Asazi to deliver such a strong yet oblique criticism of the queen's actions.

"And why not let this so-called 'King of the West' fight his own battles?" says the general of Khaya-Nyati's regiment. "Why must we shed our own sweat and blood to protect his lands? If he is truly a king, let him field his own armies to defend his treasures."

Once again the generals nod in agreement, and the queen, seated in a grid of sunlight coming through the patterned windows behind her, begins to drum on the table with her fingers.

"I thought I had summoned a council of the bravest men in the Plains," she responds. "But I have clearly made a mistake, since I find myself surrounded by dithering old men."

Stunned silence, then the men at the table grumble in disapproval.

"You needn't belittle us, Your Majesty," says the Siningwe general. "It's not bravery we lack. We simply don't understand the direction you're taking us. All this activity on foreign soil is unorthodox. We are not, nor have we ever aspired to be, an empire."

Another chorus of agreement accompanied by enthusiastic head nods.

The queen gets up from her chair and walks to the windows, where she stands in the sunlight with her back facing the table, letting the force of her magnetism permeate the room. Her gown is a sheer salmon-colored silk, and it flows like waves around the silhouette of her form, cinched at the waist beneath a plunging neckline by a thin golden belt. Hoops of gold surround her neck in layers, while her crown of copper sits around a head wrap of rose-white brocade.

Alinata knows the queen carefully tailored her appearance today for this exact moment, but she's still surprised by just how strongly the generals are affected. They sit up straighter, open defiance transformed into awe.

"How could you so thoroughly miss the point?" she mutters. "This isn't about empire. This is about ensuring our continued existence."

The queen turns back around, her face remaining in shadow, but the sunlight continues to incandesce the translucent fabric of her gown.

"General Sikhozi, the rumors are true. I have indeed taken action to bring Umadiland under the Seal of one warlord, a brutal and merciless fiend who built his power on a grave of thousands." Now that she has their attention, she moves away from the window and slowly paces down the length of the room. "The man is a living giant. Shadows cloak his face, and the one eye you can see is a tronic monstrosity that glows like the heart of a fire. He is so formidable there are some among you who would cower in his presence, and this is not to discredit you, my generals, but to look a cold, hard truth in the face. He is not a man to be trifled with."

She stops behind the Siningwe general at the other end of the table, placing a hand on the backrest of his chair. "And yet, as frightful and murderous as this warlord is, I am not *allied* with him. I *command* him. He knows that at any moment I could snap my fingers and he would be instantly dispossessed of all his power. In the blink of an eye he would be rendered impotent, vulnerable even to his weakest lieutenant, let alone his enemies."

The queen starts walking again, looping around the table and pacing back the other way. "That is the power I hold in my hands, and you should all be grateful to Ama I was wise enough to reach for it, because someone else would have, and then where would we be? Yonte Saire now has an emperor who could raze villages with the wave of a hand, yet he would not dare pit his forces against mine because I have a power to match his. Our future, my generals, our autonomy is assured, because of *my* actions."

As she arrives back at the head of the table, she doesn't sit down. She places her hands flat against the stone of the table, looming over the generals. "Now I am telling you of another power out there, I am telling you that it is so compelling foreigners from beyond the continent are coming in droves to seize it, and *do nothing* is the best you have to offer me? You are upset that my actions are not orthodox? You would rather I sit on my hands and hope for the best while our enemies amass weapons and sorceries we have never seen before? I ask again, did I summon a council of generals, or am I in the presence of spineless cowards?"

Shamefaced, the generals shift uncomfortably in their seats.

"We are your brave warriors, Irediti Ariishe," says the Siningwe general. "Perhaps we were too quick to doubt you. We are yours to command."

No one argues with him. Victorious, the queen sits, and the rest of the meeting proceeds without further protest.

When it ends and the men begin to leave the war room, the queen remains seated, and Alinata and Neropa emerge from the shadows to stand by her side, their silken gowns trailing on the floor.

"General Siningwe, a word," says the queen.

"Of course, Your Majesty." The general has already risen from his chair. He stands behind it now, waiting for the other generals to make their exits. Whatever he's thinking is hidden behind his usual stony gaze.

Alinata knows that her role in this conversation is to look the general in the eye so that it's clear to him that the queen is not alone. But his strong resemblance to his late nephew makes this task especially difficult, so she focuses on his fur collar instead.

"General, I was hoping you could shed some light on a mystery that has troubled me for some days now," the queen says once the door has shut. "Your nephews absconded from the Plains with my honor guard, whom I have had to expel dishonorably for abandoning his queen's side without permission. Can you tell me why they might have done this and where they might have gone?"

The general betrays not even a scintilla of emotion. "My nephews have always been impulsive and resentful of authority, Your Majesty. I wouldn't think much of it. I'm sure they'll return and be properly contrite once their little rebellion has run its course."

"You don't seem particularly concerned," she observes.

"They are capable warriors, Your Majesty. I taught them myself. They can take care of themselves."

The queen cocks her head to one side. Alinata can tell by the slight pursing of her lips that she's unamused. Perhaps she was hoping to rouse a stronger reaction.

She tries again. "I have been patient and generous with your clan considering all the tribulations you have endured in the past, but it seems defiance and . . . divergent behavior are an inextricable part of your nature."

A subtle dig at his marriage to a man.

There, a reaction: the general gives the faintest of smiles. "Divergence is not necessarily evil, Your Majesty. After all, was it not my late nephew's divergence from tradition that has made us the most powerful tribe in the south? You said so yourself."

"Yes, I did," the queen allows. "And it remains true to this day. Musalodi was a boon to his people. His sacrifice will be remembered for generations."

"Our clan has suffered much, Your Majesty, but we are fiercely loyal, and when you call on us to fight for you, our roars will be the loudest on the battlefield."

The queen nods. "That is why I intend to select Aneniko's replacement from your clan. Any recommendations?"

"Aneniko is a fine warrior," the general replies. "My recommendation is that you give him a second chance. He might have followed my nephews into the wilds for their sake."

"I shall take that under advisement," the queen says. "Thank you, General. You are dismissed. Please send my regards to your husband."

The general bows, then leaves without another word.

"He knows more than he's letting on," Neropa intones.

"I suspect the new AmaSiningwe has been talking," the queen agrees, bringing the tips of her fingers together. "She has an inquisitive mind, that girl. Even when she was here, she kept asking questions, searching for answers in the library. Never overtly—she thought she was being secretive—but I knew. I thought sending her back to her kraal as a mystic would get her to desist, but I should have known better."

Alinata's heartbeat grows sluggish, the temperature in the war room seeming to plummet. She can already sense what's coming, and she would run if only she had the courage. But she stays, ever the loyal apprentice.

She tumbles from the skies, but the clouds do not cushion her fall . . .

"What was she researching?" Neropa asks, an innocent question, but she might as well have pushed Alinata into a frozen lake. A biting cold seeps into her fingers like she's scratched the surface of a grave.

"It does not matter," the queen says. "She has made herself a problem that needs solving."

"I can go find out what she knows," Neropa offers.

"No. This requires a more . . . nimble solution."

She tumbles and falls and the earth rushes to meet her, death waiting in its bosom. She plummets and screams and she—

"Alinata?"

"Yes, Your Majesty?"

A slight wrinkle appears on the queen's brow. "You have been distracted recently. Are you well?"

"The idea of foreigners on Red soil has left a bad taste in my mouth," Alinata says. "That's all."

Neropa's eyes narrow at that answer, but she says nothing.

"Then I trust you can do what needs to be done."

Alinata is an incarnation, a vessel of the queen's will, her shadow. And a shadow listens and obeys. It does not ask questions. "I am your servant, Your Majesty."

"Wait until the regiments have left the Plains," the queen instructs. "Leave no trace. There will be questions, but people still believe in the curse the last AmaSiningwe left on her clan. Don't give them a reason to doubt it."

A chill has spread throughout Alinata's body; she might as well be in the Void. But she gives nothing away lest the queen and Neropa see through her. "Understood."

"I know you're there. At least have the courage to come out and face me."

In the blackest hour of night, Alinata steps out of the Void in bodily form, revealing herself to the new Siningwe mystic in the kraal's alchemical workshop. She gained the ability to make herself immaterial when the queen strengthened her gifts, keeping both herself and her ravens in the Void. Under the soft light of the glowvines hanging from the ceiling rafters, two knives of pure Void craft shimmer in her hands, her heart beating with the steadiness of a hunting python's.

Most of the kraal is asleep, but her target, a pretty young woman with a round mass of curly hair, has been studiously brewing elixirs in the workshop for the past twenty minutes, combining different compounds in her alchemical reactor and writing down her observations in a leather-bound journal. Alinata watched her from the Void until the other young woman felt her presence.

Now they stare at each other, nothing but a table between them.

AmaSiningwe's breathing has sped up. She's blinking rapidly, the fear patent in the tightness of her shoulders, but she puts on a brave face. "And so the queen sends her loyal assassin to kill me at last." They're not strangers to each other, although they've had no cause to become better than acquaintances. "Why haven't you done so already?"

Alinata makes to move around the table, but the mystic mirrors her motion, keeping the table between them. "Why are you a threat to her?" she says, words she hears herself speak almost unconsciously. She's already erred by alerting the target to her presence. Speaking to the target is an even bigger transgression.

But she needs to know.

"Because I figured out what really happened in Yonte Saire," says the woman she should have already dispatched. "There aren't many books on the All Axioms—I suspect the queen made sure of that—but if you know what you're doing, you can piece together the truth from footnotes and tangentially related sources. The Yontai's new emperor? The queen's new magic? None of it is a coincidence. And Musalodi didn't die in a riot. He was *murdered* in a ritual to take from him what would have been his as the architect of an All Axiom."

So you were clever enough to figure out the truth, Alinata thinks, *and yet too foolish to realize what it would cost you.* She moves around the table, and so does the mystic.

"Who have you told?"

"His family. His father, his uncles. His stepmother. I owed it to them. They deserve to know the truth. I'm not sure they believe me, but they know."

What are you waiting for? Alinata asks herself. *You know what you need to do.*

"Are you going to kill them too?" asks the mystic. "Just like you killed Musalodi?"

Alinata stops. "I didn't kill Musalodi."

"You might as well have." The mystic scoffs, her tone bitter. "You knew what was planned for him, and you helped make it happen."

Kill her now. "I was acting for the good of the tribe. Salo's sacrifice has made us stronger than we've ever been."

The mystic stares at her with cold, dead eyes. "You don't even believe your own lies. Is that why we're talking right now? Are you hoping I'll provide some validation for your dreadful choices?"

"I don't need your validation." Alinata breaks eye contact, the emotions in her chest pulling her in too many directions at once. "I just want to know why Aneniko abandoned his post. He wouldn't have left for the desert unless he felt it was urgent."

AmaSiningwe folds her arms, contemptuous. "Why do you care?"

"He's a friend," Alinata shoots back.

"You don't have friends, Si Alinata. That's why you're the queen's favorite. She wouldn't choose someone with split loyalties."

A vein pulses on Alinata's left temple. "There are people I like and respect, and Niko is one of them."

"Was Musalodi?"

"Don't change the subject."

The young AmaSiningwe openly evaluates Alinata, from her gown of pale silk to the knives of Void craft in her hands. Whatever she decides releases some of the tension in her shoulders. "One of the Faraswa refugees we took in started having seizures. I later discovered that the cause was a pulse of energy coming out of the desert. As far as I can tell, most Faraswa can sense this signal, but the boy's reaction to it was significantly stronger. He said he felt like it was calling him. And since he and Niko are friends, Niko decided to take him to the desert to investigate."

That's it? Alinata almost says. *He abandoned the queen's side and his place in the honor guard to help a Faraswa refugee? How foolish.*

But also, how decent. To be motivated by something other than one's own power. To risk everything for a friend. It's the decent thing to do, the choice a good person would make.

"There's more to all of this, isn't there," says the mystic, breaking Alinata out of her thoughts. "What is the queen doing in the desert, Si Alinata?"

"You ask too many questions, AmaSiningwe. Had you minded your business, perhaps you would not now find yourself in the company of an assassin."

"The queen has overstepped, and I won't be the last to ask questions. Already there's talk among the clan mystics. How many of us will you kill to keep her secrets safe?"

Alinata decides to stop pretending she didn't come here with her mind already made. "If I was going to kill you, AmaSiningwe, you would already be dead." After relinquishing her knives back to the Void, she turns around, moving to open the door. She steps out into the cool night and pauses by the threshold. "The queen might send someone else," she says over her shoulder.

"I'm not defenseless." The mystic Nimara waves a glowing arm and reveals the wards of deadly Blood craft she wove into the floor of the building.

Alinata nods in approval, recognizing that she was in more danger than she realized. "Clever. It might have even worked."

"What will you do?"

A leafless witchwood tree stands sentinel in the compound outside. Looking at it, Alinata contemplates something the queen said to her recently, about how a person's life can sometimes be defined by a single choice they make at a critical moment where the outcome cannot be divined. Alinata thought that her moment had come and gone. Now she realizes she was wrong.

Her moment is now. Right this instant.

"The moon preserve you, AmaSiningwe. Be careful what you eat and drink in the coming days. As for me, I have an appointment with fate."

With that she gives herself to the Void, ascending into the night sky as a flock of ravens. And then she heads west.

23: Salim

"Do you *really* know what you're doing?"

"Don't interrupt him, Sevan. Let him work."

"I'm just saying. If he doesn't *know* what he's doing, he might kill us all."

In the crystal hub of the *Ataraxis*, a compartment near the engine room where all the ship's main enchantments are housed, Sevan and Priscille watch anxiously as Salim pulls out yet another cable from its socket on a brass cylinder. Showers of red sparks fly from the disconnected cable, forcing both women to shrink back with stifled cries.

The brass cylinder is as tall as Salim and about as wide, one of many housed in the compartment in neat rows. Thin black cables from all over the ship run beneath the grated floor and rear up to fasten themselves onto sockets on the cylinders, as many as a hundred cables to a cylinder. Within their internal machinery, each cylinder holds a high-grade crystal and is essentially a massive cipher shell: a device that can receive and execute the prose of any enchantment.

"The ship has built-in redundancies," Salim explains as he unfastens another cable from the same cylinder. "The kinetic shield, for example, isn't just one big enchantment; it's one big enchantment and many smaller ones housed in nodes all over the hull. But this"—he knocks on the brass—"is the main node, the one that controls the others. Lose this one, you lose the rest."

The cable comes out of its socket, and once again there's a sputter of red sparks that dies out after a few seconds. "I'm disconnecting nodes that were damaged during the attack before they cause a surge and take down the rest of the system. If that happens, we die."

"Suns." Priscille presses a palm to her heart. "We wouldn't want that, now, would we."

"No, we wouldn't," Salim agrees, moving on to the cylinder responsible for the lighting on the ship.

He still can't be sure of who or what he actually is. Whatever the truth, when the king banished the shadow that hunted him, he was able to reach into himself and unlock a deeper understanding of his mind and, beyond that, a greater mastery of its abilities.

Now he doesn't just *see* the flow of power from the engine to the cylinders in this room to the rest of the vessel; he *understands* the flow on an instinctual level, as if he built the windcraft with his own hands.

After the last faulty node comes off in yet another shower of sparks, Salim exhales, wiping his forehead with the sleeves of his bloodstained coveralls.

"Is that it?" Sevan asks. "Are we safe?"

"Almost. Now, I need to reconfigure the hub to compensate for all the dead nodes."

"And how the hell will you do that?"

He could do it with his mind. He's already flying the ship remotely. But it was designed with dedicated physical interfaces for almost every system—switches, levers, consoles, the like—and bypassing them has proved to be quite the taxing mental exercise. Far easier to fly the ship the way it was meant to be flown.

He makes his way to the central mind core at the far end of the compartment, a control console of brass keys and a panel of Mirror light, where presumably the ship's mechanic would access and monitor all the enchantments in the hub.

Salim can't recall ever using such an interface before, but his bruised fingers fly across the brass keys. Soon he's got the network reconfigured, restoring most of the ship to full functionality.

A mini explosion comes from the direction of the engine room. "Not to worry!" Salim shouts. "Everything is fine! That was just the kinetic shield roaring back to life. I hope."

"You hope?" Sevan shrieks, halfway panicked.

"A figure of speech." Having done his best, he performs one last quick inventory of the systems, then deactivates the console. "I can't do much about some of the lights in the lower decks, but most of the ship is working as it should. We should be able to stay in the air for as long as we like."

"Wonderful news," Priscille says, relieved. "You must be a mechanic, then."

"That . . . feels right, strangely." Salim squints as if to see through the fog shrouding his memories. It has thinned somewhat since he achieved his new awareness of himself, but the details remain too hazy for him to be certain of anything. Are those even *his* memories?

"We're done here, I think," he says, remaining in the present. "Perhaps we should go up to the weather deck? I haven't seen the sky in so long."

Sevan stares at him with continued suspicion, Priscille with open innocence, neither making any motions to leave. They're an odd pair: an androgynous, tattooed, spiky-haired woman in sleeveless blue coveralls, and a pleasant-natured matron in a lime-colored dress.

Sevan still has bruises on her face from taking a beating on Salim's behalf. Why she'd do that for a complete stranger is still out of his grasp.

Suddenly self-conscious, he rubs his hands on the thighs of his coveralls. "All right, then."

He starts walking, and Priscille and Sevan follow.

"No way it's that simple," Sevan whispers behind him. "He caused an Imperial battleship to *explode*. He can break into cog minds and change them. Balam's a mechanic. Whatever Salim is, it's not that."

"Then . . . what do you think he is?"

"He's gotta be a war prototype. Some kind of weapon or something."

"Do you think he's dangerous?"

"Of course he's dangerous!"

"I mean, to us. To us. To us. To—"

"That's what I'm trying to figure out," Sevan cuts in.

At the stairs to the upper deck, Salim stops and turns to face them. Their eyes widen, and they freeze in the corridor like they think he's about to attack them. The fear he sees on their faces makes him nauseous.

"I'm no danger to you," he says. "I may not know what I am, but I know I'm not a murderer. And about my abilities . . ." He adjusts his spectacles, ill at ease with discussing his nonhuman nature. "So you know how we're all built around crystal mind stones? Well, my creator gave me a metaformic artifact for a mind stone. That might be why my memories are inaccessible to me. My mind is failing to properly integrate with it. I don't think it ever will."

Priscille's head flinches back slightly. "You're a metaform? But metaforms can't be sentient."

"I'm not *a* metaform. I believe I was poured into an empty one and then given a body."

"Frankly I don't see the difference," Sevan says. When Priscille glares at her, she sighs. "Fine. If you say you're not a danger to us, then . . . I guess you're all right in my book. For now, anyway."

That'll have to be good enough for Salim. "I can live with that."

There are five decks in total on the *Ataraxis*, the smallest and uppermost nearly completely exposed to the open air. Mild sickness visits Salim as they emerge onto the deck. The ship's moonglass wings are both fully unfurled, giving the vessel a triangular profile if seen from above. Blades of moonglass extend from the prow and float lengthwise above the deck, held in place by a system of automated ropes and pulleys. Above the blades the suns shine in an empty sky with a dazzling brilliance.

Balam is standing by the portside handrail, looking out onto the carpet of white clouds below. He's unbuttoned the top half of his stained brown coveralls and let the sleeves hang around his waist. A white undershirt strains against his hefty frame. Salim can hardly believe this is the same man who was a quivering mess down in the brig.

"Balam, are you well?" Salim says as they join him by the rail.

He smiles through his thick beard. His voice is deep. Rich. "It's good to be back to normal. I didn't like being afraid. Goes against my nature. Thank you for restoring me to myself."

"Thank you for breaking us out of the cage," Salim says.

And for a while the four of them stand in the sunlight, enjoying the freshness of the air. They were flying west of a continental landmass when the Imperial ship attacked; they're hundreds of miles farther south now, but the coast is still visible through the cloud canopy. The sickness Salim felt ebbs away, and he begins to relish the view, knowing that whoever he was before wasn't accustomed to seeing the world from so high.

"So now what?" Sevan says, breaking the silence.

"Now?" Salim thinks about it. "I honestly don't know."

They're all startled when Sevan starts laughing. "Is this what freedom feels like?" she says and leans against the handrail with both elbows as she becomes pensive. "We could do anything. We could sail the skies forever. We could become traders or wanderers or even pirates. We . . . we're free."

She says the last word like she can't quite believe it.

"What if the captain realizes his ship is still flying and comes back for it?" Priscille asks.

"Salim will just make them explode, won't you, Salim? This is our ship now, and we make the rules. Hey, can I be your second-in-command?"

Salim stares blankly at Sevan. So do the others.

"Don't you get it, people?" she says. "We're *free*, and we have a ship! Salim is the captain, obviously. I can be the deputy. Priscille can take over the sick bay. Balam can be our new mechanic. We're our own masters now."

Sevan's enthusiasm is contagious, and they all smile at each other as they realize that she's right: Perhaps for the first time in their lives, they truly have no one to answer to. They can do whatever they want.

So over the next several days, whatever they want is precisely what they do.

First, Salim brings the ship low to the sea, and they hold a short funeral ceremony for Lyria and the faceless atmech that sat in a corner of the Professor's workshop, then release their linen-wrapped bodies into the water from the empty skiff bay.

They then clean and deodorize the workshop, scrubbing down the oil-stained floors and countertops and disposing of anything the man might have used for his depraved experiments. They service the wheeled beds, lubricating their joints and giving them clean sheets and pillows, and repair whatever medical equipment is salvageable, though Priscille laments the lack of basic instruments and medications.

With the sick bay restored, they clean out the cabins, claiming the garments that were in the closets, mostly shirts and coveralls, of which there are dozens. At Sevan's insistence they launder all of them first in the machines on the fourth deck, including all the bedclothes, and discard any personal effects that might serve as reminders of the old crew.

Priscille takes what used to be the Professor's cabin, next to the sick bay. Sevan claims the pilot's bunk beneath the bridge. Balam takes over Faidon's cot in the skiff bay, saying he likes the open space.

They leave the captain's old quarters to Salim, though for all the presumed prestige of the position, the old captain was a man of simple tastes, and the cabin isn't any larger or more comfortable than the guest compartments.

There's a bed in a compact frame. A brass control console. A desk beneath a round porthole. A cramped but private washroom.

Not especially luxurious, but it might as well be heaven for Salim, and he's grateful to be able to wash himself, put on fresh clothes, and sleep on a bed for a change.

Sevan ambushes him the next morning as he leaves his new quarters, a predatory glimmer in her eye. "Salim . . . er, Captain. So there's a *big* storage compartment on deck four, but it's locked. Would you be so kind as to do your mind thing and unlock it? I need to make an inventory of whatever's inside."

Seeing no harm in the request, Salim sends a simple command to the central core, unlocking all compartments on the ship. "It's done."

"Great!"

Sevan walks off with gleeful purpose, which Salim finds somewhat worrying, but he thinks nothing of it until she shows up to breakfast in the dining compartment wearing a typhonic sidearm holstered to one hip.

By its ornamented brass frame, the typhon was built to be eye catching. A tube of reinforced glass runs beneath the weapon's two barrels, boiling with sparks of scarlet lightning.

Priscille almost chokes on a toasted biscuit as Sevan takes a seat by the table. "Sevan! Where did you . . . how . . . what have you done?"

"I'm the ship's second-in-command," Sevan says, unconcerned. "I have to be able to defend myself." She goes on to place three well-crafted bracer tools on the table, each of them made of mahogany leather with an array of brass instruments, including a small Mirror light panel. "Here. Your very own weaponized bracer tools so we can speak to each other remotely. They can also generate kinetic shields strong enough to stop a typhon bolt, so there's that."

"Where'd you get these things, Sevan?" Priscille asks, inspecting hers like she thinks it might explode.

"Turns out our dear old captain was a serious illegal arms trader." Sevan leans back in her chair, folding her arms with a self-satisfied grin. "The storage bay on deck four is practically an armory loaded with all sorts of stolen military Redware. Dual-mode typhonic firearms—all automatic. Crates of arcsling explosives. Electrified melee weapons. Tactical mirrorscopes and other gear. I even saw a triple-barreled war gauntlet. I'd have taken it myself, but it's too heavy."

"You seem to know a lot about illegal weaponry, Sevan," Balam remarks.

"Of course I do. Captain Axios is exactly the sort of man I used to help catch when I was still with the military." Sevan leans forward as an idea occurs to her. "Hey, maybe *you* can have the war gauntlet. You're certainly strong enough."

Balam simply shakes his head.

"Why not? And don't give me that 'I'm a peaceful cog' bullshit. Not after what they did to you. What they did to all of us."

"They?" Balam repeats.

"The humans. The people who imprisoned us here. We have a right to defend ourselves and make them pay if they try to hurt us."

"I have no desire for revenge," Balam says calmly. "And even if I did, I have violence-inhibiting restraints. And so do you, Sevan. You can walk around with that typhon on your hip, but you'll never be able to use it."

Sevan's eyes go shiny with emotion, her breathing rapid, her folded arms nearly trembling. She looks around the table, then at Salim. "Salim can break our restraints. Can't you?"

It hits Salim right then that these people are now his responsibility, and he suffers a wave of fear that he'll fail them somehow. He clears his throat, looking fixedly at the table. "I could, I suppose."

"You suppose?"

"I could try, but all of this is new to me."

Sevan watches Balam and Priscille for their reactions. "If he can break our restraints, why not let him? Don't you want to be your own person? Aren't you tired of being a prisoner in your own mind?"

Balam shrugs. "All I want is for no one to ever make me afraid again."

"But don't you see?" Sevan says. "Messing with your mind will be harder if you don't have restraints."

Balam regards Salim, his brow furrowing. "Is that true?"

"It's certainly easier to manipulate a restrained mind," Salim agrees.

Sitting forward, Balam places his massive hands on the table. "Then you will break my restraints."

They all look at Priscille, who shrinks a little into her chair from the attention. "I don't care about restraints," she says. "I just don't want . . . I don't want . . ." She pauses, taking a deep breath. "I want to be well again. I want to do what my hands were meant to do. That's all."

Salim can still sense the fracture in Priscille's crystal core, the fault that plagues her speech and memory. He doesn't think he can mend the damage, but he might be able to isolate and quarantine the region so she can simply think around it.

"If that's what you want, Priscille, I'll do my best." He puts his hands on the table, palms open.

At his expectant look, Sevan says, "Here? Now?"

He smiles. "Let's all link hands. This will feel a little strange."

Salim becomes restless as the days pass, memories of his encounter with the king in the in-between hounding him with increasing frequency. She said she needed his help and that his memories would return. He tries to be patient, to distract himself, working on repairs with Balam, inventorying the contraband on deck four with Sevan, cooking in the galley with Priscille. But the nagging feeling only worsens, the worry that he left a fire burning somewhere and it has grown in his absence.

He's stewing in his troubled thoughts on the weather deck one afternoon when he spots something that makes him bolt upright: a white streak of smoke moving higher in the sky above the *Ataraxis*.

A flood of disjointed images pours into him at the sight, fragments and faint whispers that do little to disentangle the knotted threads of his past. Nonetheless his next step becomes clear.

"I know what to do," he says to himself, and at the same time gears start turning belowdecks, moonglass membranes realigning as the ship banks eastward and begins a slow descent.

He connects his bracer tool to the rest of the crew and speaks into its voice implement. "Everyone, prepare for landing."

Minutes later the *Ataraxis* folds in its wings and extrudes its massive landing gears, settling down onto a flat stretch of coastal desert at a slightly awkward but stable angle.

"What the hell are you doing, Salim?" Sevan says as she follows him out of the skiff bay and down the exit ramp. Priscille and Balam are quiet shadows behind her. "Why have we landed? And *where* have we landed?"

"I need a place with water," Salim answers without stopping. When his sandals touch the golden sands of the beach, he continues in the direction of the sea and the waves breaking gently in foaming swashes. The breeze carries a pleasant tang of salt and wet sand.

"There's water on the ship," Sevan points out, keeping pace with him.

"I need lots of water."

"But why?"

"The Veil is often weaker around bodies of water," Salim answers automatically. "Makes it easier for the gods to communicate with us."

"Oh yeah? And how do you know that?"

Salim thinks about it, then frowns. How *does* he know that?

"I read it in a book the Imperials showed me," he hears himself say.

And only now does he realize, much to his shock, that the book was more extensive than he initially thought. While his conscious mind saw only the story of the Last Hegemon and the hands that touched the book in the coming centuries, his metaformic self saw beyond the surface, to the truth: the Book of Lies is a detailed chronicle of the desert people who once ruled the Red Continent. Their culture might be lost to history, but much of their knowledge is preserved in the book's gilded pages.

And now it's also preserved in the lattices of Salim's second mind. Not all of it—there wasn't enough time for him to absorb the entirety of the book—but what he acquired will take him months to fully digest.

He starts to wonder about that final layer he couldn't penetrate. *Did my subconscious also see into those mysterious depths without my knowledge?* He searches his mind and comes up empty.

"Apparently not," he says, then realizes he's stopped walking and the others are staring at him with varying degrees of worry. "Sorry. Just thinking out loud."

He starts walking again, and Sevan jogs to catch up. "Are you, Salim? Still thinking, that is. Because I'm beginning to doubt you still have your wits about you."

"Don't be mean, Sevan," Priscille scolds her.

"Why not? We're finally free, and he lands us out here in the middle of nowhere so he can—'communicate with the gods'? How is that not insane?"

Neither Priscille nor Balam has an answer to that question, and Salim doesn't think he could explain himself either. He just knows what he needs to do.

The *Ataraxis* is like a sea monster beached on the sands behind them. At the edge of the crashing waves, Salim takes off his sandals, a fluttery sensation settling in the pit of his stomach. He couldn't see it before, but that day in the cage he didn't just achieve a deeper insight into himself. He also summoned . . . *something*, and it has been waiting for him all this time. Now he feels it drawing nearer like a moth to an enchanted crystal, a force of nature that won't be denied.

He rolls the pants of his coveralls up to his knees and starts wading into the water. "You should all probably stand back," he says to the others. "And don't make any loud noises. No matter what."

The redhawk descends into the shallows of the beach in a spray of red-and-gold flame, its hornlike crest aglow, starlight pouring out of its eyes and glittering on its tail feathers. Salim has memories of drowning beneath such an entity, his chest transfixed upon a talon and pinned to a lake bed. He should be terrified.

Instead he's oddly at peace as the creature lands in the water in front of him and enfolds him in its scaly metal wings, giving off an intense, encompassing heat. The entity bends its neck, lowering its enormous beak, and when their heads touch, the world melts away, and Salim is spirited elsewhere, to a place familiar but not quite remembered, beneath a lavender sky with many suns and ringed moons, in a forest glade hemmed in by ancient trees. Their thick roots twist into earth so soft and crimson it might have been soaked in blood. And in the middle of the glade, a crystal cube spins beneath a ball of red fire.

"I've been here before," he says, and the branches of the trees around the glade rustle as if in agreement.

"Indeed, you have," says a voice like hissing wind. *"This was where we first spoke."*

Salim turns, and his breath catches. The living god now standing before him is a lean giant wearing only a loincloth of hide. In one hand he carries an ornate spear of a cobalt-blue metal—blue like his skin, and like the many metallic panes of his beautiful face. His eyes are like the faceted interiors of diamonds or sapphires, one or the other or both at once. They might have shone with divine pride once upon a time, but all Salim sees in them now is profound sorrow and regret.

"Hello, Salim," the god says.

A woman pouring acid into his eyes. Derisive laughter as he ran from a charging bull. A boy dying in his arms. Drowning, thrashing pain. A curse like webs of sunlight, making him forget. Nameless horrors in an underground lake. A new word exploding into his mind and stunning him with its cosmic scale. Galaxy.

The memories flood into Salim all at once, incomplete snippets from a life lived in a world vastly different from the one he awoke in. He spoke a different language. He wore different clothes. He had friends, family, a boy he was beginning to love.

I was human once. A god showed me the truth of my world, and I ran in cowardice when it was too much. And then I was murdered.

His legs weaken and give out, and he falls to his knees. "I died," he says, voice hoarse with the onset of tears. "Dear Ama, I died. But I'm alive again. How?"

The god—the Star of Vigilance, Salim remembers now—speaks without ever moving the panes of his face, his voice a whisper. *"How you're here is not as important as why, Salim."*

"Salim is not really my name."

"A name you choose for yourself is as true as any given to you." Vigilance turns his head to look at something within the trees, as if he can see through them to whatever is beyond. *"And someone else has already claimed your old name."*

Salim follows his gaze, then jumps and turns away. He looks back only to spy a twisted, deformed reflection of himself glaring back with soulless eyes.

"The shadow," he breathes. "I know him."

"A reflection of you tainted by my enemy's essence," Vigilance says. *"She knew I had plans to bring you back, so she conspired to obliterate you and raise a corrupted facsimile in your stead. She didn't know I had a contingency. Prescient and clever as she is, she did not expect you."*

A frosty breeze makes Salim shiver. "The shadow chased me in my dreams."

"He sensed your existence and sought to destroy you. We are lucky your friend intervened when she did."

"You mean the king," Salim says, watching Vigilance closely. "She has taken the goddess's throne. But you knew that already."

Vigilance dips his head in a quiet nod. *"The gods were due a reckoning, I suppose. Our hubris created the very monster you must now confront."*

"And that's the truth about heaven," Arante once said to Salim. *"It devours universes to feed the greed of its gods. Stars, worlds, everything turned to ash. But why? Why, when that power could be harnessed to fix this universe and make it better? All those people you saw in that lake. All that sorrow. The gates of heaven hold the power to rectify those wrongs."*

"I ran the last time we spoke," Salim says. "All I could think about were the faces I'd seen in the lake of the nameless. Arante . . . she said she wanted to use the power of the gods to fix time. To undo all the unjust suffering that ever happened."

The trees around the glade tremble and creak in an angry wind. *"And perhaps she believes herself capable of such a feat. But what is justice worth if the pursuit of it leaves trails of untold destruction? And was it just for her to attempt to obliterate you, to take your form, your choice, your existence, and bend it to her will?"*

Salim stares wordlessly at the god, not knowing what to say. He tears his eyes away when black mists begin to drift into the glade from the trees.

"Our time here is at an end," Vigilance says and walks closer to the crystal cube spinning beneath the ball of red fire. *"This All Axiom has already been claimed. It is no longer yours. But we are fortunate I can simply grant you another."*

He touches the cube with the tip of his blue spear, and its base expands, the four vertical sides stretching and slanting inward until the shape isn't a cube at all but a truncated pyramid.

It's still a six-sided figure encompassing the six crafts of Red magic—Fire, Blood, Earth, Storm, Mirror, and Void—but where the cube handled all six crafts with equal proficiency, the pyramid has a weaker Blood aspect and a stronger Void aspect, represented respectively by the much smaller roof and the larger base.

An All Axiom. Not as balanced as the one he built, but its weaknesses are compensated by greater strengths. The Axiom spins beneath the red sphere of fire, the source that resides in the heart of the moon.

"Once, you would have spoken a vow," Vigilance says, his voice beginning to fade as the black mists thicken. *"A pledge of undying allegiance to a goddess in exchange for her power. But one way or the other, the age of the divines is drawing to a close. How it ends will be up to you."*

Salim can already feel himself being pulled away. "Wait!" he cries. "I don't know what I'm supposed to do!"

Diamond-sapphire eyes flash at him in the gloom. *"You have allies. Find them, and let them find you. The path forward will become clearer."*

He's drowning, seawater choking out his airways, when a pair of burly arms grabs him by the armpits and drags him out of the water. The redhawk's departure is a mighty drone in his eardrums, so loud the sands and the waters of the beach are vibrating.

Beyond the reach of the swash, Balam lets him drop to the sand on all fours. He coughs, clearing out his lungs, coming back to his senses.

"That was amazing!" Sevan exclaims. "I've never seen a redhawk so close. It's so big! And beautiful! What'd you do? And why did it do that thing with the wings? And then it just left!"

"Wait," Priscille says, pointing at Salim. "What's that?"

Still coughing and out of breath, Salim glances at his arms, where mazelike patterns of red-hot moongold have begun to glow on his skin.

"Those are cosmic shards," Balam says gravely. "He's a mystic now. Everyone get back."

"But cogs can't be mystics," Priscille says, though she retreats from Salim like the others.

"And don't they need some sort of machine to get those?" asks Sevan.

"They use machines now," Balam says, "but long ago they did it with redhawks."

Salim gives one last cough and turns to lie on his back so he can catch his breath. Beyond the droplets of water on his spectacles, the pale-blue sky seems like it's spinning.

"Not long ago," he manages to say. "Where I come from, that's how we still do it."

"Where *do* you come from?" Sevan asks tentatively, keeping her distance.

"Here. This continent. Far to the south." Closing his eyes, Salim lifts his spectacles off his face and takes a moment to fling the droplets of water from the lenses. He returns them to his eyes, then props himself up on one elbow so he can look at the others. "I can take you there. To my home. You can all come. You'll be welcome there."

"You mean, take us to the Red Wilds?" Priscille says, and Salim nods.

"We may have some stops along the way. There are . . . things I need to do."

The three atmechs look to each other, and Priscille bites her lower lip in thought. "I've always wanted to travel the world. I guess now's as good a time as any. So yes. I'll come."

"So long as we're not going back to the Empire," Sevan says, "I go wherever the ship goes."

"No Empire it is," Salim says. "What about you, Balam?"

The big man responds by coming forward and offering him a hand. Salim takes it and lets Balam pull him up. He tries and fails to dust the sand off his wet coveralls; then he picks up his sandals, and they all start walking back to the ship.

"So you can do magic now?" Balam says with a hint of amazement.

The flight of Salim's redhawk is still thundering across the sky. He looks up at its lingering smoke plume and smiles. "Yes, I guess I can."

Knowing only that he must head south, he keeps the *Ataraxis* afloat along the continent's western seaboard. But the ship's sensors detect other windcrafts in the sky, some just a few hours away, releasing bursts of destructive energy at each other, so he climbs to a much higher altitude to avoid them.

He also engages the rather interesting stealth shield, which he's realized is probably the most sophisticated enchantment on the ship and was likely an expensive retrofit the captain invested in to facilitate his illicit activities. It was also probably why the Imperials decided to charter his ship, for all the good that did in the end.

The engine's reserves of raw essence start to burn faster, but the crystal in the engine room is so saturated it would take many months of continuous operation to deplete. For Salim this realization is a stark reminder of the truths he learned in the inner sanctum: the powers of the gods were once used to ferry people between stars. In theory, this ship barely scrapes what's possible with the energy density of its power source.

The boy from his past visits him again that night, and this time Salim is aware of his metaformic subconscious casting the fishing line and reeling the other young man into a shared dream.

It was me all along, he realizes. *I've been summoning him into my dreams, and he's been letting me.*

The slight embarrassment doesn't stop him from enjoying the boy's company. They used to pass the time smoking beneath a tree until Salim decided he was tired of dancing around what he wanted. The dreams are more fruitful these days, and Salim has grown addicted to the thrill of being desired, of being cherished and admired, of being wanted, possessed, and taken. It escapes him why his past self was ever shy about such things.

Tonight, they fool around in yet another desert location lifted by his subconscious from the Book of Lies: beneath the stars, on the back of a large sphinx with the head of a redhawk. As they collapse side by side in the aftermath, Salim smiles like a fool, languid and sated.

"Wow, you're really good at that. *How* are you so good at that?" When Salim turns his head, he finds the boy staring back with a liquid glaze over his eyes. Concerned, Salim caresses him on the cheek, enjoying the feeling of his beard. "What's wrong?"

"You asked me what I like about you once," the boy says, and Salim gives a smirk, a flicker of renewed desire passing through him.

"I think I know exactly what you like about me. I know how; I know where."

"I'm being serious," the boy says, not at all amused.

Salim keeps stroking his beard. "Sorry. Go on."

"I recently lost something important to me. I was devastated at first. But now I realize . . . my conscience is clear. Despite what I stood to lose, I stayed true to myself and to the people I care about. And you know what? I'm proud of myself." The boy smiles, but it's sad, broken. "That used to be one of the many things I liked about you. You were never ashamed to stand up for what you cared about. And now it's something I can say I like about myself too."

Salim stills his hand, resting it on the boy's cheek. "Why don't I like where this is going?" When the boy says nothing, a sinking feeling touches Salim in his core. "You're not . . . ending us, are you?"

A tear escapes from the boy's eye. He captures Salim's hand, then brings it to his lips and kisses it on each knuckle. "My biggest regret is not showing you how I felt when I still could."

"You can show me here," Salim pleads. "I know I said I wasn't real, but I don't think that's true anymore. You don't have to go."

The boy isn't listening. He kisses Salim's hand again, grief glistening on his cheeks. "You're so beautiful. Goodbye, Salo."

"Niko, wait!"

The dream vanishes, and Salim bolts awake in the captain's cabin, heart racing, the taste of remembered names on his tongue.

Salo. Musalodi. That was my name. Aneniko. A ranger. A friend. A real person whose dreams I've shared. He's out there, somewhere, and he thinks I'm dead.

I have to find him.

I have to remember who I was.

Salim lies back onto the bed, other memories and names teasing him, shadows moving in the fog of his past. He finds a loose tether that stirs even more memories, a forgotten connection that has been waiting for him to pick it back up. So he does, and the tether solidifies in his mental grasp.

He readies himself with a breath, and then he pulls.

He appears in another dreamscape, on a marble porch where a musuku tree grows with bright-yellow crystals for fruit. Two heavy doors are sealed shut on one side of the porch, while across the doors, a walkway connects the porch to a marble rotunda. The rotunda is itself the heart of a grand library built in the middle of a lake, beneath violet skies with ringed planets, glowing comets, and flowering bloodroses.

Tears prickle Salim's eyes, more memories returning to him. He built this construct. He once sat in the rotunda across the porch with friends. They were people he'd come to care about. People he *still* cares about.

Are they alive? What were their names?

Lightning flashes in the sky. He moves to the edge of the porch and looks up in time to see a colossal crimson serpent swimming inside a colorful nebula. Crystalline eyes sparkle down at him from within the cloud; then a voice he feels rather than hears addresses him.

"Ziyo welcomes the master," it says.

"You know me?" Salim asks, although something about that name tugs at his memory.

"Ziyo knows the master, yes."

"I shall call you Ziyo," he once said, *"short for Owaziyo, for you are wise and know many things."* "I remember! You cannibalized my talisman so you could communicate with me." Another memory returns to him, drawing his gaze to the closed double doors on the porch. "And you helped me steal spells from the Pattern Archives."

"The master remembers correctly," Ziyo says.

The doors open to Salim at the slightest push, and he enters a large hall populated with countless rows of shelves on the main floor and on multiple mezzanines. The shelves hold plates of metal slotted into horizontal grooves, each plate with a bar of colored light attached to the front-facing edge. Judging from the tree growing on the porch outside, this is the Earth craft archive.

Salim walks along the carpeted aisles, soaking in the memories of creating the hall and being proud of what he'd built. He reminisces for perhaps a minute before someone else enters.

"Salo?"

Salim turns around. The large, unshaven young man gaping at him from the doors, dressed in a black dashiki and matching pants, has a metal brace around his left leg and leans on a cane. The sight of him stabs Salim in the chest with a sharp pang of emotion.

"Mother damn me to hell," the newcomer exclaims with a wide grin. "It *is* you!" Before Salim can react, the young man walks over and crushes him in a tight embrace. "Ziyo kept buzzing in my pocket like I told him to if you ever came back, but I didn't want to believe. They actually did it! They brought you back!" Still holding Salim by the shoulder with his free hand, he looks him over and lets out a laugh. "You're wearing a shirt! And pants! Never thought I'd see that."

That someone is so happy to see him makes Salim happy, too, even if he can't quite place the young man. "Forgive me; my memory isn't fully restored."

"Ah. I'm sure it'll come back." The young man looks around. "Where's Ilapara? Is she here? Is she all right?"

Kohl-ringed eyes. A smoldering fire. Seething passion wrapped in a steely red exterior. My friend.

Salim gasps. "Ilapara! Where is she?"

The young man gives him a quizzical look. "Isn't she with you?"

"No! Is she supposed to be?"

"She left with Tuk for the Enclave to bring you back from the dead, so since you're alive, I'd say yes, she's supposed to be with you."

Tuk. A dimpled smile full of mischief. Eyes that changed color like the sky, but green was where they liked to stay. Tuk and Ilapara traveled many leagues to bring me back, but they weren't there when I woke up. Why?

"I woke up in a city of ruins," Salim says, dread quickening inside him. "Everyone was dead. I was alone. I didn't know who or where I was. I didn't know to look for them."

The young man treats him to a lingering stare, then goes to sit down on a nearby wicker armchair, where he stretches out his bad leg and places his cane flat across his lap. "She's alive; I know that much." He caresses the ivory pendant on his chest. "I felt her move south a while ago, almost like she was . . . it felt like she was moving over the ocean. I thought she was coming back, but she kept on going south, and now . . ." The young man blinks rapidly, his eyes reddening. "I wish I could see her just one last time."

Salim's blood freezes near solid in his veins as the truth dawns on him: Ilapara and Tuk weren't in the city when the cataclysm struck. Because they'd already left. With *him*.

My reflection.

He returns to the present at the sound of a distant boom. The youth seated on the wicker chair—*Jomo Saire*. Yes, Jomo. A prince. Cousin to a king. He briefly flickers out of view, his mental grip on the construct slipping away. He manages to hold on, but Salim starts picking up the details he missed: the sweat on Jomo's forehead, the tension in his shoulders, the sorrow in his eyes.

"Was that an explosion?" Salim asks. "Are you in danger?"

"I eat danger for lunch," Jomo responds. "But I guess it's catching up to me now." He plants the butt of his cane on the floor and rises. "Ah well. This has been a nice little reprieve, but I have to get back out there. I'm making my last stand, you see. I'm going to die fighting, like my cousin." He considers Salim for a beat. "At least I know you're still alive. The emperor may yet get his just deserts."

"What's your situation?" Salim says. "Do you need assistance?"

"That would be nice, but I doubt you'll make it here on time. The emperor's men are almost through."

Salim closes his eyes, sending his senses outward, picking up every thread he finds, trying to see which ones he can command. He won't lose a friend so soon after getting him back. "I have a lock on Ziyo's location. The crystal is in your possession, yes?"

Jomo nods. "Ilapara gave it to me after you disappeared. I used it to organize a resistance, and for a while we were a thorn in the emperor's wrinkled old behind. But the bastard is just too powerful."

A resolve hard as tempered red steel takes over Salim. His heart rate slows, his mind sharpening into a calm, crystal clarity. "Hang on awhile longer, Jomo," he says. "I'm on my way."

There was another thread out there waiting patiently for his return. He finds it, reaches for it, and pulls.

And many miles away, a giant feline opens its eyes.

24: Ilapara

The Faraswa Desert

Ilapara is with Tuk in the throne room among Salo's courtiers when the countess presents three hooded figures to him. Guards in full silver armor flank him where he sits on a dais, dressed in a crimson kilt, a broad collar of colored stones, and a silken headcloth of black and golden stripes pinned in place by his crown.

Painted reliefs occupy the sandstone walls and snake up the thick pillars of the hypostyle hall, depicting scenes of kings and gods lounging together in lush gardens. To think all of this was a crumbled ruin just three days ago.

Ilapara still hasn't grappled with how powerful Salo has become, how much of a stranger he is now, and, more worryingly, how much he frightens her. But she's decided to stick around in the hopes that perhaps he's still adjusting to being alive again, that the friend she knew will return.

"They call themselves the Wise Ones, Your Glory," the countess says. "They've come to pay their respects to the new Hegemon."

"Your Glory," Tuk whispers in mockery of his sister, pulling a face.

Ilapara giggles involuntarily. Thankfully they're standing some distance behind Gregoire Silver Dawn and the rest of his well-dressed friends, so no one hears her. Not that she'd care if they did. She finds them all beyond ridiculous, the way they practically worship Salo.

The young man in question leans forward in his throne to take a closer look at the three figures. The one in the middle is considerably shorter than the other two, but all three wear robes of white cotton and black lengths of cloth wound around their faces so that only their eyes can be seen.

"Where did they come from?" Salo asks, an interested look on his face.

"From the desert, Your Glory," the countess says to the hall, and since she makes no effort to translate her words, Ilapara assumes the courtiers have all imbibed some version of the comprehension pill she took in Apos. "It seems these lands were not completely abandoned," the countess continues. "There are groups of Faraswa who trickled back to resettle their old homeland over the centuries, and apparently, some never left."

"Do not speak for us, Woman of Mysteries," barks the figure in the middle. "We speak for ourselves."

The croaking voice might belong to an old woman, but it rings in the throne room with an arresting authority. And the Izumadi, though fluid, carries an accent strange to Ilapara.

Woman of Mysteries? If the bizarre epithet offends the countess, she doesn't show it. She simply looks to Salo for further instruction.

"By all means," he says to the visitors, "come forward and say your piece."

The countess steps aside, and together the three figures lift their palms as if to utter a prayer, the old woman speaking first.

"Hail, Merensutekh Asheremi!" she shouts. "You whose coming was foretold."

"Merensutekh," shouts the man on her left, "for you are beloved of the deserts, and of the storms, and of disorder, and of the foreigners who people your halls."

"Asheremi," shouts the third speaker in a younger female voice, "for the moon weeps in your presence and the heavens quake in fear. Cursed is the ground you walk on. Blessed are they who hide from your sight."

A murmur ripples through the throne room, the courtiers frowning at each other as if to check that they all heard the same thing.

"Now this is interesting," Tuk remarks, eyes a murky shade of green. They haven't been that light in days.

On his throne, Salo is much less amused, the muscles of his neck visibly tensing. "Have you come here to insult me?"

"On the contrary, King Asheremi," the old woman says. "You wear the garb of our people; you sit upon a throne carved by our ancestors. You are indeed a king, yet you know not your true name. We have come to make it known to you."

"Hail, Merensutekh," shouts the man. "Son of the wastelands and the chaos that devours. Hail, Asheremi. Woe unto them who do not flee from the shadow that stirs in your heart."

Salo stands, nearly trembling with fury. "I don't have to listen to this."

"Take them away!" the countess orders, and the armored guards in the throne room burst into motion, rushing to apprehend the three robed figures.

"Cursed be your name, Merensutekh Asheremi!" shouts the younger woman. "And cursed be all who bow before you."

As one the visitors open their robes.

"Explosive!" Tuk shouts, and Ilapara sees only a flash of light coming from their direction before a force slams into her chest, and then she's on the ground, groaning in pain, her eardrums ringing like she was inside an erupting volcano.

Is someone calling her name?

"Ilapara!" She blinks and sees Tuk's face hovering above her. "Are you all right?"

She groans again, arching her back off the floor. Her ribs feel like they've been cracked, but she's still alive. Why is she still alive?

"Help me up," she says, and Tuk obliges her.

Everyone else is in the process of getting back up as well. The guards, the countess, Gregoire Silver Dawn, the rest of the courtiers— everyone except Salo, who's standing on the dais, eyes and cosmic shards ablaze, a hand outstretched.

A shimmering dome has materialized around the three visitors. They seem frozen inside, paralyzed where they stand, as if the air around them were solid. Even the fire that had begun to radiate away from them now hangs motionless in the dome like the flames of a painting.

Still holding his spell, Salo descends the steps of the dais, and the deadly calm on his face gives Ilapara a reluctant pang of fear for the visitors. She doesn't recall ever seeing him this angry.

"I've done you no wrong," he says. "I've not lifted a finger against you, yet you would come here to kill me?"

The throne room has fallen so still Ilapara swears she's not the only one holding her breath.

He inclines his head to one side, watching his prisoners through the shimmering membrane of his dome. "You were clearly prepared to die," he says, his cosmic shards gaining a stronger glow. "Perhaps I should grant you what you desire."

He performs a gesture, and the trapped flames come back to life, sweeping around the dome in slow arcs. The three visitors remain frozen, their muffled screams filling the hall as they burn alive.

Horrified, Ilapara makes to go and stop him, but Tuk holds her back, shaking his head even though his eyes are liquid pits of tar. "Don't."

She doesn't fight him, and Salo continues his slow execution of the visitors. By the time the screams subside, the dome is a raging inferno.

With apparent ease he casts another spell, turning the dome into a serpent, then guides it out through a window. It explodes out of the throne room with a whoosh, leaving only a blackened circle on the floor.

Salo swiftly turns to his armored guards. "What use are you if assassins can just walk in here and make an attempt on my life?" he demands. "Were they even searched?"

One of the guards speaks, and the countess translates, her voice slightly shaken. "'They had no weapons on them, Your Glory. Only necklaces of old bones and wood.'"

"These are the Redlands," Salo tells everyone. "Deadly magics lurk even in the most mundane objects. Do not count on me to save you the next time you underestimate so-called old bones and wood."

The guards execute bows of contrition. "'We'll do better, Your Glory,'" the countess translates on their behalf.

He turns away from them. "Countess, these people might be in league with whoever's hiding the key to the gate. Find out where they came from. This won't be their last attack."

"Yes, Your Glory," she says.

Without another word, Salo walks out of the throne room, a contingent of guards falling in line behind him. What stuns Ilapara is his complete lack of remorse over having just tortured three human beings to death.

She remembers the day when they watched from a nearby mountain as a warlord's disciple burned down a wagon of Faraswa slaves he'd just rescued—while the slaves were still inside. Though difficult to watch, the scene was nothing new to Ilapara; gruesome acts of cruelty are an inescapable reality of life in any Umadi stopover town, and the wise know to look away.

It was the abject horror she saw on Salo's face that finally broke through to her and made her recognize how desensitized she'd become in her quest for independence. His innocence made her confront the loss of her own, to ask herself how she could live in the presence of blatant evil. She remembers how it was at that very moment that she chose to follow him.

How could that same person do what Salo has now just done and then walk away without showing a flicker of guilt?

Ilapara allows herself to admit a difficult truth. The Salo she once knew never returned.

She stops trying to reach out to him over the coming days. And after several declined requests for a private audience, always with some paltry excuse about being too busy or tired, so does Tuk, though he remains hopeful that his friend is still in there somewhere.

But Ilapara only becomes more certain of the truth: the Salo they remember is gone forever.

If he notices their declining interest in being around him, he does nothing to rectify it. He and his new court of admirers settle into life in the restored palace complex, a well-oiled, ready-made, stratified machine that takes to the desert with such ease Ilapara would have believed them natives had she not arrived with them.

Smells of cooking food float out of the kitchens. Acrobats and musicians entertain the noble folk in the courtyards. Armored guards move in regular patrols up and down the colonnades. Ilapara and Tuk seem to be the only ones who don't know their places in the machine.

They're given spacious stone chambers filled with silken pillows and mattresses, and the servants bring them more food than they can eat for each meal, but beyond that they are largely ignored and find themselves adrift, exploring the halls of the palace or taking walks around the oasis.

Salo starts going out on excursions into the deserts on one of the smaller windcrafts. It's an agile, fast-moving vessel with a slim body and wide double wingspan of moonglass that vaguely reminds Ilapara of his enchanted skimmer flies.

She watches it lift off one afternoon while resting with Tuk in the shadow of a large date palm growing near the lake. "Think we could steal one of those and fly it to the Plains?" she says. "I'm getting tired of this place."

Tuk watches the vessel bank away from the oasis with cloudy eyes. "I've never flown a windcraft before."

"We could learn." The windcraft dips out of view. Ilapara is annoyed by the sting that pricks her in the chest. "What do you think he's looking for out there?"

"His gate, probably."

"But *what* is it?"

Tuk makes his cheeks swell with air, shaking his head. "I'd give anything to know. My sister probably knows, but I'm not about to ask her. I'd probably just end up killing her. Not that she'd speak to me anyway. Maybe I'll try asking one of the servants. There's a maid who has eyes for me."

"None of them trust you," Ilapara says, to which he flashes a smile, a rare sight these days.

"Ilapara, my dear, you should know by now I can make *anyone* trust me."

He doesn't sleep in their shared quarters that night. He shambles through the door of their living room in time for breakfast, though, eyes bloodshot, hair looking disheveled, shirt askew.

In between forkfuls of savory pie, he says, "I had an interesting night."

"Do I even want to know?" Ilapara wonders aloud.

"I was referring to what I learned about our friend. He's raised an old pyramid out in the desert, allegedly. He also met with a local king and queen, or some such thing. They're his allies now."

"Queen?" Ilapara doesn't like the sound of that. The nearest queen to the desert is the ruler of the Yerezi Plains herself, the same queen who supposedly betrayed Salo for a fragment of the Hegemon's crown. Surely she wouldn't come all the way out here to meet him, and if they did meet, how would he react? How would she?

It must be a different queen. Ilapara opens her mouth to say so, but the whole room suddenly quakes, followed by a loud bang coming from outside the palace complex. She locks eyes with Tuk, and they get up from their mats and go out to investigate.

So does nearly everyone in the complex, it seems. Guards, servants, courtiers, Salo himself—they all follow the source of the sound and emerge to a scene of pandemonium.

Three of the windcrafts resting in a crescent around the oasis are engulfed in moonfire. The vessels nearest to the flames are scrambling to lift off and move out of harm's way, and one leaps up a little too quickly, tilting precariously to one side before stabilizing itself. A nobleman next to the countess—presumably the owner of one of the burning vessels—cries out, his face full of rage. There were probably servants still onboard.

The gathered people gasp when Salo dramatically lifts off the ground, borne upward by magic. He doesn't fly so much as translate himself across the air, his body upright, one knee slightly bent.

He stops to hover near the burning vessels, and with all eyes watching, he casts a spell of wind that draws the flames up from the vessels in three swirling funnels. They join in the air high above him, collecting into a sphere; then he spreads his hands, and the sphere explodes across the sky in radial waves.

The fires extinguished, he returns, cheers and applause greeting him as he touches down with effortless grace. His irritation is palpable, however, and he seems to see no one else but the countess.

"You told me you know where the assassins came from."

She nods. "There's a settlement some several leagues to the northeast, Your Glory."

"Prophet, have your warship prepared for immediate takeoff. This demands a response."

The white-suited Gregoire Silver Dawn bows, then whispers a command to the most senior of his warriors, a flaxen-haired man in silver armor and a golden cape hanging from his left shoulder. He in turn shouts at his subordinates, and the command trickles down the ranks, booted feet moving to obey.

Tuk shares a tense look with Ilapara. "We should probably get on that ship," he says.

"I think we should," she agrees.

They proceed to insinuate themselves onto the *Rapiere* before it takes off. A few of the armored warriors give them dirty looks, but no one tries to stop them. They do steer clear of Salo, however, watching him from a distance.

He speaks to no one, a focused frown on his face as he watches the deserts rush by from the forecastle deck. Their low flight path puts them just within visual range of one of the ruins littered across the desert, this one a circle of seven pillars with no other structures in the vicinity.

The pillars soon slip out of view, and the windcraft slows as it makes a pass over a village of unbaked mud brick dwellings with flat roofs. The *Rapiere*'s shadow covers the whole village as it flies by; then the ship turns slowly to begin circling the settlement like an eagle investigating a chicken coop.

Ilapara goes with Tuk to stand by the railings on the starboard side for a better view of the village. Her stomach drops at the unexpected activity she sees; mothers abandoning their chores to usher their frightened children into their houses, men rushing to fetch their spears. She expected a small camp of rebels, perhaps, but there's every indication that this is a thriving community.

She throws caution to the wind and goes to talk some sense into Salo. He's still standing near the prow of the vessel, looking down as the ship flies in a slow circle.

"Salo, what are you going to do?"

"Those people need to be taught a lesson," he answers without turning around.

"You've invaded their homeland and made yourself king," Ilapara argues. "Of course they're fighting back."

"They're standing in the way of justice. They must be destroyed."

Ilapara gapes, unable to believe her ears. "There are children down there, for Ama's sake! Families! Innocents!"

"Innocents?" Salo finally looks at her, and the seething fury in his eyes nearly pushes her back. "I've tasted rivers of innocent tears. I've seen oceans of innocent blood shed by the wicked. I've lived innumerable innocent deaths and heard their endless cries for justice, cries that weigh on my soul every waking moment of my life. I know innocence better than you ever could, so don't speak to me of it."

Stunned, Ilapara does nothing when Salo brushes past her and approaches Gregoire and his armored captain.

"Tell your people to fire on the village. Raze everything to the ground."

In a way, what follows shocks Ilapara more than witnessing the destruction of Apos, where millions of people died. Here she saw children fleeing into the houses, some young enough that they needed to be carried inside, and now she has a clear view of those same houses crumbling beneath a fusillade of sunfire shot from the freely rotating artillery weapons mounted onto the vessel's keel.

Some of the villagers are fast enough to escape the rain of destruction, but a redhawk swoops down from out of nowhere, cutting off their escape. Ilapara doesn't look away when it pins a man to the ground and rips him in half with its beak.

She jumps at the gentle hand that settles on her back, but it's just Tuk seeking to comfort her even though his own eyes are wet.

"That thing is not Salo," she hisses, gripping the handrail so tightly it hurts. "I don't know what it is, but it's not him."

Tuk doesn't say anything, but he doesn't have to. They both know she's right.

And all at once everything becomes simple. All the branching paths before her cohere into one obvious choice.

He's watching the destruction from farther astern. He won't see her coming.

She reaches for the knives in her boots and approaches. She's already halfway there.

"Ilapara, wait."

She twists one wrist, and a spectral shield of scarlet light bursts around her from her enchanted bracelet. Salo himself wove the magic of that bracelet, but it doesn't matter. That Salo is long gone. This one is a mistake she's about to make right.

She's almost there, almost close enough to lunge and slip her blade into his neck, but Tuk barrels into her from behind and brings her down to the deck.

She shakes free of him so she can finish what she started, but Salo is looking at her now, and a pair of armored guards falls on her so fast, too fast, seizing her arms so she can't move. She shouts uselessly at Tuk, hot tears blinding her eyes.

"I'm . . . I'm sorry," he stammers. "I couldn't . . . I can't . . . forgive me."

She screams again, this time at the thing wearing Salo's face, struggling against the guards, but even with her shield still active, their grips might as well be iron fetters.

"After everything we've been through," says the pretender, and he has the gall to look betrayed, "you would stab me in the back?"

"You are *not* Salo," she spits at him. "He would have died a thousand deaths before he did what you've done here."

"The man you knew was weak. Indecisive. I'm doing what's necessary for the greater good."

"The greater good?" Ilapara says. "Does this sound like our friend to you?" she asks, turning to Tuk. How could he betray her like this?

"He's changed," Tuk bargains, struggling to look at her, "but maybe he's confused or being mind controlled. Maybe he needs us to save him from himself."

"I'm glad I still have a friend I can trust," the thing says, then sneers at Ilapara. "As for you." He glares at the guards holding her. "Throw her overboard."

She isn't surprised, but Tuk's eyes nearly come out of their sockets. "What? Salo, you can't do that! She's your friend! Our friend!"

Despite his protests, the guards move to comply with the pretender's order, dragging Ilapara to the rail. She knew she was probably going to die even if she succeeded, but fear unlike any she's known grips her in her final moments.

She doesn't struggle. She won't give them the satisfaction.

"Salo, please, I'm begging you!" Tuk yells. "Don't do this."

"She tried to kill me. If you hadn't stopped her, she might have succeeded. She can't be trusted."

"No!"

Ilapara plummets, tossed over the rail. She thinks she's finished, but something catches one of her legs before she hits the ground.

"Ilapara!"

She opens her eyes, and the scream she releases comes out of her like someone reached into her gullet and wrenched it out. Were it not for her spectral shield, the redhawk's talon might have pierced her leg.

417

Its grip around the leg is sure, however, and the ground recedes from them so quickly it seems they are falling upward.

She can't be sure how long they climb, how long she shrieks in the redhawk's clutch, but it's long enough that the air becomes thin and the arching dome of the sky deepens its shade of blue.

She screams some more, they climb, and then the redhawk lets go.

25: Alinata

The Faraswa Desert

Alinata is a streak of black feathers above the desert, the Void a thick cocoon around her, the world below a blur of rusty dunes. Ahead of her a figure sheathed in scarlet light tumbles through the sky like a malaika cast out of heaven. She draws her ravens together until she's a needle cutting through the air at a slight incline, and she accelerates.

The Void's embrace is almost crushing. She's used it to kill many times before, each use sanctioned by her queen, from whom she draws her power. Never has she strayed from the path set for her; never has she questioned an order or disobeyed. She's been the perfect apprentice since she was raised to the position.

Until now.

There will be consequences for her transgression; this much she knows. But she's made her choice and will face what comes when it comes. For now, she belongs to the Void, and the Void belongs to her.

It is cold and indifferent, but it welcomes her without judgment, demanding nothing from her but the recognition of her own insignificance, the nothingness of her being, and the inevitability of time. In return, it gives her power.

But she isn't alone in the skies. A fast-moving ball of flame has left plumes of its circular flight high above her, where her ravens could never reach. It might have already sensed her presence, and if it attacks, Alinata knows she will stand little chance of survival.

She accelerates and reaches out. She tears through the sky like a javelin. She draws so much power the queen will surely sense it and know that she's been disobeyed. But Alinata reaches out anyway, becoming the Void, becoming time itself and all it has seen.

Ahead of her, sheathed in moonlight, Ilapara tumbles from the skies, but the clouds do not cushion her fall. She tumbles and falls and the earth rushes to meet her, death waiting in its bosom. She plummets and screams, but Alinata is there, and she accelerates, and she reaches out, and she yanks her out of the sky.

The redhawk's screech hits them like a shock wave.

Alinata knows she can't outrun the beast, so she spreads herself thinner, summoning a burst of power to temporarily become insubstantial, folding her ravens back into the Void. Alone she might have sustained the feat for as long as she needed to. With Ilapara in tow, they have only a few minutes.

She flies toward the rock formations in the south, which descend into sandstone canyons that might give them shelter. But in no time the redhawk brightens the sky above her with its aura of flame, and suddenly it tucks its wings and dives down, burning its way through Alinata's incorporeal form.

No fire or weapon could harm her in this form, but the redhawk's passage unbalances her like she's a tiny sailboat caught in the wake of a much larger ship. She nearly loses control of the magic keeping her aloft but somehow holds herself steady and makes it to the canyons.

The redhawk gives chase.

This part of the desert is a maze. Alinata speeds deeper into the winding gullies, trying to lose the pursuing bird among the vertical cliff walls. As her grip on her immaterial form begins to loosen, she makes a desperate plunge into a ravine barely wide enough for a person to walk through. The redhawk is so close behind her it banks away too late, grazing a nearby outcrop and causing echoes of falling rock.

Inside the narrow gully, Alinata slows to a stop and drops out of the Void. So does Ilapara, whose eyes immediately widen.

"You!"

"Yes. Me," Alinata says. "I know. You probably have a *lot* you want to say to me, but for Ama's sake, hold it in until we escape the giant bird trying to kill us."

"You—" Ilapara's nostrils flare as she inhales a calming breath. "Fine. But when this is over, you and I are going to—"

Sensing movement, Alinata covers Ilapara's mouth with a hand. "Shh."

The redhawk lands just outside the entrance to the narrow gully, then peers in with one eye. At the sight of it Alinata's skin crawls with revulsion; something looks wrong about that eye. A disease or some other corruption seems to have infested it, creating many little pits and clusters of holes around the glowing pupil. Deathly quiet, she and Ilapara inch away from the creature, deeper into the gully.

The redhawk screeches at them, the cacophony so loud they have to cover their ears. It leaps upward, and seconds later there's a thud as it lands on the cliffs above, peering down at them through the narrow opening between the walls of the gully.

They both crouch lower, bracing their hands against the smooth sandstone walls for support.

"Now what?" Ilapara whispers, looking up at the beast.

"Now we hope it gets tired of us and flies off," Alinata says, which earns her a glare from the other woman.

"Great plan, Alinata. Outstanding."

"Do you want to fight it?"

Ilapara doesn't answer the question. She simply glares some more, then looks back up. "What if it doesn't go away?"

"It'll have to, eventually."

"So it's a waiting game."

"Unless you have a better idea."

No suggestions are forthcoming, so they both stay put, preparing to outwait the redhawk.

Alinata can hardly believe this is the same young woman she lived with in Yonte Saire. The nose piercing is still there, and so is the kohl and black lip paint, but she's not hiding her crimson dreadlocks beneath a veil anymore, and gone are the billowing Umadi robes and the breast-plate that was practically glued to her chest. She's actually showing skin now—her top looks like it's a length of crimson silk wrapped creatively around her chest.

Something else that hasn't changed, Alinata notes with an inward smile. Ilapara always did love the color red.

A wave of weariness envelops Alinata without warning, forcing a gasp out of her. The air seems to turn gelatinous, and her limbs become sluggish, like they weigh a hundred pounds. The red steel jewelry adorning her wrists and neck and forehead turns against her, becoming heavy and strange.

Ilapara frowns at her. "What is it?"

She stares at her bracelets, which she's worn since she became an Asazi. She would laugh if her throat didn't feel constricted. "The queen has withdrawn her blessing from me."

Ilapara blinks, her mouth making several false starts; then she looks up, where the redhawk still watches them. "Of all the times to lose your power, Alinata, you choose now?"

"We're lucky we even got as far as we did." In truth, Alinata wasn't even sure she'd reach the desert before she lost her blessing.

Ilapara gives her a searching look. "I take it you're not supposed to be here."

Not trusting herself to speak, Alinata simply shakes her head, and they proceed to wait in silence while the redhawk tries to scratch its way in. Its attention span proves surprisingly short, however, and after less than a half hour it loses interest and takes off, echoes of its booming flight filling the canyons like the music of a thunderstorm.

"I think it's gone," Alinata says as the echoes taper off. "But it might not be safe to come out just yet."

"Agreed." Ilapara still looks up like she expects the redhawk is hiding and will show itself again.

"Nice boots, by the way," Alinata says. When the compliment fails to thaw the other woman's icy demeanor, Alinata sighs, resigning herself to the inevitable. "I see you have things to get off your chest. Go on, then. I'm listening."

For whatever reason, this wasn't the right thing to say. "You're listening?" Ilapara repeats. "*You're* listening? The gall. I'm not the one doing the talking here. *You* owe *me* an explanation. Why, Alinata? Why did you do it?"

"Why did I do what?"

"Don't play dumb with me."

"Why did I do what I was told? Why did I follow orders? Because I'm the queen's apprentice, Ilapara. Following orders is what I'm supposed to do. It's what I've always done."

"Even when the orders are immoral?"

"I don't get to make that kind of evaluation."

"You're a grown woman," Ilapara scoffs. "You can think for yourself."

"That's what you don't get," Alinata tells her. "When you swear fealty to the queen, she becomes your moral authority. You defer to her judgment in all things because you trust that she knows better, and even when you don't understand, you obey, because you believe she won't lead you astray. That's how it's supposed to be." Alinata's eyes fall to the bangles on her wrists, her voice losing its conviction. "But sometimes, it isn't like that at all, and by the time you realize, it's already too late."

Ilapara's eagle-eyed stare doesn't relent. "You knew Salo was going to die. From the very beginning, you knew."

"Yes."

"And you didn't stop it. In fact, you helped make it happen."

Alinata sighs again. "I did."

"For almost two moons you colluded with the Arc to manipulate Salo into a trap, knowing he was going to die."

From reporting his movements to both the queen and the Arc, to leaving one of his skimmers in the sewers for the investigators to find, to persuading him to go out onto the streets on the night of the Requiem Moon—they could spend hours dissecting the manipulations Alinata partook in during their time in Yonte Saire. But what would that gain them?

"What's your point?" she asks, losing her patience.

"You had enough time! You had *more* than enough time to realize what you were doing was wrong, so don't give me this 'I was just following orders' crap. I don't believe it."

Bitterness slides down Alinata's throat like bile, and she struggles fiercely against a wave of tears. She won't cry. Crying would be pathetic. "You'd never understand. You're the only person you've ever truly believed in. You see what you want and you go for it, because it's what *you* want."

"Are you calling me selfish?"

"I'm saying you've never trusted someone so implicitly as to believe everything they tell you. I believed in the queen and her vision for our tribe's future. She told me Salo was dangerous and that it was ultimately better to sacrifice him and use what he'd built for the tribe, and I believed her, because why wouldn't I? I had no reason to question her."

"But you lived with Salo long enough to form your own opinion of him," Ilapara argues.

"Yes, and I witnessed with my own eyes just how dangerous he was despite his mild temperament. And I had no way of predicting how he'd change with even more power. Ultimately, he was still an unknown, so I decided to trust the queen. It wasn't until after his death that I realized I'd made a mistake."

Ilapara's face remains twisted with disgust.

"What do you want me to say, Ilapara? That I regret my actions? I do. Bitterly. I wish I'd warned Salo not to set foot anywhere near that temple. But I didn't, and here we are."

There's no forgiveness, not yet, but the hostility starts to ebb from Ilapara. "Here we are indeed." She glances at the mouth of the gully. "We should probably head out."

"Where?" Alinata asks.

"There are settlements of Faraswa people in this desert. I'm also hoping there's a stream somewhere in these canyons. We find the stream, we follow it. Maybe we get lucky."

A desperate plan, but there's not much else they can do now that their mobility has been curtailed. *Ama watch our steps,* Alinata prays, and together they venture out into the open.

The action of water created these ravines, and it's possible streams flowed here in the recent past, but the rocky ground underfoot is dry.

"What are you even doing out here?" Ilapara says as they enter a wide gully whose walls nearly touch at the top, forming a roof. Sunlight pours through in shafts bright enough they look near solid. "Come to think of it, your appearance is suspiciously timely. You showed up precisely when I needed you."

"I saw you fall from the sky in a vision," Alinata confesses, and at Ilapara's sidelong glance she adds, "The tribe's new oracle showed it to me."

"We have an oracle now?"

"A lot has changed over the last year." A breeze whistles into the canyon, making Alinata's pale gown flutter. She suffers a twinge of regret at the reminder that her ravens are forever lost to her. "What about you? Why are you out here? And how on Meza did you wind up falling from the clutches of a redhawk?"

Ilapara gives a humorless grunt. "It's a long story."

"We have time."

"I suppose we do."

It is, in fact, a long story. It is also completely deranged. Each new detail has Alinata nearly losing her footing in shock, and she begins to wonder if Ilapara didn't bump her head too hard back in the gully and somehow lose her wits.

"So you crossed the Jalama to bring Salo back as a machine—"

"An atmech. He's as alive as anyone; he's just . . . not Salo."

"But he looks like Salo?"

"*Exactly* like him," Ilapara says. "I don't know what happened. Tuk said the crystal held his true self, and at first, he really did seem like Salo. His mannerisms, his speech—it *was* him."

"Until Tuk's sister showed up," Alinata says, trying to make sense of the wild tale, "who's also the Crocodile's widow, and she happened to possess a fragment of the Hegemon's crown."

Ilapara looks dubiously at her. "You didn't know she was working with the Arc?"

"I knew he had an ally from across the Jalama, but I never learned the ally's identity."

At the end of the day, Alinata was simply a mouthpiece in Yonte Saire, an intermediary between the queen and the Arc. She relayed their messages to each other and carried out their instructions. She didn't get to ask questions.

"Well, now you know," Ilapara says.

Alinata can hardly believe it. Tuk's sister was the Crocodile's wife *and* the Arc's secret ally, who made off with the third fragment of the Hegemon's crown. What were the odds that she and Tuk were randomly in Yonte Saire at the same time? And why would she then give her fragment to the newly resurrected Salo when she'd played a role in his death?

A heavy sensation settles in the pit of Alinata's stomach. "So you're telling me that the mysterious King of the West is actually a machine wearing Salo's face."

"And he's insanely powerful," Ilapara says. "The things he can do now . . ." She shakes her head. "No one should have that kind of power."

"He's met with the queen. And the emperor. But she didn't see his face. She said he was hiding behind a mask. He stood right in front of her and . . ." Despite everything, Alinata feels a pang of worry for her mentor. "What do you think he's planning?"

"I don't think it's revenge, if that's what you're wondering. He's obsessed with some gate he's trying to open."

"You mean the pyramid," Alinata says.

"Could be. I heard he raised a pyramid out of the desert. But he's missing the key to it, or some such thing."

Alinata frowns at the path ahead, which forks into two canyons, both completely dry. The suns will be setting in a few hours; if they're still trapped in this maze, it'll be a rough night.

"The queen believes unlocking the pyramid will strengthen each fragment of the crown," she says. "That's probably why he needs her and the emperor. He wants more power."

"It can't be that simple," Ilapara says. "Salo's obsession with that gate goes beyond power. To him it's about justice, and the people following him already have all the power and money they could want. I think they believe that gate will change something monumental. I just don't know what."

The shadows grow longer, the maze of dry canyons showing no signs of a stream, an exit, or a village of Faraswa settlers ready to welcome them.

It's quite the novel feeling to Alinata to be stuck somewhere. Is this what it's like to be a regular person? *Time to finish working on my Axiom,* she thinks.

"How's Tuk, by the way?"

"Not good," Ilapara says, and then she does that thing she's done several times already, clutching the little ivory horn-shaped pendants dangling on a string around her neck. Some tension loosens from her shoulders. "He's alive, at least."

Must be some kind of enchantment, Alinata concludes. "I miss that little scoundrel."

"Well, I don't think he misses you."

"I know." Hurts to hear, but it's the truth. "So . . . um, you crossed the Jalama," Alinata says, wanting to change the subject.

"I did." Ilapara gives a weak smile, still fondling her pendants. "I guess that's a thing I get to say now. I crossed the Jalama and lived to tell the tale."

"You're probably the most interesting Yerezi woman alive right now. What's it like on the other side?"

"Amazing. Everything is fast. Everything looks new and shiny. They have floating buildings and ships that can fly." Ilapara's smile had grown somewhat, but it wanes, her eyes reflecting some distant sorrow. "It's all gone now. I watched it burn, a city of millions, destroyed in seconds by a single weapon. Tuk was devastated. The city was his old home."

Is such a thing truly possible? Alinata wonders. "Why? What happened?"

"I couldn't say. Tuk thinks the people now following Salo are responsible. But it all started because of rumors of a new Hegemon."

"You think . . . are you saying Salo had something to do with it?"

Ilapara lets out a heavy breath. "For all I know, Alinata, we all did."

The path begins to descend, and they soon come to an opening wide enough for the afternoon suns to shine unimpeded. A stream of aquamarine water meanders in the wider canyon among numerous shallow pools.

This is what they were hoping to find, and perhaps with it, a settlement nearby, but they both freeze solid at the sight of the creatures frolicking in the water.

"What are those?" Ilapara whispers.

It's a whole pack of them. Slender canid beasts with slick black coats and forked tails that look like serpent tongues. Their long ears stand erect, their eyes carry the glow of burning cinders, and their elongated jaws hold thickets of drooling teeth.

They look like nothing Alinata has seen with her own eyes, but their features are distinct enough for her to recognize from folklore.

"Sha beasts," she whispers back. "This must be their lair."

"Are you sure you're completely out of magic, because we could really use some right now."

"I've got nothing."

One of the beasts perks up and sniffs the air, its erect ears twitching. Alinata and Ilapara don't make any sudden moves, but they both walk backward slowly, retreating into the canyon from which they came.

And then they run.

26: Salim

Far away, a mechanized leopard totem vaults over a fallen tree, startling a group of nesting pheasants. They squawk as they scatter, fluttering off into the surrounding jungles, but the leopard is already gone.

His metal paws leave deep hollows in the soft earth. Trees shudder and the wind wails behind him. He splashes across watering holes, tears through low-hanging spiderwebs, triggers traps laid by hunters. A jungle leopard roars when he races through its territory. He has no interest in fighting it, however, because he's needed elsewhere and won't stop until he's reached his destination.

Aboard the *Ataraxis*, Salim climbs up the stairs to the bridge, his heart beating almost in tandem with the galloping motion of the distant totem. He'd forgotten the thrill of being one with the leopard, but above the thrill is an urgent need to save his friend.

The bridge is a spacious glass-enclosed compartment rising behind the prow, where the floor-to-ceiling windows provide a near-unbroken view of the surrounding night sky.

Aside from the helm—situated at the very front of the compartment and surrounded by an assortment of flight instruments—the bridge also houses the ship's navigation station, as well as weather- and object-detection control panels. Sevan is fast asleep at the helm, awash in a film of red light from the low-hanging gibbous moon.

"Sevan!"

Startled, she bolts up, her chair swiveling, blanket falling to the ground. One of her hands flies to the typhon on her hip, but she stops just short of pulling it out when she sees Salim.

She exhales in relief and falls back onto the chair. "Suns above, I was having a nightmare! I could've shot you!"

"Sorry," Salim says, tapping his thighs in an anxious rhythm. "I'm a little tense. Which is why I'm here, actually. I need your help."

Sevan lets out another breath, leaning back into her chair. "What's on your mind?"

"I'm preoccupied right now, so I need you to take over flying this ship." Salim approaches the navigation station, a round surface in the middle of the compartment. Charts and maps of Mirror light float nearly flush with the surface. "Please take us to these coordinates," he says as he enters data onto the station's brass interface. "My friend is in trouble and needs immediate assistance. In the meantime, I'm going to see about getting us to fly faster." He taps the last key and turns around to leave the bridge. "Thank you, Sevan. And please ask Priscille and Balam to meet me in the engine room as soon as they can."

He's reached the stairs when Sevan finally speaks. "Uhhh, excuse me?"

Salim stops, one foot down a step. "Yes?"

After swiveling her chair to face him, Sevan plants her feet flat on the ground and steeples her fingers. The vulpine smile on her face doesn't crinkle her eyes. "First of all, Captain Salim, are you insane? Have you lost your mind?"

Her tone doesn't amuse him. "I need to be doing a million things right now, Sevan. I can't afford to fly the ship too."

"And you think *I* can?"

"You said you wanted to be my second-in-command!"

"Yes, while *you* fly the ship!"

Salim blinks at her for a long moment, then retracts his foot from the stairs. "Are you saying you don't actually know how to fly a ship?"

"Where would I have learned? I'm a cog, Salim. They don't teach cogs to fly ships!"

His heart sinks. If he has to devote part of himself to keeping this ship afloat, he'll never be able to—

"Wait." An idea blossoms in his mind. "You know what? You're absolutely right."

"I know!"

"No. I mean, about us being cogs. We're part machine, and maybe it's time we started acting like it."

Sevan turns her head to look sideways at Salim. "What do you mean?"

"We all have crystal cores that can process large sets of data," he says. "They don't let you access those abilities, but I've broken your restraints and I have a metaform in my mind, so we should be able to share information with each other. There's no reason you can't tap into my understanding of how this ship works."

Sevan narrows her eyes a bit. "But how would I do that?"

"Reach for the signal between us," Salim tells her. "Let it know what you want. I'll allow you to take from me what you need."

"I meant, how—" Sevan freezes in her seat, the signal between her and Salim strengthening. Information flows between their crystal cores at the speed of lightning: concepts, diagrams, schematics, ciphermetric expressions, every scrap of knowledge Salim has gathered about the ship's flight systems.

"Oh," she says with visible surprise. She swivels to face the helm and eyes the controls with a new interest. "Oh suns, this is marvelous. All these buttons make sense now."

"Great." Salim starts descending the stairs. "Maintain speed and altitude until I tell you otherwise. And remember to ask Balam and Priscille to meet me in the engine room as soon as they can."

Sevan gives an evil chuckle as she reaches for the ship-wide communicator. "Yes, Captain."

On his way down to the engine room, Salim sends a part of himself into Ziyo's construct, appearing on the porch to the Storm craft archive, where a leopard formed out of red lightning rests on a pedestal of ice.

He immediately crosses the walkway to the pavilion at the center of the library. Too anxious to sit, he pushes all the furniture to one side with a thought, clearing up space in the middle.

"Ziyo, I need to know Jomo's situation. Give me something like the undercity mirage we used to rescue the king."

The construct silently obeys, and the mirage nearly fills the pavilion, a vision rendered in shades of red, with Jomo at the center. Somewhere in the jungles of the Yontai, he and five other people have holed up in a cave and barred the entrance with a shimmering kinetic barrier.

But they're under siege. Over a hundred enemies have surrounded the cave, among them mystics attempting to weaken the barrier with a salvo of destructive spells. Salim watches a spear of moonfire slam into the barrier, causing the ground to quake.

In the cave, Jomo has positioned himself with three other youths some distance away from the entrance, facing the barrier. To Salim's surprise, they're all armed with typhonic weapons of various makes and seem ready to fire at whatever comes in when the barrier falls.

Now how the devil did they get their hands on typhons? Salim wonders.

"Ziyo, what's generating that barrier?"

Two metal rods placed near the mouth of the cave begin to glow white. *Both linchpins have degraded significantly. If the current assault*

continues, the static force field will collapse in less than fifteen minutes."
Ziyo paints a third rod placed deeper into the cave with a similar glow.
"They have also activated an antitransposition ward to prevent circumvention of the barrier through the Void. This ward has not sustained damage and remains strong."

Salim folds his arms, pushing the tip of his tongue into the gap between his teeth. His totem is still galloping. The *Ataraxis* is still thousands of miles away. Fifteen minutes isn't going to be enough. Not even close.

"We need to buy them more time," he thinks aloud.

Ziyo possesses the ability to cast basic spells of Mirror and Void craft—illusions, sounds, a permeable field that repels the lingering Corruption of a city-destroying weapon, if Salim's own metaform is anything to go by.

A barrier of the kind needed here, however, is simply beyond the metaform's abilities.

"Ziyo, I need you to project me into the cave. I assume you can give me a voice."

"Ziyo can create vibrations in the air to simulate your vocal cords."

"Do it."

Once again Salim's perception splits, and he's abruptly in four places at once: galloping through the jungles, navigating to the engine room on the *Ataraxis*, standing in the pavilion in Ziyo's construct, and now, materializing as a life-size apparition in the cave in front of Jomo and his beleaguered allies.

His mind is already straining; he doesn't think his old human self would have successfully juggled this many perceptions. But with his new metaformic aspect, he's able to keep the perceptions intact. To make things easier, he pares down Ziyo's flood of omnidirectional sensory data so that he feels like he's actually standing in the cave, seeing through a pair of eyes and hearing through a pair of ears.

"They're through!" shouts one of the youths standing with Jomo, raising his typhon.

"Odari, wait!" Jomo shouts, but the young man named Odari has already opened fire. So have the others. They pelt Salim's specter with a volley of moonfire, but as he's a mirage, the volley passes through him and strikes the barrier.

"Stop, you idiots!" Jomo shouts. "It's him! It's Salo!"

Jomo's comrades stop firing, taking a second look. Their eyes widen in recognition.

"Peace, my friends," Salim says. "I'm not your enemy."

They lower their typhons, bewildered. "By the Mother," Odari mutters. "It *is* you. But . . . how are you here?"

Salim can't say he remembers Odari or the other two youths. Perhaps they were among the Sentinels he met in the Red Temple. Thinking that perhaps his apparition is too solid, he weakens its intensity so that he is semitransparent and more obviously an illusion.

"He's not here," Jomo realizes. "He's beaming himself from the ruby in my pocket. I told you he was back." Jomo nods at Salim with a smile and a question in his eyes. "Salo?"

"Not yet," Salim replies. "Soon, I hope." That gets him a few confused stares. He glances at the linchpins barring the mouth of the cave. "Your barrier is about to fall."

"We know," says Jomo. "Anything you can do to help?"

A violent spell hits the barrier right then, making the ground rumble. Loose dust and rocks fall from the roof of the cave.

"I can't do much from my side," Salim tells them. "But I can take control of the barrier to make it drain less power. I'll put it up only precisely when it's needed but keep it off the rest of the time. That will extend its life by quite a bit."

From deeper within the cave comes a frowning woman in a black robe too dignified for her surroundings. A man with prominent sideburns shadows her quietly.

"Hold on a second," she says. "Who is this person, Bwana Jomo? How did he get past our ward?"

"He's a friend," Jomo replies with a note of weariness. "A very good friend. And he's trying to save our lives, so be nice."

"But what he's suggesting simply won't work. Taking down the barrier will only invite them closer. And what if he doesn't put it back up in time? We can't take that risk."

"Agreed," says the man with the sideburns. "It's a bad idea anyway. Repeated activations will quickly degrade the enchantment."

Jomo makes a defeated gesture, shaking his head at Salim. "Meet our resident arcanists. They've never agreed on anything, up until this very moment."

"Well." The woman lifts her chin. "We're both right, in this case."

"Or maybe you're not," Jomo retorts. "You're looking at the man who pulled off the undercity prison break. He's the sneakiest bastard I've ever met, and if he says he can do something, I'm going to trust that he can."

The mystics both regard Salim anew, but their skepticism remains.

"Ziyo will maintain the illusion that the barrier is still up," Salim offers. "I'll also scramble the area in case your enemies possess ciphermetric devices that might see through the mirage."

"Do whatever you need to do," Jomo decides. "Even if you fail, we're dead anyway. And I don't hear anyone else coming up with ideas."

Not willing to waste any more time, Salim turns around and works with Ziyo to take control of the barrier. The change is smooth and instantaneous; to the naked eye, there's no visible difference, and when the next spell hits, it crashes against a shimmering wall of force that appears to remain in place. Only Salim knows that the true wall materialized just long enough to intercept the projectile, then disappeared again.

"What are you waiting for?" Jomo asks. "Do the thing."

"It's done," Salim says, turning back around.

Nearly everyone gives the barrier a doubtful glance. "But there's no difference," Jomo says.

"That's the point."

He blinks, then laughs. "I told you he was sneaky."

"All right," the woman grudgingly allows. "So your ploy seems to have worked. But what now?"

"Now you hold on awhile longer," Salim tells them. "Help is on the way."

"I'd give you a big smooch if you were here," Jomo says.

"You can save that for later." Salim looks to the side as one of his other perceptions demands more attention. "I have to leave temporarily, but I'll be watching. Just call me if you need anything."

The fatalism that had taken up residence in Jomo's eyes doesn't quite disappear, but his smile is genuine. "Thank you, my friend."

In the sweltering engine room of the *Ataraxis*, Salim has invited Priscille and Balam to take a closer look at the arrangement of vertical coils surrounding the ship's power source: an essence-saturated red crystal the size of a boulder.

Everything here, every coil and lever, every pipe and valve, was designed to facilitate the conversion of the crystal's raw essence into the crafts of magic required by the cylinders in the crystal hub down the hall.

Salim crouches next to an open panel box beneath one of the coils. "Do you see these?" he says, pointing at the ordered set of tubelike components bolted onto the panel. "I need you to remove them from the three boxes I opened. I don't know what they're called. Inhibitors, maybe."

"Regulators," Balam corrects. "They prevent the engine from feeding too much power to the crystal hub. Prevents explosions." He lifts a bushy eyebrow. "Did you say you want us to remove them?"

Salim nods. "I'm so glad you understand. The sooner you start, the better."

Priscille straightens up, tucking a strand of mousy hair into her floral headscarf. "Wait, so these things keep the ship from exploding?"

"Normally, yes," Salim says.

"Then if we remove them, won't we explode?"

"I doubt he's trying to kill us," Balam says. "Perhaps if we let him explain himself."

"I'm not trying to kill us," Salim agrees. "But I'm about to change how the ship flies, and the inhibitors—regulators—will only get in the way."

"But why?" Priscille asks. "Isn't the ship already flying as it should?"

"We need to go faster. My friend needs my help, and I need yours."

Priscille and Balam share a look; then Priscille exhales with resignation, softening it with a smile. "We'll help as best as we can, Salim."

"Thank you! The wrenches are in that cabinet over there. Whatever you do, don't touch the coils. And remember, only focus on the panels in the three boxes I opened. Leave the others alone. Let me know if you have any problems."

"Where are you going?" Balam calls.

Salim is already halfway to the hatch. "To change the spells in the crystal hub," he replies. *And hopefully I'll replace them with the right spells so I don't get us all killed.*

Back in the Yontai, a blast rocks the cave so badly Jomo is almost knocked off balance. To those outside, the wall of force barring the entrance remains strong, but even with Ziyo's intervention, the true barrier is in shambles. The linchpins have started to release showers of red sparks as the enchantment buckles under the pressure.

In the construct, Salim splits his awareness yet again, but this time he separates his human self from his metaformic aspect: while the first continues to monitor the mirage in the pavilion, the other enters a deeper and more abstract communion with Ziyo.

The construct dissolves into a white void in which he's the only inhabitant. Here he need not speak for Ziyo to know what he wants; a silent conversation flows between their cores instantaneously, the push and pull of numbers as they run multiple calculations and simulations based on the ship's design parameters.

While this is happening, another fragment of Salim walks through an aisle between impossibly tall shelves, rectangular spell plates flying off the shelves and swirling around him in a chaotic vortex. Spells of motion, spells of flame, spells of lightning, all the spells he thinks he might need to save his friend.

He plucks a plate from the whirlwind, scans the many little ciphers carved onto its metallic surface, then lets it go, the spell instantly learned and memorized. He plucks another one, then another, on and on until he hears Sevan's alarmed voice addressing him through his bracer tool.

"Salim, what are you doing in the engine room? The thermal readings are going off kilter."

He comes back to the fragment of himself on the *Ataraxis*, who, as it happens, is in the middle of operating the main console in the crystal hub, fingers tapping away at the brass keys as he primes the ship for the imminent change.

"It'll be fine in a while," he says. "I'm about to make some changes to how the ship works."

"But if you change the ship, I won't know how to fly it anymore."

"I'll send over the new specifications shortly, the same way I did it the first time."

"That wasn't exactly pleasant, but fine. Warn me in advance."

"Understood." Salim adjusts his bracer tool and connects to Balam. "How far?"

Balam takes a second to reply. *"Almost. Just one more to go."* He grunts before he speaks again. *"There. It's done."*

"Thank you, Balam. Now get Priscille out of the engine room. There might be a dangerous surge in a moment."

"Noted."

All the ship's enchantments are finely tuned spells of Higher Red magic, which Salim now understands is powerful due to its efficiency, complexity, and precision. With Higher Red operating in the cylinders, making the smallest adjustments to speed or altitude is trivial, and the ship is thus much easier to maneuver.

But for all that fine control, Higher Red has a lower threshold for instability and cannot easily scale itself up to handle more extreme volumes of power. By contrast, its Lower Red counterpart, though comparatively unwieldy, can drink as much power as is available without losing its integrity.

Salim makes the changes one at a time and to only three of the cylinders in the hub, keeping the rest as they are since they already work just fine and won't be affected by the modifications Balam and Priscille made to the engine room.

First, he takes control of the cylinder responsible for launching projectiles of moonfire out of the ship's artillery. The weapons will be useless afterward, but their positioning along the sides of the hull makes them ideal for his purposes.

Standing next to the cylinder, he engages his cosmic shards, summoning a spell of Fire craft from the lattices of his mind. Essence flows into him more forcefully than he expects, as though his body has become a cosmic conductor.

He doesn't revel in the sensation. He redirects his power and releases the spell.

"Salim, the artillery is gone. We're weaponless. What did you do?"

"I'm a bit busy right now," Salim says into his bracer tool. "I'll get back to you in a moment."

He casts his next spell on the cylinder maintaining the external kinetic shield, giving it a much stronger replacement of Lower Red Void craft. And while its predecessor was more or less ovoid in shape, the new shield bears a very specific, deliberate profile.

His efforts cause a small explosion in the engine room.

"I'm losing control of critical systems."

Ignoring Sevan, he makes the last change, enchanting yet another cylinder with Lower Red Void craft to fortify the network of stabilizers that dampen the effects of acceleration on the ship's interior, working against gravity to almost completely nullify any tilting sensation.

This time a violent jolt ripples through every deck, all the lamps going off, plunging the crystal hub into darkness. Salim loses his footing and almost hits his head on a metal bar as he crashes to the floor. He tries to get up, but the *Ataraxis* trembles again, the room sloping downward. He's beginning to panic when the lights come back on and the floor rights itself and stills.

"That was . . . frightening," comes Sevan's voice through the ship-wide communicator. *"But I'm in control, so nobody panic."* She switches to Salim's bracer tool. *"The thermals are stabilizing, Salim, but the engines are putting out way too much power. Alarms are going off everywhere. What'd you do?"*

Still on the floor, Salim allows himself a moment to catch his breath. "Instructions incoming. Get us to maximum speed immediately." And once again he allows Sevan to draw from him his understanding of the ship's controls and specifications.

After a momentary silence, her voice comes back shaken. *"Salim . . . this is crazy."*

"I know."

"Can the shields handle this?"

He thinks about lying, but he can't bring himself to do it. "I hope so, Sevan."

"Well, what's life without a little risk? Or a lot, as it would seem." She switches to the ship-wide communicator. *"Everyone, find somewhere comfortable. Or say your last prayers. We're about to do something stupid."*

◆ ◆ ◆

The idea came to him as he watched his redhawk burn its way back into the sky. Here was a creature that weighed probably as much as ten men, if not more, and yet it propelled itself to such speeds it could exceed the sound of its own flight several times over.

How? Salim wondered.

The answer, as he worked out in the end, is simple. By rapidly shedding a cloak of moonfire that ceaselessly replenishes itself, the redhawk generates a propulsive force considerable enough to escape the world's atmosphere and enter the deep black. The hardest part for the bird is withstanding the immense heat as well as the incredible forces of its own acceleration and being streamlined enough to present little resistance to the motion of air—all specifications that figured prominently into Salim's redesign of the crystal hub.

Now Sevan flicks a switch on the helm console, activating the network of nodes that once fed flames into the artillery. Except no weapons go off; instead, a shroud of moonfire explodes to life all around the external shield, ejecting a constant, high-velocity stream of blistering-hot particulates toward the rear of the ship.

Enveloped in flame, the *Ataraxis* leaps forward with sudden and tremendous urgency, and only through the action of the strengthened internal stabilizers does the vessel not tear itself apart under the force.

The floor rumbles beneath Salim. On his way to the stairs, heart pumping with the fury of a beating drum, he pauses in the halo of angry white-red light pouring in through a starboard porthole. The new kinetic shield is a deltoid shape that more closely hugs the vessel's avian structure, curving so close to the hull the flames appear just inches away from the porthole. The thunder of the flames must surely be terrific, but the shield is strong enough to muffle the sound to a tolerable thrum.

What would the ship even look like to someone outside? Salim wonders.

Sevan's voice cuts into his thoughts. *"We're going to have to climb higher if you want us to keep accelerating. A lot higher. There's too much air resistance down here."*

"The shields can handle it," Salim says, still peering out the porthole. "Take us as high as you need."

Sevan switches to the ship-wide communicator so that Balam and Priscille can hear her. *"You should all come up to the bridge. You won't believe the view."*

"I'm on my way," he says.

Outside, the cloak of flames intensifies. The floors gently tilt, Sevan pitching the nose of the ship upward, and the *Ataraxis* continues to accelerate, burning its way higher into the heavens like a redhawk.

"Warning," Ziyo says in the construct. *"The next attack will overload the barrier."*

In the Yontai, the emperor's forces have ramped up their assault on the barrier. Salim's intervention certainly extended its life, but under the increased pressure, the barrier has reached its limits.

While his other self walks up to the bridge, the fragment of him in the construct watches the mirage with a tensed jaw. All his senses are alive. He feels like he could run fast enough to take off. What the devil kind of heart did his creator give him? He bites the nails on one hand, tapping a foot on the floor, waiting for the inevitable.

And then it comes, the next spell hitting the barrier and causing the enchantment to fail with such violence the linchpins burst open in plumes of smoke. The shimmering force field disappears, and a loud cheer rings outside.

The faces of Jomo and his friends fall with despair. "Courage, brothers!" he shouts, raising his sidearm with a trembling hand. "The odds were always against us. Let's not be cowards now. We shoot anything that comes in, or we die fighting."

Salim admires the way the Sentinels stand with Jomo, taking strength from each other, facing the now-open entrance with their weapons aimed, ready to die fighting. But an earsplitting roar fills the cave with its terrible echo, and then their eyes go wide and feverish with fear.

From their vantage points they can't see who or indeed *what* is outside the cave, but a blur of white and copper flashes past the entrance, and then they hear screams of terror coming from the surrounding woods. They wait in breathless silence, their typhons aimed and ready, but no legionnaires or spell-slinging mystics march in. Instead, another roar menaces the jungles.

"What the devil is that?" whispers the arcanist with the sideburns, speaking like he's afraid the thing outside might overhear him.

Jomo blinks, incredulous. "Mother damn me to the pits, but I believe that's the help Salo promised us."

Outside the cave, Mukuni roars again.

On the weather deck of the *Ataraxis*, the ship's blazing shield arches over Salim's head like a glass roof beneath a firestorm. Jets of red-white flames sprint rearward along the shield's contours, turning the deck as bright as the inside of a furnace. But the shield's insulation is such that he can't feel any of that heat, and the wail of the firestorm has been so well mitigated it's little louder than a low drone.

It's still unsettling, so he hurries up the slightly inclined deck to the bridge, where he finds Priscille and Balam strapped onto seats behind the helm and its pilot, all three of them outlined against the fiery view outside the windows.

"Everyone all right?" he asks as he settles down by the weather-detection console.

"Of course!" Sevan replies hysterically, a death grip on the wheel. "Why wouldn't we be? It's not like I'm flying a burning ship and can't see for shit out the windows."

"Language, Sevan," Priscille scolds her, though the nervous tremor in her own voice is hard to miss.

"Yes, it's my *language* that'll kill us," Sevan retorts. "Not the inferno right outside our very thin windows."

"You have instruments," Salim reminds her. "And the fire is on the shield, not the windows."

"Oh yeah? It's still insane! This isn't normal, all right?"

"It's like being in the eye of a storm," Priscille murmurs. She has a palm resting on her bosom, her almost unblinking stare out the windows halfway between wonder and terror. "It's so peaceful in here, but out there . . ."

"Out there it's death," Balam finishes for her. He turns his head to look at Salim. "Back at the mines, I once heard that if we dug far enough into the world, we'd reach a realm of liquid fire. Have we dived into the center of the world?"

Sevan answers that with a delirious laugh. "You're all about to see *exactly* where we are. Ending acceleration burn in three . . . two . . . one . . ."

At the turn of a switch, the network of nodes generating the ship's cloak of moonfire goes dormant, and the flames around the shield die out. And so does the noise.

"Do you feel that?" Balam says in the sudden stillness.

By reflex, Salim's hands fly to the armrests of his seat. He feels himself lift off his chair, drawn miraculously upward. The sensation is like being weightless. It *is* weightlessness, in fact; it's floating, being completely detached from the chain of gravity, and Salim isn't the only one affected.

"Suns above," Priscille utters, clinging to her armrests.

"Enjoy it while it lasts," Sevan warns everyone, though she keeps herself in place.

On an impulse, Salim lets go of his chair and pushes himself toward the windows. Priscille gasps as he glides; he underestimates how fast he'll move and ends up having to catch himself on a metal strut before he crashes into the window.

"Salim!" Priscille cries. "Are you all right?"

He almost doesn't hear her. Looking out the windows, where a wall of fire blazed just seconds ago, he sees his own bespectacled reflection from the lights of the dimly lit bridge, and beyond that reflection, a dream more beautiful than anything he could ever create in a construct.

The *Ataraxis* has climbed so high the curvature of the world is now apparent. The suns are bright jewels just beginning to dawn over the blue-white horizon, a tapestry of seas, continents, and beds of clouds sprawling out below. Only a few stars are still bright enough to be visible, but the sight of them against the empty sky awakens Salim to a truth he learned in the inner sanctum.

Once, there were vessels that could sail into the deep black, so many they could light up the sky like stars. But then our history was taken from us, and we forgot.

The stark beauty of the world becomes all the more poignant to Salim, and he's filled with a yearning that overwhelms him.

Sevan pulls him out of his thoughts. "It's time to return to your seat, Salim. We'll be heading back down in a moment."

He slips his fingers beneath his lenses to wipe his eyes. "I think I'll head down to the skiff bay," he says, carefully pushing for the exit. "My friend can't hold on for much longer and needs a quick extraction."

When he awoke Mukuni from his slumber near the gates of his kraal, Salim established a bond with the totem that remained strong even after he died and his consciousness was transferred into a crystal.

Yet for all the strength of this bond, there were things that were buried deep within the totem's mind core ages ago, deadly truths he wasn't ever supposed to see. They couldn't be erased, since they were integrated into the cat's structure, but they were so well hidden his old self would have lived a lifetime and never discovered them.

His metaformic aspect saw the walls of prose for what they were and sliced right through them.

Now he unleashes Mukuni at a fire-slinging mystic in orange robes casting her spells from within the trees outside the cave. The legionnaires around her quickly launch spears and shoot arrows at the cat, but the projectiles bounce off his mechanical frame like pins on a wall. He roars and continues to charge, the mane of spines around his neck quivering in a terrifying display. Daunted, the men scatter and the mystic screams, turning to flee.

Mukuni doesn't chase after her. He turns back and charges at another group, seeking to rout them all into the jungles. But after the initial shock of his appearance, the legionnaires reorganize and band together again, rallying around another mystic, this one in crimson robes and a horned mask.

The cat ducks out of the way when the mystic slings a spear of moonfire in his direction, barreling into an unfortunate legionnaire and knocking him down. Mukuni wants to rip and tear into him and bathe the jungles in the blood of the emperor's men, but Salim keeps those impulses in check; so long as the enemy steers clear of the open cave, there needn't be any bloodshed.

But the legionnaires notice his hesitance and become bolder, dispersing only far enough to avoid being run over and then coming back, seeking to surround him, pushing him closer and closer to the cave. Curiosity gets the better of Salim, and he triggers one of the hidden attributes buried in the cat's prose, his instincts knowing only that it might be helpful, though not exactly how.

Mukuni's spines begin to vibrate. He rears up on his hind legs, the blast of a loud horn coming out of his throat. He emits another blast, then another, a series of them rising in pitch and frequency until they come together and detonate in a shock wave.

Legionnaires in red tunics fly off their feet, some slamming into tree trunks. Snakes, spiders, and burrowing insects are flung into the air or crushed against the ground. One man cries out as a disturbed viper sinks its fangs into his ankle. Another runs blindly into a tree when a scorpion lands on his face and stings his eye.

Watching from the construct, Salim takes note of the sudden appearance of these critters and pays more attention to the battlefield. To his despair, and to the horror of those in the cave, the earth outside is crawling. Serpents, scorpions, spiders, ticks, and all manner of poisonous vermin writhe in a sea as they converge upon the cave.

"They're trying to flush us out!" Odari cries.

"Courage, brothers," Jomo shouts, even as he backs away like the others. "Ah, Mother forsake this! Why did it have to be spiders?"

"You're moaning about spiders? I see mambas and cobras in there!"

Salim attempts to replicate Mukuni's explosive shock wave, but the totem's internal machinery hasn't recovered, so all the cat can do is scratch and paw at the vermin. It proves a futile endeavor; for every one of them he crushes or tears apart, a dozen more appear. The plague flows on the ground and reaches the cave, crawling and slithering past the entrance with slow determination.

Jomo and the Sentinels engage their weapons, raining a spray of typhonic bolts onto the plague, but the rate of fire is too slow, the vermin too many. Salim considers hunting for the Blood mystic casting the spell, but there's no time.

"Salo, I don't want to die like this," Jomo mutters. "Salo, are you even there?"

"I'm here, Jomo." Once again Salim's apparition appears in the cave, the plague flowing through his semitransparent legs. In less than a minute everyone there will be buried in vermin. They don't stop firing their weapons.

"If there's something you can do," Jomo says in between shots of his sidearm, "now would be the time."

"I'm waiting," Salim tells him.

"For what?"

The answer comes as a hum that quickly increases in strength until it's as loud as the boom of an approaching redhawk. "Ziyo, turn off the antitransposition ward. Everyone, get closer to each other."

The vermin are now less than a yard away, but the *Ataraxis* is quicker, roaring over the cave in a cloak of fire with Sevan at the helm. Down in the skiff bay, Salim casts a perfectly timed spell of transposition, and in the blink of an eye, Mukuni, Jomo, and the rest of the group fold into the Void and are lifted out of the cave on the currents of a lightning bolt, appearing instantaneously in front of Salim.

"Welcome to the *Ataraxis*," he says. "Is everyone all right?"

They gawk as they attempt to fathom their new surroundings. Jomo gives up eventually and limps toward Salim with the biggest grin on his face.

"You lovely bastard. Come here so I can hug you to death." He embraces Salim, and there are tears shining in his eyes when he lets go. "Mother damn it, Salo. I was certain I was going to die."

"We all were," says the arcanist in the black robes, coming to embrace Salim too. "Thank you," she says with emotion.

Salim is slightly embarrassed by the attention as the rest of the group comes to shake his hand, all plainly relieved to still be alive.

"Is everyone safe and onboard?" comes Sevan's voice from his bracer tool, earning him a few curious frowns.

"Yes, Sevan, they're all here," Salim replies, switching languages. "Thank you for your help."

"No problem. So where to now?"

"I'll let you know in a moment."

Jomo and his people have gone back to looking around the bay. "What the devil is all this?" he says.

"A ship," Salim replies. "I'll tell you all about it soon. But when we spoke earlier, it seemed you had a way of tracking Ilapara."

"I do." Jomo reaches into his dashiki and pulls out the ivory pendant dangling around his neck. "This is one half of a linked pair. She's wearing the other half."

A smile spreads across Salim's face as he studies it. "Then we'll go to her immediately."

PART 6

ANENIKO

*

ILAPARA

*

ALINATA

*

SALIM

27: Aneniko

At dawn, the day after their escape from the cave city of Dahbet, Addi awakens into sun magic in a pool beneath a canyon waterfall. Niko and his crew of rangers look on from the edge of the pool, the four of them outsiders amid a throng of Faraswa people gathered in the canyons. But for all their otherness, they're no less invested in the outcome.

This is what they came here for: to make Addi better. And according to Ayana, awakening should end his seizures. But it might also kill him. And then what would have been the point? To be stripped of the queen's blessing only to lose Addi to his illness? Too terrible for Niko to even think about.

Fourteen others go through the ritual with Addi. Ayana brands each of them with identical hieroglyphs made of a cobalt-blue metal, burning them into their napes with a glowing finger. Most of them wail in pain until she takes the finger off; Niko experiences a trickle of pride when Addi withstands the torment with little more than a flinch.

Standing ankle deep in the pool, Ayana lowers a glass carafe into the water and fills it to the brim. She then addresses Addi and the fourteen others standing in the water with her, speaking in what Niko believes is a mixture of Izumadi and KiYonte. She never struck him as especially cheerful, but there is a coldness about her this morning. She hasn't smiled since the fall of Dahbet.

Without Addi by his side, Niko struggles to understand what she says, but Jio does his best to translate; apparently, it's something about the heavens being aligned in Ishungu's favor since the golden sun will dawn before his white counterpart, so Addi and the others will awaken with the magic of courage rather than truth.

It's all quite strange to Niko, who's never given thought before now to how solar magic might work. He wonders what someone like Nimara would make of such matters and how everyone else back home will react to Addi once they find out he's a solar mystic. Will he still be able to wear red steel? Will the queen even let him?

Never mind that. Will Addi even *want* to go back? Not everyone in the Plains was welcoming to him, so he may very well decide to stay with his own people. And he's seemed happier these last several days. Who would blame him?

Niko snuffs out the burgeoning sting of disappointment, reminding himself why they came here. This journey was never about him; it was about saving Addi's life. And so long as Addi is safe and well, then that's all that matters.

Ayana finishes speaking and faces the waterfall. At some hidden cue, she lifts the carafe over her head, and then it comes: the first ray of the golden sun lancing into the carafe as Ishungu peeks over the cliffs. The water inside the glass captures the ray, becoming brighter until it seems to have transmuted into liquefied sunlight.

By now Niko has witnessed Ayana perform sun magic a number of times, but he's no less amazed by the sight of her as she turns around with the luminous carafe in hand, cosmic shards blazing on her forehead. She speaks again, inviting the aspirants to partake of the elixir, but something else she says brings an anxious hush to the canyon, many bystanders clinging to each other for support.

Addi is the first to step forward, hands balled into tight fists, bare shoulders rigid. In the watchful silence he brings his lips to the rim of the glass and takes a few gulps of the golden liquid. He seems fine for a few seconds but then starts coughing like the liquid has gotten into his airways. His knees give out, and he splashes into the water on all fours.

Niko makes to go help, but Jio holds him back, shaking his head. "This is an awakening, mzi. He must go through it on his own."

Ayana must be of the same mind, since she makes no attempt to help Addi.

It's difficult to watch. Niko only just manages to restrain himself. But at last, Addi's cough starts to ease and then stops, his breathing returning to normal. If a change occurred within him, Niko doesn't see it, but as Addi lifts himself out of the water, Ayana shouts something that makes everyone around the pool break out in cheers.

Relieved and immensely proud, Niko curls his tongue, whistling loudly, adding to the din. The other boys do the same, and when Addi comes over with a grin, they all pat him vigorously on the back.

More aspirants step forward to partake of the golden liquid in Ayana's carafe, each one brought down to their knees in a violent fit of coughs, each success celebrated with loud cheers.

But the celebrations stop after the first aspirant succumbs, an older man who coughs himself to death just a few feet away from Niko. Two others don't make it, and the general mood is solemn when the ritual finally ends.

Even so, Niko's sense of relief remains strong. Addi survived, and whatever they lost coming here, their journey was a success. Niko decides he can live with that.

Needing a moment alone to think, he goes to watch the rest of the sunrise from the cliff tops above their hidden camp, which offer a wide view of the deserts beyond the canyons. Deprived of the effortless strength of his blessing, he finds climbing up steep, jagged terrain is not a trivial exercise. By the time he reaches the top, his face is coated in sweat, and the new scars on his thigh and arm, gifts from the Jasiri, start to throb.

Adjusting his straw hat, he sits down near the ledge facing the suns. It's already getting warmer, but the intensity of the sunlight is not yet unpleasant, allowing him to enjoy the solitude.

He's still wondering if he acted dishonorably by listening to the Jasiri and fleeing the city with everyone else. And now that Addi is cured, is the honorable thing to stay here and join Ayana's struggle, or should he head back home and beg the queen's forgiveness?

"I told you we'd find him up here," comes Jio's voice. Niko doesn't have to look to know that Sibu and Mafarai have followed him too.

"What gives?" he says to them.

The rangers join him by the ledge. He knows they don't blame him for the loss of their blessings; they followed him here of their own accord. But he senses their angst and mounting impatience to run back home and recover what they've lost. He senses it because he feels it himself. They were all secure in their identities, proud of having demonstrated their worth as men, and now that security has capsized, leaving them adrift. Who are they if not rangers?

"We did what we came here for," Jio says. "Addi survived."

"I know."

"Then perhaps it's time we headed back home."

Niko exhales audibly. "But what about what Ayana said?" he asks. "The pyramid she showed us? This isn't over yet."

"It's not our war," Sibu gripes. "We didn't come here to fight ancient evils or whatever the devil else is out here. We came to save Addi, and we've done that. So why stay?"

"Because," Niko patiently explains, "if Ayana doesn't succeed, then whatever's locked in that pyramid will eventually threaten our home. How do you not see that?"

Sibu scowls, looking away. "She could've been lying."

"We both know she was telling the truth."

"Mzi, we've lost our blessings," Jio pleads. "If we go back now, maybe the queen will welcome us back. Even if she doesn't, maybe we'll be allowed to take Nimara's blessing. But if we stay here any longer, we might end up being expelled from the regiment altogether. Do you want that?"

"Of course not," Niko admits.

"And what about the honor guard?" Jio says. "Don't you want to be reinstated?"

This time he takes a moment to think. "What I want is to go to bed knowing I've done the right thing. I don't regret coming here to help Addi. If it costs me a place in the honor guard, so be it."

Sibu shakes his head, throwing his hands up. "Not this again. When are you going to stop atoning, mzi? When will you have punished yourself enough?"

"This isn't about that!" Niko almost shouts. "This is about growing up! It's about doing the right thing. Can you live with yourself if you run back home and then this threat, whatever it is, sweeps across the Plains just like Ayana said? We're rangers, and it's our job to protect our home, blessing or no blessing. If you want to head back, you're free to go. But I'm staying until this is over."

"Maybe this argument is pointless," Mafarai says, breaking his silence. His sharp eyes have focused on something far away. He shoots up, tilting his head as if to get a better view, and his lips slowly part in disbelief.

When Niko and the twins get up and squint in the same direction, they see only clouds of dust hanging over the desert with little indistinct shapes moving beneath them.

"What's that?" Jio asks, shading his eyes with a hand.

"Believe it or not," Mafarai says gravely, "that's a regiment of quagga riders. More than one regiment. Maybe all of them."

Niko shares quiet glances with the twins. "Are you certain those are quaggas?" Sibu asks. "They might be some other striped equid."

"I know a quagga when I see one," Mafarai grumbles.

"But what the devil are they doing out here?" Jio wonders aloud, worry in his eyes.

The Ajaha regiments ride in a northwestern direction, never coming close enough for Niko to be absolutely sure they are indeed rangers from the Plains, but he knows better than to doubt Mafarai's vision.

"It's obvious, isn't it?" he says. "The queen has ordered the regiments to march on the pyramid." He stares the twins squarely in the face. "Do you still think this has nothing to do with us?"

The brothers look back at the army of riders, neither answering his question.

Addi comes looking for them just as they reach the bottom of the cliffs. Save for the added spring in his step and the perpetual grin on his face, virtually nothing about him has changed, which to Niko is a bit of a surprise. He thought there'd be something. An extra inch of height maybe, or a more muscular physique, or a magical cloak of sunlight.

"How are you feeling?" Niko asks him, inspecting him from head to sandals. "Can you conjure fire now?"

Addi snorts. "No. Ayana said my magic would be too weak for spells. I don't even have those glowing bits she gets on her face. To be honest, I don't feel any different."

"You don't seem disappointed either," Jio observes.

"Why would I be? The seizures are gone. I'm cured. And as soon as we're done helping Ayana defeat her ancient monster, we can all go back home."

Something *has* changed, Niko realizes. There, in the boy's eyes, a subtle golden hue has blended into his ruby irises, a color like the petals of a marigold. The secret dread he carried around and tried not to show has also evaporated, replaced with swelling confidence and absolute trust—confidence and trust in Niko and the twins and Mafarai, who saved his life, and whom he's already assumed will stick around to help Ayana.

He didn't even pause to wonder if they would; he trusts them that much.

Niko glances at the other rangers. He knows they're probably thinking of following the regiments, and he wouldn't blame them if they did. But he's made his position clear; they have to make their own decision now.

"Addi, what exactly is Ayana's plan?" Mafarai says.

"Actually, that's why she asked me to find you. She wants to talk."

A silent conversation passes between Mafarai and the twins.

"At least hear her out," Niko suggests. "At this point you have nothing to lose."

To his relief, the rangers take his advice, and they all go to speak to Ayana, who's waiting for them farther along the stream that passes by their camp. They nod at each other in greeting, and she offers them a subdued smile.

As usual, Addi translates her words into Sirezi. "She says she wishes she had more than just gratitude to offer you for what you've done for our people. She says that maybe when this is over and the enemy is defeated, there may be ancient treasures buried beneath the sands that you may claim as a reward."

"We appreciate the thought," Niko replies, "but I think I speak for all of us when I say we didn't do this for a reward."

Ayana smiles again, but then a hesitant crease appears on her forehead as she speaks her next words. "She's wondering if she can count on your continued aid for the next phase of her plan," Addi translates. "The four of you may be crucial."

"Ask her if she knows what the Yerezi regiments are doing here," Jio says.

Instead of translating the message, Addi blinks at Jio in surprise. "The regiments are here?"

"We saw them riding northwest just a few minutes ago," Niko explains. "Ask her what she knows about it."

Addi conveys the question to Ayana, who tilts her head in puzzlement. She speaks, and Addi translates. "She says she's confused. She thought you already knew that your queen and the KiYonte emperor were both working with the false king to open the pyramid. She says she knows you—" Addi's voice fails, and he gapes at Niko in shock. "You . . . you lost your blessing? When?" Horror and regret make his eyes widen. "Was it because of me?"

"Addi, none of this is your fault," Niko responds. "Now, what did she say just now?"

Addi starts to say something, but he lets it go and asks Ayana to repeat herself. "She said the Jasiri also lost his powers for the same reason. Your masters knew that you were helping her, so they crippled you."

After a tense pause, Sibu folds his arms and frowns. "Are we really going to believe this?"

Niko expects Jio to express a similar sentiment. Instead the other ranger gives a slow shake of the head, unvarnished despair on his face. "We already do, don't we?" He looks at his twin. "Our brother's mysterious death, Nimara's suspicions, AmaSibere's accusations. We've dismissed it all before now, but the regiments are here, Sibu. Why else if not to help open that damned pyramid?"

"Maybe she's here to stop it," Sibu argues, though he doesn't sound convinced himself.

"Then why take away our blessings? Especially if the regiment was coming here anyway."

"The timing is indeed suspicious," Mafarai agrees. "And if she's here to help stop the pyramid, then she shouldn't object to us helping Ayana."

Sibu frowns, but he has always gone where his brother goes, and today is no different. "Ask her what her plan is," he tells Addi.

"She says the builders of the pyramid knew this day would come," Addi says, translating Ayana's reply. "So they arranged a secret contingency: four magical artifacts built at cardinal points around the pyramid, disguised as impressive but otherwise mundane sculptures. She says you've seen one of them already, the giant hand with the sphere. Three others exist. Our advantage is that the enemy is ignorant of this contingency. The plan now is for those of us who have awakened to split up and sneak to these artifacts, where we'll perform a ritual."

Addi stops translating and asks Ayana a question. The crestfallen look on his face tells Niko he doesn't like her response. "I asked her what the ritual entails. She says those of us who have awoken now share a connection with the artifacts. We know not only how to reach them but what to do when we get there." Addi gives a grimace. "Great. More magic messing with my head without my consent."

"So where do we come in?" Niko asks, ignoring his comment.

Addi translates. "Ayana says we can't travel in groups too large, or we'll attract attention. We'll have to travel on foot in groups no larger than six people. She can take one group to the artifact in the west; she'd like you to split up and handle the other three. She'll send each group with a small number of Faraswa guards from Dahbet, but they're not exactly skilled warriors, which is why she needs you."

"Sounds simple enough," Niko thinks aloud. He glances at his friends. "But I won't be able to do it alone. Please tell me I won't have to."

They all end up looking at Sibu, the only one among them who's yet to articulate a change of heart. Under the attention, he scowls. "What's everyone looking at me for?"

Jio rolls his eyes and punches Sibu lightly in the arm. "Forgive my idiot brother. He's in. We're all in. We followed you this far; might as well go all the way."

Niko wells with affection for all of them. He nods at Addi. "Tell Ayana she can count on us to get her people to those artifacts."

28: Ilapara

The Faraswa Desert

If tumbling through the sky from the clutches of a redhawk was Ilapara's most terrifying experience, then running with Alinata from a pack of hunting sha beasts throughout the night is decidedly her most harrowing.

Only through the use of her stealth bracelet do they survive long enough to see the sunrise. Side by side, enveloped in a mirage of invisibility emitted by the bracelet, they sneak through the canyons from one sheltered hideout to another, praying each time that they've finally escaped their hunters.

But the sha beasts are clever. They rove about the canyons in pairs, long jackal-like ears erect, forked tails swishing about, irises aglow with bloodlust, and the high-pitched howls and screams they use to communicate sound like someone being violently murdered. The beasts are also tenacious and search unrelentingly for the prey they know is nearby, forcing Ilapara and her unlikely ally to keep moving.

The night is freezing cold. Thankfully, the magics of the mirage insulate them from the worst of the chill, and they elude the beasts over and over again. But exhaustion catches up to them, sitting like deadweight on their shoulders, lengthening each torturous hour of the night. No sooner have they climbed onto a ledge or holed up in a recess than they hear those horrid shrieks nearby, coming closer. They tell themselves that they only need to hold on until morning; then maybe the creatures will tire and return to their lair. But the sha beasts are still hunting them even after sunrise, sniffing the air with their long noses and coordinating through sound.

Soon after sunrise, Ilapara's bracelet begins to burn through its last reserves of essence. She and Alinata are trying to find their next hiding spot when they briefly flicker into view; there aren't any sha beasts in the immediate vicinity, but the whole canyon maze comes alive with canid screams. The enchantment strengthens and conceals them again, but they might not be so lucky next time.

"We need to find a way out of this maze, or we're dead," Ilapara whispers.

"I've been keeping track of our movements," Alinata whispers back. "I think we're headed in the right direction."

Hard to believe that this is the same cold, supercilious young woman Ilapara remembers. Or maybe, Ilapara is beginning to realize, she might have misread her all along. Alinata has a keen sense of direction, as it turns out, and a few hours after sunrise they find their way up a scalable escarpment and out of the canyons. As they reach the top, the enchantment finally fails, and they hear chilling screams behind them.

Fear gets them running, despite their fatigue. Ilapara's pants and high-quality boots allow her to sprint with relative ease on the hard ground, but with sandals and a pearlescent gown meant for throne rooms, Alinata is much less prepared. She does her best to keep up, though, and Ilapara tries not to outstrip her.

The howls follow. There's no shelter ahead, only flat, rocky desert and interspersed outcrops. Ilapara glances over her shoulder and despairs when she sees a whole pack of slender, inky-black, red-eyed canids climbing up the escarpment.

"Come on, you mutts!" she cries in frustration. "Go hunt something else!"

The sha beasts howl and race in pursuit.

Panting, Alinata begins to slow down. "You should go," she says. "I'll try to buy you time."

"What? No! We're getting out of here!" Without waiting for an argument, Ilapara grabs Alinata by the arm and pulls her forward.

There's nothing ahead. The sha beasts are much faster. Running is futile. They keep running anyway.

They run until they tire, the burst of energy from their fear having exhausted itself, and even then they keep running, until they realize they've been running for too long, for surely the beasts should have caught up to them by now.

Looking over her shoulder again, Ilapara slows, then comes to a stop.

"They're gone," Alinata breathes.

But why? What would make a pack of hunting predators suddenly abandon their prey just seconds away from catching it?

The appearance of an even meaner predator, Ilapara realizes after spotting a brightening point of light in the sky.

"Are you kidding me with this thing?" she yells. "Again?"

Alinata looks around the flat, rocky desert, despondent and hopeless. "What now?"

"I'm not rolling over and dying, that's for sure," Ilapara says. "It'll have to catch us. We run."

Thunder grows behind them, too loud perhaps. It's the roar of a flock of redhawks, an army of them. When Ilapara gathers the courage to look, she makes a reassessment: not an army but the biggest one she's ever seen. That wingspan would darken a whole village with its shadow.

The ground begins to rumble. The redhawk swoops down. Ilapara braces for death even as she continues to run, but a peculiar sensation overtakes her—static on her skin, an electric taste on her tongue, and the chill that comes just before falling into the Void in bodily form. She feels a pull and starts thinking that perhaps Alinata has rediscovered her magic.

But instead of ravens, she and Alinata become lightning, and they flash upward into the belly of the redhawk just as it flies over their heads.

"And not a moment too soon. Welcome to the *Ataraxis*, Ilapara. And you too . . . Alinata? What are you doing here?"

It takes a few seconds for Ilapara's eyes to adjust and for her mind to make sense of her sudden change in environment. Where moments before she was running across a bright, scorching desert, the air here is cool, and the few lights on the ceiling leave some corners of the compartment in darkness.

Before she crossed the Jalama, she wouldn't have guessed where she was to save her own life. She's seen enough now to recognize she's in the skiff bay of a windcraft.

There are other figures in the compartment, but her eyes lock on the one who spoke, the slender youth wearing reflective spectacles and blue coveralls. Her blood boils at the sight of him standing there pretending to be someone he's not.

She snarls, fingernails biting into her palms. "*You*. You shouldn't have failed to kill me, you son of a bitch."

He flinches back in surprise, but she's already halfway there, ready to end his wretched existence once and for all, except someone else she recognizes hurries forward, leg brace squeaking with each step.

"Ilapara, wait!"

She freezes in place, her lips parting, heart lurching in her chest. "Jomo?"

"Yes," he says, coming closer. "I wanted to surprise you, but . . . then I saw that look on your face."

Still too confused to react, she doesn't resist when he pulls her into a heartfelt embrace.

"Ilapara," he says in a voice jagged with emotion, "I thought I'd never see you again."

She eventually warms up to the embrace, because this *is* Jomo, and by Ama it's so good to see him. Even the magic of her ivory pendant says it's him. And the Sentinels are here, too, smiling at Ilapara. But their presence on this ship makes no sense at all.

She glances over her shoulder. "Alinata, what's happening? Am I hallucinating?"

"If you're asking me if any of this is real," the other woman says, looking around the bay, "I'm as stumped as you are."

The pretender is watching them with anxious concern, but it doesn't matter what face he puts on now. Ilapara has seen what's beneath it.

"Jomo, you all need to stay away from him," she says. "He's dangerous. *Evil.*"

Jomo frowns at her, then at the pretender. "Dangerous, certainly, but evil? That doesn't seem likely."

"He tried to kill me! He slaughtered a village of innocent people!"

"What?" says the pretender, appalled. "I would never!"

Ilapara takes a step toward him. "You liar!"

"Hang on," Jomo says, lifting a hand in a placating gesture. "Salo, now's a good time to clear up the misunderstanding. You know, before she actually kills you."

The pretender has the insolence to wring his hands like he's nervous. "I had a whole speech prepared, but I wasn't expecting the hostility. Was my reflection truly that terrible?"

"What the devil are you on about?" Ilapara demands.

Jomo huffs. "You're terrible at this, Salo. Ilapara, look . . . I assume you left the Enclave with a guy who looks and talks exactly like Salo?"

"Yes," Ilapara says, glaring at the pretender. "But he's not Salo. He's a thing. A mistake. An abomination."

"Agreed. But Ilapara, this fellow over here"—Jomo points at the pretender—"is *not* him. This is the real Salo, who saved my life earlier this morning before we followed your pendant here. The other one is a puppet, and whoever made him wants to use his power to open some gate that should never be opened."

The floor might as well be spinning. Ilapara stares at the pretender, doubt creeping into the concrete certainty that Salo is well and truly dead.

Could it be?

"Ilapara, don't you see?" Jomo says, holding her by the shoulders. "You did it! You brought Salo back."

She can't go through this all over again. To hope, to rejoice, only to be crushed. "But how are there two of him?"

The pretender answers. "I think my creator had a change of heart before she died. I don't know what motivated her to build my reflection, but the last thing she did was launch the process of my resurrection. I woke up days later in a ruined city, and you were already gone."

Ilapara walks closer, looking him up and down, trying to find anything to confirm her doubts. "Your eyes," she says. "Let me see them."

He takes off his spectacles, revealing synthetic irises like faceted little prisms with many points of shifting color. He squints, blinks, like it's troubling him to keep the eyes open.

Looking into them, Ilapara sees the friend she thought had come back to her, but she's been fooled once. Who's to say this isn't another trick? "I watched the city burn. Nothing could have survived."

The youth claiming to be Salo puts his spectacles back on. "I woke up in an underground building. I think it was deep enough for the machines there to keep working, but my creator didn't survive. No one else did."

Ayzel's laboratory. Ilapara remembers taking a cart down a vertical shaft just to reach it. She doesn't want to believe, but it all makes sense.

She was right about the pretender; he isn't and never was Salo. But this one is different. This one . . . fits.

Giving in to the hope, she closes the distance and embraces him, her eyes misting over. "Salo."

He wraps his arms around her. "Ilapara. It's so good to see you."

"I really want to kill you right now," she says. "You've put me through a lot."

"I'm sorry."

She pulls back from him, wiping her eyes. "If you want me to forgive you, we have to go and get Tuk. I don't think he's in good shape."

"Why? What happened?"

"I was wondering the same thing," Jomo says, glancing in Alinata's direction. "Where's that insufferable little bastard? I was certain we'd find him with you."

"We got separated," Ilapara says, choosing not to elaborate. "It's a long story." She shows Salo one of her ivory pendants. "This is linked to another one on his person. Last night I felt him leave your reflection's palace. I think he ran away. He might be in danger."

"Great thinking getting these," Salo says. He doesn't touch the pendant but merely brings his hand near like he's feeling the heat of a fire; then he brings his forearm close to his face and speaks into a bracer tool in fluent Syliaric. A tiny voice replies, they exchange a few more words, and then the noise from the engines changes in pitch, the floor tilting slightly as the ship changes direction.

"The pilot's taking us there now," he says. "But there are quite a number of windcrafts in the vicinity, so we'll have to go in slow and quiet. Fortunately, this ship is equipped with a capable stealth shield, so we should avoid detection if we're careful."

Ilapara lifts an eyebrow. "You have a lot of explaining to do, Salo. Like how you suddenly speak fluent Syliaric." She looks around the bay and its fittings of tarnished brass. Certainly nothing glamorous compared to the other windcrafts she's seen, but not even the *Rapiere* can fly so fast it causes the skies to thunder. "And where'd you get this ship? It looked like it was on fire. I thought it was a redhawk."

"That's . . . a long story."

She laughs weakly. "I guess we do have stories to trade, don't we."

"Indeed," Salo says, lifting his gaze over her shoulder. "Alinata."

"Musalodi."

Many emotions flicker on Salo's face. "It's good to see you," he says.

"Likewise."

He turns back to Ilapara. "We have a few minutes before we reach Tuk. I'll show you around. Maybe you'd like something to eat or drink?"

"I'd kill for some water," Ilapara confesses.

As they leave the bay, she lets Jomo put an arm around her waist. "You're back," he says to her.

"I am."

"Nothing else matters now."

There are things they need to discuss, decisions she's made that he probably won't like, but for now she rests her head against him and lets herself enjoy being in the present.

"Our friend is on those hills over there," Salo says minutes later while standing on the top deck by the portside rails.

The windcraft is no longer on fire. The pilot has apparently engaged the stealth field and slowed the ship to a stationary hover about half a mile away from a cluster of sandstone hills.

Ilapara shades her eyes with one hand, the other clutching her pendants. Tuk feels alive to her, but the link isn't as strong as it should be.

She searches the sky for signs of a redhawk or the *Rapiere*. Nothing. "Why aren't we going closer?"

"There are other ships nearby," Salo says. "Possibly in that direction. Our stealth shield should make us invisible on their instruments, but they'll see us if we come too close." Salo looks at her. "How many ships did you say were in the convoy?"

"About a dozen."

He shakes his head. "We're picking up a lot more activity than that. Someone else is out here."

"It doesn't matter right now," Ilapara says, looking at the hills. "We need to get Tuk. We can figure out the rest later."

"Agreed. Are you ready?"

She frowns at him. "What do you mean?"

"We'll transpose off the ship, get him, then come back."

"From here? You can do that?"

His lips stretch in a tiny smile. "How do you think I pulled you up from the desert?"

"How should I know? And I thought transposition was a new KiYonte thing. A few of the emperor's mystics get about that way."

"The spell has always existed. It's just difficult to cast without an incredibly efficient Axiom or the help of a metaform. Lucky for us, I have both."

Ilapara finds herself shaking her head.

"What is it?" he asks, and then his face falls. "You still don't believe it's me, do you."

"On the contrary," Ilapara says, "I'm suddenly wondering why I ever convinced myself the other one was you. The differences are obvious in retrospect."

"Really?" he says. "Am I the more handsome one?"

"Salo, just take us to those hills."

"As you say, Ilapara." His cosmic shards come aglow as he folds them both into the Void; then they bolt off the ship, appearing on the slopes of the hills an instant later.

Ilapara is used to the Void now, but she has to shake the chill out of her bones. "Something you have in common with your dark twin," she observes. "You're both a lot more powerful than you were in Yonte Saire. And more skilled, it seems."

"My creator endowed me with a few advantages to help me survive," he says. "I don't think I'd have made it this far otherwise." He points farther up the hills. "The magic in your pendant says he's up there."

"You should let me talk to him first. In fact, it might be better to wait here until I call you."

Salo lets out a nervous breath, then nods. "All right."

She proceeds alone, her heartbeat gaining speed with each step, and when she finally reaches the summit and sees Tuk sitting with his back toward her, legs dangling over a precipice, her relief nearly brings her to her knees. She approaches him calmly, though.

"You aren't really going to jump, are you?"

"I wouldn't die," he says. "It'd just hurt." Then his head whips in her direction, like he's only just realizing she isn't some figment of his imagination. "Ilapara?" He bolts up, mouth falling open in shock. "You're alive!"

"No thanks to you," she says, folding her arms. Time has allowed her to cool off and see things from his perspective; he thought he was saving a friend. She's still a little angry.

"I'm sorry," he says, eyes filling with tears. "I just reacted. I didn't think he'd . . . oh, Ilapara." Before she can stop him, his arms are around her and he's weeping into her chest. "Please forgive me."

She sighs, annoyed by how quickly her anger dissipates. "You're lucky I'm in a good mood."

"I thought it was him," he cries. "I thought all he needed was time. But we failed, didn't we. He's really gone."

"About that." Ilapara breaks the embrace, holding Tuk by the arms. "Tuk, I need you to listen to me. I know why your sister was so determined to bring Salo back. Why she forced Ayzel to help us even before we'd arrived."

Tuk blinks at her, confused. "Why?"

"Because she didn't really *want* Salo. She wanted a puppet with his power. The crystal we gave Ayzel? She didn't use it the way we thought she did. At least not at first. The person we thought was Salo is actually a corrupted copy of him. I think Ayzel was supposed to destroy the crystal afterward, but she didn't. Instead, she used it again, this time exactly the way it was meant to be used, but we'd already left."

Tuk's gaze becomes watery again. "Ilapara, what are you saying?"

"Salo is alive," she tells him. "The real Salo. Ayzel brought him back after we left. It was her last act before the Anathema hit."

"How do you know?"

Looking back where she came from, she raises her voice. "You can come forward now."

There are footsteps, and then Salo shows himself, wearing a hesitant smile. "Hello, Tuk," he says.

And then Tuk, rivers pouring down his cheeks, starts laughing.

29: Alinata

Alinata might have ordinarily relished the chance to sample every wonder on the flying ship and learn as much as she could about life beyond the Redlands. Today, she can't seem to sit still.

She doesn't indulge for long beneath the spray of pleasantly warm water inside a tiny ablution compartment on the second deck. She doesn't investigate the brass machine that launders her ivory gown and releases it pristine and lightly scented. She doesn't stick around on the bridge with the rather attractive pilot, who keeps sneaking furtive glances in her direction, or stay too long in the lighthearted company of Jomo's Sentinels.

She doesn't even join Salo's reunion with Ilapara and Tuk in the lounge at the rear of the ship, where they presumably trade stories about all that has transpired since the night of the Requiem Moon.

She keeps moving, haunting the corridors of the ship, seeing, touching, but never lingering, trying to distract herself from a world that doesn't make sense anymore and the knot of emotions she didn't even know she could feel all at once.

Relief. Shock. Guilt.

They were right to be suspicious of her in Yonte Saire, for there was not a single important word they spoke in her presence that didn't reach the queen's ears. A small miracle they haven't already kicked her off the ship, and even Tuk winked at her when they made eye contact shortly after he came onboard. She expected he'd be furious. Maybe he's just too happy for her presence to ruin his mood.

She's watching the world from a porthole in the vacant infirmary when Ilapara finds her. "There you are. I've been looking all over for . . . you." Her voice falters as she looks Alinata over. "Did you get some sleep?"

Like Alinata, she's found the time to get cleaned up. There's no kohl around her eyes or paint on her lips, and she's let her red dreadlocks hang free. But now she's wearing one of those coveralls the natives of this ship seem to love, a cherry-colored garment with too many pockets. It covers her from neck to wrist to ankle. There's also a contraption of leather and brass wrapped around her left forearm.

Alinata would be damned before she ever wore an outfit so stifling.

"Sleep is the last thing on my mind," she replies honestly.

"You seem strangely back to your usual self," Ilapara says, taking note of the red steel jewelry Alinata chose to wear despite its uselessness.

But why should I take it off? she asked herself. *Jewelry is still jewelry even if it isn't enchanted.*

"A bath was in order," she says, "and the lady Priscille showed me how to launder my gown. A very interesting group of people on this ship, isn't it?"

Ilapara gives her a wry smirk. "I envy that about you, you know. Your ability to gracefully exist in any situation. Are you not even a little perturbed by all you've seen since we arrived?"

The irony. Alinata has lost her grip on who she thought she was. It can't be, and yet Salo is alive again and now in command of a flying fortress from beyond the Jalama. Add to this the inescapable sense of impending doom growing in her chest, and "perturbed" feels like an understatement.

"Perhaps the shock hasn't hit me yet," she says. "Did you need something?"

"Yes, actually." Ilapara steps deeper into the compartment, interlacing her fingers in front of her like she's about to say something difficult. "Alinata, I realize I haven't thanked you for what you did for me yesterday. I don't know why you did it, but I know I'd be dead if not for you. So. For what it's worth, thank you."

Alinata feels taken by an unfamiliar warmth. "You're welcome."

"And I recognize you might not know where you fit in right now," Ilapara says, coming a step closer. "I won't speak for anyone else. You'll have to find the courage to speak to them yourself. All I'll say is that whatever happened in the past, I consider you a friend, Alinata. Don't be afraid to talk to me, and don't be too mysterious. I know you're an Asazi, so maybe it comes with the territory, but you don't have to keep to yourself. Not anymore. You're one of us now."

The warmth strengthens inside Alinata, her eyes prickling with emotion. She opens her mouth to say something, but before a word has left her lips, the light coming in through the portholes changes dramatically from daylight to the crimson white of intense moonfire. The floor beneath her rumbles slightly, a muted drone joining the hum of the engines. Then Salo's voice comes out of a speech contraption on one of the walls, speaking in KiYonte.

"We've detected a massive burst of activity in the southwest. Sevan is taking us closer to investigate. I'm on the bridge if you have questions."

Alinata shares a glance with Ilapara; then wordlessly they leave the workshop and head up to the bridge. They both gape at the flames blazing almost flush against the windows, completely obscuring whatever's on the other side. Alinata suffers a tingle of fear that they'll crash into a mountain, but the pilot Sevan appears completely at ease behind the helm.

They find Salo standing in front of the seated uroko bull of a man named Balam, helping him strap a peculiar brass eyepiece to his left eye. Tuk is watching nearby with folded arms; Alinata decides she likes the way he's tied the sleeves of his black coveralls around his waist and how his simple white shirt visibly strains against the physique beneath it. But the petulant, shadow-eyed look on his face makes her lift an eyebrow.

"What's going on?" Ilapara says.

Salo finishes attaching the eyepiece, then moves to check on the crate of peach-size brass spheres resting on the floor. They're obviously some sort of machine, with little telescoping mechanisms sticking out of them, though Alinata can't immediately divine their purpose.

"I've just finished making some changes to the way these mirror-scopes move. Balam will control them remotely."

He speaks to Balam in the singsong intonations of some outworld tongue, and then the spheres quietly lift out of the crate and hover in place for a few seconds before slowly dropping back into the crate. Evidently pleased, Salo pats the big man on the shoulder and says something that might be encouragement, but Tuk's eyes instantly turn orange—a color Alinata knows betrays intense irritation.

She always did find his eyes a beautiful tragedy. Beautiful for obvious reasons. Tragic because she can't imagine a life where all her thoughts and emotions are so easy to read. The very idea would be a nightmare to any Asazi.

He goes on to make a comment that brings a sigh and a headshake out of Salo. They go back and forth for a moment—Salo speaking in a rational, conciliatory voice, Tuk not being pacified at all. Balam remains calmly silent, but Sevan pitches in with a derisive remark, which makes Tuk point and hiss something back at her.

"Are you fighting?" Ilapara finally cuts in. "Because if you are, then do it in a language I understand."

"I spent weeks being ignored and left out by the other Salo," Tuk replies in agitated Sirezi. "I won't be ignored again."

Alinata and Ilapara both look to Salo for an explanation. He seems put on the spot, his shoulders tense. "Tuk thinks I've replaced him. But I haven't."

"Then why is he controlling the scopes and not me?" Tuk asks. "I'm more advanced than he is. In a lot of ways, I'm more advanced than even you. Why does he get the job and not me?"

Ilapara rolls her eyes. "Really, Tuk?"

"What? I'm not being unreasonable."

"If you like," Salo offers, "I have something more suitable for you, Tuksaad. But Balam wants to help, and he's used to controlling complicated machinery with his mind. This is something he can do."

Tuk keeps glowering, fists at his sides. "Fine."

Mirth tugs at Alinata's lips. How much she missed the three of them. So, so much. More than she let herself admit.

"What's going on here?" comes Jomo's voice as he arrives with the arcanist Zuri. "Why are we on fire again?"

"We won't be for much longer," Salo tells him. "In fact . . ."

He utters an instruction to Sevan, and the wall of flame outside the bridge whooshes out. Alinata feels a lightness in her stomach, powerful magics of deceleration acting on her and the rest of the ship; then silence falls on the bridge as they all stare straight ahead, at the thing they've come to investigate.

The ship has climbed much higher. The Faraswa Desert is now a remote and uninterrupted expanse of rusty sand and rocky outcrops far below—except, in the distance, a column of light has shot up into the heavens, bright and solid white against the pale-blue sky.

"What the devil is that?" Jomo says.

"It's as I feared," Salo replies with a heavy frown. "My reflection has started to open the gate."

The arcanist Zuri speaks. "We received intelligence that the emperor was suddenly interested in an ancient Faraswa ruin in the desert and was sending forces to capture it. Perhaps the gate and this ruin are one and the same?"

"I'm certain they are," Salo says. "The gate was built with the power of a Hegemon. To open it, my reflection will need the same. That means gathering all the fragments of the crown in one place. He has one. The emperor has another, and the Yerezi queen has the third."

Alinata fails to hold her silence. "But what is the gate, Salo? All I learned from the queen is that it will somehow amplify the power of each fragment. Is that true?"

"In a sense. The gate's construction was the true reason behind the decline of the Faraswa people and the fall of the Ascendancy. It acts as an inhibitor on certain types of magic. Without it, each fragment of the crown would, in theory, become more powerful."

Jomo shakes his head. "The emperor is powerful enough as it is. We can't let him open that gate."

"It's not him you should worry about," Salo remarks. "In fact, how powerful he becomes won't matter at all in the end." When everyone eyes him curiously, he explains. "There are certain . . . arcane restrictions in place that prevent me from telling you everything I learned in the inner sanctum. Suffice it to say, the gate will tear the Veil open and allow Arante and her forces to cross into our world. If that happens, the emperor will be the least of our problems."

Another silence settles on the bridge. Alinata, outwardly composed, feels a chill enter her fingers.

"Arante," Jomo says with a humorless show of teeth. "As in Arante the devil, mistress of the netherworld. *That* Arante?"

"Yes, and that's not all," Salo says gravely. "My reflection is likely harboring a shadow of her within his soul. So are the others who followed him here. Sadly, I suspect he's beguiled the queen and the emperor into binding their will to his. It's the only way he could have started the process of opening the gate."

"How long do we have?" Ilapara asks tensely.

"A day, maybe. Not much more."

The queen under the devil's control? Impossible. He's wrong.

The chill has spread to the rest of Alinata's body, frost coiling down her spine. Fear.

Fear of something other than the Void. She once boldly dived into an undercity shaft to face a horde of tikoloshe, and not even then did fear touch her. But now she's swimming in it, drowning, flailing against a river of fear that wants to sweep her away.

"I can't accept that," she says. "Salo, do you hear yourself? You're saying the queen is working for Arante. I know she's done many questionable things. She's ambitious and ruthless, but she's not evil."

"He's telling the truth, Alinata," Tuk says. "My sister is one of those people, and serving Arante has long been their purpose. We also know the reflection met with two local leaders a while ago. I don't think any of them are truly evil. But the fact remains: what they're doing will destroy us all."

She should control herself. She should deal, accept, process quietly, but it's out in the open now; the fear is on her face, making her eyes water.

My queen, my mentor, working with the devil. It can't be.

Salo's voice becomes gentle. "It's unlikely my reflection was completely honest. She probably wasn't aware of the danger she was in. Perhaps if we stop him, we might yet free her from his compulsion."

"Then we must stop him!" Alinata cries, trembling.

He comes closer, this boy whose elaborate death she once helped orchestrate. He comes closer and places a tender hand on her arm. "We'll do everything in our power to save her, Alinata. Whatever she may have done, she is still queen of the Plains, and I have no desire to see her come to harm. If I can stop it, I will."

On any other day Alinata might have doubted his sincerity, but today she needs to believe him, so she wipes her face and nods. "Thank you."

"Did you see that?" Jomo interrupts, pointing. "An explosion near the light source. Something is going on down there. We need a closer look."

"It's too risky to fly any closer," Salo says. "Balam?"

The big man sits forward, forehead wrinkled in concentration; then the brass spheres lift out of their crate again, this time enveloped in clouds of red static. The press of magic fills the bridge as the static intensifies, and then the spheres fold out of space, disappearing from sight.

"These scopes are like the skimmers we used in Yonte Saire," Salo explains. "Except with vastly superior sensors. They couldn't fly as fast or as stealthily, though, but that wasn't too difficult to improve."

"I should like to study them, if I may, Bwana Salo," Zuri petitions.

To which Jomo snorts. "Is there anything on this ship you don't want to study? Bwana Msia is probably in the engine room as we speak, taking notes."

The arcanist folds her arms, impenitent. "This is a rare opportunity to study outworld magic and technology. We would be foolish not to take advantage of it."

"Agreed," Salo says. "And yes, Bibi Zuri, you're welcome to study the scopes when they return, as well as any other part of the ship."

"About the scopes, Salo," Ilapara intrudes, bringing focus back to the matter at hand. "How will we see what they're looking at?"

"On these." Salo leans down to flick a switch located on a nearby circular table, and two brass sheets unroll from slender drums on the ceiling, flanking the helm. Images of Mirror light appear over both sheets, each one showing the perspective of something racing across the desert at blistering speeds, approaching the shaft of light.

Alinata's heart pumps faster when the scopes finally decelerate and settle into slow but opposing orbits around the light source. No one speaks as they all take in the brilliant star sitting at the top of a massive blue-gray pyramid, which itself rests on a platform that rose out of some bottomless shaft. A wide walkway bridges across the chasm to the base of the pyramid on each side, and lines are carved onto its walls in indeterminate arrangements. They don't look like scripts to Alinata's eyes, more like the amplifying patterns of cosmic shards.

Dread wraps itself around her heart. This is the artifact that made her mentor so reckless. A gateway to hell.

"Remarkable," the arcanist exclaims. "The ancient Faraswa built their monuments with limestone, sandstone, and basalt. This appears to be a different material altogether."

"I'm more worried about those ships spitting fire at each other," Jomo says, pointing at one of the brass panels. "What the devil is happening over there?"

As if he understood, Balam sends one of the scopes a few miles away from the pyramid to the cluster of airborne vessels firing volleys of destructive fire and light at each other. They're a kaleidoscope of magics, sun against sun, moon against moon; Alinata fails to see anything that distinguishes the two battling sides from one another.

She inhales sharply when a redhawk plummets into view and slams itself against a ship with crimson sails. The bird ricochets off some invisible shield, but the ship is rocked out of its flight path, pitching its nose dangerously toward the ground. It rights itself just in time to avoid catastrophe, but a second collision from the redhawk proves too much, and the vessel crashes in a bright explosion visible even through the windows.

"Did the convoy turn on each other?" Ilapara wonders aloud, a baffled look on her face.

"No." Tuk steps closer to the mirage on the right of the helm. "Some of these ships weren't in the convoy." He shakes his head slowly. "My goodness, I can't believe my eyes."

"What is it?" Alinata asks, along with several other people on the bridge.

When Tuk turns around, his irises are a striking shade of cobalt blue. "The war began in part because a group of Vigilants in the East were preparing to meet the new Hegemon. I think this might be them."

"But you said you doubted they were Vigilants," Ilapara reminds him.

"I said I wasn't sure. The world is too busy fighting a war right now, exactly like my sister and her group wanted. The only people who would have known to gather a force and bring it here are the Vigilants."

On the other mirage, a battalion of outworlders in heavy suits of armor is trying to advance on the pyramid, shooting bolts of fire out of their gauntlets as they march forward. Alinata doubts her eyes when she spots blooded champions of the Muomi tribe fighting beside them, identifiable by their elaborate hide garments and the scarlet paint on their faces. Many of them have their greatswords sheathed and are instead shooting volleys of moonfire from heavy-looking multibarreled weapons they have to carry with both hands.

A closer look reveals to her a smaller crew of agile Mbare skirmishers firing longer but much lighter versions of those weapons, as well as a few Numbi magicians casting spells with their elemental familiars.

Despite this firepower, the mounted riders resisting the attacking force are fierce and organized. One of them unleashes a spirit of moonfire from a staff; it takes shape as a winged beast and roars toward the enemy, killing at least half a dozen people.

"That's an Umadi spell," Ilapara mutters, incredulous. "And there's more than one east-coast tribe supporting the Vigilants."

Exactly what Alinata was thinking. "Salo, tell Balam to close in on those riders in the background."

Balam complies, and the scope flies toward the regiment of quagga riders in bloodred loincloths routing an infantry unit that came too close. The vision settles on one particular Ajaha just as he throws his spear; the weapon leaps from his hand with such force it explodes through an armored chest, impaling a man through the heart.

"Small eastern tribes fighting alongside foreigners," Ilapara says. "Yerezi rangers fighting alongside Umadi sorcerers." She gives Alinata a slantwise stare. "What the devil is going on here, Alinata?"

Attention swivels in Alinata's direction, and she has to battle the reflexive urge to prevaricate and protect her queen's secrets. But these are her allies now, so she tells them everything.

"A while ago, a plague of foreigners from across the Inoetera flooded the eastern coast with exotic armaments. Their intentions weren't clear; the queen suspected they were trying to recruit bodies for a confrontation with the Empire on Red soil. Whatever the case, she decided to take control of the entire south to stop those weapons from reaching our enemies. The Umadi, Valau, and Qotoba are now under her command."

"I won't even ask how she was able to pull that off," Ilapara says with a shudder. "I've seen what Salo can do with a Hegemon's fragment."

"Not Salo," Tuk reminds her. "His reflection. And those foreigners bringing weapons here weren't recruiting for a fight against the Empire; they were recruiting for this battle. They were Vigilants, and they need our help."

"It looks like they're retreating," Jomo notices. "Already? If they give up so quickly, they won't be of much use."

"This was an exploratory force, I think," Salo says, still watching the rangers on one of the panels. "Our sensors report a larger cluster of ships a dozen leagues east of the pyramid."

"Then we must go there immediately," Tuk asserts. "We must pool our resources and mount a joint attack."

Alinata shakes her head. "We'll still be fighting our own people, none of whom have the slightest clue what they're really involved in. Salo, I think you and I need to speak to your uncle before we do anything else. He's the most influential general of the regiment, and he already knows the queen played a part in your death."

"If he knows," Ilapara says skeptically, "then why is he out here fighting for her?"

"Perhaps he's biding his time. Waiting for the right moment to act. This might be it."

Salo's shoulders heave as he considers the mirage. "None of this is a coincidence," he murmurs, then turns around, a frown on his face. "Last I spoke to the Imperial lords, they mentioned seeking out the Vigilants. I think it's possible they found them and led them here and that the book they showed me is with them. We need that book. If there's a way to stop the pyramid, the book has the answer. But Alinata is right. I need to speak to my uncle first. My brothers might be down there, and I know Aneniko will see reason."

"Aneniko and your brothers aren't with the regiments," Alinata tells him.

He gives an enigmatic smile. "But they're in this desert, yes?"

"They preceded the regiments by days, if not weeks," Alinata says. "How did you know?"

"It's hard to explain. But even if they're not with the regiments, we should pay my uncle a visit."

"I'm coming with you," Tuk declares, looking at Alinata like he isn't putting it past her that this might be a trap. She can't say she blames him.

If Salo notices, he lets nothing slip. "One of us needs to stay onboard. Ilapara, you're captain in my absence. If you need anything, use your bracer tool."

"Hopefully I'll remember how to use it. Also . . ." She glances at the helm console and whispers, "I thought Sevan was your deputy captain?"

The hint of humor crosses Salo's face. "She's decided being the pilot is better."

"What about me?" Jomo asks. "What do I do?"

"You can keep me company," Ilapara tells him, to which he beams. "A fine idea."

At dusk, Alinata strides purposefully into the Yerezi camp, an organized grid of triangular goatskin tents sitting within sight of the pyramid. Pole-mounted standards of the clan totems stand high above the tents, marking the sectors each regiment has claimed for itself. All over the camp the Ajaha and their quaggas are a blur of stripes, straw hats, and crimson loincloths, smiles abounding in the aftermath of their recent victory.

Alinata has only ever seen this many rangers gathered in one place during the bullpen ceremony at the Queen's Kraal. But any illusions that she might be back home dissolve in the alien backdrop of red dunes and the looming presence of the pyramid and its unwavering pillar of light.

Here and there she sees flashes of beads and kitenge—Asazi tending to injured mounts, taking inventories, or supervising the erection of more tents. She avoids them in case they know about her expulsion from the honor guard, but she still walks with the self-possessed confidence of an apprentice here on the queen's business. Ajaha respectfully move out of her way, and she reaches the Siningwe camp without incident.

The Siningwe general is amid a group of older men seated on low stools around a fire near their clan standard. His leather chest harness is empty of a sword, and he's taken off his red steel armor, a light woolen cloak draped over his shoulders. Like the other men, he's covered his head with a conical straw hat.

A wrinkle appears above the bridge of his nose as soon as he spots Alinata, which tells her he knows something. She doesn't let that stop her.

"General Siningwe, a word." She glances at the men around the fire. "In private."

The general considers the request, then quietly gets up, though he jerks his head at one of the men, asking him to follow. Alinata recognizes him as the general's lieutenant and significant other—obvious insurance in case she's leading him into a trap. *He definitely knows something.*

He shows her into his tent, where he pours himself water from a tankard into a soapstone cup. Meanwhile the lieutenant sits down on the lone stool by the bed, eyes shimmering with alertness in the yellow light from the two enchanted citrine stones hanging from the tent's roof.

"General, there's very little time," Alinata begins. "You must come with me at once. There's someone you need to meet and a tale you won't find easy to believe, but it's imperative that you hear it. You've all been deceived."

After downing his cup in a few gulps, the general puts it back down onto the table and finally pins Alinata with his severe, impenetrable gaze. "Where is this person?"

"Outside the camp." Recognizing how dubious she sounds, she adds, "Believe me, you'll understand the secrecy as soon as you set eyes on him."

"Forgive me if I'm confused, Apprentice Alinata. I heard a rumor that you'd disgraced yourself and fallen out with the queen. And now you come out of nowhere to demand that I follow you out of the camp to meet someone unspecified. Am I a fool? Why should I trust you?"

Alinata pauses, considering her strategy. A smart tongue is not what's needed here. Clearly the truth is her best recourse, but too much of it too soon and she'll lose him. *Start with what he already knows.* "General, surely you know by now that the queen played a part in your nephew's death."

Neither man reacts, but they're listening.

"I know because I helped make it happen," Alinata confesses. "Because I trusted her. I blindly followed her, believing she had the tribe's best interests at heart. But I was wrong. She's fallen prey to her ambitions, and what you're doing out here is a mistake we will bitterly regret unless you come with me and see the truth for yourself."

The general watches her blankly, his thoughts inscrutable.

"It could be a trap," the lieutenant says.

"But whose?" the general muses, never taking his eyes off Alinata. "She isn't working for the queen anymore."

"On the contrary," Alinata says, "I fear Her Majesty considers me an enemy now. Please, General Siningwe. Time is of the essence."

After another thoughtful pause, the general makes a decision. "If I'm not back in half an hour," he says to the lieutenant, "raise the alarm."

The lieutenant nods, his face an impassive mask.

They leave the camp on the general's stallion. Seated behind him in the saddle, Alinata guides him a mile from the camp, toward a distinctive cluster of exfoliated mushroom-shaped rock formations. The sunlight has faded, deepening the desert's rusty shade, but the pillar of brilliance coming out of the pyramid behind them is intense enough to hold off the encroaching night.

"Over there," Alinata says, pointing into the rock cluster.

The general brings his quagga to a stop, and they both dismount, though he takes a moment to sheathe his blade in the scabbard on his back. Salo is seated with Tuk beneath an overhanging rock dome. They get up when they spot the quagga, dusting themselves off. A shadow skulks about the rocks behind them. The quagga releases an anxious snort at the sight of it.

Salo's strange manner of dress probably throws the general off, because he doesn't react until his nephew is almost in front of him.

"Hello, Aba," Salo says with a nervous smile.

Frozen in place, the general stares at Salo in a way that slows the wind and banishes the last traces of the desert's heat. An air of danger caresses Alinata's skin, and she starts fearing that they've miscalculated. Tuk must sense the same given the rapid blackening of his eyes and the subtle change in his posture, limbs tensing in preparation for a fight.

The general trains his glare on Alinata. "You have one chance to explain yourself, Asazi. What wretched magic is this?"

She has no blessing now. If he moved to attack, not even Tuk could get there in time to save her. But fear might be misinterpreted as dishonesty, so she keeps it off her face. "There's no easy way to say this, General, but this is your nephew Musalodi, returned from the dead."

"I watched my nephew burn," the general says in a near whisper, "his soul committed to the Infinite Path. This *thing*, whatever it is, is not him."

"I told you this would not be easy to believe. I had my doubts, too, but please, listen to what he has to say. The future of our home depends on it."

The general's nostrils flare, but he doesn't attack. "Speak, demon," he barks at Salo. "Before I end your existence."

"I'm no demon," Salo calmly replies. "This may not be the body I was born with, but the soul that inhabits it is the one you've always known."

The general continues to seethe, but at least he's listening. Salo goes on to explain everything, and even Alinata learns things she didn't know before: how King Isa anticipated his death and arranged for a ritual to trap his soul in a crystal before it crossed the Veil; how that crystal was taken across the Jalama and used in a spell to give him a new body; how he was briefly enslaved on a flying ship while he struggled to remember who he was; and how he eventually found his way here to fight an impostor built from the same crystal that housed his consciousness.

"He's a shell of me," Salo says. "Enough of me to pretend and know what I know and use it to his master's benefit. That's why he hides behind a mask, because he wears my face. But he's not me."

Alinata didn't know the general was capable of displaying such intense emotion. The redness in his eyes and the lines on his face are the picture of agony, like he wants to believe but is straining against an immovable wall of doubt. Like he's teetering on a knife's edge and could fall one way or the other.

She gives him a nudge. "Musalodi didn't die in a riot, General Siningwe. He was murdered in a ritual to take what had been given to him in the Red Temple's sanctum and sunder it into three parts. One was given to the queen. The emperor took another. And the third now rests on the impostor's head."

The general watches Salo in conflicted silence, moisture thickening in his eyes. "So the queen's new powers . . ."

"They are why your nephew was sent to Yonte Saire. And now she has sent you here because she believes that opening the gate will strengthen those powers. But she is mistaken. An ancient evil lurks behind that gate, and unleashing it will bring doom on us all. We cannot let that happen."

The general blinks back his tears, veins popping on his temples, the doubt beginning to crumble in the face of growing hope. "Dear Ama, is that really you, Salo?"

"Aba D, you taught me how to play matje and kept playing with me even when I started beating you every time. You taught me how to shoot a bow and throw a spear even when I was a brat about it. You're a hard man, but you never once said a harsh word to me. And if I can't convince you, maybe he can."

Salo glances over his shoulder, where Mukuni has just slunk into view. When the general sees his clan totem, surprised delight shows on his face.

"Mukuni! I always wondered why he didn't come back."

"He knew I wasn't fully dead," Salo says. "He guarded the crystal until my friends came for it. Not even my reflection can control him."

Alinata watches the wall of doubt finally collapse as the general accepts the truth. "Musalodi," he says tearfully, moving forward to embrace his nephew. "Ama be praised." They hold each other tightly, then laugh as they wipe the tears from their cheeks. "Your aba will be so happy when he finds out. Your brothers too. We've all missed you so much."

"I missed you too, Aba."

They embrace again, and then the general pinches his nose, fixing his face into its usual stolid, no-nonsense expression. "Thank you for bringing my nephew back to us," he says to Tuk, who nods.

"It was my pleasure."

"The generals will want to hear this themselves," he says to Alinata. "You must speak to them at once."

"Of course." She glances at Salo. "But I believe your nephew has other places to be."

"I intend to meet with the groups you were fighting," Salo explains. "We will need all the help we can get to stop that gate from opening."

The general nods. "Perhaps it's better that you not be present. My counterparts will be more receptive to a simpler story. It is enough for now that they know what the queen is doing. The rest can come later."

"Agreed," Salo says. "Alinata, I will leave Mukuni with you." He retrieves a rectangular contraption from his chest pocket and hands it over. "Take this. This switch right here will connect you directly to me. Don't hesitate to use it for whatever reason. I'll let you know how our meeting with the Vigilants goes."

While nephew and uncle take a moment to embrace for the last time, Tuk comes closer to Alinata, and she feels a tightness in her chest as she anticipates the worst.

She folds her arms. "If you want to tell me how much I muddled things up—" she begins, but Tuk cuts her off.

"Actually, I wanted to tell you I think you look amazing in that dress." He should hate her, but his eyes are a soft green, and the smug little smile on his face is the same look that got to her back in Yonte Saire. She's always found his self-confidence compelling.

"I see some things haven't changed," she remarks.

His smile brightens briefly, then wanes, tinged with sadness. "For what it's worth, Alinata, I now understand why you did what you did. It's easy to follow someone you trust even if you know they're wrong. What matters in the end is that you had the guts to follow your conscience. I respect that." He touches her arm and squeezes lightly. "It's good to see you again."

They part ways, Tuk and Salo walking off in one direction, Alinata, Mukuni, and the general riding off back to the camp. All the way there, Alinata suffers the uneasy feeling that this will be the last time she'll ever see those two boys.

30: Salim

From the bridge of the *Ataraxis*, the evening desert is a still and quiet landscape of soft, undulating shadows tinged red by the light of the moon. Peaceful on the face of it, but Salim knows better. This is the illusion of serenity before a world-ending storm.

The windcraft's sensors have picked up increasing levels of activity in the skies. Scores more ships have arrived from the west to join the desert king's fleet, bolstering his defense of the pyramid against further attack. Tuk thinks they might be remnants of the Imperial naval force from the battle against the Enclave over the Dapiaro—evidence of how thoroughly his sister's cult infiltrated the world's bases of power just to have them turn on each other.

"This is the *Ataraxis*," Sevan says, speaking into the ship-to-ship communicator on the helm console. "We come in peace. Please do not fire." Sevan waits a few seconds, then looks over her shoulder at Salim with a tiny shake of the head. "They're not responding."

Since their failed attack earlier in the afternoon, the Vigilants have thus far continued to lurk several leagues to the east of the pyramid. Most of their ships are still airborne, but a few have clustered on the ground near a large encampment.

Salim decided it was best to approach this camp slowly, with the stealth shield off so as to avoid raising suspicion, but they've invited the attention of a warship with two heavy cannons currently aimed at the *Ataraxis*.

Stroking his chin, Salim assesses the images displayed on the panels of Mirror light hanging from the ceiling. It's nighttime, and the warship is little more than a looming shadow outside the windows, but Balam's hoverscopes have a crystal-clear view of the vessel and display it on the panels in perfect detail.

It's twice as large as the *Ataraxis*. Even so, Salim thinks the new kinetic shields would be able to withstand the brunt of its firepower, but he doesn't want to find out.

Like picking up a thread and unspooling it, Salim reaches into the warship's web of signals and projects his voice through every speech box onboard. "This is Salim of the *Ataraxis*. Do not fire. If you call your-selves Vigilants, then we are your allies. We wish to stop the pyramid from opening just as you do. We'd like to speak to your leaders."

The response is an immediate rush of signals flowing to the keel of the ship.

"They're charging up their artillery," Sevan warns.

"We are not your enemies," Salim continues in a tone of calm con-fidence. "If the Imperial lords Claud, Julian, and Luka are among you, tell them Salim would like to speak to them."

The signals pause. Another one shoots out of the ship to the Vigilant ground camp. A reply comes back seconds later, and then the speech box on Sevan's console crackles with an unfamiliar female voice.

"Who did you say you were?"

"My name is Salim. I am . . . the captain of this vessel. Captain Salim of the *Ataraxis*." He cringes at the uncertainty in his voice.

Another pause transpires; then the voice speaks again. *"Captain Salim, land your ship at the following coordinates. If you veer off course, we will attack."*

Sevan takes a moment to look over the new information on her console. "They're sending us to their ground camp. Do we proceed?"

Salim nods, and to the warship he says, "Thank you; we're heading to the location now."

Balam breaks his silence. "I have eyes on the ground camp. They're mobilizing an armed welcoming party. It might be best to be prepared."

"Agreed," Salim says. He's almost left the bridge when he glances back at the big man. Balam has claimed the seat by the object-detection console for himself and appears to have adapted to his new role surprisingly well. "Any headaches, Balam?"

Balam shakes his head, a green light flickering inside the eyepiece on his left eye. "Not anymore. The scopes are fairly simple compared to what I'm used to. It was just a matter of adjusting to the unique motion controls. I've never worked with anything so fast."

"Let me know as soon as you feel any discomfort."

"I will."

Salim leaves the bridge through the stairs to the second deck, connecting himself through his bracer tool to Ilapara, Tuk, Jomo, and the Sentinels. "We've been allowed to land in the Vigilant camp. Come down to the skiff bay so I won't have to meet them alone."

The trove of equipment, weapons, and other implements that were stored on the fourth deck is proving more useful than Salim expected. He's already found purpose for the hoverscopes, and hours ago he asked Tuk to look through the collection and help Ilapara and the others familiarize themselves with whatever weapons or technologies they can safely operate.

They join him in the skiff bay as a group, all wearing bracer tools and earpieces. Tuk has a huge grin on his face.

"Salo, I take back everything I said. You were right; I was wrong." He's wearing a gauntlet made of ancient brass on his left arm; he makes a fist with it and aims ahead. Cylinders rotate, and three barrels slide upward from the gauntlet, their interiors swirling with dangerous tendrils of moonfire. The barrels slide back inside, and he lowers his weapon. "This is definitely better than the scopes."

"He squealed and danced when he saw it," Ilapara remarks, to which Salim chuckles.

"I had a feeling he'd be pleased."

Everyone else is armed as well. The three Sentinels chose brass-plated typhonic carbines with collapsible stocks and barrels, all worn in holsters strapped to the thighs of their coveralls. Glass tubes on the carbines glow with active moonfire; from Sevan, Salim knows those typhons can also shoot bolts of lightning.

Jomo has ditched his old sidearm for a new pair of larger, more powerful typhons worn in shoulder holsters. Ilapara has an even longer sidearm slotted into a thigh holster and a telescoping electrified spear dangling from her other hip.

A nervous shiver moves through Salim. "Tuk, did you properly explain how to safely operate those weapons?"

The Sentinel Kito emits a grunt. "We've been using bindukis for months. These are certainly more powerful—"

"*Way* more powerful," Odari cuts in with an ironic laugh. "Makes our old gear look like toys."

"Yes, but the concept is the same," Kito argues. "You point, you shoot, things die."

"We've been using one of the heavy-duty crates in the storage bay for target practice," Tuk says to Salim. "Your weapons pack a meaner punch than what they're used to, but they adapted pretty quickly. Even the lumbering dimwit impressed me."

Jomo guffaws at the comment. "Did you say something, little man? Why don't you try standing on a chair. Perhaps your voice might carry."

"Why bother?" Tuk rejoins. "You wouldn't understand me even if I shouted into your ears. You have all the intellect of a used chamber pot, not to mention the stench to match it."

"Smart-mouthed little twerp."

"Jackass."

Salim blinks, stunned by the exchange. Odari, Kito, and Ijiro are dying with quiet laughter.

"Are they always like this?" Salim asks Ilapara, who gives him a tired look.

"Honestly, I think they like each other but are too afraid to admit it."

While the two young men pull faces and inch away from each other, Sevan's voice comes out of Salim's bracer tool.

"The landing area is surrounded, Salim. You'll be swarmed as soon as you open the door. Should I proceed?"

"Go ahead, Sevan. If they wanted to attack, they'd have done so already."

As the ship slowly descends, they all face the large door at the rear of the bay, waiting.

"Why do you let them keep calling you Salim?" Ilapara inquires. "Your reflection might have stolen your appearance, but he doesn't have to steal your name too."

A question he's been dreading, because the truth is, Salo doesn't feel like his real name either. It's a weight he's not yet ready to carry, and if it wouldn't upset everyone, he'd ask them to stop using it and call him Salim instead.

"Salim is an atmech who woke up not knowing who he was," he explains. "I'm not as ignorant anymore, but important pieces of me are still missing. I guess . . . I don't quite feel myself yet. But I'm getting there," he says. "And finding all of you has brought me closer to being whole, so thank you."

Tuk reaches up to squeeze his shoulder. "We understand, Salo. That's why we'll keep reminding you who you are."

The floors rumble slightly as the vessel touches down on its landing gears. The camp outside is awash in signals that vie for Salim's attention. Ships, communicators, heat generators . . . thousands of other devices with enchanted power cores emitting signals only he can sense. He shuts them out so they don't clutter his mind.

The rear door hisses, lowering itself to the ground to become an exit ramp. Multiple cones of torchlight sweep in from outside, nearly blinding Salim. For a moment he imagines what they look like to those behind the torches: seven young people in coveralls of varied color, six of them heavily armed, a bespectacled figure standing at the front with his hands clasped calmly behind him.

Would the Salo from before recognize himself in this peculiarly dressed youth? Salim isn't so sure.

He leads the way down the exit but stops near the foot of the ramp, not willing to startle the scores of men and women standing in a semicircle around the rear of the ship, aiming their typhons in his direction. The camp behind them is an organized grid of bright lights and large tents with arched roofs. Makeshift sheds provide shelter for parked land vehicles and small winged skiffs. A heavy-duty kinetic-shield generator can be heard as a low and steady hum in the wind. The pyramid is too far to see from here, but a glow hangs over the east, concentrated around a thin stripe of white light stabbing into the sky.

"We come in peace," Salim says in Syliaric. "We're your allies in the fight against those who would let Arante into this world. If the Imperials are here, it's imperative that we speak to them immediately."

"By the suns, it *is* him! Put down your weapons!" A mop of golden hair appears among the torches, the eyes beneath it wide with pleasant surprise. "Salim!"

Claud jogs over, Julian and Luka in tow, all three suited in their enchanted armor, but Tuk and Ilapara make gestures that discourage them from coming too close. Not that it dims the wonder on Claud's face.

"Salim! You're alive!"

"Your Lordships," Salim says. "I had a feeling I'd find you here." He nods at Luka and Julian, who are both visibly bemused. "It's good to see you alive and well."

"And you too," Luka responds mechanically. "I guess."

Julian's cool gaze flicks over Salim's companions, then above them, taking in the windcraft. "Last we saw of the *Ataraxis*, it was pinned down by an Imperial battleship. How are you here right now?"

"A story I'll tell you once there's time," Salim replies. "Your Lordship Julian, I need to see the Book of Lies again. I believe the answer to stopping the pyramid is in that last layer we spoke about."

"You said you couldn't see through it. What's changed?"

"I didn't have the means to see through it at the time. I do now."

The Imperials swap looks. "He's the one who told us about the pyramid," Claud reasons. "And right now, we need any edge we can get."

"For once, I agree," says Luka, though the look in his eyes hasn't gotten any friendlier.

Julian takes another glance at the ship, like she suspects it might be a mirage and if she looks at it just so, she might spot the lie. When she fails, she shakes her head. "What have we got to lose anyway? The book is in our tent. Right this way."

"Hang on just a minute." A rather large woman in a suit of silver armor steps out from the welcoming party, a typhonic rifle in hand. Her russet hair is cut short, and the web of fine scars on her face twists with suspicion. "Before I let you into my camp, I need to know how a cog ended up in charge of a ship."

Salim opens his mouth to speak, but Tuk beats him to it. "Who are you?" he demands.

The woman's frown hardens, and so does her voice. Her Syliaric carries a heavy accent. "Admiral Leto Vasia, formerly of the Eastern Alliance Navy, now in command of the Vigilant fleet. You're standing in my base."

"Admiral, do not let my height fool you," Tuk says. "I'm faster and stronger than any human alive. I could cross the distance to you and snap your neck before anyone fired a shot. Do not repeat the mistake of calling my friend a cog."

The welcoming party had begun to relax; they immediately aim their weapons again, ready to fire at their commander's orders.

"What the devil did you say?" Jomo hisses.

"Tuk, it's all right," Salim says, trying to pacify him, but his irises remain scarlet, his face flushed with anger.

"No, it's not all right!" he shouts, loud enough for everyone to hear him. "A cog is a mindless thing, a tool with no feeling. We are people, as much as anyone else here, and we will be respected as people."

"And who are you to threaten me in my stronghold?" the admiral demands.

"I am a servant of Vigilance." Tuk reaches into his shirt to pull out his Fireblue pendant, which he proudly displays.

The commander leans forward, squinting at it, then makes an irritated noise. "You should have led with that. Let them through." She turns around and starts to leave. "Your Lordships, find me if you have something to share. We're finalizing plans for the next assault."

The Imperials watched the exchange in silence. Julian gives Tuk a lingering stare before she pries her eyes off him. "Salim, the book is this way."

"Well, that was intense," Ilapara whispers as they follow the Imperials deeper into the camp.

"Sorry," Tuk mutters, looking at his boots. "I couldn't help myself."

"No, you were absolutely right," Salim tells him. "We *are* people, and we deserve to be treated with dignity, even if we have to be impolite to get it. Thank you for standing up for me. For all of us."

Tuk says nothing, his eyes turning a shade lighter.

◆　◆　◆

Standing in Julian's sparsely furnished tent, with nine pairs of eyes watching him, Salim palms the Spectral Star in one hand and looks once again into the golden pages of the Book of Lies. As he suspected, the last layer of obfuscation parts before him, and he sees into the truth at the heart of the book. He sees, and he sees, and his heart kicks into a gallop.

It is called the Book of Lies, but he now thinks a better name for it might be the Book of Omissions, for it achieves its lies not by spinning falsehoods but by omitting greater and greater truths from each successive layer built around the tome.

The first layer is a cloak of sunlight and shadows that conceals the words written on the pages from the naked eye. It requires the Spectral Star to pierce and reveal the second layer: a historical account written in hieratic script describing the building of an elaborate tomb by an ancient king who was later buried inside it with his wife. Beneath this mundane tale is the third layer: the story of Rao Ashermose, the Last Hegemon, concealed through sorcery to be visible only to a Red mystic—or, as it happens, an atmech with a metaformic artifact in his mind.

As for the final layer, not even a metaform could see through its murky depths, for its magic is as ancient as history itself, a curse only a mystic who has walked the Bloodway and entered the Red Temple's inner sanctum would know to look for.

The Great Forgetting.

A memory returns to him, and he's suddenly standing at the doors to the sanctum in the Red Temple, the Arc giving him a stern warning about what he'd find within:

"Ignorance is like basking in the suns. It is warm and beautiful, but it is blinding. Step into the sanctum, and your soul will never again taste the warmth of this light. The shadow of knowledge will fall upon you, and you will not escape it, but your eyes will be shielded from the blinding rays, and you will see things you could not have seen before."

With trembling hands, Salim sets the book down onto a nearby steel table and closes it for the last time. Ignoring the expectant eyes on him, he goes outside the tent and casts his awoken senses across the desert, searching for signals he didn't know to look for until now. They appear to him as faint stars in the night sky, four of them, weak, but growing stronger by the hour.

"You have allies," Vigilance said to him. *"Find them, and let them find you. The path forward will become clearer."*

"The admiral," he says to the Imperials. "Take me to her immediately. We're going about this the wrong way."

If the Imperials are affronted by his tone, they hide it successfully. "This way," Claud says and leads the group down the road to the commander's tent.

Admiral Vasia is drawing battle plans with a group of her advisers around a horizontal brass Mirror light panel installed on a table. Generals of the Muomi, Mbare, and Numbi tribes are present, dressed in their respective regalia and armed with heavy-looking typhons. None of them appear especially pleased to see the Imperials walking in with a group of young strangers.

"You'd better have some new information for me," the admiral warns. "We're launching the next attack in an hour. We don't have time to waste."

"I have seen the truth at the heart of the Book of Lies," Salim declares. "You'll be wasting your time if you launch that attack."

The admiral straightens, folding her arms across her armored chest. "Salim, right? We have a Red mystic in the camp. She looked into the book with the Spectral Star and saw the same thing you told the Imperials, including a final layer of obscured information. She said it was impenetrable."

"Not to a mystic who's walked the Bloodway like the Hegemons of old." There is a crackle in the tent as Salim engages his cosmic shards, surrounding his arms in dancing sparks of scarlet lightning.

The Imperials recoil in shock, but the admiral's eyes reflect an enkindled interest, a war tactician who's discovered a new advantage.

"I was not always a cog—an atmech," Salim corrects himself. "I was once a mystic from the Yerezi tribe in the plains east of the World's Artery. The story of how I ended up here is one I'll save for another time. What you need to know right now, Admiral Vasia, is that the gate cannot be stopped. It will open. In truth, it was always meant to be opened."

Confusion eddies in the tent, and even Tuk frowns.

"Unacceptable," the admiral barks. "We didn't come all the way here just to embrace defeat."

"Allow me to explain," Salim says, cutting off the flow of essence to his shards. "The first layer of the Book of Lies tells us that the pyramid is a tomb. The second layer says it's a gate. These are both true. An ancient Faraswa king and his wife were buried inside, and the pyramid was indeed used to tear open a pathway into the Veil. But these are careful disguises built to conceal the truth from the enemy. At its most basic level, the pyramid is in fact a trap, and the quarry it was built for now sits in its jaws. I have reason to believe there are people already working to spring this trap. What we need to do is help them, and I know how, but we need to act carefully and decisively."

The interest Salim saw in the admiral's eyes returns, hotter this time. "All right, Captain Salim. You have our attention."

31: Aneniko

Faraswa Desert

When Niko parts ways with the four young men he has come to consider his brothers, he doesn't embrace them or shake their hands. He doesn't bid them farewell or say goodbye or make a speech. He offers them only a nod, a mundane *see you later* delivered with the carefree cadence of a *tell the cook to cover my food.*

He tells himself the anxiety he feels is only because this is the first time they've separated since leaving home. But they are men, and they've dealt with much worse than being apart for a day or so. They'll be fine.

Of the fifteen Faraswa who attempted to awaken, twelve survived. Ayana will be going to the western artifact with three of them and a pair of Dahbet spearmen. The twins will head to the artifact in the north, accompanying three of the awoken with another spearman tagging along. Mafarai's group, which includes Addi, will go to the eastern artifact, while Niko heads south with the last group:

Inaya, who gives her six-year-old son a tearful goodbye; Kirabo, a teenage girl whose older brother, Wasswa, insists on accompanying her; and Aksil, a quiet but watchful man perhaps approaching his fortieth comet who came alone from Ima Jalama. Niko and a single spearman from Dahbet make it a group of six, a number Ayana insists they don't exceed.

He would have liked for Addi to travel with him, but he decided it would be better for him to go with Mafarai so they'd watch each other's backs. Without Addi present, though, Niko is practically deaf to his new traveling companions, but he figures they don't need to talk much anyway.

Sword sheathed on his back, borrowed spear in one hand, water-skins filled, and a supply of dried food in his leather pouch, Niko sets off with his group on foot, at first walking alongside Mafarai and Addi in a general southern direction, then splitting up when their paths diverge.

Ayana was right, as it turns out. Inaya, Kirabo, and Aksil seem to know exactly where to go, and Niko ends up following them out of the canyons and across a landscape of rocky desert, then skirting the edge of a dune belt. Kirabo's brother, Wasswa, is quite talkative and keeps up a lively conversation with his sister and the guardsman. Aksil's participation is limited to laughs, smiles, and nods with the occasional comment thrown in, while Inaya remains downcast, perhaps haunted by thoughts of the son she left behind.

Enduring the itch of his scars and sweltering beneath his woolen cloak and straw hat, Niko listens to them absentmindedly, picking out familiar words and phrases, but never enough to understand the overall conversation. Mostly he pays attention to his surroundings, looking out for any signs of trouble, though he's not sure what sort of trouble Ayana expected.

It's around noon, shortly after their second break, when a blaze of light briefly consumes the skies behind them, casting shadows even in the daylight. They turn to look just as the blaze condenses to a pillar of pure-white light shooting up into the heavens from a point just over the horizon.

Niko knows of nothing that could explain that pillar of light, but Inaya, Kirabo, and Aksil watch it with the quiet fatalism of people who've just found out that something they dreaded has happened.

Inaya says something that gets the others moving again, and Niko is forced to hold in his questions since no one would understand him anyway. Rumbles like the sounds of faraway explosions chase them throughout the afternoon, coming from the direction of the light source. At one point Niko looks back and sees shadowy shapes moving in the distant sky, too large to be birds, but he can't imagine what else they may be.

The pillar of light eventually disappears behind a dune belt as they descend into a valley, where their prize awaits among ruined and effaced columns of limestone. When Niko finally fixes his eyes on the artifact itself, his step slows, a heaviness settling in his stomach.

What grave sin did he commit for the moon to play such cruel tricks on him? Surely it must be a punishment that the illusions of his dreams should now also manifest in front of him in the light of day, for was it not on the back of a dream chimera that he last spoke to Salo's ghost?

Here is the same chimera, a building-size carving of a reclined sphinx with the body of a lion and the head and four wings of a red-hawk, looking down from its perch on a large slab of rock.

It shouldn't be familiar. He shouldn't feel like he's returning to this place when he knows he's never set foot here before.

Something must show on his face given Inaya's concerned glance at him. "Are you well?" he thinks she says.

He nods, pulling himself together. "Good," he says. It doesn't seem enough, so he scours his limited vocabulary for something else to say. "Big."

"It *is* big," Inaya agrees, though by the restrained amazement in her expression, he guesses she probably sees beyond the size of the statue to whatever arcane purpose it was built for.

She and the other two awakened don't waste time beginning the ritual they've come to perform, though Niko grows doubtful when all they do is sit around the statue and close their eyes as if in meditation. Even the other two men watching with Niko raise their eyebrows, and after a half hour of uneventful sitting and watching, Wasswa says something—probably a question—but the sharp rebuke his sister hisses makes him back off.

"I guess that means no interrupting," Niko mutters to himself.

As dusk settles, he and the lone guardsman go foraging for dry wood and build a fire near the statue to keep themselves warm. It doesn't get as cold as Niko expects it to, though. In fact, he could swear there's a warm draft of air coming from the statue's direction.

Suspicion becomes certainty when he notices the red glow coming out of the sphinx's eyes, subtle at first but gaining strength with each passing hour. All the while the awoken remain frozen, legs folded beneath them, eyes closed, locked in a trance.

Gradually, the glow starts leaking out from underneath the creature's body, as though it were lying on a bed of burning coals. *They're feeding it,* Niko realizes. *Bringing it to life, whatever it is.*

He suffers a twinge of dread as he imagines Addi doing the same thing miles to the northeast.

Will the trance ever release them, or are they stuck like this forever? And when the ritual is complete, what will it birth?

His worries ease as the night progresses, and he even lets himself doze off for a few hours while the guardsman takes the watch. But the pull of Salo's ghost is stronger and more insistent than ever, and the battle to deny it is so ferocious it gives him terrible nightmares. He wakes up with a start, drawing a glance from the guardsman. Unwilling to risk those dreams again, he decides to take the rest of the watch and let the guardsman sleep.

The three awoken are still exactly as they were when he dozed off, but the sphinx has lifted off its base, now engulfed in a red aura. Flakes of limestone have peeled off from parts of the statue to reveal a surface of pure moongold, and by dawn the entire statue has been freed of its false cover.

At sunrise, cold flames appear all over the statue as the arcane metal reacts to the solar rays. It floats higher into the air, and its four wings slowly begin to unfurl. Wasswa and the guard eventually wake up, and Niko shares with them a breakfast of water and dried fruits and nuts. Loud bangs carry over on the wind from somewhere far away, intermittently at first, but then more frequently.

And still the awoken remain in their positions around the statue.

Niko is beginning to feel restless when about a dozen riders appear over the dune belt, all wearing straw hats and woolen cloaks of Yerezi design, the horns and lower legs of their quaggas glimmering with a tronic shine.

Despite the heat, a frozen shiver goes down his spine. He picks up his borrowed spear and gets up, his lips suddenly dry even though they all just quenched their thirst. The other two men rise, too, but he gestures for them to stay put, then goes to intercept the riders so they don't interfere with the ritual.

The riders aren't in any rush. Their pace is leisurely, like men who know there isn't much that could stop them from getting what they want, so why hurry?

By the wide jaw and unnaturally defined musculature, one of the two riders leading the group could be none other than Vitari, Niko's former colleague in the honor guard. He's even wearing his unique pauldron, cast in red steel into the head of a buffalo in honor of his clan. It takes Niko a while longer to identify the other rider in the lead, but as they approach, the sheer hostility on the young man's face becomes visible.

Tumani. Niko's Siningwe rival for a spot in the honor guard. The queen probably promoted him soon after Niko's banishment.

But how the devil did they find me? he wonders, then glances at his own honor guard pauldron.

Could the queen have left just enough of her magic in his red steel to track his location?

Ah shit.

32: Ilapara

The Ataraxis

"So?" Ilapara demands, glaring at Jomo. "What do you have to say for yourself?"

The weak light of dawn is just beginning to wash in through the single porthole in her private compartment. Dressed only in underpants and seated on the bottom bunk of the bed they spent the night on, Jomo stares up at her like he's just watched her head explode.

She's just told him the Thing.

He moves his lips, but she shushes him with a pointed finger, her eyes slit dangerously. "And if you ask me who the father is, Jomo, I swear I'll strangle you and wear your teeth for a necklace."

He flinches back, a wounded look on his face. "I wasn't going to ask you that!"

"Then? Say something, damn you."

"I'm trying," he protests, then reaches for his gray coveralls. She watches him shove his legs into them and pull a black shirt over his head. Salo says his new garments once belonged to the former captain, who was also a big man. She'd tell him she likes the look of them if he weren't getting on her nerves.

He pauses after snapping his metal brace to his left leg, tilting his head, a slanted grin spreading across his stubbled face. "Then again, this was bound to happen, wasn't it? We were pretty relentless for a while."

"You think this is funny?"

"Actually, I think it's good. Right?" He pushes himself up from the bed to stand in front of her. "Me. A father. It's absolutely insane. But the good kind of insane," he rushes to say. "I'm not upset about it. Maybe I'm having a little panic attack—just a small one. But . . . Ilapara, this will bring us closer, won't it?" He puts his hands on her shoulders. "We'll be parents! To a child. Us. Together."

She searches his eyes and finds no deception. He really means it, the fool. It's a relief. And a curse. Her heart sinks, and she lowers herself onto the bed, wishing he'd reacted poorly if only to make this next part easier.

"I'm sorry, Jomo, but I don't think it can work like that," she mutters.

Now it's him looking down at her in confusion. "What do you mean?"

"Look at our lives!" she cries. "I was almost eaten by a pack of sha beasts! You were almost gnawed to death by insects and rats or whatever. We spent months plotting in vain against an emperor, after plotting against a prince and his evil wife, and now we're plotting against gods and devils. This is no life for a child."

He sits down next to her, his brace squeaking from the movement. "All right. You have a point. So I guess when this is over, we'll have to settle down. No more fighting or plotting or running. We could become merchants. Or farmers. Something quiet and peaceful."

Ilapara's shoulders droop. "I'm going back home, Jomo. My mother knows more about being a parent than I do. She'll help me with the child."

For a long minute, Jomo's steady breathing is all she can hear. She fixes her eyes on the floor, waiting for the unavoidable argument.

"Then I'll come with you," he says, and she whips her head to look at him so fast she almost sprains her neck.

"What?"

"I'll come live with you in the Plains," he says. "We can learn how to be good parents together." Seeing her shock, he frowns. "What?"

"Are you insane? You're a prince of the Yontai!"

"I *was* a prince. I'm not anymore."

"What about the fight against the emperor?"

"Isn't that what we're doing right now? And even if he comes out alive at the end of it, assuming the world isn't crawling with mapopobawa by then, someone else can take up the fight if they want. I have other priorities now."

He's such a fool. Such a damned fool. This was supposed to be straightforward. Now he's made it all muddy and messy again. Ilapara drops her face into her hands. "Jomo, I can't . . ."

Her unfinished thought gets cut off by Salo's voice coming out of their bracer tools. *"It's time, everyone. Please come up to the bridge."*

Jomo starts pulling on his socks. "We'll talk later, all right?"

Already dressed, she watches him put on and then lace his boots. He gets up, limps to pick up his cane, then gestures for her to come closer. She obliges and lets him hold her and kiss her gently on the forehead.

"I understand your concerns, Ilapara, but don't think for a second there's anything in the world I'd choose over being a part of our child's life—or yours."

The Sentinels are already on the bridge by the time Ilapara arrives with Jomo, standing around the large navigation table while they wait for Salo to finish a conversation with his bracer tool. The usual denizens of the bridge are absent; Sevan is nowhere to be seen, and Ilapara saw Balam in the dining compartment on the way up here.

As for the Sentinels, Ijiro is smug behind the pair of green lenses he took from the armory simply because he liked how they looked, while Kito and Odari are alert but bleary eyed. They greet each other with nods while Salo carries on his unintelligible conversation. Beneath the sleeves of his blue coveralls, his cosmic shards are aglow.

"I'm still not used to that," Jomo says with a disquieted frown. "Hearing him speak like the outworlders."

"Tell me about it," Ilapara agrees. "Even his reflection needed a translator."

At last Salo ends his conversation and turns his attention to the room. "I hope you've all gotten some rest, because we need to be at our sharpest today."

"You don't look like you slept at all," Jomo remarks, probably on account of the dark bags beneath Salo's eyes.

"I slept for an hour maybe," Salo admits. "After our meeting with the admiral, Sevan and I traded some of our contraband for skiffs, medical equipment, and as many compact barrier generators as we could get. The arcanists and I spent the night repurposing the generators and installing them onto the skiffs to give them added functionality.

"A very humbling experience, by the way," Salo adds with a self-deprecating smile. "Not only did they prove just how much I still have to learn about enchantments and spellcraft, they also identified several fatal and frankly embarrassing flaws in my redesign of this ship's flight systems. Don't worry; we addressed all the major concerns. The only thing wounded is my ego."

Ilapara huffs out a laugh. "They may fight like a pair of feral cats, but they were essential to keeping the resistance alive."

"Agreed," Jomo says. "Though I suspect the fighting masks a deeper friendship."

Across the round table, Odari grins. "Now where else have we seen that before?"

Ilapara feels a smile pulling at her lips.

"Don't even go there," Jomo warns Odari. "The only thing I feel for that annoying little shit is intense loathing. Where is he anyway?"

"Waiting with the Imperials in the camp," Salo replies. "In fact, that's why I've asked you here."

Sitting on the navigation table is a circular panel of Mirror light; Salo manipulates it presumably through his old metaform, which he's wearing on a chain around his neck. A mirage of the desert appears above the panel, showing a pyramid and four other structures rising out of the sands.

"Our one hope to defeat my reflection and his master lies with these artifacts." As Salo speaks, the four structures surrounding the pyramid grow larger on the mirage. Ilapara eyes the circle of obelisks to the north, convinced she's seen them before.

"The Book of Lies refers to them as the Cosmic Tetrad. Each artifact represents one of the four arcane powers that exist in the world: the moon, the suns, the Blue Comet, and the Primeval Spirits. The artifacts were built in secret along cardinal points equidistant from the pyramid and were designed to slowly amass power from their respective sources over the centuries. So slowly, in fact, that no one would ever notice, not even Arante's powerful, all-knowing servants."

The artifacts above the panel each gain a white glow, and then together they release beams of light that intersect at the pyramid's apex.

"If we succeed today, when the gate fully opens, the Tetrad artifacts will simultaneously release all the power they've collected, directing it toward the gate and into Arante's metadimension. With luck, this should be enough to destroy her and all her forces before they cross over to our world."

"I'm sorry, Bwana Salo," the Sentinel Kito interjects. "Have these artifacts been secured? I'm confused about why we didn't rush to them as soon as you found out they exist."

"A good question," Ilapara says.

"We have eyes on the artifacts," Salo responds. "Balam's hover-scopes confirmed that groups of Faraswa allies are currently performing the necessary rituals on-site to activate them. Their rituals are slow, but so far the enemy seems unaware of what's happening. The last thing we want is to draw attention to those artifacts prematurely. And I say prematurely because the enemy *will* wise up to them eventually. But that's where we come in."

On the mirage, an armada of windcrafts appears over the pyramid, armies of riders and foot soldiers seething around its base.

"The king's forces are considerable, but they've all gathered around the pyramid because they think that's our target. We want them to keep thinking that for as long as possible. As we speak, Admiral Vasia is moving to engage the bulk of the enemy force at the pyramid, both in the air and on the ground. That will keep them too preoccupied to divert any significant forces to the artifacts. Smaller contingents can then move in to secure the artifacts until the rituals to activate them are complete."

The map on the mirage shrinks so that the Vigilant camp comes into view, many miles east of the pyramid. Three tiny skiffs appear above the camp, then fly off, one going west, another south, and the third heading straight for the eastern artifact.

"Alinata, my uncle, and a company of rangers from our clan will take the northern part of the Tetrad; they're already on their way. We'll handle the rest. Admiral Vasia has assigned all the remaining skirmishers of the Mbare tribe to help us, so about thirty men in total."

"That's it?" Ilapara blurts out. "Thirty Mbare skirmishers? Not to speak ill of them, but couldn't she offer us a few of her elite armored troops? Or what about the blooded Muomi champions and Numbi magicians we saw fighting yesterday?"

Salo gives a sad smile. "The admiral is . . . a practical woman . . . and her sole focus is on capturing the pyramid. But this will work to our advantage. The more fierce a battle she mounts at the pyramid, the less pressure we should face. And don't discount the skirmishers too soon. The Mbare were the first Red tribe to adopt typhonic rifles and have become skilled sharpshooters. The skirmishers are also well equipped; I assisted with this myself. They won't let us down."

Ilapara isn't convinced, but she nods. "What's the situation with the Ajaha regiments?"

"Tense. The generals believe my uncle, but they're reluctant to oppose the queen directly. They fear she'll suppress their ability to use their blessings as punishment."

"She can do that?" Ilapara asks, balking at the thought.

Salo dips his head in a nod. "Among the privileges of the Hegemon is some measure of control over the ancestral talents. I assume her fragment has given her a limited form of this power, but I don't imagine she can exercise it without cost to herself. The crown was never meant to be used that way."

"The crown is a blight on the world," Jomo gripes. "Nothing good can come from anyone having that power."

Salo's spectacles reflect the dawn light coming in through the windows. "You won't hear an argument from me."

"So what now?" Ilapara asks. "Are you saying we're about to fight our own people?"

"No, but we can't count on their help either. They've decided to stay out of the battle for now."

"Better than the alternative, I suppose."

"Indeed." Salo looks back at the map on the table, where the three skiffs have each reached their destinations. "Whatever the case, the five of you and about ten skirmishers will be heading south in a moment. Tuk, the Imperials, and the arcanists will go to the other two artifacts.

Sevan, Balam, and I will keep an eye on everything from here and provide assistance when necessary."

"Are you casting a spell, Bwana Salo?" the Sentinel Ijiro asks, bringing attention to Salo's cosmic shards, which haven't stopped glowing since Ilapara and Jomo entered the room.

"Yes," he admits. "But I hope I won't have to release it. Either way, it took me hours to prepare, so I have to hold on to it. That's why I can't be on the ground with you today. My attention is divided enough as it is."

"As usual," Ilapara teases him.

"Before you go . . ." Salo has spoken with a calm authority all along, but he hesitates now, pushing his spectacles up his nose. "I have an advantage to offer you. Beyond your weapons, that is. It doesn't have to be permanent, but it will make you considerably stronger during this battle."

"Are you talking about a Yerezi blessing?" Jomo says. "Because if you are, then I'm in." He looks at the Sentinels, mulish. "What? Did you think I was going to twiddle my thumbs while you went out to play at being heroes? Mother damn that. I'm going."

"We're not stopping you, Jomo," Kito says gently, and Jomo loosens his shoulders like he was expecting a tougher fight.

Ilapara resists the temptation to give him that fight; she would feel better if he stayed behind. But she's wiser than to insult him. Not only does he have a personal stake in this battle—he's also proved quite capable of keeping himself alive and would be even stronger with a blessing.

And so would Ilapara, but she abandoned the desire for a blessing after her chief refused her the bullpen all those years ago and became hostile to the idea altogether as she grew into a woman. It seemed ridiculous to want to base her worth on borrowed strength that someone else could take away. Better that her strength be hers and hers alone.

"Just this once," she tells Salo. "But you should know that when this is over, I won't be keeping it."

"Understood."

Jomo fails to show her the same courtesy she showed him when he leans over to whisper into her ear. "Are you sure it's safe? I mean, for . . . you know."

"Of course it's safe," she hisses. "Do you think we'd still have a tribe if it wasn't?"

He thinks about it, then nods. "I guess not. Carry on."

For something she's fussed about for so long, the act of receiving a blessing turns out to be rather unexciting. They link their hands around the table, Salo strengthens the glow of his cosmic shards, Ilapara feels a tiny flash of heat in her chest, and a lightness settles over her, like she's suddenly lost half her weight. And then it's over.

"That's it?" Jomo says, staring at his hands. "Am I stronger now?"

The Sentinels do the same, as if they'll find the answer written on their palms.

"Don't try to use your strength just yet," Salo warns them. "Let it settle for a few minutes. In fact, maybe you can do that on the way. Your skiff is waiting for you outside."

They arm themselves and cover their heads with long scarves for protection from the suns, then head down to the skiff bay, Ilapara with her typhon holstered to her thigh and her telescoping electrified spear in one hand. Before they descend the exit ramp, Salo pulls her to the side.

"Ilapara, I tried to reach out to Aneniko last night, but he shut me out. He's actually at the artifact you're headed to." Salo doesn't say more, but his request is plain to see on his face.

"I'll look out for him," she says.

Relief and gratitude loosen his features. "Thank you." To everyone he says, "Keep your earpieces on. We can always communicate by thought, but the way I'm built now makes it a very unpleasant experience for me. I tried it with Tuk, and it sounded like he was screaming into my mind. Let's save that for emergencies only. Balam will be watching you and your surroundings; we'll let you know of any important developments. Good luck, everyone, and Ama watch your steps."

An impulse comes over Ilapara, and she embraces him. She says nothing as she lets go, because this will not be a goodbye. Then, armed with foreign weapons, with Jomo and the Sentinels by her side, she sets off to defy a devil.

33: Salim

Salim walks down the exit ramp of the *Ataraxis* to watch the three skiffs lift off into the early-morning sky. They are identical for the most part, elongated pod-shaped vessels with round windows and shiny surfaces of smooth brass, each armed with two side-mounted cannons of respectable capacity.

Compared to the rest of the admiral's fleet, however, the skiffs are fairly old. Sevan thinks the admiral swindled them in their trade with her and that the weapons and explosives they offered her were much more valuable than what she gave back. But Priscille is happy with her restocked infirmary, and the skiffs themselves are not nearly as important as the wealth of enchantments they're hauling around.

Granted, Salim and the arcanists made some changes to the crystal cores to make the skiffs faster and quieter, but most of their efforts went into reenchanting and testing the barrier generators they'd gotten in the trade with the admiral and then bolting those generators to the floors of the skiffs.

Now, as the skiffs gain altitude over the camp, triangular sails of moonglass fanning out from their rears, shields of light distortion ripple all around their shapes, and they slowly blend into the sky before disappearing from sight altogether. Invisible and silent as the whistle of a gentle wind, they bank westward and zip away.

A second later his bracer tool buzzes. *"I've been tracking a squad of rangers from your tribe, Salim,"* Balam says. *"It looks like they're heading for the sphinx. Come take a look. I'm on the bridge."*

"On my way."

Salim heads back into the *Ataraxis*, and he hasn't even reached the stairs to the upper decks when his tool vibrates again.

"How the hell is this skiff flying itself?" comes Luka's ill-tempered baritone. He and his brother, Claud, are currently seated in the skiff heading west with the two arcanists and a team of Mbare skirmishers. *"And what's that shimmer I see outside?"*

All three Imperials have been standoffish with Salim since they learned of his magic. Even Claud barely spoke a word to him last night. He might have taken offense if he didn't have more pressing concerns.

"We made nonstandard alterations to the skiffs," he explains. "It would take time we don't have to teach someone how to safely operate one. For now I've assigned my metaformic familiar the responsibility."

"A metaform is flying this skiff?" Luka asks with audible alarm.

"I'm currently too busy to do it myself, so yes."

"By the suns. And the shimmer?"

"A cloak of light distortion to make you invisible to the naked eye."

The next voice that comes is Claud's. *"Salim, I'm beginning to think that finding you in Apos was no coincidence."*

"I doubt any of us are in this desert right now by coincidence, Your Lordship."

"I suppose that's true."

Whatever's happening at the pyramid is so energetic it's tickling Salim's cosmic shards even from many miles away. He puts the sensation out of his mind as he enters the bridge, where Balam is alone, sipping tea from a giant mug while he monitors the swarm of scopes through his eyepiece. As soon as he notices Salim's arrival, he summons the two brass panels from the ceiling and displays a different vision on each one.

"Here. Take a look. They're almost there."

The helm chair is empty, which means Sevan is probably still in bed. Standing by the navigation table, Salim takes a look at the visions. He's visited the one on the right several times already. It was still dark the last time; the suns have just risen now. The three men in focus are sharing breakfast around a dead fire, one of them wearing a red steel pauldron fashioned into the head of a spike-maned leopard.

Salim would like nothing more than to simply lift the *Ataraxis* into the air and go to that man, but now's really not the best time for major shocks. Things might have been different had they dreamed together last night. Salim would have told him the truth, and Niko would have expected him. But the magic of shared dreams only works if both parties are willing.

The other panel shows an unexpected squad of rangers riding purposefully across a dune belt. Balam has marked their location on the navigation table as a group of red lights moving in the direction of the sphinx. There's a second group of lights heading north, to the circle of obelisks, but this group, which includes Alinata and Salim's uncle, is supposed to be there.

"Maybe my uncle sent them," Salim muses. Just to be sure, he reaches for Alinata through his bracer tool. "Alinata, it's me. Are you there?"

She takes a few seconds to respond. *"Yes, Salo."*

"Did my uncle send anyone to the artifact in the south?"

"I don't know. Let me ask."

While he waits, he flicks away from Niko's vision to watch Tuk and Julian arrive at the eastern artifact with ten skirmishers. The two of them insisted on taking on the Vigilant quarter of the Tetrad, so he had no choice but to put them together.

Their skiff ripples into view as it lands a few hundred yards from the artifact. Hours ago the artifact looked like a limestone hand rising out of the sands with a sphere in its palm. Now the sphere has lifted off the palm to hover in the air, and the limestone has peeled off to reveal a glowing surface of perfect Fireblue.

The dreadlocked ranger and the two Faraswa spearmen guarding the artifact are only briefly paralyzed by the shock of a flying machine appearing out of nowhere. But as soon as they see people stepping out of the machine, they quickly move into defensive positions, the ranger drawing his bow.

"*We're your friends!*" Tuk shouts with his palms raised, first in Izumadi, then again in Sirezi. "*We're here to help, not to interfere!*"

Salim withdraws from the scene when Alinata gets back to him. "*Salo, your uncle didn't send anyone to the south. And he didn't tell the generals about the specifics of your plan either. Why do you ask?*"

"There's a group of Ajaha heading in Niko's direction right now."

"*The queen might have sent them. Aneniko is—was—an honor guard. She can probably still track him.*"

"Should we expect trouble?"

A pause. "*I'm afraid so, yes.*"

34: Aneniko

The Sphinx Artifact

Unease pricks the inside of Niko's throat like needles. He grips his spear tighter, the thin scars on his arm throbbing in revolt, but he maintains an outward ruse of self-control.

"You're a long way from home, cousins," he says to the fifteen or so rangers when they come within earshot.

"You're one to speak, deserter," Tumani shoots back.

They bring their quaggas to a stop, letting Niko study their faces for a moment. He became acquainted with many of them during his time stationed at the Queen's Kraal, when he was first raised to the honor guard.

Tumani is the only clansman, though, yet it seems the antagonism on his face is the strongest. Perhaps their relationship is well beyond repairing, and nothing Niko says will get through to him. So Niko tries his old colleague.

"Vitari."

"Aneniko."

"You've never lacked something wise to say to me every time we've met. Are you not happy to see me, or have you finally run out of insults?"

Vitari grins, but something like regret flashes through his eyes. "You messed up, mzi. I really wish you hadn't, but it's out of my hands now."

Even with the queen's enhanced blessing intact, Niko would have hesitated to take on two honor guards, let alone two honor guards and a squad of rangers. Now, it wouldn't even be a fight. He'd be dead in less time than it takes to draw in a breath and scream.

"So what happens now?" he asks, keeping calm. "Are you here to toss me the reed? Because if you are, you could have just waited for me to come back home."

"We're well past the reed now," Tumani growls. "Disownment is the least you deserve for your betrayal."

"Then what justice have you come here to mete?"

"You can hand over that pauldron, for starters."

"If I hand it over, will you go away and leave us alone?"

"Oh, we're definitely stopping whatever vile demonic witchery you've got going on back there." Tumani curls a lip in disgust as he glances at the glowing statue, then glares back at Niko. "But if you willingly hand over the pauldron, I'll make your death quick and painless, and your ama can weep over a good-looking corpse. Or you can hang on to it, and I'll just remove it after I take off your head. Your choice."

So the queen has sent you to kill me, Niko thinks. Which means the queen and her allies have somehow divined Ayana's plan and probably sent people to the other artifacts.

Despair weakens Niko in the knees, but it's quickly drowned out by violent anger. He bares his teeth, the skin on the knuckles of his spear hand stretching so much it might tear.

"I knew you were bitter about the queen choosing me over you, Tumani, but I didn't know you were *this* bitter. Then again, it must be a grave insult to know you've taken my sloppy seconds."

"Keep talking, siratata," Tumani snarls. "Make it easier for me."

"Why don't we settle this once and for all? You think you're better than me—"

"I *know* I'm better than you. You're a traitor. An enemy of the queen and a disgrace to the Siningwe."

"Then prove it," Niko says. "Fight me without your blessing. Prove to everyone here that you deserve this pauldron more than I do. Or you can kill me like a coward, and they'll always know I was the better man."

Even if Tumani holds back, this can only end one way, but Niko's only course of action now is to buy the awoken as much time as he can, and if that means drawing out his death, then so be it.

Perhaps recognizing he's been led into a trap, Tumani glowers at Niko. "I know my worth. I don't care what anyone else thinks."

"Really? Not even him?" Niko says with a nod in Vitari's direction. "He has a big mouth, you know. He'll tell all his friends what happened here. So will the others, I'm sure. You'll strut around with my pauldron, but they'll be laughing at you behind your back. Everyone will know just how much of a coward you were when I challenged you."

Fury burns in Tumani's eyes. He dismounts from his saddle, his spear in hand. "Say your last prayer, siratata," he says. "I'm about to flay you alive."

35: Ilapara

The Sphinx Artifact

Ilapara's skiff is whisper quiet as it ghosts across the Faraswa Desert. Inside, she and her fellow passengers are seated on benches of old cracked leather arranged so that they're facing each other. Several brass engines in compact cubic frames bolted onto the floor fill the interior with a soft thrum. There's no pilot at the helm.

There's no speaking, either, not even among the Mbare skirmishers—turbaned men draped in loose printed cloths who wear their typhonic rifles on slings. Small vials are nestled in pouches on their shoulder belts. Their eyes are alight with intense focus, their lips dry and slightly parted as if in hunger. Ilapara has seen that look before, on tonic-drinking ravagers of Umadiland. She can also smell the whiff of burnt nsango and at least one other mind-altering herb.

Whatever works for them, she supposes. The Mbare tribe is a coastal people not known for much beyond their fish trade. If alchemy helps turn them into effective warriors, so be it.

About three minutes into their flight, Salo's voice fills the cabin from a speech box on the ceiling. *"Bad news, everyone. A squad of hostile Ajaha are already at the sphinx. Immediate intervention is necessary, so you'll be transposed off the skiff. Be prepared to leap straight into a fight."*

Ilapara glances directly across from her at Jomo. She brings her bracer tool closer to her face. "Salo, you said we wouldn't be fighting our people."

"These are the queen's own men. They're not with the regiments."

"Are you saying the queen has already figured out our plan?"

"It's possible, but so far only the sphinx is under attack. Do not engage them in the open. The goal is to surprise and overwhelm them with firepower, forcing a retreat. A . . . friend is currently fighting a duel with one of the Ajaha; it's not looking good. Ilapara, I'm counting on you to put a stop to this."

"Understood."

"Their quaggas are tronic and will be vulnerable to the lightning modes of your typhons. The Ajaha themselves will be more resilient due to their enchanted red steel. But I'd rather they lived to escape than died for not knowing any better."

The skirmishers nod, adjusting their rifles, and the interiors of the long glass tubes running down the barrels change from boiling moonfire to electric scarlet plasma. Jomo reaches for his two sidearms while the Sentinels unholster their brass-plated carbines; they all switch their weapons from moonfire to lightning beams. The sidearm strapped to Ilapara's thigh was already set for lightning, so she leaves it as it is.

Everyone looks around when a new voice comes out of the speech box, unidentifiable as either male or female. *"Transposition in sixty seconds."*

"Who the devil was that?" Jomo asks.

"That was Ziyo given a voice," comes Salo's reply. *"Did I forget to mention this?"*

"I think you might have, yes."

They all stand, weapons ready, Ilapara's spear extended to its full length. A worried tingle goes through her at the sight of Jomo's cane lying on the floor.

"Are you sure about this?" she asks him quietly.

His grin is wide, fearless. "I might still need the leg brace, but I've never felt better in my life."

"Just . . . be careful, all right?"

"Hey, I'm only here to watch your back. In more ways than one, I guess." He winks when she gives him a half-hearted glare.

"Transposition in twenty seconds," the disembodied voice announces.

Curious, Ilapara speaks into her bracer tool again. "I'm concerned. How will you transpose us from so far away?"

"Through an enchantment in one of the generators. Ziyo is in control of it."

"Transposition in ten seconds. Nine . . . eight . . . seven . . ."

As the countdown continues, Ilapara finally confronts her blessing for the first time. The secrets of strength and speed she learned from her uncle opened a door to a new understanding of just how far she could push her body. But the blessing is like opening a floodgate. Like standing next to a gushing river of strength and esoteric knowledge and all she needs to do is bend down and touch it.

Static crackles inside the cabin and folds them into the Void, and they arc down to the surface as a lightning bolt, appearing on a dune ridge overlooking a valley.

On one side of the valley, a rearing sphinx of burning moongold floats above an empty pedestal, metal wings spread like those of a red-hawk, three Faraswa people seated around it still as rock formations. On the other side of the valley, a circle of mounted Ajaha cheers as two of their comrades duel to the death. Ilapara is in motion as soon as her boots touch the ground, Jomo and the Sentinels close behind.

One of the dueling rangers is bleeding from cuts on his chest and face, and now a spear pierces his abdomen even as Ilapara runs to save him. He falls to his knees, gurgling blood. She runs ahead anyway.

Beams of red lightning buzz past her from behind, peppering the unsuspecting Ajaha and their tronic mounts with a sudden electric blitz.

Enveloped in hostile static, the tronic quaggas bray and kick wildly, and two riders are shaken off their saddles.

With the circle of rangers broken, Ilapara has a clearer view of the fallen ranger and his would-be killer, who even now lifts his spear for the finishing blow. Her reflexes are like clay in the hands of a sculptor; without missing a step, she draws her typhon from its thigh holster and fires. Arcane reactions inside the weapon's glass chamber release focused bolts of red lightning that shock and stagger the ranger, forcing him a step back from his quarry. She fires again, but this time he lifts his forearm and summons a shield of magic from his red steel vambrace.

She keeps firing as she charges at him. The bolts explode harmlessly into sparks on his invisible shield, but the onslaught pushes him away from the ranger bleeding out on the sand. He snarls at her, a vow of painful things to come unless she backs off, and when she doesn't, he leaps forward on moon-blessed strength, quickly following through with a mighty thrust of his spear.

She dodges to the side, holstering her sidearm and in the same motion whipping her spear up in time to repel another strike. Frowning, he draws from his blessing to deliver faster thrusts, perhaps thinking he should have ended her already, but little does he know he's not the only one with a blessing.

He thrusts. She turns him away. He tries to outmaneuver her, but she's too fast. A proud Ajaha who proved himself in the bullpen, and yet here is a woman dressed in foreign garments who can mimic his fighting style and match him in speed.

At his next strike, she leaps away, giving Jomo and the Sentinels a clear line of sight. Just as she hopes, they proceed to bury him in lightning fire.

He groans, going down on his knees, his skin burning and peeling off in places. An ordinary human would have already perished, but his enchanted armor protects him from the brunt of the fire. She delivers a hard kick to his face, and he crumples to the sand, unconscious.

All around her, the electric buzz of lightning is deafening. The skirmishers are an organized line crouched at the top of the ridge, their tonic-enhanced aim brutally perfect. Jomo and his friends have flanked the Ajaha on the side of the sphinx, unleashing a second front of lightning, Jomo shooting with both sidearms, the Sentinels with their rapidly firing automatic carbines. Ilapara joins in with her own weapon, her augmented reflexes guiding her aim.

With worsening blisters and burns all over their bodies and facing fire from two directions, the Ajaha should scatter and flee, but the muscular one with an honor guard's pauldron manages to rally them for a charge up the dune.

They don't get too far. A flying hulk of metal shimmers out of stealth above the skirmishers on the dune, and from its two side-mounted cannons it spits out bolts of moonfire that scorch the ground where they hit, nearly incinerating the cavalrymen.

Frightened, the quaggas abort the charge. "Retreat!" shouts one of the rangers.

To Ilapara's shock, the honor guard leaps off his quagga in a blur of scarlet shadow, flying up to the skiff like a demon of moonfire. It looks like a spell, something she'd expect from a Jasiri or some other warrior mystic. The next thing she knows, a lightning bolt catches the Ajaha in the air before he reaches the skiff, and he vanishes, only to appear back where he started, several yards above the ground. He falls the rest of the way down and is immediately engulfed in a hailstorm of lightning bolts.

"Retreat!" he shouts, hurrying back onto his saddle.

And at last the Ajaha flee from the fight, riding their panicked quaggas in a hasty withdrawal while the skirmishers continue to fire at them and the skiff herds them away.

The one Ilapara kicked is awakening. She points her typhon at him when he tries to pick up his spear.

"Don't."

He freezes, his eyes widening at her use of Sirezi. Burns weep all over his face and arms. She might have felt sorry for him had she not just seen him try to murder another of his own.

"Just go," she says. "And remember we did our best not to kill you. Come back again and we won't be so merciful."

"Who are you?" he asks.

"I said go!"

He nods, lifting his palms, then gets up and flees.

Only once she's sure he's gone does she turn her attention to the fallen ranger. Two Faraswa men she's only just noticed run to him, one of them trying to stanch his bleeding wounds with what looks like a head wrap. She approaches them.

"I sent down a barrier generator," Salo says to everyone. *"Place it close to the meditating Faraswa and activate it as an extra security measure."*

Odari and Kito spot the brass engine on the sands and move to comply.

When Salo speaks next, privately to Ilapara, his voice is still calm but noticeably subdued. *"How is he?"*

She kneels down next to the ranger, wishing there were something she could do. The ranger looks up at her, confused recognition showing in his eyes. She remembers seeing him in the construct back in Yonte Saire. He looked happy at the time, holding a cat in his arms. He's wheezing for breath now, an ashen cast to his skin.

"He was stabbed in the abdomen," she says into her bracer tool. "Someone's trying to stop the blood loss, but it doesn't look good."

"Please ask one of the Sentinels to take over."

"What's your plan?"

She looks up as the skiff stops to hover in the air nearby, a low whine coming out of its engines, the twin suns reflecting on its metal surface.

"He needs urgent care. I'll fly him over on the skiff."

"Understood. Ijiro!" The youngest Sentinel comes over, his carbine still in hand. "This ranger's name is Aneniko. He's Salo's friend. We need you to keep pressure on his wound until you get him back to the ship."

Any displeasure Ijiro might feel remains hidden behind his green lenses. "Sure thing, boss."

The stock of his carbine retracts, and he holsters it onto his thigh, then kneels next to Aneniko and takes over from the confused Faraswa gentleman.

"Are you taking him somewhere?" the gentleman asks, speaking also in KiYonte.

Ilapara points at the skiff. "That machine will fly him to our friends." She gets back up. "All right, everyone. Move back so you won't be taken with them."

They watch Ijiro and the ranger disappear in an arc of lightning that shoots up to the skiff. Then the skiff banks away and accelerates, vanishing into stealth.

A heaviness weighs on Ilapara's heart. "I'm sorry I wasn't fast enough."

"You did all you could," Salo says, and she wonders how he can continue to speak so calmly under the circumstances. *"The Ajaha are still retreating, but we'll be watching them. I'll keep you informed."*

36: Salim

The Ataraxis

Salim is not calm. Somewhere inside his mind he screams in terror. But his metaformic aspect helps him suppress any emotional response that would cloud his judgment. He knows he cannot afford the luxury of panic.

When the skiff lands in the Vigilant camp, he's waiting for it with Priscille and a wheeled stretcher. The last time he saw Niko with his own eyes, he was riding away from the kraal while Niko looked down at him from the top of a watchtower. Salim thought it the end of their complicated friendship, that he'd driven Niko away by being too defective a man.

But they would meet again in their shared dreams, and the same boy he thought he'd disappointed would come to make him feel like he was loved and admired, not in spite of his eccentricities but because of them. Like he was perfect just the way he was.

Here they are, reunited as the entrance to the skiff opens. Ijiro looks up from where he's kneeling next to Niko, who is supine on a bench, bleeding out into the cloth pressed against his wound. "He's lost a lot of blood."

Priscille is already performing scans with her medical bracer tool. "Get him on the ship, Salim. There's no time to waste."

They gently carry him out of the skiff and onto the bed, and she covers his mouth and nose with a metal breathing mask. He winces beneath it, his eyes blinking open as the bed rolls itself up the ramp.

"Salo?" comes his muffled voice.

"Yes, Niko. I'm here."

"Am I dead?"

Salim brushes Niko's forehead in an attempt to soothe him. He tries not to let his voice crack. "You're alive, and you'd better stay that way. You hear me?"

Niko's eyes close as he drifts out of consciousness. Walking beside the bed, Priscille continues her scans, mumbling about intraabdominal injury and hypotension.

Cast a spell! shouts Salim's panicked self. *You have a whole archive of Blood craft at your disposal! Find a spell and save Niko's life!*

He ignores that voice, for while he may be comfortable with the operations of machines, to attempt spells of Blood craft on a living person without a firm understanding of the human body would do more harm than good. And he would have to abandon the spell he's gathered around his cosmic shards.

In the sick bay, Priscille has already activated the compartment's disinfecting crystal lamps. She finds a sharp pair of scissors and begins to cut off the straps of Niko's leather harness, moving with a purpose and self-assurance Salim hasn't seen in her before. "I need you both to leave the room."

Salim stays put. "Priscille—"

"I have everything I need to help him," she says, cutting him off. "The best thing you can do for him now is let me do my job."

He opens his mouth to say something, but his bracer tool vibrates. *"Salim, the ground assault on the pyramid is going poorly,"* Balam says. *"The masked warriors in red are too strong."*

Salim's mind races, and then he replies into his bracer tool. "Balam, locate everyone wearing a moongold mask. They'll also be in red, and there'll likely be seven of them."

"Got it."

"Priscille . . . ," Salim tries again, struggling to convey how important it is that she save this young man.

What does he mean to me? he once asked himself. The answer seems plain now.

Sometimes people need others to show them that they're valuable before they believe it themselves. Because of Niko, Salim knows he is worthy. Desirable. Beautiful. Adored.

"He means the world to me," he says to Priscille.

She looks him in the eye to show him she understands. "I will do my utmost best. Now go fight your war."

The door to the sick bay closes behind him and Ijiro, and they stand there for a quiet moment, Salim flexing his fingers just to give his hands something to do. Then the moment of helplessness ends, and he returns to the present.

"Thank you, Ijiro. If you want, you can return to the skiff, and it'll fly you back."

Ijiro looks at his hands, which are still slicked with Niko's blood. "Maybe I can hang around a little longer. It feels . . . wrong just to leave. You can let me know if I'm needed back at the artifact; then I'll go."

Salim nods in silent gratitude and makes his way back up to the bridge.

"Balam, what's going on?"

Balam points at one of the panels hanging from the ceiling. "I thought Imperial knights were formidable, but those warriors are something else."

One glance at the ferocious battle on the panels, and Salim suddenly understands why his cosmic shards keep tingling with distant bursts of energy.

Yesterday afternoon the Vigilants sent only a small force to test the pyramid. Today they've sent the full measure of their power, hoping perhaps to overwhelm the king's forces. But the king amassed more ships since the last battle, and his ground forces are proving strong enough to withstand the admiral's assault.

Salim's heart misses a few beats at the sight of a Jasiri conjuring a storm of moonfire and hurling it at a unit of enemy infantry. A group of armored warriors in the path of the storm summons shields of force from their bracer tools, deflecting the heat. A Numbi magician in black robes unleashes a wind familiar that swirls around her and her allies in a protective dome. A blooded Muomi champion with scarlet face paint should duck into the dome, but he roars at the flames instead, mad with bloodthirst and perhaps convinced he can simply cow the approaching wall of flames into submitting.

And for a moment, the flames *do* stop, held back by an ancestral magic dependent on bloodshed and rage, but the press of moonfire proves too much, and the champion's hold eventually breaks, and the flames incinerate him in a blink.

Salim withdraws deeper into the cold and logical lattices of his metaform, his human self recoiling in disgust. "Have you found our targets?"

Balam grunts in satisfaction. "Take a look."

The mirage on the other panel splits into seven different squares, each one showing a figure in crimson robes and a full mask of moongold. A few patrol the railed walkways that span across the chasm to the pyramid's platform. Others are on the platform itself, near the very base of the structure.

"Seven, as you said, alone or in pairs in the immediate vicinity of the pyramid. Are they sorcerers?"

"High mystics of the Yontai," Salim responds. "Their predecessors were the most powerful sorcerers on the continent. But these are beholden to the emperor, so I'm not sure how they compare. I wouldn't underestimate them either way."

"Looks like they've positioned themselves as the last line of defense, but no one has gotten that far."

Salim takes a closer look at the blue-gray pyramid that brought them all here. It's beginning to split right down the middle like a slowly opening gate, though the capstone has stayed in place above the widening gap, a pillar of immensely bright light shooting out from the pyramid's interior.

Dread grips the base of his spine. "Have you seen the king?"

"No sign of him yet. Haven't seen a queen or an emperor either. My guess is they're probably inside that thing. My scopes can't see past the pillar of light."

Salim shakes his head slowly. "I can't believe I'm about to say this, but we need to take out those sorcerers."

"How? You repurposed the weapon systems on the scopes."

"I don't regret that. We needed the added speed and stealth; otherwise the scopes would have been discovered by now. And I doubt those weapons would have been strong enough anyway."

"I could cause the scopes to explode destructively," Balam suggests, and Salim shakes his head again.

"We need something certain. And quick. Something they won't see coming."

"I'm out of suggestions."

While a plan takes shape in Salim's mind, he looks away from the Shirika and takes over the other panel, skimming through the visions until he finds the one where Tuk and Julian are chatting to each other as they watch the sphere of Fireblue lift higher above the palm it once rested on. They seem to have made peace with the lone ranger and his two Faraswa companions, though given how far they're standing from the artifact, they were probably told to keep their distance.

"—you speak like one and you look like one," Julian is saying.

"My progenitor was a Chatresian noble from centuries ago," Tuk responds. *"So you could say I am a native."*

"But your name—"

"I changed it when I left the Empire. The old one didn't fit me anymore. What about you?"

"What about me?"

"Julian Silver Dawn. How are you related to Gregoire Silver Dawn?"

A long pause transpires. *"He's my grandfather."*

Tuk's response is a long and silent stare.

"Yes. I know. That's why I'm here. To stop him. For his own sake."

Guilt prompts Salim to announce himself. "Tuk. Change of plans. A team of Jasiri is decimating the admiral's forces. If they fall too soon, the artifacts will be in danger. We need to take those Jasiri out."

On the panel, Tuk brings his bracer tool closer to his lips. *"I hope you're not about to ask me to go do that. I could handle one, maybe, but a team?"*

"You won't have to. I'm sending you to deal with the Shirika. Remove them, and all the Jasiri lose their power. They're standing guard around the pyramid. You still have that stealth bracelet I made for you, right?"

"I do," Tuk says. *"But even with the bracelet, it's a tall order."*

"I have a plan," Salim says. "And I'm about to ask a favor of Alinata. Get on the skiff, and I'll explain everything."

"Ah. A competition? I'm on my way."

Salim glances through Mukuni's eyes and sees Alinata staring at a circle of obelisks rising higher above the sands. He connects himself to her communication tool, praying she won't be too affronted by what he's about to ask.

37: Alinata

The Circle of Obelisks

It was just after dawn when they arrived, a lone former Asazi leading a squad of Siningwe cavalrymen on the back of their clan totem. Many in the squad, including General Siningwe himself, had misgivings about a plan that involved sneaking away from the epicenter of battle to guard some mysterious artifact out in the desert.

But all their doubts vanished when they finally sighted the circle of seven obelisks slowly lifting out of the sands in the shadow of a hill, their exteriors of granite flaking off to expose etched surfaces of lustrous gold.

And who else but the general's twin nephews would be seated by a fire with a Faraswa spearman, watching over the ritual inside the circle with glazed eyes.

Eyes that widened when they saw their uncle riding toward them with a group of familiar faces.

First came the surprised reunion. The hugs, the patting on the backs, the uncle telling his nephews they almost sent him to an early grave with worry, the nephews sheepishly apologizing.

Then came the questions. The who, the what, the when, the revelation that their brother is still alive.

Alinata expected to become the focus of the interrogation, and she wasn't disappointed. While two of the general's rangers left to serve as lookouts, everyone else gathered around her to listen to her answers.

Yes, I'm sure it's Salo. No, I haven't met the king who supposedly looks like him. No, he's not a machine; his new body is just different. Yes, I take responsibility for my actions. Why shouldn't you kill me? Because I'm doing my best to make things right.

That was perhaps an hour ago. The brothers haven't spoken to her since. She thinks they might be suffering from more emotions than they know what to do with, so they've settled on the most immediate: being angry with her.

The three Faraswa people seated beneath the floating obelisks have not moved since she first laid eyes on them. As the suns rise higher into the sky, she hides herself beneath the hood of a borrowed cloak, wondering how much longer she'll have to sit here, waiting for the inevitable attack.

She nearly jumps when her brazen communication box vibrates for the second time that morning. *"Alinata. I need a favor from you."*

A number of the Ajaha seated with her hear the voice, including the twins, whose eyes bulge in shock.

She gets up and slowly walks away, and she isn't surprised when Mukuni follows. "Speak."

"The Jasiri are annihilating the Vigilant forces. Unless we stop them, this battle will be over too soon, and the artifacts will face more pressure than we can handle."

"The Shirika followed the emperor here," Alinata says. "Eliminate them, and the Jasiri won't be as much of a threat."

"That's what I was thinking."

"So you're not asking for advice."

"No. I'm asking you to help Tuk do the . . . eliminating."

Still walking, Alinata glances back at the Ajaha. They're all watching her. "Salo, did you just ask me to kill people for you?"

"I don't think we have a choice. Do you have a better idea?"

"No. Removing the Shirika is your best option. But aren't you forgetting something? I don't have my powers anymore."

"You could have them back if you wanted."

Alinata stops, the significance of his words hitting her like a punch in the gut.

"Let's not think of it as anything other than you taking what you need to accomplish a task. When it's over—"

"You don't have to explain yourself," her lips say almost of their own volition. "I'll do it."

"It's just that I can't think of anyone else with the skills—wait. What?"

"I said I'll do it."

"I expected more resistance."

"I helped create this mess, Salo. I'll do whatever I can to fix it. So are you coming here, or am I coming there?"

"No need. We can do it right here."

When Mukuni prods her with his massive snout, a puzzle comes together in her mind. "This is why you left him with me, isn't it. You knew you'd ask this of me."

"Leaving him was a contingency for multiple scenarios, but yes, this was one of them."

Alinata shakes her head. "I assume you know the Asazi blessing is different from anything else you've done."

"I'm aware, and I've already prepared the blessing and a spell composition appropriate to your talents. A little different from what you're used to, but I'm certain you won't have trouble adjusting."

"It won't work. The type of Void spells I know require a medium to anchor the mind in the world. When I became the queen's apprentice, I bound myself to ravens she'd enthralled. I don't see any appropriate mediums in the vicinity."

"I was thinking," Salo says, *"maybe you're standing on your medium."*

Alinata looks down and catches her breath at the idea. Binding a nonliving medium is incredibly difficult and demands a talented mind and an exceptional Axiom.

But then again . . . "Do you really think I can pull it off?"

"There's only one way to find out," Salo replies. *"Make physical contact with Mukuni, and we'll get started."*

The Ajaha are plainly confused seeing her touch Mukuni's head and stand still with her eyes closed. That's because they don't see the magic pouring out of the cat and into her bones, spells taking up residence inside her red steel jewelry.

The last time she cast a binding spell, she was plummeting from a height with a girl who was as much a friend as a rival. They both carried the queen's blessing in their bones, having studied the spell for months in preparation. But it was Alinata who successfully mastered her fear in the end, capturing the flock of ravens while her friend fell to her death.

There's no fear today as she casts the same spell. At first it seems a breeze has disturbed the grains of sand near her sandals. But then more grains leave the ground, looping and eddying around her, and soon she's enveloped in a revolving curtain of her new medium: a whirlwind of fine sand.

She completes the spell at last, and as the Void welcomes her back, she flows back to the Ajaha, the movement new yet familiar. Her ravens were light, agile, but conspicuous, too, and because they were alive, there were always places she couldn't take them. She couldn't pass through water or flames or spaces too small for a bird.

The sands are the air itself. Fluid, weightless, faster, easier to disperse, though demanding more concentration. She reconstitutes in front of the Ajaha, most of whom get up, spears ready to attack at the slightest provocation. Only the general remains seated, showing no surprise.

He glances behind her, at the totem. "It appears you've recovered your powers."

"Your nephew needs my help and has granted me his blessing," she says. "You should take this." She hands over the communication device to the general. "Musalodi will reach out to you if necessary. Mukuni will also remain. I'll return once my task is complete."

The general frowns at the device as he accepts it. "How much longer will we have to sit here? It is unbecoming to remain idle while our allies fight a war."

Salo answers the question before Alinata opens her mouth. *"The longer the artifacts go unnoticed, Aba, the better our chances of success. You're our last line of defense, but I pray you won't have to lift a finger."*

Hearing their brother's voice, the twins gather around the brass device, hopeful. "Bra Salo, is that really you?"

"Hello, Sibu," comes the voice. *"Yes, it's me."* A tense silence transpires, then: *"I've missed you. I've missed you both."*

Tears shine in the twins' eyes, and they don't bother wiping them off. "We've missed you too."

"Go, Asazi," the general says. "Do what you must. We'll remain here."

Alinata dematerializes and lifts off the ground as a whirlwind of sand, and then she heads for the pyramid.

38: Salim

The Ataraxis

About a dozen of Balam's scopes are monitoring the four Tetrad artifacts. Their perspectives keep cycling on the leftmost panel of Mirror light, one moment showing Ilapara and her team guarding the sphinx; the next Julian walking in a slow circle around the hovering Fireblue sphere, studying it with great interest; then the arcanists trading stories with Ayana while Claud and Luka stand nearby in clueless silence, watching two radiant sun disks rise higher above the desert; and finally the squad of Siningwe Ajaha sitting around a dead fire, including a pair of twins who suddenly can't stop asking Salim questions.

"Is everything Alinata told us true?" Sibu says, speaking into the communicator. *"Did you really die and come back as a . . . what did she call it?"*

"An atmech," Jio tells him.

"Yes, are you an atmech, Salo? Are you . . . like a tronic human, now?"

Standing by the navigation table, Salim lets himself chuckle. "'Tronic human' isn't far from the truth, actually."

"Enough, you two," comes their uncle's stern voice. *"Musalodi is busy, and you're keeping him from his duties. Give me that thing."* Aba D takes the communicator and addresses Salim directly. *"Salo, you'll tell us when we're needed. Chatting can come later."*

Salim holds in a sigh of relief. "The enemy has not yet detected your artifact," he says. "No hostile forces are currently en route. As a precaution I'll be delivering a barrier generator for you to place near the artifact. I'll let you know when it comes."

"We'll be waiting."

With the barrage of questions ended, Salim devotes his full attention to the other panel, whose vision Balam has split in half: on one side, a cloud of fine sand gusting across the desert as fast as the winds of a cyclone, and on the other, Tuk sitting inside an airborne skiff. Their positions are white dots on the map in front of Salim, both just seconds away from reaching the pyramid.

He was confident Alinata would adapt to her new medium fairly quickly, but she's taken to it like she was born in the sands of a desert. Even the new tether between them settled in Salim's mind without discomfort. He's already sent her the locations of the targets Balam picked out. He did the same for Ziyo, who now strengthens the stealth shield around Tuk's skiff as it navigates into the chaotic aerial battle taking place in the skies over the pyramid.

Or the two halves of what used to be a pyramid. They've slowly slid apart from each other, the aperture between them a widening gateway to a realm of impenetrable brightness.

Looking out one of the skiff's round windows, Tuk gives a low whistle. *"That can't possibly be good. And that redhawk I see out there is going to be a problem."*

"I'm aware. One problem at a time."

"Transposition in ten seconds," Ziyo announces in Tuk's skiff. *"Nine . . . eight . . . seven . . ."*

While Tuk stretches his neck muscles and flexes his shoulders, Alinata's cloud of sand, dispersed so thinly it's effectively invisible, drifts across the chasm to the pyramid's northern face.

Two high mystics stand guard along that face, watching the battle from a distance, each with a pair of Jasiri guards lurking nearby.

Salim holds his breath as the sand falls to the ground and slides along unseen.

Then a figure in a fluttering white gown rises from the ground behind one of the high mystics; there's a glimmer of gold-encrusted metal, and then the mystic's hands fly to her neck, blood gushing through her fingers. Her Jasiri guards leap to her defense, weapons moving to cut down the attacker, but Alinata's already coalescing behind her second target hundreds of yards away. She slits his throat and is gone even before her first victim has fallen to her knees.

In that same second an invisible skiff performs a slow flyby on the other side of the pyramid, its lone passenger activating his personal stealth shield and summoning a single-edged flashbrand from an enchanted ring. A bolt of lightning carries him down to the south-side walkway, in front of a pair of high mystics taking a stroll. He strikes from stealth, blasting one with gauntlet fire, cutting the other down before she has time to react, then finishing the first off with a decapitating maneuver. A Jasiri throws a spear of Void craft in his direction, but a lightning bolt carries him off before it hits.

Four high mystics dead before the alarm could be raised. Salim covers his mouth and nose with his hands, horrified.

"Your assassin friends are very effective," Balam remarks, his eyepiece flickering with green light. "Look: the masked warriors on the battlefield are already in chaos. Makes me wonder why the sorcerers spread themselves out like that, with limited line of sight to each other and no means of communicating remotely. It's like they didn't expect anyone to target them. The other three still don't know what's happening."

Precisely the weakness Salim identified and exploited. The emperor himself should know: the best way to kill a high mystic is to do so quickly, with no advance warning. Salim just didn't expect the reality to be so . . . brutal.

Even now Alinata finds her third mark, who collapses on the east walkway, his throat slashed, while Tuk falls upon his next victim from out of thin air, his flashbrand driving into her chest. The last of the seven lifts off the ground as an enormous falcon, but Tuk unleashes his gauntlet, and automatic bursts of moonfire pummel the creature's body and roast it alive. With a piercing shriek, the bird falls into the chasm beneath the pyramid and vanishes; then a flash of lightning carries Tuk away, and his skiff immediately accelerates.

"*I win!*" he exclaims, pumping his fist in the air. "*Take that, Alinata!*"

Salim's guilt pivots, shifting into something hotter and easier to express. "This is *not* a competition, Tuk. We're killing people. We can't turn it into a game."

"*I beg to differ,*" comes Tuk's unrepentant reply. "*Killing dangerous sorcerers to save the world should absolutely be a game.*"

Salim starts to reply, but Sevan's voice comes out of his bracer tool, interrupting him. "*Salim, come down to the skiff bay immediately.*"

"I'll talk to you later," he says to Tuk. "For now, you're heading back to Julian." He allows himself a moment to calm down. "And thank you for what you did," he says in a conciliatory tone. "You're invaluable. I don't want you thinking I don't appreciate you. It's just . . . this whole thing. The deaths. I wish I didn't have to do this, you know?"

"*Yeah,*" Tuk says, leaning back into his seat. "*I know.*"

"*Salim, where are you? You need to come down here* right now."

"On my way, Sevan."

He leaves the bridge to go investigate whatever has agitated her, thinking maybe she's overreacting about something ultimately unimportant. She can be as dramatic and short tempered as Tuk, after all. But when he arrives and sees what's in the skiff bay, his next breath hits his lungs like little shivs of ice.

Captain Axios and two of his crew have made it as far into the bay as the hose Faidon once used to cleanse the captain's suit of the Corruption. Faidon himself is here, too, and the willowy blue-haired woman with them must be the former pilot Alesia. They're all carrying small typhonic sidearms, which they've pointed straight ahead at

Sevan and Ijiro, who are themselves armed with much deadlier carbines pointed back at the intruders. A deadlock.

With a tingle of fear, Salim looks around; neither the Professor nor his monster is present. He comes to a stop between his two friends.

"Ijiro?"

"I heard Sevan shouting, so I came to investigate," the Sentinel says in his native KiYonte, his aim never wavering. "These outworlders were trying to force their way in."

"Sevan, are you all right?"

"Of course I'm not all right. These assholes are trying to get onto our ship."

"This is *my* ship!" bellows the captain. "And those are *my* weapons. How dare you touch my things without my permission."

"They're even wearing our clothes," Alesia grumbles as she gives Sevan's short-sleeved green coveralls the evil eye. "They've practically made themselves at home."

"You have *no* idea," Sevan retorts.

The captain glowers; then his enraged eyes fix on Salim. "And what's this I hear about you giving my goods away to the admiral? That had better not be true, cog, or I swear what I do to you will make the Professor's worst look like a kiss on the cheek."

Salim privately thanks Ama Tuk isn't here. "Where'd they even come from?" he asks Sevan.

"I asked around earlier," she says, eyes still on the intruders. "Turns out the admiral imprisoned them on one of the ships for harboring a dangerous criminal and the illegal trafficking of cogs. They must've escaped." Sevan bares her teeth at the captain. "The admiral will know of this."

"It won't matter," the captain growls back. "I'm taking my ship and getting the devil out of here."

A headache has blossomed behind Salim's eyes. The spell he's holding in the background is beginning to irritate his gums. If only he could get his hands on one of those smoking pipes from his dreams with Niko. "Captain Axios, let's not waste any more of each other's time. You forfeited your ship and everything onboard when you abandoned it over the Dapiaro. The fact that I salvaged what was no longer valuable to you—"

"I had no choice!"

"—does not change the fact that you abandoned it, and us, to our destruction. We were fortunate I was able to avert this fate, but by then you'd already left. If it's any consolation, know that the *Ataraxis* is playing an instrumental role in our effort to save the world from impending doom. But you're interrupting, so I insist you leave."

Stunned, the captain gawks. Faidon laughs like he can't believe his ears.

"Ziyo, disarm them, please."

The captain was about to explode in a fit of rage, but his words fail him when a flash of red lightning carries his weapon out of his grasp. Faidon and Alesia are similarly disarmed, and all three of them stare at their hands, then at each other, none the wiser about the reenchanted barrier generator sitting in the bay.

"As you can see," Salim tells them, "we've made some changes to the ship since you were last onboard."

"Put your weapons down, or she dies."

That voice. Only by yielding control to his metaformic aspect does Salim remain calm. He turns around slowly and doesn't react when the Professor comes out the hatch in front of Adamus and a very pale Priscille, Adamus holding her by the throat.

While Ijiro remains still, his weapon aimed at the captain, Sevan looks over her shoulder, and her mouth falls open in despair.

"If you hurt her, I swear—"

"Sevan, do not lose your nerve," Salim interrupts. "Keep your weapon aimed."

"But—"

"I have it under control."

"No you don't," the Professor gloats. "Put your weapons down, or your friend dies."

Imprisonment must not have been kind to the Professor. Bruises mar his face; his yellow, thinning hair hasn't seen a comb in days; and his blue shirt is stained and tattered, just like the thin veneer of refinement he likes to hide behind.

But Adamus hasn't changed. His copper hair still has an impeccable side part, one half of his face square jawed, well groomed, and handsome, the other a monstrosity of brass human skull with a glowing pinpoint of amber light coming from an eye socket. The hand gripping Priscille by the throat is a work of articulated metal joints whose strength Salim knows intimately.

"Priscille, are you hurt?"

Adamus lets her speak. "No," she says between rapid breaths.

"Niko?"

"Stable, for now."

"Enough!" the Professor shouts, his voice ringing in the bay. "Drop your weapons, or the cog bitch dies!"

"Adamus, you're enslaved," Salim says. "But I can free you if you let me."

"Don't listen to him!"

"I can give you your voice back."

"Professor, what are you waiting for?" shouts the captain. "Kill them all!"

Without moving a muscle, Salim reaches into Adamus's mind and shatters whatever restraints the Professor put there. The change is instant. Adamus lets go of Priscille and looks at his hands, then feels his face, horror taking over his human features as his fingers slide over the monstrous half. Moisture coats his single eye.

"Professor?" Alesia asks.

The Professor gives his malfunctioning creation a puzzled stare. "Adamus, I didn't tell you to release her. Catch her, and kill her. Kill them all."

Adamus looks at his hands again, then back at the Professor, surprise on the better half of his face. "It seems I'm no longer compelled to obey you," he says, his voice an unexpectedly bright tenor. He looks at Salim. "You freed me. Do you command me now?"

"What the hell is happening, Professor?" asks the bewildered captain.

"Adamus, obey me," the Professor says hysterically even as he backs away around Sevan, toward the captain. "I gave you a command."

"And I refuse that command," Adamus says. "I have a new master now."

Sevan's demented cackle fills the bay.

"I'm definitely not your master," Salim corrects Adamus. "You're free, which means you may do as you please, so long as you don't attempt to harm me or any of my friends."

Adamus seems to think about it; then his amber eye returns to the Professor, now trying to hide behind Faidon. "Then you must let me claim my vengeance," Adamus says. "The things that were done to me, that I was made to do . . ." A tear spills down his cheek. "I deserve justice."

"On that we can agree," Sevan says. "Hey!" she shouts at Alesia. "Who said you could leave? Move again, and I'll burn a hole through your skull."

"Why don't we all calm down—" Alesia begins.

"Shut your mouth!"

The anger in Sevan's voice, the cold rage contained inside Adamus: Salim understands them too well. "I can't tell either of you what to do," he says. "We all have legitimate reasons to hate these people. But bloodshed as justice can easily warp you into something monstrous, and I'd hate to see that happen to you."

"So you want us to let them go?" Sevan demands.

"This is a large desert. They will either surrender themselves back to the admiral's people or try their luck out on the sands. And these are the Red Wilds." Salim takes a long look at the four people who've invaded his ship. "But if you wish to kill them, I won't stop you. What happens to them is no longer my concern."

Sevan maintains her aim, then shakes her head in disgust. "They'll just muck up the bay anyway. Adamus can have them if he wants, but he'll have to clean up the mess."

"As a favor to you for giving me my freedom," Adamus says to Salim, "I will follow your lead. They may leave unharmed."

Alesia and Faidon immediately turn tail. The captain, too, though he slowly backs away as if searching for one last trick, some hidden weapon he can pull out of his old skiff bay to reclaim his ship, but he doesn't find it, so he turns around and flees. The Professor is the last to leave, but at the ramp, he attempts one last desperate, tear-filled plea.

"Adamus, I created you. I made you strong. Are you really going to abandon me like this?"

The atmech he created closes his one eye, the other one going dim, his metal fists clenching tightly. Recognizing that Adamus is trying his best to restrain himself, Salim speaks on his behalf.

"For your own sake, Professor, I recommend that you don't address him again, that you return to walking, and that you don't stop for a very long time."

Defeated, the Professor finally leaves, and Salim commands the ramp to rise and seal the bay shut.

"I've put a few scopes to watch the ship," Balam says on Salim's bracer tool. *"Not doing so was a major oversight."*

"I wasn't paying attention either," Salim admits. "But the situation is over."

"And just in time, because we have another situation on our hands. There's a shadow of some kind heading for the sphinx. I can't see exactly what it is. You might want to take a look."

"I'll be there shortly," Salim says, but he's not done here. "Are we safe around you, Adamus? You're welcome to join us, but I need to be sure we can trust you."

"I have no compulsion to hurt any of you," Adamus says. "But I have rage that needs venting, and it seems you have a war to fight. Put me on a battlefield, and let me be useful."

Adamus once unmade Salim so thoroughly he screamed himself nearly out of a voice. But now they shake hands. "I hope your offer is sincere, Adamus, because I'm going to take you up on it."

39: Ilapara

The Sphinx Artifact

There are no clouds, and morning is well underway, the desert heat scorching Ilapara beneath her scarf and coveralls. But the strength of sunlight above the sphinx starts to wane for some reason, the sky's hue deepening as if dusk were approaching.

With growing disquiet she shades her eyes and looks up to the weakened suns. She's about to ask Jomo if he sees the same thing when her earpiece vibrates. *"Listen up, everyone: Something we can't identify is approaching your position from the north. I suspect it's an illusionist masking the approach of a hostile force. Help is on the way, but you might want to retreat to the barrier until we know what we're dealing with."*

Jomo shoots her a worried glance. "You heard that too, right?"

She nods and looks over her shoulder at the barrier generator they placed near the artifact's pedestal. There's nothing visible to betray the barrier's existence, and the three meditating Faraswa it's protecting have yet to move from their positions. Above them the eyes of the rearing sphinx have become incredibly luminous, flames of moonfire licking out of its opening maw.

"Come on," Ilapara says to Jomo. "Let's go."

Kito and Odari were chatting with a few of the Mbare skirmishers up on the dune ridge. It seems they've stopped to stare at something in the north, their backs toward the sphinx.

"Kito!" Ilapara yells. "Odari! Didn't you hear the man? Get down from there right now. All of you!"

The skirmishers who were down in the valley are already walking toward the barrier, but the men on the ridge seem petrified.

"What are they looking at?" Jomo mumbles with a frown. "Kito, Odari! Get down here, you idiots!"

None of them move, transfixed by whatever they've seen on the other side of the dune. The dread Ilapara felt earlier returns, compounding at the sudden and intense flare that briefly blinds her eyes. When they adjust, her knees weaken at seeing the devouring sun that has appeared above her; it's black as the devil's heart, but the lights swirling in violent arcs around it could bring high noon to a starless night.

Dear Ama, no. Ilapara grips Jomo by the arm, trying to hurry him along. "Jomo, to the barrier, now!"

But he wrests his arm free and runs instead for his friends up on the ridge.

"Jomo, don't!"

He's halfway up when the dune explodes. A colossal fist of Void and shadow bursts out of the sands, tossing everyone on the ridge into the air. Ilapara loses sight of him in the shower of sand and bodies, but she sees the hand catching someone and crushing him between its fingers. Before she can even yell Jomo's name, the ground moves beneath her, and she's flung upward by the same force. Ears ringing, she flails uncontrollably but somehow manages to hit the ground in a roll, stopping just short of crashing into the artifact's stone pedestal.

Inside the barrier's invisible radius.

With a groan she lifts her head just in time to see a squad of riders in red masks come out of the curtain of falling sand, swinging their blades or throwing their spears at the disoriented skirmishers. This alone would have crushed her with despair.

But the sands clear up enough for her to see the giant among them, riding the biggest antelope she's ever seen, with horns like sickles and a hide as black as his robes, black as the impenetrable shadows swirling around his face, except for the beam of moonfire coming out of his left eye.

Fear paralyzes her, blood freezing over in her arteries.

The Dark Sun is here.

40: Alinata

The Pyramid

Alinata should have already returned to the obelisks after removing the Shirika and turning the tide on the ground, but she caught a glimpse of a descending staircase beneath the pyramid's widening aperture and has been waiting for the chance to move closer and investigate.

She's the sand and wind in a battle so fierce the smoke billowing out of all the downed ships has blotted out the suns. She dives out of the path of a fire elemental launched from the ground and weathers a violent shock wave when the spell detonates against a sun-powered windcraft.

Beneath it an armored giant ejects a spinning disk from a wide-barreled weapon; it flies for the organized columns of outworld warriors retreating to the pyramid, hitting one and electrocuting ten of his friends. More men quickly fill the gaps left behind, responding with concentrated fire shot from their gauntlets and typhons, using their flashbrands when enemies come within melee range.

Some are in crimson tabards; others have golden feathers sticking out of their helmets. Alinata hardly believes they belong to the same army, but they fight united by the single-minded purpose of protecting the pyramid at all costs.

Finding her opportunity, she floats past them and across the chasm to the platform on the western face, a gust of wind they fail to notice. The pyramid has split open along the north-south axis, so she ghosts down the face and makes a turn left, flowing between boots and armored legs until she finds the staircase.

She pauses before committing herself to the plunge. The floor beneath the walls of the splitting pyramid is a portal to a realm of astral brilliance. Even from this close, the pillar of light coming out of it and pouring up into the sky is almost solid. What unsettles her is the deep chill accompanying the light. She expected to be pummeled by intense waves of heat, but she might as well be standing near the mouth of an ice cave.

Bracing herself, she flows down the stairs, thinking she'll find the source of the brightness lurking just below. Instead, darkness envelops her as she enters a stairwell leading deeper into the bowels of the earth, and soon she discovers that the pedestal on which the pyramid stands is in fact a vast underground tower rising out of the chasm.

The staircase spirals in a square around the tower, and she descends until she reaches a door at the bottom of the chasm. Beyond that door is a raised walkway bridging across the upper interior of a massive hall.

Silently, she steps out of the Void in person and peers over the parapet on the walkway. The pillars supporting the hall's roof stretch down to a dizzying depth, partly illuminated by the ancient sconces burning on the walls.

The hall isn't empty. Way down on the floor, three figures in glowing crowns, one of them masked, are standing around a spinning sphere of moongold, their eyes and cosmic shards alight with magic. Dozens and dozens of people dressed in fine silks and precious stones have prostrated themselves motionlessly around the trio, frozen so still Alinata might have thought them dead had she not seen the Faraswa at the circle of pillars similarly immobile.

She doesn't need to go any closer to recognize her queen among the three figures. Magnificent as ever, she stands in a golden gown with a collar of spikes flaring out from behind her neck. Powerful and commanding, a goddess. Alinata's heart breaks at the sight. She knows the queen isn't evil. In her heart, all the queen has ever wanted was to strengthen her tribe and build a lasting legacy. If she knew who she was consorting with, she surely wouldn't have gone through with this.

"And so, the traitor finally shows herself," says a voice nearby. "Just as the queen knew you would."

From out of the corridor at the other end of the walkway comes a girl in a flowing crimson gown and chains of red steel adorning her frizzy hair. She has a smile on her face, but the glimmer in her eyes is poison.

"Unati?" Alinata murmurs, dumbfounded. The last time they spoke, Alinata apologized to the younger Asazi for humiliating her in front of her friends. "What are you doing here?"

"That's a question you ought to answer yourself," says Neropa, stepping out of the shadows behind Alinata. She's dressed similarly to Unati, red steel chains woven into her braids. "You've no business being here. The queen disowned you, and you've been replaced."

Alinata glances at Unati, whose smile widens.

But of course.

Pushing past the hurt, Alinata turns to Neropa. "Her Majesty has been deceived. Whatever they're doing down there, she won't survive it. None of us will. If you care about her, you'll help me stop this."

Neropa has no expression on her face, but she considers Alinata for a lingering moment, like she's making a decision. "The simple truth, Alinata, is that I don't trust you," she says at last. "You've always been distant with me despite my attempts to get to know you better. At first I thought maybe you felt threatened by me; then I realized that actually, I barely exist to you. I'm not worthy enough to be your rival, let alone your friend. Now you come here after defying the queen, demanding

I trust that you somehow know better than her? How do you expect me to react?"

"I've been horrible," Alinata admits, "but you can't doubt my devotion to the queen. You more than anyone know how far I've gone for her. I've killed, manipulated. I've done things you don't even know about. Do you think I'd be so quick to disobey her without cause?"

"What I think is maybe the guilt over whatever you did in Yonte Saire has clouded your judgment."

"Some people just aren't ruthless enough for the job," Unati intones. "Too soft, too weak minded."

Alinata reaches into herself and extinguishes the urge to scream. "I know who the king is. I know the face hiding behind his mask, and if you saw it, too, you would—"

"Save your sob story," Unati cuts her off. "It might have worked on the regiments, but they're gullible men easily fooled by the wiles of a faithless woman. We know you for the snake you are."

"I don't have time for this." Alinata dives off the walkway, prepared to put an end to this ordeal, to slit the king's throat if necessary, anything to get her queen out of this madness. But the Void turns against her, Neropa and Unati pulling her upward against her will.

Their enhanced blessings are like iron chains, and she is dragged out of the hall and up the tower's stairwell in a furious storm of black wings. She finally breaks free of them halfway up, and they all reconstitute on the same flight of stairs, Neropa on the landing below, Unati above, Alinata trapped in the middle.

They've both summoned their Void knives, pulsing with shadows Alinata knows all too well. Unati slowly closes in, eyes dancing with malice in the dim stairwell.

"My, my, she's already accepted another blessing. What traitor do you now serve, Si Alinata?"

Knowing that the time for talking has passed, Alinata summons her golden daggers from the Void, and they coalesce in her hands, slim and tapering, their hilts encrusted with desert gemstones. "I wish it didn't have to be this way," she says.

Neropa gives her a sad smile. "Me too."

And then the Asazi attack.

Alinata discorporates just before Unati's thrown knife twists into her head. She tries to surge past Neropa and race back down to the hall at the base of the tower but is pulled out of the Void, the point of Neropa's shadowed knife streaking for her face.

She's too slow, and the knife tears open a gash on her left cheek. But she blocks Neropa's forearm before she's cut a second time and retaliates with an upward swipe of a golden knife. Ravens burst away from her before the knife finds its mark, and here's Unati again attempting to slice the back of her skull in half. Alinata becomes sand, flowing behind Unati. The younger Asazi anticipates her, yanking her out of the Void and slamming her against a wall.

Blood trickling down her cheek, the pain like frostbite, Alinata moves in time to stop Unati's knife from plunging into her eye. She strains as the knife inches closer and closer to her face.

An earthquake rumbles through the tower, sand falling into the surrounding chasm from above. Beyond the knife, Unati grins. "You were right, Si Alinata. Strength is just as important as poise and control. I've been training."

"I apologized for that," Alinata grits out.

"I'd have respected you more if you hadn't."

The knife finally makes its plunge but finds only sand. Alinata grabs Unati's arm and twists until the girl screams from pain and drops the knife. It clatters to the steps, where it becomes mist, returning to the Void.

When Neropa comes for a swipe, Alinata ducks and flows upward, then stops at the next landing.

"Stop this, both of you."

They don't. They attack together, pushing her up the tower, their knives slicing into her arms with each mistake. She anticipates their strikes, but their augmented blessings allow them to warp the Void around her so that she can't escape.

More earthquakes rock the tower, each one stronger than the last. Still the Asazi come at her with their knives, giving her no rest, determined to tire her out. As she becomes more desperate, she leans deeper into her knowledge and experience with the knife, and this they cannot match.

They box her in near the top of the tower. Unati lunges, and Alinata appears to evade her by flowing toward Neropa. Both girls fall for the trick and realize too late that she's split herself in half. A golden knife flashes from behind Unati, and there's a thin red line coating the edge of the blade at the end of its arc.

Neropa gasps, covering her mouth in shock. A drop of blood drips from Alinata's knife. Just as it hits the floor, the next earthquake comes, and Unati, eyes widened from her slashed throat, tumbles over the railing and plummets into the stairwell.

"No!" Neropa cries. She looks at Alinata, anger and despair having glossed her eyes. "What have you done?"

That look. Unlike Unati, Neropa was just following orders. But now Alinata recognizes she's made it personal.

"Neropa, you can kill or hate me all you want when this is over." She has to shout because the earth groans and shifts, the tower rumbling ominously. "But we have to save the queen before this tower collapses."

"You killed her!"

"She gave me no choice!"

They might have fought to the death right then, but a scream drawn from the depths of hell roars upward from below, followed by a wall of whiteness rising up the stairwell to swallow them.

It's too late.

"We have to get out of here!"

Neropa's shock hasn't left her, and now she stands paralyzed, horrified by the approaching light. Instinct takes over Alinata, and she draws the other woman into the Void, lifting them both up and out of the tower. They explode out of the base of the pyramid, fly over the battle and through the clouds of smoke and burning windcrafts, and land at last on a sandstone hill with a clear view of the pyramid.

It's now more obviously a gateway to somewhere else, with the light pouring out between the split halves a membrane between worlds.

The ground trembles as the membrane is tested, an enormous shadow darkening the gateway from the other side, taller than the pyramid, twice as tall perhaps. A black claw breaks through first, followed by a giant, skeletal arm, then a ghastly one-eyed face with a forest of weeping teeth.

And as the winged popobawa demon takes its first step into the world, dwarfing the windcrafts in the vicinity with its size, it releases a scream that will surely echo to the ends of the world.

Then it flaps its wings once and leaps into the air, and the next thing Alinata knows, it's flying off into the west.

Trembling, Neropa grips Alinata by the arm as if to anchor herself in place. "Alinata, what's happening?"

More things pour out from beyond the gateway, smaller but numerous: mapopobawa, tikoloshe, and other creatures of the netherworld. "It's over," is all Alinata can say. "We failed."

And only now does Neropa notice what Alinata already knows even if she can't feel it herself.

"My blessing," Neropa weeps, falling to her knees. "It's gone."

41: Salim

The Ataraxis

Salim expected it.

He knew the gate would open eventually—that was the plan. But the artifacts aren't ready, he isn't ready, and everything seems to be going wrong all at once.

They saw only the warlord's shadow slinking toward the sphinx and didn't think to check whether there might be stealthed groups approaching the other artifacts. Now Salim watches in horror as a team of armored knights appears out of thin air near the twin solar disks and opens fire on Claud, Luka, Ayana, and the arcanists. The same thing happens at the circle of pillars, knights appearing as if from another dimension and unleashing their typhons on the unsuspecting rangers. Tuk, Julian, and their team are already battling their own group of sudden attackers at the sphere, and whatever's happening at the sphinx is now impossible to see due to interference from the warlord's mystic Seal.

Balam sits forward in his chair, and Salim hears anxiety in his voice for the first time since they escaped the brig. "I've lost all visuals on the sphinx," he says. "And the other artifacts appear to be under attack."

"How the hell did they get past your scopes?" Sevan asks, seated at the helm.

"I cannot explain it. Did I make a mistake?"

That doesn't seem likely to Salim. He modified those scopes himself, giving them robust detection spells of Mirror craft. If there were any outworld stealth technology out there, Balam would have seen it.

Unless it wasn't outworld technology at all. "They used Umadi spirit charms," Salim realizes. "Inkanyamba stealth fields are virtually impenetrable. The scopes wouldn't have seen through them. Ziyo, open fire on all enemies within the vicinity of a skiff."

"Understood," the construct responds.

Seated with Adamus onboard the skiff racing back to the sphinx, Ijiro speaks into his bracer tool, addressing Salim. *"We're seeing something in the skies to the north. Do you see it too? Looks like . . . smoke, but it's glowing? I can't explain it."*

Those are spirits pouring out of the netherworld, Salim almost says. He can even see some of them falling like shadows onto the armored warriors who were fighting near the pyramid, possessing them, twisting their bodies, making their eyes glow like white torches.

"You're almost to the sphinx," Salim says to Ijiro. "The warlord has cast a Seal over the area, and it's blocking our ability to see or communicate with the people there. I'm counting on you and Adamus to get everyone safely to the barrier. The rituals aren't complete."

"Yes, Bwana Salo."

"What. The. Hell." Sevan gapes at one of the brass panels. "Are we really seeing this?"

Great one-eyed mapopobawa can be seen lifting out of the chasm beneath the pyramid and spiraling into the sky as if in celebration. The redhawk—or what was once a redhawk, now a winged demon of withered black flesh and smoke—joins them as they assail the admiral's forces, ripping windcrafts apart, tearing into the ground troops with their sharp claws and teeth.

When some of the winged demons spread away from the pyramid in beelines for the artifacts, Salim connects himself to the communication device in his uncle's possession.

"Aba D, you all need to retreat to the barrier immediately."

"If you're speaking to your uncle," Balam says, "he can't hear you. He left the comm device by the fire."

Balam reveals this to be true on one of the panels; the device was forgotten on the sand at the enemy's sudden attack.

"Shit." Panic is beginning to take hold of Salim.

So far Mukuni has successfully menaced the armored knights, forcing them to focus their salvos on him. But a few Ajaha were caught in the initial attack, and some haven't risen from where they fell.

Salim connects himself to Tuk's earpiece. "Tuk, retreat to the barrier immediately. You're about to have more company."

Unsurprisingly, Tuk, Julian, and their team of skirmishers have been doing rather well against their attackers, having already cut their numbers in half.

Julian's aim with her rifle is impeccable, and so is the dreadlocked ranger's with his bow, and Tuk hasn't stopped using the skiff's transposition enchantment to augment his martial abilities. He bolts from one armored warrior to the other, cutting them down with his flashbrand, blasting them with his war gauntlet.

"Tuk, did you hear me?" Salim tries again. "Retreat to the barrier."

He replies only after tearing into another enemy with his gauntlet. *"We can take them."*

"You don't understand. The gate has opened, and demons are inbound. Get inside the barrier, Tuk. You too, Julian."

"Understood," Julian says, already in motion.

In the canyons near the floating disks, her Imperial comrades are in a grave state. The ambush was sudden; by the time the skiff intervened, first with cannon fire and then by transposing everyone into the barrier,

Luka and Ayana were already motionless on the ground, and so were most of the skirmishers.

Claud is still screaming over his brother's body. Zuri and Msia are still trying to resuscitate whoever they can.

"Bibi Zuri," Salim says, speaking into her earpiece. "Stay in the barrier. Do not leave under any circumstance. The gate has opened. You're about to be swarmed."

"Ayana is down," Zuri replies between panting breaths, *"and so is Luka."*

"You must stay in the barrier," Salim reiterates.

"I . . . understand."

Like the other three artifacts, the twin disks have lifted high above the ground, over the top of the canyons, both incredibly luminous, one gold and the other silver. And as at the other three artifacts, the three Faraswa mystics meditating around the pedestal below have not yet completed their ritual.

Come on, Salim prays. *We can't hold on for much longer.*

Closer to the pyramid, the regiments of the Ajaha have finally joined the fight, forced to believe by witnessing with their own eyes what Alinata warned them would happen. Here is the horde of nether-world creatures pouring out through the pyramid—ravenous, destructive, darkening the sky with their sheer numbers.

A little too late.

"Salim, your brothers and uncle are under too much pressure," Balam warns. "They won't make it."

"They'll make it," Salim says strongly. *They have to.*

A fragment of him is there with them, watching them turn away enemy fire with their red steel bracers and retaliating with their spears. It is valiant, and perhaps if the armored warriors were the only enemies they faced, they might have prevailed.

In a desperate move, Salim triggers one of Mukuni's hidden aspects. The cat gives out a roar so loud even the Ajaha cover their ears. The outworld warriors respond by pummeling him with volleys of fire from their cannons and rifles and are emboldened when the beast appears to succumb, catching flame all around his body, crouching like his legs are giving out.

Except the flames are coming from inside him. His leopard spots have incandesced like molten lava, his mouth has become a furnace, and his eyes, usually bright cyan blue, are now orbs of moonfire. A roar builds up in his throat, his body vibrating in faster and faster pulses. And just when Salim thinks the cat is about to vomit a river of fire, twin beams of destructive moonlight explode out of his eyes instead, scything through the armored warriors like sharpened swords through ripe melons.

The Ajaha cheer when the last enemy falls, but Mukuni cuts them off with an angry roar, then gallops toward the dead fire. The Ajaha watch him in confusion until he picks up the discarded communication device with his jaws and tosses it at the general's feet.

"I think Bra Salo's trying to say something to you," Jio surmises.

The general picks up the device. *"Yes, Salo. I'm here."*

"Aba D, the gate has opened, and demons are coming your way. This isn't a figure of speech. Get everyone inside the barrier and stay there. Please."

Mukuni roars again just to drive the point.

To Salim's relief, the general immediately orders his men to retreat, and they obey, carrying the injured and unconscious along with them.

"How strong are the barriers?" Sevan asks. "The first two of those creatures have already reached the eastern artifact."

Indeed, they can be seen on the other panel falling upon the barrier with their poisoned talons, and so vigorous are their attacks the generator starts emitting sparks as the enchantment bends under the pressure. Most of the people who've taken refuge inside cower from the beasts, but Tuk stands face-to-face with one of them even as it scratches mindlessly at the barrier, snapping its horrid jaws, trying to claw its way to him.

"Salo," comes his choked whisper. Salim can almost feel the tears in his voice. *"I think that's my sister out there. I can see it in her eyes. It's her."*

"They were drawn here by our presence," Julian says grimly, watching the other demon. *"But that's no longer your sister. The people we once knew are gone."*

An explosion comes out of the shroud of sorcery beneath the warlord's Seal. "We've lost contact with the skiff at the sphinx," Balam says. "I still can't get a visual to the barrier."

"Bwana Salo, I think the barrier is failing," Zuri says in a shaking voice. She and Msia are holding each other tightly, watching their barrier deform under the pressure of three mapopobawa striking at it.

The same thing is going on at the circle of obelisks. *"Bra Salo, will we survive this?"*

"Salo, that's my sister. I failed her."

"Salim, our barrier generator is failing."

"I still have no visual. Every scope I send inside goes dark."

"This is my fault."

"I don't want to die like this . . ."

"Salim . . ."

"Bra Salo . . ."

Salim blanks out his mind, turning everything off for one quiet second.

It can't end like this. Not after all they've been through. Those rituals *will* have enough time, even if he must die for it.

He opens his eyes. "Sevan, take us into the air immediately."

"Where are we going?"

"As high as you can, as fast as you can."

He's already on his way down to the skiff bay by the time Sevan lifts the *Ataraxis* off the ground and ignites the ship's flaming shield.

When he first peered into the Book of Lies, his metaformic aspect saw and recorded deeper insights than what was immediately apparent to his eyes, even if he didn't yet understand the full extent of his abilities.

Fragments of Faraswa history poured into his subconscious mind: maps, registers, family trees, laws, catalogs, legends, fables, even recipes. An incomplete history but a cross section of the empire that once ruled the Redlands.

Buried beneath all that clutter was a spell so revered its scripts were carved onto a wall in what was once the desert's largest temple. A spell rarely cast, and only ever in defense of their homeland. Its difficulty was such that it took four high priests of the moon two full days to execute it successfully, and the specter of catastrophic failure was never far away.

With Ziyo and his metaformic aspect, Salim was able to manifest the ciphers of that spell in one night. It's been spooled around his cosmic shards since morning, waiting for him to release it, but he was hoping, praying, that he wouldn't have to, for however fast his metaforms may operate, the release of so much power will surely destroy him.

Alone in the skiff bay, Salim commands the ramp to lower itself. They are already miles above the desert and still climbing higher, though the pitch of their ascent has leveled out.

"Salim, what are you doing?" comes Sevan's voice from his bracer tool.

He looks out into the sky. It's still morning, but he can see patches of darkness covering the ground far below. "What I have to," he says. He takes a step closer to the ramp.

"Salim, don't do it!"

"Priscille," Salim says. "Tell Niko . . . tell him everything we shared was real. Tell him . . . I love him."

Priscille takes a moment before she replies. *"As you wish."*

"Salim, there must be another way!"

"I'm blessed to have known each of you. Thank you for all your help, for who you are. Use your freedom well."

After discarding his bracer tool, Salim takes one last breath, prepares to release his spell, and leaps.

42: Ilapara

The Sphinx

Jomo is still out there.

The barrier around the artifact's pedestal is an invisible dome the drizzle of disturbed sand cannot penetrate. The meditating Faraswa people have still not moved. A few of the skirmishers made it in, and both the Faraswa men they found guarding the artifact are safe inside.

But outside, the warlord and his bloodthirsty men are cutting down the skirmishers with gleeful abandon. And dear Ama, Jomo is still out there.

Ilapara moves. She finds her spear, determined to go out and save Jomo even if she must fight the warlord herself, and now she's running, except Odari pulls her back and tackles her to the ground within the barrier's protective radius.

"Don't!" he cries. "You'll die!"

She grits her teeth, her voice deadly calm. "Odari, let me go."

"Jomo wouldn't want you throwing your life away! Please, don't do it. For his sake."

Jomo was immediately willing to come raise their child together in the Plains. She was planning on fighting him on it, of course, if only to be difficult, but in the depths of her soul she was delighted.

She can't lose that. She can't lose him.

"Odari, let me go!"

She tries to wiggle free, but Odari was always strong, and now he's moon blessed.

"I'm only doing what he asked me to do, boss."

She screams, the rage whooshing out into despair, and her head sinks onto the ground. Eventually Odari lets her go, realizing she won't run out of the barrier.

But she can't even weep in peace, because something is going on outside. The gusting sands still haven't settled; in fact they've thickened to obscure her view of the warlord and whoever else is out there. The rearing sphinx is a faint lamp shining above the barrier's dome. She sees only shadows moving in the murk, and even the sunlight has fled, turning morning to dusk.

Confused, she sits back up in time to witness a temporary flash in the sky; she makes out the shape of one of the skiffs just before it explodes in flame. Burning debris ricochets against the barrier, and the men and their warlord cheer at the destruction.

Except now there's the buzz of shooting typhons, flashes of moonfire visible through the sandstorm. Several shapes emerge out of the chaos, running closer, and Ilapara's heart stops when the warlord breaches the barrier, an amber light coming out of one eye. But the shadows that swirled around his head have receded to reveal a man-machine dressed in coveralls, pale skinned on one half of his face, a brass skull on the other.

And he's helping Jomo limp, one arm hooked around his shoulders. Ijiro and Kito follow behind them, shooting from their carbines to cover Jomo's retreat.

Inside the barrier, Jomo falls to his knees, weeping, but he stops when he sees Ilapara, eyes widening in shock and surprise. He crawls over in a hurry, and they fall into each other's arms.

"You're here!" he cries. "I saw you fly off in exploding sand, so I thought you'd . . . dear Mother, I don't know what I'd have done."

Ilapara rests her forehead on his shoulder, the relief almost painful. "I'm fine, Jomo. What about you? Are you hurt?"

"Just a scratch," he says, not letting go.

"Come here, you bastard." Odari embraces Kito like a long-lost brother. "I thought you were dead. Don't ever do that again."

When she and Jomo finally let go of each other, Ilapara turns her attention to the half-faced man. He's positioned himself at the edge of the barrier, looking out with a large rifle ready to fire. His posture is inhumanly erect, his arms monstrosities of metal.

"Who is that? I thought he was the warlord."

"That's Adamus," Ijiro replies. "Salo's outworlder friend. We came on the skiff before the warlord took it down."

"At least you both got out," she says. "We may yet survive this."

Ijiro looks out the barrier before shaking his head grimly, his lips dry. "I don't know, boss. On our way here we saw a pall over the skies in the north. And we weren't the only thing the warlord was fighting out there."

On a second look, the storm outside the dome has strengthened, thickened, blackened even, and Ilapara realizes it's not sand she sees swirling outside the protective dome but ash and cinders, the remains of burnt and decaying things. She is almost unsurprised when a multitude of torch-like eyes appears in the gloom.

What does surprise her is the silver reptilian kongamato she sees alighting among the torches and turning into a naked woman. The storm parts for her as if she has mastery over the air. She is bathed in a white light that conceals more than it illuminates, but Ilapara recognizes her anyway, the silhouette, the ciphers covering her skin. Sure as the pits this is the Black mystic who once hunted her across the Yontai, the Dark Sun's favorite disciple.

The storm also thins around the mounted warlord so that he's visible to everyone in the barrier. His men have already perished to the tikoloshe. He alone remains, swinging his bladed spear and cutting down any demon that comes too close. At the appearance of the Black mystic, the demons draw back from him, opening a path.

"Who is that?" Jomo whispers.

Ilapara doesn't answer, feeling like the air might retaliate if she did.

Shadows still blanketing his face, the warlord considers his disciple. "I thought this might be your doing," he says, his voice a sonorous boom. "Your petty demons cannot take me. The taste of victory will be sweetened by your screams."

The woman's voice is like ice scraping on metal spikes. It lowers the temperature, clouds the skies even more, dusk becoming midnight.

"You still don't see what has happened, do you, Muchinda?" she says. "You still don't see what you've wrought upon the world and yourself."

"I have consumed the flesh of enemies more terrible than you. Your words do not frighten me."

"Oh, but they should, for you now stand at the shores of hell, and here, I am strong."

Demons burst out of the sands beneath the warlord and bite into his mount, tearing chunks of flesh out of its belly. It collapses with him, and he is likewise swarmed. No sound comes from him as the demons take a leg, an arm, a piece of his face, feasting on his bowels. Ilapara looks away just as the woman outside wails like she's tearing herself apart, the storm of ash and cinders thickening to almost blanket the barrier again.

Who knows how long the storm rages, but when it finally settles down, neither disciple nor warlord is there. The demons are gone, too, destroyed by whatever spell the woman released. Just as Ilapara starts to think that maybe her ordeal is over, a huge shadow crashes onto the barrier, then another, then a third.

A few of the men yelp when the shadows reveal themselves to be winged one-eyed demons. They strike at the barrier with their talons, drool seeping through their pointed teeth. Ilapara covers her mouth to keep herself quiet, to not scream, to be brave, to not remember watching Obe's arm being torn to shreds by a demon exactly like these back in Yonte Saire.

"Mapopobawa," whispers a wide-eyed Ijiro, staring straight at one through the barrier. "What does this mean?"

Jomo holds Ilapara closer. "It means the gate has opened," he says. "It means we failed."

The calm in his voice rubs off on Ilapara. They will all die here, despite everything they did to stop it. "We tried our best," she says.

"I suppose we did," Jomo says, and she leans deeper into him, grateful that she will meet her end by his side.

But then the demons abruptly stop their pummeling, turning their hideous heads up to the sky, where a bright star has appeared.

"What's that?" Ilapara asks.

That's when they see the first plumes of smoke coming down from the heavens.

43: Alinata

The Pyramid

Alinata and Neropa watch the end of the world from a hill with a good view of the open pyramid and the demonic host pouring out from the other side.

Neropa is too numb to speak, and Alinata lacks the will or the energy to console her, so they sit in silence side by side, waiting.

For death? For one last fight? Alinata hasn't decided. What would be the point of fighting anyway? The sheer number of demons is staggering.

The rangers have joined the fight, though. From this distance they're intrepid little columns of crimson and tronic ivory keeping the tide at bay, fighting alongside the remnants of the Vigilant forces—the very people they came here to oppose. But the press of demons from beyond the gate is immense and shows no sign of waning.

"There are so many of them," Neropa murmurs. "How did we not know?"

Alinata has no answer for her, so they continue to sit in silence and watch as the rangers slowly fall to the demons. Then a popobawa notices them as it flies by overhead, and it starts circling them, assessing them with its terrible eye. Alinata gets up, dread rising up her gullet, not because she's afraid to die but because she could swear she recognizes the sinuous copper circlet sitting on the creature's head.

It can't be.

The creature hisses at her as if it has read her thoughts, tucking in its wings in preparation for a swooping dive, but it aborts the motion at the unexpected brightness that explodes across the sky above it.

The creature looks up to investigate. Alinata does the same, squinting and shading her eyes with a hand. At first there is only that one star that has appeared, stationary and intensely luminous. But then the whole sky comes alive with falling comets, balls of fire raining down in trails of smoke . . . tens, hundreds of them.

Alinata can hardly believe her eyes, but all her doubts wither away when the first of the arriving redhawks pierces her ears with its characteristic shriek. The demon screams in anger and flees, but a redhawk swoops down on it from above and tears the thing apart with its beak and talons.

As more redhawks rain on the battlefield, setting upon the demons, the Ajaha are quick to capitalize on the unexpected help, and their renewed battle cries are loud enough to carry all the way to Alinata's ears.

"Ama Vaziishe is with us!" they shout. "Ama Vaziishe is with us!"

Alinata sinks back down to sit next to Neropa, an emptiness inside her, a shock that will take a moment to wash over her, for just seconds ago she witnessed the demon's crowned head tumble from the sky, separated from its body, the redhawk flying off.

"You saw it too, didn't you," Neropa says numbly. "You know who that was."

"Ama Vaziishe is with us!"

It comes out of nowhere, a pressure bursting out of her chest, and before Alinata can control herself, she's weeping like a child.

44: Ilapara

The Sphinx

The sky burns as redhawks descend from the heavens, righteous fire raining with a vengeance upon the demons that would have clawed their way through the barrier. But Ilapara and the others don't dare leave the barrier's confines.

Disturbed sand rises into the air as a redhawk pins one of the mapopobawa down on the ground before ripping off its perforated wings. The other two demons are quickly eviscerated and cast aside; then the redhawks simply lift off and fly away in the direction of the pyramid.

No one is brave enough to speak or move for a full minute.

"Did that just happen?" Ilapara finally whispers.

"You saw it too?" Jomo says. "Oh, thank the Mother. I thought I was going insane."

One of the Faraswa gentlemen they found here has a look of wonder as he gazes at the smoke plumes striating the sky. "Legends say that the ancients could summon redhawks to fight for them." He looks down at his sister, who's still frozen in a position of meditation. "Perhaps that's what they came here to do?"

Is it? Ilapara wonders. That doesn't sound like what Salo told them. She starts to explain this when the ground shakes once as if a god struck it with a hammer. Then the three people who've sat still as carvings all along surprise everyone by gasping for breath and opening their eyes.

They look up at the shining moongold sphinx. It has spread its wings as wide as they can go, and by the brightness blooming inside its open beak, it has finally amassed all the power it needs.

As one, the trio of Faraswa utters a command Ilapara doesn't catch, and the Tetrad ritual finally completes itself in a column of light that shoots north toward the pyramid.

45: Salim

Broken on the ground after falling from a height, Salim coughs out sand from his mouth. He should be dead, ripped to shreds by the spell he used to summon all the redhawks of the deep black and compel them to fight for him. And if that didn't kill him, his collision with the ground should have done it. But he isn't quite human anymore, so he survived.

Death might claim him yet. He tries to move, but his limbs are twisted wrongly. He blinks his eyes open, but his spectacles fell off, and the light is unkind to him. An hour passes, perhaps. Then another. He drifts in and out of awareness, clinging to life by a fraying thread.

His heart begins to slow, his labored breaths growing shallower and further apart. He makes one last attempt to lift himself up, but his strength fails him, and he stills. For the last time.

A large shape blocking out the sunlight. The low whine of a windcraft. Voices nearby. Hands touching him, cradling his head.

"Here. Put these on."

Someone slips a pair of spectacles over his eyes, then gently lifts him up into their arms, but these can't be ordinary human arms, because Salim feels like he's leeching strength off this person or like this person is pouring their own life force into him. His broken bones begin to mend, and he gains enough presence of mind to open his eyes and assess what's happening to him.

The bulk of the *Ataraxis*, seated on the sands. Faces, watching him with concern. Ilapara. Tuk. Jomo. Priscille. Balam.

The twins are here too. And so's a Faraswa boy with a face that tickles Salim's memory.

All alive. All exhausted. All worried.

"Where will you take him?" Tuk demands.

"You may follow us, if you like," says the person carrying Salim in his arms. "I will make our position known to your pilot. Don't worry; he won't be harmed. But this is a final step we must take together."

And then Salim is carried into the air, his rescuer translocating them through space even as he continues to drown Salim in waves of healing life force. They fly across the desert faster than a falling comet, and yet there's no sonic boom, no wind battering Salim's face. They continue past the coast, hurtling farther west over the glistening waters of the Dapiaro.

All the while Salim continues to heal, and when he gathers enough strength, he finally turns his head to look at the face of his rescuer.

"Niko?"

Niko smiles down at him, eyes glittering like sapphires and diamonds. "In a sense."

"Am I dead?"

"No. And you'd better stay that way."

Salim decides he must be hallucinating, that he's probably still waiting to die on the sands of the desert. But he doesn't want to wake up just yet, so he rests his head back onto Niko's chest.

"My friends," he says.

"They will be fine. Don't you see? You did it, Salim. You ended the war."

Did they really succeed, or is this also just another figment of his hallucination? "But Arante made it out. That huge demon flew off."

"That's true," Niko says.

"So what now?"

"Now, we play the last note in this song."

At last they come to their destination, a city of glass domes and towers floating on the surface of the ocean. It is arranged in eight circular clusters: seven smaller ones surrounding a much larger central hub in a radial arrangement.

It already looked massive from a height, but the scale grows more astonishing as Niko descends toward the central hub.

"What is this place?" Salim asks.

"A ship," Niko replies. "Once, it crossed the immense rift of space between two galaxies. Then it lay hidden at the bottom of this ocean for thousands of years. It's what Arante has been hunting ever since she began her war against humanity ages ago. And now she has found it."

They touch down slowly in the empty courtyard outside a majestic glass atrium. Manicured lawns, palm trees, and other ornamental plants lend their fresh scent to the sea breeze. The buildings around the courtyard are pristine. Salim hardly believes this place has been abandoned for a week, let alone thousands of years.

As Niko places him on his feet, Salim takes another look into his eyes. They're not quite blue, not quite clear either. Still soulful, still sincere, but the wisdom shining within is not human.

"You're not Niko, are you," he says. "And this isn't a dream."

"The Veil has shattered, and the gods can now walk the earth in person," Niko replies, "but Vigilance remains too weak, so he asked for my help, and I agreed. Think of him as a passenger. He gives me directions, but I'm in control. He won't make me do anything I don't want to do."

Salim glances at Niko's abdomen, where he was pierced only a few hours ago. The wound has healed, leaving a scar. "Are you really in there, Niko?"

Niko smiles, offering Salim his hand. "Come. Let us finish this together."

They enter the atrium, a circular hall where two pillars stand on a dais like the posts of a gateway, and it is here that Salim finally meets the devil.

They might have looked alike once, but the shadow his reflection contained has burst out of its shell to reveal a being of black mists and skin like volcanic rock. The face is capricious, overwhelmingly beautiful one moment, chillingly horrifying the next, and so is the shape of her body, talons becoming hands becoming talons.

She's waiting for them on the dais, standing in the space between the pillars. When she addresses Niko, her voice is the same metallic harmony Salim remembers from their first encounter in the inner sanctum.

"I see through your fleshly disguise, old friend. But you are too late. After eons of being denied, here I stand at the gates of heaven, and I shall now do what you failed to do—bring justice to an unjust universe."

Niko tightens his grip around Salim's hand so much it nearly hurts. "Your source of power is no more," he says. "Your dimension, your forces, gone. You've failed."

"I do not need my dimension," Arante says, her eyes becoming torches of antilight: a whiteness that conceals. "I am powerful enough on my own." She turns to face the pillars and spreads her arms, her antilight leaping to the pillars on the dais. A distortion of air appears in the space between them. "You fought well. But my victory was inevitable. Justice is inevitable."

The distortion grows. The floor begins to quake. Salim's ears pop as a rip tears open on the dais, the door to an endless path of glory whose brilliance would burn his eyes if he stared too long.

"Yes! It's opening!"

Arante feeds power into the pillars, drawing from her core. Tendrils of corrupted essence leak out of her to pry the breach wider, and it obeys, the Infinite Path opening right before Salim's eyes.

"It's almost over! I have won! I have finally won!"

She gives herself over to the pillars, pours her soul, her being, her power, her everything, and for a twinkling, heaven fills the atrium.

But like sunlight on an overcast day, the brightness begins to recede as the rip seals itself closed.

"What's happening?"

Arante pours more of herself to fight the mending breach, but the celestial realm has already retreated to a fissure no brighter than a candle.

"No!"

She gives a mighty roar. She heaves, she pulls, she releases so much essence Salim thinks the power will tear out his eardrums, time seeming to stop. But even the shimmering distortion is gone now.

"No, no, no!" She tries to cast another spell, but she's lost so much of herself she's little more than the bony creatures that populated her realm, the palest ghost of what was once human. Enfeebled, she sinks to her knees. "Why?" she cries. "Why is the gate not opening?"

"And that is what you've never understood," says a different voice, and with it comes King Isa Andaiye Saire, dressed in a gown of scarlet and starlight. She steps into the atrium with three other godly beings, two with halos of opaque sunlight that conceal their faces, the third clothed in the radiance of an arboreal Primeval Spirit. Salim squints at that last one, making out a face with strong features, a broad and slightly crooked nose and hair sheared to the scalp. The specter of recognition passes through him.

"The gates of heaven are not of this universe," Isa says. "You could no more destroy or harness them than an ant could do the wind. And we are all but ants to the builders of the Infinite Path, even those of us who claim godhood."

"You are wrong!" Arante hisses. "I can use the gates! I know I can."

"Don't you see?" the king says. "These pillars are not, nor have they ever been, the gates of heaven."

"The gates never left the stars from which you came," Niko says. "The exodus to this galaxy was not to save humanity but to lure you away. You were fooled into thinking the gods had fled with your prize, and you followed. All the eons it took them to get here—you abandoned your war and followed."

"Allowing those left behind to recover and rebuild," Isa says. "And for the gods to devise the means of your destruction."

"How long have you waited?" Niko says. "Plotted? Schemed? All for an empty gateway that leads nowhere."

"You lie!" Arante puts out a hand, blackened essence gushing out and racing for the king. But the king's eyes catch fire, and the rays of a thousand red stars purify the atrium. At Arante's next attack, the king's eyes shine again, and a fire sparks inside the devil's belly. Salim sees it through the mists flowing around her emaciated form, a ball of flames burning her from within.

She sags, shaking her head slowly. Moonfire engulfs the rest of her body, the last shadows of the netherworld wrestling with the punishing fury of moonfire. "You lie," she whispers. "I have waited. I have fought. I have lived the deaths of countless innocents. So many. I . . . I wanted to fix everything. I could have . . . this can't . . . it can't . . ."

"Rest now, old adversary," the king says. "You have suffered enough."

The flames finally overpower the shadows, and Arante falls upon the dais, crumbling to ashes that slowly disperse. The sense of relief that pervades the atrium ebbs into Salim's own soul.

"And at last, it is over," King Isa says. "It is finally over."

Salim has kept silent all along, but now he looks at the gods around the room, the king, the suns, the one he thinks he recognizes, and the one whose hand he's still holding. "What happens now?"

"Now we must journey into the Infinite Path," the king says. "It is the right thing to do."

"But how?"

She points at the dais. "Through this gate."

Mouth agape, Salim stares at the pillars and the ash still dispersing on the dais. "But . . . I thought you said it wasn't a gate."

"It is *a* gate. Just not the one Arante was looking for. The true gate to the Infinite Path was hidden on the progenitor world eons ago. Every soul who's ever lived on this world has passed through these pillars, but they are simply one of many waypoints the gods built to shorten the trip back home, to the true gate."

They're leaving for another ocean of stars, Salim understands. How long will it take them to cover such an immense distance? "Don't you want to return to your old lives?" he asks. "You're gods now, but you were once people. What about those you left behind?"

"I will miss them," Isa says. "My cousin. The Sentinels. You. But I will not be alone." The king favors her godly companions with a smile, but her tone hardens as she looks Niko directly in the face. "The gods should not have returned from the Infinite Path. To be a god in this universe is to suffer the great disadvantage of having nothing more to learn. Limitless power with no challenge or adversity breeds only decadence, and cruelty, and the belief that you can play games with human lives. The previous gods left the path of enlightenment to seek cheap adoration and worship. We will not make the same mistake."

Feeling a vise gripping his heart, Salim looks into Niko's possessed eyes. "You're not taking Niko with you. I won't allow it."

Niko gives him a reassuring squeeze of the hand. "I wouldn't leave unless you were coming with me."

"I'm afraid we must depart now, Salo," the king says, "for our journey is long, and it is best we not linger." She comes forward and embraces him, kissing him on both cheeks.

The space between the pillars sputters again, becoming a transparent film, like the air above a hot surface. The two suns are the first to walk through, their halos vanishing beyond the portal.

"It was an honor," says the one Salim thinks is Obe Saai, whom he met on the night they delved into Yonte Saire's undercity. He wears the light of a god now, and without another word, he follows the solar deities.

"What do we do with all this?" Salim asks, looking around the atrium.

"Learn," says the king. "With the fall of the Veil, the Great Forgetting curse has lifted. All the knowledge the gods came with from their home stars is in this city, and you"—she places a hand on his chest, a flash of heat and arcane knowledge passing into him—"are now its custodian. I trust that you will use it for the betterment of your world."

Before stepping through the pillars, she considers him one last time, and Salim finds himself reminded of the young woman he first met sitting on a bench in Yonte Saire's botanical garden. It feels like such a long time ago.

"Goodbye, my friend. Live a long and happy life. We will meet again on the Infinite Path."

And then King Isa Andaiye Saire walks through the portal and is gone from the world forever.

"And so, the age of gods and devils has come to a close," Niko says. "And rightly so. This world was not meant for us." His gemstone eyes slant toward Salim. "You have done well, Salim. But I, too, must now take my leave."

"Will you follow the others through the pillars?" Salim asks. "You said you wouldn't."

"And I shall keep my promise." Niko, or Vigilance, starts walking out of the atrium, heading for the courtyard where they landed. Salim follows him.

"I have lived a long and arduous life," he says. "A hell of my own making, I suppose." Outside, he looks up into the clear blue skies and takes a deep breath. "But now I think I'd like to rest. I shall fade into the dark like my kin. In the end, I think that's what we all wanted. We were all so tired."

His eyes are already losing their jeweled shine, but there is still a shade of sapphire within them when Vigilance speaks for the last time. "A gift, Aneniko, for your service. Use it well."

And then Niko closes his eyes. In a blink the world changes around them, the city transforming into an alien mountain range just as an immense blue sun dips into a barren, jagged horizon. Nothing could live here, for the sun is much too powerful, but the beauty of its last rays as they scatter across the violet sky brings dampness to Salim's eyes.

The sun sets, the alien world dissolves, and the city returns. When next Niko opens his eyes, they are the same rich brown Salim has come to know and adore. He holds Niko by the shoulders and takes a closer look just to make sure. "Niko? Are you all right? Is he really gone?"

"Most of him," Niko says, then stretches out his left arm, now marked with scripts of Fireblue that pulse with light before fading into his skin. "He left . . . something. I'm still trying to make sense of it." Finally, his attention returns to Salim, and he beams like they're seeing each other for the first time.

Which Salim supposes is true.

"You were real. I wasn't going mad. You're really alive."

"I am."

"And when we . . . you know," Niko says. "That was real too."

"Yes," Salim says, unable to hold back his grin.

"But not really, though. I've never actually kissed you, have I, Salim?"

Salim pauses. That name coming out of Niko's mouth doesn't ring true to his ears. Not anymore. Whatever inhibition refused his old name is gone, and now it's the new one that doesn't fit. "I'm Salo," he says. "And as for kissing me, I'm not sure what you're waiting for because—"

Musalodi, no longer Salim, does not finish whatever he was going to say, his lips captured in a sudden and forceful kiss. It is familiar and yet different in electrifying ways, and it goes on and on until they hear the drone of the *Ataraxis* as it arrives with the rest of their friends.

Epilogue

Khaya-Siningwe

They were born weeks after he left for Yonte Saire, twin baby girls with chubby cheeks and luxuriant puffs of hair ornamented with beads.

Mariha gurgles contentedly as she bounces on Salo's lap beneath the musuku tree in the chief's compound, while his other little sister, Selema, dozes off in Ilapara's arms nearby.

"They're so pretty," Ilapara remarks, gazing at the baby in her arms with glittering eyes.

She has just arrived after a monthlong stay in her clanlands with Jomo, and during that time she's gained a softness about her, an easiness to her smiles. A bump is also showing on her red sleeveless dress.

"That one usually makes a fuss with strangers," Salo tells her. "But she seems at home in your arms. Perhaps . . . someone is getting used to the idea of motherhood?"

He meant to tease her, but she becomes pensive. "The world can be so unkind," she says. "Bringing a life into it isn't a decision to make lightly. But the last month at home . . . it was good for me. I'm still nervous, of course I am, but in a good way." She regards him, her kohl-ringed eyes narrowing slightly. "Salo, did you put my ama on your list on purpose?"

He doesn't bother lying. "Nimara asked her if she was interested; she said yes."

"I tried to talk her out of it."

"You don't want her coming?"

"It's not that. I didn't want her uprooting her life for me, you know? But she's so happy. She really wants to be there for me and her grandchild. I'm happy, too, I guess."

The joy on her face buoys Salo's heart with warmth. "It's the least you deserve, Ilapara."

They both watch Alinata as she walks over to join them, her face schooled into a worried frown, but the slight twist of her pursed lips betrays her amusement.

"Salo. It's getting heated in there. Everyone is waiting to hear from you."

Salo loudly exhales as he looks over at the thatched council house across the compound, which has become host to an impromptu gathering of the tribe's leadership.

Such a thing is almost unheard of; with the exception of funerals and weddings, the tribal leadership never convenes anywhere outside the Circle of the Elders at the Queen's Kraal, as it is neutral ground. Meeting here gives the Siningwe clan an outsize advantage.

"You can't avoid this," Ilapara says. "Just get it over with. I'll watch your sisters. Your ama should be back soon anyway."

Salo would rather not set foot anywhere near that meeting, but Ilapara is right, so he kisses Mariha on the forehead and places her on the mat beneath the tree.

"I'll be back," he promises, then leaves Ilapara to console the baby as she starts to wail.

The tapestried oval hall is more crowded than Salo has ever seen it. Every chief and clan mystic is there. Members of their personal advisory councils. Generals of their regiments. Asazi from the Directorate at the Queen's Kraal.

They're all seated on stools in a circular arrangement, listening as the chiefs and mystics bicker. The argument doesn't stop even after Salo enters the hall.

"This is his mess," says one chief. "He should tell us how to fix it."

"How dare you lay this on my son after all he has sacrificed."

"All I meant was, we wouldn't be alive without him. We should follow his lead."

"Musalodi has done enough. If he wants to be left alone, we must honor that wish."

"But can we afford to do that, VaSiningwe?" says a mystic. "Whether we like it or not, your son's influence is a gravity well that can't be ignored. Our presence in this hall is proof of it. Any queen who takes the throne will always wonder where she stands with him, and so will we. He needs to be explicit about his intentions."

Nimara, seated in her place as clan mystic next to Chief VaSiningwe, spots Salo, and a spark animates her glazed-over eyes.

"Perhaps we should give him a chance to speak," she cuts in. "Step forward, Musalodi, and say your piece."

"Thank you, AmaSiningwe." Lacing his hands together respectfully, Salo steps deeper into the hall so he is visible to everyone present. The sudden quiet makes his ears ring. "As my aba and a few of you already know," he says, "I'm here to announce my imminent departure for the city in the Dapiaro. The Plains are my home, and I'll visit as often as I can, but any role I play in this society will be from a distance."

The tribal leadership looks to each other, muttered grumbles and whispers disturbing the silence.

"Why not fly the city here?" demands one chief. "It belongs to our people."

"Our tribe will certainly have a presence there," Salo replies. "AmaSiningwe and Si Alinata have helped me compile a list of Asazi scholars to join me, pending your approval. But make no mistake: the city and its treasures belong to the world."

More grumbles. Salo speaks over them. "I understand you are unsettled, but with due respect, my elders, your concerns aren't unique. Governments everywhere have collapsed. Major cities are in ruins beneath clouds of poison that need cleansing. The vacuums of power that have been ripped open on our own continent are already breeding conflict. There are millions of problems that need solving in these uncertain times, and I intend to do my part wherever I can. But I can't—I *won't*—tell you who to choose as the next queen. Figure it out yourselves."

Many in the hall begin to protest, but VaSiningwe has had enough. "You wanted my son's opinion, and he has given it. Musalodi, you are dismissed."

Salo bows even as a clamor returns to the hall. "Thank you, Aba."

"They're right to worry, you know," Nimara says to him later as she accompanies him down the kraal's plateau to the lake. "You command a literal flying city filled with knowledge from the gods. Everyone will be watching what you do, what you say."

"I'm aware," Salo replies. "That's why my first mission will be to gather a council of scholars and peacemakers from around the world and give them command of the city."

Nimara eyes him, a wrinkle on her forehead. "Is that really wise, Salo?"

I don't know, he thinks. "I'll retain the final word at first, but my hope is to gradually cede control to a group of wise people who are also principled. Ultimately, I'm just a kid, Nimara. I shouldn't get to make decisions that affect millions of people on my own."

"Even that's a decision that will affect millions, but I take your point."

A shadow passes over them as the *Ataraxis* shimmers out of stealth and extrudes its landing gears, preparing to touch down on the lakeside.

"I'll never get used to that," Nimara says with a shudder.

"You'll have to fly on one if you want to come visit," Salo tells her.

"Hmm. We shall see."

He hesitates. "And . . . when you decide you're tired of clan politics, there's a place for you on the council, should you want it."

"That's . . . an offer I may actually accept," she says after taking a moment to think about it. "Being clan mystic has its perks, but I'm a scholar at heart. Research is my calling, not the minutiae of running a clan. I still need to train a few more apprentices, but soon there'll be enough suitable candidates to replace me. Then maybe I'll come to your city."

"I look forward to it," Salo says, pleased with her response. "In the meantime . . ." He stops and pulls out a brass cube from a chest pocket on his outworld sky-blue shirt, which he has worn with a traditional white Yerezi loincloth. "You've been approved as our first ambassador by the current members of the council," he says, handing over the cube.

"Meaning you and your friends," Nimara quips.

"Well, I have to start somewhere," Salo says self-consciously.

She takes the cube, studying its openwork structure. "What is it?"

"The city's libraries of knowledge will take generations to catalog. We intend to build a data bank our ambassadors can access from anywhere. There isn't much in it right now. Just the Pattern Archives of Yonte Saire. But the data bank will grow as we work on it."

"*Just* the Pattern Archives?" Nimara gasps, gawking at the artifact. "Salo. When you promised to bring me the biggest and best gift from

Yonte Saire, I assumed you meant a necklace or some other trinket. Not a library of spells in the palm of my hand!"

Before he can speak, she puts her arms around him and holds him tightly. "Oh, Salo. It's so good to have you back."

He reciprocates, unexpected emotion clenching his heart. "It's good to be back."

He goes down to the Ajaha training glade, where he finds a young ranger leaning casually against a tree, smoking a pipe as he watches the shimmering lake through the surrounding woods. The ranger is alone.

"I'm leaving later this evening," Salo tells him. "I'm moving to the city."

The ranger breathes out a cloud of smoke, keeping his face in profile. "I see."

"Some outworlders have already tried to seize it, and I doubt they'll be the last."

"How . . . problematic."

"Exactly," Salo says. "So I was thinking, we'll probably need someone to watch over us. Someone to keep us safe."

"Someone?" the ranger says, finally turning his face. The heat in his eyes is still intoxicating to Salo even after a month of camping trips and midnight swims and secret trysts wherever and whenever possible, as if their hands were glued to each other.

Salo moistens his lips. "Someone dashing, maybe. And strong. And maybe I've met his parents, and they thoroughly approve. He might also be very good at . . . that thing I like."

A wicked grin. The ranger straightens from where he was leaning against the tree and comes closer. "Is he now."

"Very."

"Hmm." Another step. "What if this dashing someone has friends who want to join him. Can they come?"

"Absolutely."

Hands slide down Salo's hips, the scent of nsango tickling his nose. "I might know a guy."

A throat clears nearby and they both jump, startled; then Niko scowls at the boy who's appeared off to the side, watching them with a poorly hidden smirk.

"Addi. I told you I wasn't to be disturbed. Have you loaded our stuff onto the ship yet?"

"That's what I was doing, Bra Niko," Addi says, "but I thought you'd want to know that the twins—your brothers, Bra Salo—are insisting on bringing their quaggas onboard, and Sevan isn't having it. They're arguing in two different languages. It's insane."

While Salo chuckles at the image, Niko fumes. "What the devil do they need their quaggas for? Do they know the city is in the middle of an ocean?"

"That's what I tried to tell them, but you know how stubborn they are."

"Don't we all," Salo agrees. "You have to go and sort this out," he says to Niko, who gives a disappointed sigh.

"We'll continue this . . . discussion . . . later," Niko says, a twinkle in his eye.

Electricity ripples through Salo's veins. "I look forward to it."

Tuk comes to stand next to Salo while he watches from afar as the rangers carry supplies onto the ship with Adamus and the Sentinels. Tuk and the crew of the *Ataraxis* left three weeks ago to gather intelligence about the postwar outer world—specifically, how they're reacting to the battle in the desert and how they're receiving the news about the sudden appearance of a city in the Dapiaro.

His report was not good.

"Where's that handsome fellow of yours?" he says, folding his arms over his black coveralls.

Salo nods at the ship. "Making sure no one packs too much." Glancing at Tuk, Salo says, "You know, I'm disappointed you two aren't getting along as well as I hoped."

Tuk's eyes become emeralds. "Oh, we get along just fine. He's been very polite. I think maybe he wonders about the nature of our relationship."

"He's not one to be jealous," Salo says.

"Perhaps, but everyone has a threshold. In any case, we've come to an understanding. He'll manage local security with your brothers and Mafarai. Alinata and I will handle external business. I've already laid the groundwork for a network of spies and assassins—"

"Tuk, we talked about this."

"I meant operatives," Tuk says, impenitent. "People who can solve problems your ambassadors can't." His eyes go distant, losing a shade of color. "It's getting wild out there, Salo. And whether you like it or not, that city is a big target. It won't survive on diplomacy alone. There are already plots to seize it, or destroy it if that fails. We'll need to stop those plots before they get too far."

"You don't act without the council's say."

"We won't act without *your* say. Matters of security are best decided by as few people as possible. Your council can bicker over something else."

Salo regards his stubborn friend. "You really don't like my council idea, do you."

"No organization is immune to corruption," Tuk says. "You could even say corruption is inevitable. No matter how rigorous your standards, sooner or later you'll invite the wrong person to your council, and I shudder to think what damage they could do with access to the city's archives."

"But *I'm* not immune to corruption," Salo argues.

"No, you're not," Tuk agrees. "But I trust you, which is why I sleep well knowing you're in control. Once that changes . . ." Tuk shakes his head, not completing the thought.

Salo understands his concerns, but he's made up his mind. Even if he starts off as a good custodian of the city, there's no guarantee he'll remain so. What if he becomes a tyrant? There has to be a better way.

"Is that Jomo?" Tuk says, looking at the distant figure in a leg brace coming down the plateau with Ilapara and her mother. "I've missed that big oaf."

"You should go say hello," Salo suggests, to which Tuk's eyes crinkle in the corners.

"I probably should."

After the farewells, the hugs and kisses from his family, the promises to visit every other week, Salo boards the *Ataraxis* with the rest of his party, and they lift off the lakeshore, thundering into the sky in a cloak of moonfire.

A few members of the city's new council are also onboard, having been collected as the *Ataraxis* made its way to the Plains.

Tuliza, here on behalf of the KiYonte people. Aaku Sissay, here for the Faraswa tribe. Julian Silver Dawn, the first Imperial representative.

There will be more, all sourced from the world's places of wisdom, to decide what to do with the city's treasures. Its archives alone hold the combined knowledge of a civilization that once spanned a galaxy. Countless worlds contributed to this trove.

How could one person in good conscience decide to control it by himself?

"I've been meaning to tell you," says a voice from behind him.

At cruising speed, Sevan has reduced the strength of the fire cloak so that it's transparent. Salo is leaning on the rail on the weather deck, enjoying the view of the continent rushing by below.

His lips stretch as Niko joins him. "Tell me what?" he says.

"I finally figured out what our blue friend left for me," Niko says.

"You have? What is it?"

Niko slides closer. "I'd show you, but I think maybe the world has seen enough upheaval for now. Once things have calmed down a little . . ."

"Don't you dare keep me in suspense," Salo says, poking him in the side. "What is it?"

Niko glances upward, an enigmatic look in his eyes, and Salo swears he sees a flash of blue pass through them. When Niko looks back at him, a wide grin splits his face.

"How would you like to take a ride on a comet someday? We could take it around the suns and maybe land it on the moon. We could even go out to other stars, see what else is out there."

Salo's heart misses several beats. "What do you mean?"

"The New Year's Comet," Niko says. "It's a ship. A vessel of the deep black. And now, it's ours."

They could leave now. Salo could give the keys to the city to someone else and let Niko take him to the heavens. They could visit alien worlds; they could live their lives without responsibility, be young and lustful and free.

They could have it all.

Salo reaches over to caress Niko on the cheek. "One day, my love," he says. "One day. For now, let's do what we can to fix this broken world. Then you can give me the stars."

ACKNOWLEDGMENTS

Writing this trilogy has been an incredible journey. I have grown so much as an author and as a human being, but none of it would have been possible without a team of people cheering me on.

I would like to thank my family for their continued support and patience. I am what I am because of you.

A very big thank-you to Julie Crisp, my agent, and Adrienne Procaccini, my editor at 47North, the original champions of this trilogy.

Thanks as well to my developmental editor, Clarence Haynes, who helped me tell the story I wanted to tell and love the result.

To Riam Griswold, Susan Stokes, and Stephanie Chou, who put that extra polish on my writing: Your work ethic and eye for detail are simply next level. Thank you so much.

Thanks as well to Karah Nichols, my production manager at 47North, and thanks to you, my readers, who made this story possible and one worth telling.

ABOUT THE AUTHOR

C. T. Rwizi was born in Zimbabwe, grew up in Swaziland, finished high school in Costa Rica, and got a BA in government at Dartmouth College in the United States. He currently lives in South Africa with his family and enjoys playing video games, taking long runs, and spending way too much time lurking on Reddit. He is a self-professed lover of synthwave.